the SECRETS of JANE

Reborn

II

First Printing Edition 2025

Copyright © 2025 by Charlotte Mallory

www.charlottemallory.com

ISBN: 979-8-9862555-8-3

Editor: Heather Creeden

www.creedreads.com

Interior Cover Art by Lulybot

Cover Design and Map by Charlotte Mallory

———◆———

WARNINGS:

Content Warning 18+: This series contains explicit scenes, depictions of war, battle violence, abduction, graphic depiction of violence, references/threats of SA (no on screen), fire and burning, drugging, and overall a very crude world.

This is the final installment of a duel POV duology with a guaranteed HEA.

❀ Created with Vellum

For all my duology lovers

Huntswood
Deadmen's Teeth
Trident's Cove
Serpent's Reach
Seafarer's Rest
Spi...
The Veil
Skull's Row
Restless Peaks
Raven's Basin
Graywatch
The Keep
Bandit's Meadow
The Black S...
Dryhill
Inkstone
Bala...
Talon's Perch
Ender's Bay
Coalfell

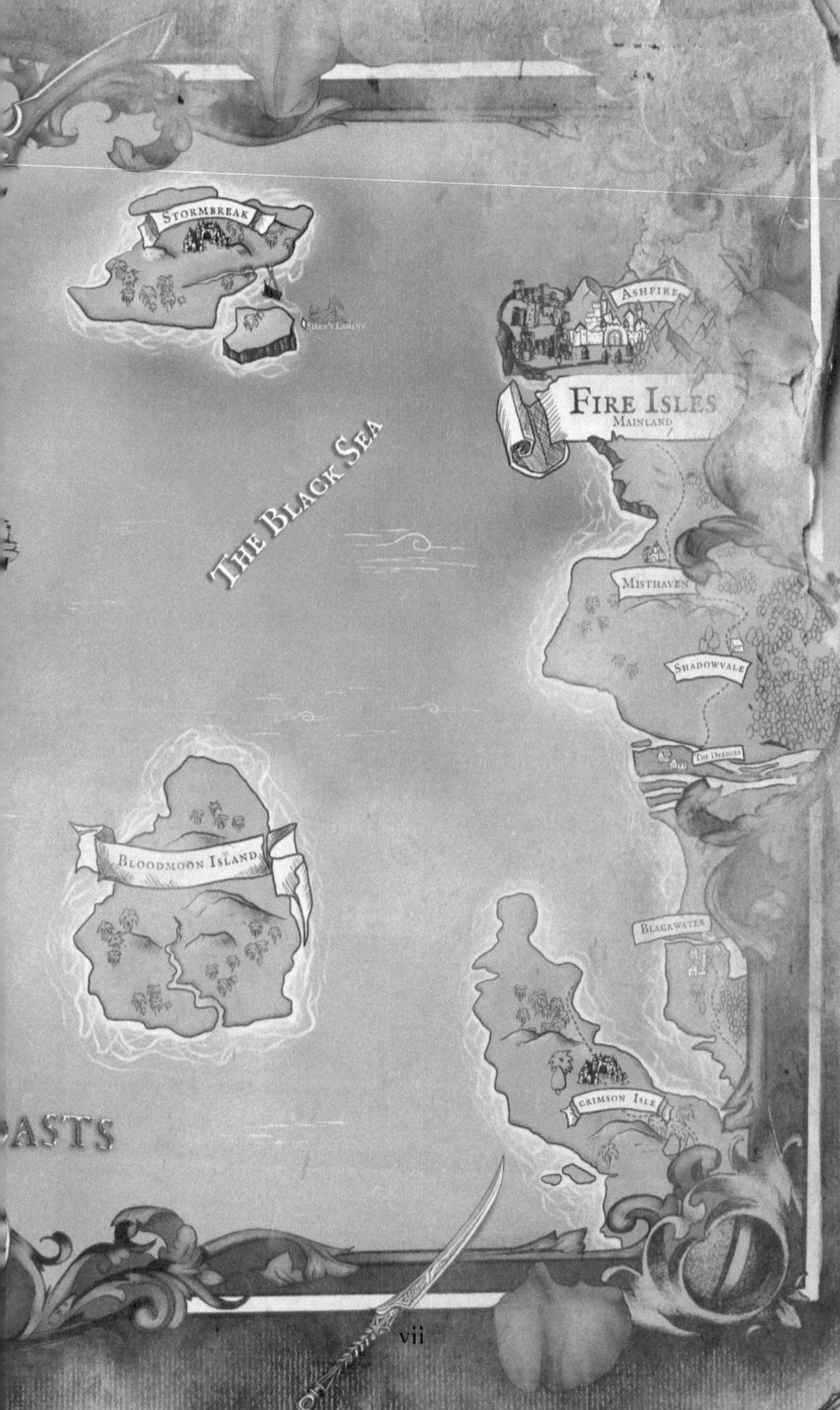

STORMBREAK
SIREN'S LAMENT
ASHFIRE
FIRE ISLES
MAINLAND
THE BLACK SEA
MISTHAVEN
SHADOWVALE
THE DREDGES
BLOODMOON ISLAND
BLACKWATER
CRIMSON ISLE
ASTS

BLACKWELL

Back when Soren visited Blackwell and felt something menacing in the room...

DON'T LOOK AT THE CORNER.

It's fucking hard pretending like there isn't a god of misery in my room, penetrating his gaze right at Soren and me. His existence to everyone else is thinner than smoke, while *I'm* the unlucky bastard that has to see him in all his terrifying glory.

Being subjected to such darkness should be considered a *sacrifice* with my efforts to secure Skull's Row. Sure, cocky cunts like Soren will drown in what's to come next, but those that comply will live a controlled, yet stable life within these walls.

A new world will be born, and I the king.

That is *my* reward for suffering.

Continuing to deny any acknowledgement of the god in the room, I fix my gaze onto Soren as he rises from his seat with a loud scooting of the chair. He downs the shot of rum and places the glass on my table, pushing it forward with weathered hands.

Sea glass eyes burn through me like hot iron piercing flesh, but I bet he gains absolutely no information. He's grossly misplacing his confidence in his senses.

It's his *true* weakness.

Hopefully by the time he learns that lesson, it will be too late for him.

"You're certain?" Soren's rough timbre breaks through the thick pause between our words.

What were we talking about?

"The bastard is a warlord," I retort, referencing our conversation once it returns to me. I inhale deeply as I put on my best face for deception. "The Basilisk is out there trying to steal land that he sees as open, but we all know it's *ours*. Someone has to go take care of this, and the Corsairs know that craggy coastline the best. To which they'll only listen to *Tempest*. So yes, I'm certain that she goes. If Basilisk gets a *foothold* in the Crimson Isles, he'll become a real problem for Skull's Row."

Almost as soon as I release those words, an uneasy chill sweeps over my body, the hairs all along my skin rising, even down to my balls.

Don't look at the corner.

If I dare glance that way, I know I can't cover the abject fear that even a drunk pirate could see. Just the mere *thought* of those onyx eyes with tiny, orange glowing pupils burning into the two of us, as if unwinding our souls, seam by seam, is enough to keep me notice-ably on edge.

They're eyes that Soren remains oblivious to; nearly *everyone* is, if *he* wants it that way.

"That's a lot of men to sacrifice for something so *petty*," Soren remarks.

He doesn't believe me.

"Tempest is the one risking it all, so if she agrees, I don't see what the others are bitching about. Including you," I snap, wanting this conversation over with.

Just let it fucking happen as Misery wants and shut up. Do we really care about the Crimson Isles? No, but Misery wants Basilisk dead, along with Tempest, and you, once he's done using you, anyway...

Soren's inscrutable eyes flash with an irritating insight that I'm growing to despise. The more he's among us, the more he's learning us, and the bastard is clearly aware that something isn't quite right. Which is impressive given that we're fucking with his powers, making it nearly impossible for me to be read.

Misery, no doubt, is aware of Soren's perception.

Soren continues to move in his stance like the floor is immeasurably uncomfortable. "If you insist, Blackwell."

Without more pushback, he heads toward the door as if he's suddenly gotten word that he has better things to do.

A faint smile tugs at my lips as I consider living in a Skull's Row where this man's body rots at the bottom of the ocean, tied to a large stone with ropes I'll force him to knot himself. Misery's restoration will be the death of the Council, and I will be there to stand in their ashes with a crown on my head, like the pompous cunts in Belstead.

My crown will be made of naprese gold and bones.

When Soren's grip is on the handle of the door, my gaze almost immediately drifts to where a shadowy figure resides, one that holds a large, black staff. Darkness eats away at any light that reaches that corner, an ebony, ethereal cloak covering the body underneath. Long, gray arms emerge from a heavy hood that covers his face. His hands are clawed and veined, slowly wrapping around the staff. His pupils are like candlelight that doesn't flicker, burning with a depth that Soren *wishes* he had.

The Zenith before me has the audacity to pause before opening the door, turning his head to stare right at the spot that *should* look empty to him. My jaw drops as I nearly back away from whatever encounter this could become; my heart rarely races this fast. I've seen my share of warfare, but the devastation that this broken god can bring is *disturbing*.

The God of Misery stares pointedly at Soren, sharp teeth glinting underneath the hood. Whether Misery is smiling or baring his fangs, I'm not certain.

Soren continues to fight his hesitation to leave, moving his attention to the door, then back to Misery, almost as if he swore he saw a ghost.

Just leave, you annoying bastard.

My shoulders heave forward with a heavy sigh as he finally fucking leaves. Did Soren see him? Or feel him?

I wait a few moments before I can breathe again, nearly panting as I do so. "You said he can't see you," I mutter, staring at the empty glass I drained my rum from, wanting to remain calm.

That was the deal—Misery uses some of my energy to conceal himself from Soren; a feat he can accomplish on his own when, and only when, he's returned to full power. In the meantime, the taxation of his energy means he requires *mine* to do it.

The shadowy figure lazily turns to face me, his eyes the only visible feature among the darkness of his face. "Nor can he hear me, which explains your tiredness as of late. I have been consuming more than usual. It would be unattainable to conceal *sensing* me, though, given our connection. I'll admit… he has remarkable control over his powers. It's rare to witness such a feat in an ordinary mortal," he replies, his voice like that of a hell hound's, if one could talk. I hate the way it wraps around the room as if his very words could grip my neck if he so desired.

I eye the glass that Soren drank out of, watching the last legs of the rum drip back down into the well of the chalice. "He doesn't trust me, or what we're doing with Tempest. He will see through it. He is a massive liability."

"The Scorpion's daughter will fix it all," Misery croons. "Soren is quite distracted by her. It's her first act of service to my cause, whether she realizes it or not."

I look at the floor in front of the fallen god, unable to call him by his true name, even in my mind—*Morvock*. It's as if every time I do, his power saturates the room; acknowledgement, or worship, nourishes his existence. I can't give him any more of what I have, though. Just because I need him, doesn't mean he doesn't scare the shit out of me.

Even *I* have to admit that what Misery plans for Jane is barbaric.

"Does Soren know who she is? That she's Ritter's daughter?" I ask, anxiously rapping my knuckles on the table.

"He was... hard to read." An otherworldly breeze chills the air, emanating Misery's distaste.

Gods I'll never get used to him.

If I were one of Misery's fanatics, I might find some demented enjoyment in being so close; to *feed* him with my own energy. But all I want is what I'm promised, then to be as far away from this fucker as possible when this is all done.

Looking out one of the windows to prevent despair from leeching under my skin, I survey the ocean skies. I imagine a day when I can sail those waters as *mine*. "I still think the others should know about who Jane really is, rather than let Soren put on this show. They're all catching on to the fact that I'm plotting something."

"And ruin good bait? The Scorpion's heart still beats, although I can't sense his location. Soren inspires many when he's out for blood. Miss Ritter will lead them both astray, and Tempest will meet her fates out in the Crimson Isles while destroying Basilisk... then we restore my body, and you will have nothing else to ask for in your lifetime."

It's like making a deal with a kraken.

Misery adds, "You may come out, now."

It's always a relief when another person interacts with Misery alongside me, as if affirming I'm not suffering from insanity. I scoot my chair on the wood to watch as a door to my private sitting room opens, revealing a *very* capable man by the name of Shade. His attire is like all the rest with leathers, buckles, weapons, and an addition of chain mail on his thighs that clink with every step.

A howler monkey with fur so black it's like a moving abyss springs out on pattering feet, its eyes two giant orbs of molten orange to match its master's. The animal leaps up onto Misery's shoulder, and I have no fucking desire to learn about *why*, out of all the animals, he has a *monkey*.

The only relevant part is that it's connected to Misery, like an extension of him. And unlike the god it's tied to, the monkey cannot take on the power of invisibility; it's often locked away in my chambers of this castle, or in Misery's.

Shade, too, lowers his gaze whenever it nears the miasmic corner. "Yes, my lord?"

Misery turns his oppressive gaze to Shade. "Do you have word on locating Ritter?"

It's so unnatural seeing someone as bold as Shade to seem almost meek; even at a young age, he feared nothing. "No, my lord. He's elusive."

A grating sound emanates from Misery that makes both Shade and I lower our heads even further. "So is your use to me, then, if that's true."

"I do believe that there's something he's doing that makes him hard to find," Shade swiftly adds.

"That is painfully obvious if *I* can't sense him," Misery snaps. "I suppose it was wishful thinking on my end, as it's not your true purpose. Both Soren and Jane will be residing at Rosmertta's in the near future. I can see *that*, at the very least, which is why you were chosen. Use that to your advantage as a guard there. Wherever Jane is, Ritter will be close. He always has been. I can sense *that* much, as well." The burning eyes shift to examine a large black ring encircling his finger, its surface glistening darkly as if forged from the depths of an abyss. "We need Soren removed, or wounded, before making an attempt. I will inform you where to be at the right time. It will be up to *you* to take advantage of it."

"Understood," Shade replies, a hunger in there that gives me some confidence he might actually succeed. He's always been impulsive, even as a child. Hopefully, it won't ruin him here.

The glowing gaze flits down as Misery reaches into his robe, pulling out an antiquated bronze pocket watch on a matching chain, fluidly opening it as he stares at worn patina. I've seen the watch up close only twice, and it doesn't read wherever north lies

It tells Misery the direction of calamity. A faint, red light slowly illuminates as it's opened and fades before he clenches it shut with a *smack*. "And beware of rubies."

GHOSTS

JANE

CRACK.

A powerful wave of thunder rides in the wake of lightning, flashing through the storage room of the bakery.

Anya stands at the threshold, running a hand over her damp, dark hair as she says, "There's a man that says he's the Scorpion."

Fear seals my lungs, the battering storm defeaning my mind. It's an energy from the seas I used to find comforting as a child, but now it just reminds me how real Skull's Row is.

How real the *Scorpion* is.

The pelting rain grows heavier, allowing me to pant without hearing it. My heart feels so visible with Soren here; he's no doubt reading a part of me that *I'm* not even familiar with anymore.

"Don't retreat." Soren's deep voice brushes against my ear.

9

I don't know if it's desperation or that he's truly earned my trust —even if a sliver of it—but by the gods do I want to let him help me carry this.

Turning my head to glance at him through the dim, stormy lighting, I quietly ask, "Is it actually him? Can you feel him?"

Being close enough to see the details of his irises, it's as if he's everywhere underneath my skin, moving his energy through me wherever he pleases. "It's probably him, Jane. I'd bet a lot of gold on it. I saw him before the strike landed."

The words don't sink in, denial guiding my mind more than any truth; the unseen wounds that beg to rip open cannot be hidden anymore, and I'm not ready.

This is too sudden.

The rough touch of the Zenith brushes against my chin, gripping me with just enough force so I can't look away from him. Soren repositions from his slight lean, his face grimacing with the movement. "Do you *want* to meet him?"

The estranged man that is connected to so many frayed edges of my soul is right outside this door, holding answers to questions that I've lost countless nights over.

"Do I—" my lips rise and close as I struggle to finish, "Do I have a *choice?*"

His scarred brow slightly perks in consideration, speckled blood dotting his face. "I can make it very difficult for him."

"What do you mean you'll make it difficult? You need to *rest.*" My heart *begs* to focus on *Soren* rather than the Scorpion. "No, you lost a lot of blood," I plainly state.

"I have many surrounding us, at all times. I don't need to do it *myself.*"

Well, he thinks of everything, doesn't he?

I almost smile at Soren's confidence, but that sentiment fails to reach my face.

The notion that I can say 'no' almost makes it more real; the power to tell the Scorpion to go away breathes life into him. In all my days of hatefully missing him, I never considered I might actually desire avoiding the betrayer.

My silence spans longer than I realize as Soren banks his head to the side. "Jane?"

"I'm—I'm frozen, I think," I mutter, blood pounding in my ears.

Staring into eyes that haunt and soothe me all at once, I wait for him to continue, to further proclaim what my heart desires—to *tell* me I want to see my father, so I can believe it.

The mere *possibility* that the truth of what happened to me is at my fingertips, terrifies me like nothing has in a long time. Words hover on my lips until they feel entirely natural to say, "Tell me what I want."

His eyes widen with intrigue as they pierce through me with greed. "What you want? What you *want* is for me to make it all go away, love. Which I could, but it's not what you *need*. It's not what is supposed to happen." His voice is steady and smooth against the wicked winds of my soul, yet grave enough that I hear the advice. "I'd get this over with."

Releasing a hot sigh, I worry my lip and avert my gaze. The warmth I wanted from Soren is now cold within a heavy loneliness. I know situations like this—I either cower, or fight. No one can change that.

"Fine," I say, tilting my head back, my lips wordlessly moving as my shoulders heavily rise and fall. "Even if briefly. Just get this part over with."

Soren's free hand gestures to Anya, to which she swiftly disappears, and my stomach might as well have fallen clear out of my asshole because I feel as hollow as a vase.

Straighten your shoulders, Jane.

As soon as they rise up, I'm slumping again. In Soren's shadow, I find that my years of conditioning and survival are so hard to recognize.

He's making me too vulnerable.

As I wait for the sound of two sets of footprints, I swear all I hear is the lighter ones of Anya until it's just her in the threshold, concern written across her face. "He's gone."

The words penetrate instantly, but my understanding is incapable. I'm on my feet before realizing, moving past Anya to stare at the doorway that *he* might have stood in. The empty threshold only brings in natural light, rain pattering on puddles outside. My legs move on their own as I bolt out of the building, my brows furrowed to help keep the wetness out of my eyes, searching for him.

What the fuck?

The initial hesitation flies away like a fragile piece of cloth I clung to, only to realize how light and useless it was against the wind. No, now I'm *pissed*.

He *owes* me. *I'm* the one that gets to decide if he leaves or not.

My concern instantly reroutes back to Soren, and I track in mud as I hurry inside. He stares right at me, blood still all over him and the floor.

"He's gone," I confirm.

"He *was* here." Soren glances down at his own blood as if it might help him concentrate better. Probably is, but just on the surrounding energies.

"Let's get you back," I suggest, motioning to Soren. I'm so tired of these games while someone *real* is in front of me. There's also an immensely heavy conclusion that my father being gone for so long means he wasn't *missing*. What if... what if he could have reached out, but he just *didn't*?

I want to feel *anything*, but I can't even cry.

After downing many ladles of water, Soren finally stands, even if slowly, and throws a cloak over his bare shoulders. He tucks part of it behind his sword to clear the hilt that his hand rests on it while giving a nod to the both of us, not even bothering to clean his skin. I cover my own head, just wanting out of here. I can bandage and clean him once at Rosmertta's.

It's almost better this way, as all the feelings of dealing with my father's supposed return can now safely settle as I follow this Zenith out of the bakery without another word.

Soren is what matters now.

Once we're back in the diluted sunlight, it's as if whatever happened is nothing but a mere rumor; no men are training, and the area is rather deserted. My heart races when I'm quite aware that everyone has probably entered some sort of agreed-upon formation in response to what happened, which means we're not safe.

My feet move one after the other, my shoes slightly soaking from the puddles, already eager to get somewhere warm and dry. *Numb it. Numb the entire thing.*

"Jane," Soren very quietly adds, slowing so as to close the space between us. "If something goes wrong in these streets, my people will appear, and two will grab you. This is a reminder that you *do not* fight them."

I nod, having been told this before. It still does something to me that he has entire formations in line for my safety, like he's truly my protector in all of this. Soren faces forward again after raking his gaze over me, and as we walk, I do a double-take when we pass a storefront nestled between larger buildings. A long, wooden sign hangs on chains that reads *Caraham Apothecary*, which gently moves within the soft breeze.

Nostalgia seeps deep into my bones as I recall the many apothecary goods that mother used, with *that* name scribed on them. "We need to visit there," I quickly say.

Soren glances over his shoulder, rain dripping down his cloaked head before peering at where I gesture. "I don't want to stop," he replies, his words carrying an extra length that I've heard from someone whose body is on the brink of exhaustion. "Something is changing in the air, and I honestly want to get the fuck out of here."

"Well, good luck trying to escape without a blood tonic. It won't take long for me to make one, but I need supplies and ingredients. I highly doubt Rosmertta's has everything, and we're right here."

I *will* get it with or without his approval. I doubt he can carry me far in this state, which means if he chucks me over his shoulder, I can probably wriggle away if necessary.

He *needs* this. I don't like how pale he is. And I'm useful for once, when all I've felt like is a burden, bounty, or just in everyone's way.

I miss carrying purpose.

Soren's gaze is heavy with concern, but his subtle gesture to Anya, followed by her course correction to the apothecary, surges a sense of hope I haven't felt in a very long time.

It's been so long since I visited a *proper* apothecary.

As soon as we commit, I run a mental list of what I need so I can be as quick as possible. We cross the wide street, veering through horse-drawn carriages as street sweepers clean up any shit left behind. It reminds me of stepping back in time, when I once would have followed my mother rather than Anya.

She's the first to step onto the wooden porch, turning the worn brass knob to open the door on its squeaky hinges, standing aside so

I can enter—there are at least a dozen people visiting. Stepping into a place that smells entirely of herbs and metal, it's immediately darker and taller than the outside appears, with a high, sloping ceiling that extends to a second story. Narrow windows grant in what little light the storm conceals. If it were sunnier, light beams would shine down below.

I'm a little sad to see they aren't hanging stained glass that the sun used to catch. Skull's Row is so gloomy and dangerous, and I used to love seeing the rare display of colors.

The weight of Soren creating deeper *thuds* on the floor tells me he's inside, and that he stops *just* behind me.

The present. Not the past.

As much as I want to explore every ingredient, I need to grab what's required and get out of here. I snag one of the wicker baskets in the front and immediately look for the first thing I can find. If I can avoid asking *anyone* for help, it's for the best. We don't want eyes on us right now, and Soren's size and visible sword are already making it impossible to blend in.

I untuck the hair behind my ears to cover the ruby earrings—I've been wearing them every day to feel closer to Mom—and pinch my earlobes to double-check they're both there.

No need to draw attention to those, either.

When I glance over my shoulder, Soren's body blocks the view, but I can see Anya standing outside through the window. My heart races a little faster, reminded that we need to be swift.

"What are you getting?" Soren asks, his gravelly rumble always penetrating my anxiety.

Facing forward, I drag my finger on a shelf in an invisible line to ground my search for dragon root. "Things I require to create a tonic my mother taught me. It helps rejuvenate your blood. It's not a miracle cure, but it helps rejuvenate the ability to be back on your feet in a week, maybe less, versus a few weeks to over a month. Especially if I can make a large batch that you can nurse over the coming days."

When I set my eyes on the stringy, dried brown strands of dragon root, I swiftly grab three bundles to put in the basket, now peering around for crushed siren's whelk.

"And how are you paying, exactly?"

A smile spreads on my face as I scan the area for oceanic objects. "I figured you'd take care of that." My gaze stops on a pestle that an older woman examines in her hands, extending her arms as if the distance makes it clearer.

Oh, a *pestle* is a good idea. Should I buy one, or hope Rosmertta has one of her own? Surely they have tools, if not the ingredients.

Get the consumable bits first. In and out. People are staring.

Soren huffs out a laugh behind me. "Have you ever even earned your own gold? Or just always take it?"

"Oh, I know how to earn my own." I glance back at him with a smirk. "But I also enjoy a good five-finger discount. Not my fault if things aren't well-guarded. *Except* for somewhere like this. Caraham deserves to be paid. He works very hard."

There's a slight play in Soren's eyes when they connect with mine. "Don't know why I expected anything else." He picks up a vial of very green liquid, and I catch the word *essence* on the side.

"Don't be so beat up I stole your coin. I used to be an *expert* pick pocket."

"At *eleven*? Or were you stealing from people at Talon's Perch, too?"

I scan the area for the familiar captain's wheel—which will indicate the section I need—with a giant smile. "Fine, I was a *prodigy* who retired at eleven. Never took much when we did. Just enough for us all to buy sweetened cream."

"There was more than one of you?" I catch the way he sounds genuinely intrigued.

"A little gang of us kids. We tried to defend those that were taken advantage of... and then steal from others that were right assholes. Or from people that just wouldn't notice it."

Saying that out loud and breathing life into an identity I've kept locked under key for so long feels like touching the wisp of a ghost.

Finally, I spot the captain's wheel on the floor, leaning against the wall—when it should be hanging—and quickly enter through the small doorway to peek around the corner. There's a decent-sized room in the back with a window and alternate door for entry, leading to another narrow street on the backside.

"Shade?" I ask before I can even process what comes out of my mouth.

The fighter from when Kathleen and I met at Rosmertta's is already watching the spot right where I stand, and I don't like the look in his eyes. There's a greed that shouldn't be directed at me, and the five men in the back all seem to be the same—the only items in their hands are all of the stabbing kind.

An immediate sense of this encounter being *entirely* above my ability is all I process, especially when one of them is within arm's reach. One man stands beside an active hearth, grabbing a boiling cauldron hanging over the fire, as if waiting for this; he even has gloves on. In the same instance, every single pair of eyes moves over my head.

My body reacts instinctively as I step in front of the threshold— even an *ounce* of their hesitation will give Soren an edge.

The man nearly drops the cauldron to try and stop his throw of what's in the pail, but it's all for nothing as boiling water soaks my body.

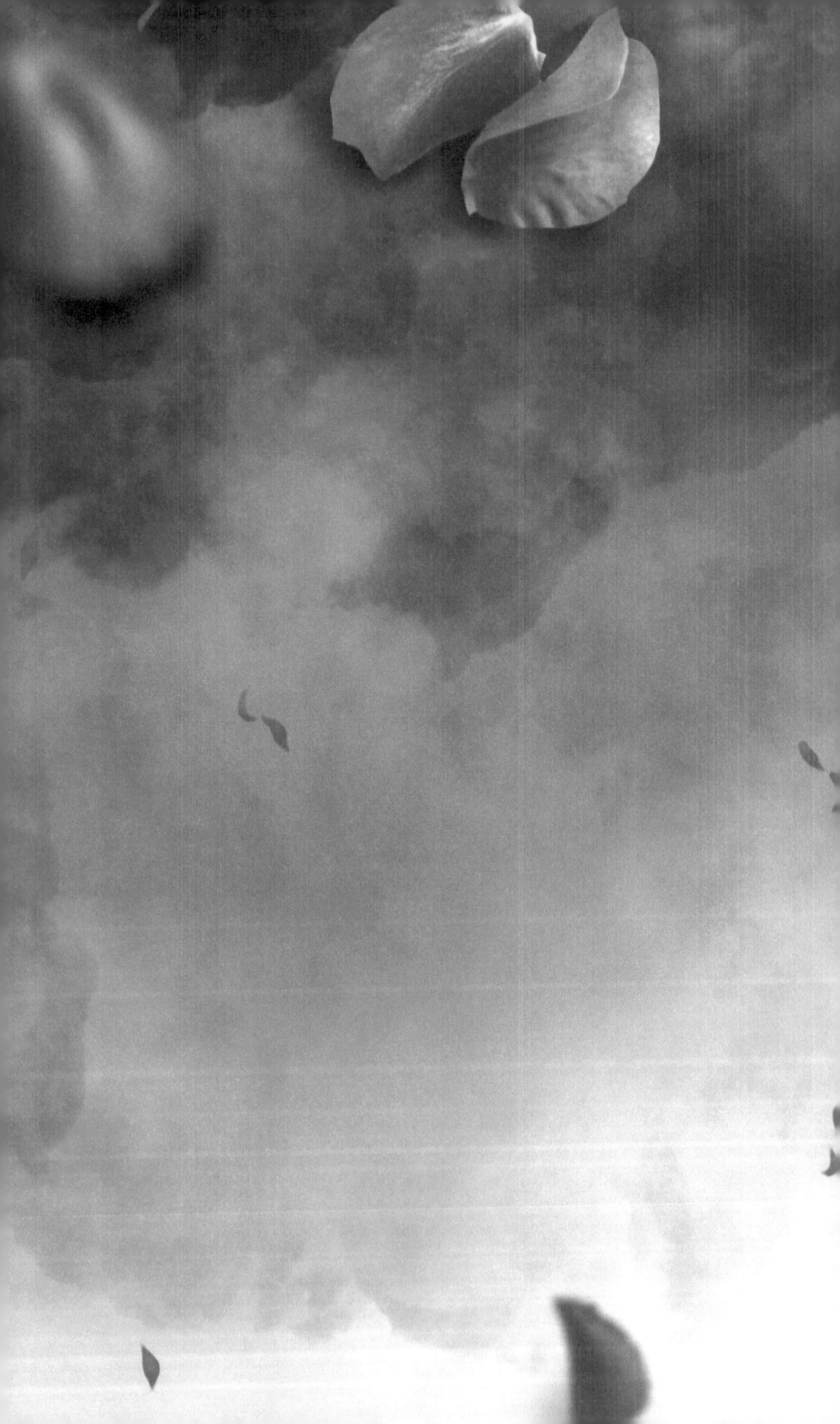

BOILING WATER

JANE

Life really does move slowly when shit gets real.

I'm not even sure what possessed me to do this, other than an instinct from all the bar fights and getting in the way of Kathleen if someone threatened her; I could always heal what's thrown at me.

That's what I told myself.

A scream tears from the depths of my chest in pure shock. I've seen boiled skin before, and even if one recovers… it's a debilitating injury that haunts someone to the grave.

Shit—fuck. Heal yourself! Now! What do I tend first? What if my hands are too injured? Are they—

I don't even have time to process as a fight breaks out; my body coils with white-hot fear. Pain flares at my scalp as I'm quickly

19

pulled down by my hair—which hurts more than my skin—and someone throws a blade so close to my head it might have sheared a few hairs off. Shade barks out furious shouts, something about 'ruining my skin,' but I—I can't feel a thing, except for the cold rain as it hits my face when I'm half-dragged, half-shoved outside through the back door that slams open. Once I'm fully in the street, another shuts the door to lock the rest inside, smacking a bar down to barricade it.

Math. Add. How many outside? Two of them… three are inside with Soren…

I'm trying to maintain balance on my feet to alleviate the searing pain at my roots, but frequently tumble as my feet struggle to keep up with the pace. The sound of a gnarly fight continues in the apothecary, thuds echoing through the wall. Glass shatters, followed by a war cry cut short, and then the sharp clang of metal on metal.

A body even smashes through the window, the man's throat slit as his head looks half-decapitated.

Not Soren. Please don't be Soren.

The burning pain ceases from my scalp as my hair is released. I'm then weightless as Shade picks me up from underneath my shoulders, walking backward. Another man secures my legs around his waist, facing forward.

What of the burns?

I try my best to examine the back of Caraham's, my face flinching as the wooden bar splits open all over the street, the door nearly bursting off its hinges as Soren lunges out of it with heavy panting, his large sword in hand, his eyes locking with mine before I lose him around a corner.

"Oh fuck, he killed Benny, Jack, and Alex! You said he was injured! I told you we shouldn't do this!" The man who holds my legs yells.

"I bet she fucking healed him," Shade replies. "We need to throw her in that wagon right behind me!"

I look up, still dazed, still dreading to experience the pain from the boiling water, concerned about moving too much in case there's fragile skin.

No pain.

I can even see the raindrops right before they fall on my face, as if there's nothing in the world to distract me. *I should be barely able to breathe.*

"She isn't burned," the other one remarks.

"Good—I'll get her in, and you hold her down in the back. We'll ride to the Spiraling Stone. We'll make it work."

I stare at the belt of the one that holds my thighs, breathing slowly as the options run through my mind. *Soren has men watching, but can I do anything?*

"Are there others, Shade?"

"It's just us," Shade confesses, his grip under my arms already digging too deeply into my skin, the pain making me wince. "I didn't want to wait. He was injured, like we needed him. He wasn't—just hurry the fuck up!"

The thin street clears out, people scattering like clockwork to avoid getting caught up in whatever the hells these men are doing with me; it's instinctual to duck low and keep out of the way—

Without warning, the man *stops.* Shade's momentum keeps my body moving as I slide out of the other man's grip, who falls to his knees.

Oh, fuck.

That asshole's head is sliced clean off.

Shade releases me, pivoting to grip my wrist and then my throat—my airway is immediately constricted, and my wrist fucking *hurts.*

When our eyes meet, Shade's intense, rage-filled eyes morph like a skin shifter's if they could shift emotions; fear *consumes* him. He looks at my jaw, or the side of it? I'm not sure, but he lets go and just *takes off,* pushing over a cart of goods behind him as the contents spill out, probably the same one he planned to chuck me in.

Someone is already grabbing underneath my arm, and I flail at being touched, my blood running so hot I can't feel the cold rain. "Stop flailing like a dying pigeon," says a voice I know all too well.

I glance up at Bones, his hair wet as rain runs down his face. Blood is splattered all over his outfit, and I look at the decapitated body that spurts out what's left of the corpse to mix with the rainwater. Bones raises an axe in his other hand, eyeing the crimson liquid on his cold steel. "Shade won't get far. Don't worry. We'll catch that cunt. Have *no* idea what he's thinking."

A woman near us selling oranges yells out, "Oi! Don't get my fruit bloodied! This street was supposed to be safer than Doggins!"

"He was taking me. Something about seeing an opening with Soren," I get out through a pant.

Bone's mismatched eyes flash with a depth of cunning that is usually hidden behind a bedlam personality. Bones completely ignores her, and it's really the first time I've seen him this concentrated. With the way he normally acts, it would be hard to guess someone calculated lives in there.

"Bones, what's happening?" I ask, searching the area for Soren. "Shade was with *Rosmertta*. He was a guard there."

"No fucking idea," he replies with a gritty tone, looking in the same direction as me. "But let's get out of the middle of the street. And if Soren doesn't appear soon, I'm giving the signal, so be ready."

As it was explained to me, Bones is expected to always appear first, keeping a skirmish to a minimum so I can be extracted with little notice, unless a cue is indicated. I don't answer him as my hands roam my neck and face. "Am I burned at all?"

He frowns, looking at me like I might have hit my head. "What, no. We have to move."

"Bones, they threw boiling water on me," I implore, trying to find *any* spot that might be blistering.

"Are you sure you're alright, dying pigeon?"

"I—I guess," I answer, dumbstruck. "I mean, I guess I am. Okay… okay, let's go."

I can figure that out later.

As we step to the side to walk along the walls, a few men move out of the alley adjacent to us, with a rather large one in the very front. Bones is swift to shove me back, releasing me to grab ahold of a second axe on his backside. *Another* set of hands are on my shoulder right away, and I see it's someone I don't know the name of, but I've seen their face countless times with Soren.

He's not alone.

The man who faces Bones is a stranger, clearly aged and beyond his prime, yet still easily matches Soren's height and thickness. His gray beard is braided and bristly, one eye completely milky. His worn leather contrasts his freshly sharpened steel—the only thing about him that doesn't look threadbare.

Slowly, a handful of similar men reveal themselves from either alley, all with the same milky eye. With each one that emerges, so does another that belongs to Soren—whether it's on a rooftop, or from down the street.

"You with Shade, old salty dog?" Bones asks.

He sucks his lip to his graying teeth and spits on the ground. "We're not with any man that runs as cowardly as him."

Each word sounds as if it's been scraped up from the bottom of his chest, finished with a rasping undertone.

"You want to clarify what you want then, or just going to stand there? We got shit to deal with," Bones says.

"He'll probably just stand there," says a new, smoky voice whose warmth contrasts so greatly with this cold weather. "Rorge doesn't have much of a personality. Unless there's tobacco."

Many heads turn to look behind us. I notice only Bones continues to face forward while I observe a woman approaching from our backside. At least both her onyx eyes match, standing out against her bronze skin. White streaks line her curly black hair, which is pulled back into a partial bun, the rest of it lying on her shoulders, the rain sitting on it in pebbles. Her leathers are well-fitted, and the blades sheathed along her are purposefully placed. "I'm Donna. Anyway, what Rorge means to say is that it's time to meet the Scorpion. No more delays. We'll deal with whatever the hells just happened outside of this. We still need to move."

So, *not* related to Shade?

"You can fuck right off if you think I'm trusting you," I reply with a tight tone, not liking that Soren doesn't seem to be visible anywhere.

"We're here to take you to the Scorpion," she explains, nodding toward us, hands in the pockets of her cloak. "He was unable to fulfill his appearance just now."

I'm starting to regret thinking that Coalfell was too boring for me. The stress of wondering what is going on, and why there are people staring at me as if I'll disappear if they blink, is beyond exhausting. Let alone why so many have their left eye completely white, as if they all lost the same sword fight.

Panting, I turn back around, *refusing* to leave without Soren, or entertain these people for a moment without his input.

There's so many watching us, but mostly from cracked curtains behind windows. *Rumors of this will spread swiftly.*

When no one moves, not even Bones, an aching solitude blooms rapidly in my chest as the stillness allows me to feel Soren's absence—

"Soren," I breathe out when the brute moves around the corner with a bloodied blade in hand, cloak gone, and his thick chest is on full display. A man trails the Zenith, also seeming to have the same milky eye. The stranger even tries to stop Soren, who scowls almost like an animal defending its space. The violence in his eyes is so different from back at Moore's Inn with that stupid mayor's cousin —this is *real* bloodshed.

Soren's gaze is all over the wet, dingy street as he strides forward, his body moving in a straight line toward me through the drizzling rain until he's close enough that his gaze snaps to me, rapidly taking me in, his chest heaving. Bones steps to the side to keep an eye on the street, Rorge clearing his throat in the background like his chest is a rumbling inferno.

Soren touches my face before trailing that hand down to expose the skin on my chest, slightly pulling my tunic side to side. "No burns..." he comments with clear relief. "You don't feel like you're in pain, either."

I didn't anticipate the way it would make me feel to have someone like him—an impossible bastard to get close to—analyzing my body as if the state of me matters. To feel me out as if my pain might hurt him, too.

"Yeah," I state, squinting when rain hits my eye, my mind so effortlessly derailed by him. "I don't know how I'm not burned. I'm glad you're okay."

Soren deeply inhales before his hand moves to the back of my neck, pulling me closer as he looks over his shoulder at the world around us. It's almost instantaneous how his touch calms my anxiety, especially as I'm pressed right up on his warm, exposed skin, breathing in his sweat while he's protecting me.

"I wouldn't hold her close like we're not taking her, Zenith,"

Rorge warns, Soren's hand still firm on my nape. "We are Ritter's men. We are here to collect her."

Collect me.

If I wasn't so damn curious about my father, I'd be more annoyed at how everyone is pulling on me, as if they'll win a prize for being the one to catch me. At least with Soren, I'll be able to tell if they're lying or not.

In all this madness, my heart leans heavily on him, completely trusting that man.

A tightening of his hand on my nape, along with pulling me even closer, feels like an acknowledgment of what I just felt for him.

"Why did he appear and leave?" Soren asks. Despite fighting what I know has to be exhaustion, his voice easily carries through the quiet street as he addresses them. "Is Shade with you? Was that why he took her just now? To take her for the Scorpion?"

"No, we're just as shocked at that man's behavior as you are. The Scorpion appeared at first because he thought it was clear," the woman named Donna answers from behind, and I glance over my shoulder once again. "But then it wasn't, so he had to abandon plans. It's been hard to approach Miss Jane without eyes on us. And clearly, they were," she explains, biting her bottom lip. "Which is why we need to go. *Now.* Shade coming for her confirms our suspicions that she's in more danger than ever because he's not working with us. He's working with *Blackwell.*"

Oh, *fuck.*

"Well, that dumb cunt will be caught shortly, if he hasn't already been." Irritation is undeniable in Soren's tone. "I want the smoke and mirrors over with, so get us out of these damn streets."

My heart nearly launches out of my chest at hearing we're doing this. "Are they actually here for him?" I quietly ask Soren. "Can you feel that they're with my dad? This isn't a trap?"

"They're all stained with his energy," Soren confirms, an edge in his tone that keeps me apprehensive. "Nothing about this feels like an illusion."

The old, leaden man who first confronted us grunts. "Your troupe can follow, but if they get in the way, we *will* create a barrier. Scorpion's orders."

Emotions hit through me like a barrel being slung around on a stormy, craggy coastline. My dad gave orders to protect me, too? I... I don't even have words for what's happening inside of me. Since when do I have so many people in my life who care this much?

Except for Kathleen... my racing heart calms. I *cannot* let my emotions get the best of me when she's probably still at Rosmertta's. I need a steady head on my shoulders if I'm to help her.

"Kathleen is at Rosmertta's. It's not safe," I quietly remark. "Someone has to get her."

"The men with me will have taken care of that."

I glance at his chest. "Really? She's a part of your plans?"

"Kathleen is a target of manipulation for you. She's heavily watched and guarded."

Oh, that makes sense.

Without much transition, the lot of us move like a current; it's an awkward integration of who walks where and what formation we take. Soren's grip loosens on me, but his hand still remains on my back. If I wasn't certain that he was feeling out every damn corner, I would be more dubious. But he can feel the energy of the environment, right? Surely his powers will hint at something being wrong?

He didn't sense Shade, though. Or did he? Is it the blood loss getting to him?

As we pass through the alleys, I notice the same people trail alongside as well in other streets, and I imagine if I were a bird to fly above, I'd see an amalgamation of people all moving in the same direction, wherever we're going. I'm now paying attention to any abnormalities, or patterns, that could indicate a signal. How will Soren's men know if they're needed? They can't *all* fit in the narrow alleys. Does he have enough?

Then again, I barely know a thing about how this world works as an adult. And now, after an agonizing era of silence and boredom in my life, two very accomplished Zenith are crossing lines, over *me*.

Best face on, Jane. It's time to see Dad.

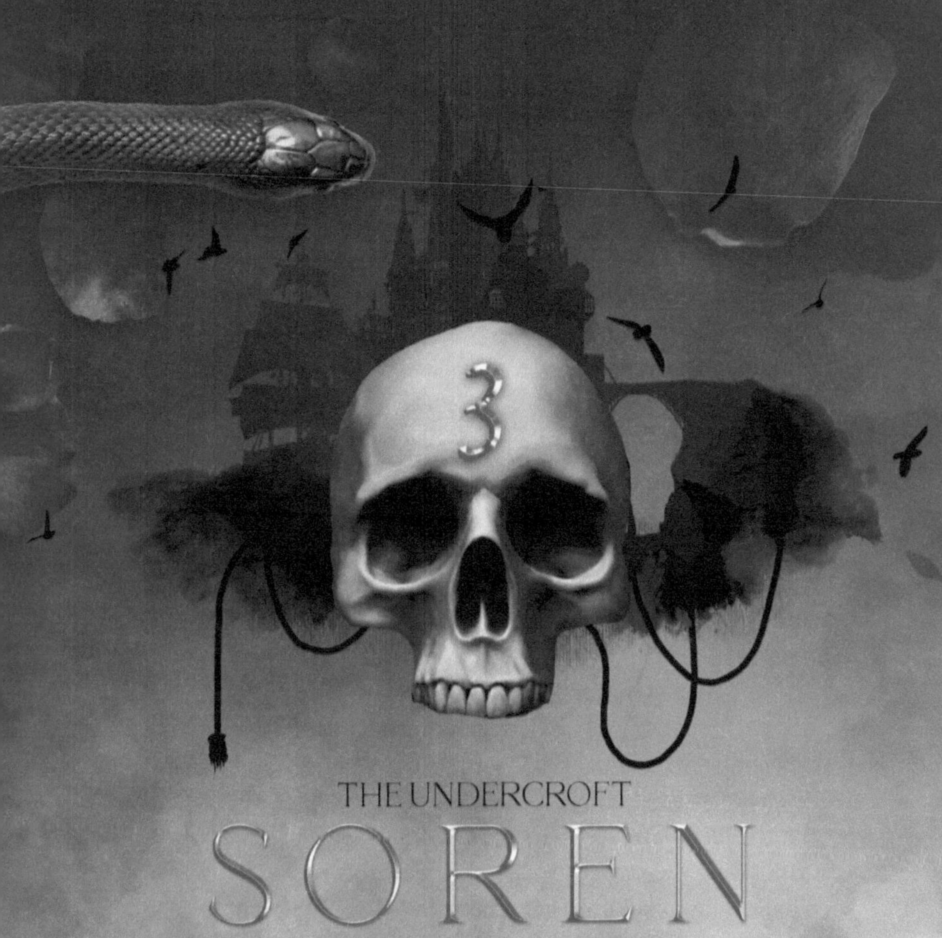

THE UNDERCROFT
SOREN

This moment is like the eerie howl as a hurricane nears—there's no telling how much time we have before the devastation strikes, only knowing that it's coming.

The scent of wet soil and stone fills my lungs as the rain continues to trickle. Bruised clouds promise that the entire day will be like this, which means *more* chilling droplets seeping through the seams of the wool cloaks that are given to us—well, more like Bones grabbed a few when he saw them.

I still don't know where we're being taken or what the hells is happening. All I do know is that everything feels entirely smooth in my chest, a confirmation that this is safe, despite my mind screaming at me that it isn't.

Then again, maybe I'm like a fucking broken clock, and I'm only right because that's what logic dictates. I didn't sense *anything* from Shade. The room felt as plain as the rest of the apothecary, the only threat or danger coming from the heavy energy that constantly surrounds *Jane*.

Many move quickly on the streets when the rain picks up, their feet landing in wet smacks. Despite the sheer number of moving souls that create an overpowering exchange of auras, I have no trouble locking onto Jane, even if her pretty hair is covered as she blends into the rest. It's as if her presence is so much louder than everyone else's, like the others are black and white while hers is a bright auburn.

I *should* throw her over my shoulder and leave this place while we still can, but my magic pulls me fiercely to face the Scorpion.

Unpacking the events at the apothecary, one detail blatantly stands out to me. "Did you heal yourself? Your skin is completely unmarred."

"No, I didn't. I… I didn't have *any* burns."

What? That makes no sense. "You should be burned, Jane. I don't know what's happening right now, but I want to leave this city *immediately* when we're done."

Fuck this place and whatever is going on. I need people I trust surrounding me, not the shady shit of Skull's Row. That was a sickening feeling to not only witness *boiling water* thrown on Jane, but to be gutted by the sensation that I failed so miserably.

I like order and efficiency, but failing to protect those I care for… Serena's face, wide-eyed and full of trust… guilt coils around my heart like iron chains. Seeing Jane being carried off by Shade was a cruel joke from the fates, as if I've been written into the same script twice.

It's the unbearable acceptance that despite all my strength and all my training, it's not enough. To make the guilt worse, she stepped in front of me with no hesitation.

"I honestly have no idea what's happening. I was *soaked*, and yet the only thing that actually hurt was him pulling on my hair," she murmurs in response, vexation, and confusion intertwining in her heart, her teeth slightly chattering.

For a moment, I thought perhaps Shade was working with the Scorpion, and that's why I didn't give a signal. Not with Bones out there. Perhaps the Scorpion wanted to steal Jane from me, and that's why he also disappeared; out of everything, the only thing I *could* feel was that dumbass meant to soak *me* with the water, not Jane. "What exactly happened?"

"Shade wanted me for something. It seemed spur of the moment. That's when Bones came in and lopped a head off. Shade then looked at me and it was like he saw a ghost before running for it. He's such a little *bitch*." She cranes her head to look up at me over her shoulder, a few wet strands of her hair stuck to her face. Her rosy cheeks and nose tell me we don't have much more time out here in this condition; we're all dressed in leathers, not wool. "And I'm angry because we *still* don't have anything for you. You need regenerative medicine, especially with all this walking. You're so pale."

Despite the agonizing pain gripping my body, I still can't control the addicting affection that Jane's concern creates within me. She'd never judge me for what I do—she'd only offer to heal, then stab any more offenders for me.

"I'll live." My breathing is labored, but that's not the point. I don't like the way Jane's safety is volatile. The existing undertone of her security being in question has never deteriorated so rapidly; it's as if I expect to see someone around the corner, waiting. *Like with Serena when she was taken...*

Like what happened just now.

My mind blanks.

I can't have that happen again.

"Should we try to leave rather than meet him?" she quietly asks, even if a part of her heart breaks at the idea. "We can only do so much before the cost is too great."

My little desert rose trusts me, even if she can't utter those words herself. My hand that rests on the back of her shoulders slides slightly up in a silent reassurance that her trust isn't unnoticed.

"No, you need this," I insist, even if it drives me mad to utter that.

There's also my own particular *selfish* inclinations—Jane's emotional wounds prevent her from fully giving herself to me. As I once told her, I'm a man before anything else, and I have my own damaged heart that relentlessly chases the things it craves. And I want the violent Zenith's daughter who is weak to me, and I want her vulnerability to *only* be for me. I want to feel her walls completely removed while the rest of the world will *never* be welcomed in.

Jane belongs to *me* now.

So, we will deal with the Scorpion and bury that for good. *Then* I can take her out of here and leave it all behind.

"What if he's..." her voice trails off, and the corner of my lip slightly curls at feeling she's embarrassed.

"*Continue.*"

Her shoulders tense. "What if he's an asshole? What if he has no good reason for what happened?"

Her sentiment damn near pulverizes through me... more than normal, even. It's as if she's learning how to *push* her heart at me.

That is very dangerous, love.

The things I'll make her confess...

"You need closure, Jane. One way or another."

"I'm worried we're doing all of this just for someone who doesn't care about me. This is possibly *idiotic*. It's just for *me*. I can move on without meeting him. I don't—I don't want to risk you at all, alright?"

"Are you growing fond of me, Jane?" I ask with a faint smile.

"I'm mostly fond of you while you're *alive*, rather than dead," she quips.

Within the whirlpool of this surrounding anarchy, this tenderness directed right at me is what *truly* takes me off guard. It's not just her words that brush against me, but the pulse of her emotion— an ache, fierce and protective, like she's holding me at arm's length and clutching me close at the same time. Or perhaps it's not the affection, no, because I've had *that* directed at me... This is different. Her emotions don't just touch mine; they settle, weaving into me with a depth so natural it feels like breathing.

I want to bottle it up. Hold it, preserve it, protect it from the chaos around us. She doesn't just feel for me. She *chooses* me, even when the stakes demand she shouldn't, and the weight of that trust sinks deeper than I'm ready to admit.

"I wish I had a more simple answer, love. But I can tell if we run from this, we *will* regret it. There's something important to your father."

She seems to accept that answer.

It's a good thing *she* can't read *me*. I'm completely on fucking edge. The small calvary here is nothing compared to the loyal legion with the snake crest at home. Maybe we can escape via ship versus land. If we can get south, beyond the Balar Coasts, there's plenty of space to recoup and organize. Write to my mother to tell her to get out and draw attention away from the families who follow me.

Death's Wing is south, and that's a loyalty bound by blood oaths, embedded in our stripes.

When a sudden shot of pain gnaws at my shoulder, I gently touch the very angry gash that's closed on my neck. Jane stopped the bleeding and even bound some of the flesh so perfectly that it forms only the faintest raise of a scar, and yet it still aches as if it's an open wound.

That stupid fucking hit.

I felt the damn strike coming; the pain seared before the blade sliced at my skin. But I knew I had to let it happen; everything told me to claim the injury. To seek out Jane, too.

Although, now I'm wondering if it's not all just a bunch of shit. Clearly, my powers are being manipulated, so what if something can influence my instinct, too?

Rorge gives a hoarse bark to those around as he stops just beneath a lantern with red glass, one that creaks on hinges and hangs over a massive, dark archway.

The fucking Undercroft?

As I glimpse at one of Ritter's men, his milky eye heightens my unease about whatever the fuck is going on here. These men have become the subject of rumors during Anya's reconnaissance, existing as a hushed whisper.

And now they're here, in broad daylight? As a *group*?

It's all too fast; no time for me to truly decipher what I feel. No time to analyze. Thank the fucking gods I can still feel *my* people surrounding us. Bones knows the Undercroft, and Anya even more so.

Even then, I *know* this is moronic. Just like with the harbors, the rules underneath this city don't apply like normal. And damning creatures haunt the tunnels.

Has Ritter been hiding there this entire time?

Jane's persistence eclipses any of her unease, already stepping forward as my hand slides off her back; I prefer to be behind her than in front—better vantage as I can see clear over her head and I'm covering her backside. This time, I'm focusing more on what I see rather than feel. Even so, there's a distortion in the air as we enter, a sensation I swear I've only felt before my sister was taken— the reason I'm here as a Zenith at all.

Every time I think I've honed in on the source of this aberration, the context turns to smoke. It's unnatural, in fact. It reminds me of Cypress and the way she fucks with all our energies.

"I promise the Undercroft won't bite," Donna says from behind. "Not with us, anyway."

"It's not the Undercroft I don't like," I grunt, moving forward, accepting we have no choice. On top of everything, I still want to know how Ritter is tied to my sister. Cypress made it clear that helping the Scorpion's daughter will guarantee answers.

I owe Serena this.

It's a long, slow descent until I can no longer hear the rain, the air thick and musty. Along the way, *wanted* posters stick to the wall, drawings of men and women that have pissed off the wrong people. Garnering a wanted poster is common throughout the lands, but for a city of thieves to post them, the actions have to be doltish, audacious, truly barbaric, or a mixture of all three.

At some point, we pass by another who drags the carcass of a donkey upward by two others, the smell absolutely foul. I'm not shocked, though. Hard to get rid of bodies when there's no soil.

Usually, the pigs are for that.

The tunnels spill out into an open cavern that spans a good three or four stories. Buildings rise haphazardly along the cavern walls, stacked precariously and connected by old wooden walkways. Their windows faintly glow, and the occasional shadow of a figure slips by. Above are large grates that filter in a bluish-gray hue of natural light that gives the Undercroft an otherworldly pallor, water dripping down in a dramatic, glimmering descent.

I always imagined this as an ancient Skull's Row, reclaimed by the cliffs it's built upon, the wood of long-forgotten structures fossilizing into stone like the old world is being slowly digested. The people here are as odd as salty legs, or the weathered bastards that rarely step onto land. There's a tangle of uneven stone pathways and rickety wooden walkways suspended over dark chasms, and I don't want to know how many drunkards or poor souls have accidentally wandered off.

The air buzzes with the murmur of deals being struck, arguments over coin, and the occasional muffled cry quickly silenced. I swear if I see an ocean imp climbing up from the bowels of this city, or a molgrin…

Jane's energy vibrates with uncertainty, anticipation, and longing, sending my gaze all around the discord of auras.

"What is it?" I ask as we momentarily stop when Donna raises a hand.

There it is—the calming effect I have on her. The reaction that I can't get enough of, as if something in my chest tells me I'm *supposed* to make her feel this way.

"This still feels safe?" she asks, gesturing to symbols of thieving guilds etched onto the wall.

"I don't know if my ability to sense anything matters anymore. I couldn't feel Shade in the other room."

She looks up at me in surprise. "*What?*"

Worrying Jane is the least of my desires right now, but I also have to give her the truth in case something happens to us. "I'll examine that later, love. Right now, these men with white eyes fit with the stories I've been hearing about down here, so I trust that. It's better than going to Rosmertta's. You and I both want answers, and this gets us off the streets, and this gets you to see daddy dearest."

She faces forward again, moving when Donna motions for us to follow. "Yes, that's right—your sister, too. He'll help you find her."

It's not just for her, Jane; it's for you.

At some point, a lanky man with unkempt gray hair sharpens his focus on Jane, a mixture of desperation and skill in his gaze. When I turn my head at him, and our eyes meet, the very pleasant reaction of fear completely washes right through him, and he steps away.

I'm quite literally her shield down here.

And I'll gladly leave a trail of blood, if necessary.

The tunnels twist and wind unpredictably—a purposeful design to confuse anyone unfamiliar down here—some so narrow you have to press your back to the cold, jagged walls to squeeze through, others opening into vast, echoing chambers where the darkness seems to stretch infinitely. The stonework is inconsistent—some walls are rough and natural, others are smoothed and adorned with faded carvings and symbols.

Darkness eventually consumes us, the only light emitting from someone carrying a torch as we take a few more turns.

I'll be fucking glad when we've stopped, my head faint from the blood loss, but my core instinct tells me I'll live. Although I don't like how far we're removed from resources. I won't be able to recover on air; I need food and water, at the minimum.

Then I feel *her*.

The fucking witch.

"Are those *rubies*?" Jane asks.

I crane my head up to notice perfectly red ruby crystals growing out of the wall like a fungus.

"Fucking hells," I grumble.

Rorge approaches a spot in the wall and pulls out a crystal neck-lace from underneath his clothes, holding it up to the stone as lines suddenly appear and glow vermilion, forming the outline of a door until the glowing disappears, and then the rock moves and bends to take on the outlined shape.

Then, he takes out an iron key to open the rusty, resistant locks.

As the heavy doors swing open, we're flooded by a rush of sounds. The once-confined space expands, revealing a tall ceiling adorned with flickering torches and mismatched candle chandeliers. Ventilation holes dot the ceilings and floors, allowing fresh air to circulate. The immense chamber is filled with rows of tables occu-pied by people who indulge in lively conversation and drinks. The scent of rich leather, spiced drinks, and polished wood fills my lungs.

And of course, all the fucking rubies growing out of the walls, glinting like bloodied glass in torchlight, and I swear they fucking *pulse*. Rows of long, sturdy tables stretch across the room. And even though it's a rough-hewn lot, there's a cohesiveness I usually find in either armies or ship crews.

The room falls silent as everyone's attention is on us. It's not just curiosity—it's expectation, a charged stillness that sharpens as their auras shift in unison. Rorge doesn't stop, continuing to guide us towards the left.

Then I feel *his* energy.

It's subtle, just like at the training grounds and the bakery. It's something I don't even have the words for, but it's the weight someone carries when they're not only a Zenith, but a respected one. Almost as if the magic of the black skull mask marks them for me.

Who would have thought that one day, I'd be bringing the Scorpion his daughter?

I'm ready to meet this bastard, so her heart can properly scar over, so I can hold it for myself.

Stone gives way to wood-covered ceilings as we enter a room that smells of aged, salty timber and candle wax. Barrels furnish the space with carved-out seats. Rope that's threaded tightly holds a candle chandelier whose smoke doesn't darken the wood above— made from the forests of Skull's Row then. Wreckage from a repurposed ship?

Not the point. I focus internally on what my body is processing. I'm aware of the location in the room that claims to harbor Ritter's energy, but I look everywhere *else* first, exploring the push and pull of those who serve him and wondering where the fuck Cypress is.

None seem surprised to see me, either. My skull mask means very little among other Zenith, other than as a last-ditch reminder that if I disappear, *many* people will hunt them down.

The three stripes on my back guarantee that.

Assurances bought with blood and oaths.

It's Jane's utter confusion staining her aura that makes me look to where I can feel *his* energy. My brows knit into a deep furrow.

"Ern?" Jane's voice is a stark difference in the room, and it all quiets.

Her eyes fixate on a man who comfortably leans on one armrest of a meticulously crafted seat fashioned from reclaimed wood and iron; the top curled into the tail of a scorpion.

The man looks *exactly* like Ern from Ern's Tavern, and it even stuns me to see him sitting in a seat that clearly doesn't belong to him, and yet everyone here acts as if it does.

I stare so intently at someone who's supposed to be a barkeep that it's *impossible* to miss the way I can't read a single thing from him.

A curt gesture from Ern empties the room.

As everyone departs, I'm even more aware that Ern is someone with a unique identity, and yet the signature of his aura is empty. *Why does Ern feel so much like the Scorpion when I didn't feel this before? Wouldn't Jane have known if Ern was her father? Is something wrong with her memory?*

And why can't I feel him?

No emotions.

No fluctuation in what he feels.

No information.

Jane's disappointment and confusion makes me angry, because if this is a rouse—

As the last person leaves the room, Ern's face changes in ways that make even *my* jaw drop. His face elongates, his nose sharpens, and his facial hair rescinds to reveal a clean face. Tattoos emerge where clear skin was.

The Scorpion.

THE SCORPION

JANE

My jaw drops from blinding uncertainty. "What the fuck."

"Of *course*," Soren growls.

It's… *him*.

My father's face.

Familial roots, miserable feelings of abandonment, and over a decade of loneliness collide into a wreckage. My breath is utterly robbed from me as I take in how the Scorpion is dressed unpretentiously in black pants with a messy gray tunic tucked into it. A long black leather coat shrouds him, one with tattered edges.

He's so simple, yet sharp, in appearance.

I have spent many nights envisioning a reunion, about how we might embrace. How I *yearned* to hear him validate everything that happened, to tell me it will be okay. Those expectations, however, leave my heart as if they never existed; I can't read his face, or make sense of the eyes that roam over me.

Distant.

He doesn't even take me in for long before sliding his mahogany gaze to Soren. "That's a careless injury," my father cooly remarks.

Bumps rise all over my skin as I exhale—it's his voice. He even drawls out his last word like he does in my memories. Crow's feet frame his dark eyes as a slight, inky smudge darkens the surrounding skin. His heavy eyebrows—*that* hasn't changed—are furrowed, his cheeks slightly gaunter, accentuating a thinner nose, a commanding, matured appearance.

The smallest, involuntary sound squeezes from my throat when I register how his face has aged in ways that indicate we missed out on *years.*

My dad is actually here.

Alive.

"What do you want?" Soren asks, unmoving.

"My daughter."

There it is—acknowledgment.

It's almost painful how long that hangs in the air, as if I'm waiting for something more profound to occur. Bafflement changes into frustration as that's all it remains, an *acknowledgment.* "Um… who exactly *are* you? You need to explain what happened with you looking like *Ern* a few moments ago."

The words sound just as bizarre as thinking them.

I glance at Soren almost instantly, feeling as if I may have admitted that I'm going crazy. His skin is balmy and pallid, his under-eyes darkened. All this walking was probably detrimental to him, and yet his gaze *burns* at my father like he's only suffered a nick to the skin.

"You're not losing your mind, Jane," Soren quietly comforts, maintaining his gaze ahead as if he's at full strength.

Clenching my fists, I turn to glare at my father in the dim lighting. It still feels like I'm addressing a hallucination, making me feel like someone has removed my entrails and wrung them so tight that I'm completely hollowed.

"I *am* Charles Ritter, Jane… *and* Ern." The Scorpion returns his gaze to mine, the intensity of his furrowed brows loosening, his eyes softening like they used to at Mother.

I shift my weight between each foot, standing in front of a legend that terrifies many just by name alone, yet all I see is a father I don't recognize. "That makes absolutely no sense," I say through thin lips, my voice breathless from adrenaline.

"It does if he's a skin shifter," Soren comments.

A… no.

No.

I had *never* considered that.

We heard about them growing up, and I honestly forgot they existed after living in Coalfell for so long. They seemed more like a fable that *might* exist only over the Black Sea, like mentions of a vampire.

I take my father in all the more as he stands there. His hair is wrong… yes, that's what's annoying me, too. Mom liked it long, and he's gone and cut it. My lips part, but I still can't actually process this. "Are you seriously saying you're a skin shifter?"

"We have a lot to go over," the Scorpion gently replies.

Soren snorts behind me. "No shit."

I prefer *his* voice over anyone else's.

The Scorpion looks at Soren over my head, any warmth that might have existed completely washing away. It reminds me that two Zenith occupy the same empty room and are both extremely capable, if not the *most* capable, at delivering carnage.

"I've been watching you," my dad remarks to Soren, as if I'm not here.

"Bet you have," Soren mocks, not an ounce of fear present.

"Blackwell knows," my father states swiftly, his eyes searching the room even as his head remains still, before our gazes connect. "About who you are, Jane. That I'm alive and somewhere in this city. We need to clear that air so you know *everything* in case this all goes under. I nearly approached you just now, but then I saw Shade in the distance and knew to back off. I have no idea why he acted so carelessly, but perhaps it was for the best if it got you down here."

My heart twists uncomfortably as this entire moment reminds me of watching someone reunite, only for one side to realize the other hasn't been thinking about them at all.

It's not terrible, but… I *wanted* more. I dreamt of more. I survived Coalfell because I *swore* to myself I'd get more than *this*. That we would have a reunion to make it all worth it.

"I need to have questions answered before we discuss *anything*, even Blackwell," I say, like he's an apparition that I only have so much time with.

He closes his eyes as if he's dreading what comes next before opening them. There's enough of a pause in his uncertainty that I notice an unfamiliar scar that slices deeply through his cheek, and my gaze lowers to his exposed neckline—new tattoos. On both sides, just barely visible. They're decorative lines that don't immediately create an image, and I stop trying to find one.

It just confirms how much he is no longer the man I *knew*.

The Scorpion finally rises from his seat, nearly matching Soren in height, as he takes a few steps forward while rolling a ring on his finger. "Jane, Ern *is* me, and has been this entire time, because I *am* a skin shifter. I always have been."

"Then how the fuck did *I* not know?" Soren asks. "I met you at Talon's Perch."

Dad motions around us. "As the rubies indicate, Cypress is *heavily* involved in this orchestration. You met exactly who she wanted you to meet."

My body twitches as if I'm possessed by tremors. Somewhere behind my consciousness, my mind pieces everything together, and seeing the painting of it for the first time—my father is a skin shifter and declares he was Ern.

"No…" I utter, moving my head around but keeping my furrowed gaze on him. "That doesn't even make sense. I mean, if that's true, that means…"

You've been in Talon's Perch this entire time.

"Yes, Jane," he confirms with a heavy sigh. "*That's* what it means."

No.

No.

That's impossible. The twisting of my heart morphs into feeling as if my entrails are sliding out of a deep wound that finally bleeds, like the one that killed my mother.

I can't…

I replay this man transforming from Ern to my father in my mind's eye, all the while touching my stomach as if I might actually find a gash there that would explain why it feels like I will collapse at any moment.

But there is no wound. No physical injury to blame for why I feel this way.

He lied to me. To my face. For years.

Even if that concept collides in my mind, not a single one sparks any bit of understanding. *"How?"* is all I manage out, in an annoyingly small voice, like it will give him the chance to take it all back. It's such a foreign, *needy* sound that I almost want to carve out my tongue.

"I've been there since a little after you arrived, Jane."

For a moment I stare off into the distance, eyeing a ruby growing out of a wall before turning to Soren, hoping that his knowledge of the world can aid in my understanding.

Soren's pale gaze lowers to meet mine. I nearly demand him to read my father like an open book until his recent wound catches my eye, the sewn flesh still angry and red. He's probably ready to sleep for two days straight, and instead, he's standing here with me. *Watching over me.*

Looking back at my father, the violence within lifts its claws, cracking from dormancy, yet I make a conscious effort to restrain myself.

For now.

"So," I state, using the same arid expression and tone as him. "You truly were there, every night, while I thought I was abandoned? Is that actually what you're telling me?"

His lips thin as if he doesn't like the accusation. "I was never far, correct."

"Ah, I see," I reply, taking a few steps near this man as he stands only a few feet from me now. "And you never reached out?" That seething heat is all the way in my throat as I give him every chance to explain the confusion away.

"No."

I can't help it.

I propel myself toward him, unleashing a torrent of blows on his chest. The impact forces the Scorpion to take the smallest step back to brace himself. As I strike my father with my other hand, my wrists ache from slamming so hard.

It's strange to touch him after so long. It's even stranger how much it breaks my heart to strike him.

It's too much. All of it is. The truth that he is *alive* and has been close the entire time, that he seems annoyed more than happy to see me—this is *not* the dad I remember.

Glancing up at his face, he doesn't seem to feel a fucking thing. I pound on his chest again like it's a wooden door, and I'm trying to get the attention of *anyone* inside.

"You *left* me!" I cry out, shoving both hands into his chest, feeling my palms dig into his body. "Now you say you were around this entire time, and even talked to me when Kathleen and I would visit! I *needed* you! I *trusted* you! That you would come for me!"

Heat sears my veins, and my cheeks flush as tears flow freely. The next time I hit his chest—without any friction from him—only a visceral sound escapes rather than any words of hurt.

When my imagination gets the best of me and plays a scenario in my head of him sitting at a table, all happy and eating a hot meal at Ern's Pub while I'm all alone in Coalfell, sleeping in the rented attic space infested with rats that I occupied for *years*...

My hand is at my hip, sliding out a dagger as I aim *right* for the heart. Right where he taught me—

My father tightly grips my wrist as my seething mixes with a shaky exhale. Through tears, I say, "I swear to all the fucking gods, if you have a second family out there and were playing daddy dearest to them while I *waited* for you, I'll send them your head myself. Ern would talk about his *family*—"

"*Jane*," the Scorpion warns.

I eye the tip of the dagger that's pointed *right* at his chest, blood trickling down my knuckles; I must have hit one of the buckles on his leather straps.

"I lied about having a family," he breathes. "It's only you. You are my only family."

I yank my hand back, and he releases me, only for it to be caught by another. The Scorpion's eyes flare with danger as I realize that Soren is behind me and holding my hand back, prompting space between my father and me.

"My daughter doesn't need protection from *me*," the Scorpion hisses.

"You're either not who you say you are, or your mental state has been altered if you think any aspect of you is *trustworthy*. Jane, of all people, won't give it so easily."

My dad's scoff is bitter and judgmental. "Don't pretend as if you *know* her."

"And stop pretending as if the last decade of her life hasn't torn her apart."

The words of recognition stroke against the angry demon in my chest, contradicting the fury that clearly leaches from feelings regarding my father. The tension in my body slightly loosens, my arm sagging even if still firmly gripped.

"And how hard would it be to remove you?" my father asks, nodding to Soren. "You're only here because of my good graces. Nothing more."

"Soren goes *nowhere*," I hotly reply, my arm tensing again. "Or you and I will *never* speak again."

There's the smallest flash of emotion in my father's eyes, but it only exists within the space of a heartbeat, potentially never at all. *It's so unlike him...* Silence settles in the room like a thick fog, like a bunch of thieves waiting to see who will stab first, to which Soren eventually releases me but positions his body slightly in front.

This is going so terribly.

No '*I missed you, Jane. I'm sorry I lied to you for over a decade.*'

No embrace.

No sheer relief that we're *finally* meeting without the skin suit of another man.

The man I remember would have stood instantly from his chair and held me for as long as I wanted him to.

I think—I think that father is *gone*.

When there's enough silence between us for me to *accept* that fact, I shake my head as the words pour out of me, "Well, if that *grand* reintroduction is over with, you need to start talking before I lose my shit and find a way to gut you, as I'm doing a *lot* to keep it together."

His harsh eyes gentle, the lines of his face momentarily giving way. His sigh is clearly burdened with regret; even *I* can see that, but he has to earn the luxury of me *believing* him. "I honestly didn't know how to come to you, Jane. I still don't even know how or where to start. I waited here in the Undercroft as Ern, as a place to begin."

He sucks in air as if he's about to continue, but nothing more comes out.

"You… you didn't know *how to come to me*?" I raise both hands, slightly leaning over as if it will make the words clearer. "You could have just *appeared*. And what do you mean starting as Ern? I would have really liked a hug first, or a 'How are you,' or a 'Why are you back in Skull's Row.' Not the *innkeeper*."

I glance up at Soren, about to demand him to read my father and strip every emotion bare so I can understand, to break through whatever barrier the Scorpion has in place. But when our eyes connect, I realize he's devouring *me* more than my dad.

With whatever finesse I have in situations like these, I try to motion to Soren what I want; I *know* he can feel that. Instead, he just nods toward my dad as if telling me to keep talking.

Nearly huffing as I look back ahead, I tap my foot and arch a brow. "You're oddly indifferent. You don't seem like the man I remember. Honestly, it would have been better if you stayed in the shadows. Then at least the imaginary version of you could have comforted me when I missed you, versus whatever you are *now*."

I expected to see him tense or even—if I was lucky—to witness his heartbreak. Instead, he merely smiles, revealing the rather straight teeth of his. It's a detail that stuck with me for so long when so many pirates from Skull's Row have teeth ravished from scurvy.

He's been in good health all this time, it seems…

My father dips his head in a single nod. "Sometimes I liked to think your tenacity was from me, but I think it was from your mother. Or more so *her* mother. That woman couldn't be molded into anything. Getting her to like me was one of my greatest feats." He turns around and walks back to his seat, sighing as he reclaims it. "The trait you got from *me* is your temper. And since now we've had the proper reintroduction, let's talk about what's important." His head slightly lowers while his fervent gaze is on me. "You're being hunted, Jane. And it's not by something that any of our men can fight."

The temper he mentioned is ablaze inside, but there's a bit of Kathleen's voice telling me to hear what he just said. *Kathleen. Make good choices for her safety, at least.* "What does that mean?"

He looks at me almost apologetically. "What I'm going to say will be a *lot* to take in."

My tutting laugh echoes as I place my hands on my hip. "Right, don't want to shock me or anything," I sarcastically reply. "Get us somewhere to sit, at least. Soren needs it."

The Scorpion nods to some of the reclaimed barrels.

"Soren needs something more substantial. Get him an actual seat," I order.

Something about that clearly pisses off my father, and Soren coughs out a chuckle that's almost enough to distract me before I point to the open space in front of us. "I'm serious. Here. Put something *real* here."

The Scorpion begrudgingly complies, his eyes narrowing as he calls out to the empty room, only for someone to appear in the threshold that gets everything moving. Whether his attitude while requesting his men to fetch something is from annoyance at me giving orders or his aversion to aiding Soren, I'm too overwhelmed to care.

The sound of hurried footsteps echoes through the room as things are set up for us. It's only when a large chair, one matching the Scorpion's, is brought out and Soren sits in it with an extra flare for drama—as if rubbing it in—that I suspect he's more so upset to accommodate the other Zenith.

"*Continue,*" I state with clear articulation, still not sitting myself.

Soren inclines his head to my dad, rolling a hand as if he's Bones and supporting my demand.

The Scorpion's gaze rakes over the floor like he's hopeful that the situation will somehow get better. "Alright, let's resume, then, about being a skin shifter. It's one of the reasons I've gotten to where I'm at. Unless there's someone like Soren nearby that can sense someone no matter what skin they wear; I can become whoever I want and infiltrate wherever I want."

"Are you—are you *common?*" I dimly ask, still completely dumbfounded.

"I am very rare over here. The reason we hear about it across the

Black Sea is because magic exists with more order there. More definition. We—those living in the Balar Coasts and its mainlands—are the bastards of people from over *there*, breeding with those that live *here*. The connection to the gods is subsequently weaker." His gaze holds mine when I'm about to interrupt, "Magic exists *here* like a broken language that only a handful are fluent in. It's why sometimes the magic seems to appear randomly, like with *me*."

To be completely honest with myself? My mind is absolutely blank. "Did Mom know?"

"Of course," he replies, almost offended by the question.

When Dad is about to speak again, I throw a hand up to silence him as I face Soren again. "Is any of this true?"

"I want to keep hearing what he has to say," he answers, still staring intently at my father while leaning his chin into his hand.

Okay, it's not a clear answer, but we can work together here. I'll keep the Scorpion talking, then.

"I wanted to tell you so badly, Jane. I wasn't permitted," Dad immediately explains with a clipped tone, pulling my attention back to him. "After I got you to Melona, I waited in Skull's Row with the skin of another man, waiting for the signal that you had made it to Coalfell. Once I received it, I shifted into another that became known as Ern in Talon's Perch, taking over the tavern, waiting even more… until it became clear I'd have to watch you turn into a woman from afar. I was even present the night the village burned down. As soon as I got word of Coalfell, I left and went through the woods, killing those that I could. You even looked in my direction, once… I hoped you'd come my way… but then you didn't." I admit I hear a tremble of emotion breaking through, only for everything to go cold in his expression before he adds, "And then I watched Soren pick you up and carry you off."

I strain to listen as the words reach my ears, their meaning sinking in, but accepting them is an entirely different, overwhelming task. "You could be lying. It doesn't make any sense. Why couldn't you approach me? Let me know it was *you*?"

With slight acknowledgment to one of the rubies growing out of the wall, the Scorpion's knuckles turn white as he calmly states, "Because of a web we're stuck in that I'm desperate to get you out of."

JANE

There's a bittersweet sensation to having so much information, and yet so overwhelming to hear what sounds like I might be in a complete pile of shit.

"What is Cypress using us for?" Soren asks, straightening his posture from a slight slump, his drifting gaze now sharpened.

My father slowly blinks before craning his head to look up at the ceiling, as if reading something unwritten up there. "The honest truth is only *she* knows. The reason I'm here, aside from seeing *Jane*, is that the fanatics in the Fire Isles, the ones going by the Order of Ash, are closing in, and I've secured somewhere across the Black Sea to escape to. It's safer there. *That's* what can't be delayed. And I want out of this city. Immediately."

No matter what, it's as if I climbed a mountain's peak, only to see the *real* peak in the distance, and I have no interest in even *attempting* it. The Order of Ash are those fire worshippers, situated on a giant island near the Balar Coasts. To have them here... It doesn't make a lot of sense. "Closing in? On who? For what? Why is Ash after me? They don't seem to ever bother us here. You said something about *Blackwell*."

"They want you, Jane, because of a power you don't know of. Or, perhaps you're aware that it exists, but don't understand it," my father answers, his voice low and full of urgency. "Fire, heat, anything that would burn the average man can't hurt you."

My lips open, and then they stay that way.

"That—that's it?" I aimlessly look all around as I raise my hands as if to grip *something*, but then they drop with heavy confusion. "That sounds useless."

Soren's grave expression momentarily breaks with a flicker of amusement, only to deadpan again. "Would make sense why you're unaffected from the boiling water."

As fascinating as that might be on any other day, it just feels like a massive distraction right now. "Okay, sure, let's say that's real. Why are we bringing it up?"

In all honesty, even if it immediately brings clarity about my lack of burns, I can't embrace the concept. It's such a random trait to learn about myself, and feels so wildly disconnected from what's happening.

"Useless to *you*, perhaps. But not to those who want you. It's from your mother's line. It's why you were hunted in the first place. Why you *both* were." He leans back in his seat, glaring at a candelabra. "There is an entity known as the God of Misery, who lives north of the Fire Isles, in lands that are so damn hot no man can walk before burning through his boots within a few steps. The further inland you go, the air will eventually burn your *lungs*." He lifts a finger to gesture at me. "*Your* lineage, and those with your powers, allow people to reach there. To visit Misery's crypts, so he can be reborn in the flesh. *Our* flesh."

"Did you just say the fucking God of Misery?" Soren asks, an intensity in his voice that makes my heart race.

"*He's* the reason we're all here," Dad grimly answers. "Blackwell. The Order of Ash. Even Cypress."

My heart thrums in my rib cage, my teeth grinding painfully into each other. Staring at the many waxy sticks that melt down the iron ore that holds them, I fixate on one in particular, observing the bright light like it's a giant, bizarre lie.

Fire? All of this for something I didn't even know I supposedly am?

Some neglected, traumatized part of my heart sorely longs for the idea that my *father*—a man I thought I lost—knows more things about me than I do. Like a parent might. Even the *suggestion* is so enticing that I'm momentarily frozen, not wanting to ruin the possibility.

Fuck it. Release the hope. It always tastes bitter in the end. Get this over with.

Nearing one of the waxy sticks, I reach out, holding my hand near the heat to feel the gentle sensation of warmth, pinching the fire, then squeezing the wick between my fingers and hold it.

I examine my skin.

Nothing. Maybe slightly pink, but there's nothing like what I witnessed in the village. It's also far from uncomfortable, reminding me of how the baths are never too warm, even if others have skin as red as cooked lobster.

There's no way…

Coalfell. My gut seizes with dread when recalling the villagers, and of Maryanne. The guilt for what happened is like poison, giving me tunnel vision as soon as it enters my veins. Almost as quickly as it appears, I shove it down so it can't drown me. *Don't focus on that now.*

My chest rises and falls, faintly shaking my head now that *everything* is heavier with my dad's statement. "I didn't realize… how did I never know? Mom never said anything," I murmur.

"You always stayed away from fires because it's what everyone else did. And she and I *planned* to tell you, but didn't want that secret out in case anyone was searching for someone like you. Kids keep secrets with each other, and you were close to your friends. It was a risk we weren't ready to take."

Focus, Jane. Don't get emotional. A god wants you for this… "I don't —you said this dumb god wants to be born in the *flesh*? I've never heard of that."

I just want things to be normal.

So badly.

I'm so burnt out by the calamity.

"Gods usually don't seek this route. The risk is insurmountable to most, requiring a forfeiture of powers for centuries. They usually manage their bidding through conduits, like Cypress. Meddling directly with us means they can be killed and cease to exist while in the limbo state that Misery is currently within."

"And he's risking all that… for what? Do you even know?"

"If grief and strife are how he gains force, and he is *greedy*, then being in the flesh allows him to ensure a reign of misery would last for centuries, if not longer. And either due to an annoying string of the fates, or shit luck, we're alive in a time where he's seeking rebirth. Fifty years earlier, and this would be your mother living this reality."

It's almost annoying how ignorant I feel. I suppose I should have focused more when Mother tried to teach me the history of our worlds, but it honestly seemed like useless stories.

Especially with a father as a Zenith.

What an idiot for a kid I was.

"So what do *I* have to do with this again, exactly?" I ask, facing him, slowly churning it all together. I so badly want to latch on to him for safety, but he still looks like a stranger to me. I can already feel my heart closing off to him. "They want *me* to go to the crypts, or something?"

"Across the Black Sea," my father begins, speaking quieter and directly to me. "They call people like you a Cinder. Just like they call *him* a Sensor." Dad lazily motions to Soren. "Fire mages hold Cinders in high esteem because they're a dying breed, and as everything is in the Balar Coasts, powers and magic are scarce here. There's nothing that indicates a Cinder, other than they don't burn, meaning they're hard to track. Which is why we didn't say anything —we figured it was best to just let you avoid fire. Misery currently wants all Cinders that can be found, and so the Fire Isles are rather aggressive in this support. He needs people like *you* to reach Misery's crypts if he ever wants his power back, so yes, I imagine he'll use you, one way or another, to get to his crypts. I still don't honestly know how they found you or your mother——"

"Did *they* kill Mom?" I interrupt, the churning of information spinning so fast the pieces aggressively collide like they've been chucked around in a hurricane.

He offers a single, somber nod—the first *true* emotion deepening the concern in his eyes; something in me breaks a little that his concern didn't involve me.

I grind the wick near my fingers to extinguish the flame, my breathing deepening with adrenaline. "*Mom* was a Cinder?"

"Any offspring of the maternal line will be a Cinder. Your grandmother was one, too. They were hunted about a hundred years ago, killed on sight. It's why your grandmother settled in Skull's Row. There's not many of you left."

I cling to every word like a man lost at sea who has finally been granted a map, although bitter to realize how much I've completely missed and can never go back. "But my naprese scar..."

"I thought that was interesting that it burned you," Dad remarks, looking down at my wrist. "It must be from its magic. I admittedly don't know much about naprese gold. They guard that very closely..." He tilts his head to the side. "Whatever that magic is doesn't matter now, though, Jane. You've been of interest to fire worshippers for some time. Cinders aren't from the Fire Isles, but an island obsessed with fire is also highly fascinated with collecting humans that don't burn. Misery is utilizing their lust for influence and flames to create a minor cult that will support him." He hesitates before adding, "That awful burning of the woman that you witnessed was probably a burst of power for him. Probably the burning of Coalfell was, too."

An icy dread settles on my shoulders, clarity striking with brutal force. I search for any emotion in him, but I just don't see it; I don't fucking see it. My lips open and close a few times before I manage out, "If they needed Cinders, why did they kill Mom?"

His sigh morphs into a grumble that emanates through his throat, sucking his lower lip to his upper teeth. "I don't know, and I ask that question nearly every day."

Blinking rapidly, I try to imagine being taken to reach some crypts to restore a god of misery. "Based on the way you talk, I'm not the only one, right? So why haven't they restored him already? Surely they don't need *every* Cinder."

Surely, there is a hole in this plan.

Something massively overlooked.

There *has* to be.

"No. They don't. But that doesn't matter for you, since they'll use you, in particular, to get Misery back to his power. It's what I've heard when I've managed to get close to them. They've been gathering Cinders for a while now, but you're of particular interest for some reason," he replies, his expression tightening again to something deadly.

Oh, great. Maybe not.

I'm just of *particular interest.*

If steam could pour out of me, this entire room would be blanketed by the thickest fog. Out of everything I could feel, I'm primarily pissed off. All the suffering, aching loneliness, and excruciating agony of mourning my family… it's suddenly gaining a name. *Motives.* The chaos of everything has so much order for the first time in my life, the gravity of what was done to me, my family, and my village now has a name… and I bet a face.

I'm even trying to picture this person in my head, the one that *leads* the Order of Ash, which leads to me biting my lip all too hard as that ugly ass face of the man who killed my mother persists through it all.

I always thought that what happened to Nora Ritter was a byproduct of living in Skull's Row and my father having enemies, not actually an execution related to a sophisticated orchestration.

She was *hunted.*

Pure murder and vengeance stain my essence; slaying the man who killed my mother isn't enough.

Not when I have direction.

Not with *understanding.*

Spreading my fingers out so my hand trails down the candelabra to extinguish the other flames, imagining each one is the beating heart of the Order of Ash, I try to breathe steadier to control myself. "So, in all of this, I was meant to be *taken* after what they did to Mom?"

I can nearly hear every heartbeat of mine as I wait for my father to answer.

"Yes. And I did *everything* to avoid that. But Misery is patient. He sees the benefit in properly cultivating the young ones, like Jesper—the leader of Ash. Misery groomed him as a child, promising to make him a fire god in his own right.

"That doesn't mean he can't force you to comply as an adult, though. It's just more effort, which is why you're still in incredible danger," he explains, a tightness in his words that gives me *some* comfort; maybe he will try to stop them.

Either way, my throat is suddenly parched, and feels as if sand is stuck in it.

Well, fuck.

I had to hide before, but now a literal god is hunting me. I'm not a damsel in distress, damnit. I don't *want* to be. The Council seems so small compared to this.

"So, why now?" I ask, trying to refocus on collecting my understanding. "What changed? Why didn't you send at least a *whisper* my way? You said—" I pause, still unable to fully process his identity this entire time "—that you were *Ern*. As in, we spoke *countless* times…"

I could say more and even have to fight back words I want to sling around like daggers, but I bite my tongue—metaphorically and physically.

The Scorpion needs to clarify *everything*.

"Circumstances that prevented me from reaching out to you are still in effect, but loosened," my father carefully says. Dad doesn't let that settle for long before looking at Soren. "Which means whatever's going on here is done now that I've returned. I'm not letting you *sit* there because I think you deserve to. I simply don't want to fight that battle right now while speaking with Jane."

"Need me to be injured this badly to finally face me?" Soren replies without missing a beat, his grating voice bringing texture to my thoughts.

Dad sneers. "Honor doesn't mean shit around here. I'll always take advantage of a weakness, especially to cull the bastards ruining *her*."

"You seem to miss the part where she's alive and well, Ritter. It *is* hard to notice such things when you're not around, though."

My father's expression grows colder with each breath. "My daughter is alive, aye, but you've been keeping her tethered."

"Because letting her out would not have been safe."

Dad scoffs, shifting even more in his seat as he sneers. "*Safety*."

"*Stop it.*" I nearly yell at the both of them, but when my rage speaks for me, it has me turning to my father instead of Soren. "I have been through a lot of shit recently, and the last thing I need is you bickering with Soren."

Dad doesn't look at me as he says, "You're surviving right now, Jane. Soren is the best anchor for that."

There's something annoying about him acting like my *father* at this moment, especially when he hasn't even asked *how I am*. "Just finish explaining whatever it is you have to tell me. Why did you bring me down here?" I ask, gesturing around before adding, "And while you're at it, explain the rubies. How is *she* tied into this? I want this all wrapped up with a pretty bow before I step a *toe* out of this room. It's the *least* you owe me."

With a deep sigh that seems to re-center him, the Scorpion looks down at his hands and remains still for a long moment. "Everything that has commenced has done so for a reason, Jane. Whether we like those reasons, or not. Cypress, for all the shit she's put us through, *did* hide you for over a decade, protecting you in that village from Misery, until for whatever reason, she's revealed you back to the world. At least, that's my assumption, or else Soren wouldn't have found you. Or the Order of Ash."

Thirst morphs into nausea, my stomach tightening. "Wait, *she's* the one that hid me?"

When our gazes connect, there's a falter of emotion once more before it's solid again. "That was the deal. She'd ensure that Ash couldn't find you, nor could Misery. And somehow, Ash *did* on the same night that Soren found you, which, again, is why I'm assuming her protection was removed. She told me I could come to you once the world knew you. Which is why I'm here now…

"Either way, that's outside of our control and not worth worrying about. Not right now. The issue at *hand* is Blackwell. I believe Misery intends for Blackwell to rule over Skull's Row and bloody the Council. It's the *true* reason that Blackwell sought *you* out, Jane. Not because of the tattoo. He wanted you captured, as instructed by his puppeteer.

"They're moving again. Ash is in Skull's Row at the behest of

Misery, while Blackwell is trying to gain control over the Council. They're connected to Blackwell somehow, too, but that secret has been guarded enough that even I can't find it. I also don't know why Ash would come for you when Blackwell sent Soren, and that's the chaos I don't like right now." He cants his head at Soren. "Speaking of all of this, you're supposed to be able to sense danger. So why in the hells have you been holed up here for weeks instead of fleeing? Even Corvus looks like he's about to leave. And Jane was nearly taken just now. It would be dangerous to assume I'm not aware of that lack of good judgment."

Soren's gaze glints with something vicious. "Blackwell has an odd, neutral aura about him that makes it nearly impossible to read his motives… just like Shade. And *you*, Ritter."

I—

What?

Clasping my hands together as I place my weight on my hip, I narrow my eyes on my father.

The hells does that mean?

Dad stiffens, something flashing in his eyes that reveals he didn't expect that. "So you're useless to bring, then," he replies. "He doesn't owe you anything, Jane. I don't trust him anyway."

I scoff. "He's clearly far from *useless*. And what does he mean that you're hard to read?"

Dad looks at me like a parent who pities their child's poor decision. "You saw that neck wound. Even the baker could have seen that coming, let alone what followed."

Soren's annoyed laugh is almost like a threat. "I felt the need to let it hit me, Ritter. Seems it has set into motion the perfect waves that need to wash over us. I'm unafraid of the damage, unlike you, who seems to be worried about pissing off his precious Blackwell. You could always try sucking his cock if you're that worried."

Dad's entire posture stiffens, and I swear his hand pulls back— even for a fraction of a moment—as if he might reach for his blade.

"*No*. We are *not* doing this right now," I interject, taking a step forward as if my being between them might change something. Even if Soren's pallor is off, I still have no doubt that someone fighting him will be punishing up until his last breath. "We need to have a plan for whatever the hells is happening here, not fight.

Blackwell, Order of Ash... I don't even honestly know if I *know* what's happening—"

I pause when I'm about to mention that my life is at risk, and that *that* is the priority. It's not even because I'm concerned about my beating heart, but rather...

I can get revenge for my mom. For what happened to me.

But my awareness of the selfishness in such a statement is almost instantaneous. I'd be asking for them to give up everything just to defend me. Especially Soren. He owes me *nothing*, which means I can't ask him to risk *everything*, not with his sister.

What of *his* revenge?

I need to let it go—all of it. If I die at their hands, it means my mother's death was for nothing. I need out of here, if I am to stay a step ahead. That's my priority.

Emotional ice settles over my heart, freezing this moment of time like it's done countless times before to help me survive. I can drop everything here and follow my father across the Black Sea—he's the only one who has any reason to *owe* me. I don't have to forgive him, but it would prevent this cunt named Misery from touching me, and maybe I could find these fire worshippers and gut every one of them.

And it would get the putrid breath of death out of everyone's shadow that seems to be haunting mine.

"Are you alright, Jane?" Dad asks.

Snapping my gaze up, I breathe sharply to steady myself. "I have a lot to process," I say with a flat tone. "Are we in danger? Sounds like everyone else is, especially if they're associated with me. Should I leave now? Is there a ship that can take me within the day?"

My father eyes me with a scrutiny that's almost familiar. "We need to make a move soon, aye. Ships across the Black Sea are rare, but we can sail to other lands as we wait for them," Dad calmly answers. "And if Soren is worth *anything*, he'll make sure to prevent you from running off if you're worried that you'll get anyone killed and would rather turn yourself over—" he holds a hand up when I'm about to defend myself "—you remained in Coalfell because of your fear of others getting hurt. You told me, or Ern, so many times that you made an oath to stay, and a few times let it slip it was to a siren. It's clear what guided your decision. While admirable, this is a very different encounter. Misery getting a hold of you will cascade a dark era over us all until any and all prosperity is forgotten. He *cannot* return to power. And for whatever reason, he's completely honed in on *you*. Which means you're not going anywhere without us knowing."

My lips press together as I don't have a single reply. The ease of shutting up tells me I'm far from complying—I just want this conversation to end so I can find my own way out.

I also need fresh air, which I can't get stuck down here.

I don't require Soren's powers to know that the behemoth's gaze is burning into my back, but I can't look at him. My world, just as swiftly as the blade that struck Mom's heart, is changed within this entire conversation.

The familiar desire to build my walls returns, telling me that if it comes down to it, Soren can become a man of my imagination, living in a place I'll visit when I'm lonely.

I can die getting the revenge I never knew I needed to seek.

Can Soren feel that at all?

A knock in the pattern of three raps fills the silence, and I glance over my shoulder with Soren in my peripheral. The two Zenith in the room stiffen in ways that only experienced, confident men do; nothing akin to jumping to their feet or looking frightened. No. Instead, I swear I can see them both holding their breath and waiting, in case a strike might come from somewhere else.

When Soren finally lifts his gaze to see who is opening the door, Dad does something… different.

My jaw drops as his features completely change. His nose, mouth, eyes, and even ears all shift like sand that's being rearranged. His hair changes from brown to blonde, his eyes now a stark green. His long nose becomes short and chunky, his upper lip much larger than the bottom. Even the scar fades, his tattoos gone.

My lips part, so many pieces of my childhood swirling together as I can't stop my mind from piecing it together.

He really is a skin shifter, isn't he?

Soren's posture remains strong, yet his eyes reveal how wound up he's becoming. Especially when Rorge enters. "Sir, we've got Evan at the door," he says, clearing his throat.

I don't know who or what Evan is, or why it makes my father stand as if he's going to leave.

"I'll be out, Rorge," Dad answers, barely moving to look my way as our eyes connect. "Rorge or Donna will be tending to you and Soren while everything gets set into motion. I understand you trust that brute right now, Jane, so I'll permit him to stay while you process everything in here. If you need anything, Rorge is outside the door."

As my father walks by me, I reach out without thought to request something, pausing just before I touch him; I can't commit to that. He doesn't flinch, or move away, and instead looks at my hand and then at me, and I retract my attempt to touch him.

It's honestly easier talking to him when he's not wearing *his* face.

"I need supplies to help Soren. That's why I was at the apothecary."

It's so odd to see something entirely emotional flash through a stranger's face when they're looking at me like I'm a long-lost relative. "I'll get those things gathered for you."

"Do you know what I need?"

"Your mother ensured I do. I'd often get it for her." The corner of his lips twitch like he might hint at a smile, but it's gone before I can even savor the concept.

The Scorpion moves quickly past Soren and out the door, as if whoever this Evan person is holds the most importance.

I'm not even jealous—just nosy about who my father really is, and to know the people he keeps around him. As the door to this makeshift throne room shuts—Rorge glaring at Soren like he's a very unwelcome guest—Soren and I are left inside, alone.

Breathing steadily, I know I have to be honest with him, and immediately. The reprieve we made over the last few weeks is now stained with this *hunt* over my head.

How can he possibly stay in my life without threatening his own?

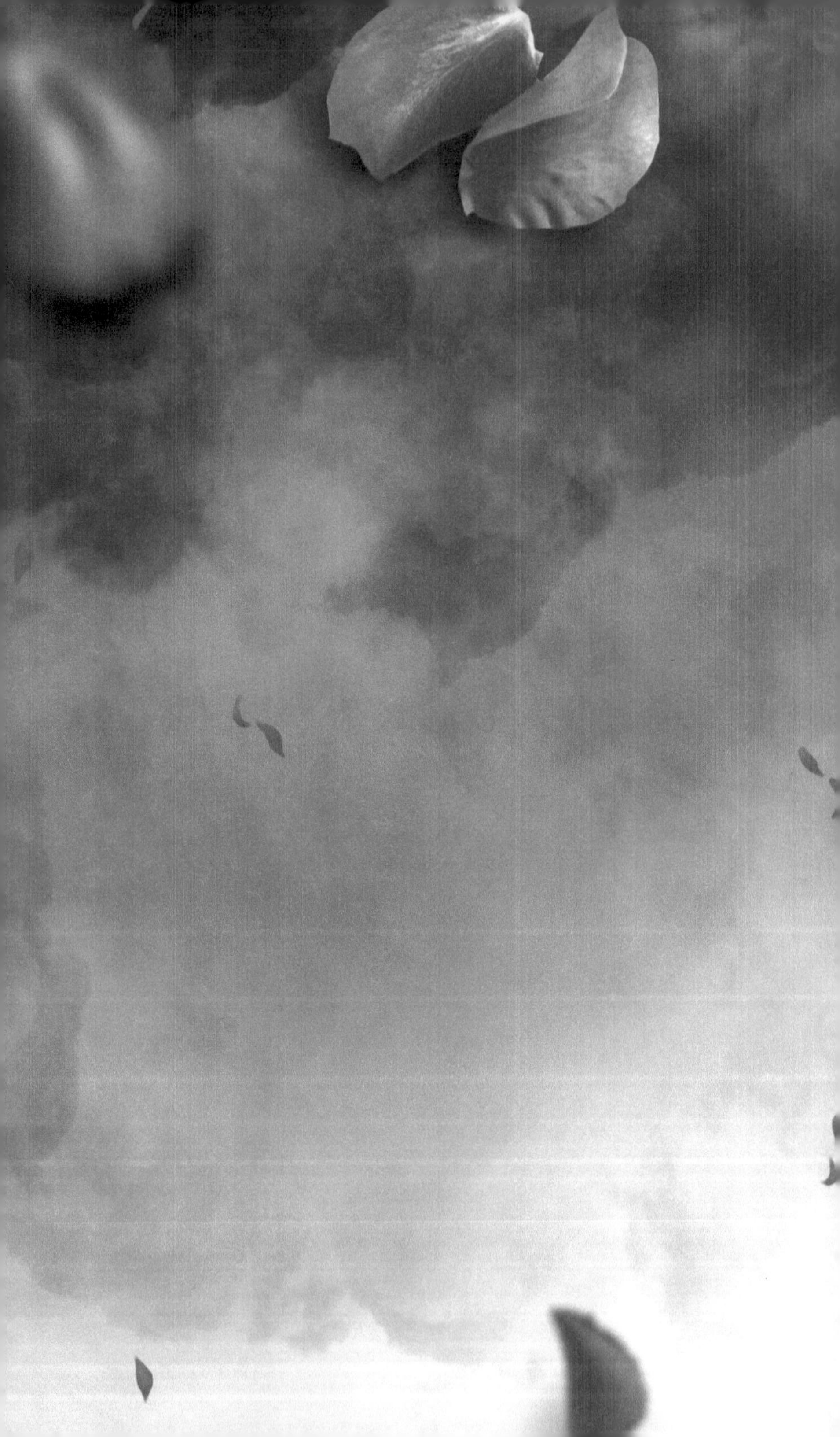

DISILLUSIONMENT
JANE

"**B**efore your heart wanders," Soren begins. "We can't trust him, yet. While I can feel aspects of him… he's *very* hard to read. Unnaturally hard. Something is shrouding him, and I'm not sure what it is, but it's similar to Blackwell. It's a fuckery that reminds me of the world across the Black Sea."

My mind is like a spider desperate to form a web, but no design *fits*. I sink into one of the barrel-shaped stools right next to Soren, the rough wood creaking, and place my face into my hands.

"Jane," Soren coaxes.

There's always the chance that Dad and Blackwell are working together, I suppose…

Could the Scorpion have been corrupted over that dangerous ocean? Were he and Blackwell corrupted together, used in tandem?

If this weird god is after me, maybe this is a very contrived plot to ensure I *won't* be leaving?

"You know," I begin, spreading my fingers slightly so he can hear me better. "Everyone talks about the Black Sea as if it's this wall that once you climb, suddenly it's an entirely different world there. It can't be *that* different, can it?"

A part of me hopes it isn't, because if so, then its magic is an enemy I know nothing about fighting.

"Maybe one day you'll cross the Black Sea, love. It depends on how the rest of this goes." My shoulders shake at hearing that term of endearment from him—the affection shakes every thought I'm trying to piece together. "But it's not a simple journey. If the ocean waters were to disappear, you would see a seabed of ships more than you would sand. If you were to survive such a journey, then aye, you'd see an entirely different world."

Okay, so I guess I'm fucked.

How can I make any decisions when I'm so ignorant of the world around me? I definitely can't take on a *god* by myself, but how do I let people help when it feels as if I want to run from my *own* shadow?

Every fiber of my being itches to get across the Black Sea to this other world and perhaps learn about the magic that might be influencing the Scorpion—if there even is one—so I can undo them. I could sell myself as a healer to anyone who needed it to make money. Maybe travel so far to the other edge of the infamous continent that Misery might give up on me.

"Jane, I can feel you searching right now for an immediate reason for it all. We hardly know any details."

Talk to him; don't shut off. I glance up at those pale, blue eyes. "Soren, you do realize you can't help me from here? If I seriously have all these people coming for me, then anyone being *near* me might die—*will* die. My own mother did, and my father is a *Zenith*. You can't be near me. *Kathleen* can't even be near me."

I state it with such clarity that someone from the outside might think I have no care for any of them. But it stems from a place where I have been able to numb myself when needed, so I can fall apart years from now when I realize what I truly lost.

I'll at least be *alive,* which means I can fulfill defending my family's honor. And hopefully all these people will move on with beating hearts, too.

Icy eyes pierce mine, almost with a force that pushes me back. "And what if everything he said was a lie? It's interesting, certainly. Aligns with some suspicions of mine. But I don't trust many things right now, *especially* since I cannot feel him."

I drop my head to stare at the ground with so much force that it nearly hurts my neck. When threatened tears burn my eyes, I bite the inside of my lip to stop them.

Why can't it be simple for once?

"Jane," he gently says.

"I, um," I begin, trying desperately to remove the deep urge to release my tears. I wipe my eyes, then rub them. "It's like the last ten years of my life have meant nothing, and my own father might as well be a stranger to me. And all that Misery nonsense aside, for the first time, I have clarity about my mother's murder and that her revenge is *not* done. That I need to make people pay for my own suffering, too. I feel... I don't know, I feel alone, and so *hateful*."

"And what of me?"

Refusing to look up, I so badly want for the fates to reveal that this man is meant to be my rock. My *true* rock, the one that a hurricane can batter while *he'd* never move.

It's a security and love I had as a child, and now it feels like a figment of my imagination; a lost fable. Maybe what I want more than anything is to experience that again, and whether Soren is planted on sand or stone is yet to be revealed to me. We only *just* crossed very deep, intimate lines...

I also can't ask that of him. How *could* I? He's not just a mercenary to hire, a lone man. He's the leader of many, and I could never guarantee his safety.

My lips part, but it's a struggle to articulate the totality of it all.

I hear him move, and yet it still startles me when Soren's firm, yet gentle, hand touches my chin to lift my head—he scooted to the edge of his seat to reach me. The desire to give my heart to him, and to not think twice about it, deepens when he looks like nothing but *strength*. I'm high on him, and this is more than physical.

Romantic thoughts flood me with his touch, ones that are

dangerously persuasive. It hurts even more because it's just a glimpse of what we *could* be.

I was so fucking close to a life I longed for.

Still leaning over, Soren's hand moves to tuck my hair behind my ear before pulling his fingers through just how I like. "You are defeated, Jane."

I don't answer. Instead, I let my gaze roam his face, memorizing every tiny detail of him, even the dark roots of his eyelashes and the spots where his stubble doesn't grow because of the scars, in case I don't get to again.

"Let's get something straight, too," Soren says, my body relaxing to the sound of his voice, even if I know better. "You didn't develop affection for me because it was *necessary* for survival." I clench my jaw, and the deep pit in my gut is nearly instantly filled. "You opened your heart to me for a *reason*, so don't remove me now. Don't act as if you suddenly have to do everything alone."

The way his gaze hardens tells me he's already pillaged every emotion of mine.

Lying is pointless to him.

"What other choice do I have? Not only is it safest for everyone, but also a lot easier to hide when it's just one person. And I'll be damned if I don't get to gut every last person involved who ruined my family."

"So you'd lead me on and then leave?" he asks, although he looks more angry than upset, like he's making a point. "I meant it when I said if someone else makes you speak of love, they won't live long, even if I have to do that to every man until I'm all that's left."

That's the romance none of the villagers were ever able to give me—I don't know if he *truly* means that, but the intensity of such a statement is so tempting. "And what good would that do?" I ask with a smile, although I know my eyes are sad.

His gaze roams my face. "Make me feel better for a moment."

For a moment.

And even though this whole conversation makes me feel better, that's what this is, though, isn't it? A moment in time, uncorrupted from what haunts me.

Gods, I'm so fucking tired of running. Of something existential controlling my life.

"If I don't run, then what else? At least over the Black Sea, it sounds like I can hide in the open. Here? I don't think I can just go back to some village and live out my life that way. That's not living. That's just growing old with no purpose." The words rest on my tongue, and the reckless side of me wins as I continue, "I'd rather die soon, after tasting the affection you gave me, than ever go back to something like Coalfell. And at least going over the Black Sea would be a *chance* to live."

I don't mention that it's a chance to live, so I may become worthy of killing others. I'll be like my father and train for ten more years, then take them all down for what they have ruined.

I'll make it my life's mission.

And there's a chance Soren might stop that, so for now, I'll keep it quiet.

There's something guarded in his gaze, vulnerability still managing to break through. We never usually get past this point of sentiment. I know for me, it's because this just seems so unrealistic. Too perfect. There's no way this can work in the context of the real world.

His eyes focus on me, but they move quickly as he takes me in. Some part of me registers what that look is—he's not confident about what he wants to say.

If Soren cares for me more than just a fleeting encounter, I almost hope he doesn't tell me how deep those emotions run. If he *really* cares about me... Gods, I don't know how much it'll break me if I have to cross the Black Sea without him.

But I will, especially if it means he lives for his sister, too.

NEGOTIATIONS

SOREN

What would Jane do if I locked her away until this all passes? It's what I've been doing as of late, hoarding her heart because, for some reason, her affection is captivating for me, just like her ruthless side that's only enamored by my violence. And this ravenous need for revenge only binds me to her, as it's a vibration that hums perfectly with mine.

Perhaps without my abilities, I might have cut my losses and walked away to focus solely on Serena, but Jane has brushed against my essence in ways I've still yet to describe.

I *know* her.

When Jane gives herself to me, her soul resonates an affection that's dying to cling to someone. I *despise* the idea of another man receiving that, no matter the logic, or lack thereof, in what I feel.

Especially knowing that someone could love her when she isn't trapped within survival.

She's a Zenith's daughter, and I fucking want that for *myself*. The *entire* package, the one when she's completely reborn.

And yet, as I look at her pretty face now, that sickening feeling of something hunting her is completely clear—if the Scorpion means what he says, then this is *nothing* like trying to keep her safe from the Council.

I remove my hand from Jane's soft hair, her walls mostly down, even if she's thinking of pushing me away. I'll let her believe she can if it gives her some sense of control.

But as long as a part of her still craves me, I'll be weak to that call.

"Someone needs to get Kathleen," she murmurs, as if the thought left her mouth as soon as it entered her mind. "I know you said people will be looking out for her, but if she gets hurt because of *me*—"

Jane aggressively toys with one of her fingers, as if considering all the things that could go wrong. It's odd to feel thoughts of Kathleen no longer bring her comfort—when I stare at Jane, I can picture a fleeting image of a blonde with no face that mixes deeply with a longing for friendship, a depth of solitude crowding her heart as if to block out the familial affection. As far as I know, she has no idea that Kathleen owes the Scorpion; I know better than to tell her that *now*.

She wants to pull away so badly, like a wounded animal who craves the pack but trusts only its own shadow.

Ah—it connects; Jane doesn't know what it's like to let others sacrifice for her. At least, not directly. Everything in me wants to tame the lone animal so she may one day smile without burden.

The instincts that seem to fail me as of late seem so powerful right now, to the point I can almost hear a voice telling me that her pain, her fears, her heart—all of it—belongs to me. That the fates crossed our paths for a reason, promising that I could give her everything of *myself* without reservation.

I've *never* experienced this before.

But every time I will my arms to move, the same powers simultaneously scream to leave her be.

The deeply protective side of me that belongs to family claws out to her, as if I'm *seeing* a future where Jane has been mine for *decades*. Like a vision, maybe... I don't see visions, though. More like imprints.

It doesn't matter, because just even the suggestion that I've found that person is enough to erupt a swell of rage that *someone* needs to suffer for what's been brutally done to Jane's life. For the family she's lost.

Space. Give her space.

Jane unequivocally needs time to process all of this—there's no argument there, even without my powers to tell me that. I've seen many faced with this exact metamorphosis, and the final result can only be driven by *her*. In that, it makes sense now why everything told me to take her down here; there was no way for her to evolve without this encounter.

While I'm speechless as I try to navigate everything that overwhelms me, an energy precedes someone entering the cleared-out throne room and, of course, declares that I'm needed. One glance at Jane and she straightens up, immediately numbing every part of her so she can remain alert.

You've been on guard for too long, love.

There's no point in trying to fight this, though. I can't read the Scorpion for shit, and yet there's no danger surrounding him; he *does* feel safe for Jane. Blackwell might have been a wall of nothingness, but the energy *around* him was dire. Putrid, even.

She'll be safe if I leave her. Probably best, too. She could use the quiet.

Standing, my heart pounds, and I know it's because I need to rest, maybe eat an entire cow's liver. Jane's determination changes to deep concern—I glance down, her hazel eyes bright with worry. I touch her cheek, apprehension flooding her as I drop the hand to give her my back.

She's safer in here than she has been since I first found her.

"Stay alert, Jane," I say, only able to concentrate on so much with how lightheaded I am. "Even if you're among your people here."

I hate to leave her; this burning desire to remain is wrapped in so many layers of wanting to know what the hells I feel when around her. Is it the fates? My own biased heart? Some other force manipulating me?

I *never* anticipated to find anything akin to this, to experience such a powerful push to a single person. Ever since entering here, it's as loud as a storm.

Clearly, it has to be the rubies. They're a magic source, aren't they? Is Cypress manipulating me so I agree to her bidding? Is it even *manipulation* if I give in without a single fight?

Later. Focus on what's here. On those around.

I'm taken along a narrow hall, stained glass windows fitted into the stone so the candlelight from whatever room it connects to can carry through—not only is there a lot of noise, but extensive energy.

I'm guided in there, the sensation of everyone's unique vibrations so much easier to define—uncertainty, curiosity, and observing me as an outlier floods the space.

For a moment, my mind warns me Ritter is about to confront me in front of his men, but my instinct tells me it's not the case. I sense privacy, as if I'd blink and the room would disappear; a sign that this room is negligible and I'll imminently be sitting somewhere quieter.

For having no fucking luck with my powers, they're suddenly as clear as polished crystal.

I pay no mind to the crowd as we walk another small corridor, ignoring the fuckers that don't mean a thing to me. A guard at the end stands next to a door that's opened for me, revealing living quarters. Scanning the area that has slightly taller ceilings, more inviting furniture than what I just sat on, and trinkets all around, I can immediately tell it belongs to Ritter, and while everything looks as if it's placed with care, it's clear that none of this is home to him.

It reminds me of how Jane felt about Coalfell, about how *I* feel about Skull's Row. True homes carry a warm energy with a lot of personhood attached. This utterly lacks that.

By the fire sits Ritter, a few drinks on the worn, wooden table in front of him.

The door shuts behind me, and finally, I'm alone with *the Scorpion.*

SOREN

No words are spoken as I near a chair across from the Scorpion, sensing an aura that is familiar—glancing down, there's a letter with a broken seal, one I recognize.

Why is Corvus writing Ritter? It's so fresh I can still feel his energy on it.

My fingers roll as I think of the ring on my forefinger with a serpent imprint and how the Council's customary wax merges with the heated ring to create something akin to naprese gold. It's a seal no man can forge, and when it's broken, it crumbles to pieces; impossible to read a letter and reseal.

An unnatural quiet surrounds us, despite Ritter being only a few feet from me—he might as well be a statue, so heavy in contrast to all the chaos outside here.

So, some part of me still works, even if I couldn't feel Shade or him. Something is being blocked within me.

Narrowing my eyes, I raise my gaze to stare right at him. I wonder if this cunt knows anything about that? Yes... he's absolutely shrouding himself, and I have no idea how or why.

"How is Jane?" he stiffly asks, sipping on a pewter mug that he taps with his forefinger.

"She's had her life ripped from her, and now you're back like you got lost on the way home. So she's coping to the best of her ability," I reply, sitting down on a moth-eaten velvet couch to alleviate feeling lightheaded.

I pour a pitcher of clear liquid, not realizing how parched I am. "Do I need to worry about poison?" The words lazily roll from my lips.

"No," he answers dryly. "You're not done being useful yet."

I drain every last drop of water, sighing with relief as I stare at the ceiling that a fucking ruby grows out of like this place is infested with rubied mold.

Ritter sets his mug down before fidgeting with one of his rings—an elaborate one that's made of silver with a hint of magic I can't decipher—his hands part as he retreats them into the pockets of his cloak.

My eyes widen as a fierce wave of so many fucking layers that are unmistakably Ritter—of the Scorpion in all his enigmatic glory; I feel as if I'm trying to breathe underwater with how much it washes over me, pulling me deeper into a sea of unspoken crevices of his soul.

I can read him just as clearly as that room I walked through. "What the fuck just changed?"

He cocks an eyebrow, arrogance in his gaze. "Not going to read me in silence?"

"Answer my question," I reiterate, my voice steady.

He scoffs, the sound dripping with condensation. "What authority do you think you have over me to make demands?"

I'm fucking your daughter.

I nearly laugh to myself, but I know that's a petty comment. No, there's one that, even after only a few *seconds* of being exposed to him that I know will crawl right underneath his skin. "Jane trusts me more than you. By a significant margin."

After having been around him with no input, the emotions emanating from Ritter are profound and... deadly. Jane trusting me more than him is like a poisonous assault to his nervous system. My survival is born and bred in a dog-eat-dog world, and there's incredible triumph in having such leverage over the Scorpion.

I'm *relevant* to him now.

Stupid fucker.

"Do I need to watch my back around you, Ritter?" I tease, so eager to rub salt deeper into the wound. "That might piss her off, you know, if you try to kill me."

He leans over slightly on one knee, rich brown eyes digging deep into me in a look forged over decades of sharpening his threats. "I've lived as another man to hide from my daughter for over a decade to ensure the cunt that killed my wife will face a *very* undignified end, and to simultaneously protect Jane for as long as I can afford to breathe." He tilts his head slightly to straighten it. "Imagine what I'd do to the man that hurts, or kills, my Jane."

Now this is utterly fascinating to finally meet *Charles Ritter*. "Will be quite challenging if you're dead, and the way this city is moving, that's a high probability for all of us. So what's your point?"

"Oh, I have ensured that in my unlikely death, vengeance will still reign." He leans back to get more comfortable in his seat. "I may be out of shape, but I still have my networks, and *many* owe me a debt." He pauses, a sense of exultation exuding from him that feels callous. "That sister of yours is your weakness—yes, I'm very aware of it. You hurt Jane, in any way, *Soren*, and I'll see to it that *she* is hurt, too." He casually looks at the rings on his fingers and the naked forefinger. "Perhaps even involve your dear mother, somehow. I'm not here to make others suffer if it's not needed, though. I'm getting too old for this reckless shit, so don't make it necessary."

My fingers twitch, knowing the exact blade I'd reach for and where I'd want to plunge it into him. Or grab one of the stone busts to smash his face in. *No, stop. What else is expected from the Scorpion?* He might have been gentle with Jane, but she has never seen her father outside that role.

He's a ruthless cunt to the rest of the world, an enemy no one wants to make. I didn't know how to bring that up to Jane, who was barely keeping herself together when she asked about him.

The Scorpion is *feared* for a reason.

And I don't like that he mentioned Serena. Or my mother.

"You know of my sister," I calmly state, as I rest the empty water cup back on the table and clear my throat.

"Oh," he squares his shoulders, glaring at me with a viciousness I'd expect from him. "*And* where she is."

My breathing grows deeper, and I control my eyes from revealing the shock flooding my system. I swear to the fucking sirens that I can feel he is speaking the truth.

In a fluid movement, my left thumb unhooks a sheath as an upside-down blade slides out from around my thigh, moving to my feet so I can catch the hilt as gravity takes it. Ritter removes one from his sleeve at nearly the same pace.

My heart pounds from blood loss, my body shot. My ego refuses to acknowledge reason, which tells me I *know* I'm not winning here. Even if I overpower an aged Scorpion, his men will kill me before mine reach me.

Maybe just *one* stab…

Grinding teeth, my knuckles are white as I grip my blade. "How the fuck do you know that."

"If you'd like to have a real conversation, let's have one *without* the metal." He looks at my hand and motions to it with his armed one. *Calm down.* Hesitantly, I slide the dagger back into its sheath and re-secure it, waiting for *any* suspicion that he might strike while my blade is away.

"Like before, let's not waste time." Ritter rolls his head around in a stretch before languidly blinking and staring me down, retaking his seat, and I do so as well. "First, let's clear up the fact that Cypress is Jane and I's great aunt from many, many generations ago. Jane doesn't know that. And I'm not proud of hiding it. To be frank, Cypress is pure poison, but she also is her own antidote. So I'll use her, knowing she won't let Jane die while I poison the rest, even if that includes myself."

I bet that witchy bitch is laughing somewhere, her ugly eyes blacked out.

"So that witch knows where my sister is, then? She probably

even knows what roof is over her head and the exact passage I'd need to take to find her," I state with clarity.

I knew Cypress was aware of my sister's wellbeing, but to really accept she knows *where* Serena is, and is using me, makes me feel like my skin is peeling away at the seam. My sister is out there, no doubt suffering, and I have to play Cypress's game with no insight as to when it'll end, and for all I know, every day that Misery is alive is another day that Serena is in pain.

I barely register him mentioning they're *related*.

Ritter gives a deep nod. "Save Jane's life, and Cypress will tell you. I'm aware you two met recently, and in her vagueness, *that's* what she meant by keeping my daughter alive. You will be given absolute clarity as to where to find your family once Misery is taken care of, and only then."

"Why in the hells does Cypress need Jane alive so much? How are you certain that Jane isn't a victim of Cypress like the rest of us, and we're not just fattening Jane up for the slaughter rather than keeping her safe?"

"I've nearly begged for that information, but all Cypress told me is that Jane is essential for Misery's return. And I don't think she'll let Jane die, or walk her to her death. She's loyal to her god *and* her bloodline."

I nearly laugh when I consider a month ago I thought Jane's name was rather simple, and her stature much too small to warrant a *Zenith* calling for her. Now, she's like a bona fide treasure who requires utmost security.

"So," I begin, languidly pointing at him. "You have a plan, surely, of what to do here? Cypress must have given *some* kind of directive as to how we fight Misery?"

His entire face hardens in the dim lighting, his eyes shining when the fire flicks in a certain direction. His jaw flexes from grinding his teeth. "No. She hasn't said a damn word in that regard. Just that we have to secure Jane."

"Then she's the most useless general in an armada I've ever met."

He smiles, but not from humor. "Except she's incredibly surgical when we remember her true allegiance is to her god, who *despises* Misery. My daughter just so happens to be *the* thing Misery requires to reclaim his body—for whatever reason—which means *all* of our survival is absolutely conditional on whether Jane's heart beats or not. So in that, we don't need to know shit. We just need to be able to follow orders."

A sardonic snicker escapes me after listening without breathing. It's ironic that two Zenith—two people who clearly want to be in charge—are left in the dark, much like those who follow us.

Every part of Ritter seems just as annoyed as I am, this room teaming with animosity directed toward the rubies that encroach upon the space.

"So then explain," I say, a thought crossing my mind, leaning forward and speaking quietly. "How do we keep Jane safe if her literal existence is what makes or breaks Misery's revival? People will come for her like she has the biggest bounty on her head."

"Precisely the reason for so much caution. Cypress is aware, and it's why she's meticulous in her execution. The Order of Ash may very well know, same with Blackwell. But they have a vested interest in keeping Jane alive, so they won't speak. But we have to get her out of the city before word spreads, if it does at all."

I nod slightly, shifting in my seat. "I still want my first question answered, that you skipped over." I slide my tongue over my teeth, my gaze lifting up at him. "Why can I feel you now?"

Ritter moves as if every minute gesture is purposeful, and as his hand dips into his pocket, there's no rush as he pulls out the ring, like this moment—the entire situation—belongs to him.

He holds up the silver jewelry. "We are all like fish, being dragged around by a lure, unaware that those who use us are so much more powerful than we can fathom," he answers, moving it around in his fingers. "Whatever magic connects all of *your* kind that allows you to see, feel, or read others can be manipulated. Cypress has made it so this ring and the ruby inside, when worn, can block prying powers, such as yours. She can control how much bleeds out, but if I take it off, its ability is moot."

I glance immediately at one of the rubies growing out of the walls, no longer 'guessing' if that's their true purpose.

Blackwell.

I nearly rise to my feet with this understanding, my racing heart staving off the exhaustion, even if it's false. The fighter in me wants to storm the castle and rip the truth from him. Staring at the rubies, I accept that Cypress is probably aware of everything in here. Perhaps even controlling Jane somehow with the earrings she wears. My gaze lands back on Ritter. "Before anything else is said, are we allies in this, or are we to become enemies?"

"I exist to ensure Jane's safety and happiness. So that answer is entirely dependent on *you*."

The lamina of his facade seems so inconsequential when I can sense out the broken, angry man underneath the confidence.

"Let's skip unnecessary chatter, then—Blackwell and Shade had the same issue as you," I say, *needing* these answers. "And you said Blackwell is working with Misery, so does that god have the same ability to block them?"

He looks off, tucking the ring back into his pocket as he says, "If that's true, then it does confirm Blackwell's direct connection to Misery. *Someone* is granting him that ability, and I doubt it's a Sensor. I've never heard of one *giving* their power to another. It's either innate, or transferred from an ethereal source. And Cypress would never help *anyone* associated with Misery."

"That bitch can't see what Blackwell is using?" I ask with a little too much attitude.

I'm so fucking ready to gut someone.

"No," he says, resolute, unaffected. "Whatever form Misery takes on now is akin to a corpse, but even then, his corpse-like state rivals Cypress, who's just a witch living off of her god's endowment. If Misery wants something hidden from her, it will be so."

I consider those words, and it's hard to imagine a deity literally among us. "I can't believe there's a god who is creating all this mayhem. It honestly sounds like a fable."

"Who knows what a god really is? All I know is that there are beings out there with powers that make us feel mortal. And you'd do well to accept this reality as quickly as possible. You're useful to Cypress in all of this, and you have good leverage with your sister. You're exactly what she wants, which means she'll drain every last drop of potential you have."

Our eyes connect, and no matter the skin he takes on, his atmospheric impression is the *Scorpion*—capable, determined, and I can't ignore how the man feels utterly broken. Like finding a priceless painting with a giant gash ripped down the middle.

He has *not* been thriving, even if he looks like it. Seems his witchy aunt is draining everything out of him, too.

"What's really happening, Ritter? You want my help? Then, reveal all the layers. And tell me everything, *before* you tell Jane."

His chin tucks into his neck, like the request disgusts him. "Why the fuck would I tell you everything, especially before Jane?"

"Her heart is in a delicate place," I respond in earnest. "I want to know what she has to take on."

"Like you fucking care." His voice is almost a growl as he leans back into his chair. "I'm honestly torn on whether it's worth killing you after this is all said and done. Jane only believes she has affection for you because survival demands it of her."

"And what would you know?"

"I've been following you both since you left Coalfell. Saw you walking her in *chains*."

"It's called putting on a show."

"You took my daughter to appease the Council." He grips the armrests tighter. "I get it. But still. Do you not think I've been trailing your shadow this entire time, *not* ready to stab your heart while you couldn't read me? To take you down when the opening is so clear and easy?"

I stare at Ritter under this novel light of judging a man I once only knew through legendary tales. What if the fucker is telling the truth? I don't get a single negative emotion from him toward Jane. Even then, I *will* dissect him as much as I can before he and Jane unveil more to each other. He is the reason her heart is wound so tightly, shredded in places she has tried to mend but failed. The way she kept looking at me when speaking to him, as if she *needed* me, fuels me with something dangerously tempting.

She knows who she is with. Who I am. The way I'd love would not be gentle, and that includes guarding her even from her father. And it seems like I'm affixed to that woman like an anchor to a ship, no matter what I do. Especially if the premonitions of her being in my future are true.

I'll absolutely go out of my way to take care of her.

"Why didn't you kill me already, if it was so easy?"

Ritter seems to mull that over. "Right before you arrived, Cypress warned me Jane would be in your company. Not when, or how. Just that she would be and not to interfere. But I *would* have killed you if you crossed a line. Too many of our kind are selfish and cruel. I wasn't going to risk it."

His proclamation to murder me hardly phases me—I'm quite used to, and expect many to take me down if they ever saw it as a benefit. One thing I note is that his passion for my death hits as deep as his words for Cypress. So, he speaks the truth about the witch, then? "How do you feel about Cypress if she was manipulating you? Why did you ever trust her?"

"I am kin, and she *always* saves her kin. Even if she fucks us over, she'll keep our hearts beating. And I wasn't ready to die. Nora—" he pauses, as if he can backtrack. But he has to know I read him just now—he grieves her *still.* "Would want me to live as long as possible to keep an eye on Jane. Even if she never saw my face again. Nora would want Jane to be safe. *Truly* safe."

I lean forward to place my elbows on my knees. "Tell me everything, Ritter. Let me do what I do best, which is piece things together. If we both want out of here with as little carnage inflicted upon us as possible, I need to know it *all.*"

It's odd to negotiate with him as if we are allies. Then again, is it really? We are both Zenith. His daughter is my charge now, especially if I want my sister back, let alone how I feel about her.

This *is* what I do among our little Council.

That changes something in him, just *barely* soothing out his irritation.

"First, tell me what you want with my daughter," he declares, the indelicacy returning in his expression. "You have known her for just over a month."

True. Even I have to remind myself of this often, and yet what I feel is profound. Does one really need to have been with someone for years before they know they'd stab a man for them? Or is it my unique magic that makes me so confident in her?

"That's personal, and you know it. So instead, how about this— you tell me the truths I want, and I'll ensure Jane believes your sincerity and trusts you once more," I offer. I wait to see how that feels, and oddly enough, my gut guides me to this being the correct path.

That piques his interest more than anything I've said so far. "We can start there."

"And one more thing," I say, knowing this is going to piss him off, but I'm claiming *this*. "I stay in her quarters."

"Oh, fuck off." I've hit such a nerve that I can tell he doesn't even believe me, although the grate in his voice says otherwise.

"You want my help to get her to trust you, and I know about Kathleen." Ritter's brown eyes are so very careful to hide the absolute annoyance brewing in his chest. "I can be very critical in how revealing that plays out. How all of it does, actually."

"How chivalrous to threaten her father."

I lean over, and I don't know why, but even now, I can't quite bite my tongue. "She doesn't want me for my chivalry."

Ritter is so conflicted he can't stand it, his body so still it could morph into a statue. I can read him so fucking clear, and he's so uncertain on how to parent a child who thinks he's been gone for over ten years, while also respecting her adult autonomy.

"I have every motivation to see her heart is beating by the end of this," I add. "I *also* don't want her alone. I kept the Council from getting to her, and I didn't even have to work that hard to do it. Don't act like I'm some petty thief."

I'll never tire of knowing when I've won in a conversation before the other person admits it. "If Jane has any hesitation, or any hint that she doesn't want you there, we *will* fight over it."

A sly smile slowly spreads on my face. "And *I* can work with that."

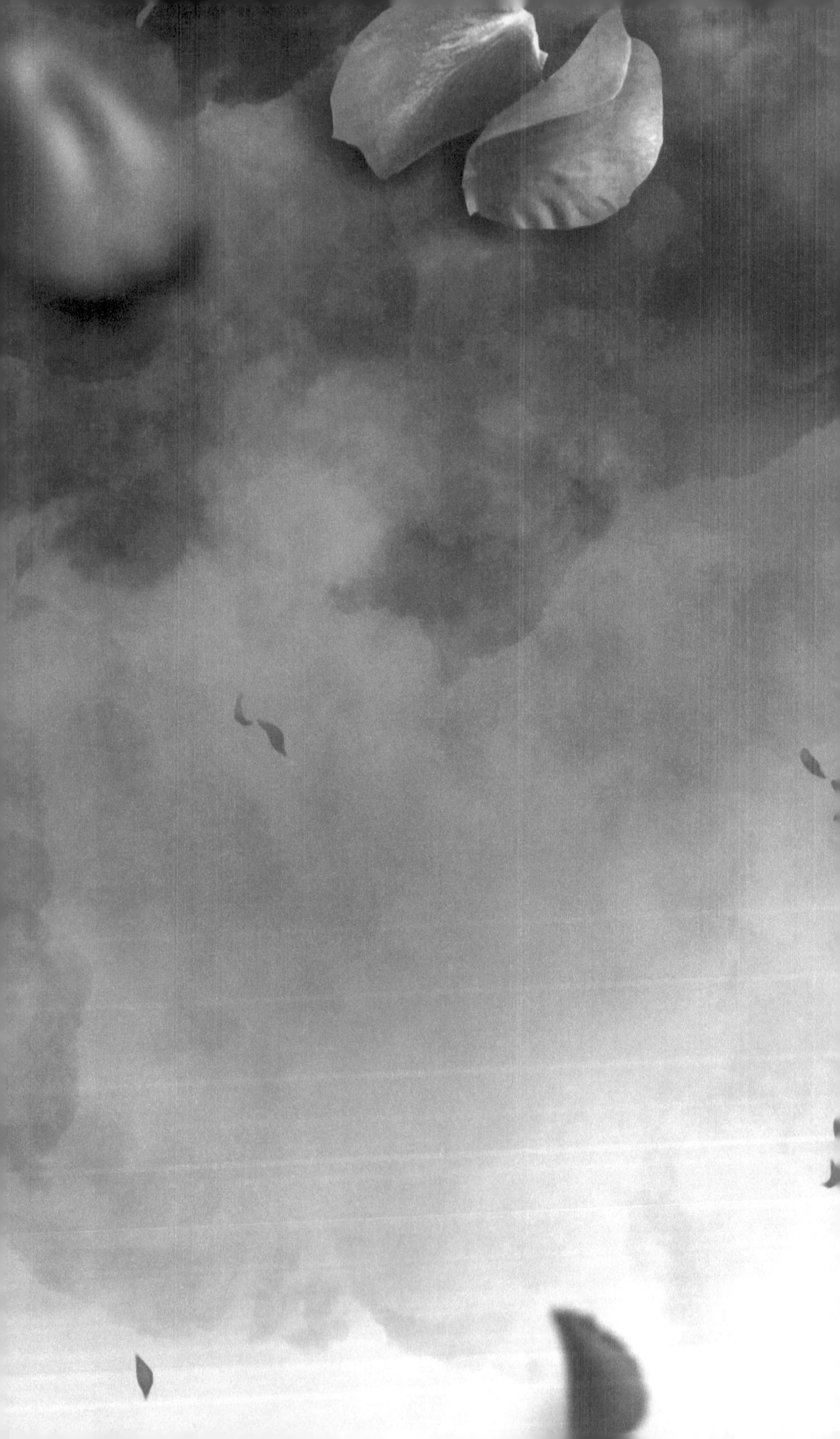

I 'm never complaining again after this is all said and done.

Every time my mind *touches* a concept of what we discussed, it dissolves like wet sand between my fingers.

My hands are restless as I twirl my hair so much it's almost a permanent ringlet. My eyes haven't moved from the dark wood of my father's seat; if I look away, it makes it all too real. I also can't stop examining every memory, wishing I could desperately go back in time to pay attention to *everything*.

What *else* is he hiding? If anything at all? How much of my childhood is true? Was Mom in on all of these secrets? Did 'Ern' ever tell me anything that was a hint? It's all just…

I'm *stunned* that everything could be explained with what Dad told me. It's actually a massive relief that I didn't make up my entire life in my head and that what happened to me *was* real. But with that comes an incredibly difficult concept—*accepting* it also means welcoming in the absolutely monstrous concept that *a god is after me.*

Every time that sinks in, my gaze wanders back to a certain detail of the chair that comforts me like nothing else has in a very long time—at the top are dahlias carved into the wood.

Mom always grabbed fresh ones when she could.

My actual family.

There doesn't seem to be any rhyme or reason when I finally make the decision to stand, approaching the chair from the side as the totality of my life settles in my heart like ash once a fire is no more than a crackle. Running my hand over the smooth wood, my fingers roll with the indents and raises. Touching the dahlias breathes so much life into someone that's so far in the past for me.

Bringing her memory back from the dead also pulls forward the image of her lying on the wooden deck with blood blooming on her peach dress. I can even see her blonde hair stuck to her jawline, everything stained in crimson.

"*Mom,*" I seethe through clenched teeth, trying to grip the carved wood, my fingers creating a squeaky whine as it slides along the polish. My vision blurs from tears, my chest constricting. "You should *be here.*"

That deep, aching loss of knowing I'll *never* see her again is a chasm in my soul, a cruel robbery of what should have been my mother's presence. Even after all this time, all this pain, all this suffering, all I have of her are stagnant mementos, like these dahlias.

I really will never see her again.

Not in this life.

I'll never share the tale of how I escaped with a siren, about Kathleen, or see her hair gain silver streaks, or smell her faint perfume, or hear her say '*Jane*' with trepidation when she thought she lost sight of me, because now that I'm older, I see how desperately she wanted to keep me safe in a city far too easy to get hurt... of how dangerous it was that my father is Charles Ritter.

My chest hurts. That same regret burns my veins like acid; if I had stabbed Mom's killer when I first saw him, right as he had grabbed his blade… I just didn't think he'd actually stab my *mother*. Dad *always* had people around—

I revoke my hand to grip my face a little *too* hard; my shudder muffled through my fingers. My fingernails dig into my cheeks, violent retribution tightening my windpipes. I want to *stab* someone.

My lips curl in as my shudder morphs into something similar to Maryanne's cries, and I slowly move away from the chair, my watery eyes unblinking as my jaw trembles, my breathing shaky. Even through this immeasurable pain, there's a calm that steadies me as if I never used to be afraid.

My purpose has never been clearer.

The entire life my family was *supposed* to relish in was utterly ruined for the *cunts* that broke us apart. Coalfell became such a new normal that its mirage temporarily blinded me, even if I remember how home is *supposed* to look.

Oh, how I will *gut* these men.

I need it—

The door to the room opens, and where I might have once spun quickly on my heels like a mouse afraid of its own tail, I instead slowly pivot, already knowing that I'd grab the candle stick next to me if I needed to use it.

The Council doesn't mean shit anymore—

What the fuck?

Cypress?

The rhythmic taps of her leather boots click on the stone floors. Faint whispers of conversations outside breech through the open door until, on rusted hinges, it shuts on its own. The rubies inside radiate like candles doused in oxygen, casting a rich red glow as if the light is filtered through stained glass.

My heart races like I'm seeing this woman for the first time. I can't stand the way she glides, or the way the whites of her eyes surround her entire iris.

"What are you doing in here," I state through tight lips, glaring at the witch.

Cypress scans the room, lingering her attention on the chair next to me, her black eyes suffused with power. "There is something that needs tending to."

A gust of wind blows through the open holes in the ceilings, lifting dirt from the floor, rustling hooks from ropes that clink along the stone, and strands of my hair twirl in my face.

The room darkens as her black irises eat away at the white, giving her two glistening onyx voids for eyes; the rubies in the walls only seem brighter, her milky pallor now almost pink from how the entirety of the room reddens. I hardly blink, afraid that any closure of my eyes will result in Cypress suddenly appearing before me when they open again.

That resilience I just felt, admittedly, is very weak right now.

How am I supposed to handle a god if I can't handle her?

"That is the appropriate thought, Jane." Cypress sits in a chair with such elegance that it's as if gravity doesn't affect her. "We have a lot to cover, don't we?"

My head slowly moves as my eyes dart around like I've drank too much coffee. *She's so fucking creepy.* "Is this really necessary?" I ask, clearing my shaky voice, vaguely pointing around. "All of this?"

"Quite, actually. It's how my magic works, Jane, and how I can read a singular wave of *everything* relevant to you. Including how I can tell that your heart is most hungry for the *truth*. I am here to confirm that your father spoke with veracity, and now, it's time that you're given *purpose*."

Oh, gods. I don't need purpose anymore if it's from *her*.

"There are very few things I'd be willing to die for," the witch continues. "And one of them is to prevent Misery from taking over the Balar Coasts. My god needs these lands. If there is one thing I do not lie about, it's my role to ensure *you* don't end up as Misery's catalyst."

When those black voids seem to peer right at me, I feel *haunted*. Soren's gaze might dig deep into me, but Cypress seems to see *through* me, like she can see my past, present, and future all in this very room.

"Now hold on," I begin with more confidence, even if she freaks me out. "You knew about him wanting *me*, then. You clearly know about *so much* and yet only tell everyone crumbs."

She weaves her bony fingers through the air. "A starving man won't seek food if I give him more than crumbs."

I scoff, loathing that she isn't fucking wrong. Which means there's a really good chance she knows exactly how all of this will go, and won't tell any of us.

She threads her fingers together and places them on a crossed knee. "Jane, you have incredibly high odds of encountering Misery. I want to protect you from his powers if that is to happen."

The recent rush of fear once again rescinds… wait, she wants to help me take on Misery? Petty vengeance is loud in my heart, telling me that if there's a way to fuck with this god, I should at least hear her out. I cross my arms, slightly shivering as some of my clothes are still damp, and it's as if *now* I can feel the temperature of the room. *Or maybe it dropped with her in it.* "I don't believe you aren't about to send me to my deathbed."

She slowly smiles, something about the humor unnerving. "It amuses me that when I'm finally being forthcoming, you refuse to trust an inch of it."

I look down as if it can give me a sense of privacy, and when I glance back up, her eyes are already boring into me with that inky stare. "What are you going to do, or with, me?"

"What I have planned will be extremely minimal."

That somehow does *nothing* to comfort me.

I glare at Cypress, and something hits me in the chest that tells me she will do whatever she wants with me, whether I like it or not. "Do the others know you're in here?"

"I'm the one that made these tunnels possible. It makes it rather easy to slip in and out."

I hesitate, almost wanting to scream at the idea, because I'm so damn tired of everything not making sense. "Why can't another god help, or something? I mean, why me?"

Her face contorts with frustration, as if the mere idea of involving anyone other than her god is the first and only thing to offend her. "Only three gods have any strength out here that are worth anything. The ocean god, *mine*, and Misery. *We* are the first line of defeating him, and seeing as how we're on land, it's rather up to *me*, then."

"And I seriously cannot run from this?"

Fuck it. It's worth one last shot of trying to avoid this.

Cypress looks around, cracking her neck before flashing that haunting gaze back at me. "The truth is, Jane, when I look at you… I see Misery's burning eyes *right* behind you."

My shoulders immediately pull upward, as if to cover my neck from chills that threaten to wash over. I even glance slightly to the side as if I might see something terrifying, but it's just more of the same floor.

My arms come out from the fold, holding my hands to the side. "Then what the *fuck* was the last ten years for?"

"The last ten years were necessary to reach *this* point in time. If my intention was to push you off a bridge onto a passing boat, it would be nonsensical to do it before the boat is even in sight. Metaphorically, the boat is currently *right* underneath us."

"Indulge me," I suggest with a weak laugh. The sound is dry and humorless. "You claim it's important I avoid Misery, and yet you're more than confident that I'll cross his path. You're clearly powerful. Why don't *you* protect me, then? You said I'm a catalyst, but I bet you won't even tell me what *that* means."

"Oh, I have protected you, Jane. I *do*. Which means if he is likely to take you, then I will continue to protect you by equipping you with what you need."

My lips tightly press together, not fully realizing that while I loathe her mystery, I also can't deny she *hasn't* helped, even if I barely understand just who she is.

"If you know the future, then why does any of this matter?" I quip.

"Free will ensures the future is in constant flux." Her smile is uncanny, as if pulled up by another. "I've become adept at reading human behavior and guessing what their next actions will be. Otherwise, I can't read the future as if it's been written in a book. No one can. Not even Misery… and to answer… no, I will not reveal what he wants with you. Not right now. It won't help anything in the immediate, and some rest could do you good."

I nearly *chortle* at her acting like she cares. Do I need her sympathy, though? Temptation tugs at me to go along with whatever she schemes, just wanting to get her out of this room. As I look away, I feel like I can't think without her eavesdropping in on *that*. "What does your god want? What is he *really* after?"

"The gods are greedy. Morvock, or Misery as the rest call him, is perpetually parched for an army of devout followers. It's said that to be in his inner circle is the opposite of what everyone else is subjected to—he provides utter luxury to those most loyal. Once he has a grip on society, everyone will be willing to kill whoever they have to in order to even *witness* a second of it, lest they return to their miserable lives." Her sigh is heavy, like it's weighed down by a thousand considerations. "*My* god," she continues, quieter now, "wants these Balar Coasts free of Morvock, or else *he* loses power. It's that simple."

The suggestion of someone having such a hold on society makes me shiver, and also feels so fictitious. "If these gods are so powerful, then why don't they just take care of this themselves? Why be so convoluted?"

"Have you ever wondered what a fish would think of a jar of rum?"

I—what?

My breathing halts as if any movement will only add to the confusion. "Come again?" I ask slowly.

She motions in the direction behind me. "Directly that way, through the stone, is where the ocean meets this city. There's a vast world in which aquatic life is born, lives, and dies within. Meanwhile, we exist on dry land. They will never know the refreshing smell of campfire smoke, and we will never know how refreshing freezing water might actually feel.

"Humans are like the fish underneath the ocean's surface, and the gods are like *us*, above the water. It's hard for them to exert perfect control when they can only skim the surface, so they have conduits like me to do it for them." She pauses and glances at me with a mixture of pity and pride in her onyx eyes. "And Misery plans to exist in the ocean without consequence... to which the Cinders, like *you*, will allow."

"No, Dad made it seem like Misery needed *me*."

Her lips tighten, her eyes widening before narrowing; I don't think she intended for that. "Then I will say this—you are uniquely qualified, in ways you do not know, to be *the* conduit for Misery. Do *not* ask me further on that." Her voice rises like a crescendo, as if to speak over my thoughts.

If I thought I felt murderous before, then I'm not quite sure how to describe the violence inside of me now. "You know how *messed up* it is to tell someone these things and then just demand that they ask *no* more questions?" I shake my head, placing my hands on my hips. "Also, I'd literally jump off a cliff before then. Hells, I can get pretty creative on how to off myself before that happens. Actually," I pause, the concept a morbid one, my hand raised slightly as my finger lazily points upward. "Why don't you just kill me now? Rob him of that? Come to think of it, why isn't there a bounty on my head? If I'm a *conduit*, as you say."

"Because no one knows other than his close followers, and your willingness to keep it that way will do great good for you," she purrs, her approval making me slightly lurch. "But I do warn you not to allow yourself to die, Jane. You partaking in Misery's undoing is *essential* to minimizing the catastrophe that otherwise would occur. Because if he takes over the Balar Coasts, then his moniker will be understood to a depth that will scar these lands for hundreds of years, if not thousands. Where he might need you to regain a human form in this *decade*, you're not essential in the grand web of the fates. Instead, it's his steadfast *focus* on you that creates an opening for his *demise*, especially with me helping you. We have *one* chance to make this happen.

"You're a distraction I have been patiently waiting for, while also maximizing your likelihood of surviving. You are, in essence, my ultimate gamble, and even if he's aware of that, I think he's too greedy to care, and too self-important to see me as a *true* threat. You dying would mean I'd have to start entirely over, and that gives him an upper hand I'm not willing to risk." She bores her gaze into me. "You die, and I can guarantee *many* on this continent will follow that same path. *Especially* those associated with you."

The only way I can describe this out-of-body experience is as if I've stumbled upon an ancient curse that exists only in nighttime folklores told next to candlelight, and it turns out it's actually real, undeniable, and utterly mind-blowing. It's so tempting to immediately believe her, because in many ways, so much is explained. But there's a resistance that screams at me that I'm an idiot for even *thinking* about considering her words.

Well, what if whatever she does to me is minimal? I can work with that.

Can I really say no to some help? "Okay... say I agree to this. Can I even take on a god? Are we sure of that? I mean... look at me."

"*Everything* has a weakness, especially in our realm. Morvock's soul is raw in this state, and I wouldn't be here if I didn't think you have incredible influence over what happens next."

It's like there's a bunch of river stones in my gut, sinking lower with each breath. My mind races with everything that's ever happened in my life, to every scar I've earned, to the latency of my teens and early twenties. It's not that I even really fear *dying*, but I dread the unknown of it all, the demand beyond my skill.

I *loathe* not knowing if I have to bury another person I love. Gods, even the thought of that makes my heart turn to lead.

My gaze only rises once I *swear* I can hear my mother's voice again, always there to comfort me in the recesses of my mind. This isn't just about me or my revenge. No, this would be for Soren's sister, and the heartache that humanizes him to me. For Maryanne and her children. If Cypress is being truthful, then it sounds like she's gambling with my life, and she's placing a *lot* of worth on that bet.

What's the worst that happens? I gain a defense against Misery? He's coming for me, so that seems like an obvious answer. "What did you want to do with me?" I quietly ask.

"I will implant something under your skin that prevents anyone from reading you," she gently replies. "The time isn't right now. Not yet. I thought it best to give you a warning, so you'd have time to really consider it. But as I said—minimal."

"I—Even *Soren*? As in, *he* couldn't read me?" The question tumbles from my lips before I can restrain myself, my voice utterly saturated with concern. *No, I love that he can read me.*

"Even him."

My breathing grows labored, my chest heaving with each inhale. "I don't want Soren to not read me."

"He will, again. One day. Once I remove it when Morvock is no longer a threat. Morvock has the same ability to read people, and it's best to prevent him from using it on you."

"But if Soren can sense when someone is blocked, won't Misery also be able to detect it in me?" I protest, examining the scenario as if it's a precious stone and I need to rule out all compromising details.

"Oh, yes. He will be able to tell, almost certainly right away. And he will not be surprised that I have taken precautions," Cypress reassures. "He will not have a choice on whether he keeps you. He *requires* you, at least, to fulfill *this* grand scheme he's plotting."

The question about what *exactly* he wants with me rests on the tip of my tongue, but I know she won't answer. She'll probably just give another fucking metaphor about a boat or some rum. I finally sit in my father's seat when it's the closest to me, and my knees are about to give out; closing my eyes, placing a hand over my face, and speaking through my fingers, "You are so exhausting."

"I should let you know that I plan to do this to you whether you like it or not. It is important you have time to mull this over, so when the time comes, you are ready."

"Such a *considerate* person," I quip, throwing her a look through my parted fingers and then focus back on my hands, only to close them again when those damn eyes are still completely black. "Do you mean for me to kill him or something? Because I want a lot more than something implanted in me for that. Like a new, special skill. Something a lot more useful than not being able to burn. Maybe a dagger that makes me stronger, or something like a Zenith's mask."

I swear I hear genuine humor in her barely audible chuckle. "All those things can and will be taken from you, if he apprehends you. And I don't know if *you* will kill him or not, but you have immense potential to be the toughest challenge he will face. If you do not hold the blade that will stab him, I have no doubt you will pass it to the person who *will*."

I'm tired of this and lean back in my father's makeshift throne, staring at the floor. "When will it happen?"

No matter the intensity of what's occurring here, there's so much relief in having a real plan. Something crafted by Cypress herself, a lifeline promised by the witch that, for better or worse, I believe might actually help me because she's desperate to make her god happy.

It's better than nothing.

"Soon, and when it feels right for me to come back to you. It's also pertinent to mention that I wouldn't tell anyone of this, either," she warns, leaving that statement to hang between us for a moment.

"If someone gets the idea that your death robs Misery of his rebirth, then you'll have the largest bounty on your head since Scarlet Ironjaw."

I frown at the name, having no freaking idea who *that* is. Cypress stands up, her gaze sweeping over me with an unreadable intensity. "I also wouldn't tell Soren about what is planned, about the fact that I intend to block the ability to feel you. Or your father. They will take that to mean Misery *will* get you, and take extreme actions that will ruin the ripples I have so carefully orchestrated. Which can, and very likely will, result in their deaths that *otherwise* could have been avoided. This plan is between you and me, because remember Jane, you're capable within your own right. It's in your blood... we'll see each other again, very soon."

My lips twitch with many replies, but nothing makes it even to a small whisper as I watch Cypress depart, the intensity of the rubies diminishing back to normal as if she never walked in.

How in the fuck do I keep this secret from someone who can read if I'm lying to him or not?

PLANNING

SOREN

Like a changing of the guards, everything is set into motion once I'm removed from Ritter's room. The act feels necessary, and yet there's a pulse of *something* brushing over me with such subtlety I barely register it. *The hells is that about?*

One of the guards looks at my wrists, as if he might want to bind them. I arch my brow, a silent challenge daring him to try. His hands fidget like he doesn't know how to approach me, until he steps back against the wall and gives up. It's evident he doesn't think it's worth it.

Damn right.

Glancing over my shoulder I see Ritter is leaving his room, and I make exaggerated efforts to move against the wall so he might pass, as if mocking his importance when we both know *I'm* the conduit to his daughter. The old man doesn't look at me as he walks by, and for an annoying moment in time, I'm a little fascinated to be *here*, negotiating and strategizing with the Scorpion while the world thinks him lost.

He *is* a legend, after all.

Ritter's energy burns through those around us, almost as if his entire aura contains more power than the rest. His presence is both magnetic and suffocating with its intensity, and I'd wish he'd put that damn ring back on.

He walks with confidence, and I get a good look at him and know the distinct weight in a gaze of a man that has seen, and done, a *lot*.

"Take Soren to the Commons. Give him blood rejuvenation if we have it and send someone to fetch replacement ingredients. Neither he nor his men are touched. They're to aid us without hesitation—" my head tilts, as I didn't fucking agree to *that* "—Soren is to remain in the Commons until I make plans to adjust our arrangement here. I need time to myself. I'll be back."

Biting my tongue is almost physical rather than metaphorical as, once again, everything swings into motion when someone tells me to move.

I momentarily almost retort, despising the way Ritter just volunteered my aid—

Stop.

My ego is not what matters here.

As I'm guided forward, I need to be prepared for it all, including letting these cunts bind my wrists, even if it pisses me off. I'm essentially in enemy territory, and that means this is an exercise in utilizing my *compliant* side, which is quite underused.

I'm essentially their bitch until I decide to fight back.

Maybe this is good for me; a bitter dose of discipline to strip me back down to what I'm here for in the first place; my sister, *not* establishing my rank as a Zenith. So that means if the Scorpion is going to bark orders like this, I'll do what I can to roll with it.

The area outside Ritter's little nest is where I'm taken, right to a cornered alcove with a blanket crudely covering a pile of hay, almost insultingly so. I lie down on it when it's clear that's where I'm staying put for the time being, and my bones feel like they can finally rest, even if the straw pokes into my skin. Closing my eyes, I open myself up fully, stretching my senses outward like unfurling tendrils. Every wavering emotion and deep fear that these men possess grows more vivid the longer I remain still.

Rorge clears his throat, and as soon as he begins speaking, the noise of this place silences. "This Zenith is supposedly our ally for now, so leave him be. I assume Scorpion wants him here so we can all keep an eye on him. Don't let him leave this corner."

The room's energy tightens as they all seem to take this responsibility seriously, and meanwhile, I lace my fingers and just let my body rest, eyes still closed. "Yes, please watch over me as I nap. Very dangerous business."

I breathe out a heavy sigh, moving my shoulders to get comfortable. A fierce wave of judgment pulses through the room, with only less than a handful who seem amused.

I breathe slowly so my heart rate can even out, not giving a shit what any of these people think. It's oddly relaxing since I know Jane is safe—I *do* trust Ritter to keep a very close eye on her. I assume my men will be informed that we're *temporarily* allies, and if not, I can tell I'll be able to pass that on soon.

One way or another, this is a clear moment of rest to regain what strength I can.

And to think.

Jane is truly the center of all this attention, isn't she? I can sense her inner fire hasn't had enough oxygen to breathe, and she needs to let these changing winds fuel her so she can ignite. Unleashing her potential is critical, so when all these fuckers come for her, she can slit their throats *herself*. The more prepared—mentally, emotionally, and physically—she is, the better we *all* are.

At the same time, she won't have the luxury to properly heal the wounds that have been ripped back open and exposed, which means patchwork for now, because we need to leave as soon as possible; to formulate a plan.

I need a plan.

My fingers tighten in their hold.

Shit. What comes next will be one of the hardest challenges I've ever faced. How is a man supposed to take on a broken god, an entire cult, *and* another Zenith all at once? Even if Ritter doesn't want to kill me *now*, it's still a conditional handshake.

And what about the detail that Cypress, that worthless cunt that she is, might *actually* be able to get me to my sister?

Protecting Jane is literally my life's purpose if what Ritter says is true, that drive layered with many different obligations. Learning that Misery is deeply entrenched in Jane's shadow quite honestly fucking unnerves me, and the way every aspect of her aura *bleeds* destruction makes sense now if that god is hunting her, and logic tells me that getting too close is dangerous as fuck.

I could very easily die in this.

Can I risk that?

What would happen to Serena if I died? Has she given up on being found? Has my sister suffered and endured abandonment for the latter half of our lives, or has she found her own peace? If I found her now, would she even be able to function? Surely, *I* can offer her something with my powers. A way to numb her trauma, even.

We're all evolving without understanding in these coasts, so what if I learned how to ease Serena's terrors? If these gods can fuck with our energies, surely I can learn how to push my powers onto another.

My death, on the other hand, will make that impossible.

That sinking feeling of considering I'll truly never see Serena again rears its head, thrashing in my chest. It's a sense of defeat that hollows me out. Cypress doesn't give a shit if I see my family again, and I know that. I could die in the exact breath that saves Jane from Misery, still fulfilling her promises.

What am I to do, though? Just leave Jane and hunt for my sister on my own as if none of this ever existed? Jane's tangible, real, and grazes against something in my chest that has me seeing and feeling shit I'm frankly unprepared for. I know, without much pushback, that there's something in the fates with her.

Some part of her is *meant* for me.

Deserting her isn't just a failure my ego dislikes, but I simply can't even consider it. I *won't* leave her.

So, what does that fucking *mean*? I can't risk my life for Jane while also ensuring I find Serena.

I mindlessly rub the rings on my fingers, running a fingertip over the snake design the Council crafted for me. I joined those assholes for their resources, so I could man a pursuit over the Black Sea to find my kin.

Literally everything I've done has been rooted in trying to find my sister.

As I try to focus on feeling out what's best, it's damn near impossible in this room, the energies swirling together while there's a foreboding danger, thick like miasma, somewhere to my right, and I know it's circling Jane.

Jane.

The idea of Misery, Blackwell, or the Order of Ash getting the tip of their *pinky* on her enrages me, because they *will* destroy her if they capture her.

The thought that I'd lie my head down in an empty bed, her soft hair gone from this world—the fire blown out that is so desperate to rumble—makes me grip my fingers so tight the circulation diminishes.

I care for her.

I *must* ensure she doesn't drown in Misery's murk—

Anya's presence spreads through the chatter of the room, and I open my eyes, her aura being one that blends easily into the background; there is no chaos inside of her, only *purpose*. Drive.

Yet I know that subtle, calm energy anywhere.

As her aura approaches me, I observe the face she wears—a woman closer to Jane's age with a messy, black braid down the middle of her head, bringing a stool over and placing a basket next to me. Mossy green eyes meet mine—so different from the usual dark brown—but I know who they really belong to. "I haven't had time to study her full mannerisms, so make it short."

A skin shifter.

Ritter and Anya are the only two that I know of with these powers in the Balar Coasts, although their type tends to avoid the shit out of me—I can spot them a league away if I know the energy they're *supposed* to have.

I sit up from lying down. My vision momentarily fades when

limited blood pulses through my veins. I still don't know the purpose of suffering that attack, especially since it's not a simple one to recover from.

It better be for a good reason.

Looking at a stranger's face, I ask, "Where is everyone?"

"More are making their way down here," she answers, pulling out tonics from the basket. "Elise has left to secure passage. Our *trusted liaison* is aware, and may do what he can to ensure an exit route. The rest are assuming their positions. I came to confirm that you are allied with the Scorpion? That's what we were just told before I entered."

"Unfortunately, that fucker is our ally for now. I'll be on a tight leash while we're in *his* domain."

"Drink that bottle, then," Anya instructs, rising to her feet, a knee cracking. "I'm going to leave before people get suspicious. Get your energy back."

"Where is the woman?" I ask, looking her body up and down to insinuate the skin suit.

"Safe. Just temporarily borrowing her flesh. She's being treated well. We assumed it would be best not to piss off Ritter *too* much."

I grunt in reply, having recalled Anya mentioning she secured someone she believed to be among Ritter, a follower who frequents Skull's Row to shop for ingredients—perfect for identity theft since she doesn't sit in one place.

At least the fates are smiling on us a *little*.

As Anya departs, I assume that this confirms Ritter doesn't have anyone like me among him too. Otherwise they'd be able to sense Anya like a murderer smeared in blood. Uncorking the small bottle given to me, I immediately bring it to my lips, grimacing when the thick liquid tastes like rust and seawater.

What a *foul* aftertaste.

I lie back down on the blanket that hay pokes through to let the magical concoction work, trying my best to ignore the assault on my tastebuds. As my exhaustion gets the best of me, my mind drifts back to Jane. If she is meant to be anything akin to permanent in my life, then I owe her that unwavering dedication I know I have.

The kind I *never* give out.

It's a weakness. A huge fucking soft spot that anyone can strike, and it would cripple me.

Gods does that make me uncomfortable.

I know I need to speak to *him* soon. He's the only one I know like me who is as skilled as I am, so maybe he'll have insight and understanding.

I'd burn the world down for someone born to be mine.

I'd burn the world down for *Jane*.

MENTORS

JANE

Gods, what a shit show.

The only silver lining has to be that while this is *over-whelming*, there's simultaneously so much relief in clarity. My gaze finds its way back to where Cypress had sat, staring there for however long until I'm slowly searching the room.

"Okay," I say to myself, tapping a hand on my thigh, "*Okay.*"

Somehow, someway, I can hide all this from Soren. *And that there will be a time when he can't feel me…*

He's *not* going to like that—

The door opens once more, and in the dim lighting enters Donna, her footsteps echoing softly against the worn stone. Both hands are in pockets of a cloak she wears—this one looks dry. "Thinking of your *own* throne?"

With a raised brow, I move my hands from the armrests when I realize what seat I'm in, scoffing slightly at the idea. *Act normal, Jane. Practice on her.* "I mean, the carvings are beautiful, but I wouldn't call it a *throne.*"

"Eh, it's his throne for now. Doesn't sit on it much, really. We'll get him a proper one once all this shit is done and over with, and we don't have to live down here like moles."

My mind is stuck deeply within what I just uncovered, and yet it wanders away just as fast when hearing someone speak about my father as if they know him. For so long, I refused to even *whisper* a hint of his identity. A deep inhale fills my lungs with musty air, with a hint of candle wax. "How long has he been down here?"

"We've centralized in these tunnels for the last five years. Although he isn't here much, like I said." She pierces a knowing gaze through me, and being this close, I notice her dark lashes are as thick as her eyebrows. "He's always off as Ern."

I still can't tell if it comforts or annoys me that he was so close for so long.

"I'm sure you all loved being here just so he could pretend to be a barkeep."

"Oh, there's no issue on our end. When your father first disappeared, we all knew something was wrong in Skull's Row. We had no problem hiding rather than sitting like an open ship at sea. We were all mostly curious to meet *you.*" I don't even know how to reply to something like that, so instead, I just sit there while staring her down. She crinkles her forehead while raising her brows, looking off again. "Plus, we know what's out there, now. We've known since we took up residence down here. It's unified us."

"You're talking about Misery?"

She dips her head in affirmation, not looking my way. "Cypress keeps us informed, with what little information she gives. The Eyeless have seen the miasma around Blackwell, so they know *that's* true, at least."

I tilt my head slightly to the side, as if it'll help me re-hear what she just said. "Eyeless?"

She vaguely points to one of her dark eyes. "The ones with a milky eye."

"Oh," I say, sitting straighter. "So you're all aware of that, then? What does it do?"

She tilts her head back and forth like she's considering what to say. "Well, where someone like Soren can feel and sense things, they can *see* the auras, especially with a patch over the normal eye. The world through the mirk is quite blurry and colorless, but they can see the energies. Whatever that means. It's some witchy shit they did over the Black Sea. It's not as intuitive as a Sensor, but they make incredible guards."

My intrigue is so momentary. Normally, I'd be more nosy, but it just feels like something else I don't want to worry about right now. "I still don't understand why everyone is *here*? Why not just leave and get as far away from this as possible?"

"Why not just tell a hurricane to blow right over you?" she retorts, as if my acumen disappoints her. "You can't do that. Misery takes over, and *all* our families are dead, and since Cypress declares you're to play one of the most critical roles in stopping him... well, we've been waiting for you. Otherwise, we'd have to uproot *everyone* who lives on these coasts, and even then, it would only be a matter of time before Misery's reign or torment leeches into other lands, and by then, he'll be so powerful it would be nearly impossible to kill him."

I rub my eye hard enough to see little lingering spots, wishing more than ever for my mother, to ask her what to do. To confide in somebody about *everything*. "I feel like I need *months* to catch up and process."

"Well, we don't have that. We have a few *weeks*, maximum. And then it will all likely happen at once, like it usually does. If it makes you feel better, we *are* leaving soon. We just want to do so with caution. There's a man known by the name of Basilisk and he was spotted recently. His *true* form."

"Who in the hells is the Basilisk? And what's a true form?"

"You really lived under a rock, didn't you?" Her scrutinous gaze really irks me.

"Yeah, I did. It's called Coalfell. Any other obvious questions?"

She snorts. "Fine, fine. I'm just used to most people knowing about the Basilisk. He's *from* here, but I guess it's been almost two decades since he roamed these lands. He's akin to a Zenith, but over the seas. His golden eyes got him that name, and how if you look into them, there's a good chance you're dead. Mostly because he's so accomplished he doesn't do his dirty work anymore, so if he shows up, you're not going to be alive for much longer. A master swordsmith, honestly. His personal circle is harder to get into than your father's. It's doesn't bode well that he was spotted nearby."

I roll a hand, feeling like I'm back as a child and being taught about the history of the world. "And what does *true form* mean?"

"Right. He's got someone shifting into his skin out in the Crimson Isles for some reason, while the *real* one is here. Your father doesn't like the uncertainty in that. Once it's ironed out, we're *then* making our move. If Basilisk is here to claim you, then we want to avoid *any* confrontation."

"Why the fuck would *he* claim me—" I raise both hands in the air, palms out, stopping when a sickening sensation weighs down my stomach; what if Basilisk is here to *kill* me? To cull Misery's revival in the exact way Cypress warned against? In that, I can see why I shouldn't tell *anyone* that Misery needs *me*, even if I don't know why myself.

"Take that up with Misery for making you so interesting to everyone. Maybe Basilisk wants to see the world burn and prefers to stand among the ashes rather than suffocate, so getting ahead of the curb, really. Wouldn't put it past him. Either way, we're taking no chances. Not with Cypress's protection being taken off of you."

I rub my chin, noting that she doesn't seem to be aware that my death would be a swift way to buy all these people a lot of peace—even if temporary. "So, what has Cypress said about me? I didn't get much myself," I ask, seeing what insight she truly has.

I know how to lie if I need to.

She looks surprised. "That's annoying she didn't say much, considering we were relying on that… she mostly just said the Scorpion's daughter will be what we need to overcome Misery, like you're some kind of key or tool, and that your safety is the priority of everyone. You know, because if you die, then we lose our chance to use whatever it is she has planned."

Ah, shit. I hate to think everyone is being misled. It's like the siren's promise all over again.

I look back down at my lap. "That's the gist of what I got." I sigh heavily. "I'm sure she'll reveal it to me, one way or another."

Fuck. I really didn't consider the way it would make me feel to lie to all these people, or at least, to lie to their *hope*.

The sharp rhythm of five knocks comes to the wooden doorframe, and Donna seems to be entirely expecting it as she turns around and heads to the door. A guard stands there, one hand lowering from rapping his knuckles and the other near the hilt of his weapon. "All clear?" she asks the man.

"Aye," he firmly answers with a practiced formality.

Another thing I'm growing rather tired of is all this waiting until someone permits me to leave a damn room. Oh, how I miss walking to the Perch when I felt like it and the freedom that the dirt road promised at night.

Kathleen…

It's her consideration that moves me forward without question, as I need to tell my father that her safety is non-negotiable. And also ask him about this Basilisk asshole, whoever he is.

I don't like those undertones.

It doesn't take long before we reach one of the Eyeless from earlier, Rorge looking down over his large, crooked nose at the both of us.

"Watch over Jane," Donna briskly commands, her black hair the last thing I see before she disappears around a corner. My heart races as I stand against the cold wall, Rorge's hands crossed in front of him while I stare at the floor. The sound of all those people nearby is getting to me, *my father's people.*

People that have been told I'm essential to Misery's downfall, and that they better keep me alive or their families will die.

It's honestly unnerving to think they would all fight over who gets to gut me first if they knew that Misery's rebirth was entirely contingent on whether I lived or died, but that my *death* would stop it, like snuffing out a candle.

Best part is, I don't even know *why.*

Donna returns when I haven't finished considering the ramifications of it all, waving for me to follow. Inhaling deeply while aggressively rubbing my tongue on the backside of my teeth, I enter what looks like a communal space that smells like brined meat, tobacco, and wood. The textures of all the chairs are a chaotic jumble, from velvet to wood to cotton, all clearly carved by different creators.

A nod to the fact they were probably stolen.

Spotting Soren is like finding an anchor in a new harbor when I locate the behemoth resting on a bed of hay; ankles crossed as he lies there, eyes closed. I don't wait for anyone else's permission and strut over straight away, only to pause a few feet from him when I remember that skin shifters exist in this world—what if this is a trap? Would that even happen among my dad's men?

No, surely not, not with the Eyeless, right?

Pale eyes flash open, and I'm not sure an imposter could quite mimic the way that gaze penetrates. "Why the hesitancy? I was enjoying your immense relief at seeing me."

A grin spreads across my face, that man slithering right under my skin.

A scarred brow raises in consideration. He motions next to him. "Sit. I'd get up, but I was told not to move a muscle, so I'm proving a point."

Glancing around, only for a moment, my ass clenches when there are at least three dozen eyes on us. It's never bothered me to really have the attention of many, but knowing they all belong to the Scorpion… I swiftly find a place to sit as if crouching down will somehow hide me, some of the hay digging through my pants. "I need to get ingredients for you," I say, never quite finding a comfortable spot. "I should probably go do that right away, actually."

"They already gave me a tonic."

Out of everything that just happened, that's the one statement that cuts *personally*. "*I* was supposed to make that," I say, as if taking the tonic of someone else breached something between us. "And you know what, who are you even sitting still for, anyway?"

He finally flashes a short-lived grin. "Don't worry, love, whoever made it means nothing to me," he teases, which does make me grin… slightly. "And there's an old woman walking around, sweeping up the place. She told me to cease all movement because I was getting hay all over. Then she smacked me with her broom when I tried to show her it wasn't *that* much."

"*What?*" I ask, barely able to control my laughter, not wanting to bring *more* attention my way. "You're clearly a *Zenith*. Your mask is right there—why did an old lady hit you with a broom?"

"I don't think she gives a shit who I am." His dark lashes part to reveal the sea glass underneath. "I'm in your daddy's world, love. The boat is already rocking, so no point in making it worse."

I try to inconspicuously search around for a woman with a broom, needing to see what she looks like. "You have a *title*."

"This isn't Belstead. Respect isn't what precedes a name. And I have a feeling that the old woman is someone all these assholes have a soft spot for, so I'm going to win her over."

I face him again, my gaze dropping to one of his bare forearms. His rough skin is covered in tattoos, from a skull to a siren, to intricate line art that scars cut through, to even a little design of braided rope, and another of an osprey.

The rest of him matches the roughened demeanor, even down to his stubble. There's no way a woman is casually hitting him with a broom. "Are you sure you're feeling alright?"

"No, actually," he growls. "There are a lot of men here who are surprised you're prettier than they thought. Can't blame them. I had the same reaction when I first saw you, but I particularly dislike that some are under the assumption they wouldn't have to fight me for you."

Oh, that sends a prickling sensation all through me.

Gods, he has a way to make me melt at the most unpredictable times, doesn't he? Especially when my gaze roams his torso and chest that's on full display, rising and falling with each breath to subtly express the power he harbors.

I can't resist teasing him. "Well, if they're paying attention, they'll see your weakness is apparently a broom."

He grins, and gods, does it unwind me when it's unburdened by his mercenary warlording side, especially the way his lips curl, slightly crooked, creating those damn feelings that make my heart fill dangerously high with emotions I can't spare right now.

I *shouldn't* spare them, anyway.

It's only stifled when, as if on cue, a woman who wears an unassuming dress and cloak steals his attention, broom in hand, with a large bag cinched around her waist. She's swatting at a rat, her faded tattooed left hand waving at it as it scurries away. "Need more traps, Davis," she comments, to which a man near her yells back, "Aye, aye, Mod."

With a huff, she straightens up and places both hands atop her broom handle, vigilantly surveying the space. When her stringent gaze lands on Soren, it flits to me and softens immediately, only to narrow back on him as if he tricked me into being there.

"You don't need to sit with him, dear Jane," she says, her voice deep and raspy like tobacco might have aged it as she makes her way over. Even if her skin is wrinkled, her dark eyes vibrate with youth.

Of course, *everyone* is watching now.

"I'm fine here, thanks," I reply with a polite tone, wondering what Soren's expression is. The man moves slightly to my back as I shift to look at Mod.

The woman frowns, twitching her nose. "Next to *him*? Oh, come now. You're with your father's people. Leave this man be."

"He might need something," I counter.

She leans over, crinkling her nose as it twitches once more, speaking quieter as if it's just for us, but there's no way Soren can't hear. "You don't fancy him, do you? That's the rumor I just heard. There are so many better options out there, especially with your lineage and how pretty you are. Really, Jane."

"That's unfair," Soren comments with that false sound of hurt in his voice. "You haven't even gotten to know me, Mod."

She shoots a burning gaze at him, her thin fingers tightly gripping her broom. "Don't call me *Mod*." She looks back at me, licking her thin lips as she straightens her worn dress out like she's wiping his words off of her. "You might not remember me, but I was the head organizer of the followers in your father's company. We keep things very tidy and running properly, and sometimes cook and help with healing or mending broken things. I'd stop by you and your mother's from time to time to bring sugared apples."

The mention of sugary, tart treats floods my taste buds as if licking a memory. "Those were *yours*?" I blink a few times. "Did I ever meet you?"

I swear when she smiles, there's an added bit of ego, as if rubbing it into Soren. "Your father kept a *very* tight circle around you, and so did your mother. I would wave a few times, but that's about it. My hair has gone white since seeing you last, so I'm sure that makes it harder to place. Age has also seemingly caught up with me when I thought I might have outran it." She addresses Soren while raising her head, as if to ensure she has to look down her nose at him. "Which is why I know you're better than *him*."

"I haven't moved a muscle, just as you asked," Soren replies. "What have I ever done to you?"

I can tell there's definitely a play in his tone, but it mixes so perfectly with his seriousness that it's clear she can't tell what he's thinking.

Mod grunts at him. "I don't like you."

"It's never too late to have a change of heart."

That just seems to make her even angrier as she rolls her eyes until they land back on me, and the smile that *almost* appeared is wiped off without thought. "You don't owe him anything, Jane. You're with your father's people now, like I said. There's so many to meet. So many to get to know. An entire world has opened up before you. You know, let's see... ah yes, over there, that's Jake, and he's the weaponsmith. So is Brett, Sam, and Cora. I bet they can get a fine, new blade made *just* for you... if you go over there, that is. I can take you even, if you're just not certain where to go."

As much as I'm confident I'm not going to be swayed by her, there's the most curious hesitation when really considering what she just said—I'm not alone. My father has his troupe; a *community*. One that I can belong to. And make my own weapons?

Swallowing thickly, I manage out, "I really should ensure Soren is okay."

She shakes her head, pity written clear across her face. "Not good enough of a hit he took if you ask me. Could have gone deeper."

Without waiting for a reply, Mod walks off with a stamp of the broom as if it helps her pivot. I dip my head low to conceal my grin, even bringing my forefinger to my nose. "I think you shouldn't turn your back on her."

Soren's long and heavy sigh precedes him, closing his eyes once more, nestling further into the hay. "*Clearly,*" his lip twitches into something like reluctant admiration. "Although I kind of like her. Her attitude stems from a deep loyalty. That's worth *everything*...

But that's not the point, Miss Jane." His pale eyes lazily lift open, the faintest lines of crow's feet deepening as they pin me in my spot. "Tell me of your plans, love. I can tell something changed."

My mind skips over Cypress as if it was a dream; I *treat* it like a dream, as that's the only way I might be able to get away with this. "I've decided I'm going to channel everything I have into wanting to kill those who ruined my life, and killed my mother," I answer, having practiced that a few times in my head already.

His brow arches in a detached amusement, as if he accepts the diversion for now. "Well, I can definitely tell you *want* revenge.. Have you ever *plotted* it before?"

"Well, yeah, of course. Like when Dicky stole my socks. *And* my shoes. I plotted a whole series of events, actually."

There's a distinguished pause that stretches between us. "What now?"

"One of the kids growing up here stole my socks. I tell you... I wanted to pluck his ears for that. It was the cold season, and he didn't even need them. Just thought it was funny. I had to walk home with frozen feet."

The corner of his mouth twitches, his restraint cracking just enough to hint at laughter. "I'm going to suggest that what you want to do now might be more complex than *that*."

There I go smiling again, helpless in his wake. "What's your point?"

"I might be good at something like this. So don't treat me like I'm not here."

There's a moment of pure peace that sits over me, a calm that is so rare it's sacred, chasing away the biting loneliness that's become my new normal since Coalfell. Being near Soren reminds me a lot of when I first met Kathleen and how every encounter always went right. He continues to make me feel things that normalize who I am, to validate the side that not many would understand. Even the jagged, unpolished edges of me.

I've never felt so... *normal*.

"So, then," I ask, leaning into this moment. "What's my first step?"

He draws in a long breath, scratching his stubbled chin to make it sound like he's rubbing sandpaper. "Well, don't get caught again, for starters," he half-jokes, his tone dipping down into something more serious. "The Shade shit proves you're being targeted. So I'd revert back to barely trusting your own shadow. Right now we are waiting for an opening to try and leave this city. So, in the meantime, I'd start practicing how to fight. Immediately."

"You think I can just start fighting *now*?"

"I'll arrange for either Anya or Bones to do it. No one else, maybe except your father. I don't know his men yet, so I don't trust *them*. Anya's your stature, so she'll have good insight. Bones is a professional and won't hold back, which is something you need. And yes, do it now. Better than not trying at all."

The absurd image of sparring with Bones floods me. "You're going to let me beat him up?"

His grin is almost feral. "You talk a big game, love. I'm sure you're capable."

I pivot, bits of hay crunching under me. "What about *you*? Why won't you teach me anything?"

He leans in slightly—the first movement *toward* me—his voice dropping to a dangerously tempting vibrato. "You want me to pin you down again?"

I look away, refraining from lightly hitting him, biting my lip with a half-smile. "I hardly think this is the time."

"There's never a better time for pleasure than while death is at the door."

That poetic thought is like a gust of wind that catches just right in one's mouth, making it hard to breathe. So much so that I have to immediately think of other things. "I think you're afraid to fight me," I reply, wanting to live in this easy conversation.

His unburdened laugh warms the space between us. "Do you just miss hitting people, Jane? Is that it?"

"I mean a *little*," I laugh out. "It sure makes me feel better."

There's enough of a pause that it's almost hard for me to ignore a table of men who seem to be talking about me, gesturing over here frequently. I nearly rise to strut over and ask what they're gossiping about when I blurt out, "Can you read them at all? Or are they silent, like my father?"

When I feel the bed of hay shift, I rotate my head to look at him once more; he's up on an elbow, looking directly at me. "About that… I *can* read him, actually. He took off a ring when he and I met just after I left." He slowly licks his bottom lip, that gaze lingering behind me more and more before he adds, "It's connected to Cypress. And I'd bet my entire coffer that Blackwell is using something similar, possibly from Misery."

The room constricts; his words are a noose around my thoughts. My pulse thunders in my throat when presented with the possibility of *knowing* my father, not considering how much I still didn't know him. "What did you feel? Is it really him?"

His demeanor is nowhere near as rushed or panicked as mine. "He's your father, Jane. And his heart is heavy."

My *dad*.

His heart is heavy? My gaze lowers as if I've been looking at my father through a mirror's reflection, only for the glass to disappear, and he's standing in the frame.

Soren's comforting presence morphs, too. Some part of me is confusingly annoyed now, as if my heart is too bare and open, and I'm not ready for him to explore that. Nor do I like the idea of him sitting and waiting for me to figure myself out. It's as if he can finally see the seam that holds me together, and I don't like that he knows how deranged its design is.

"I'm sorry you're stuck in this, by the way," I murmur, my voice strained. "Sitting in a bed of hay isn't exactly worth your time."

When I face him, his eyes deepen with that same hidden depth that seems reserved only for him—for now. "*You're* stuck in it, too."

Inhaling deeply, I stare back down at my hands, a bruise already forming around my wrist where Shade grabbed me. A small glance through my lashes shows Soren watching me, pure displeasure overtaking his face as he stares at my wrists, although I think that's just the emotions that escape, where I imagine something more savage plays out in his mind.

"I suppose that's true. I often just feel like everyone is stuck *because* of me." I give a half-chuckle, not wanting to think about Shade right now. Or any of it. I want conversations that have no purpose. "Anyway… did you know someone like you is called a Sensor?"

His head rises, but his gaze remains on my wrist, a callousness slowly erasing as a warmer expression overtakes it, but I can tell he's *far* from forgetting these bruises.

"My old mentor never mentioned it. Didn't know I had a proper name," he replies, and I love that he knows I need a conversation like this.

"*Mentor?*" I ask, my curiosity piquing.

"Another Sensor, like me," he answers, although his voice tells me his mind is still elsewhere.

My attention, on the other hand, is stuck on my spiraling imagination, considering Soren as a mentee, fascinated by this side of him. What was a young Soren like? I bet he had a mouth on him. And who in the hells was in *charge* of such a bastard? "Well, who is it? What was their name?"

He licks his bottom lip. "A man named The Basilisk."

INTERROGATION

SOREN

Jane's heart flickers around in that chest, small emotions creeping through only to be suffocated like they shouldn't have escaped.

Lies.

She's covering up something.

"You heard of the Basilisk?" I ask.

"Donna mentioned him." Her reply is fast, and her stare waivers.

"And what *about*?" I want to grab the back of her hair so badly so I can stare into those hazel eyes and find the truth—I can read someone the best when their heartbeat is nearly right next to mine.

I don't like, in any capacity, that Jane is hiding something from me. Not now. If I'm to fight even the thinnest sliver of a shadow that gets near her, I need to know *everything*.

She can't stop looking out at the room, sometimes even adjusting her position as if it matters. She's never had to worry about appearance before. From what we've talked about, it sounds like she's always had to *hide* her identity, even as a child, not embrace it.

That discomfort doesn't help with getting to her truth.

"Well, Donna said that the Basilisk is rumored to be in the Crimson Isles, but I guess it's a skin shifter, and he's *here*, in Skull's Row."

Well, it seems like Ritter has good intel. That's not enough, though. Why does it feel like Jane has something *else* to share, like that secretive truth is hiding behind the Basilisk?

She tuts slightly, leaning in. "So what do you mean he was your *mentor*?"

I'll indulge her. "He's ten years my senior and was in Death's Wing when I joined. He trained me in nearly all I know, especially given he's a *Sensor*. I guess we're called that now."

Her gaze stares intently at mine, as if she's trying to summon every ounce of will to try and read me like I read her. "I don't—but Donna spoke of him like it's a bad thing. Do the others know?"

"I don't believe they do, but it's also not a secret. I haven't seen him in fifteen years, so whatever he's doing now is not related to me."

I had heard he was here, but have no fucking idea as to why. Seeing him away from his lands is enough to make one's mind spin; he *never* leaves. Not anymore. "I think it's time we get some privacy," I suggest, even though it's more of an order.

"Where? Even if you can move, I don't even know where to go."

"You have a room here. Not that you'll be there long with how fast things are operating, but we have a lot to discuss. And I'm growing tired of these prattling idiots." I glare at those around that are starting to get too obvious in their nosy fucking ways.

There's such a wave of relief within Jane at the suggestion of us getting privacy that I don't care what she has to say; I'm done lying here now that the dust is settling.

Rising to my feet is already easier than earlier, my movements having been reduced to an unsteady mess. My shallow, uneven breathing is composed now. So far, one of my absolute favorite perks of being high-ranking, or surrounded by those with the damn titles I loathe, is they do come with access to many necessities.

We'll need it.

When I'm on my feet, the rowdiness ebbs like a receding tide, many hands drifting instinctually to their weapon. Rorge—sitting in a chair—doesn't move at first, lifting only his gaze to examine the disruption. He might be old, but his clearcut stare tells me he's far from useless. His loud cough disrupts the silence, clearing his throat as he stands and nears me, running a hand over his wiry beard. "Why're you standing?"

"Jane would like to retire to her room."

Jane pops up at being mentioned, about to protest just on the sheer principle of being spoken for, but I can tell she's also curious. Tired, even? "Yes, *I* would like to go to my room now," she says, looking up at me.

Rorge sucks his lips to his teeth, taking me in before he gives a languid blink and nods to follow him. As soon as I step forward, Rorge peers over his shoulder. "Only her."

"I'm going with her. *Everywhere,*" I reply, speaking for Ritter, since he spoke for me. "And that's non-negotiable. Ask your leader if you're worried."

Rorge's dry lips part, and I can tell he's uncertain if I mean what I said or not. His weathered face, marked by years of harsh living, deadpans as he narrows his one good eye while the other, veined and milky, stares right at me as if he can *see* my aura. I've witnessed enough in this world to know that, to one end or another, he can read me somehow.

Fascinating.

"Alright," he grumbles, turning around as if that's all he needed for permission.

Jane watches us as if every minute detail will be important later.

Even if I know my ego isn't relevant here, that bastard inflates when the energy of the room is now keened on *me,* and I swear some of them are considering the skull mask.

They've been stuck down here for too long.

Rorge takes us through more of the same stony corridors, the rubies and their reddish cast, something I accept now.

The thick wooden door that Rorge nears is studded with iron, the knob creaking as the door opens. There's warm light from many candles and a burning hearth pooling across the room. Two chairs and a table are placed next to the fire, a bed with fur and wool blankets resting underneath a singular painting of an ocean at dawn. Weapons are neatly organized with gleaming edges on a table adjacent to a singular chair; medical supplies are spread out, an empty bag hanging limply off the arm.

It's a sparse, small room, but it has all the necessities.

My heart thuds in my chest as my body begs to recover, like it's tempted to sleep deeply for three days.

"Your father has arranged the materials you requested, along with weaponry that he recommends you add to your person. There are latrines where I showed you, along with barrels of water you can use to refresh your pitcher."

Jane hardly looks my way as she nears the medical supplies, grabs a small bottle, one of four, and then looks at me earnestly. Her hazel eyes are fierce and *alive*, and I can tell how much it means to her to help me in this way.

The longer our energies collide, the more I feel innately protective of her. And it's *then* that I know, that without Serena, I'd be saying 'fuck it' and throw everything I have to protect Jane just because I *want* to, just like she *wants* to take care of me. It's the same driving force I had before learning about what truly haunts her.

On my own, I crave a deep bond, something only for *me* to enjoy. Is it truly as simple as love that I seek? Is it *that* persuasive?

Rorge's clearing of his throat echoes against the walls. "We will know if you're in danger, Jane. If *he* hurts you, or you don't want him here, we will know. And we'll remove him."

The roguish part of Jane eyes Rorge like his words are so foreign it might as well be another language, but the desolate side of her that craves community is just as touched. "Thank you," she replies, as if she's uncertain how to reply to such a statement. "Also, we need food. I don't need much, but Soren will need red meat, preferably a liver pie. Maybe some pickled eggs. And a bone broth stew, if you have it."

"Can do, ma'am."

That's right, my desert rose. Her taking care of me, even if the exchange is mundane, is such a subtle gesture that stirs something deep within me. I don't think I have much control over it anymore.

When the door shuts, and it's just our energies moving through the room—a sensation I'm quite addicted to—I sit in a rather unsteady chair near the fire, the warmth gently radiating to my left as I watch Jane to my right. She's going through all the medical supplies.

With how much she enjoys purpose, it's astonishing she survived that village for so long.

"Why did he call me ma'am?" she asks, holding up some roots to look at them near a candle. "I don't think anyone's called me *ma'am.*"

"You're the daughter of his leader," I reply, closing my eyes momentarily to deeply breathe and center myself. "Plus, those milky-eye bastards are high in rank, which means showing respect to you means more to them than the others."

She's quiet as she considers that. "Oh, I found out what they are, by the way. They're called the Eyeless."

My eyes flash open, narrowing my gaze on her, lifting my head forward. "What the hells did you do while in that room? You seemed to have learned quite a bit."

Her face deadpans, placing the root back on the table and moving it around in a nervous fidget. The smallest flutter of a truth is drowned out by other thoughts, my powers smothering her so greatly I can tell she's pushing them down on purpose. Did someone assault her? But her energy doesn't feel like assault.

My heart reluctantly races, even if it's exhausted.

"Donna talked to me for a bit," she quietly answers, picking up something else and focusing so hard on it; it's clear she's trying to prevent anything else from entering her mind.

"*Jane,*" I say, the sound almost harsh. "What else happened?" There's a stutter in her energy, her back still to me, and a piece of the truth is exposed for too long, confirming that she *is* hiding something, and it's dark. *Damning.* "Did someone do something to you?"

I'm about to stand when she releases a deep exhale. "No, I'm fine. Nothing bad happened at all—I... I need time to figure out what all I'm learning."

"*Jane.*" I finally rise to my feet.

She turns around. "It's alright. Really."

"You might have your secrets, but if you *ever* hide if someone hurt you, I will strip your energy bare until I find out what happened, and I promise, you won't like *that* process."

The statement takes her so aback, and also brushes against something *very* neglected that it has an effect that leaves her speechless.

But I mean it.

The shit with Shade hasn't fully settled on me yet, and I cannot handle the idea of something happening to her and her *hiding* it.

It's what Serena did, and then she was gone.

"It's alright, Soren," she says gently, turning to face me. "Really. I spoke with someone else, but it's a lot about my family, and my history, and I just… I need to process the allegations."

I swear to all the gods there's a flash of red in my mind's vision, followed by dark, black eyes, and it's more clear than ever she's speaking of Cypress. "Jane, I can't help you if there's *any* detail hidden from me."

The pleading in her eyes, along with the way I feel she wants to give me *everything*, contradicts that it's *nothing*. The more our energies meld in the space, I can't deny that the rubies have to be powering my senses, one way or another.

I absolutely hate how witches can obscure everything I rely on for clarity.

"I know you can read me, so I know there's no point in lying. But I… it's too soon. I really do have to sit on what was told to me."

"This is what happened to my sister," I admit, raking a hand through my hair and looking to the side. I hesitate, but when those words strike through her like her armor is made of silk, I add, "If I had known that the man who took her had spoken to her the day before, and told her he was there as a merchant, and that there was a *lord* traveling with him, I could have told her he's full of shit, and all he had in his cart was a bunch of coal."

Jane's gaze roams the floor, her face puzzled as she ever so slowly approaches me. "Wait, why a lord?"

My eyes roll, pressing my lips together as I glance at the crackling fire, hating the way it feels to speak of this to *anyone*. "Serena thought those in Belstead were interesting." The heaviness in my heart gains an unexpected lightness as the corner of my lips tugs upward. "She's a gentler soul. Not made for Skull's Row, or any of us. It's why—It's why I can't handle the idea of awful things happening to her, other than she's my sister. Out of everyone, it would break her the most."

There's the expected pity from Jane, the kind that I loathed for so long. Someone's pity changes nothing. But then there's a determination in Jane that mirrors what she feels when thinking of Kathleen. "Then I'll help you find her. When this is all done, obviously."

I glance over to see she's right next to me, and I'm eye level with her navel, her loose tunic partially tucked into her leather pants. There are ripples in the energy of this room that surrounds her, perhaps even emanating from her, almost as if through each one, I can see a different future; it's a novel effect that takes me off-guard. One of those paths removes this woman from my life, nearly guaranteeing *my* survival—something tells me the Scorpion won't wander far from Jane and will die protecting her, despite his threats.

Through another ripple presents an obscure future where I place all bets on Jane, and give her every inch of my commitment—it's warm, inviting. Almost familiar, even, like it will fill in all the cracks of my soul. And yet there's a risk, a *massive* one. As if to choose her means my death.

Death doesn't mean shit to me if I get to *live*.

I can no longer just take Jane and find my sister. No, I have to *choose*. Surrendering myself to Jane means accepting I may never live to save my sister. As my gaze takes in the details of her belt and the slightly bent frame, I think of the smooth skin underneath her raggedy clothes.

Maybe it's because I'm drained, but I can't fight the way she gets to me right now. The way a deeper, lonely side of me is desperate to release everything I've lived for since my sister disappeared and wants to take pride in dying for something *tangible*.

No matter which path I choose, there *will* be regret. Misery and his cunts have ensured that. I know better than to hope I'll live; I either will, or I won't, but planning beyond that is reckless. At least, it *is* for someone like me that knows I can't just fucking *hope* I live for Serena.

Jane is patient as I wade through this overwhelming experience before asking, "What's wrong? Did you learn something else?"

Her voice is velvet against the coarseness of my life. As I deeply inhale, I touch the outside of her thigh, right where a hilt for a blade is tied around her. My Jane would survive being taken and would thrive under the pressure of revenge.

My sigh is heavy as I consider what I'm about to say, and so is my heart. "I want you to make me a deal."

The energy within her stirs uncomfortably. "I want to hear it first."

My smile stretches without thought, raising a hand to touch her hip, running my thumb along the fastenings of her holster. "If I don't survive what's coming, will you vow to find my sister for me?"

The calm drive that fueled her shifts to a familiar anxiety. "Why? What have you learned? You can't die. Why would you even suggest that?"

I grip her hip and finally look up at her, her concerned gaze roaming all over my face. "Love, what's haunting you is not something one army can fight. I don't even know what a plan would look like. All I *do* know is that what your father says sounds true to me, and to destroy this asshole named Misery, it will be a war." I tilt my head. "Which means dying. Quite a few will, I'm sure of it. And I don't trust Cypress to keep my heart beating by the end of this, but I do believe she intends to ensure yours does. You have to agree that if I can't help my sister, you'll find her and let her know I never stopped looking."

It's the only compromise I can think of. I get to throw everything I have at Jane without reservation, and *someone* will search for my sister when this is done.

And for a small moment of my life, I get to enjoy something that's *only* for me.

Sorrow and dread wash over her, just like when she saw me bleeding back in the bakery. And then a wave of guilt washes through her so fiercely it nearly removes all other sentiments, and I'm not sure where it comes from. "Then," she says, looking around, breathing heavily. "Then go. Don't be a part of this. Don't risk yourself to *that* degree."

Retraction. I don't blame her. The destruction that will follow her is quite terrifying.

"I trust you to find a way to follow through if I can't, and you could maybe even relate to her, about losing a part of your life."

There it is—the energy that has fueled her life blooms, just ever so more, in the name of my life's purpose. When it's clear I'm not letting go of her as I grip her hip tighter, she gives a quick huff.

She doesn't move.

If anything, her body stiffens, and all the warmth that was right here rescinds. She turns her head as if she wants to look away, but it gets stuck as she can't take her eyes off of me, like too many questions hit her at once. "It kills me you're stuck in this because of me, even if I'm stuck in it too. You shouldn't be worrying about your actual death over me."

Now my guilt mounts slightly more, knowing that even if I hated her, I'm tied to her with Cypress. But I don't want to tell her, because at the same time, the guilt doesn't destroy me. It's all to protect the heart of my desert rose, and so she doesn't have to question my motives.

"It is what it is, Jane. I imagine Cypress has worked endlessly to get our paths to cross, because I bet she knew once I touched you, you'd have your father *and* me willing to do what's necessary to prevent them from having you."

Her heart returns to me, even if cautiously. "Stop saying you're going to die," she mumbles.

"Agree to the deal."

So much comes my way that I swear I can nearly hear her voice in my mind, and it takes me aback. In such a swift wave, one where she's saddened by something I don't have access to, overpowered by her just wanting this to all to be left behind.

I lick my lips before saying, "Whatever you're hiding, you have three days before I'll demand it from you." She looks at me like I invaded more than she expected. "In the meantime, make this deal with me so I can let go of it and know that Serena will one day be told I didn't forget her."

It works.

She has a desire to fight for this that will be as strong as her own, and I really do trust Jane can figure this out.

"What do you want out of this, Soren? Out of you and me?"

It's something she's longed to ask, but didn't want the possible disappointment that men like me are so prone to delivering. My hand moves to her navel, sliding my fingers under her shirt to feel the warmth of her skin. I can nearly physically feel the affection she harbors right in my palm. "What I want? All my men have someone to think about when they die. I'd like that for myself."

More than ever, the sliver of transparency into her *true* heart opens, as if she's allowing herself to give in. A hand of hers raises to my cheek, her other hand mimicking the action—I'm not used to someone touching me like this, not with my face.

Jane usually is only ever physically affectionate after I've initiated.

The pressure of her palms moves my face up, and she looks me dead in the eyes. "I already told you, you go and die on me, and I'm bringing you back just to slap you for it. It's not a part of what's going to happen."

I don't know if it's the damn tonic I drank earlier, Cypress's rubies making me fall for her more, or if this is just how this shit works, but my body is alive with something new. "We can't control our death, love. But we can control how we live."

"I just—I can't lose anyone else."

"Then you'll never gain anyone, either."

Her eyes vibrate back and forth so much it's as if she isn't even looking at me. I raise a hand and grab one of hers, pulling it from my face to my lips to gently kiss her slightly cold fingers. There's so much desire emitting from her, so much joy at something so gentle.

The sensation of being able to explore every minute change of her heart is impossible to put a price on; I'm the foundation she can lay her new identity with, and she's embracing it at this very moment.

I need this validation, too.

I need to not just feel adoration, but to *be* loved.

Pulling her down, I press my lips into hers, a warm puff of air escaping her nose. Jane's weight slowly shifts to leaning into me, and I already know how to make her body *sing*. Wrapping my arm around her waist, her bones nearly melt at my strength, so weak to being small with *me*. I pull her other leg around so she's forced to sit in my lap. I fucking love how powerful that makes me feel, her warm lips moving with mine, teeth slightly clashing as my tongue dips deep into her mouth, a moan spilling from her throat. Each second that passes, her heart is ripped more open than before. It's maddeningly addicting to kiss a woman that means so much to me.

Being low on blood doesn't seem to matter as my cock has no issues hardening, pressing against my pants. My hands glide down to Jane's hips, digging my fingers into her body to drop her further into my lap, her pussy *right* over where it belongs. Her moan vibrates into my mouth, and my eyes part to see hers slightly rolling behind partially closed lids. "I have an idea," she moans into the kiss. Something mischievous crosses her gaze, those pupils blown. "You need to take it easy."

When she tries to wriggle away, my first instinct is to tighten my grip until a wave of her energy makes it seem like she wants to choke on my cock. I let her loose almost as soon as I understand, groaning deeply as my legs spread while her fingers work at the lacing of my pants. I grab her hand, and when our gazes meet, I can *feel* how whatever expression I have makes her unwind.

"I want it *all* removed. *Your* clothes," I instruct, looking over her body.

She gives a wolfish grin, biting her bottom lip as she pulls off her shirt, auburn hair rippling back down; her nipples are hard, and her flesh is so perfectly supple. I undo my pants and belt, taking in every inch of a body that bends so easily for me. She's just as swift to remove her shoes and pants, purposely turning to the side as she bends over to reach her ankles, her pink pussy on full display. "This better?" she purrs.

"You have no idea," I say, hearing my voice drop an octave, wanting to slide my cock in between that perfect slit that I know is warm, wet, and ready to clench down hard on me.

I nearly growl when she turns around, although Jane is on her knees before I can pick her up and pin her against the wall, taking in my cock with those pretty lips, looking up at me.

Fucking hells.

One of my hands glides through her hair, watching my cock disappear into her mouth, over and over, the warmth of it making my eyes roll. Her jaw drops to accommodate more as I brush against the back of her throat. Her hands grip both my legs to steady herself, and my labored breathing morphs into slow groans, momentarily wishing I was in the Commons so they could all see *who* this woman strips so easily for, and whose cock hollows out her cheeks.

Whose cum will be sliding down her throat.

"You are gorgeous between my thighs." I grip her hair and hold her there, Jane nearly gagging, getting a high off of the way her vulnerability is at its peak. I rock my hips slightly so she can get air into her lungs. Her tongue flicks back and forth, and I grunt. "You want my cum, Jane?"

She moans into the flesh that nearly chokes her, and I grip her hair tighter with another partial roll of my eyes. "Such a good fucking girl. After this, I'm going to bring you close to the edge before stopping. Then bring you closer once more, and stop just before. Then, I'll make you collapse."

It's when her eyes roll at that notion that I grunt, breathing raggedly, baring my teeth. "And you'll fucking swallow every drop of me," I grind out, pivoting the wrist of my free hand so my palm grips the front of her neck. "And I want to feel it."

I come as soon as I feel her neck muscles swallow her own saliva, her warm mouth remaining wrapped around me, draining me down her throat, swallowing happily as I feel those muscles *drink* every drop in her mouth.

That clarity after emptying one's balls is like nothing else, the hair in my hand suddenly feeling soft, belonging to a woman I don't just want to claim physically, but I want her *heart*. Sliding my hand up along her chin before moving it back to my side, the other loosens its grip on her hair. She wipes at her lips, the fire glinting against them.

This clarity also means I can read her without my horny ass getting ahead of itself. She's so ready and open for me, but once again, she doesn't want to initiate.

One day, she will.

For now, I'll enjoy guiding her. She's trusting me to take care of that desire, to edge *right* at the precipice before it's too much.

"On the bed. On your back," I say, standing.

Jane smiles as she stands, strutting over in a sway of her perfect ass, sliding into the fur and elegantly rolling to her back.

She's so queenly in her movements when she's completely confident, as if she knows I won't disappoint her here.

I ensure all my clothes are removed, not saying another word as I place a knee on the bed, hooking an arm underneath the small of her back, gripping her inner thigh with my other hand to push her wide open, dipping down to lick her wet pussy, my tongue sliding right where my cock will stretch her later, up to her clit, tasting the mess that was made all because she sucked me off.

That clarity is fucking fading already.

I want her cunt filled with my cum, for her to smell of sex. She gasps when I *suck*, her hands now moving all over, from her face, to my hair, to my arm.

Fucking her endlessly in Rosmertta's was deliciously carnal, a release we both needed. But I can feel so much built-up emotion inside of her that mixes with her rising orgasm, and frankly, it melds with my own heart.

It's different to do this with someone's body that you know, their pleasure so much more than a flare of ego.

It crosses my mind to get *one* answer out of her in this position, as she seems to hear me best when like this. I pause when I can feel her reaching her edge, as if her body emanates euphoria.

She whimpers when she realizes I've stopped.

"I can tell you're hiding something very large from me, Jane," I say, admiring her perfect cunt while I feel her energy shift.

She even grunts, looking down with disappointment when I flick my gaze up. I grip her and push her thigh open even further as she tries to see what physical leverage she might have, but that disappears almost instantly.

She can't move, her legs spread, and her body so utterly exposed.

"That's not what I want to hear right now," she says.

"I told you, I'm going to bring you to the edge, multiple times before you're allowed to collapse. I mean it when I say you have three days to keep this information to yourself." I raise my head back further. "No more."

She loves it, even if she hates it. She pushes that uncomfortable appreciation toward me, telling me in every way but with her own mouth that she *is* keeping something, and she might not even want to.

I can tell that ripping the truth from her is more comforting of a notion than not. My hand from her inner thigh slides down, two fingers slipping right inside of her smooth heat as she gasps and leans her head back. I pump in and out, the muscles of my forearms flexing as I give her one languid lick over her clit. "Don't think I'm done asking."

"We can't just fuck normally, can we?" she breathes out.

I smile into her pussy, breathing her in. "One day, we'll make love without any barriers, beautiful. Until then, it's not my fault this is the best way to get you to confess things."

I suck harder, pumping more. This impending orgasm is stronger than earlier, her body more desperate. Her hand clings to my arm, her other on her stomach. Her thighs stiffen, some of Jane's breathing hitching as she tries to fall into that rhythm that will bring her to climax. I risk it when I suck as long as possible, *right* before pulling my fingers out and backing off her, so not even the brush of my breath can stimulate her.

"Oh, you *asshole*," she groans, looking down at me. "Keep going. We can talk later."

"I want to know who was in that room." I look at her with a gaze that has worked very well on her so far, doing everything I can to drive home that this is not something I take lightly.

"You know," she leans up on her elbows. "If this is how you interrogate, I can see why they always send you." Then her eyes flare, and I grin as I feel what she's thinking before she adds, "If you touch another woman for an interrogation, even slightly, I'll–"

"Send me her head before cutting off my cock. I'm aware, darling."

Her tightened expression loosens into almost a laugh, and there's even an emotion that takes her by surprise, as if she finds that confusingly endearing. My gaze falls down her body, staring for a moment at the black skull tattoo on her chest, to her pussy that makes me groan just looking at it.

I slowly slide two fingers back in, imagining it's my cock that's already hardening again before glaring back up at her. "Who was it, Jane? You *will* tell me that, at the very least."

"Why?" she pants with upturned brows. "I can't say it."

Oh, that pisses me off. And her expression flashes with surprise as she no doubt realizes that was the wrong thing to tell me. "If you want to hide things from your lover, then I'm the wrong one. Not when your safety is concerned."

I graze her clit with my thumb, pulling gently upward with my two fingers to massage the spot that makes her completely fall apart, her arms nearly giving out at the sudden rush of pleasure.

She lays flat once more into the fur. "Cypress," she quietly confesses. "She came to visit me."

My growl lacks any sensuality.

Nonetheless, I lean down and kiss her *right* where all nerves come to life. "Good girl, Jane."

My cock remains rock hard even if I'm pissed, and I swear I can fucking come one more time. Shit, I don't even care about coming, I just want to be buried inside of her. To further make the point that she *should* open up to me, and that I can make her feel safe, to dig it deep into her mind that I'm someone she can fall apart to, and I know being wrapped against my body is where she feels that the most.

I'll deal with the Cypress shit later.

I gently lick her clit as my fingers work, her body *flooding* with ecstasy as I'm sensing she's nearly throbbing. It's such a high that my dick is perfectly ready to go again, and I *will*, once she comes for me. Her muscles clench my fingers, trying to grab ahold of that pleasure that I might take away again. Jane arches her back as she holds her breath. I can't get enough of watching her face as it contorts with impatience, until it all washes over her, a loud moan escaping her, her pussy pulsating on my fingers.

I smile.

She squirms as I gently continue, and I find it so fucking sexy when she does. I back off when I can't take it anymore and wipe my face with my hand, only to position myself over her, spreading her legs and shoving my cock into her perfect warmth as my eyes roll, my hands digging into her thighs.

She moans deeply.

I look down and watch as her pussy stretches to fit me, our flesh interlocking. I slowly rock my hips as I lift my gaze to stare into her eyes, her hair spread all over the pillow, her cheeks flushed.

I lean over and kiss her, slowly fucking her as our bodies intertwine, one of my arms bracing me so I don't crush her. I enjoy pushing as deep as she'll take me, kissing her gently as our noses brush against each other. Jane wraps her arms around me, one hand settling on the back of my neck. I'm not sure how much time passes until I'm spilling into her, coming with our mouths pressed against each other.

Those romantic words that she craves settle so easily on my tongue, but not yet. It's not the right time.

Our hearts speak through the physical, not with what spills from our lips.

As we lie there, our beating hearts slow as we enter this peaceful aftermath that has grown more special to me than I expected. She looks like she's about to say something.

Our gazes connect, so close that I can see the tiniest variations of colors in her irises, streaks of green mingling with the bronze.

"Whenever this is all done," she says, her fingers gently scratching the nape of my scalp. "I'll do everything I can to find your sister. I promise that." My eyes widen. "And I won't leave her until she's safe."

My brows furrow, those words striking at such a vulnerable part of me I'm completely unprepared to handle it.

I've become so skilled at many things, but *this* isn't one of them. So, instead, I search her heart for what she wants to hear, and it's effortless for me to reply, "Then you have all of me."

LITTLE ROGUE

JANE

I refuse to acknowledge the part of me that is fucked up and may have enjoyed the way it felt to have Soren pin me down, to frame it from an angle of *caring* about me, as if I matter. I don't care if that's not healthy—I'm not a healthy person, and I don't know if I ever will be.

If I even *want* to be.

I don't know this man as if it's been years, but I'm pretty confident in saying his expressions are everything—I think he means it that he doesn't want me to hide anything from him.

And not because he's nosy, but he wants to help.

While I lie there in the bed, staring at the ceiling that's barely lit by the dwindling hearth, I'm pretty certain Soren's asleep. We've eaten, washed off our bodies, and now he's resting. I roll my head over to stare at the side of his face, fascinated with how mundane he is when he sleeps. How much he's just a man who has had to cull so many parts of his soul to thicken it enough to weather this world.

A man with fears.

I want to ask so many questions about his sister, about the girl who was fascinated with a world outside of here while someone like me always dreamed of returning.

I let my guilt spill out while he sleeps, mulling over what Cypress said. My heart will shatter a little when he realizes he will not only be unable to read me, but that Misery might get his hands on me, too… and I knew. The whole time, I knew, and I will have hid that from him.

How much are Cypress's warnings true? How much would telling Soren *truly* disrupt everything? I have no desire to be difficult and hide things because I don't want to hurt him. But I do know that there are forces here at work, and I need to respect their boundaries.

I'm also not dumb enough to think Soren wouldn't take imme-diate action. He'd absolutely inform the Scorpion, and then I'd have *two* Zenith trying to wedge their way between what's *supposed* to happen.

I don't even care what the fates have planned for me at this point with Misery, not if it's the best chance for *survival*. I want to make sure Kathleen is safe, that Soren *won't* die, and that I somehow live to help him recover Serena. Cypress nearly promised that, but I have to see myself as a weapon, not some noble sacrifice. I have to choose her words of warning over satisfying Soren's concerns.

Soren's head slightly rolls to face me, his eyes still closed, slowly drawing out long breaths. I stare at him without any reservation in this peaceful silence. I barely scraped the surface of seeing his *true* heart, and by the gods, do I want it all. I want *him*.

Rising from the bed is something I finally commit to, wrapping myself in one of the many blankets here, and sit right in front of the diminishing fire. I jump when my ass touches the cold stone floor, re-positioning so it's on the inside of the fluffy fur before I get comfortable.

I stare at the crackle, remembering that I forgot to ask Cypress about being a Cinder. Is that important? Useful at all? Or is it just something about me that's as relevant as my hair color?

I reach out to stick my hand in one of the small flames, a burn never charring my flesh. It oddly makes me start to cry, to think of Maryanne and the villagers. I could have saved so many more people if I'd known I didn't have to be afraid of burning. Would have been *great* to know about that back then.

Mindlessly, my hand lowers to do something I've never quite done, and I rest it on the burning log, touching the white, ashen parts that are ready to flake off, lined with a glowing smolder. It's just *really* warm, like it might start burning me if I'm not careful, but nothing amounts from there.

The yearning for my mother, to ask her about her experience as a Cinder *and* a healer, is like floating in a body of water and constantly being taken under, wondering if I'll ever surface again.

It's so immensely unfair I don't have her, and I'll never be able to ask her questions about life. About *hers*.

The bed shifts—I glance over my shoulder to see pale eyes staring at me. I try to cork every emotion I just felt so he won't have to worry, not while he needs to recover. Not while I'm still mulling over it all. This is something that requires delicacy, not blabbing away like a gossiper after too much ale.

"Go back to sleep," I gently say. "I'm just playing with fire."

He gives a crooked grin, and his eyes gently close. I know he's absolutely exhausted, and his body no doubt has to be *begging* to sleep. I rarely see him like this, which just confirms how much he needs to focus on himself. At least for the next few days.

And in that, once I feel like Soren is slumbering once more, I move to one of the chairs, unable to return to the bed just yet, settling in as I stare at Soren. It feels a little creepy, but who knows when I'll be able to do this again? What if visions of this are the only thing to get me through what's to come? What if this is one of the last few good days of my life? I know how fleeting they can be…

If there's one thing I regret about my mother's death, it's that I didn't spend enough time etching more moments inside my brain like a tattoo.

Yes, I'll unabashedly enjoy this quiet for now. Because tomorrow, I start training. Until my legs fall off.

I will do whatever it takes to protect this man and keep him in my life, and *also* fuck over this god named Misery..

THE WOODEN BLADE cracks against my calf, stinging as my buckling knee sends me to the ground.

My fingers clamp tight on the training sword, pivoting while falling, the act more instinctual already after doing it countless times. On the ground, I parry the next blow as the two pieces of wood clack against each other.

The iron grip I thought I had means nothing as the training blade flies out of my hand.

"In sword fighting, your strength is not in brute force, dying pigeon," Bones remarks, standing above me, pointing at me with his wooden weapon. "You're not quite strong enough to take the pressure of someone else's blade right now."

I snarl at Bones, panting as I reach over to grab mine. Gritting my teeth, I rise to my feet, wiping at my sweaty brow. "So just don't parry, then? I don't know what else I'm supposed to do."

"Wouldn't say that, but you held the sword up like that was your only tactic and that it might actually work," he remarks, raising the tip of his to motion to me. "You *should* have deflected my blade, but *also* had your other hand ready to grab one of the smaller blades on your chest to stab me in the thigh with."

I nearly roll my eyes, as I'm too fucking tired to implement something like *that*. I glance around the storage room that's been partially cleared for fighters to keep in *somewhat* shape down here. The fire lanterns above us aren't as optimal as the sun, and I'm already growing tired of being down here. "So what's my strength then? Let's just start focusing on that. We've been sparring like this for three days."

"We're *starting* here because you need to know how this feels, so your instinct doesn't go to it. You can't evade attacks if you're not used to it." Bones strides in his spot, his armor removed to leave only his leathers and cotton shirt. "From what you've shared, you're used to the streets as a child, or the taverns at Coalfell. Not active combat. How many times have you been able to overpower me?"

I breathe heavily, eyeing a box that I'd really like to sit on right now. "None... *yet.*"

"Precisely." He eyes the space as he talks. "Your fighting tactic stems from something you're already used to—element of surprise, and very close quarters. Very pirate-like in style, but you're using none of the evasion. If you're up against a fucker in armor, just literally dance around until his arms get tired of swinging a long sword. Again, *evasion.* I've been waiting to see if that would spark on its own, but, well, can't all be winners. You take pain well, though."

I tut, walking over to the pail of water for a drink, sliding the wooden blade under my armpit to hold it, catching the faintest reflection in the water's smooth surface—I look as good as I feel. "Then these last three days have been a waste."

I admit I could have said something prior to now, but I also wanted to give it a real shot. It wasn't until today that I started to realize I might not be as good at sparring as I thought. I can't even be mad at Bones for his criticisms, because he's not *wrong.*

I've hardly been able to land a hit on him.

"Ha! A *waste.* So many men would pay their entire inheritance to train with me for three solid days, and you're getting it for *free.* Which also includes cheap shots." Bones is advancing on me fast enough that I drop the cup of water, pull out the sword, and wonder what the hells do I do as he lifts his like he might swing it—how do I focus on evasion versus taking the hit?

"What—" I bend backward to avoid the strike, stepping back, grinning when it worked.

"You're not watching my footwork," he chides, coming in again, and I use my hand to grab the wood, so damn tired of it hitting me or knocking *my* blade out of my hands. The sting from the contact travels into my bones, but it's also when I realize Bones is slightly open, and I heavily prod his chest with my training sword.

"*Ha!*" I exclaim.

His mismatched eyes flash with pride as the action seems to wind him, coughing slightly as he takes a few steps back. "There you are," he says through a strained voice, rubbing his chest. "Might not have a left hand if that was a real sword, but that's for another day. You'll just have to get good at sewing yourself back together, so maybe just keep leaning into that."

I place a hand over my stomach where Anya stabbed me, sliding it off so as not to make it obvious. "I hate blades."

"Well, there will be many slashing at you. Not a great time to hate them," he warns, although there's such a lightheartedness to him. "Let's take a break and eat. I smell food."

Limping with a lower leg that no doubt needs a lot of healing magic put into it, I lay the sword against a box in silent agreement. "You didn't have to hit my leg that hard."

"On the contrary. Your body will remember that sting."

"Maybe I'm not meant for combat," I remark. "I prefer the stealthy stuff."

"Too bad, little rogue. Even thieves need to know how to fight."

For a moment, I consider making an excuse not to join him in the Commons, in case Soren is in there. Today is the third day since we arrived down here, and Soren has yet to ask me about what Cypress wanted with me. I can't shake the way Cypress said that telling them will likely result in their deaths. It doesn't make any sense, yet that witch *never* does. Which means I'm leaving it all be for now, including not questioning Soren on anything further related to Basilisk, or any of his history, in case Soren wants to use *that* moment to dig deeper.

I've just been a good little healer, taking care of him and then spending the rest of my time training.

My father has also been as available as he always was—a ghost. We haven't spoken *once*. Can't say I've wanted to complain, though. Keeping a distance from *both* of them is better for me so I can focus.

At least, I'm attempting to. I've poured nearly all my energy into *trying* to beat the shit out of Bones, but he's admittedly quite impressive on his feet, even with a training sword.

"You're deep in thought again," Bones says as we're already at one of the small tables in the Commons, the sound of everyone around me appearing as if there was a fog hiding them.

I glance up to catch Bones's steady gaze as we settle in at the empty table. Based on what hangs off a hook on the wall—a large piece of wood painted yellow with a black stripe running through— it's apparently midday, and stew is almost ready. It's how they all tell time down here: a black stripe signifying food will be ready within the hour.

"It's hard not to let my mind wander when I don't even remember what the sun looks like," I retort, looking up at a few of the hanging lanterns before dropping my gaze to Bones. He has the *smallest* bruise on his chin from where I got him earlier. "That will turn a nice purple," I say, nodding to him.

"*You'd* have a lot more if you didn't heal them all," he counters, looking around as if his attention has completely wandered away, until it's clear he spots a pitcher of water.

"Must be real proud to overpower someone like me," I say, my voice lifting just enough to carry over the crowd that gathers for a warm meal. He strides over to grab the pitcher and a few cups, sitting back down with a little *bounce* from the force.

"I don't have any pride," he comments. "I just want what I want."

I try not to laugh, biting my bottom lip as I glance around the dark space with warm fire lighting it. I can't deny the bastard is a *little* funny.

A *little* bit.

My wandering gaze lands on Soren as if he's magnetic to me; he's speaking with one of the weaponsmiths Mod pointed out. His black tunic that's too long is tucked into his leather pants that have a thick belt cinching around his entire waist, his weapons properly adorning him—probably over there discussing getting a new one made. He looks so refreshed compared to the alley with Shade.

Which makes me nervous, because that means he'll have a lot more energy to wear me down. He glances back at me as if he can feel that, and I reach for the cup of water, my cheeks reddening.

Gods, I dread him asking about what Cypress said.

How can I tell that man that revealing what happened can likely cause his death? I'm starting to loath that with all the more, because why did she give me this burden to carry? I want nothing more than to tell Soren.

That man legitimately slept for nearly two days straight, only awake to fill his belly with food or water, drinking a blood tonic every morning. What am I going to do if he holds me to that declaration of the third day? What can I possibly tell him so he doesn't do it? If he finds out, he's going to lose his mind. And his life.

I'm getting *really* tired of secrets.

I'm still trying to decide how I really fit into all of this. That's what a leader would do, isn't it? Know when to act independently? If Misery wants *me*, then why shouldn't I go to him? I know damn well if my father was told that including others would kill them, he would go on his own. Get right up close and personal, before striking. So would Soren.

With Cypress supporting me, I feel as if I have a *chance*.

What if telling Soren helps, though… gives me someone to strategize with?

"Did we ever figure out what happened with Shade?" I blurt out, trying to think of something else. *Anything* else, because I can sense Soren is still watching me.

Bones's expression hardens instantly. "Oh, we're on it. Given strict orders to capture him as unharmed as possible, because Soren wants to inflict it all. I personally think he means to make a message out of Shade. But I can't share those details."

"And you're certain that Kathleen is alright? I don't want her near *anywhere* that affiliates with Shade."

He starts twirling one of his rings in between his fingers. "Kitten is where she needs to be, and I won't share that, either." His mismatched eyes flash at me. "She said you wouldn't take that for an answer, by the way. So I'm already *extra* prepared to tell you *no*."

I inhale, not quite sure what I want to say but I'm far from satisfied. *She knows me well.* He holds up a hand as if sensing my protest. "I'm not saying where she is, so you can stop. She truly has been put somewhere very safe. She's a massive target to get to you, and both your daddy and Soren want her as impossible to find as buried treasure."

I hate the idea of having to open up to Bones, to give him a fraction of my vulnerability, but I may not have any other choice. I lean over slightly on the table. "Bones, I feel really weird having no idea where my closest friend is."

"Perfectly reasonable," he casually replies, looking to the side as one of the followers brings over a bowl of stew and fresh bread. The woman looks at me and smiles warmly, while cautiously eyeing

Bones. The rest of the crew all rise to stand in line for it—we don't have to, apparently—and the woman is gone just as fast as she arrived. "But that's *also* why you can't know. Just think of it as protecting her. If you knew about Kitten, and if someone like Soren gets ahold of you, they'll rip that information right out of you. *Then* all that person has to do is find and threaten Kathleen, and your savior complex won't be able to say no, and then we're all fucked."

"I do *not*—" I halt, not having seen the conversation taking *that* direction.

He raises his brows, shifting so he's facing his steaming bowl of food. "I've got zero judgment for it. I get it. But that *is* your biggest weakness. Soren's technically a target, too, but they kidnap him, and they'll have Death's Wing after him, along with his people. And he'd be hard as shit to crack. No, it's better to take Kitten if they want to get to you."

I tap my finger on the table, watching him bring the spoon to his lips before blowing on it. My mouth parts at times, until I manage out, "Who put you in charge of analyzing me?"

"Soren, when he told me to train you."

My jaw drops; not really meaning that question. I was just being sarcastic. "Wait, seriously? You know what, where is Anya while we're at it? She was supposed to help. It's just been you for the last three days. Maybe it's time to switch it up."

He shrugs, ripping some bread into pieces and dipping it into the broth, the crumbly bread slowly turning soggy in his fingers. "There's nothing wrong with that. Kathleen loves my company, and you love Kathleen," he calmly says, almost smugly.

I grab a piece of bread as my hunger betrays my irritation, my stomach obscenely grumbling at the smell of onion beef stew. I rip apart the baked goodness more aggressively than is probably necessary, the little pockets of air creating swirls where it pulled apart. "Whatever... I wouldn't say no to someone else coming over. Maybe we should invite one of these people to the table? Or would that interrupt your *analysis* of me?"

"You know they won't come over here."

I hotly sigh. He's not wrong. So far, no one has approached us when we've sat here for food between training sessions. It was apparently Soren's orders that, for some reason, my father's men agreed to. That doesn't stop them from staring, probably because they see me training all day if they pass the storage room and wonder why I fight like a flopping fish.

I've never really had a sense of shame, though. They don't know what I face, and I'll be damned if I let another moment go by that isn't about helping me prepare for what's coming.

I owe Soren.

I won't let him down.

Doesn't mean I don't appreciate that I've properly got to be aware of a reputation to live up to, however that works.

Bones tears into another piece of bread as he smirks. "But seriously, you need to work on over-gripping your dagger. It's what you're doing right now to your spoon."

I glance down, my brows furrowing when I see that I am, indeed, gripping it as if hanging on for dear life.

"I like a firm grip," I comment, relaxing my fingers as the stiffness releases. "Don't make any sexual jokes."

He grins mischievously. "Who me? I would *never*." He licks his lips, straightening up again. "Anyway, this is important because your grip is something you can work on without a partner. I'd still focus mostly on evasion, but having the right grip could be the difference between life and death." He takes another bite, the remainder of the bread dripping into the broth. "But if, and when, shit gets real, there won't be time to heal or recover. It's all about muscle memory, so being aware at all times, even eating your soup, is pragmatic."

Pragmatic. I loosen my grip, trying to eat my soup with loose fingers. Can't believe I'm being lectured about pragmatism by *Bones*. "Are you nervous at all?" I ask.

He cants his head to the side. "No point in being nervous. I'll either live, or I'll die." He seems to consider something else, sucking on a thumb. "Really, it's mostly Kathleen I worry about. I've stashed her away pretty good, but I really don't like not being able to tell what's happening on an hour-to-hour basis."

It's hard not to laugh like he's a squirrel stashing away his nuts. I don't reply as I scarf the meal down. The savory onions are so perfectly delicious after all that exertion today, even through my anxious nausea. And honestly, there's something that actually makes me feel a little better about Bones with his statement.

Maybe I can let go of my worry for Kathleen, for now. Just focus on training. On how to fight a *god*.

No fucking pressure.

"I'm getting stiff again," I say, starting to feel the beating of our sessions settle in my muscles. "You can hold back a little, you know, and I'll still get the same message."

"Try saying that to the enemy," he says, pretending to be looking at someone. "Yes, sir, please wait a moment while I stretch before you stab me. Oh, and I need this splinter removed. Maybe grab a drink while we wait, and some tweezers."

I quirk a smile, shoving my mouth with more soup before I can't hold back a laugh. He's so damn annoying, especially when he's right. Then I point my empty spoon at him. "You know you mock that, but I bet it would work for a *second*. Like you said, element of surprise. Think about it, they're going to hear the question and wonder what's going on, and *that's* when you stab."

He shrugs, although his smile shows he's a *little* approving. "You know what, I'll give it a try next time I'm about to gut someone." He downs his water, setting the cup down with a heavy sigh. "How is Soren healing, by the way? Looks alive today."

"Mostly just sleeping. The tonics will do that. Today is the first day he has real color in his face, as you've noticed. He'll be *feeling* back to normal in a few days, although I wouldn't recommend him to get stabbed again. The tonics replace the *sensation* of being drained, but he's still low on blood."

He shakes his head. "Must be odd to see that man sleep so much when he basically never does."

Huh.

Come to think of it, Soren is always up before I wake, and I never bothered to ask *when* he left the bed. He just always seemed busy. "He really does run on very little sleep, doesn't he?"

"Wait, you don't—Oh, then maybe I shouldn't say more."

I frown, tilting my head. "Say more about what?"

"If you don't know, I'm not telling you."

I growl with exasperation, glaring at him. "This must be what it's like to have siblings."

"I'm the middle child, myself."

I grunt, shaking my head, although that just brings to life the stiffness in my neck—I need a massage from a healer, like the ones I give to Soren, where I can channel magic into his muscles.

It's hard to be completely mad at Bones, especially since I can't deny he's actually helped an *immense* amount with my fighting style—

The sonance of scratching chairs makes me look up. There's a sudden shift in the room's energy, and I glance at the main entry to the room to see my father standing in the threshold.

The air is stolen from my lungs to see him without warning, still absolutely not used to the Scorpion making random appearances like this, especially when he's been gone for the last three days. He's a man that might make the room quiet, but I have the fondest memories from a childhood with a warm father, even if I feel so confused about him now. I want so badly to demand to know why he's as distant as ever, but my heart is simply too exhausted to ask further.

He silently surveys the room, and maybe I also feel different since he looks so *altered* with the shorter hair and tattoos.

It's not clear who he's motioning to when his hand moves, until a few people walk in behind him, one of them guiding Anya with a blade at her neck.

What the hells?

In true Anya fashion, she doesn't even seem bothered.

Bones slightly scoots back in his chair, his demeanor mirroring the alleyway. I nearly do the same, feeling like I actually can contribute *something* now—wait, he would be attacking my *dad*.

"You said we were possibly allies," my father states, addressing someone across the room. Sharply turning my head, my breathing quickens as Soren is intently watching the Scorpion.

Oh no, what the fuck is happening?

What are they doing?

My body tenses when they're rough with Anya, pulling on her hair to straighten out her neck, stretching the vulnerability of her throat. Dad unsheathes a blade that glints in the warm lighting, indenting Anya's cheek with it, who merely sneers in response. "Then explain *her*."

"Only if you state clearly what you want rather than being so *vague*," Soren replies without missing a beat, hostility clear in his voice, although he hasn't moved from his position, still leaning against a table.

I nearly rise to my feet in shock when one of my dad's eyes slowly turns milky like Rorge's, in a fascinatingly grotesque way. "I can see she's not mine. So where is the original, and who is *she*?"

What the hells—so Dad is like one of them?

"Remove the blade and put her down, Ritter, and we'll have a *real* conversation. Because if you slit her throat, we'll become like the Ballad of the Blood, and then this will all be fucking useless. Don't be an idiot." Soren's bitter tone is *cutting*, despite how calm he makes himself seem.

"Maeve has been with us for a very long time," Dad responds, and a woman comes out from behind them, sort of awkwardly trying to make her way in as if she's reluctant to be here. "Which also made it easy to find her, and then locate your skin shifter. Which would be something you'd want to inform an ally, no?"

Skin—Anya?

Is *she* a skin shifter?

My sensation of being lost returns to me, feeling so small against all these people who are capable of so much; meanwhile, I can barely hit Bones with a training sword. Oh, but at least my *skin won't burn*.

So fucking useful, right?

My father inhales through his nose, his eyes nearly rolling with his blink as he faces the one holding Anya, nodding.

The man releases her, and she slowly steps away from him as if he were a mere nuisance. "It was necessary for reconnaissance," Anya states, adjusting one of her bracers. "You'd have done the same. She's unharmed, as you can see."

My father ignores her as he holds an arm out in Anya's direction to indicate her, and then faces Soren, who I don't know if he's even blinked. "Anyone else I need to know about? Any *more* of my people missing?"

"She's the only one," Soren tightly replies.

A certain hatred crosses my father's eyes, although that expression is immediately replaced with concern and confusion; the same reaction washes over the room as the rubies in the wall and ceiling glow, much like when I was alone with Cypress.

A red cast settles on us all.

"This is why, sir," the one named Maeve says unconfidently, her voice shaking. "I didn't come to you. I wasn't treated poorly, but I stayed put. The witch told me when I came back is when we'd have to leave. And when, well, when things will get *hard*."

Immediately, my father's gaze darts over to me, the expression so vividly similar to when he found me on our front porch, clenching my mom all those years ago. My dad then looks back at the men behind him. "Send a raven to Tempest. It's time we leave Skull's Row. We move to the sea."

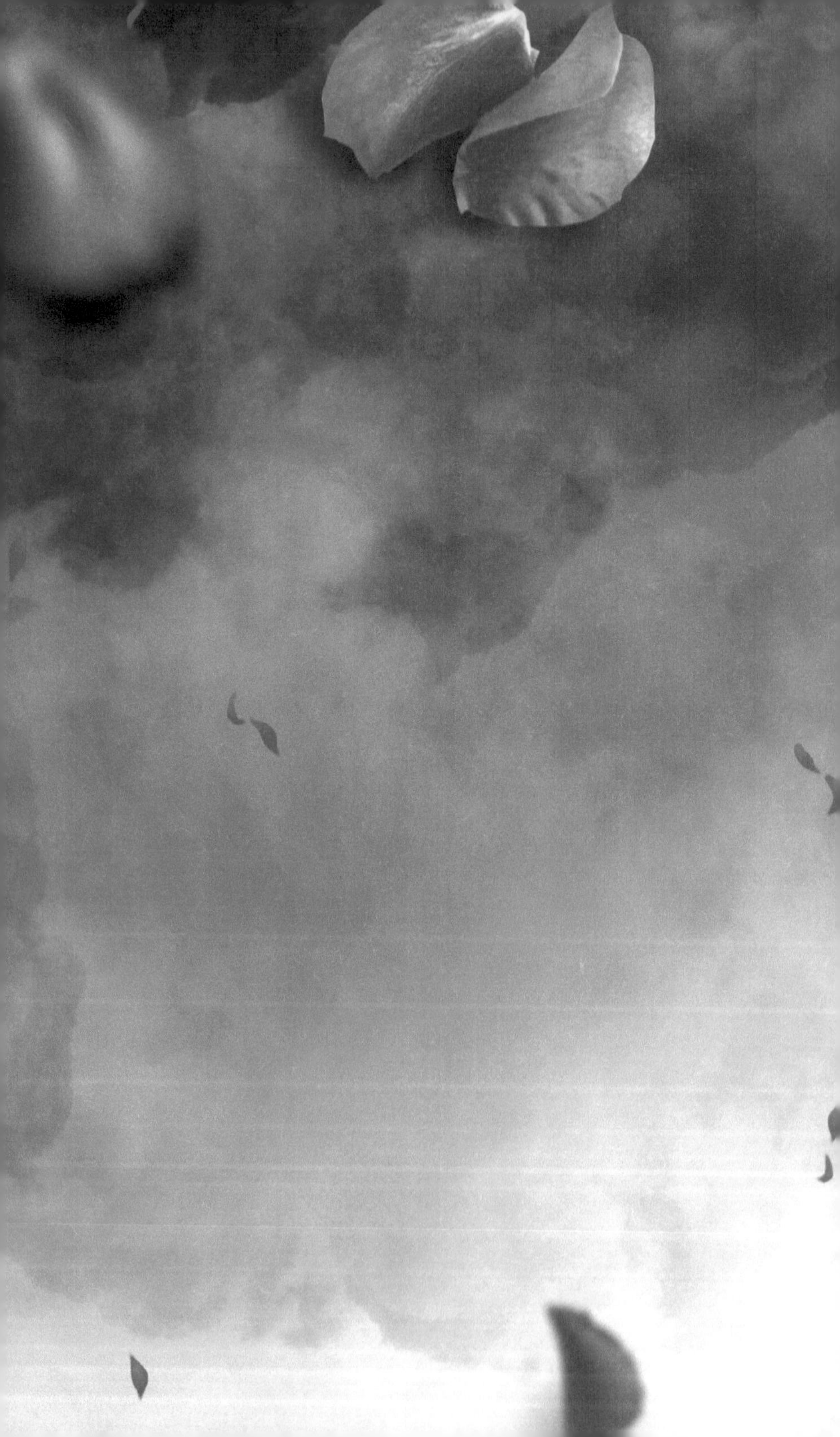

BRAIDS

JANE

Pain radiates at my scalp, my eyes clenching shut, and my nose crinkling. "You're so rough," I grind out.

Rather than pausing, Donna only pulls tighter, working with a ruthless efficiency. "You'll thank me later to have the hair out of your face."

Never did I think getting ready to leave would involve braiding my hair. The design is tightly woven down the center of my scalp. I wish Soren was capable of doing more than loose braids, or I'd have asked him to do this for me. At least he might be able to make the pain *fun*. In the same breath, if he could do them, I doubt he would. There's too much that needs to be done in such a short amount of time.

"Ruby earrings?" Donna asks from behind me.

I raise my hands to my ears, fingers brushing against the metal casing and gemstone. "They're in."

A requirement from the witch.

"Good," she replies, my neck stiffening to keep my head still. "You're almost ready."

Almost. There's such an unspoken promise there that she has no idea what she just alluded to. The notion that this all turns utterly sour has been at the forefront, side, and back of my mind, along with another consideration—*What if Misery doesn't have to catch me?* Cypress didn't say it was indefinite, just highly likely, and that she can't control free will.

What if there is an out here?

What if there's a choice I can make that changes it all?

"Have you ever been on a pirate ship?" she asks, pulling me from the haze of my worries.

"Is it different from a normal ship?"

"Oh, yes," she laughs. "They look out for their own, and only their own. Don't trust a single one of them. And follow their rules. They're very serious about their agreed-upon laws."

Noted. "Where are we going, exactly?"

"Tempest hasn't shared that."

It's strange how I actually feel better having spoken to Cypress. If I didn't have context for what's out there haunting me, I honestly would be fleeing during this escape. It's simply entirely too uncomfortable to consider all these people working to *protect* me. If it was just for my own life, I'd see it as an absolute waste of theirs.

But not with what Cypress said. If I die, then it makes it all worse, somehow. So I have to live, and I very well can't protect myself, *by* myself.

There has to be a way I can reduce the deaths while somehow avoiding getting caught…

I wince in silence as Donna is *rough*, because I do agree that I'll want this hair out of my eyes, and it'll be a lot harder for someone to yank on, like with Shade—the pain subsides as Donna is finally working on the free braid, wrapping up her task quite quickly before she says, "There, all done. Functional and fierce. Now get your boots on."

As I stand, I touch the top of my lightly aching head; the braid is so foreign, yet relieving. It's a skill I never really learned myself, always keeping my hair short and with bangs as a kid. Then, in Coalfell, it didn't matter.

I near my boots, sitting back down to slide them over wool socks. "So, is everyone expecting me to have a plan?"

Glancing up at her, she leans over, an elbow on each knee, giving me the faintest smile. "Well, since no one can get close enough to chat with you, rumors do spread. I think quite a few are under the impression you know what to do. At least, that your father does."

My fingers are quick with the laces, tightening the boot. "Do *you* think he does?"

"I think this god wants you dead, am I wrong in that?"

There's a hesitancy in her voice, and I can tell that my fishing for information may be too obvious. "Well, he definitely can't do what he needs with me if I'm alive," I half-lie, standing when both of my boots are secured.

"If killing you brings about something devastating, then it's clear we just need to keep you alive and safe while a plan is made. He's getting greedy, which is scary as shit for us, but it also means there *will* be an opening. I imagine fighting a god requires *another* one... which is why Cypress is so relevant... I don't know. Maybe the ocean god can do something?" She glances my way. "Are *you* worried?"

It's funny because I've been asking everyone that exact question, and this is one of the first times someone is asking *me*. Then again, Soren doesn't *need* to ask questions when it concerns my heart. "I'm worried for the people who will die."

"That's not your responsibility," Donna reassures, and I cross my arms as I watch her stand before she stretches her body. "It's the fault of this asshole, Misery, and also Blackwell for being a dingleberry and going along with this."

"A *dingleberry*?" I ask with a quiver of my lips.

She tilts her head. "It's a word my family used growing up. Mostly when speaking to the children. Although Blackwell is such an idiot, he might as well only have the smarts of a kid. Even *that* might be too generous."

This time, I let a laugh out; the moment of peace rather appreciated. We're in the room that's been assigned to me, one that no longer has any signs of Soren. "So seriously, what does he gain in all of this? Blackwell, I mean? It's still mind-boggling that he would risk everything for a god who he has to know doesn't give a shit about him."

She shrugs. "In his eyes, he gains all of Skull's Row. But he's a twat for thinking that's worth anything. If he so much as farts in the wrong direction when Misery is reigning, he'll kill him without hesitation. It's just like you said. Which is why he's a fucking dingleberry."

My laugh escapes me again, and this time Donna joins, too. She even nods to the door, and I know it's time to follow her out of here. *I hate leaving the sanctuaries Soren makes in these rooms...* "We're all just trying our best to mitigate the damage," she says, opening it, ignorant of the raging battle inside me. "It's just annoying when others join in to make the fight all that more complicated."

"Well, isn't everyone acting so unlike Skull's Row." A slight tease is in my voice. "You know, since Skull's Row isn't really known for this kind of *brave* behavior. To look out for others."

I think of my mom as I say that. Of how she loved the architecture of this city, the excitement of it all, and even the freedom, but *loathed* the selfishness. She would probably laugh at the irony of everyone acting like knights in a song.

"It's the natural order of things, isn't it?"

"Is it?" I rebuke, standing in the hallway that red rubies still light.

Donna rings a bell, to which Rorge looks around the corner and holds up a hand—not yet. "My job among your father is to be the people person," Donna explains. "And if there's one thing I see repeated over and over again, it's that most humans cannot resist the call of purpose. What'll happen, if I have to guess, is this entire situation we're all stuck in will pass and some peace will settle for a while, and we will have defeated Misery. Skull's Row will live through the subsequent changes. Then as people forget what almost happened here, they'll go back to thieving like this is all a fable. I mean, it *will* be a fable, to them."

My mind is *not* ready for that kind of philosophy. "It's hard to imagine it that way when my mother's death is a part of what caused it all." My gaze snaps to her, feeling like I shouldn't have mentioned my mother in such a way. I'm so used to secrecy, I'm not sure what can be shared anymore.

There's the slightest twitch to her umber eyes, as if indicating her mind refocusing on a new path. "I'm sorry for your family's suffering," she replies, her voice smoother and smokier in an attempt to comfort.

My gaze falls to the floor, a chill washing over me as I'm not used to my neck being so exposed in the back. "Me too."

The only regret of leaving this city is that I won't be able to visit the Silver District. There's something permanent in this feeling of us departing, like even if I came back, would it be too dangerous for me? Would people recognize and ransom me?

That's if I even survive.

Gooseflesh rises on my arms again as I'm so nervous for what has yet to happen that it makes me sick.

Faint echoes of many moving people make their way to this hallway, and that's when Rorge faces us to deliver an approved nod.

"So, remember," Donna says, walking ahead of me and speaking over her shoulder. "You are to *never* be alone. Either myself, Rorge, Bones, or Anya should be with you, or your father or Soren. Preferably a mixture of us all." She looks back ahead, her black hair half braided at the top, the rest still down. "I'm sure those ruby earrings will help keep Cypress alerted as well, wherever she is."

My heart pounds when we reach the end of the rest, the area alight with a need to move, to pack, to *prepare*. The sound of heavy armor makes this all sink in—so far I've only really seen reinforced leathers, maybe some armored pieces here or there.

At least three dozen are covered in metal.

There's a rotation as Anya is placed on 'keep track of Jane' duty while Donna secures arrangements, Rorge standing near to keep an eye on everyone. I pad my body with layers and weapons, and ensure my laces are tied extra tight before placing my back against a wall.

It's apparently imperative that I don't leave the *entirety* of me open, if possible.

When it's far too quiet between Anya and me, even the area itself is loud, I say, "So, a skin shifter." I glance over at Anya, who is wearing her usual attire with some metal shoulder plates, metal on her thighs, and thicker vambraces.

"Not as useful of a skill now that your father has outed me," she remarks, her arms crossed while her dark eyes scan the open area. Her slicked-black hair is fuller than normal, the few strands in her face now brushing past her nose.

"How many times have I interacted with you and didn't know it?" I joke, leaning into the cold stone behind me. I don't know what to do with my hands as an energy of utter nervousness floods me.

"Only once." Her lips curve into the faintest smirk.

My jaw drops, not thinking she actually did. "Wait, who was it?"

"*That's* ruining the fun in it," she replies smoothly. Her usual serious expression shifts to something more contemplative. "Did you find Bones useful? I hope you gained a skill or two while I was gone."

"Not sure I'd call it *useful*. Couldn't hit him to save my life."

Her smile sharpens, an approved chuckle confusing me. "You know, the time you kicked him in the nose is one of the first direct hits he's had in years."

"What?"

"It's true. There are many people in this city who would pay a lot of money to spar with him. I don't know what the hells to call his magic, if he even has it, but he's damn near impossible to hit. Unusually difficult. Even *he* thinks it's hilarious."

I furrow my brows, trying to recall back to when I kicked him in the face. "Really?"

"*I* was going to do some sparring with you, but Bones insisted the time was best spent trying to hit him. If you're training to attack an unhittable target, you're more likely to land a strike against a normal man. Especially since very few are as skilled as Soren or Bones." She reaches up, absentmindedly rubbing one of her earlobes, a small speck of gold barely existing as an earring there. "It's actually how he used to make his money before Soren. He was either training people, or hired as an assassin."

It never once crossed my mind to wonder how these people all met.

"Well, how did he meet Soren?"

Her faint but unmistakable smirk returns. "Someone paid him to kill Soren."

My breath catches. "*What?*"

"Bones tried, but met his match because Soren always saw every strike coming. Soren couldn't land a single hit on Bones, either. So, after what I'm told was an unreasonably long stalemate of trying to kill one another, they both agreed to take a break. Soren then offered to double what he was being paid, and Bones just loved that. Now, he's more loyal than a dog."

I smile widely, despite myself. "Why are you telling me all of this?"

There's a pause, and she looks me in the eye. "Because you shouldn't judge your skill against Bones. Not even Soren can stab him. Nick him, maybe. But that's it. You might be inexperienced, but it's not like you haven't been in a fight. You know how to recover. You know how to handle pain. Don't forget that."

Oh. I glance down, not sure what to do with that sincerity. "Well, thanks. That does help." I know it's a bold question, but now I can't stop wondering, "How did *you* meet Soren?"

Glancing back at her, I notice the corner of her mouth tightens. "Through necessity. But that's a story for another time."

I still can't figure Anya out. Or her motives. But I don't press, because I also understand that not every story can be told or shared. It makes me feel like there might even be an allyship here, at least until she stops assuming I'm bad for Soren, or that I want something from him.

Even that kind of worry seems distant now.

My heart races slightly faster when Bones and Donna approach, the crowd moving around them as if they're stones among the sea. Bones strides with a roughness that belies how, well, *graceful*, he can be on his feet; his boots even scuff along the floor. Contrasting him is Donna scanning the environment like a first mate ensuring the ship is in order.

A creaking, heavy door pulls my attention in the opposite direction, Soren's authority breaking through the air with an effect that's so entirely impossible to describe, but is felt so immediately it makes even *my* back straighten. I'll never quite get over the way his sheer size, mixing with an impossibly pale gaze that peels away at people's emotions, commands a room. He is completely covered in full, thick leather armor, with quite a few shining metal pieces added.

As much as the red leather was haunting to witness in Coalfell, there's something imposing about him donned in all black. Mismatched, stolen rings on his fingers stand out even more against the darkness of his attire, hair, and stubble.

I asked him about where his red leather was, and according to him, it's primarily ceremonial, worn for official tasks or making an appearance in Skull's Row.

This muted outfit is for actual warfare.

It's not lost on me that only a few days ago, Mod was hitting Soren with a broom, and now he walks among them like a revered Zenith. Even if I lack the necessary powers to read someone, even *I* can feel the reality of everything—Dad is distinguished, but Soren is replacing that generation. Much like the miners back in Coalfell when the young boys started to turn into young men. Even if they wanted to fight him based on their loyalties, no one here can deny Soren holds a place among this world.

Soren approaches us, scanning everyone with a gaze I now recognize—he's sensing out the space and the people within, to whatever degree he does. Those piercing eyes flash back at me, barely softening, although it's enough for me. "It's time to go, Jane."

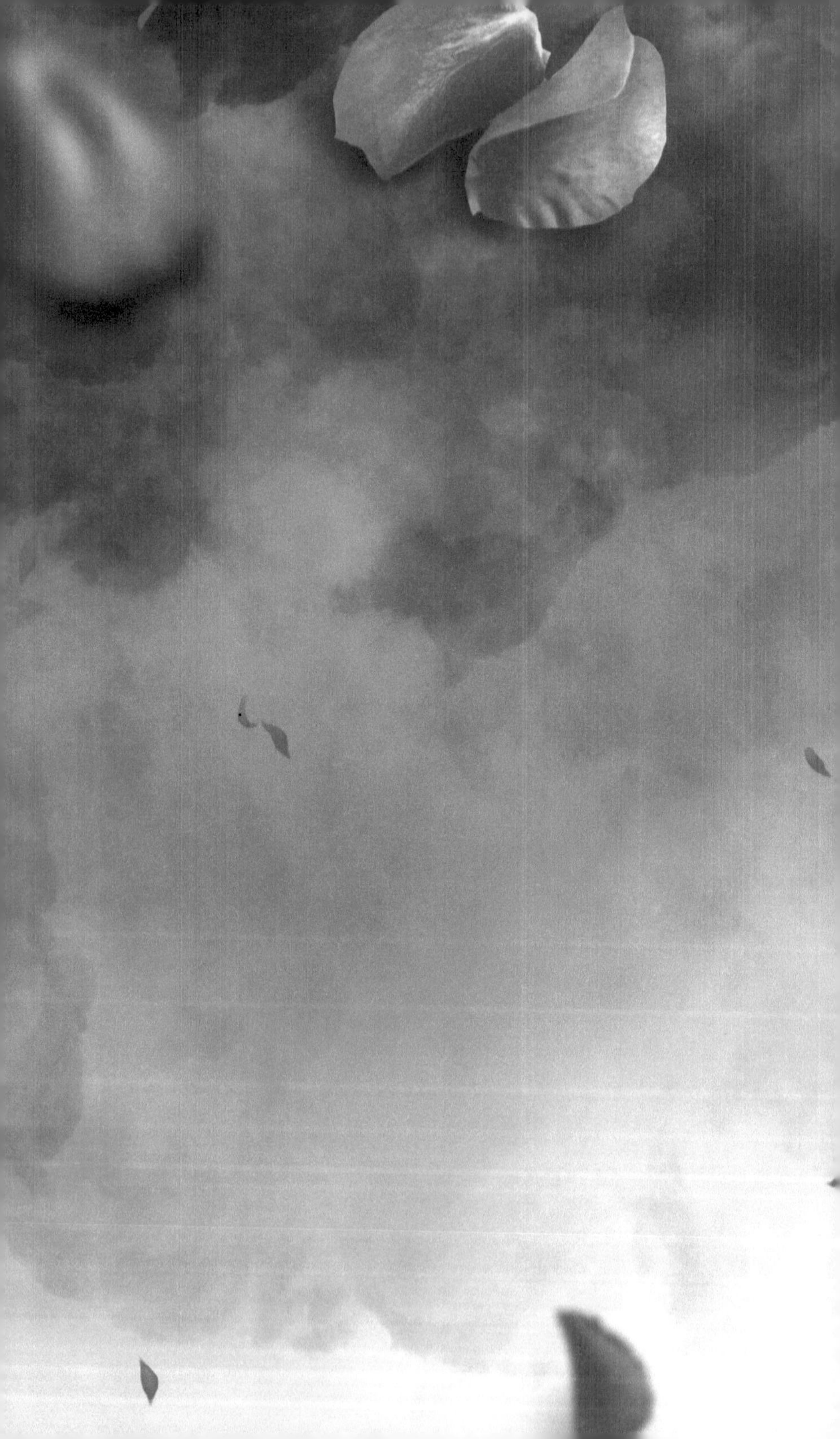

I straighten my shoulders with purpose, padding the dagger at my right hip that I'm most familiar with. I eye the stubble of a man who has broken down so many of my barriers; such a subtle detail, and yet it's *him*, especially on his right jaw, where a segment is missing from a scar.

There are moments like these where I can tell, years from now, I'll revisit them in my heart. Just like the baths that mom had drawn for me, the calm before the storm. I can only hope that when I visit them for comfort, Soren is still alive. Still right around a corner, waiting on me.

He reaches a hand out, those powerful fingers landing some-where between my neck and shoulder, and he leans in—he smells so much like oiled metal. "I honestly can't promise things will be okay once we leave here. You're to go with your father, since he can shift into another whereas I'm harder to hide," he quietly warns in my ear. "But you're not alone, love. If we get separated at all, I know how to find you. Do you understand?"

His gritty voice is absolute perfection to me, and I can't resist leaning my cheek into his—*fuck*, that means something to me, to the lost girl that grew up not knowing how to find her family. I click my tongue, agreeing with that but also *not* liking this. "Where will you be if I'm with my father?"

"Close," he reassures, his tone soothing.

To my shock, as he pulls back, his warm lips and stubble graze my forehead, then he surveys the space before we all follow him, his deadly stare returning after softening for me.

There's something to being so public with such gentle affection that makes this all worth it.

But as I start to reach the entrance, I become paralyzed.

A cold chill snakes down my spine as if I want to scream to everyone to not leave and beg the gods to pause time—I have too much to do. Too many questions for my father, too much time with Soren that I have yet to spend, and I still have Kathleen to see.

Without a doubt, there are people in this room who are already marked for death. Just like my mother was before she stepped out onto our front patio that connected to the streets.

It's as if I can see that all over again, the light of the outside world flooding my vision in a memory.

If only I could go back to the moment *before* she entered the sunlight, to tell her to stay. To ask her about being a Cinder, to learn where *she* grew up. To ask her when she knew that Dad was a skin shifter.

Donna loudly says, "We're finally leaving this fucking place!" The people around cheer, some raising their weapons. My gaze latches to the back of Soren's head when it's clear I'm the only one that's nervous; his hair tied back into a low bun, ready for a fight.

Gods, I wish I was more powerful. That I was *useful*. That I could do more than just not be *burned*.

I want to do *so much* right now, and yet I can't. I physically can't.

As if pulled over by the very earrings I wear, my head moves to a ruby in the wall. *That's not entirely true…*

No. I'm not yet prepared to give up on finding an alternative—

"Jane, you'll be with the Scorpion," Soren says, indicating a man who looks *exactly* like Ern, down to the facial hair.

That penetrates through absolutely every ounce of fear I have. My subconscious wants to momentarily ask him what he's doing here, and ask how he is.

Despite everything I feel, I almost laugh at the way he's dressed. "It's not right seeing Ern dressed like an assassin," I quietly remark, looking him over. I made the comment more for Soren, given that I still haven't had a conversation with my dad since I got here, but it's Ern—well, my father—that replies with, "I thought to walk beside you with a face you at least somewhat recognize."

That suggestion pierces a soft spot in my heart, tempting me with the notion that he might actually care. Although the hole is entirely too small to matter.

"I don't understand you, or why you don't seem interested in me, but promise me you won't die," I grind out, that humor fleeting. "I have a *lot* of questions, and you owe me."

Ern's eyes soften, and it's truly messing with me to think it's my *dad* when I feel like I know *this* person more than him. "We both know we can't promise that. It's why I did what I did with Cypress, because that's the closest I can get to promising I'll take care of you."

Take care of me.

My jaw clenches shut, my eyes vibrating back and forth as I look all over a face that hid my father for so long.

'I'll take care of you.'

He said that once before, didn't he… with my head burrowed in his neck as I sobbed when he carried me away, my mother's blood still on my hands from when I tried to heal her. I remember how much he smelled like the ocean.

"Again, we have a lot to cover," I say, clearing my throat. "Just don't die, alright?"

"I'll try."

My heart numbs itself again, just wanting to get all this over with so we can be on the other side—the sound of a raven makes me narrow my eyes. What—why…

The double door that separates this space from the rest of Skull's Row cracks open, seemingly on its own accord, as a black bird enters the space, its feathers splayed out as it glides over to an unlit torch, perching on the metal with a curling of its feet. The eyes are completely red like a white rat's, its head turning with an unnatural acuity as it looks at my father.

"It's time to go," my dad loudly proclaims. "You're with me, Jane. Soren and the rest will trail behind."

I glance back at Soren, already despising the mere *suggestion* of this distance. What if we get separated? How am I supposed to find him among the sea of people, hells, the *vastness* of this continent?

I know he can look for me, but I don't want to have to sit and wait again. My chest constricts with rapid breathing, feeling like this is losing my father all over—

"Let's go," Ern commands—my *dad*. The raven flies out of the space, and I've been around long enough to be aware that a chain of actions has started, like igniting the wick of a candle that can never be put out.

Following Ern, my dissociation is strong as I keep glancing back at Soren whose lips part, almost as if he is about to tell them to wait —is there hurt in his eyes?

It doesn't matter, as Donna gently touches my shoulder and guides me forward.

An ache in my chest blooms from roots that have entrenched in my soul before, wishing at least Anya or Bones was with me.

They could find Soren, no doubt, so I wouldn't have to wait. Or wonder.

The comfort from everything Soren has given me is completely ruined by an uncontrollable sense of betrayal. I went so long without loving anyone—save for Kathleen—and now I find I don't know what to do with all these feelings.

Facing ahead as I follow a man I've thought about nearly every single day, it's utterly confusing when, deep down, I choose Soren. I want to stay with *him*. Or maybe I've already lived through losing my father, so it's a pain I don't fear.

I can't do it again with someone else.

"You're with us, Jane, because I can look like another," Dad explains, as if he knows what plagues my heart. "I can't read much past that from you, but I can see your aura grows thicker with betrayal the further we walk."

Oh, shit, I forgot about that.

"I can't lose him like I lost you," I say, the desperately lonely part of me speaking to him with slight poison on my tongue. "I don't..."

I don't want to do this.

Maryanne's voice screams at me: *COWARD.*

That's when he pauses and looks back at me, his face morphing into the Scorpion. It's the first sentiment in his eyes, aside from when he spoke about Mother. Surprise and grief haunt his mahogany stare, and honestly, I'd rather look at *him* than Ern.

It makes me feel better to look at a man that I *know* is capable. Someone that might be able to get me back to Soren.

"Jane, when this is all done, it's *done*. Rest is coming for you li—" he pauses, a humorous expression momentarily winning out. "Was about to call you little menace."

I'm so jumbled inside I don't even know what to do with that. That once would have made me cry because it's a name he called me as a kid, and I *loved* it. "I'm still little, and a menace. Guess I never outgrew it," I reply, although my voice is completely void of emotion.

It's weird interacting with him like this.

He dips his chin in a nod, the face of Ern returning, like he knows to move past that. "This truly is almost done. The hardest part is coming, but it *will* pass."

My mind scatters in the vastness that's my misery, searching for something *truly* solid to hold onto. Surprisingly, it's when Soren's sister enters my mind that I feel some semblance of control.

Soren needs me to be strong so I can deliver my word. I'll take care of his heart if I am to take care of anything.

Even if I'm not ready for this.

⸺⸺◈⸺⸺

LEAVING the sanctuary that Cypress carved out is *not* like I first imagined it would be. My nerves scream like freed banshees who have been gagged—every movement from somebody else sends me on edge.

I brush one hand against rough walls when we pass through and around people, my other hand resting on the hilt of my dagger. I don't know where Soren is, or his men, or even my father's men. Just that Ern guides me, and Donna trails behind. Those clad in armor wear cloaks buttoned down to their waist in *some* concealment, but I've lost them in the crowd.

Distant shouts and clanging of metal keeps the underground streets alive, firelight our only illumination whether from braziers or through windows of homes and shops.

"Hood," Donna instructs from behind. As casually as possible, I raise mine over my head. Dad's brown hair remains visible, and I'm actually grateful that if he does have to wear the face of another, he looks like Ern because it's easy to keep track of him. Ern's face looks back at me, motioning to walk alongside him.

"The auras are different," he says. "Keep closer."

"So you can see things?"

"It's easier when the milky eye is out," he replies, tapping at the temple housing the eye that was recently a milky orb. "But yes, I can see if anyone has Misery's miasma clinging to them. Or anyone from Ash. I haven't seen it *here* yet, but there's a distortion I don't like."

I keep glancing up at the sharp lines of his profile. "So can we talk at all?" I carelessly ask.

What if it's one of the last times I can speak to him?

"Quietly."

The single word is a cautious permission, and I seize that opportunity. "I never met your men." I eye what appears to be a homeless man sleeping in a bundle of soiled furs, a filthy film on his skin, although now I can't help but wonder if he's just a skin shifter spying on the world around them. "I didn't even know you had any."

"I didn't want you growing up too close in my shadow," he explains, his tone guarded as he continues to focus ahead of him.

"I wanted to, you know," I say, nostalgia nipping at my heart when we step out onto a much wider street that horses clack their hooves on, carriages attached to them. "I knew you were a, you know, important person, and that everyone revered your type. It was fun keeping it a secret, but I also was bursting at the seams to tell everyone."

My gang of friends no doubt suspected *something*, but we were all in it for our own interest, one way or another. It was never safe to confide in them, and I knew that. Kathleen was honestly the first person I opened up to, and even then, she never knew my secrets until *recently*.

"Your mother was against it," he answers, partially looking over his shoulder at me, and I wish he looked like himself when he said that. "I was, too."

My gaze drops down to the cobblestone. I don't want to speak about Mom to him, not when he looks like Ern.

"Is there a reason you haven't hugged me once?" I pluck the question from a random thought passing by.

His silence makes me regret asking, dreading that he might only have something unsavory to answer me with. "Yes," he finally replies. "I can't say more."

My throat tightens, but I nod, clinging to the hope that, for once, it's not all negative. That someone's motive isn't soured, or selfish.

"So you were seriously, you know, the *man* at the tavern this whole time?" I ask, still not fully certain about giving away details like that when I have no idea who could be listening. Mentioning *Ern* might be a poor decision.

"It was so much harder than you can imagine to see you broken, and not tell you the truth." He glances down at me, his voice carrying an edge of heartache, the kind that's nearly impossible to mimic. "*Nothing* has broken me like that, Jane. Nothing."

Questions. Focus on those while you can. "How did you live knowing you knew mom's killers?"

"I could have fought them. Chased after them. Probably would have killed them. But then I'd risk making you an orphan and completely unprotected. Your mother would have ensured my torture in the afterlife if I abandoned you for rage."

A shattered childhood resurfaces, and it's pretty damn hard to ask my father questions when they're all burdened with traumatic memories.

"Why did you have my chest branded, with *your* design?"

"Cypress told me to," he flippantly answers. "Said it would serve more than one purpose."

Any answer relating to Cypress means I won't get to know more than whatever surface-level explanation she's given.

"Alright… well, why did you not teach me of the gods much?" I sidestep a pile of shit in a bucket, nearly vomiting at the stench. *Some* things I'm not used to. "I had no idea they actually influenced things. Always just sounded like something we mentioned in passing but never really followed."

"Well, because that's how I see it, in my book. They seem to answer to very few, and you can't change what they want. They don't give a shit if we hurt. What's the point of knowing them, then?"

"Sounds like a shit deal that they have power, and we don't."

"That's why I never gave it thought. Cypress, on the other hand, is so entrenched with hers that she's like his literal right hand." His glance at me is quick, but our gazes still connect. "*You* have one, you know. With your healing powers."

That revelation nearly stops my feet in their tracks. "Mom never mentioned it," I mutter nearly so fast the words have no space between them. "Or, well, I kind of remember a blue candle, but that's it."

"There's an entire ritual with the blue candle. It can aid with the healing powers."

I glare at him in the dim lighting. "No one has mentioned that to me."

His eyes move all over in their sockets, which is so interesting because, for Soren, his gaze usually steadies rather than searches. "You lived in Coalfell as a healer. They don't have healers out there, not trained ones, and *they're* the only ones that use the candle— properly educated healers get hired out left and right, or live in the cities. It makes sense they wouldn't tell you. I thought about mentioning it in passing, but I honestly didn't want you to use it so as not to draw attention to yourself."

Torches highlight the cracks and bumps of the walls, a few walking *too* close to me, like they might want to steal my things.

I had never once considered there are various levels of healers. Well shit, now I want to live just so I can learn *that*.

When a woman strides by and glares at me with hardly any other interpretation, I partially pull out my dagger. *No, idiot, what if she's a distraction?*

Quickly, I step to the side so only the wall of a building is to my left. A glance over my shoulder reveals a scabrous man suspiciously closing in on us. Before that man can make another move, my father turns around, Donna's hand quietly moving to the blade at her thigh.

The Scorpion, as Ern, speaks. "You touch her, and I'll cut off your ears and then your tongue."

The man pauses.

I raise my brows as we slow down as if to say, 'Sorry, can't stop him.'

The woman comes into view, Donna watching her with calm anticipation. The woman's dark eyes flash with concern as she draws her lips tight, waving a dismissive hand. "Let's go, Adam. There'll be other fresh ones."

The pair disperse almost as quickly as they appeared, disappearing behind two opposing carriages crossing the street. When I meet Donna's eyes, I spin on my heels and follow my father once more like nothing happened.

We just need to get out of here.

Even if this place has been forbidden since I was a child, so far, it doesn't seem much different than Skull's Row—"Hold on," I demand, getting so close I nearly step on the back of his heels. "Did you have me watched the entire time I was a kid? I was never able to sneak down here."

"You had many handlers that you never met. Mod was one. They're all keeping a distance in case they're recognized."

Makes sense, I guess.

It's easy to get lost in the detail of the carved stone once we near the more centralized part of this multi-layered maze. It reminds me of the Spiraling Stone, just underground, and one of my persisting thoughts is how many chisels were needed to carve so much of it.

My eyes widen when I swear I spot the soft illumination of true sunlight, the hues of the buildings and carved pillars gaining a subtle blue. *That massive grate, that's right. I bet we're nearing it.* "Why does this place exist like this? This is immense."

"When Skull's Row was founded, it was just a bunch of pirates looking for refuge," he replies, maintaining hawkish eye contact with someone else as they pass us by. "Some of them moved into the cave network to weather out the storms, and before they knew it, this city exploded in growth. Piracy couldn't maintain what was growing, so a new economy emerged in trade routes. Which meant bigger, stronger buildings could be built, and these caves became a place for all things hidden."

There are remnants of lives lived in all corners, many things weathered and forgotten as new inhabitants carry on with their own tales while I'm busy making a mad dash for my life, hunted by something they can't even fathom.

It really feels like I don't know this place at all, which used to live in a romanticized bubble in my mind. What did I do all day, as a kid? Did I really never ask more about how that city came to be, or why certain districts had different flares than others? I can almost recall the sun on my face as I ran about the Silver District, my lips always chapped. Whenever Dad was home, we'd spend all of our time practicing how to sharpen blades, throwing them, spotting a pickpocketer from a league away, and also playing pranks on locals.

Mom would take me to homes to assist in births, or to the Infirmary to heal injuries; it's actually where I met pirates who could afford to be transported inland. Some days, we went to the apothecary, and she was always teaching me how to heal.

I never felt the need to ask more.

"Why do I feel like I was never really taught about Skull's Row?" I ask. "I know I didn't ask about it, but nobody ever told me, either."

A deep sigh escapes his lips. "Your mother fell in love with *me*, not me being a Zenith," he admits.

I bittersweetly smile at the idea of my mother as a young woman, in love with a violent man. "Why did you become one?"

"I had a lot of anger in my youth and enjoyed killing," he freely admits. "Then I liked the riches. *Then*, I liked the security of the power it offered." He pauses as a group of kids chases a rat, one of them throwing a rock at it as the other screams. "By the time I *feared* what having that kind of power means, I was entirely entrenched in this world. Nora and I talked about leaving many times, you know." He looks at me, my heart catching at hearing her shortened name. "Going across the Black Sea. Having Tempest take us—she was the only one your mother trusted to travel with." His expression darkens, and even if he has the face of another man, I can tell it's *him*. "And then everything happened that tore us apart."

My gods, does it feel better than I could ever have imagined to hold such clarity? I really did have a normal family, at least normal to *me*; just a mother and father who dreamed of more, like so many in Coalfell, although many of them spoke of Belstead as their reprieve, or north into the vast woods.

Very few ever wanted to even *visit* Skull's Row.

Once we're bathed in a beaming ray of sunshine from the giant grate above us, I have to squint when looking up at the pattern, the natural light searing what feels like my entire eyeball. When I quickly lower my head to protect my vision, little spots from the light clouding everything I see.

I feel like a mole accidentally surfacing from its tunnels.

When the spots finally fade is when we come to a halt at a very long, stoney bridge. A man sits on a barrel and waves for people to stop, a table next to him with a pitcher of some kind, and a mug he drinks from. I peer around my father, repositioning my hood to keep my face hidden as much as possible while still being able to see.

That bridge looks utterly terrifying.

The entire thing is made of stone, tall pillars with crisscrossing rope as the side barriers, which has some gaping holes in places where someone could tumble right off and down into the black abyss below. Craning my neck upward, I guess it's better than what connects the different tiers—long, low-dipping wooden bridges.

I'd rather walk on solid material.

"Why are we waiting?" I ask, the three of us standing among a small collection of people.

"Crowd control. That bridge can only carry so much, and there's a caravan coming our way."

Sure enough, a donkey carrying a small wagon leads a seven-carriage convoy, all moving very slowly to cross. "How did we get stuck if we had a magical know-it-all tell us when it's the perfect time to move? Or did we just walk too slow?"

"I imagine the timing of this is larger than we can understand." He crosses a hand over his wrist, leaning in to quietly add, "Although yes, this is quite annoying."

I didn't realize how much walking made it feel like we were progressing, even to somewhere unknown. Now, we're planted *right* next to a tavern where many sit outside—probably basking in the scarce sunlight—drinking, no, *draining*, their horns. I can't help but watch in horrific anticipation as one man sprawls his hand out on the wooden table, and another uses a blade to stab in-between each finger. It's a game I saw played as a child, and one that produced carnage that my mother had me heal countless times so I could learn.

The sound of a blade hitting a table seems to grow louder in my head as I know the man will miss the longer they play, as they always do—the man's hand is punctured.

Many hoot and holler.

The one with the blade in his hand cries out in pain, frantically nodding for someone to pull it out. When he does, blood spills everywhere.

Without even thinking, I almost step forward, about to roll my eyes and tell him he's an idiot as I close the wound with my magic.

Dad leans over. "Don't even think about it. Healers don't frequent down here without everyone noticing. We don't need the eyes on us."

"I didn't—sorry," I mumble.

Checking on the bridge to refocus, they're all finally on the stone pathway, but still moving annoyingly slowly, probably trying to avoid getting too close to the rope that's the 'border.'

Glancing back at the man with the bleeding hand, my gaze flits to another who seems keen on staring at us. I don't maintain eye contact, as that seems to be a recurring theme around here. Until I move only my eyes to look back at him, and he's staring right at me.

My heart triples in its pulse.

There's something to him that appears more astute than the rest, like Soren—he looks well muscled, and there are too many straps on his body for weapons to be just a normal spectator of this place. My body stiffens when he rises from his corner, and I swear he's making his way to us. "Dad," I breathe through my mouth. I'm already considering the ways Dad will probably attack him—because I'm not stupid enough to take someone head-on when a skilled killer is right next to me, including Donna. I'll be prepared to come in from behind to stab the stranger, like Bones told me to do, then assess any wounds any of us might have.

"I'm aware," he states, his voice steady.

"We just ride it out, then?" I ask, looking back at the bridge, the little donkey finally almost crossing over.

"We're not alone. If this escalates, we'll deal with it. Either way, we're waiting here until we're given the all-clear to leave. Fights happen all the time, but ones comprising of entire gangs of trained fighters is *not* common. We need to not draw attention."

The man continues to near us, moving through the rowdy chatter like a breeze—if I wasn't so on edge, there's a chance I'd completely miss him. Well, maybe not. He's taller than most, and his chin-length black hair is partially pulled back like Donna's, his scruff slightly thicker than Soren's; he just *looks* like a mercenary. The more I take him in, the more I can't mistake that his clothes are *very* well-fitted, black metal armor on his shoulders, forearms, and chest.

Just like Soren, this man has eyes that pierce right through a person—

No.

Oh… oh no.

His eyes are a bright gold, and there's a controlled chaos about him.

That's when it dawns on me—The Basilisk.

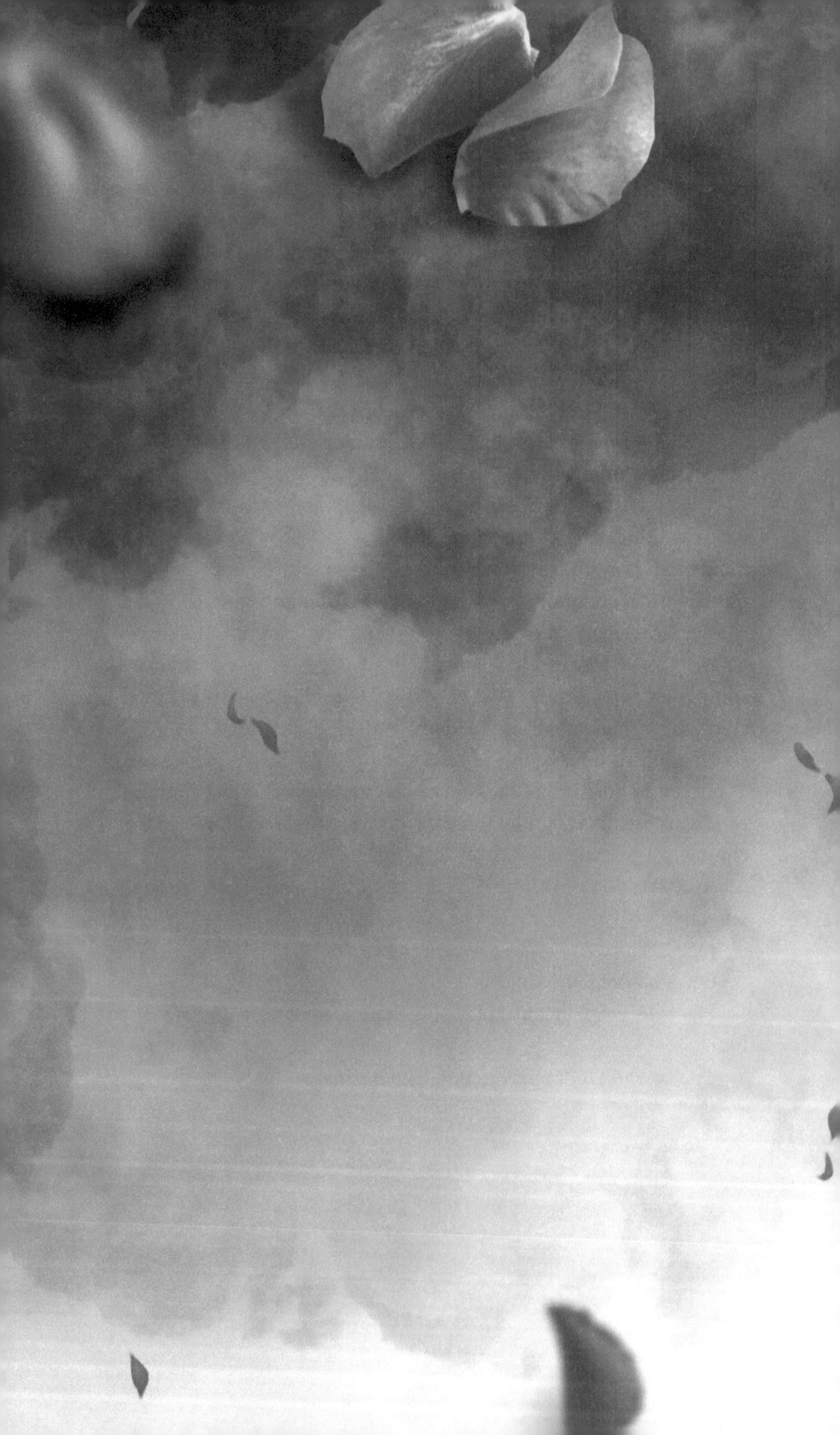

THE GRAPNEL

JANE

Dad doesn't shift a single inch of his posture.

"Do we run?" I ask Donna, since she knows of the Basilisk. She's flitting her gaze between the two men, like she's waiting for a verdict. And just like Bones in the alleyway, Donna's sociable mien is replaced with a cutthroat glare.

"No," the Scorpion replies.

"Sir, I don't trust this," Donna presses with a low tone.

The golden-eyed man tilts his head to the side when he can't be but ten feet away, looking at us with an unnerving intensity that confuses what I should feel; *this* is a man who trained *Soren*.

That absolutely fascinates me.

But I am also uncomfortable with the fact that Soren hasn't

spoken to him in fifteen years. That's a *lot* of time for loyalties to sway, especially harboring the warnings Donna gave about him.

Many clear the space around Basilisk, and some don't even look up to notice his eyes. The weaponry and armor speak for itself. When Basilisk stops approaching, he languidly blinks before looking at my dad. "You're unusually readable."

"What?" my father asks.

Oh, Soren never confirmed Basilisk was a *Sensor*, too. I bet Dad doesn't know. Did Soren say it was a secret? *I don't remember.*

The golden gaze shifts to me, and I feel the weight of it like it's a physical thing. He studies me as if trying to solve a very important puzzle as the sound of clacking hooves is behind us, fucking finally. It shouldn't be much longer before that bridge is cleared.

Basilisk gives his attention to my dad once more. "You know, I've been hearing a lot about you lately. And *her*." He finally flashes a faint, crooked grin, the act indenting the laugh lines around his mouth and scruff. "It's fascinating to see the rumors don't disappoint."

My heart nearly bursts out to the point I worry I might have to catch it.

"You don't leave your lands anymore," Dad replies. "Not unless there's something that calls for your personal touch. And that's more rare than the shadow cat that follows you. So why the fuck are you here, and why are you confronting us? You're supposed to be in the Crimson Isles."

A… *what* follows him?

His gaze moves behind us, but I don't pivot an *inch*, in case it's to get us to look over our shoulders. "I think I'm on the right path." He steps forward to avoid being accidentally bumped into without looking behind him. "I've got a skin shifter in the Crimson Isles dressing up as me. Seemed worth the effort. It's quite difficult to find one of you."

A feline walks behind him; the cat bigger than any house cat, its eyes as bright gold as his. I swear a faint wisp shrouds the cat that mimics hair when underwater. "Aren't you curious, Jane, about the spreading word surrounding your name?"

Donna steps slightly in front of me, and my father remains stolid, like he did when meeting Soren.

"Nope. Not one bit," I say before thinking, just wanting him to move on.

His eyes narrow on me, and he grunts, "Doubt it. A lot of chaos has spun up around you. You're the topic of *many* conversations."

I—is he right? Well, I mean, I'm sure the villagers are all talking. Those at Ern's Tavern no doubt spread that word like a disease, and I suppose those at the Spiraling Stone are possibly talking. The Noirs, even.

Shit.

My breathing quickens, licking my dry lips as all I want to do is flee. I hate this feeling that Skull's Row creates, like bugs crawling underneath my skin.

Basilisk's molten, golden eyes harden. "When that last carriage has crossed, you'll want to run."

He doesn't have to tell me twice. I nearly nudge my father when all he does is stand there. I steal a peek at the line of carriages, only three more still having to make their way over. What are we waiting for, actually? We can just cross around those people. We're definitely not the first ones to break the rules around here.

"He's one of the best swordsmen out there," Dad quietly warns, although I don't hear any tone of being impressed. "Don't engage with him in the slightest, Jane. Or run without word. This is *dangerous.*"

"I'm trying to *leave*, not engage."

"You can't see it, but that raven from earlier is on the other side of that bridge and has yet to caw. We are not to cross until we hear it."

"What if that cat ate it to distract us, or something else happened to it? We could be waiting for nothing."

Basilisk notices I motioned to his feline, who rubs against his leg, its long, pointy ears pulled back in an expression I don't know how to read, given Mom was allergic to cats. "I don't suggest speaking about my cat in front of me when I can't hear what you're saying about her," Basilisk says.

My mouth parts, about to ask if he's serious, when he replies, "Oh, I'm very serious. The last person to do that had their skull turned into a bowl for Jasmine to eat out of."

The cat's head perks to the side, rubbing its head on his leg at what has to be in a response to him saying its name.

A blade manifests from Dad's sleeve, some onlookers giving us slightly more space, but no one is concerned—if anything, they're all focused on staying away from the golden-eyed man. "Idle threats are not being disregarded. So if you want to threaten us, use your fucking words and let us know if this is going to get bloody or not."

"Good to see you're taking this seriously," Basilisk replies, his gilded gaze looking over our shoulders. "People are looking for her, and that's the last carriage. Your raven is about to—" he tilts his head as a raven caws. He scrunches his nose. "I would definitely *run*."

As soon as the bird makes its sound, Dad's entire energy morphs into action as his hand is on my back, glancing down at me. *"Now."*

He guides me to the rocky bridge, and I find a pace between running and walking without hesitation, still wondering what the fuck Basilisk wants while being happy to be away from another Sensor. I can only take so much of that kind of invasion from another. *And it's the wrong man.*

Donna yells from behind, "Sir, that's not good news. Every rumor surrounding him suggests he's here for *her*."

Well.

She could have told *me* that.

"Cypress said to move when the raven cawed, so that's what we're sticking to. If she didn't see Basilisk," he takes in a deep breath, "Then she would have appeared in one way or another just now. We ignore him."

The earrings dangle at my earlobes, the sensation so abnormal and distracting, just like the wind at the nape of my neck. Knowing what Cypress told me, I do believe that she lives to serve her god. Which means, for better or worse, my safety is her priority; until she's done using me.

Crossing the bridge is a terrifying experience, a slight draft tugging at my cloak that whips up from the abyss below. The rope slightly sways like masts on a ship, and I keep focusing on placing one foot in front of the next.

"*FASTER!*" Donna shouts. "Ropes are falling. Don't look back!"

My legs pump on command; I had this discussion with more

than one person that if I'm given an order of urgency, the extra second to question it could cost *everything*.

There's zero hesitation as I run like I'm back in a flaming Coalfell, so I can finally turn around...

Commotion greets me on the other side of the bridge, many of the onlookers shouting and covering their mouths; a *lot* of expletives. Panting with burning lungs, I finally see one of the wooden pillars is hanging sideways, its rope severed so it eerily dangles down into nothingness.

My dad and Donna make it across, my subsequent exhale carrying so much relief.

I rub one of my eyes when it appears that the *Basilisk* starts crossing the bridge, walking confidently as his cat follows his wake. The man swings his long sword to lop at each pole, the ropes releasing as the straw-bound barrier slowly collapses, covering the bridge in ruin. People scream with fury, many starting to cross the bridge from behind, weapons drawn, only for one of the men to get caught in the ropes, then scream in terror as he's sent over the edge. I watch in abject awe and incredulity to see one completely plummet down into the darkness—not as lucky to get caught in the ropes as the others—his screams echoing far beyond when he's last visible. The surviving ones swing and dangle, their pillar of support already cracking under their collective weight as they scramble to get back on the bridge.

The screaming from the blackness is abruptly quieted.

So much shouting, screaming, and chaos erupts. The Basilisk continues forward with more confident swipes of his sword, a few on our side debating on who will move forward to challenge him first. *"That's a shadow cat! Their fangs have venom. You got an antidote?"*

"I swear to the fucking sirens that's the Basilisk. I'm not going first!"

Just as quickly as they were to get lost in an uproar, the people start scattering like mice as Basilisk crosses beyond halfway.

Then it hits me—"The others," I urge, knowing that we're one of the first to cross, if not *the* first. "How will they cross?"

My father's arm is placed in front of my chest, slowly nudging me to keep moving. "We get you to the ship. That's the priority."

"The *others*," I reiterate, not willing to leave Soren.

Ern's eyes are sterner than I've ever seen them, the display distracting me because he looks so much like my father even though his actual face hasn't changed. "If Soren can't figure this shit out, then he's not worthy of you—" fear displaces stringency as Dad looks across the bridge. "I sense a Zenith. It's not Soren."

"I said to *run!*" Basilisk bellows, his deep voice echoing over the crevice.

Dad urges me forward, genuine concern emanating from him like heat from a forge. The three of us break into a sprint, feet pounding against uneven stone as we navigate through a crowd of people.

"If the Zenith are down here," Donna manages out, her voice uneven from all the rushing, "They could be up top, too... and Basilisk... just cut off the main escape route."

Oh.

Shit.

It doesn't stop me, though. Dad is right that Soren will be relying on us to act as directed. At least, I hope so.

I hope he's not stuck.

We're on a hurried path for so long that my ability to pump my legs starts to fail me, my lungs burning so much it brings tears to my eyes. A sharp, aching stab in my side begins to slow me down. *I'm out of shape.*

And then, the *stairs*. They appear in maddening bursts—a short, steep set here, another long winding one there. It's good that we're moving up, but damn, this is more than I've moved in a long time, and my calves are even starting to protest. The stony ceiling is slowly getting lower, too, bringing on claustrophobia.

Glancing at Donna, she moves with precision, but even her breaths come hard and fast. Dad moves like a man possessed, his focus unbreakable.

Donna's gaze finds mine when I keep looking around, my head growing dizzy. "Keep moving," she commands, her face slick with sweat.

One more step.

One more set of stairs...

It seems to happen all at once.

Without any clear source of enemies, Dad's primary blade is

removed from behind his back, countering an attack from someone charging at us through an alley. Scraping metal and grunts surge a new round of adrenaline through me. Donna has both her short swords out in a flash, fighting off her own assailants.

Metal pierces flesh, blood splattering all over. Some wounds are of my people, and other, more fatal ones, are inflicted on those who pounced.

Quickly, I'm the only one without any injury.

My short sword is in my hand, although I know I have to be careful. I'm not trained; the stint with Bones was for last-minute muscle memory, not to train in the offensive.

Watching my father fight is terrifying, both in how easily he cuts through others and how much I can't stand when there's a close call. I've seen this happen all too many times, and I know all it takes is one misstep, one exhausted raise of an arm that's too slow…

Balancing staying out of the way and wanting to keep these men off of my father is made impossible when one attacker's eyes lock with mine. I grip my sword but then loosen it as I hear Bones in my mind: *You're not your father or Donna. Barrel roll your ass around until they're tired.*

Okay, evasion.

The man comes near me, sidestepping when one of the fights nearly takes him out, my father glancing our way—it's enough to embolden me.

Don't worry about me, Dad. I can heal my wounds if this gets nasty.

Whether he can feel that or not, I'm not certain, but if his powers are anything like Soren's, then maybe he can tell I'm at least confident, which seems like half the battle.

I step back on the street, trying to glance at his footing when possible. "You're wanted alive, woman. Don't make us fight you."

"Best I can do is dead."

He snarls, falsely lunging at me, to which I immediately pounce back, smiling with certainty. The three days with Bones were for *something*, then.

Terror streaks through the man's bloodshot eyes before he takes a few steps back, focused on something behind me—a golden-eyed brute moves unnaturally quick, a long sword pulverizing the man through his chest as he turns around to try and run away, which slices down through his abdomen. He collapses, Basilisk raising a blade with one hand that I couldn't lift with two. The cat named Jasmine gently struts over and starts drinking the blood as if the freshness is a delicacy.

My father comes near, my heart racing when I try to look for who he was fighting—four dead bodies are strewn about the street, Donna removing her blade from the neck of a fifth one. Dad is covered in blood, panting like how I was on those steps. "You a fucking enemy or what?" Dad asks Basilisk, wiping his face with his forearm, blood smearing.

It's odd how quickly I've associated Ern's more ragged face with my father's identity.

"Usually depends on who's paying and who has offended me. Presently, I'm not your enemy," Basilisk replies, wiping his blade on the dark cloak of a dead man, seemingly unbothered by Donna's glare as she still grips her weapons like she's ready to fight him.

"You ruined that bridge," I say, and he slowly looks down at me.

"Saw that, did you?" His words are as saturated in sarcasm as he wipes the dead man's clothes with his blade.

"*Others* needed that bridge." Meeting his gaze is unnerving, knowing what he can feel within me.

"There are other exits; they just have worse things than Misery's lapdogs haunting them," he coolly replies. "We need to keep moving."

So, he knows of Misery?

"Why are you helping?" Dad asks.

"I owe someone a favor. You'd be surprised what debts can make a man do, including traveling across dangerous seas and returning to a home he'd rather leave behind."

"I don't trust you," Donna replies through tight lips, her stance still aggressive, her shoulder shoving into someone who is too busy staring at one of the bodies, asking who is going to clean this up. "You better share your damn good reason for being near us. Someone like you doesn't owe favors like these."

"Poor timing for trust issues," Basilisk replies, clearly unfazed, spinning his finger. "Like I said, let's keep moving."

"I don't know what the fuck he wants," Dad says, glancing at

Donna, "but everything about his aura is clean. We need to hit Third Row's tunnel system if we want to be topside in time."

Basilisk's eyes gleam. "No can do. It's infested with Blackwell's men." He motions to a street that's darker than the rest, and much less traveled. "We need to go there, and follow the claw markings in the walls. Should spill us out near the ports."

Jasmine meows, leaving little bloody paw prints as she stalks around, strutting down to where her master just pointed.

Donna laughs, some blood staining the spaces between her teeth. "You hear this dumbass? Follow him through the *Grapnel?*"

My eyes widen when I finally piece together what he's propositioning. Threats of places like the Grapnel were made whenever I'd demand to come down here as a kid; scratch marks are all along those corridors, like grapnel being thrown and then digging into the sides.

Creatures make those marks.

"Once you're done pissing your pants, we can get moving," Basilisk replies. "They're creatures of the ocean, coastal really, and Tempest is waiting on us. They'll leave us alone."

"You're with Tempest," Dad states, more than asks.

"I'm aiding her cause, which is to get Miss Jane to her ship. They'll let us through for that."

Donna eyes my dad. "Tempest doesn't have that kind of sway, does she?"

"She might," my father breathes out, and nods to the darker alley.

Before Donna can respond, Jasmine hisses in a direction that doesn't seem to have anything other than someone bringing an empty carriage, *also* complaining loudly about the bodies.

"She's hissing because shit we don't want to fight is that way."

Donna says, "Well, we could have had two dozen with us if only a bridge had been available."

"I slowed down that Zenith for you. So you're welcome," Basilisk replies, glaring at my father who seems to have a nonverbal conversation with the old mentor. Donna is clearly confused, but also looking at my father for guidance, much like Anya would for Soren, everyone's shoulders heavily rising and falling, save for Basilisk's.

A single nod comes from the Scorpion before he faces the entrance of the grapnel. "Let's go."

Donna is about to protest, but a scream from nearby sends us all moving forward, my legs shaking from exhaustion.

Entering down this pathway is like walking through a veil, the static noise diminishing into nearly nothing, the shadows almost alive with the faintest hum. Torches are sparse, and I wonder for a moment who lights them, but that consideration flies away as soon as it lands.

We're all silent, except for the sound of our breathing. Basilisk is told to lead the way so we can all keep an eye on him.

The torches slowly change colors the longer we walk, until they're nearly crystal blue. Again, I don't question why or how that works, and just follow a man who once trained Soren, hoping to all the gods he is here to help.

When we pass by other crossroads, the empty tunnels make the hair on my neck crawl, as if waiting for something to come to life in them. There's even a skeleton lying on the ground, worn clothes hanging off the bones.

"Fucker got lost," Basilisk mutters, his grumbling voice almost making me *hush* him. I don't even think anything is following us, but the idea alone is enough to freak me out.

Then, we stop.

The faintest, *clicking* sound echoes all around, followed by a guttural growl, and I swear I hear clacking claws.

Jasmine jumps up onto Basilisk's shoulder, settling around his neck like a scarf.

My blood turns to ice when there's a *second* wave of clicks, growls, and claws.

Basilisk looks back at us, his molten eyes nearly glowing. "I know I said Tempest is on our side, and these creatures revere her, but I really think we should at least *jog*."

We all move without thought, my legs finding a second wind from literally nothing. We're in a dangerous labyrinth, and the passages we run past are growing wider, darker.

I actually shudder when one of them has *eyes* peering out.

Dad's hand is on my back as we continue to move, my vision

tunneling onto the Basilisk while he guides us through the forbidden underbelly of Skull's Row.

I nearly gag when a rotten stench saturates the corridors until we near a section much like the Undercroft where light bleeds in from a grate so incredibly high up.

It shines down on a mountain of bones.

My skin nearly melts off my body, my jaw dropping so I can nearly taste the rot when I see copious amounts of legs moving in the light among the pile, eyes flashing our way as many heads of creatures I can hardly process look at us.

It's as if someone took the torso of a thin, emaciated human with stringy hair and placed it on a large body with many legs.

Their eyes glint white like a dog's in the moon. Hissing and clicking fill the space and Basilisk, very quietly, says, "Keep. Moving."

I focus on his back and continue to do so, my eyes drying from being unable to blink. Why the fuck are these things living underneath Skull's Row?

As we follow him, a few of these creatures walk aside us, looking at us. Their stench so foul I grow dizzy. They scutter ahead swiftly, then look back, watching as we continue. Every time one does, I shudder and get closer to my father. A few heads get so close to ours, tears from utter fright clouds my vision.

The sight is *shocking*.

One gets so close to my face its wispy, white hair touches my shoulder, the sheen to its skin so *clammy*. A flash of red illuminates across its face, and it *screams* at me, my earrings glowing like a torch light. The others come to its aid, and Basilisk shouts, "Fucking run for it!"

We bolt until we come across a round gate, the bars embedded into the stone. Basilisk works at the necklace around his neck, holding it to the lock, muttering words under his breath.

Dad and Donna shield me, both drawing their weapons as the weird creatures screech in the background, filling the space with their bodies as they all scurry our way, mouths baring their fangs, black tongues unfurling.

My pulse thrums in my ears, the seconds stretching into an eternity. Finally, with a soft *click*, the grate door swings open.

"Let's go!" Basilisk shouts, moving with such speed to get through, and shuts the grate behind us. The creatures slam into the metal, their skeletal arms and claws reaching through the bars, screeching at us like a horde of undying creatures.

"Don't stop," Dad says, his voice steady in this chaos.

The tunnel twists and turns as the screeching dies down, and when I start to smell the salty air of the ocean, I nearly want to cry with joy.

We come across a wooden door with cracks that sunlight streaks through in little beams, and Basilisk opens it without issue.

The sunlight is *blinding*, and I gasp for the fresh air like... well, like I've been underground for days.

I lean against a wall, sliding down to relax my legs and breathe in the cool ocean air.

The eerie grip of the Undercroft refuses to let go completely, even once sunlight washes over us, my body shivering from the way my sweat-infused clothes begin to dry.

Probably doesn't help that I'm sitting underneath a red lantern like it's a reminder of what's fucking down there. Opening my eyes, my father is standing in front of me, and Donna is surveying the area, much like Basilisk.

"Your cat," I say, noticing she's gone.

"Shadow cat," Basilisk corrects. "Can't kill them in the shadows, but you can in the sun. She already took off as soon as we exited—"

My dad and Basilisk both draw their blades at the same time, Donna and I scrambling to get our weapons out, searching for whatever set these men off.

"*Matthias*," Father hisses, transforming into his actual self.

"This one is different from who I felt earlier," Basilisk warns.

I take in the environment more, the space reminding me of a pier city with all the wood and netting, although I can't see the ocean in any direction. Looking at my back, it's a tall, natural stone wall of the cliffs with a small, wooden door covering the only entry.

It's like we just emerged from a service door to the hellscape we fled from.

"This way," Basilisk urges, guiding us to the right and down through tent-covered stalls.

"Tempest's port is the other way," Dad instructs.

"Soren is in *this* direction!" he glances over his shoulder. "And he's got a lot more people."

Dad picks up his pace, urging me forward.

Soren? My gods, I actually forgot about them in our escape. That's when, through one of the alleys, a man emerges who looks just like the pale blonde from the Council, more men matching his speed and halting with the same intensity.

Basilisk doesn't stop, barreling toward them and parrying immediately with two of them, catching them all off guard.

Even Matthias looks at him like he's crazy before adhering his Zenith mask to his face.

Dad lunges forward, striking at Matthias, who yells out when he barely avoids being gutted. Fear grips me almost immediately, knowing that he's risking everything right now. Matthias is twenty years younger, and in more shape.

Even so, my father demonstrates that he has *years* of training. The blows are so forceful, the dodges so swift, and hair cutting close, I don't know what to do. I want to help, step in, and do what I can.

But this isn't a fight for me. I could make it worse.

What's worse than him dying?

In the distance, I hear screams and scuffles. A hoard of horsemen ride fast toward us. In the front is a man wearing a black skull mask. But when I glance back at my father, my braid whipping around my neck, it might be too late. We're tired and just escaped near death, *more* than once.

My body shakes as if it's been shocked by an eel when I see a blade pierce right through my dad's shoulder, his echoing cries stretching through the streets, the blade sinking further as Matthias *twists*.

THE UNDERDECK

SOREN

N*o.*

Wherever Jane is, something catastrophic is happening.

I kick Phantom's sides even harder, riding as fast as I fucking can. I paid a lot of money to stow this horse somewhere rather inconspicuous with one of my men until I was officially out of Skull's Row, and he could be ridden home.

Even with all my planning, it might not be enough.

We twist and turn upward through this coastal village that's right outside the pirating ports. Grabbing the black skull mask at my hip, I adorn it on my face, the material adhering to me. *Everything* evolves into utter clarity: my body stronger, my ability to grip Phantom with my thighs easier.

Jane, and her frantic heart, shines like a beacon during a storm. We round a corner and that woman's energy is so palpable I can almost *smell* her. Commotion fills the narrow streets up ahead, Phantom piling through any fucking idiot in my way, not giving a shit who it is, his hooves stamping into a few bodies on the ground that he knocks over.

I don't care about *anyone* when I see *her*.

A blade pierces right through Ritter's shoulder, with Matthias standing slightly over him, holding the weapon.

I can't—*Jane*.

While his attention is focused on Ritter, she lunges at Matthias's back. Ritter stabs the Zenith in the stomach—still pierced in his own shoulder—while Jane's initial attack lands a dagger right above his collarbone. She yanks *hard* as skin stretches and blood sprays out, the liquid coating his armor. His black skull mask conceals his expression, but his aura deciphers as *petrified*.

Gripping his lower neck with one hand, glistening blood pulses through his fingers, while his other dagger slices right at Jane.

My body freezes, my breathing hitching, the mere *suggestion* of her being seriously injured ripping at my sanity. I'm not a man who does well feeling powerless.

Jane's yelps morphs into a wince, placing a hand on her hip.

Phantom charges forward right through a carriage of goods, Phantom bursts through the wood, the war horse trained for this, and I *swear* if it's too late—most of the men that follow Matthias look on in shock to see he's slumped on one knee and profusely bleeding, their attention honing in on *Jane*.

They can all fuck themselves.

I grab a throwing knife from Phantom's harness, sit up slightly, leveling my hand, and throw with as much force as I can muster, the powers of my mask channeling into the blade to send it further than any normal man is capable.

I aim right for the group, knowing it'll pierce *one*—when it strikes one of the bastards in the neck, it draws all of their attention to him before arriving at *me*.

Basilisk steps in after dropping his long sword, grabbing Jane by the waist, and hoisting her up to get her out of the way. Their blood thirst diminishes when they realize I'm not alone, and relief rejuvenates me when I'm close enough to dismount Phantom while he still moves, hitting the street as my knees intentionally buckle so I can roll forward. Carrying the momentum without hurting or slowing myself down, I rise to my feet, drawing out two swords, cutting away at flesh and armor.

I channel my focus on slaying the ones who might run, my body moving with the practiced finesse of fighting with brute force and relying on my powers to guide me, feeding off of the intention from each opposing strike.

When my steel slices at a forearm, the thrill of battle pulses through my veins, and clearly his; I recognize this cunt as a man that's akin to Bones, the asshole transforming into a feral animal in his assault.

But there's no time for this, and I'm bigger than him.

When he strikes again, his sword slides against mine as I kick my heel right into his liver. He collapses to catch his breath, and in that same labored inhale I slit his throat, that very blade pivoting in my hand to rise in a counterstrike.

These men are swiftly outnumbered when at least double their amount arrives on horse.

"Cut down every last one of them!" I demand, the mask amplifying my voice. The clashing of steel reverberates in the confined space, each strike echoing like crisp lightning in my ears.

I scan the vicinity when enough of my people enter the fray, fear spreading through the street as wet grunts mix in with the sounds of battle, many trying to flee but get struck down or hunted out. There's never a lot crying out in pain; barbarism tends to silence someone before they realize what's happened. Just like with Matthias, who was mostly a Zenith because of his connections, and the land he held.

Good fucking riddance.

I near the dying Zenith when a glance at Jane tells me she's fine —six of my people surround her, including Basilisk who many are clearly too afraid to strike. Matthias continues to grip his neck, pressing hard on the wound. Disbelief clouds his dying mind, his shoulder rising and falling heavily. He can barely lift his head to peer at me, his eyes so wide the whites are visible around the entire iris. "It was a poor decision to injure Jane."

No one will hurt her without suffering immeasurable pain or death. Not anymore.

Not with me in her shadow.

With no forgiveness, I swing my sword with full force as Matthias's head cleanly lobs off. Grabbing him by the hair he so prized, the scalp is still warm as I break off a pole of a nearby tent and spike the wood through the severed head with a *crunch*. In a pile of melons being sold, I lodge the spiked head. When I glance up, my gaze connects with a merchant who blanches, her eyes fluttering before collapsing.

Anyone looking on might think she's squeamish, but that pulse of primal fear as I looked directly into her eyes is what did her in. I survey the rest surrounding us. "Keep your tongues tied until sundown, and you won't be spiked like him. Until then, leave his head as a warning."

Ritter holds his hand to his shoulder, removing it to look at the blood that wets his palm before reapplying pressure. "Reset yourselves!" I yell to my men. "And if Anya isn't here by the time your blades are cleaned, we're moving!"

I approach Basilisk, the man slightly older in appearance than we last met but hasn't changed much otherwise. Any oddness to seeing him is absolved in the ability to connect with another sensor. The capacity to communicate deeply with him is unnerving when he's been a stranger for so long, a man with deep insight to my younger, more volatile self.

None of that matters right now, though, for some reason, he's here for us. And I trust it. I can deal with the *why* later.

He releases Jane, who winces when back on her feet, her hands at her side. As soon as she's got her bearings, everything screams in her to rush over to her father, that wave of desperation colliding with me. I stick out an arm and grab her outer shoulder, my back to Ritter as she faces him. "Heal yourself first."

She looks at me with the same intensity that she just looked at Matthias. I tilt my head, doubling down. "Yourself. *First.*"

My voice is more grating and intense than I intend for it to be. But shit is about to escalate, and I'll be damned if we move forward without getting her healed.

She doesn't fight me, and the hand on her bleeding hip glows blue; Jane continuously glances toward her father. Her hazel eyes are stuck in shock, staring blankly ahead like those who suffer from *horrors*.

That beast in my chest that's overly protective is eager to get Jane far away from here; to gift her those nights of safety that helped her heal. Her eyes close to concentrate, strands of auburn hair stuck to her face. The bleeding stops rather quickly, probably indicative of being mostly surface level. My arm is still across her, some of Jane's weight leaning into me, and I'm sure she's overcome with exhaustion.

Get her out of here.

I glance up at Basilisk, whose golden eyes watch with immense curiosity. "What path did you take to get here?" I ask, just to confirm it.

"The grapnel."

My eyes widen, even if it's obvious with what door they came out of, even if I could feel that's where they'd go; it's still a dangerous fucking path. "The molgrin infest those tunnels."

Jane's ear nearly twitches at that detail, like the name gives life to an awful memory. I grip her shoulder tighter, almost pulling her into me.

"We're aware," Basilisk comments, leaning on a wall with his arms crossed.

When Jane's eyes open once more when her injuries are healed, she nearly bolts to her father in a desperate attempt to begin tending to his wounds, but I hold onto as I say, "Heal what you can, and once it's not life-threatening, we're moving."

When she nods, I release her as she hurries across the street to the Scorpion, to which I'm not far behind. Ritter motions to the bleeding wound in his shoulder. "Just stop the bleeding, honey. I'll be fine—I'm okay."

Without hesitation, Jane's wrists are already glowing blue as she reaches for his wound.

A few gasps pervade, and I glance over to see all the commoners of the street are focused on the spiked head. Matthias's mask slowly slides off his face, having completely hardened, an expression of horror revealed as the mask hits the ground. The gold decorations melt into a puddle underneath, only to harden into a molten mess.

Fascinating.

I've never seen that in person. We're told the mask is completely useless once we die.

"I'll be okay. I promise," Ritter reiterates, pulling me back as he reassures Jane, the bleeding indeed slowing. I can tell it means everything to her to be able to save a parent this time, and it's probably for the best that he actually looks like himself rather than Ern.

Giving them my back, Anya's energy grazes against my powers as I focus on searching where she approaches from; I spot her white horse among the crowd that parts with more effort than when I stormed in, as if merely touching Anya might kill them.

I can see now why everything in me screamed to send her. When we caught wind of the bridge being destroyed, and that more than one Zenith was confronting us, I knew there was no point in Jane escaping the Undercroft if what awaited her on the other side were blades.

Which meant sending Anya ahead to scout out the best path to Tempest's ship, while I moved as fast as I could to reach her to avoid getting stuck here.

She surveys the scene until she's right up on me, pulling on her horse's reins, looking down. "We have to leave, *now*. Blackwell has sent everyone, and he's manning his ships. There's *one* path that can take us to Tempest without issue, but it's a matter of time before it's overcrowded with their fucking henchmen." Anya's usual resolute determination is shaken when she spots Matthias's ugly head. "Did you kill him?"

The murder of a Zenith isn't going to go over well.

"Jane did," I answer, glancing at her as she removes her hands to examine her father's wound.

Anya snorts, surprise washing over her. "Great. Now she'll have a real bounty on her head." The fleeting humor fades, her face deadpanning as she dismounts, the stirrups clinking. "We need to leave the horses, too. We're going to take the cliff's boardwalks—*oh.*"

Anya's focus draws me to see that among the bodies are two of *my* men. My priorities shift as I move to their side, glancing at both their faces; their eyes are wide, unblinking, and jaws slacked, carelessly open. Their vibrations in this world are silent. "They died quickly, sir," one of mine solemnly says, who was already standing near them.

Mads and Silas.

We don't have time.

Guilt strains my focus, knowing I have to make this call. "Take their effects, leave the bodies."

With a whistle, every one of my people focus on me, and I motion for Michael, who hurries over. I lean toward his ear to speak quietly, "We're taking the cliff boardwalks, down to the Underdeck, so we can board the Sea Wolf. Start with Rogers and tell him to get Phantom out of this city and up north."

In a swift series of movements, another man who lives as a stablemaster back in my lands approaches Phantom; the man that will now tend to my horse while I cannot. Anytime I'm away from my war horse, Rogers is with him. I touch the nose of the black beast, looking him in the eyes, an odd sense of guilt pinching my heart to think I very well could die and leave him without a master. He's a stallion who hates bowing to anyone but me.

I understand him, in that way. Fuck authority.

"Don't bite Rogers again. He's your path to safety... and if I don't return, they'll set you free, alright?" Phantom breathes harder, leaning into my hand. "Ride hard, my friend. Be safe."

Rogers kicks Phantom's hips, turning him around, and I step away when the horse seems to fight the command from a rider that's not me. Rogers says, "I'm going to find a heavy merchant carriage and attach him to it. See if that works to get him out unnoticed, if it doesn't spook the horse. I'll take care of him, sir."

I nod once, watching my horse be ridden off, sentiment an odd feeling in my chest, which makes me look at the men that haven't moved; not even to breathe.

So swiftly, they're gone.

It won't be in vain.

Basilisk moves among the crowd, reclaiming his long sword, the shiny metal glinting in the sunlight where it's not marred with blood. He's probably the only person, other than Cypress, to *know* my pain. My rage. A vulnerability that will either prove to be comforting, or a massive risk and fucking annoyance.

Approaching Basilisk, I ask, "What are you doing here?"

His jaw clenches before he looks at me, the lines around his eyes deeper than we last saw each other, but it only adds to his intense demeanor, really. "I'm here to protect my cat, if you must know."

That's so abstract of a comment that I completely ignore it, focusing instead on his aura. It's like it was fifteen years ago, except maybe more focused. Less aggressive; no, the aggression still exists, but it's *honed*.

It's hard not to notice he has new scars, or that a few streaks in his dark hair are whitening. He's still young enough to not look aged like Ritter, but just wisened.

"Are you going to be useful to me or not?" I ask, as there's no time for familiarity.

"I saved your woman." He casually flits his gaze to Jane. "*Ah*, don't get angry. I don't seduce the women of friends."

The fucking womanizer; his difficult personality seems to make women pine for him all the more, even down to his harem back home.

What the man does in his own time has no effect on me, but when he refers to what is *mine*, I can't help but feel defensive. I do my best to focus on not giving away my emotions toward Jane—a much harder feat given Basilisk is as capable as I am to know the *truth*. Some rumors even say he has a rotating harem wherever he lives, tucked deep within his private life.

"Don't make this personal, Rasmus," I warn, the use of his real name bringing out the callous side reserved for the rest of the world.

"Don't fucking call me that, and it won't be personal," he retorts, his desire to stab me quite intense.

I smirk under the mask. "Then you trail at the end, and I'll lead."

"If you say so, *Zenith*."

That man used to be immeasurably difficult to talk to, let alone be personal with. Yet once he allows someone in, he's a different human being. I just don't know which one we have following us, even if his energy feels like it's here to help.

"We'll speak later," Basilisk remarks.

That's enough for now.

It's difficult to switch between people, but there are many

relying on me and my decisions. *Jane. The priority is always her.* Approaching Jane is like nearing the failure I fear, my magic honed so much onto her that I can feel the miserable memories of losing her mother as it stirs up my emotions of losing Serena. Her father almost dying, in the same manner, has not just reopened a wound; it nearly crippled her.

I *hate* not being able to keep her safe from the world, even from heartache. "Let's go, love. Are you too tired on your feet?"

She straightens up, the pet name softening her anxiety. "No, no. I can walk."

I waste no more time, ushering everyone forward with Anya guiding me, Ritter changing his face once again to another man instead of Ern, although it's not as extreme of a transformation. His hair darkens into raven locks, his eyes glinting with a brighter hue, and mostly, his nose and jaw alter their shape.

"We need to move, and make it fast," I say, the pace of everyone increasing to a rhythm that hovers between walking and jogging.

A familiar metallic, salty taste fills the air, the dampness of the nearby ocean reassuring us that we're at the edge of this merchant village, even if we can't see the docks.

Michael aids Ritter as we move while Jane reaches into her small pouch to give her father a blood tonic. Michael seems to be fucking thrilled to aid an old legend, like this is one last step he needs to be fulfilled in life. Ritter drinks the tonic as we move. "I'm good," he says to Michael.

Michael replies, "If you say so. We need to be swift now that a Zenith was killed."

Jane's hazel eyes widen with sudden realization as we move further to the rocky walls of the cliffs, and she dashes a glance back my way then at Michael, avoiding stepping on an apple that falls off a cart. "Well, the bastard shouldn't have stabbed my dad."

Jane can't see or feel it, but something in that statement is almost healing for Ritter.

A woman steps forward through the chaos of the market, wearing a worn woolen coat, yelling at passersby about her shells of a spotted snail and how she has tonics made from its venom.

My eyes trail to the back of Jane's head, who watches the crowd alertly. Once, I would have thought the precaution unnecessary—

not with how her safety seems to matter more to my magic than my own life. But now I know that it's nearly impossible to spot the blank spaces in a giant crowd unless I'm *searching* for them.

Anyone could be an issue, and I don't have time to decipher *who*.

We just need to get to the harbor.

Jane continues to glance at her father as we move, eyeing his shoulder like she's worried she didn't do enough. Well, I guess I have to protect the old fucker, too, for Jane's sake.

He can't die on my watch, not until this is all in the past and Jane's heart is healed from everything that's happened to her. Not until I'm so entrenched in her soul that my presence will *always* soothe her.

A black banner with the pirating skull is visible once we round a street corner, hanging above a wooden walkway. Skulls dipped in gold hang on the side of the pillars, along with ropes and netting.

I fucking hate pirates, so goddamn unreliable and backstabbing in nature. Like the fucker who raped my mother to make me.

Thank the gods, he was a pirate of another coast, so I don't have to come across the flag he sailed under because I can't miss a step right now. The scent of saltwater is so strong that it overrides my annoyances—getting away from here *also* means getting away from the pirates in this bay; I'd rather be among a crew I know. And that water is our best chance of freedom, even if it comes with the assaulting smell of fish.

Right before we pass underneath the banner, we're upon an exotic trader of cloaks—silks, fine wool, and embroidered cotton. I grab a thick wool cloak as if it's free. "Jane," I say. She slows to look back at me, and I hand it to her. "To keep warm and cover your hair."

Relief floods her more than her eyes reveal, and she's quick to throw it over her shoulders. I can even hear someone yelling about their cloak behind me, but unless they're willing to fight me, it's as good as gone. When the path hikes up, and we crest at the top…

The ocean's horizon is clear in view.

We're at the very top of a monstrous wooden construction that reminds me of a god having to make a city out of broken piers and ships, one who has no concept of how even surfaces work. Down below the weather-beaten cliffs, after what will be a difficult descent to navigate, is an inlet of sails and ships, and we must be fifty stories above seawater.

Magic pulses faintly through its bones, as if daring gravity to intervene, buildings overhanging each other.

I can see a crevice that splits the cliffs. That will lead to the entrance for the docks—it's a shadowy gorge with rope bridges crisscrossing the chasm, the Underdeck. "Let me lead from here," I command the few in front of me. "Jane, stay very close behind me."

I move in front of her, because these peers can arguably be more dangerous than the city, like roaming alone on Carver's or the Undercroft.

Tempest's ship sits out at sea, near the harbor, clear even from here—the infamous Sea Wolf. To many who frequent these piers, that ship is a status symbol of the most elite pirates, a life's goal to sail among it. I can imagine the details of the wolf's head at the front of the hull, the paint worn from all the trips. It's one of the only ships that can handle the Black Sea without losing a single sail, let alone escaping with a crew that survives.

If it's at sea, then we have to catch one of the longboats that will take us to her, and then we can get the fuck out of here.

Descending swiftly is risky at best, everything fucking uneven or worn and slick. The planks creak underfoot like they'll splinter at any moment. More than once, I turn around for Jane, offering my hand for stability so we don't slow the momentum. She's the only one here who hasn't been to these ports, and navigating the rickety platforms requires experience.

Our hurried steps take us past a large structure that looks like the rest of it merges deep into the cliffside, the energy changing as we're forced to weave through a cluster of nosy pirates—cotton shirts hang loose over tattooed bodies, cutlasses glinting at their hips. The already narrow walkways are hemmed by multi-tiered shanties stacked haphazardly on top of each other, and these assholes are blocking the only clear way forward, one of them with a wooden pegleg.

They don't hide their curiosity, or their disdain.

"You seem to be—" one of them starts, his voice dripping with mockery.

I simultaneously unsheathe both my swords, not slowing down. When my gaze connects with the man, his confidence crumbles like wet sand, his posture wilting as he steps to the side, and the others follow in discontent.

"He's covered in blood, don't be a fuckwit," one says to another.

A greasy pirate looks at Jane, or at least, I can tell one of them is eyeing someone behind me with more interest than I care to feel. As soon as I give him my full attention, swords still in hand, he throws his hands up to show they're empty and swiftly backs away, averting his gaze down.

That's fucking right.

This pattern repeats as we move through to the misty Underdeck, especially passing one of the lodges that's filled with hammocks, even out on the deck; the place is layered with marauders and outlaws. Some are more finely dressed in a cocky display of confidence that no one will try to steal the clothes off their back. Even the brothel is questionable, like the lot is about to seduce their way into our pockets, the perfume that saturates their building as potent as the scales in a fish market.

We're getting closer.

The journey feels endless, every step carrying what feels like a hundred prying eyes. We finally make it to one of the lowest levels. Adjacent to our pathway is a small, oceanic river in one of the crevices of the stony cliffs. The towering harbor now is completely above us, their surfaces dotted with glowing lanterns and windows. Rounding a corner, I glance up to see a sign hanging on rusty hinges, denoting a market for fishing hooks.

Shit.

A nasty collective of pirates has made a home right around this bend, their residence established over a bridge; their longboats are anchored in the narrow waters right next to us, so they're definitely home. They frequently perch their asses on a deck—*there they are.*

They adorn featureless, black masks that are slightly in the shape of an animal skull with subtle ridges, their fingers all stained black in an uneven fade to their wrists as if dipped into the shadows. Their bare arms are layered with intentional, small scars revealing a pattern of how many they've killed in an open ledger of death.

Blades of Zanos.

Aside from being hired swords, they're one of the very few who can cross the Black Sea, and *also* have knowledge of the harbors and ports. It's a complete mystery how they acquired their vessel, which defies the odds, as not even Tempest knows.

They're ruthless cutthroats who like to demand tolls down here. When I look up at four of them, not one of them seems interested in us—thankfully—except maybe morbidly curious about what we're doing and why we're all covered in sweat and blood.

I swear those fuckers all have to be classified as insane before earning their mask.

I'm so fucking ready to be out of here.

When we walk under a two-story footbridge with pirating flags hanging down them, cold chills of relief wash over me. Ahead, the official harbor stretches into view; we pass by ships pulled completely out of the water as barnacles are scraped off the bottom like beasts being flayed alive. The floors creak underneath our feet, worn by relentless waves, sea water sprays, and boots.

We're so damn close.

At least forty vessels are anchored in port or pulled out for cleaning. There are only two flights of stairs we need to descend to be on the piers themselves—

I'm overwhelmed with the sensation of something so incredibly *foul* behind us, but I ignore it to scan for any of the longboats that have the wolf's head at the hull, but I don't see one. My heart races faster, everything telling me *below*, but looking down only reveals the wood.

The foul sensation slithers up my spine, the undeniable rot nearly identical to the corner I felt back in Blackwell's room.

No.

He's here.

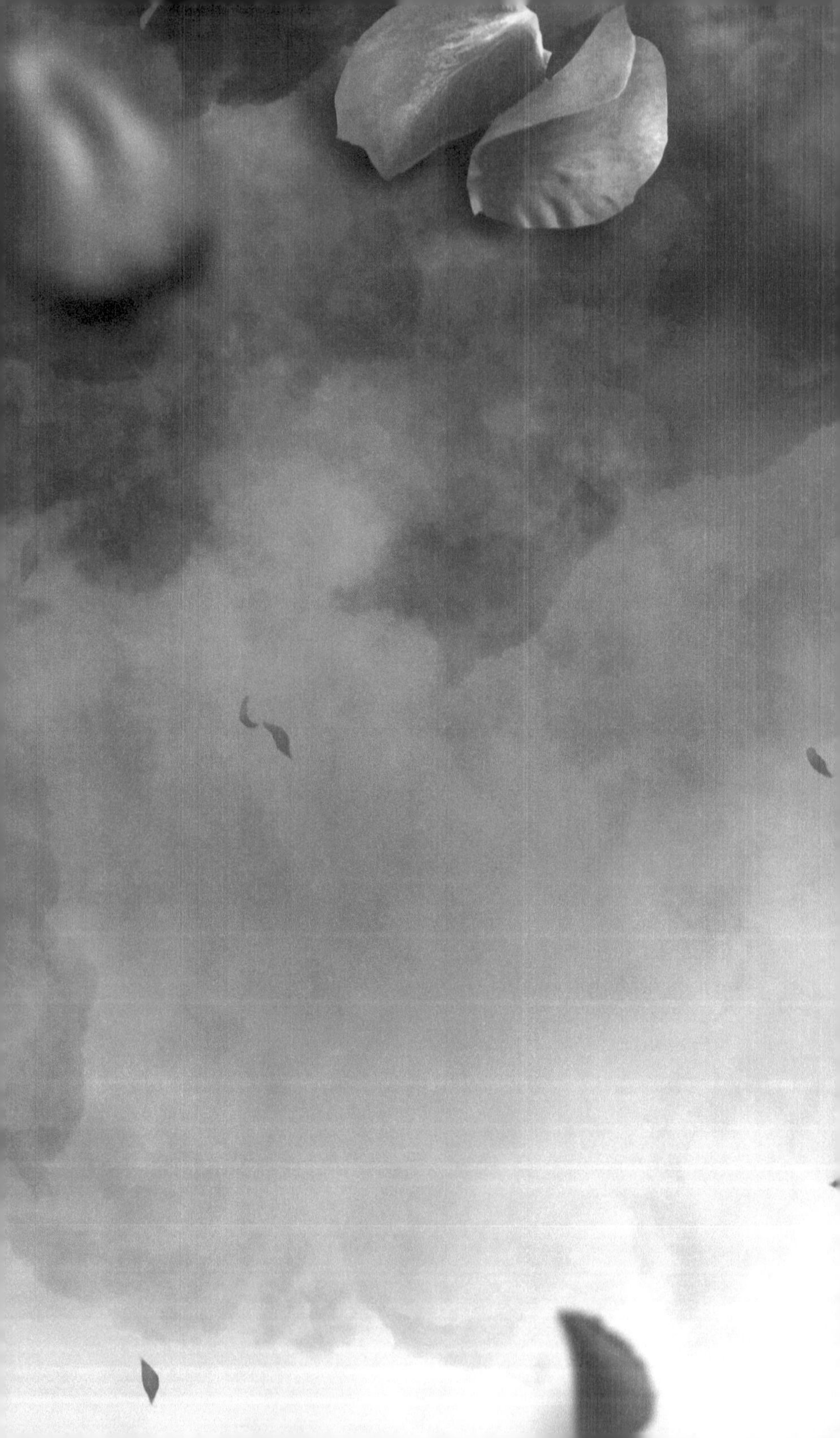

JANE

We just need to leave.
We just need to leave.
We just need—

Soren looks over his shoulder as I'm slightly above him on a set of stairs, the massive man terrifying with that mask on, the skin around his eyes smudged with black ink to emphasize the pale blue.

It's like the further we get to the possibility of fleeing, the more *that* part of my mind can register how unfairly seductive Soren is, all violently wrapped up in his armor and weapons, let alone the loose strands of dark hair that get in his vision. It's only more pronounced that he basically saved me by showing up at the right time—

When our gazes connect, and he's lost in the sea of his Zenith ways, his eyes are entirely cold, and… alarmed?

I follow his line of vision that he just looked at, dread consuming every inch of my skeleton when, probably ten stories higher on a stoney ledge behind many wooden columns, is a cavernous entrance—

Blackwell.

My heart races when next to him is something that sticks out from the shadows, the wind catching the edges of a cloak, two orange, glowing lights disturbingly haunting and I have no idea why.

Everyone in our party catches on, even Basilisk, who looks up at the very end of this chain of humans and then swiftly at Soren.

What the fuck are those glowing dots?

"Get in!" shouts a voice I don't recognize.

We all glance down to see what appears to be longboats emerging from underneath these docks, like pulling out something from below a bed. There's got to be at least six, all of them already half-filled with what appears to be pirates.

Tempest.

She's in the first boat, commanding her men, who are tossing ropes to those on the piers, working with finesse; thick ropes hoop over the cleats with precision.

When I crane my head back up, Blackwell and whatever those lights were are gone.

Soren's deep, angry voice yells, "Get Jane on Tempest's boat! I don't care how it's done!"

It's like I've been smacked by a wave as everyone moves so I can jump down a few steps at a time, barely touching the wood until I'm on the pier, a few of Tempest's pirates grabbing me like I'm a bag of loot, nearly tossing me on, only for others to catch and balance me, strong hands grabbing all over.

The rest that join us cascade down the port, and there's the sound of a *screech*, but it's not loud, just… everywhere.

An arm wraps around my neck, one that's covered in a leather sleeve, although it's not a forceful action; this person smells like a floral, balmy oil. A few thin, black dreads are in my peripheral.

"I know you're out there, you miserable cunt!" Tempest yells out, and it's clear that she's the one who grips me. The men all jump onto the boats, Soren landing on Tempest's, along with my dad, Donna and Anya. Basilisk takes up the seat of another, and so does Rorge.

Once full, they are immediately cast off, the ocean waves making us rock as we float among the craggy sea water.

Tempest's arm is still wrapped around me, and Soren is looking over his shoulder at the cliffside. "He was in that cavern," he states, nodding to where I saw.

"Blackwell?" I ask.

"*Misery*," Tempest answers. "He's letting us all see him for some reason."

If the cold ocean winds weren't enough to raise the hairs on my body, that certainly does the trick. That… that was *Misery*?

"Why did he back off?" Donna asks, her voice full of alert.

It dawns on me that there's not a single person rowing, and yet the boat is moving with ease toward the Sea Wolf, even avoiding the jagged stone that sea foam sprays around.

"He senses another god, and he lost his opportunity. He was simply too late."

The screeching *bellows* from the cavern, an orange glow emanating as the sound of men yelling follows it, almost like they're being tortured. It's absolutely fucking terrifying to think that the very god radiating that wrath is the one that wants *me*.

"What other god did he feel?" Donna asks.

The men on the boat all snicker, the pirates carrying a cocky demeanor.

"Ta'Kan." Tempest releases me, telling me to sit before explaining, "The ocean god."

My eyes widen, recalling Cypress mentioning the god of the ocean. My gaze is latched to that cavern as my back is to the Sea Wolf, feeling like I'm actually safe in these salty waters.

"Charles," Tempest says. I look at Dad, whose appearance is of himself. "You don't look good."

He grunts, reaching his hand out into the water to wipe his face, the ocean dripping off his chin. "Not surprising. Matthias stabbed me."

"*Oh*," she breathes out, sounding genuinely surprised. "Did he?"

Dad inhales deeply, running his tongue over his front teeth before nodding to me. "Then Jane killed him."

I immediately look over my shoulder at Tempest, catching that her crew's interest has drastically increased. Her dark gaze is enigmatic as always, if not possibly a little more intrigued than usual. I face back ahead at the harbor, my gaze landing back on Soren, the man so out of place with how, in his own way, with that mask, he looks like a god of war.

"Well, I'll keep my back guarded, then," Tempest teases.

I never thought twice about the implications of killing a *Zenith*. His title was absent from my mind when I attacked, only seeing that my father was about to be murdered.

Just another damn thing to worry about.

We pass by other massive ships, the water lapping against their wooden bodies, and I still have no idea how we're moving without oars. Or that Misery wouldn't even *attempt* to claim me even though I'm still in this harbor.

There's genuinely no way I trust any of this.

And yet... we continue to slowly sail away.

It isn't until we're officially out in the water that we truly take in what we just did. I have to admit, this place is damn near impressive, even if the crowd we walked through were as inviting as vultures near a dead body; I can see why Dad never let me down here, let alone the Undercroft. I wouldn't put it past some of these people to try and take a Zenith's daughter for ransom.

I'm grateful I get to see this place before departing, at least from this angle. The amount of seagulls flying around, along with the waves, creates so much movement and life, especially with all the activity of people tending to the docks. Deep groans of the ships fascinate me, trying to imagine those vessels as the only source of "land" when in the open ocean.

Let alone during a storm.

Hells, even one of the ships has a giant hole in the side. Like what could possibly have caused that? Also, how did it make it home?

Home.

I lift my gaze to where the silhouette of the Silver District is located, then back to the empty cavern. Sure, I'm naturally freaked out by that fucker. But I'm *angry* more than anything.

His selfishness ruined my life, stole my mother, and now could harm or kill those around me.

One of the men on this longship, who wears a necklace made of wolf teeth around his neck—now I'm noticing they *all* do—looks at Tempest over my head. "Are we sure he let us go that easily?"

"No," she replies from behind. "They're scheming something, but so are we. There's a reason I'm mandating keeping your blades sharpened."

Silence befalls the longboat, which rides with the waves, the power of the ocean welling around us as the cliffs of Skull's Row become more clear. The Spiraling Stone looms high overhead the entire time. That dark castle is so vast, so many little dots lining the walls where windows are, reflecting the sun against the roughness of the walls where some have glass. They even descend all the way down to the rocky base.

Bringing the cloak around me to cut out the freezing air, my breathing halts when I recognize what I see at the base of the castle —cut out of the stone are wide open strips that are almost like balconies.

Cells.

Prison cells.

Some have iron bars for those who are wanted alive, whereas others are wide open in case the prisoner decides to end it themselves.

My gaze falls back to my dad, to the man who connects me to every aspect of *that* world, whose face is the one I recognize. Even if his hair is different from when I was a child, it somehow already fits him. He looks paler than I'd prefer, and I don't know how I'll be able to make any more blood tonics when we're out here, or going to wherever we're being taken. It's sort of a luxury limited to being within the city.

Soren's gaze is lowered, and I know that look—he's feeling out everything around him. Deciphering every pulse of whatever it is that he senses.

Glancing over my shoulder once again, Tempest is sitting down, her dark eyes scanning the scene. I quickly notice she has her nails a different color, the reddish tone complementing the dark brown of her skin, the golden rings adorning her thinner fingers even more extravagant in contrast.

How in the hells did she get her *nails* a different color?

She clears her throat and looks at my father. "You got hit easily," she comments.

The men on the ship that belong to her all face my dad.

Dad still has the strength to glare at Tempest as if he's willing to brawl right here in this small ass boat. "I've been living my life as a barkeep. You try not killing on the regular for a decade and see how well you fare."

She smiles approvingly at him. "Glad it wasn't fatal, Charles. And no need to worry for now, Soren—" pale eyes flash up at her. "We got wind that Blackwell is preparing ships. He can try to follow, but he will fail." She leans back confidently. "Let Misery come, too. I can't damage that decrepit bastard on land, but the seas will aid me."

As we get further into the water, the frigid sprays start to seep through the wool. This longboat traverses the larger swells with ease as we sail out to a monstrous ship that looms over us like a giant among ants. A carving of a wolf's head casts long shadows, pearls for eyes the size of my body, glinting in the sun. Its mouth hangs open, and the sharp teeth all look like they've been coated with metal.

Just the head alone is massive–the size of a *house*. I squint and swear I even see a few windows in the lower level of the fur. Well can't imagine what Tempest's quarters look like on the back end— sure enough, it's incredibly elaborate. The carving of sirens surrounds the entire bottom of the multi-tiered back, windows inset within thick carvings. I can't see the full backside, but even from here, I spot at least two bay windows.

It amazes me to think that there are people who were born and died in Coalfell, never leaving to see how much of the world exists. *They wouldn't be privy to this part, anyway.*

The sense of importance makes me straighten my back, wanting to appear as if I belong here. I killed a Zenith, didn't I? Sure, he was already distracted and didn't see me coming, but I can say I did it.

All to protect my Zenith *father.*

I can do this.

When we're near the ship, ropes are dropped down with a flapping roll. Without any steering, the boats turn to the side and line up to the Sea Wolf.

A few men from each longboat grab the ropes and immediately fix them to iron hooks, shouting up that we're ready. Our boat gives a jerk as we're slowly taken out of the water, rising alongside a painted hull.

Once pulled up from the side, quite a few small ladders wait for us that are only a handful of rungs. "Go on, Jane," Tempest urges, motioning to one as she climbs another. It freaks me out a little to think my grip can slip, and I'd plummet below.

I haven't really gone swimming a whole lot in my life... Soren's presence behind me quickly eases my worries.

Climbing is swift, and when I crest over the side, all I can think is that the entire sun-kissed deck is *massive*. I have to look firmly left or right just to see the entirety of it. The sails are gigantic, black strips of fabric. There's so much rope, and they're all so *thick*.

My feet thud on hollow-sounding floors as I gain my footing. Everyone is dressed differently than on land—breeches, looser, billowing tunics, nearly all wearing bandanas, and most are in shoes rather than boots, belts strewn about their bodies to affix many things to. Plain wool jackets are adorned by over half. Tempest is already speaking to a man, her own coat sharply contrasting the rest in how detailed and clean it is. "Misery was spotted in those caves. So was Blackwell. This ship is on war duty. Spread the word."

"Aye, ma'am."

Soren climbs over right behind me, and so do more of his men, and there's an awkward separation of people before Tempest yells, "You greet these people as if they're an extra body to help us fight Blackwell and that *miasma* that follows him, because that's exactly what they are. You'll be thankful for them when the time comes. Keep your swords sheathed and mind your manners." She then faces me with the sun behind her head. She flashes a grin, a few of her golden teeth shining. "Welcome aboard the Sea Wolf, Jane. Hope you have sea legs."

THE PIRATE QUEEN

SOREN

Boarding the Sea Wolf allows my mind to finally accept what just happened; what we just escaped.

The gravity of abandoning my men's dead bodies in the streets weighs deeply on me. Their death bought me the time to breathe in this air. It's hard not to think about how they deserve better—a burial, burning their bodies, *something*.

It always feels wrong to know that the dead don't get to see what they died for, even if every single one of us is aware our bodies might never be laid to rest.

Not with war.

"You can take off your mask," Ritter says.

The two of us are standing at the ship's helm, watching Skull's Row harbor as it's left behind us, and my gaze is wherever Mads

219

and Silas are. The sound of waves crashing against the Sea Wolf fills our ears, mingling with the distant cries of seagulls that will soon be gone. Jane is secured down in Tempest's quarters while the crew prepares for warfare, her energy felt securely below me.

"It enhances my powers, and I'm currently using them." I glance at him, a briny breeze moving loose strands of hair into my eyes. "I haven't seen you use *your* mask."

"It's currently in use, as well. That purpose is not for you to know."

My attention returns ahead, glad to have more ocean between us and Skull's Row, even if the Spiraling Stone is still stationed high over us. Once the sun dips below the horizon, this place will be lost over the ocean's surface line.

"So, is Jane safe in the captain's quarters?" Ritter asks, more like confirming something rather than inquiring.

"About as safe as she was in that tunneled nest Cypress built… Something dark still haunts her."

His sigh is heavy. "I can see it, too."

Oh yeah, the eye shit. "So how the fuck does *that* work?"

For a moment, he looks like he won't tell me, but he seems to realize the value of being honest. "Your power," he begins, choosing his words carefully, "as far as I'm aware, taps into the essence of the energies around us. You can *sense* it. With mine, it's essentially a broken version of yourself. A forced magic that we acquired over the Black Sea. With the Seeing Eye visible, I can *see* if energies align, but I can't get more than that. When I look at Jane, traces of a putrid darkness surround her, one when I look at Blackwell, he's saturated in it… it *has* to be Misery."

Hearing it from another somehow makes it worse, as if acknowledging how damning this is for Jane.

"Speaking of that," I say, crossing my arms as the leather stretches. "You ever killed a god before?"

His laugh is short and sharp. "Not yet." His humor fades, Ritter shifting his stance to straighten himself, then looks at me in my periphery. "I assume you're aware that there's no point in meddling your emotions with my daughter if all of our lives are on the line, and your focus is your sister."

Oh, fucking great. He wants to talk about *this*.

"It does go against logic."

"And with your powers, I know enough to know that your magic tells you when not to associate with someone. And yet you continue to do the things you do."

"I'm not spelling it out for you," I snap, my voice grittier. "Nor am I going to sound it out, act it out, or fucking make any comment about it."

His snicker contrasts the fierce side of his heart, the one that exists solely for Jane. "All I'm getting at is if your powers can tell you not to associate with someone, then I'm curious if they can tell you *to* associate with a person."

"What's your point?"

"You could easily wait until this is all said and done before entwining any emotions. You're not a romantic. So something is telling you to do it, or there's *other* motives."

That makes more sense, at least with what he's getting at. I inhale deeply, my teeth grinding. I can't tell him I don't even know what's going on. About how my magic latches to Jane like she's destined for me, and right now, her heart demands affection, even if she doesn't see it like that, and I am weak to that call. The taste of longing coats my tongue as I struggle to articulate the inexplicable connection between her and me. No matter how loud the chaos of the unknown is, I feel utterly compelled to give her everything I have; I'm living recklessly, because I fucking want to.

No fucking way I tell him any of that.

So, I remain quiet.

"It's not lost on me that Basilisk has appeared," Ritter continues. "And I'm aware he was in Death's Wing, just like you," he adds, like explaining something complex in a simplified manner.

"I have no idea why he's here."

Ritter slides his hands into his leather coat, tilting his head to the side. "He mentioned something about his cat."

I frown, since he said the same with me, to which I honestly didn't believe. He didn't have a pet last time I saw him—not an *animal*, at least. "Does he really have a *cat?*"

"Don't touch it, or he'll kill you. *Jasmine* is very real."

My movements are momentarily suspended, even down to the

blinking. Then, my head cocks to the side, my lips parting. What the hells is that about?

Ritter turns to face me, but I still don't shift. "Jane needs to focus on surviving, and if she's busy navigating a confused heart, that will fuck us all over. Including you. Which is why Basilisk appearing is suspicious as all hells, especially since *you* won't talk."

I finally move my head to look into his eyes. "You threatening me, or what? Be clear about it."

"I'm trying to understand what surrounds my daughter."

Reasonable, but he's asking for too much. "I'm not answering anything beyond what I've already said."

I don't care if he's looking out for his daughter. I don't talk about my heart to anyone, which means giving it to Jane is still as confusing for me as it is for the rest of the world, especially since I do it without question. Just because I crave warmth doesn't mean I know how to describe what it's like to finally have it, or why I want it in the first place.

Ritter turns even more, but it's just then that Tempest's energy appears behind us. On land, she feels like any other Zenith—capable, difficult, and dangerous. Here... I look over my shoulder, and there's something almost ethereal about her. She reminds me of Cypress, as if her energy is the *source* of ripples, ricocheting off the rest of us.

We both face the pirate queen, whose leather jacket is embroidered with elegant filigree, something she rarely wears on land. "So, let's be direct. Misery is hunting Jane; that's confirmed."

"Did you know prior to now?" Ritter asks.

Her smile is feline in nature, the truth in her soul as blended together as ever; impossible for me to decipher *details*. "I know a lot, Charles Ritter." Her nearly black irises flit to mine. "You're an interesting wild card, Soren. Blackwell didn't like you having her," she laughs, revealing two golden teeth that, unlike other pirates, I know hers are naprese. "No, he wanted Jane chained up just like Misery asked for. But he couldn't step too far out of line, or it would unnerve the rest, and Misery was not ready to make such a disruption." She steps nearer, her energy so *potent*. "He underestimated the role you're playing."

"You know this how?" Ritter asks immediately, almost *for* me.

Her languid blink combines with shifting her gaze to him. "My men tortured the one named Shade."

My hand instinctively drops down to my sword's hilt, the cold metal grounding me. "What did you do?"

"Your man Bones brought him here, just as you requested when the rest fled. Shade was brought to us on the other side of the pier and immediately taken to Sea Wolf," she answers, which makes sense why I felt Bones on here before we even boarded, along with Shade. I just didn't realize they'd begin torturing him so swiftly. "I just got done getting the insights they've acquired so far. Don't worry. He's still on board and I thought to let you handle the rest."

My veins run cold at the gauntlet thrown at me. *Bones better have been in that room.*

Tempest faces the Scorpion once more, "So... are you officially out of hiding, Charles?"

"Aye," he groans out, inflecting the end of that word as if it's obvious.

"And what is the plan? The reason for it all?" she asks, waving her hand around.

"I told you, a while ago, that I needed Jane safe—"

She interjects, still rolling her hand— "That when I'd see the ruby earrings, I knew to act.... Even if I hate the rubied witch being involved."

Oh.

That's *interesting.* The ruby earrings, back in the Pit...

"For whatever reason, Jane being a Cinder is important to Misery. It's what started all of this, back when I had Melona take her to safety," Ritter immediately answers.

Her eyes widen, and it's the first time I've seen her genuinely surprised, as if Ritter knew all the right things to say to catch her interest. "Cinder? Those are... this is what started it all? Is that related to Nora being killed? She would have been one, too."

"Yes."

"Why does Misery need a Cinder? And why were you in hiding for so long? You could never answer me in the letters."

Her gaze burns at him like the act itself might command his obedience.

Definitely don't intend to piss off the captain of the ship any time soon.

Ritter glances my way, and I get the message that this is private. "I took a lot of oaths that required a lot of specific behaviors, and one of them was to remain a mystery until it was time."

Tempest licks her broad lips. "So…" she begins, lacing her fingers. "We either protect Jane and hope that we fuck with Misery, or we give her to Misery in order to spare losing resources and men?"

Ritter's entire being is flooded with murder at the mention of sacrificing Jane. "If Misery has his way, he plans to take over the Balar Coasts, and it will be centuries before they're reclaimed, if *ever*."

The bodies of my men cross my mind, knowing they died for that very cause. That more of us will, too.

Tempest's eyes flare, her meddled aura unifying in her sense of betrayal. "Interesting. Maybe that's why Blackwell really wanted me in the Crimson Isles, to get my ships out of these ports… and what information is this all based on?"

He groans, as if he's a child that is about to admit *they* were the one that lost their parent's very precious item. "Cypress."

Tempest's eyes flash with true murder, much like how my body does if someone references my sister. "You bring that witch near me, and I'll feed you to the ocean. Those earrings are the most I will tolerate."

I lean my head forward. "You find her among us, and I'll help feed her to whatever the fuck you want."

Tempest doesn't seem entirely pleased, but is willing to let it go. Thank the fucking gods she can't read me like I can read her, even if she's enigmatic. She'd know that Cypress is so ingrained in this we might as well be encrusted with rubies.

Tempest moves on. "So, why did they kill Nora if they want Cinders?"

"They want Jane for something in particular, as in Misery wants Cinders, but Jane is targeted *directly*. I honestly don't know what that is," Ritter answers.

She nods, looking away like she's far from accepting that answer as the closing of this conversation, but also wants to process it on her own.

"And since I saved your hide just now, how about a deal that your army back home will be used if we need feet on soil?" she asks, tilting her head.

He hardly reveals any emotion. "I already assumed as much."

"Then you can all go below deck and rest, and tomorrow morning we interrogate Shade. We're leaving him overnight with no sleep or food, and I want the port to be out of view before we begin dissecting him further, to distance ourselves from Misery, in case he can hear any remnants of him. We can discuss what happens next once on my island. I'll fetch Jane for you… and for now, Charles, we are even."

With that, the pirate queen's back is to us, the crew around her eyeing us with scrutiny but I can tell they're slightly terrified for what comes, and yet thrilled to be a part of something *large*.

Perhaps it's time to make Jane tell me what Cypress promised her, to claim clarity in *everything*.

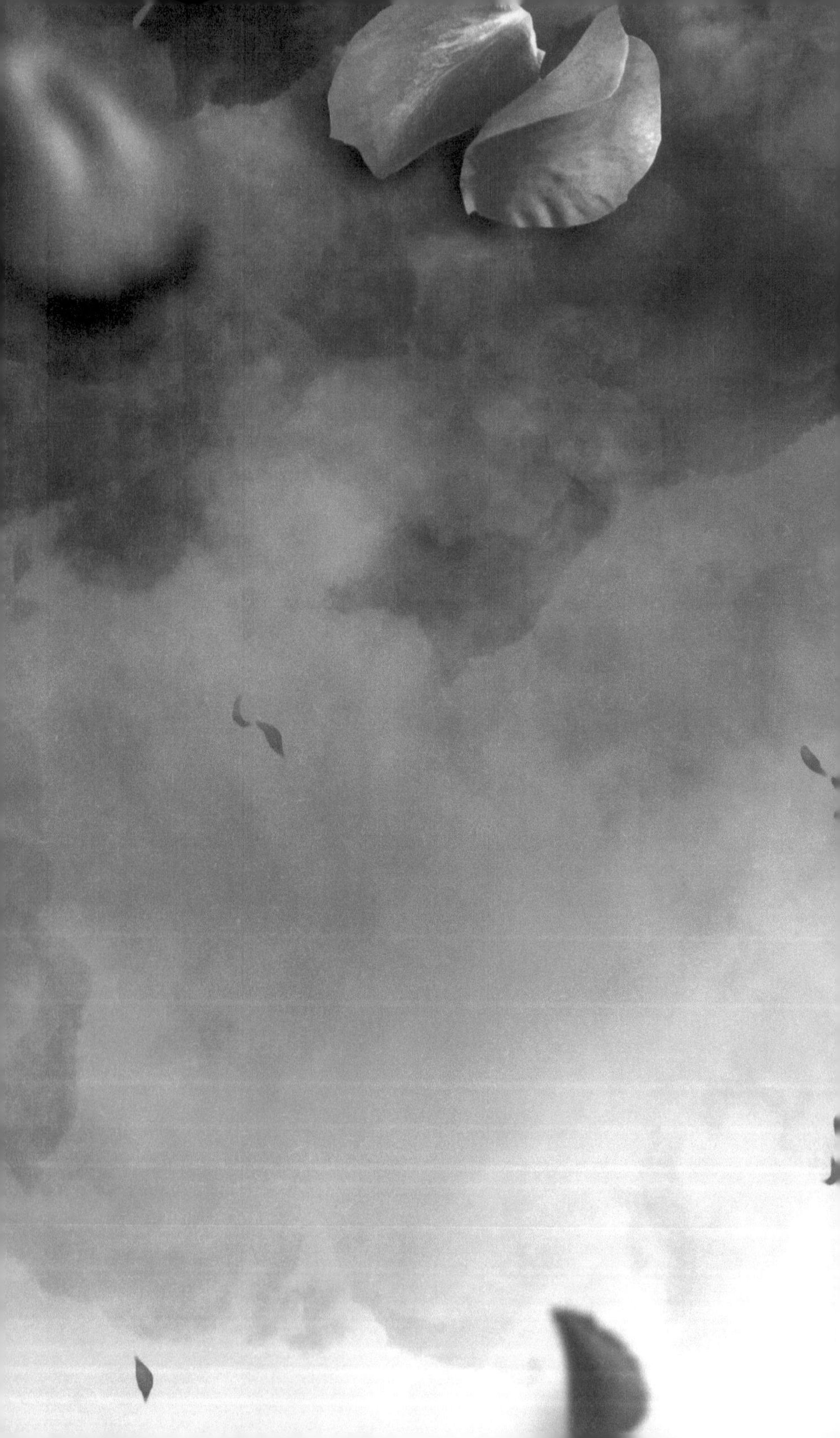

HAMMOCKS

JANE

Well, I think I prefer land. And if I have to hear one more joke about my sea legs, or lack thereof, I'm going to stab someone. I've only been in here for a short amount of time, and it's all anyone can comment on when I don't sway properly with the ship. Especially when I was being taken to the captain's quarters, and the ship steered pretty sharp—in *my* opinion—and I was the only one to wobble with it.

I'm sitting here, in what seems to be a waiting room in Tempest's portion of the ship. I don't know much about these layouts, but I'm pretty certain it isn't common for this to be so large. There's even a circular window that perfectly frames the view of the ocean. It's taller than *me*—which, perhaps, is not as significant as it feels. The rest of the room is still opulent for a ship, though, with a candle

227

chandelier hanging on a chain, and there are carvings of sirens throughout the walls.

Staring through the window, the view slightly shifting side to side, Skull's Row is clear as day, officially behind us.

It's actually quite amazing to see it from this angle, with the Spiraling Stone rising high above the cliffs.

I release a slow, purposeful sigh as this reality settles over me.

We escaped.

Over ten years since my mother was ripped from this world, I'm actually leaving all that shit behind. What's next is arguably worse, but *damn*, my anchored life in Coalfell felt like change was insurmountable for so incredibly long.

Now, it's just a memory. A long, leaden memory.

I wish I got to see Kathleen before we left.

A few sets of footsteps precede the door to the room opening, and only one set enters: Tempest.

She struts in confidentially, the door shutting behind her. "Your people are here to collect you, Jane, and take you to your quarters. You were here for safekeeping while matters got settled."

I stand right away, because out of everyone I've met, she really does feel the most like a *queen*. It makes me want to behave, which is a first. "This is a beautiful ship," I comment, not sure what I want to talk about with Tempest, but I also don't want to leave her. She seems like a treasure trove of information.

"Took many years to carve," she smoothly answers, removing her leather long coat, the buckles clinking.

"Thank you for helping us," I add, bending my knees to help with any sway so I don't embarrass myself in front of her, especially when it moves enough to make the chandelier tip a little to the right.

"The moment that people in Skull's Row catch wind that Blackwell is seeking you out, let alone Misery hunting you, people will either be out to kill you or turn you in and hope there's a ransom. You wouldn't last long enough to drain a pint of ale." She hangs her coat on a hook in the wall, her white tunic more fitted than the rest.

"Well, true, but that also means I just put you and your crew at risk."

She smiles as she faces me, a roguish gleam in her eyes. "We're pirates. They're used to it. As long as there's time aboard the ship, and something to raid in the end, they'll be happy."

There's something calming and inviting about her honestly, and I've been curious about this world since I was a kid.

"What..." I begin, although the question is honestly random and out of nowhere. "What do you, well, I know it's random, but, what do you raid? Other pirate ships?"

Her grin widens. "Pirating for *us* is about money, and ultimately, the treasures of the world. My ship has quarters to allow for passage for those who pay. Over half our income's from that; otherwise, we target shipments to Belstead all along the south, and those have become more popular for my kind." She frowns, the enjoyment of that thought clearly leaving her. "It's almost a shame, as they're starting to invent new, long-range weaponry. Removes the personal sacrifice of having to fight in close quarters."

Long-range? That's such an interesting aspect, and yet it feels so useless to me. Only hunters used bows and arrows, the weapons banned in Skull's Row, and that's the only knowledge of *long-range* that I know of. *Prioritize surviving.* "Why are you helping us?"

"Your father saved my daughter, once. She would absolutely be dead without him. I owe him by saving his child in return—to an extent. Your condition is much more demanding than his was to save mine. I'll help as long as I can, although I consider my debt fully paid."

A daughter? I want to ask more, but when our gazes connect, it's as if she senses what I want to ask. "Go rest, Jane. You'll need it. It can be tiring outrunning a god."

"You have experience?" I ask with heavy sarcasm.

She smiles mischievously. "Of a certain kind."

⟡

ANYA LEADS me past the mess deck, my stomach growling at the smell of meat and onions. The moment we step through the door toward the private quarters, I reach for the wall to regain balance.

"I've already put in word to have whatever they're serving

brought to your room," Anya comment. "Soren is waiting in there in the meantime."

I nod, although she doesn't see that. "Where's my dad, by the way?"

"He's with Tempest now, I believe. He was going in after you."

I hate that I don't see him at all, like he's avoiding me intentionally. We managed to survive those creepy ass creatures together, and I'd just like to know how he is. Is his shoulder healing? It's just… weird, not to have him check on me. "Where's Bones?"

"Do you care about him now?" she teases.

"He knows where my friend is," I quip.

"He got here early, with a delivery. He's quite safe." Her tone dips back into tedium.

We pass by a few areas that are a collection of hammocks, and then at the end of the extremely narrow hallway are seven doors, three on either side, and one in the back.

Anya guides me to the solitary one, nodding at the gilded handle. I enter the room, quickly shutting the rickety door when I spot Soren inside, wiping off the smudge around his eyes.

The sight of him in front of me eases the fear that had been gnawing at my insides. The space is small, but after seeing where the rest sleep, this is a luxury to have such privacy. The room has two hammocks, a small table nailed into the floor with a large, corked container, and an empty bowl. The way Soren uses it suggests we pour water in, gingerly, to avoid spilling out.

"Are there no beds?"

He laughs, the towel scraping against his stubble. "Better not ask that among the crew, or they'll never let you live that down." He glances my way, his eyes tired, his lashes slightly darkened from the paint, or ink, he used. "There's hardly a bed on any ship. They get wet and rot, and this will help stave off seasickness."

I peek out the small window we're afforded, seeing nothing but the empty ocean. There's something about being alone down here that makes it feel like we officially escaped. "I can't believe we really made it out of there." I glance at his back, the man's powerful body moving to remove his weapons and armor. "Are you alright?" I ask, thinking maybe he's injured and said nothing.

He looks over at me with that pale gaze, smirking. "I'm fine, love. Taking off this constricting shit. We'll be at sea for at least two weeks, and Tempest has other clothes to wear that are better for the sea. Mold will grow, believe it or not. Damages the leather."

If it weren't for the darkness hanging over me, I almost might laugh at how interesting that is.

He grins slightly. "You think it's funny?"

"No," I quip, straightening my back, moving to a hammock to inspect it. "I just always thought pirates were fascinating as a kid, but I was never allowed near them. Never even realized they might be dressed differently because of the ocean."

He pauses for a moment, like something crosses his mind that he might share, but tucks it back away. "There are bandanas, too. Keeps the salt off your hair."

It's so hard to hide the excitement of wearing a bandana on a pirate ship, let alone the *Sea Wolf*.

"It's nice to feel you happy about something for once," he loosely comments. "Take off your clothes. Dry them out and put these on."

I rock my hip to the side. "What if we're ambushed? Those clothes don't look as protective."

"*No one* challenges the Sea Wolf in open water."

"Blackwell has a god on his ship."

Soren unbuckles his pants, still staring me down, those forearms working in distracting ways. He walks near me in the confined space, speaking lowly, "There are rumors that Tempest is entwined with the ocean god herself. Misery can't touch her out here." He leans in slightly. "Don't repeat that. Don't know what her crew knows, or what's just a rumor."

I'm a lost cause, because even the man simply undressing is an event of temptation. Everything he does is done with this undertone of cocky confidence that I find so annoyingly provocative.

It's not even thoughts of Misery that repress what I feel, but more so, I can't stand to think I'm wasting time on a ship when I could be training. I feel like a treasured jewel everyone keeps delicately passing around, and not a person whose heart festers with revenge. Or a person who has time to engage in anything romantic with another.

Especially after our escape just now.

Soren slides his belt out in a fluid motion that it completely pulls me out of a trance… maybe just an *hour* with him. He places it on a hook on the wall and then comes over to touch my hair. It's so damn calming that I have this overwhelming need to bury my face into him and pretend like none of this has happened. Staring at his muscled chest donning the Zenith tattoo brings me right back to all the times we spent alone in rooms such as these.

"Until we're back on land, enjoy the safety of being on the Sea Wolf. There's nothing safer on the ocean. We're only docking because we can't hide on the waters forever. At least Tempest needs to resupply for that, if it comes down to it."

I want to be vulnerable with someone, and desire Kathleen without thought, from habit. He grips my hair and pulls my head to the side. "You can be vulnerable with *me*."

I can't help but smile, my bones melting at how uncouth he can be, especially when he wants a part of me.

"I feel like this is why I've been running for my whole life, and I also can't escape it. While *also* feeling like I just want to breathe every breath with the intention to kill Misery."

He seems to think on that, a dark approval lacing in his gaze. "I've lived with that very revenge for years, Jane. I know what it means. You can join in on the mock combat when it happens on deck, and we can plot whatever, too. It doesn't have to be wasted time."

I stare into his gaze that darkens, knitted brows crowning them, and I give him a questioning expression. "Does it bother you to let that go? That revenge?"

Soren's gaze roams my face before pulling back to sit on his hammock, his entire abdomen flexing as he sits. "No. I trust you'll find her, and that's the important part. If anything, the world is playing out in ways that make sense now.

"I tried to befriend Matthias, actually. Slowly, because of his connection across the Black Sea, where I thought my sister was. Until my instinct screamed to stay away from him. Now I know why." He chuckles, and I start to remove the top layers of my clothes while he watches. "Can't believe you're a Zenith slayer. Didn't realize the danger I was in back in the Black House."

My attempt to stifle a laugh is a complete failure. "I kept telling you, you were lucky I was bound."

A crooked grin spreads across his face before he looks down to laugh more, then flits that icy gaze right back up at me, tilting his head slightly. "Would you kill a Zenith for me?" he asks, although it's more like a fun question than something serious, like he's curious what I'd say.

"I'm taking on a miserable god so you can live and see your family. A Zenith would just be calamity."

He looks at me—*really* looks at me—like even though he has scourged my soul, he still wants more. I didn't mean for that comment to affect him, but it's enough that he motions with his fingers for me to near him.

An impish grin unintentionally plasters itself right on my face, removing my shirt at the *perfect* moment so once I'm in relative arm's length, he leans over to wrap that powerful grip around me like looped rope. His lips fiercely press into mine, scruff rubbing against my face in a collision of desire that is layered with emotions I don't think I'm prepared to feel. He tugs me closer until I'm nestled between his thighs as he leans further into the hammock. His radiating heat envelopes me, our flesh warm when pressed together, and it dawns on me that I'm not just kissing him for sex, but purely for comfort.

Being wrapped in his deadly arms is a safety no amount of coin can buy.

As I embrace that feeling, his grip on me grows firmer, his tongue spreading my lips, my hands roaming his thick shoulders and neck. What used to be a foreign touch is so familiar now, his hands so rough against my skin, but I love it; any other way, and it wouldn't be *him*.

The remainder of our clothes are discarded easily, having seen the shapes of each other many times by now. I just want him bare, so my skin can be against his warmth. There's nothing like being cold all day, craving heat, to then get it from another.

He makes me feel genuinely taken care of, that gratitude swelling with each kiss, my heart so wide and open to him that the sinking feeling from earlier, of the thoughts about losing him, weighs deep in my belly.

I can't lose him.

I *can't* live the rest of my days without having this.

Words that seem to slip off the tongue too easily when emotions are high nearly spill out, but he can feel it—shit. I can't even hide *that*.

He smiles into the kiss, his hands roaming the expanse of my bare back, down to my ass cheek as he squeezes it hard, his fingers gripping deeper and lower, just barely grazing against my pussy. We grow wilder, and hungrier, riding this wave of passion together, and I crave deeply to hear him say the things I feel.

He's right—warfare is the *best* time to be like this with another.

My world is utterly consumed with him, my weight placed entirely on him, the hammock surprisingly taking the both of us, his legs still balancing us while planting his feet on the floor. My thighs spread around him as his cock presses between our stomachs; positioned just right, his cock slides against my clit. *Gods, he's the best escape.* I let my heart wander dangerously in feelings that could destroy me forever if he abuses them.

And this time, I don't soften that, and instead simply embrace it, because I want to.

As our bodies move against each other with an intoxicating rhythm, I can taste the tang of salt on his skin. Soren lifts me by placing both hands on my ass, his cock hard and ready to pierce.

"Say you're mine, Jane," he says, gripping my hips to line me up with him. Even if I'm on top, I'm nowhere near being in control. "And *mean* it, in more than flesh."

Fuck, that turns me on in ways that ignite my heart. "You know I'm yours, Soren." I hover my nose close to his, my pussy still ready to be filled with him. "Tell *me* you're mine."

His eyes flare with desire, and his cock slides in so quickly, a gasp escapes my lips, rolling into a moan when my body feels so *full*. That sound deepens when my body lowers even further, so my clit grazes against his veined skin. I try to be quiet because I assume these walls aren't terribly thick, and this is between *us* right now.

His arm wraps around my back, the other still gripping my rear to keep me in place and help me rock with him. "My fixation has belonged to you since I first saw you tear apart that room," he says, finding a rhythm as flesh connects. A few pants are shared. "Whatever magic is in me is so focused on you, love, I have no control over it," he grunts, breathing raggedly. "I'm yours whether *you* like it or not." The greed and vulnerability that bleed from his face completely undo me. "Which means you have the power to break me, Jane. *No one* has that."

His unyielding cock drives into me, his muscled chest heaving as his arms flex with each stroke of his hips into me.

"*Soren,*" I moan, giving him all of me, a tingling electricity shooting throughout.

I've never made love or anything like this, but this has to be what it is. Or fuck it, I don't care. The rough hammock is an odd sensation when my arm or leg grazes against it, and yet I love how foreign this place is while he's the only thing I know.

I arch my back as he's unwavering in how deep he fucks me. "Fuck me until you come, Jane."

Well, that helps surge pleasure through me, my hips rocking so my clit rubs against him, my eyes partially rolling as a deep and fulfilling pleasure hits me square inside. Holy shit, this feels good.

His eyes are locked with mine, searing my skin with their intensity. He hasn't quite looked at me like this before, as if the confession of him being mine has unleashed a more possessive side.

"Use me, Jane. Fuck my cock like it's yours." The hammock rocks with us, my gasps turning to whimpers as I clench around his cock. His bruising grip on my hips pushes me harder to the edge, tightening every time I tense or hold my breath to catch that wave of ecstasy. Then it strikes me, that feeling that just a little more... my eyes widen, but my focus blurs, Soren's eyes so fierce they may as well brand me.

After my orgasm floods my body, clenching his cock like it's meant to be there, Soren works solely for his own pleasure and pushes so hard into me that I gasp, my pussy completely devouring every inch of him. I dip my chin to glance at the crevice where our skin is flush, watching his stomach contract as he spills into me, panting in my face.

There's so much satisfaction inside my body that I want to slap him.

Soren keeps us this way by not letting me budge an inch, and I cave while laying my head on his shoulder, his stubbled jaw at my forehead. His hand caresses the curve of my ass, and I swear I feel his heart beating against mine as his cock rests inside of my body.

My entire being is wide open to him, this man successfully cradling my heart in his hand.

We finally reposition, and somehow, we both end up fitting in one hammock. "I'm shocked this isn't breaking," I say, my body melting against his.

"I asked for this room because this one handles heavier weight."

Once I'm no longer afraid of it breaking, I close my eyes as our bodies hang in the air, the hammock ensuring we're properly intertwined. It's absolutely perfect; I love lying next to him. I can't help it.

Is falling for a man as simple as this? It feels like something *more* needs to happen, a big epiphany. These feelings blossomed on their own accord without much transition.

That caress gently grips my hair, and he kisses my head. He pauses for a while, his breath warm against my scalp. "I'm sorry today shook you, with your father."

My eyes part, and I stare at the details of his skin that's taught around muscles. "My dad acts like I don't matter, and yet I can't stand the idea of him dying."

"You *do* matter to him. I can tell. I think there's a reason he's doing what he's doing." My head rises and falls when his chest pulses with a laugh. "He keeps asking what I want with you."

I grin ear to ear, although more so at the thought of Soren being pressed about his feelings for me. "Oh, I'd love to hear that answer."

He chuckles, the sound deep and masculine. "Wouldn't be much. I won't tell him shit. He doesn't get to see that side of me. No one does, except you."

He leans forward and kisses my forehead while circling his rough finger on my exposed shoulder. I nestle my face closer to his chest, kissing his skin. The moment is so much tender than before, my eyes closing with ease as if this moment is meant to be. As I let feelings bleed out that can only be described as love, he continues to gently touch me as we sway in the hammock as the ship sails.

MEMORIES

SOREN

The quarters we've been given face the ocean, which looks entirely too calm for the storm I know awaits. It's such a gentle roll of the waves, softly caressing this ship.

When I look down at this wild, yet beautiful creature, I smile without reservation while no one's watching.

She lifts her heavy gaze, her hair falling past her shoulder. I love how rough everything around her is compared to how soft her body is. "Can I ask you things about your life?" she asks.

I stiffen for a moment, not having expected that. Boring my gaze into her, all I feel is a genuine desire to connect with someone right now. "You want to know about me?"

What joy filled her now partially fades. "What if something happens, and it's all I have left of you?"

There's something about that statement that punches clear through any armor I have left to shield me from her. She says that as if it matters. It's been a while since I considered my death directly impacting someone—emotionally—other than my mother.

And now, apparently, this woman with a Zenith tattoo would use memories of me as her comfort. I'm completely weak for that. To read someone's heart to the depth that I can, and feel that true desire in return, when you *want* it but it's not something that can be forced, is a sensation so alluring it scares me. "You can ask whatever you want."

She relaxes more, and I stroke a finger down her shoulder, hovering my lips over her head and breathing her in as she lies back down on my chest.

"What's your favorite childhood memory?" she asks, her arms limp across my chest.

"*That* matters to you?"

She slightly knees me as the hammock sways more, and I can't help but gently laugh before hearing her persistent voice, "Answer it."

I think on it, finding the past so bittersweet, a place I don't like to frequent anymore. But there's something about her, about this moment. *She's comforting to me.* "It was right before Serena was taken," I state, recalling the last time I felt truly happy while still feeling like a child—before I was forced to become a man. "I was proving myself to Death's Wing at about twelve, and killed a man for them. They let me have his coin bag for doing it so quickly— which was easy with my powers. I used that money to buy us our first real feast. We ate so much, Serena threw up." I chuckle, only for the humor to fade as I wonder if *she* thinks of that day, wherever she is. "I can still smell how salty the pork was, and remember how the fat dripped over the table."

I touch Jane's hair, feeling guilty as I recall my family. I only joined the Council of Zenith to find Serena, and now that plan has blown up in my face.

'*I'll help you find her...*'

It still hurts to think it won't be *me*, but I cannot abandon this woman in my arms. Somehow, that might hurt more.

"What did you eat at the feast?" she softly asks, and if I was able to see in front of her, I'd bet that her eyes were closing.

"A pig roast, and potatoes with butter and cream. Our mother baked the fluffiest biscuits, and then we had two pies for dessert."

Peace fills her heart, so soothing against my chest. I want to guard this sensation as long as my heart beats, my grip on her skin digging slightly deeper.

With a dramatic sigh, she continues, "Do you ever see yourself settling down? Would the people that follow you be okay with that?"

I raise a hand to stroke her hair, eyeing a strand as it wraps loosely around my finger. "I don't think it's shocking to any of them that one day, I'd want to settle. It's a natural evolution for us all. Their primary motive is safety in numbers. It's a dark fucking world outside of Belstead, and even then, some warlords are creeping in on those lands. I live near water and it's harder to siege, and I don't struggle for a second to make hard decisions, even if they're *distasteful*. As long as I continue to make them, they'll be there for me."

All it does is soothe Jane, and it's why she feels so faultless against me. "Why aren't you a pirate with the way you talk?"

I stiffen, but decide to get it over with. "My father was a pirate."

I bet her pretty little eyes are open now.

She's intrigued, and sorrowful. Perhaps even slightly bashful for realizing how personal of a question that was. "What if you run into him?"

"I already tried. He was dead before I got to him." I run my fingertips against her skull. "Otherwise, I'd have killed him myself."

Acceptance.

The Zenith princess not only is molded for me, but she accepts me. She shifts slightly so her body closes in all the space between us, my cock hardening, even though I don't plan to use it again so soon. I'm enjoying the gentleness.

"I don't think I could live with peace," she confesses. "I desire it, sure, but I know I'd get bored."

"Which is why you're with me, because that's how I'm built, too."

Something profound blooms inside of her, and I realize we've never outright stated we're together. It deepens whatever she feels for me—*security*. I want to give her more. "After this, I think we will go across the Black Sea with Basilisk, to look for Serena and get away for a moment. Explore, which I know you want to do."

Her walls are nearly non-existent at this point, and I can tell how much she wants what I just offered. *That's it, love. Such a good girl.* "Is that his real name?"

"No." I glance up at the ceiling, then out the window. "It's Rasmus. He has a small kingdom out there. He's also someone that can make very hard decisions very quickly, which is what all men really want to follow."

A cool breeze enters the room through the open window, her shivering against me, making my cock twitch even more. I want to be the man who knows her body better than she does. Even if she hated me, she'd always have to crawl back if she wanted to properly be tended to, to feel my touch that would know every inch of her and how to make her come over, and over.

Owning this part of her is a triumph nothing else will satiate.

THE ROSE DAGGER

JANE

The breaking of dawn brings an empty stomach and dry lips. My body nearly collapses from exhaustion in his arms once sleep took over; he even placed a blanket over me at some point, although I'm alone in the hammock now. I'm not used to rolling out of these things and nearly fall over to see the man is already dressed for the day.

"You don't sleep much," I say, noting that he still dons most of his weapons. "Also, why did you move me?"

"I need less than most people."

Before, I might have prodded about what I learned from Bones, but I almost don't even care if he doesn't want to tell me. Knowing wouldn't change anything, and Soren is the type of man who will live a life with many secrets.

I understand how important they can be to keep—Cypress's desire to put a ruby into my skin creeps in; I shut that off and even tell myself it was made up, just so I can avoid letting *any* feelings about it move to Soren.

I swear he was going to ask me about it, right before I fell asleep. But he didn't, and I'm not sure why. If anything, him not asking almost has the opposite effect and makes me *want* to tell him.

He lays out rags to clean ourselves with, and I do a quick pass over my body after all that sweat and cold ocean water that got on my skin. "Why haven't you asked more about Cypress?" I finally utter, unable to handle it any longer. If the witch *really* wanted me not to speak, she would have made it more obvious. Cursed me a little; *something.*

Soren also hands me clothes my size, staring me down. "I don't have a clear answer for you, Jane. Everything within me tells me not to."

"What?" I wasn't anticipating that, dressing slowly as I think that over. "That's different."

His sigh mixes with a growl like he hates the mere *idea* of this conversation. "If I *trust* what I feel, I can only imagine that whatever Cypress told you might actually be best kept without saying a word to me. But then that means trusting Cypress, and I *hate* that."

That changes *everything* within me. "She did make it seem like you shouldn't know, Soren. Like it would make things *worse.*"

That man stares me down, his broad shoulders rising and falling as he hardly blinks. "Do *you* think it would?"

My eyes move around as if trying to track a fly, completely taken aback by this sense of responsibility. Would him knowing he can't read me hurt this? In many ways, *no.* It makes logical sense. If I fall into enemy hands, for *any* reason, being cut off from them would only help. But it might drive Soren mad, sending him into an even *more* protective mode to keep me out of Misery's hands.

Cypress thinks I'm useful and that my actions can *help.* And I can't tell if me withholding that is just to please some neglected pride within myself, or true strategy. "Can I think on it?" I ask.

He gives a curt nod, before motioning a bandana in my direction. I wrap it around my hair, and he adjusts from behind, the fabric rustling my braided hair until it's situated. My outfit is essentially everything I normally wear just looser, and he even aids me into a bodice to keep my breasts in place. There's no way I'm moving about with floppy tits, as a certain blonde would put it. I smile sadly when her face enters my mind, and as Soren's tying the back. "What is it?"

"I miss Kathleen," I admit without reservation. "She's the one that taught me about finding a *properly* fitting bodice and how comfortable they can be."

"She's very safe where she is."

There's not a lot more said because I'm tired of worrying, and at some point, I have to hope for the best. It kills me to think I may never get to see her again, but imagining her face in my mind's eye makes me feel like she would be majorly pissed if all I did was wallow when I'm sailing on a *pirate ship.*

I'll keep my head up for you, Kathleen. We promised we'd share these stories one day.

The two of us make our way to the mess deck, and I follow closely in his shadow. My presence garners a lot of attention, and so does Soren's, a sea of gazes bouncing between us. Especially when he has to duck to avoid certain beams.

"What do they eat here?" I ask, passing by one man sweeping the deck.

"The swaying of a ship means fires aren't the safest. So, biscuits, dried meats, and beans. Stews when it's calm."

Don't complain. "Delicious."

He smiles at me. "Do you miss being spoiled, Jane?"

"That's your fault. And at least I like beans."

"Well, maybe you'll enjoy yourself on board, then."

The hustle and bustle of the crew is captivating, especially since I feel completely removed from danger with Soren here. They all remind me of the coal miners, where each person has a role to keep the rest flowing.

A man passes Soren, one that looks to belong to him, handing over something wrapped in leather. The Zenith takes it as if nothing occurred, indicating to our table—one of the few in here—which is also bolted into the ground. The behemoth sits across from me, my back to the ship's wall. I can't spot my dad anywhere when I survey the space, which feels cramped with the low ceiling.

"Where is my dad?" I ask, feeling like a lost kid since he's the second person I've asked this about.

"Around here, somewhere. Felt him earlier." A man who definitely belongs to Tempest nears us with a bowl of beans, and some biscuits wrapped in linen, crumbs dusting the table's surface. His skin is kissed so much from the sun he may as well have been smothered by it; his nose and cheeks are red, his hands as dry as sand. A chained necklace with a wolf pendant dangles as he bends over to place the food on our table. "Tempest says if you need any more food, let us know, sir. Not much of a selection, but we do have plenty of it."

He turns around just as quickly as he appeared, swaying fluidly like he knows the exact motion the ship will make.

Casually lifting his fork packed with beans, Soren sucks in his lips before pressing them together. "I hate beans."

The comment incites a small, high-pitched laugh out of me, which only continues to roll into a full one; I didn't expect his weakness to be a *legume*. I take a large mouthful, surprised it has some of the same seasonings that Mom used to use. "I think they're delicious."

The clinking of utensils on plates and laughter from those around gives us a sense of privacy as he forces himself to eat. I lean over on my elbows. "You better eat all of that. I bet you need a massive amount."

"Just like training back in the day when I ate shit food."

After a few large bites that he forces down, he rests his fork on the table and reaches down to the wrapped leather handed to him, sliding it across the table to me. "The blacksmith with your father was adamant he'd get this made before we left. He handed it to me after we parted back in the Undercroft."

"What is it?" I ask, looking at the soft, brown leather.

"I don't know, almost like it's difficult to open and find out," he sarcastically replies.

I throw him a look like I'd hit him if he were closer. Reaching out, I unwind it until a sheathed dagger is revealed, along with a holster for the thigh. At the center of the hilt is a rose, with what looks like tiny vines wrapping around each side. The sheath is bright red, with bronze fastenings at the top and bottom. "What…"

"I had him make you a dagger. You were so worried about being useless," Soren clarifies, leaning over and drinking some water. "Figured it was worth getting you something that shows you're not. You're your father's daughter, that's for fucking sure after everything I've felt. You should have your own weapon fit for someone of his rank. Of *your* rank."

If I thought I felt romantic things for this man, this takes it to another realm I didn't know existed. My fingers gently roam the smooth blade, utterly amazed at how beautiful it is.

"You…" I start, connecting my gaze with his. Pride gleams in his eyes, like he knows he did well. "I don't—thank you." I glance back down at it. "What if I lose it?"

"Why would you lose it?"

If Misery takes me… "There could be a fight, and it gets knocked out of my hands."

My heart races when I still have no idea how to tell if Cypress's warnings are valid or not. It would be so *nice* to get Soren's opinion on what she said to me.

"Then we'll make you another one. Use it for now. It's from the strongest steel in Skull's Row."

It's the first time in a while that my desire to cry is for everything *but* something that aches. "This is nice of you."

"I can be nice," he comments, his grating voice low and almost seductive.

What the hells is he doing? I'm nearly blushing over here. "I don't have anything for you."

"That's not how gifts work, Jane."

"Can't believe I'm getting taught about gift-giving from you," I mumble, turning the blade over in my hand. "This is gorgeous, and thoughtful, Soren."

"Red is a color I tend to prefer," he replies so smoothly I half-wonder if he's about to ask for a favor after buttering me up.

But then his face hardens to the shell it was when we first met as he looks over his shoulder.

Basilisk approaches through the crowd of the room. "Don't mean to interrupt what seems to be a very good conversation," he says, placing both hands on the table to lean over; they're just as worn as Soren's, and a shade darker. "We learned something from

Shade that seems… *relevant*. Think you should go down and take over."

Soren's posture stiffens, his shoulders flexing underneath the loose fabric. "Glad they fucking involved me *again*," he replies, clearly pissed.

Shade?

"Tempest wanted one more word with him before you were brought down. I'm here to retrieve you." He glances my way; he and Soren so much alike in demeanor and attire. "I could watch her for you."

"Jane comes too," he immediately replies.

My brows raise as I look between the two.

Basilisk moves his gaze back at Soren. "He might not speak easily," he says, as if to hint at something.

"And she needs to know what's happening. It's sort of relevant to her," he sarcastically replies before glancing my way. "Unless you don't want to."

My fingers curl around the dagger's hilt. I'd like to slit his throat for nearly ripping my hair out, but I know that will get us nowhere. "I can handle it. He worked with Misery, right? I definitely want to hear those answers."

The dread that tragedy will strike us all resurfaces, but honestly, there's something to Soren having this dagger made for me that makes it feel like I will be alright.

A sentiment to show that I'm *not* alone.

That has to count for something, right?

I drown out the worry of knowing that whatever comes next it won't be easy. Or remotely safe. But that's fucking Skull's Row, isn't it? I also can't ignore how there has to be a weakness within Misery. If he does take me, I'm the only one that can get close to him and not die. At least, he needs my heart beating to use me however his sick mind needs to, which means an opening.

An opening that Cypress is meddling in—the acceptance that being close to Misery might be the only way we ruin him sits on my shoulders like a weight that won't let me stand. It's not like I can get close without being *taken*.

Later. Focus on Shade.

I immediately begin wrapping the holster around my right

thigh, affixing the dagger to my leg before standing with Soren, whose eyes are back in his mercenary gaze. I fall into a comfortable silence as I'm ready to follow them, knowing that somewhere in my mind, to truly save lives, I might have to offer myself, and the fucker named Shade has information I need. I'll need everything I can get before facing Misery.

I'm ready to kill this stupid god and be worthy of the tattoo on my chest so I can finally live without worrying who is in my shadow for once.

SHADE
SOREN

Everything in my gut tells me the conversation with Shade will begin the true unraveling of the chaos that surrounds us, and that once it starts, it will *spiral*.

The only concern I have is that my powers are quiet. There's no denying those rubies escalated everything, but even *this* is tame. Normally, when my sedated intuition contrasts with my restless heart, it means I need to let things play out.

But I don't want to.

I want to *plan*. I want to be in *control*.

Jane is close behind me, her heart altering so much with that dagger. There wasn't even the intention to open her up—I just wanted her to have something that proved she *does* belong. That she's capable and worthy.

She's open to me like she is with Kathleen.

I will take care of her.

The ship's shadow envelopes us as we're taken below to the storage level. Pain, agony, and dread fill the belly of this ship, and it all comes from one source. I pause to glance at Jane, who radiates determination. It's even a little concerning how well she wears that pirate's bandana. "This will not be pretty."

Hazel eyes peer through lashes to connect with mine. "Neither was clinging to my dying mother. I need to know who to hurt."

Her ire feels more tempered, the frayed edges of it burned away. It's the person I knew my powers sensed was within, and I fucking adore it.

When we enter the room that no more than five men occupy, both Ritter and Tempest are present, along with Bones and two who belong to this ship. Shade's eyes flash my way, and his energy warps into chaos. "You're fucking serious?"

Tempest sits down on a box labeled *rope*. "Please, Soren, do your work." She spreads her legs and leans over to rest her elbows on each knee.

Shade's eyes flash with something I know gives him away—he's been caught. No lies will work anymore. Whatever truth he's terrified to reveal is going to be exposed.

"This is all rather rude," he states, his bound hands between his thighs. "Didn't even bother asking me anything before clearly assuming the worst. You've all already asked me all the questions I can answer. Is this necessary?"

He's still as indiscernible as before, although it's interesting I can sense the general things that plague him, just with no specifications.

A magic wearing off?

"Why couldn't I read you earlier," I casually ask, as if telling him the weather. Basilisk shuts the door to this room while Jane stands behind me.

"I will die with sealed lips." Blood sputters out from what looks like blunt force trauma to the face. Bones rolls his fingers like he's revving them back to life, and I have a feeling I know who did it.

"Strip him," I command. "Completely. He's hiding something, and I want it all removed."

The betrayer grunts, his body stiffening as Bones and the others begin to cut his clothes off, shredding them like beggars searching for hidden gold. Tempest and Ritter both watch on, and Jane does so from behind, while Basilisk stalks from the shadows, his golden eyes glinting like metal. It's then that I sense a creature before noticing another set of golden eyes, but more round and only a foot off the ground—*later*.

Shade thrashes, his face reddening. "Where's my fucking digni-ty?" he shouts as they yank his boots off and cut at his pants.

"Yes, I have a reputation for giving a shit about *dignity*," I reply coolly, my gaze unwavering, reprioritizing his torture. As Shade is stripped of his last piece of clothing—a wool sock—I feel that pang of sympathy that nearly always creeps up when I know that one day, this is how *I'm* going to die, no doubt: attacked, mauled, or mutilated.

But who the fuck cares when my fate is already damned to an end like this? "I still can't read you," I state.

"Well," Bones says, running a hand through his short hair, his mismatched gaze downward at Shade. "I can see why he was a lady's man."

A few snigger, and I fight the temptation to pinch the bridge of my nose. Even Tempest gives a chuckle.

"Can't help but look at my cock?" Shade mocks.

"It's hard to miss when it's basically a third leg."

The tension around lightens, although not from me. I still can't feel shit from Shade. "It has to be underneath his skin," I say, looking over the interlocking scars and tattoos. Something from Jane emanates behind me, a discomfort that seems out of place. I tuck that away and save the concept for later, trying to detach from her.

His legs fidget at my words, and that's all the confirmation I need. "Poke and prod and see if you feel anything around his scar that might be a foreign body." Our gazes connect when I say, "Or we can sever you limb by limb, shred them apart over sieves, and see what we find. Jane can heal your mutilation, so no need to worry about that killing you. All you need is a brain and heart to function."

Shade's chest heaves, strings of saliva stretching when he pants. "You won't get me to talk with such barbarism. I'm a fucking gladi-ator. I can handle pain."

They all say that, but everyone talks once the flaying starts, especially if a healer can keep them alive and awake. I squat down, the man starting to shiver. No doubt the wood is frigid, and his entire being rattled. "There's no such thing as pushing through pain when you're sleep-deprived. You are forcing me to do that to you. I *will* get what I want before we leave the ship. You know no one is rescuing you."

All it takes is a nod of my head for Bones to grab an arm, the other man putting the heel of his boot into Shade's shoulder to press him against the pillar, all while I watch, still squatting down.

"Let me, *give you a hand,*" Bones mocks, gripping Shade's wrists.

Shade's panting grows panicked. "You won't break me. But they *will* break your little toy behind you. You cut off my fucking arm, and I *definitely* won't help you there."

I backhand him so hard it nearly sprains my wrist, his head hanging limp in a daze, his cheek bleeding from one of my rings.

"Must be embarrassing for a gladiator to be backhanded like that. Someone get some water," Bones chides.

It doesn't take long before someone is dumping water over Shade, his naked body jolting. He sharply inhales, his teeth chattering.

My head pivots as if honing in on something—among the calmer, excited energy, bleeds something entirely wrought with fear and dread. I narrow my eyes on Shade, and it's like a vast ocean of one's soul opens up before it closes back off.

Something faltered in the magic that binds him.

I lean forward to grab his chin and shake his head, to which he groans. I laugh. "It's in his fucking teeth. Someone, hold his head still."

It takes two to hold him still enough that I can pry his bleeding mouth open by shoving a block of wood in, sliding it around until I spot a golden tooth. It looks like any other, but I can feel something emanating from it—if anything, it looks loosened with how it bleeds.

Basilisk steps into the dim lighting. "Now that's fascinating. It's a suppressant."

"You're familiar with that?" I ask, looking up at him.

"Not as common over here, but they're everywhere across the

ocean. There's more of us over there, too. So there's a natural counter. It's only the second one I've seen over here."

I glance up at Tempest. "You have any smithing pliers? Or anyone on board that handles tooth extraction?"

"Aye… Fred, take care of that," she says, still leaning on her knees, and one of the men takes off quickly.

We don't wait for long before someone is back with dental tools. Shade beginning to hyperventilate over the wooden block still shoved into his mouth.

The belly of the ship becomes an echo of blood-curdling screams, muffled by the wood in his mouth. When the tooth is removed—his cries morphing into shrieks—Shade slumps over once more when they release him, blood spilling out of his mouth. His chest rapidly rises and falls.

Immediately, I can feel the depths of Shade, every corner of his fears revealing themselves to me. Taking the bloody tooth encased in metal to a nearby lantern, I hold it up so it glints in the light—naprese gold.

Blackwell.

I don't understand. How can he possibly use our metal to create this effect? Tempest has naprese caps, but to imbue them with *other* magic… When Shade comes to with a slow, hoarse groan, I can read him beautifully, handing the tooth to Bones to hold it for now. "So… now that *that* is out of the way."

The truth bleeds out in his aura like how his mouth does, the man spitting multiple times to clear it. "I'm still," he says through a pant. "Not talking."

Squatting down once more, I lock eyes with his frantic ones, gripping his chin tightly and feeling the warmth of his trickling blood on my fingers. "You are protecting someone," I state, as if reading a map that finally makes sense. "How original."

His dark brows upturn. "Are you really going to be pissed that I am choosing someone I love over you?" he asks, his voice cracking with exhaustion. "I'm desperate, you cunt."

I raise an eyebrow. "So are we."

"Is there any way that I live?" he pleads, reeking of anguish. Some last bit of survival breaks through the warrior's facade.

His gaze swiftly flicks over my shoulder, and I follow the direction to see that he looks up at Jane, who watches very carefully.

"You should understand, Shade," I slowly say, looking back at him. "That I am going to learn what is happening to you. The duration, and extent, of your torture is completely within your control." *Blackwell.* I get Blackwell and another dark figure, who has to be Misery. "Unless you're waiting on someone to rescue you." His eyes flash up at me. "In these circumstances, I sometimes have the patience to break a man. We, unfortunately, do not possess that time, which means I'll have to threaten *another* whose pain would break you. It will not take me long to learn who that is to you, and it just takes one hawk to reach the right people from here."

There it is. A flash of heat and worry, but as I invade his energy and look over his scars, I know when I'm across from someone who will take *weeks* to break.

He will take time.

I stand, my leather crinkling with the motion. I still don't understand *how* Blackwell did it, or why, but if Ritter is doing something similar, then this is also not impossible. And Basilisk says this is more common across the sea.

I should have known. Triumphant magic is only dominating until someone learns to manipulate it.

"If I die," he sputters out. "Without telling a word of what was done to me by Misery, then people I care about live. The words that come out of my mouth matter, no matter what happens to my flesh."

Misery floods Shade again, that sense of impending nothingness one of the heaviest burdens I've ever sensed from another: death. He's aware he will not see anyone else that he loves, nor will his body get a chance to recover. Shit, he probably won't even get one last drink of water.

His energy reeks of a determination that will be like chipping away at stone, but it's only held up by fear. I get no sense that he's loyal to Blackwell, but more so loyal to the deal that he's being offered. I inhale deeply, thinking of something interesting. "Tell me what I want, and I can find a way to hide you from Misery. I'll use the same method with the tooth, but with another magic he cannot penetrate."

I'll use Cypress's shit like the way she uses me. If it doesn't work, then, well, it's not my problem. I need to know what Jane is up against, and I get the sense he just wants *safety*.

His eyes vibrate around in his skull, his expression turning despondent. "Misery will kill me if he gets his hands on me. It's better I die, knowing I didn't speak."

Ritter hands me his ring. "Not if you wear this."

I can't help but almost snort that Ritter caught on that fast to what I'm offering; he's actually kind of useful.

"What is it?" Shade asks.

Ritter says, "What I've been wearing for ten years so no one can find me."

He is absolutely sold on that, looking at Ritter with reverence. *Oh*, so he looks up to the Scorpion, then? Is that possibly why he wanted to get a close look at Jane in Rosmertta's?

"Why did you take Jane in the alley?" I ask.

"Because you had been struck," he answers with a weakened voice, defeated. "It was a stupid fucking move. I thought it was a good opening. And if I could have handed Jane to *them*, without a single fight, and knowing Ritter was always nearby, then I'd be..." he trails off, like the reminder of his failure physically pains him. "I'm a fighter. Not a strategist. *Clearly*."

My gnarly injury is what brought him out of the shadows?

It's making a whole lot of fucking sense now. I knew to trust my gut, but sometimes, I can't interpret the meaning or implications. And if everything in me screamed to take the hit, then something in the fates wanted Shade to cross my path in such a manner.

Which means he might harbor information that could save our collective asses; my powers do tend to lean toward self-preservation.

"*And?*" I coax.

"Misery wants Jane, as I'm sure you've guessed. He's promised Blackwell the entirety of Skull's Row. Misery is the one making it so you can't read any of us," he says, the words flowing out like he's desperate to purge the sickness of lies from his body.

Ritter says, "Not useful enough information."

He looks panicked, bouncing his gaze around between us all; he doesn't fear death, but he is broken by the idea of leaving someone behind. "Please. I—I know what he wants with Jane," he says, eyeing the pocket Ritter slides the ring into.

"And why would you know that?" Ritter asks. "I couldn't even find out, and I was *close*."

"I've been in the rooms during conversations. He... he uses me for strength when it's too much for Blackwell."

"For *strength*?"

"He's like a succubus, but worse. He can only function based on stealing energy from someone." He has so much relief telling others this. "I'm Blackwell's nephew; very estranged, but we're related. And for some reason our bodies are good sources of energy. We don't burn out like the others do. I—I think my uncle doesn't understand Misery is using us. That he only chose us because we're good for him. He's lost in the high of ruling over this place. And Misery is growing weaker by being away from his land. More desperate."

"So, then, what are his plans with Jane?" I ask.

Sounds like we just need to outlast Misery until he's too weakened to mean anything.

Shade swallows thickly, rolling his eyes under his blink as if to refocus his gaze. "Two things." He's truly nervous to say this, and I can feel Jane get closer. "First, well... he, um... he needs her skin."

"*What?*"

"Once in his lands, he plans to flay her alive and use that skin for his rebirth. He won't look like Jane, but he needs whatever magic is in her blood. He just kept saying it has *her* magic, and it will make him impossible for *her* to kill, whoever *she* is. And if he doesn't get Jane before he has to return to his lands, it will be another generation before he can return. It's optimal *now*, and he doesn't want to wait."

Ritter and I look at each other. Is this Jane being related to Cypress? The Scorpion reeks of fear for his daughter, but I can tell these answers give him some semblance of purpose, too.

"What does that process look like?" I ask, facing him again. "How long would it take? Would he do it immediately?"

I need to know what time we have. Is it something immediate, or would we have time to save her? I don't plan for her to get taken, but I'm also not a man to get caught off guard, either.

I thrive on plans.

"It would be a long process. She has to be willing. *Very* willing, or else the magic won't transfer properly. It's why he wants her as quickly as he can get her, but again, he's weak. He doesn't want to make a move unless he's certain he can get her all the way north without anyone stopping him. It's risky otherwise. It's why he let you have her for a bit... it would have caused too much of a stir among the Council. There are those loyal to Ritter in there, and I'm sure some guessed who she was as soon as they saw her. Letting you have her appeared the most normal, meanwhile, I kept an eye on her when she came to Rosmertta's, because Misery said there *would* be an opening..."

My mind rushes with considering every avenue that this can go wrong for us, feeling Jane out over my shoulder. "And what is the second thing he wants her for?"

"They want as many offspring as possible that are Cinders," he quickly gets out. "Since making her willing will take time... I've heard them state they might as well use her to make more Cinders in the process."

My rage flares, standing as I look at Jane, the thought of her stomach swelling with an abomination of Ash striking at a mania I didn't know existed within me.

Jane doesn't even seem fazed, despite her father looking at Shade like he might rip his balls off. She slowly tells him, "Well, I'll never let *that* happen. Tell me, why did you come talk to me back at Rosmertta's?"

"It, well... I wanted to meet the person Misery is fixated on," he answers, which is most of the truth; the rest of it is related to Ritter, like I guessed.

"And?" I coax again.

There's a dehumanized feeling in him, like he's embarrassed this is all turning out in such a manner. "I admired Ritter when I was younger. I wanted to see his daughter."

I face Tempest. "What do you want to do with him? That's all he knows. His knowledge of Misery and Blackwell is shallow, which means he hasn't been around for long enough to gain deeper insight."

It's almost paralyzing to think of what Misery intends to do with Jane, and I want this over with so I can start plotting with everyone in this room. My heart pounds so feverishly, I start pacing.

Tempest inhales deeply, looking him over. "Then we are done. I don't want him to have that ring, though. Let's give him to the sirens. They'll judge his worth, and if he's got a rotten soul or not. If he doesn't, he'll be released when Misery is no longer a threat. That's the safest thing to do with him."

Panic explodes inside of Shade, more petrified of that than death. "No, no, please. Not the sirens. Not coral skin, not their curse..."

It's said that the sirens take men they dislike into their waters, affixing them to the stones below; metamorphosis takes over as they slowly lose bodily needs, coral growing out of their bodies that the sirens use. But the mind never dulls.

One just remains there, forever.

The siren's curse.

Tempest stands, her head held high. "There's nothing to fear if your heart is true," she says, like telling a child not to fear the dark. "Let's go. Get this over with. We have many things to consider."

We all follow as Shade is led, while screaming for mercy, to the top of the deck. The sunlight nearly blinds me, and I'm reminded why so many wear an eyepatch. "We offer him to the sirens!" Tempest shouts. The pirates are all smiling like they're feeding a prized pet, some clanking against metal and others stamping their feet to a rhythm.

Tempest pulls out a small pendant from underneath her shirt and blows on it. I don't hear a fucking thing, but it seems to work as the crew start cheering when looking overboard.

Shade shouts, blood stained on his chin, neck and chest. I can't resist and look overboard; it's a far drop, but I can see many heads sticking out of the water, a mesmerizing crooning brushing against my ears coming from the sirens.

Without hesitation, Shade is tossed overboard, screaming all the way down until the waves consume him.

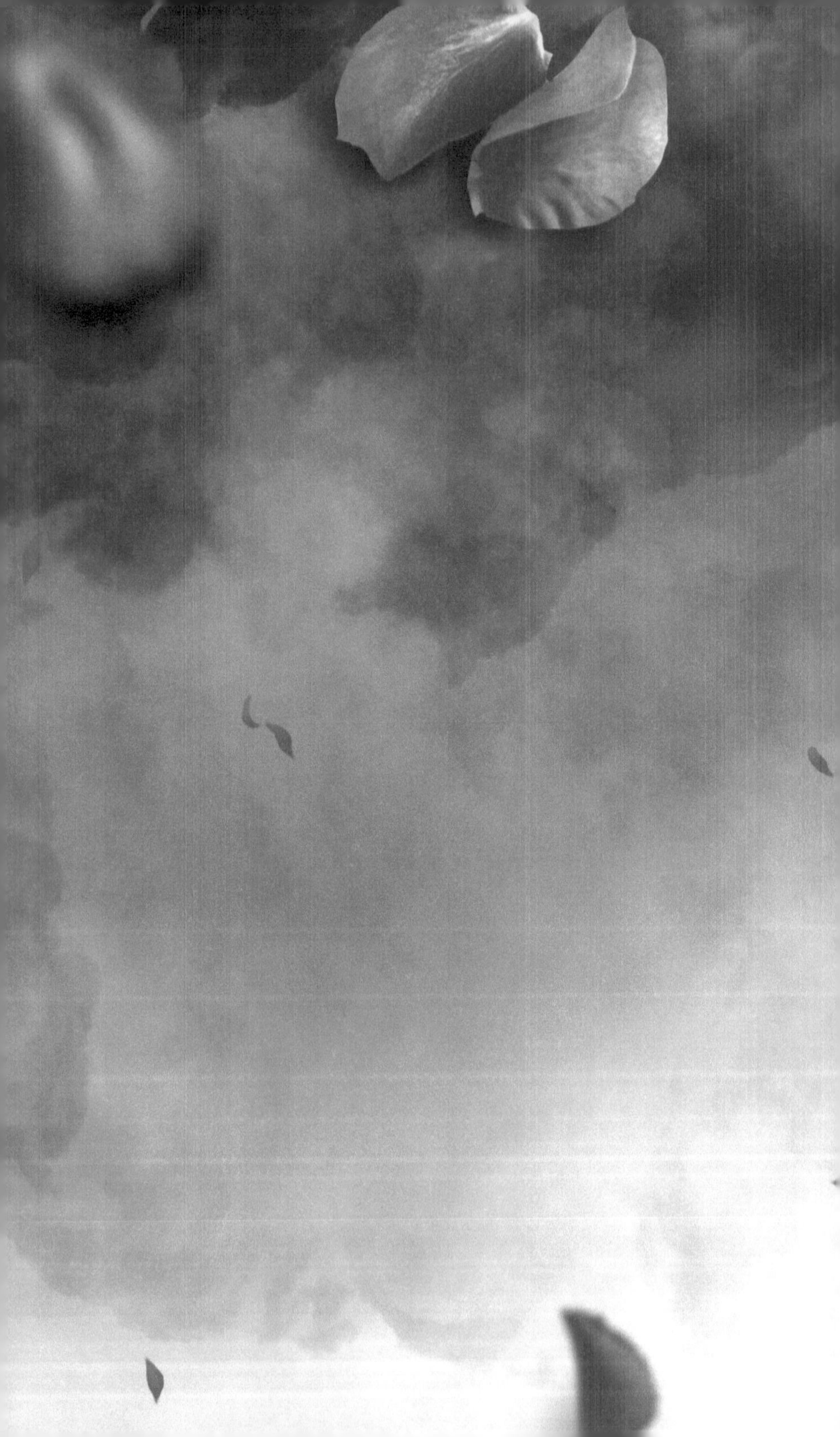

STORMBREAK

JANE

Two weeks later

We're landing today.

The sun kisses the horizon of an island that belongs to Tempest, a soft glow lighting our way. A mist lies on the morning ocean and wraps around us like we're ghosts entering the afterlife. It's hard to see anything outside the harbor that we enter. I breathe in the wet air as I stare at the cloud surrounding us that's so soft, compared to the harsh, dark waters below that look like moving slate from up here.

There's a sense of peace in this moment that feels like a precipice.

The distant sound of waves crashing against the ship makes me think of Shade, and I'm a little shocked it's already been two weeks since that entire event. My mind constantly wanders to him, realizing how he's just another piece of calamity in all of this, even though he still had a life himself. He was someone's kid, maybe even a father. Someone's family, doing what he thought he had to.

He died in a way I was positive would take me when I first met Soren.

At least, I assume he's dead. I don't know what the sirens decided, as I didn't get to see them much before they disappeared back underwater. Tempest said they'll be made aware of the verdict when this is all said and done.

The stranger part is that he really hasn't been talked about since, like tossing him over was another part of the routine, like finding a rat and sicking a cat on it.

I don't let my mind focus for too long on it, because he's a man who made his decisions. For better or for worse, it didn't work for him.

It's how our world is.

Glancing up, Tempest stands at the ship's helm, staring at a lighthouse whose burning flames guide her home. A network of weather-worn docks and wharves sprawl outward through the mist, every inch of it owned by this pirate queen.

Being on her ship is a trip I'll never forget, that's for sure.

It was quiet, overall, and I did, in fact, partake in many mock sparrings. Soren trained pretty much the majority of the time, grumpily eating his beans to help him maintain his energy and girth.

Dad was enigmatic as always, and I guess that's the new father I have to get used to. It's so different from when I was a kid, but it's honestly not important now. I'm focused solely on what I have to do to destroy everyone who thinks they'll use me like I'm a puppet.

That miserable cunt of a god seriously thinks he can use my skin, and *breed* me like I'm a fucking bitch in heat? The concept is so laughable, it doesn't even worry me.

Death will be greeted like an old friend if that happens.

My hair gently tugs in the wind, the strands dry and salty; I didn't braid it much while on this ship, because my arms grow too tired when I have to do it again for the fifth time. Braziers and torches are lit among the sandy shores, pine and palm trees scattering over the land. High up on a cliff's edge is a giant flag with the outline of a red siren on it—what I've been told is the original Jolly Roger. On the dark side of the island, in the morning sun's shadow, is what looks like a verdant jungle through the haze.

The pirate queen's personal dock is unmistakable as it comes into view, a stretch of obsidian-black wood extending out into the bay.

Honestly, the primary thing I really notice is that it doesn't seem overly fortified.

As the crew aligns the ship to glide into the dock, the scent of salt and jungle fills the air, mingling with the faint, acrid smell of burning pitch and sea-soaked wood. The island hums with latent energy, or maybe that's just the mist.

The Sea Wolf creaks and groans as over a dozen fat ropes are tossed over the edge, landing with loud thuds on the pier as men below use them to wrap around cleats.

Soren stands a few feet away, and Bones peers over to look at me before sauntering closer. He grabs the rails of the boat, leaning down a few times before facing me. "Bet you didn't expect to be around a bunch of pirates in all this."

I allow a half-smile. "I've had fun on this ship." I look out at the dock again, noticing a wolf's head carved out of wood on one of the buildings. "Why is it a wolf, by the way? Sort of random, given the whole *ocean* image."

"From the way I hear it, Tempest grew up in the Huntswoods. There are a bunch of wolves out there, and she *claims* they were her first true friend." He raises his brow. "Wouldn't put it past her. She leads like an alpha wolf."

The people on deck start to move to a long, wooden plank that connects with the pier. Soren waits for me, looking me over before eyeing the island. We traverse this narrow strip of wood, and I struggle slightly with my balance. Once down on the piers, I can't believe I'm actually dizzy the longer I stand there, like I can't seem to find the right footing.

"Welcome to Stormbreak" Soren says behind me.

I swear the air smells like saltwater and *rum*. There's even singing from somewhere nearby. The place is a mismatched ramshackle that reminds me of the harbor at Skull's Row, but more tropical.

I turn around when I hear a thumping on the ship, like a low drum coming from the very top, but it has to be the remaining men stomping their feet. Tempest begins her descent, wearing her leather long coat. A solid gold line is painted down her face in contrast against her dark skin. Quite a few pirates begin walking down the shoreline, hollering for her.

Her skull mask is at her hip, the design *so* different from Soren's or my dad's—the forehead is covered entirely in seamless gold, all pointing down to form the same golden line that's on her face. Shiny gold metal is perfectly painted on her lips, and also a solid, thick line around the eyes. When she gets closer, I can see that there are many ornate patterns, but they're all black, so the only smooth surface is where the metal cuts through.

Once ashore, she grins at her men. "We drink tonight! I have a feeling a hurricane is coming," she says grimly. "And if we're lucky, a god's coffers are up for pillaging."

Cheering erupts, many chatting with a camaraderie I do *not* see in the streets of home. Tempest strides away as many holler, her boots striking the wooden steps with purpose.

My body is sore from all the training, but I do feel stronger and more capable than before, even if my head still spins. I follow Tempest when I'm guided that way, Dad somewhere behind, along with Donna, Rorge, and his people.

"I think Jane has land legs," Soren says from behind me, although it's clear he's speaking to Tempest when she turns around and I stop, her dark gaze looking me over.

"I'll have someone bring you *leggings*."

"What?"

"It's what we call the tonic that will help," she says, pointing at my head, spinning her finger around. "You're wobbling. It happens to the best of us. It's hard transitioning from the motion of the ship to something stagnant. A shot of that will clear it up for you."

Without skipping a beat, she smoothly faces ahead again, guiding us through and away from the wharf. The salty tang of the air mingles with the richer, earthier scent of damp wood and the faint smokiness of torches burning in iron sconces once we're further inland. It's so humid, too, and I quickly miss the breeze that would frequent the deck.

To one side, a group of pirates huddle around a weathered table beneath an overhang, their laughter loud as they toss dice and slap down coins with calloused hands, all pausing to silence and lower their heads as Tempest passes. A parrot perched on the shoulder of one squawks something unintelligible and seems to mimic them, too.

Brightly colored sails are repurposed as awnings or hammocks, shading market stalls laden with exotic goods—gleaming pearls, polished bones carved into trinkets, and bottles of strange liquids, and even one woman is selling shriveled hands. Another vendor waves a stick of roasted meat through the air, the smell making my stomach grumble despite my nerves, desperate to eat *fresh* meat. Somewhere nearby, a blacksmith hammers at glowing metal with a rhythmic clang.

It never dawned on me that there would be an ecosystem of merchants here. I don't even really think I gave it much thought, to consider a kingdom belonging to *one* person.

Tempest doesn't pause for anything, weaving through the chaos with so much belonging that I cannot imagine living a life where *everyone* knows me, and they live on *my* land. I struggle to keep up, nearly tripping when I sidestep a burly pirate dragging a net filled with wriggling, silver-scaled fish. He grunts a half-apology before barking at a kid to haul over a barrel of salt.

The bustling life of Tempest's harbor finally fades as we climb a winding path toward the more wooded part of the island, the surrounding sand morphing slightly into soil around our walkway. Tempest points out a single-story shanty with a roof made of woven palm leaves and shutters painted a faded, peeling red. It's nestled among a cluster of similar homes, overlooking the sea from its perch on a rocky rise.

"There are nicely arranged shanties that way," she says, motioning with her hand. "It's where all your men can stay, Soren. Provisions will be provided. *This* home here will be for you and Miss Jane."

It's interesting that this time, there's no *need* for Soren and me to be housed together. I'm not his prisoner, nor his bounty. There's clearly space for us to have our own separate quarters and yet she's automatically pairing us together.

Clearly, I wouldn't have it any other way. I need that man's invasion of my heart at night to sleep soundly.

The door creaks open when she guides us in, revealing a sparsely furnished room with three hammocks strung on ceiling beams. A table dominates the opposite wall, its surface strewn with a scatter of crumpled maps, half-burnt candles, and empty bottles. The air is slightly musty but tolerable, the space dimly lit from the morning light that pours through the cracks of shuttered windows. Tempest steps inside and opens the shutters—no glass for the windows. "You'll want the hammocks to sleep in to help with the dizziness. A shot of *leggings* is already in place inside, the one with the green cork. We usually keep it here." She looks me up and down, smirking. "The pirate look works for you."

I stare after her as she leaves the shanty, the sound of her speaking to others getting drowned out the further she moves away from us. Behind me, Soren's voice cuts through my thoughts. "Are you alright to stay in here, by yourself? Everything about this island feels neutral to me, and while it's peaceful, I want to get things arranged."

I glance over my shoulder, managing a faint smile. "Of course. I'm just a little dizzy, like my legs can't catch any balance."

"It's why Skull's harbor is a clusterfuck of levels that all seem like they move. It's easier to walk on that than hard land." He leans forward to brush his lips against my forehead, more so my bandana, in a fleeting moment of tenderness. "I need to ensure everyone is settled properly. And the men need a proper moment of silence for those that died, probably a round of ale or rum. You can come to that, but you *should* rest for a moment and let that shot work. There will be a dozen of your father's men outside while I'm gone. He already agreed to it."

It's so odd to think my dad and Soren are talking about me when I'm not around, even arranging my safety. Just over two months ago, it was only Kathleen looking out for my shadow…

Gods that hits me hard.

I fucking miss her.

I nod at Soren, my smile lessening. "Yeah, go ahead. I'm going to drink that leg stuff and lie down in a hammock for a bit."

Soren hesitates, that space between words where something more might be spoken opening between us, but he turns to leave, his stride purposeful as the door swings shut behind him. I've gotten used to him needing to depart quickly, his people relying on his presence.

"We're at Stormbreak, but don't let down your guard," Soren says, and it's clear he's speaking to those who are stationed outside. *"Be as quiet as possible, so Jane can rest. The nights are about to become very long. My men will be here to rotate out with you shortly."* That's the last I hear of him as I spot Soren walking away through a crack in the shutters near the front.

The shanty settles into quietness as I'm left alone, save for the faint creak of wood expanding and contracting under the island's humidity.

Uncorking the bottle and downing the liquid in one go, my face scrunches and my body gives a little shudder, a sharp, earthy tang of crushed leaves, followed by a jarring spice that burns like fire—or what I *imagine* it feels like to be singed, now that I realize I'll never truly know. It's smoothed over by an unexpected creaminess, almost like milk, but it sure as hells won't be something I reach for frequently. Grimacing, I wipe my mouth with the back of my hand and sink into the nearest hammock. It sways gently as I let my body relax into it. Sure enough, the motion is quite soothing in comparison to a floor that seems far too stable.

I close my eyes, trying to ground myself. The dizziness slowly starts to ebb, my breathing slowing. When I open them again, the morning light has shifted, painting the room in streaks of amber and gray through the window Tempest opened, the one that overlooks the ocean.

A shadow flits across the wall, along with the sound of flapping, feathery wings.

I fall out of the hammock in a panic, landing only *slightly* gracefully. My heart races as black feathers flap fiercely inside the shanty. A raven banks a sharp left before landing on the table, its crimson eyes gleaming, unnaturally burning with intelligence.

I don't have enough time to register what I'm experiencing

before feathers dissolve into smoke, its body twisting, elongating, reforming into something altogether more human.

Cypress.

She settles into her form like she might if she were floating underwater, her black eyes teeming with unsettling, predatory energy. "Hello, Jane," she says, her voice carrying the faintest other-worldly echo.

Fuck.

IT'S TIME

JANE

"**W**hat are you *doing* in here? They'll be here any moment," I say through tight lips, glaring at the witch. My gaze shifts to the door, expecting the outside men to come barreling inside at any moment.

"Don't worry about them. They won't be aware of this meeting occurring. I'm sure you can guess why I'm here?"

My heart races, a sinking sensation pulling down on my stomach. It's more than obvious why she's here, but it also makes my blood fiercely pound through my veins. Everything has been *good*. My father is weirdly distant, but I feel peace now, like there's a real closure there. My heart burns for Soren in ways I didn't know it could. Bones is actually kind of funny, and Anya doesn't seem to hate me.

Things were looking *up.*

"I'm sure," I say, my soul saddened. So much can go so wrong with whatever she has planned. If she's here, then she suspects Misery is near, I bet. Or else why protect me, now?

A vigorous gust sweeps through the open window, fluttering the fabric of the hammocks and gently moving strands of my hair. The room actually darkens as Cypress's obsidian irises alter into shining black voids for eyes.

Once, that would have affected me greatly. It even did, back in the Undercroft.

The *show* has very little influence on me now, just wanting to get this over with.

Facing the witch, her eyes are already boring into me. "Well? Are you here to put something in my skin?"

Silence.

I glare at Cypress, and something hits me in the chest that tells me she will do whatever she wants, whether I like it or not. "Does it matter that we have a plan now?" I ask.

She tilts her head. "What kind of plan?"

I swallow thickly, rubbing my face as I say, "Shade, a gladiator from Skull's Row, was working for Misery. We interrogated him on Tempest's ship. He told us what Misery wants." I point at her. "Did you know he was after my skin? The magic in my veins? Oh, and they want to breed me. So that's fun."

The smallest smile tugs at her lips. "There is something special in your veins, my dear Jane. And don't worry about the latter; that will not happen. I do not foresee it in any of my visions."

"Well, still, I don't want to risk my *skin* getting used. Shade said Misery is growing really weak, and will need to go back to his lands soon. So we're just going to wait him out."

The small smile slowly unfurls into a larger one. "You cannot wait Misery out. What will happen is he will grow more tenacious and risky. Which means *lives*, Jane. Blackwell originally sending Soren for you was Misery's first attempt to have you. He did not take you then and there because it would have been hard to leave the harbor without many following. In numbers, Misery does not have strength. Not in the Balar Coasts. Not in his current state.

"Misery *was* planning to attack Rosmertta's, because he was running out of time. And now that you wasted two more weeks on that ship, he is willing to use what remaining influence he has to take you in whatever way deems necessary." She raises a brow. "The remaining power he has can wipe out everyone at this camp before they know it."

"He'd have to get here first."

Anything recognizable as human is gone from her face. "He already is."

My head juts out slightly, a hand rising to my chest as if I felt her steal the air from my lungs. "He *what*?"

"As I said, he will use everything he has right now. You do not want him to be able to read your heart or soul if he's near you. Silence will be your greatest shield."

A sickening sensation twists my heart at realizing how deep this failure is. "How did he get here? How does Tempest not sense him?"

"If I had to guess, he's draining his followers until their life is gone. It's potent, but taxing. He will need significant rest after this. I only know he's here because I'm keeping the closest eye on him."

"He can't sense you?"

"I'm using my own sacrifices to ensure that's true," she grimly replies.

That bleak reality momentarily settles on me, truly hearing what she just meant. "What if I refuse?"

"Then I will do this to you while you're unconscious." Her abject gaze holds no space for *any* remorse.

"We seriously can't try to outrun him?" I cannot believe I bought into that plan with such confidence, only for it to turn to smoke.

"Not when he is already here."

"No—I just… It doesn't feel right just letting you do this. This isn't right. *None* of it is."

I want to yell. What if I screamed as loudly as possible? Would it be worth it? Could Soren hear me, then? Anyone, other than Cypress?

I don't fully hear her when she says Misery is *here*. Honestly, it sounds like a fucking lie to me. Sure, if he showed up on that shoreline outside my window, I might tell her just get it done with because I'll take *anything* I can get to fight him.

Soren. There's regret now, in not telling him. And yet my mind screams it wouldn't have made a difference. How can *they* stop Cypress?

I'm about to bolt for the door, the trust issues returning as all I know is I'm being *used.*

Moving my knees to lift my feet—they're stuck.

What the—

Shit.

Rubies climb up my legs through the floor, stopping at my calves, bolting me to the shanty.

My racing heart mixes with my panting breath, glancing between her and the door. "You're offering me to him, aren't you?" I ask with more panic than I'd like in my voice, nearly falling over when my balance is off, but I can't move my feet to counter.

"Jane, if you're in an alley that only has two exits with no other way to escape... and at one end lies your freedom, while the other contains your mother's killer before he reaches your home all those years ago, which would you choose?"

All movements cease and my breathing becomes shallow as I glare at her. "Don't use my family like this."

She nods. "I'll answer for you. You'd choose the killer, to stop him from getting to your mother." She holds up a hand when she senses my protest. "I truly do admit that these circumstances *are* different. They are much more akin to you seeing your mother's killer and having no idea what he is about to do. You'd choose freedom without question, as any sane person would."

Out of everything she's said so far, this holds my attention the most.

Cypress rises to her feet, mine still stuck in gemstones. "I am going to go ahead and perform this act, seeing as how I do not believe you will trust me to be honest—and no need for guilt for not sharing this, as I asked. You know why you didn't, and it's not because you're being a hero." She walks to my backside, my jaw trembling from how anxious I am. "Your father made the exact same deal to save your life. If it makes you feel any better, if you had told any of them the truth, I would have removed you from them immediately."

She pushes my head down, my body shaking when that barrier

between us is broken. Her power behind me, even if it's unseen, is almost as palpable as being drowned in mist.

"I'm aware Soren didn't press you further, either. Do you think that wasn't for a reason?"

"He said he didn't feel like he should, and... I dropped it after that. He left it up to me." I'm about to become incensed if this turns out to have been a poor decision.

"Because the fates told him not to, through his powers. His moment of action is not yet to come, and to know would have ruined what he *will* do. The actions he will take that will benefit us all the most."

Soren... she's using him, too.

She prods at my hairline at the nape of my neck, and holy shit do I just want this over with. "I will numb what I can, but I am putting a ruby directly underneath your skin. You will then reach back and heal it. It will block the ability for anyone to sense you, and will kill you if removed—" she places a hand on my head to keep me from rising, the back of my thighs straining with how I'm holding myself up at this slight lean "—which has a purpose of preventing Morvock from doing so himself."

"Did—did you just say it would kill me? Why couldn't you share those details *before hand!*"

Ignoring me, she places something cold on my skin. I feel the slicing of flesh, my shoulders tensing as my mouth opens in a silent scream; I'm more terrified of the unknown than the pain. The slight numbness has the unsettling feeling of frostbitten metal in winter. It's when she shoves something under my skin that the pain is so unnerving I want to vomit, the sensation beyond violating as the foreign object presses on nerves that radiate all through my shoulders. I can't help it when I jerk away, to which she doesn't stop me, because, well, I don't have anywhere to go.

"You can heal it now."

Well... do I feel anything? Any sense of mind control from Cypress? A warm wetness at the back of my neck tells me I need to heal my wound.

Cypress grins with utter triumph. "I can't feel you at all."

The rubies rescind down into the floor like spores withering away, and I stumble over until I catch myself on the table, my palm slamming into the edge. Reaching back, my fingertips graze against a lump under my skin, to which I swiftly pull my hand away, disturbed by the sensation. "What do you mean *you* can't feel it? It's *your* magic! Did something go wrong?"

"I have been working on that stone in particular for over five years now. I wanted it so strong that even *I* couldn't sense it."

My stomach drops, not ready to heal the skin and sew it in. "You can get it out, right?"

"Yes, of course. I would guard that spot with your life, though. There's no question that if another tries to do so, you will instantly die, like taking your heart from your ribs. The process to harvest your skin will require your heart still beating, right up until you drink a potion that keeps your skin fresh for an entire cycling of the sun and moon… but he can't use that until you are in his lands, and they're currently unreachable until the next solar eclipse, which happens to be three weeks from now."

I hold my hands out, my left one bloodied. "That is *incredibly* relevant information. You seriously didn't fucking tell us that before *now?*"

Her words of warning lodge into my brain, and even then, I can't quite *comprehend* them. That if I were to give myself to Misery and do *nothing*, that he'd actually use me and my body to create a really fucked up re-birth. It's almost like being afraid of sharks but still on land—the threat is so far away that it's negligible. Hearing it from Shade was unnerving, but having *her* confirm it brings a new reality to it.

I really do have to fight a *god*.

"Heal your neck, Jane."

I feel gross. Like I let her do something to me that I'm embarrassed to admit, and the thought of sealing it in myself is almost too much.

"*Jane*," she presses, her thin brow perching.

"What if you can't get it out?"

"Does it matter? Are you willing to risk the lives of those you love over that stone?"

Fucking bitch. I bet she can't get it out. I bet, after all of this, I'll be stuck like this, because why would she care? As long as her god gets what he wants, why would she?

Too late now.

Probably better to heal it rather than risk it falling out and killing me—what a stupid death that would be. I place my hand on the back of my neck with such aggression I nearly smack myself, sending healing energy into the wound while closing my eyes.

My hand flops down to my side once the deed is done, and I sigh. "Can you at least tell me why he wants *me*? Shade said there was a reason. There's something about *me*. Even you said there's something in my blood."

Her eyes look comforting, but in a way that only makes me feel worse about myself. It's like the act is very foreign and uncomfortable for her. "You will find out in due time. I promise, for what it's worth, that this is all to help you. The less he can feel you, the more freedom you'll have if you're near him. The less you know, the more he can't use your mind against you." She inhales deeply and slowly looks out the window. "If I exposed the details of what I see is likely to happen, it would ruin your behavior too greatly. And that behavior, as I see it now, is what will allow you to survive.

"There is *one* thing I can tell you, though—" my gaze hones in on her, and I don't even blink "—once he has you, as he is *close*, your goal from then on out is to free the sirens."

My lips part, only for a sad exhale to leave them. "Is that code for something else?"

"I won't say more. I can't," she says, shaking her head. "I know that's frustrating. Right now, what I see for you is if I don't reveal more, you will have the best chance to derail Misery so greatly that he will make severe mistakes. And freeing the sirens is like opening up a massive hole in the bottom of a ship in an open ocean—it will be only a matter of time before it sinks. Your role is to create that opening that will sink Misery and all of his plans, and *no one* else can do it but you."

A glance at the entrance is like tempting a drowning man with fresh air. I want to bolt, *so* badly. What if she's full of shit?

I hesitate to move… what if she's *not*?

"I struggle to believe you," I say, looking at the floor. "Because I'm not an idiot, and I'm not driven by ego, Cypress. I know that it's not right for *me* to be chosen."

There's a long pause from her, long enough that when I glance up, she truly seems deep in thought. "You are the only one, Jane, with skin that cannot burn and a magic that *is* useful. *And* Misery *cannot* kill you." She shrugs, but it's more out of pity than to mock me. "Mix that with your temperament, your motives, those that surround you... it's a web of the fates that I *cannot* describe to someone who can't see it.

"It's time for me to go, though. You will have until this hourglass drops its last piece of sand before Soren will realize something is wrong, and he *will* immediately seek you out. If that happens, then he will become calamity in Misery's wrath." Onyx eyes connect with mine as she pulls out an hourglass as tall as my hand, made of gold. Her shoulders rise and fall with a sigh as she places it on the table, turning it over so the red stand starts to trickle down. "Yes... I think I will tell you this, too... Morvock is Soren's god."

My lips wordlessly part, my blinks slow. "He's *what?*"

"When gods exist, their powers can sometimes enter this realm. Oftentimes through us mortals that can use that god's powers. Morvock has relinquished his *true* title as a god and would rather rule here as a god emperor. Sensors have an origin in something much darker than being an empath... the entire point of this, Jane, is that Morvock has the ability to completely break Soren without much effort, even if their connection is severely broken. Soren *cannot* be near him if you want him to live, and *that's* why he could never know what's about to happen. I couldn't tell you earlier, because I bet he'd sense that within you." The witch stands, some sympathy in her eyes. "What happens next is entirely up to you."

The witch morphs, like scrunching up a blanket into a ball, except she's a collection of feathers until a raven's shape is clear, the bird taking flight out the open window.

My neck starts to hurt, like a deep scratch once the soreness sets in.

I immediately begin to feel wrong, as if I cheated on Soren, knowing if he barges in right now, he won't be able to feel me, and that I know of his god. What will Soren do when he finds out what has happened here? It's not like I can just let him open me up and read how my intentions are genuine. How I was afraid of what Cypress would do if others intervened, and how apparently, I *can't* let him near me.

Perhaps, more than anything, my inaction stems from… well, maybe some part of me *wanted* this.

This is *my* revenge.

My father and Soren… they're both important people *no one* crosses without watching their backs. I know damn well they'd do anything to have an advantage in a battle, no matter the cost to themselves, so why can't I?

The red sand builds the smallest mound at the bottom.

Well, shit, where do I go? What do I do? Can I run to Soren and tell him everything? Can I possibly tell him of what I learned, and make him promise to just walk the fuck away? Tell him who his god is, and explain that *that's* why he can't be near me?

No, he would never allow that.

Nearing the window, all I see is a calm ocean, the sound of the waves so innocuous.

I glance back at the hourglass before surveying the shanty, everything eerily *still*, except for the small stream of sand. Tapping my hand on the wooden sill, I give a scoffed laugh. "Okay… so, uh, what now?"

My eyes shoot wide open when I think I hear something.

Sticking my head out the window, the faint hum in the air comes from the jungle nearby, when it's now clear that what I hear is the sound of sirens singing in the distance…

INTO THE JUNGLE
JANE

Gently placing my hand on the rough wood, I hold my breath, angling my head slightly to hear better. The song of sirens is absolutely out there, and as I slowly peer through the window, I swear that rather than coming from the ocean, it's coming from the *jungle.*

I know that's not right. My stomach drops, like someone trying to outrun a tiger only to realize they've been hunted across an entire ocean.

How the fuck is he here? Already?

There's no way this isn't *not* Misery's doing.

My feet are immobile, wanting to run to my father and demand he tell me *everything.* I want to know about Cypress, about what he really thinks—wait. *That's* what I want; I want to make an *informed* decision.

Cypress is the opposite of clarity. I still can't shake that it seems like I'm being tricked into this, that she's leading me astray on purpose.

As if having someone tap on my shoulder, I sharply steal a glance at the hourglass; it's over halfway filled. My heart races with anxiety. What if I choose not to go? Would Soren truly fall that easily to Misery?

No. Why am I even willing to risk that? Misery wants *me.* Clearly, he's not going to kill me. Not right away.

Okay, what do I fear about going, other than the obvious?

I cant my head, as if conceding to a point; I fear that being taken means everyone here will overreact and suffer in an attempt to come for me.

Or that I'm being influenced by bravado and not logic.

The sand... make a decision.

"Okay," I say to myself, my voice shaking. "Let's just climb out the window. Start there."

The idea of leaving without any note of explanation sounds like a terrible fate to deliver to my father or Soren; rushing over to the table, I find that it actually has a very worn quill and barely any ink left. On the back of a map I don't bother to look at, I begin penning my farewell note.

At least this might give them some peace in knowing why I chose this.

Signing my name is... odd. Heavy. Like I just realized what I committed to. I glance down at my thigh, pulling out the rose dagger. I hold it in my hands, taking in the beautiful design.

He gave this to me thinking I'd be with them at all times, not taken. Like fucking hells I'll let them lose this. They'll strip it off me as soon as they've got ropes on my wrist, and probably toss it into the ocean.

No time to look at it any longer.

I place it beside the note, repositioning it a few times, wondering if I should add anything about why I'm leaving the blade. But it seems obvious, especially since I asked about it already.

The singing grows louder.

I feel rushed, like I need to evacuate but don't have anything ready.

GO!

I rush to the window, climbing out as my knees scrape against the shanty until I'm dangling. I release my grip and land with ease, moving to the jungle almost right away.

The single action has my heart racing and breaking all at once, just like the letter. What if this doesn't have a happy ending? What if I lose everyone? What if I never get to say goodbye?

Soren will be coming back to an empty room.

Fuck.

That hurts.

So then destroy them for doing this to everyone. This isn't your doing.

I'm breathing rapidly, stopping just near the outline of the trees and underbrush, the ethereal music of the sirens making it seem like I'm hallucinating.

Glancing back at the shanty shows a bunch of guards lying on the ground. *Fuck.*

Something in that solidifies this for me. Those are my *father's* men. *My* people, in one way or another. Even if they're just temporarily incapacitated, they're caught up in the whirlpool of my life.

Why the fuck would I let others sacrifice themselves to protect me like this? I'll kill myself before Misery has a chance to actually use my body. And I know that if we *all* take him on, so many more will die. Especially if Cypress is right, and Misery is Soren's *true* weakness.

I can get close, though. I *will* be close.

He needs me willing, right?

I'm not just some maiden who needs protection. I'm literally the daughter of a revered Zenith, with the skull tattoo on my own chest. This might be unfair, but it is what it is. Misery is hunting me, which means that at some point, we *will* clash.

I stare at the damp soil beneath my feet, then at the big leafy plants casting dark shadows without a care in the world.

"My men have someone to think about when they die... I'd like that."

I smile as tears blur my vision.

At least I have people to think about.

Go. It's either you, or Soren. He cannot confront Misery, and if Cypress is right, then that god is in this jungle. Soren still has his sister to see. Don't risk that.

Perhaps I'm an idiot, but the idea of that man dying for me threatens my sanity like nothing else ever has. Him not existing, on my behalf, feels like someone is genuinely ripping a part of my heart out.

I take a single step closer to the jungle, having to push a leaf the size of my arm out of the way, hardly blinking as I peer into the verdant underbrush. I knew how to numb it all in Coalfell, having learned the art of detachment among those coal miners.

I will do it here.

Stepping through the cracks of twigs underneath, I'm reminded why I hate the forests—so many things hide in here that I can't see. At least in the streets, I know the nooks and crannies, and that my biggest threat is a human.

Every minute sound out here is so foreign to me, even the damn squirrels scraping their sharp claws on the bark. That's not even addressing the many weird noises coming from the canopies, or the echoing *hoots* and animal sounds along the branches.

I've never heard so much life yet felt so alone.

My body freezes mid-movement, even my fingers that are stuck in a partial grasp of a branch I was reaching for—there are people up ahead, all silent and looking around. Dressed in leathers, weapons, and cotton tunics.

I immediately recognize Blackwell among them.

Oh that *fucker*, I want to rush over there and stab him in the eyes for killing Maryanne.

But there's a hooded figure among them, who is facing me, and he makes every ounce of my blood run cold. The sound of sirens emanates from that circle—with absolutely no sirens present—the singing dying down until there's nothing left but the jungle's ambiance.

I consider bolting back, calling for Cypress before bringing Dad or Soren into this. At the same time, if there are things Cypress can do that not even Soren or my father can fight, what would challenging *Misery* be like for them? What could *he* do?

He's fucking staring right at me.

I glare at the nearly black void that he creates, as if the sun avoids touching him, those orange circles clearly his eyes.

One by one, the others all turn to face me. Blackwell has a primal look on his ugly face. "Ah, well, she seems to have listened to the siren's singing."

I lick my lips, tasting salt and dirt. Bitterness creeps up my throat as if I ate a rotten apple, but I move forward nonetheless. It's not as terrifying to be upon them as I thought it would be; it just feels like fate.

Like we all knew this would happen.

"I hear you want me," I state.

The hood gives a single nod, creepy dark fingers tightening their grip on the wooden staff he holds. It's almost uncomfortable to look at the gnarled heartwood, like the thing gives off a manifestation of sorrow and despair.

I observe it, forcing myself to learn as many details as possible— what looks like old runes are carved into the black stained wood, and at its crown is a twisted knot that grips around what looks like a black stone the size of my fist; it reminds me of flint.

I decide then and there that I fucking hate anything related to the gods, or their magic. It doesn't matter if they think our lives don't matter; we *do*.

My mother did.

Soren's sister *does*.

I take another step, this time with more confidence.

Blackwell nears me as well, rubbing his hands together, then looks at who has to be Misery. "Is she alone?" he asks.

"No," the hooded figure croaks out, his voice emanating as if his mouth were the depths of a cave that his words echo from. I fail to hide my disgust at the thought of *him* skinning me alive to use my flesh to don anything that remotely resembles humanity.

Then it sinks in.

I'm not alone?

My heart drops, and I turn around, skimming for the forests. I don't even care if I give them my back or vulnerability.

Who is it?

There's a scuffle a few feet over in the underbrush, and I see some men stand and skirmish as another—female?—lets out a muffled grunt. Then, the men start dragging someone into the woods.

These seconds are painfully long as I wait to see who they pull through… Anya.

No.

Does that mean that Soren is nearby? If he is, there's no reality where he wouldn't barrel through these woods to help—I'm about to scream, but that's when I'm tackled like when I first met the Zenith; my body hits the ground so hard I scrape the dirt with my teeth, the air in my lungs expelled from the weight of whoever is on top of me.

My instincts scream to fight back, to kick. To curse at them as if it's the only words I know. As I struggle while they bind my hands with rope, I can tell I've changed.

I already know how I will play this one.

I let them bind me how they see fit. Let them think that they have the upper hand. I learned a lot when being Soren's little pet, and now I know how to *truly* submit—there's no threat of saving lives now. If anything, submission will save lives.

So I can burn it.

Burn them all.

I hear someone near me, I can *sense* him, too. Dirty, worn boots are in my peripheral while someone continues to pin me down. A tattered cloak enters my vision, the energy from him emanating in ways that make Cypress look like a child playing at gods.

"Cypress has meddled with her," he states, his staff shifting its imprint in the ground.

"How?" Blackwell asks.

"I cannot feel her."

His staff lifts and presses against my cheek to hold my face into the dirt floor. I almost want to laugh at how utterly unafraid I am to die. There's a sense of being whole now, knowing my father is still out there, and that he didn't abandon me. That Kathleen is my friend, and that Soren showed me I can love myself and the violence within.

"What did she do to you?" he asks.

"I'm not answering that," I reply.

Anya is chucked to my side, grunting through the cloth tied around her mouth.

"Antony, examine what is at her neck. Something that doesn't belong to her is there. There area is stained with poison."

The sound of someone nearing me precedes the sudden sensation of being touched, and I hate myself for flinching when he does. "There's a lump. Something hard in there."

"Answer me," Misery grates. "Or we will force-feed your friend's heart to you as it still beats."

"There's a ruby in there," I admit without hesitation. "If you take it out, Cypress said it would kill me. Instantly. So… please don't."

Everyone is so still they might as well be statues, until Misery's staff is lifted off my cheek. "Turn her over," the god commands.

I'm violently flipped over by what appears to be Blackwell. Misery peers down at me, my eyes widening in absolute terror when I meet his gaze this close.

I can't see anything other than two tiny glowing circles, the color of a burning sunset. "Your lover is an offshoot of the powers I harbor," he says, lowering his head. "Of the powers I *give*. He's a bastardization of my magic but, admittedly, talented. Just like Cypress is to her god. Whatever she has done to you, I *will* undo. And Soren cannot save you. Not with *me* around."

I'm honestly terrified looking at him, nearly wincing when I swear I see the outline of his face. But the thought of what he has planned for me makes me fight. I don't respond and simply stare him down. *Get used to him.*

Blackwell asks, "*You're* the god that gives Soren his powers?" His voice is full of absolute awe, almost like he learned the funniest thing about someone.

Well, it seems Cypress wasn't lying about that.

"I *was*," Misery answers. "In this mortal state of mine, his powers will take on a mind of their own." The staff hits the ground near my head, and I flinch. "Render her and the other incapacitated. I want to move quickly. We will examine what Cypress has put into her skin when she is unconscious."

"There's no need—"

It's all black.

NOT AGAIN

SOREN

The rum burns as it slides down my throat, a poor distraction for the sense of wrongness clawing at my gut. The communal space buzzes with quiet murmurs and laughter, but it all feels distant, muffled—until the unease blooms into something sharper. Something visceral.

The glass tumbles from my hand as I stand abruptly, scanning the room for something I can't name. *Jane.*

Ritter catches my movement, his sharp eyes narrowing. "What is it?"

I don't answer him. My chest tightens as I close my eyes, reaching for the faint thread that connects me to her—the tether that exists with or without our consent. *It's quiet. Too quiet.* The world narrows, and all I hear is my heart pounding like war drums in my ears.

"*Jane*," I murmur, barely audible. My voice grows louder, rising like a storm. "Jane."

Ritter is on his feet in an instant, following me as I tear out of the space. The humid air slams into me like a wall, my boots digging against the dirt as I make for the shanty where she should be. Where she *has* to be.

But it's wrong. Everything about this is wrong.

The building feels like a corpse, hollow and dead. The space where Jane's presence should light up like a beacon is nothing but emptiness.

"No," I whisper, shaking my head. The pressure in my chest is unbearable now.

Not again. Not this.

"JANE!" My voice scratches against my throat as I roar her name. The sound bounces off the nearby structures, mocking me with its void. I rush forward, nearly tripping over a body sprawled in the dirt; one of Ritter's men. He doesn't move. Another lies close by, their faces slack in unconsciousness—or worse.

I don't stop to check. My boot splinters the door as I crash through, frantically scanning the room.

Empty.

My breathing is ragged, my hands trembling from fear and rage as I search the space, trying to reclaim any inkling of her aura.

"No, no, no…" The words spill from my lips like a prayer to the fucking gods who never listen.

Ritter steps in behind me, his presence as heavy as an anchor. "Where is my *daughter*?" His voice is low, dangerous.

I don't answer him. My eyes fall to the floor—and freeze. Blood.

I drop to my knees, touching the dark stain. It's dry. Old. My heart lurches as I close my eyes, forcing myself to feel for something, *anything*. But the energy is blocked, like a severed limb.

"There's an obstruction," I whisper, more to myself than Ritter.

"Where is my *daughter!*" Ritter snarls, his own desperation cracking through his stoic mask.

I rise on unsteady legs, my gaze snapping to the window. Something pulls me there, a shadow of an instinct that refuses to let me rest. I stagger outside through the front door, my chest heaving as I glance at the ground.

"Footprints," I say hoarsely, pointing to the faint marks in the dirt.

Ritter crouches down, his face pale. "One set."

One set.

It makes no sense. Why would she leave?

Why would she leave me?

My breath comes in sharp, shallow bursts as the tracks lead toward the dense jungle. The air feels heavier here, oppressive, like the very trees mock my every step. There's no trace of Anya either, who I told to keep watch, for *my* sake.

"Round everyone up," I growl, my voice raw with fury and anguish. My hand falls to the hilt of my sword, fingers curling around it like a lifeline. "I'm going to look for her."

"*Soren*," Ritter says, his voice tight with warning, but I don't stop.

My mind screams with images of Jane—her laugh, her auburn hair splayed on the pillow when she sleeps, her fire that I use to keep myself warm inside—all slipping through my fingers like sand. The jungle swallows me whole as I plunge into its depths, the weight of failure and fear dragging me down like I exist within an abyss.

I can't lose her. Not her, too.

Not again.

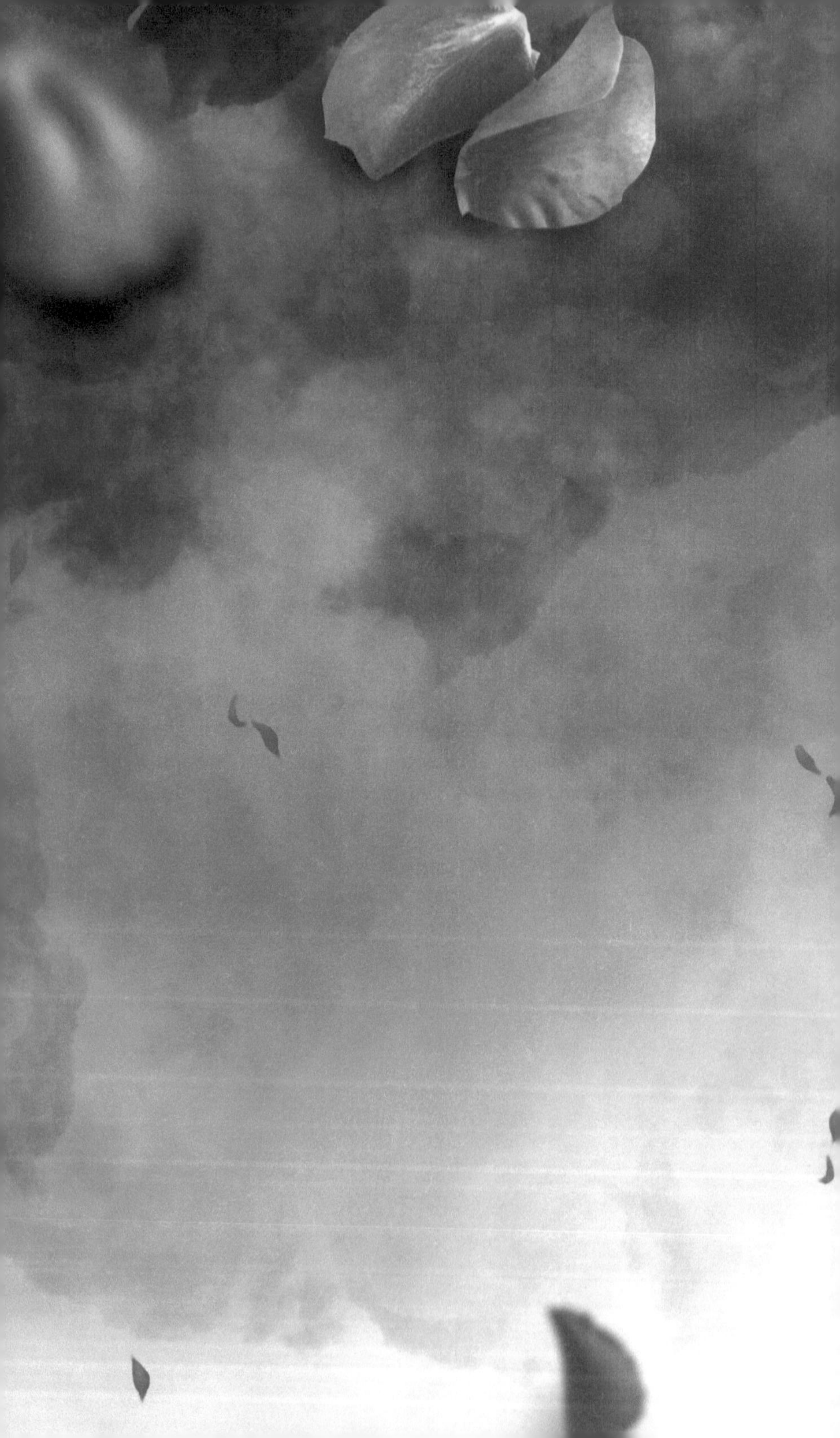

HOSTAGE AGAIN

JANE

For a fleeting moment, there's peace.

Then, my body aches, my head pounds, and I'm aware of the rhythmic sway beneath me. A rocking motion. Gentle, almost soothing—if it weren't for the stench of sweat mingling with the salt in the air.

When I crack open my eyes further, the peace shatters.

The ocean. Sea Wolf. Skull's Row. Dad. Soren. My breath quickens as I glance around, taking in faces I've never seen before. My racing pulse makes my head pound. Anya is on the other end of the boat with a gag still in her mouth, her eyes squinting against the glare of the sun.

I press my lips together; no gag. I jiggle my wrists, but they're bound. I swear to the gods if—my movement stops when I spot the

297

blue tattoos on my wrists. *Gods. Magic.* Is *mine* actually out there, somewhere? Does it even matter? I don't remember the goddess's name.

And how useful is a healing deity in times like this?

"Where are we?" I croak out, struggling to focus.

I'm so tired of waking up parched. Just because I didn't want to live in a pacifist's village, doesn't mean I wanted *this.*

Blackwell leans over me, smug as always, his scruff thicker than when I last saw him. "Your man isn't here for your salvation," he sneers before leaning back to pivot on his bench seat to face Anya, who glares at him with a burning defiance. "Nor is he here for you," he taunts. "Don't even know why he has you. You're quite easy to overpower."

Anya lunges at him, although it goes nowhere with how bound she is, her ropes tied to hooks in this longboat. Blackwell backhands her, the boat rocking with the action as Anya bleeds from a busted lip, staining the gag.

For one, terrible second, my mind flashes to wondering if that's how I looked when Soren first took me. What the hells am I going to do with Anya? She wasn't supposed to be here. This plan required that I go by *myself,* so I didn't have to worry about others.

I try to see if we are far from land—a small part of me hoping we only just left. That maybe we can still be saved.

Blackwell sighs as he reaches into a pouch, pulling out a small, opaque vial and shakes it lightly, meeting my gaze. "Misery wants you knocked out until we land, but with *this.*" He leans over to dangle it in my face. "Open up, you need to consume it."

I barely manage the smallest struggle before my shoulders are held down by someone behind me, Blackwell pinching my nose until I take a breath, draining a liquid into my mouth as I choke on it.

Within a few more moments, I'm out again.

❖

I WAKE up to being chucked onto hard sand. Pain radiates from every bruise and cut that covers my body. After a few gritty bites, I decide that I prefer dirt in my mouth. Hands yank me to my feet. My legs tremble beneath me, barely able to hold my weight. A shove sends me stumbling forward.

My head must have been hit hard the first time they knocked me out, because I seem to forget about my plan and throw a kick as hard as I can behind me in a moment of lucid movement; a real nice donkey kick. My foot collides hard with someone—Blackwell—and he falls square on his ass. Anya moans through her gag as she's shoved onto land, as if to tell me to quit.

The men around laugh.

I spit on the ground to get the sand out of my mouth. "Stop fucking being rough with me. I'm clearly not fighting you."

Blackwell's eyes flare as he stands, his jaw tightening, wiping the sand off of his body as he glares at me like he did when he ordered Maryanne to be burned—cold, calculated, and cruel.

The transition from him trying to collect himself to beating the shit out of me occurs within seconds.

The agony is a blur as adrenaline kicks in like an old friend to numb the rest of the assault, hitting, slapping, punching, or shoving me into the sand. Without my hands, I can only do so much to defend myself. What hurts the worst is when his knee collides with my stomach *just* right, dropping me to my knees as I struggle to breathe.

"*Enough,*" Misery commands.

Pain morphs into delirium as I slump over, adrenaline not strong enough of a drug. It aches so much deeper than the skin, my heart hurting just to beat. I'm hauled up and carried like dead weight for a long time while fading in and out of consciousness, the world darkening around me.

Eventually, I'm thrown onto the ground again; this time, it's dirt. There seem to be more people, and some horses, but that's all I can register.

Someone's boot presses into my shoulder to turn me onto my back. The sky above looks like it might beckon the night soon. The bindings around my wrist are cut, and I inhale sharply, my hands held out like I'm not sure what to do with them. *I can't think, and all I taste is blood and dirt.* Blackwell's ugly face enters my line of vision, leaning down over me. "Not able to handle the pain? You want to be a part of Skull's Row *so badly,*" he says, spitting on my chest. "Disappointing, really. Your father must be so disappointed with how weak you are." My eyes widen, and I try to focus on Blackwell, but he continues to blur, my head still spinning. "His daughter is *so* disappointing."

The pain in my soul is fleeting when I can't even remember why I'm here, breathing heavily as I just lie there.

"Heal yourself before we move further."

I struggle to move my neck, but force myself so I can locate Anya. I don't know what happened, but she looks worse than when she was on the boat.

Things blend and fade together, and the next thing I am aware of is a woman hovering over me with tattoos on her forehead and chin, one hand on either side of my skull until clarity returns. I almost regret this because I'm more aware of the pain, *everything* aching like I fell over the Sea Wolf and smacked right into the water's surface.

The more I feel, the more I groan.

I move my head so I can find—there she is; Anya lies there with labored breathing, all by herself. I feel an immense sense of gratitude that I'm not alone, all the while being wracked with guilt that she's enduring whatever the hells is happening to us.

As soon as I'm able to move to my knees, I push the healer off of me to crawl over to Anya, leaning down next to her. Glancing around, I try to understand where I'm at—we're in some wooded area again, and this reminds me a little more of what Coalfell looked like.

Not helpful at all.

Focusing back down on Anya, her nose, lips, and chin are stained in blood, and her usual stoic eyes are enraged and swollen, her gag now out and dangling around her neck. "Heal *yourself.*"

"You need some, too," I breathlessly say, squinting from the splitting headache.

I want to ask Anya so many questions that she'd probably bite me to get me to shut up. I know that we're being watched, but what the hells is she doing here? A quick glance tells me that Misery stares at us through the impending darkness that dusk brings, the flickering glow of his eyes emanating like a wick of a candle that picks up steam.

Gods I can't wait to kill him.

And I'm really fucking happy he can't feel that from me.

Anya's breathing evens out as I focus on healing her chest, her ribs giving off the sensation of being broken; I can feel a fractured energy in my palms. Well what the fuck do I do with her here? Where is *my* plan in all of this? I know I came here for a reason, but honestly, I had to see the lay of the land before concocting a *real* strategy. Something that is much harder to do when I'm constantly drugged to sleep.

According to Cypress, I have to free the sirens, and I don't even know what that means.

And what will Soren think when he realizes Anya is missing, too? Will he blame me? I can't lose Anya, not on my watch.

⟡

THE ROUGH BARK of the tree digs into my back as I sit against it, bound once more. I tilt my head back, staring up at the night sky through the dense web of branches; my body is a mess, and the humidity just makes it all worse with how sticky I am. Anya sits next to me, our shoulders pressed together—a small anchor in this oppressive darkness.

Beyond us, a campfire crackles and pops, twisting smoke coiling into the air. Its amber glow is like an island of camaraderie we're deliberately being kept away from, the men's shadow stretching and elongating on the jungle floor.

Around the camp, totems stand tall, their crude carvings casting jagged silhouettes against the trees. Misery can apparently creep on the energies around us with it, like Cypress can with her rubies.

So far, I've been rather quiet and compliant, observing. Misery doesn't move much, like a hawk perching and *watching*. Blackwell commands the space when the miserable god is stagnant, and it's clear that man enjoys his title; always laughing at his own jokes, telling people he'll consider their words like he's granted them a gift, and orders people around as if it's obvious he wouldn't lift a finger.

My focus veers to watching the man that is on guard duty for the two of us. I've overheard that we're a day's ride away from Ashfire, the castle for the Order of Ash, which means Anya and I sit here like prisoners.

An idea begins to bloom as I try to think of a way to be alone with Anya, even for a moment. I've been watching this man closely, noting his every movement, every nervous tick. He's squeamish—I can use that.

My heart races, hoping this will work—just as I'm about to enact my plan, the guard rises. "I'm going to get Benny. You both smell like shit."

Well, I was about to piss myself, but apparently our stench already does the job. So far, I've taken to soiling what I wear rather than letting anyone near me. The more feral, the better.

And there's no way I'm undressing regularly in front of them.

I lean closer to Anya, and she acts like she might scoot away. "No, stop. I need to talk to you," I say, knowing that at any moment, someone else will be out here. "Why are you here? What happened?"

Anya sighs with annoyance and leans in quickly, as if admitting that yes, this is an opportune moment to speak. She's so close to my ear it feels moist. "First, you stink. Secondly, I have a piece of Soren's mask embedded in my skin. He can track me. Same with Bones. He got the idea when he learned of your father's ring," she whispers, her voice so low it's almost drowned out by the jungle sounds. "I mean, honestly, I don't know if it works or not. We haven't tried it before. But I thought it was worth it, rather than have you be taken without a single tracing effect."

My eyes widen with understanding. "He sent you?"

"No. I came on my own. Would have yelled for help, but they would have been gone by then with Misery. Thought it was worth the risk. They always need prisoners when looking for collateral." There's a pause before she adds, "You need to leave at any chance you get."

I begin to shake my head but stop when I realize I might smack into her face with how close we are. "Not without you."

She pulls back slightly, the faint warmth of her breath replaced by the cooler, damp air of the jungle. "You idiot, I'm doing this for Soren," she says sharply, her words cutting like a knife through the dense night. "Don't waste my efforts on some noble gesture."

"I'm not just running away and leaving you," I assert, my body stiffening when I see someone look our way.

In the distance, I hear a shout, "Leave 'em and let's eat! Just keep an eye on 'em. What's the worst they can do?"

She leans back in, still speaking quietly. "I'm *capable*, Jane. I can escape when I need to. You know that." I get the tone that she's trying to say things without explicitly saying them.

Skin shifter.

"What are your plans if you're not rescued for a few *months*?" she asks.

I examine her face. In the dim light, her skin is pale and drawn, a sharp contrast to the dark swelling around her left eye. The blood-shot whites brutalize her injury further.

"Cypress told me it will only be a few weeks. She gave me a *task*, and I'm going to do it." My voice falters for a moment before I continue, quieter this time. "I don't want to sit and hope. I didn't come to be rescued."

"Then spend this time plotting."

The camp near us is alive with the sound of laughter and coarse jokes as the men feast, ripping chunks of meat from the spits. The grease drips onto the fire, hissing and spitting with each drop, sending curls of black smoke into the humid air. In the shadows, Misery sits apart from the others, those spying candle eyes locked onto us.

"I will. I'm observing as much as I can," I say.

"Well, do it quickly, before Soren burns these people down. I want to ensure they're *ruined*."

How badly I want that.

It might be for the best if he does that, and not just for me. How long can Anya's beating heart be useful to them? Other than function as blackmail against me? Killing her would be extremely standard practice, once she becomes just another mouth to feed.

"You don't think I'm stupid for walking into this?" I ask.

Her sighs carry a lot of unspoken opinions. "Not with what I overheard. Not if Misery is Soren's god. He would have died, I'm certain of it."

I look back up at the stars once more, the anxiety that I chose poorly greatly easing.

How does Soren do any of this? Manage the weight of everyone's lives against his decisions? One wrong move, and *poof*—everyone is dead.

He's relying on me, though. They all are, whether they realize it or not.

I just wish I got to say a proper goodbye.

AFTERMATH

SOREN

A few hours earlier…

The jungle is disorienting, not made better by the foliage cancelling out so much of the sunlight. It reminds me of being so far beneath the ocean's surface that it's hard to tell which direction is up. No jungle has ever felt like this.

Something is wrong.

It breaks me to consider I *know* why this is wrong, even if I'm trying to avoid it.

Misery.

He seriously fucking took her, and he left a magic to disorient me. There's only one set of tracks, and I know Jane's heart. She didn't go to him because she wanted to. Something forced her hand.

The realization cuts unrelentingly deeper than any blade. *Don't use magic; it makes it worse.* It's nearly impossible to obey that

307

concept. My soul screams to unleash everything I have, to scorch this jungle to ash if it means finding her.

Focusing on the foliage around with my eyes and ears, deadening the well of magic in my chest, it helps lower whatever effect is placed upon me here. It's all made fucking worse since my mind is one thread away from spiraling; he has Jane.

My sister and Jane have both been taken from me.

I move in the direction that I can weed out as the right one, to where Jane was, my magic never truly turning off, which might also be why this forest is so oppressive.

Trying to emanate my magic once more, just to test my theory, that pressure around my ribs returns—I stop, my gaze burning in the direction where I know I need to go, before moving again while trying to deaden a part of me that's never been quieted before. It's like pushing against hurricane winds; even breathing is strenuous.

The moment my boots hit the grass of a clearing, the pressure around me is so unbearable my vision spins. I collapse to one knee, gasping as though the jungle itself is choking me.

I can see the dirt is disturbed, and more than by animals. My fingers eagerly dust away at twigs, footprints made by boots. With squinting eyes, I look around until I see—no.

There's a long, auburn piece of hair. I pick it up; the length is right.

Jane.

The scream that rips out of my throat is primal, raw, and utterly devoid of restraint, echoing through the jungle, the sound entirely made up of *rage*.

They don't know what they've done.

If Jane thought she wanted revenge, it's nothing compared to what they've just unleashed in me.

⋅⋅◈⋅⋅

EXITING the clearing was the only option I had, given I could barely stand, and I needed people searching *now*. Tempest needs to be made aware, too, because how did Misery make it here? We barely set foot on this island.

This whole place needs to be on guard. Every person examined for being a traitor.

Ritter stands there, along with many more, including Bones and Basilisk. Anya is missing—the piece of my mask tells me just as much, and yet I didn't see any of *her* tracks, either.

"He took her," I rasp, my voice hoarse. "I couldn't do shit. The jungle affects my magic. Hard to focus. There's a clearing; Jane's hair was there. Many footprints. I don't know how."

Ritter doesn't need more before he barks out to his people to follow in, his voice cutting through the air like a whip. Donna yells out at the rest to follow her as Ritter leans in before departing, "There's a note. Left it in the shanty."

I focus on nothing else, even moving through my people without addressing them as I near the shanty where I left Jane, the absolute void of the place making me want to rip the hearts out of anyone who aided in this. I shove the door open to scan the area for a note. Normally, I'd have felt that there was something waiting for me.

Even *that's* gone.

There's a piece of parchment with a scrawled note made with the hurried lines of someone who didn't have time, next to her dagger —*fuck*.

'*What happens if I lose it?*'

I immediately pick it up, denting the sides of the map she wrote on.

> Soren,
>
> Perhaps some will see this as reckless. Cypress has given me a task, and it's one that I was not allowed to share with you. Your involvement— or any of the others— would have lead to death and I could not risk it.
>
> I don't know where they're taking me. Only that I can hear the siren's song deep within the jungle and that it will lead me straight to them.
>
> Which means they're here.

So, I will go.

You should know that she put a ruby under my skin, right at my neck. It will prevent anyone from reading me, including Misery. Including you. I didn't have a choice in the matter.

If something happens to me, just know that I, too, now have someone to think about in this suffering. Thank you for that gift.

With more love than I can describe,

Jane

With more love…

The weight of that statement, beautifully unbearable, crashes into me.

A sound escapes me—a low, guttural growl of pain and fury, the kind of noise that tears out of a man when the world has ripped away what matters most.

My breathing morphs into panting, my body full of so much energy and yet nowhere for it to go. "I'll find you," I whisper, staring at her name, my voice breaking, barely more than a rasp. "I swear to all the fucking sirens in the ocean, I'll find you, Jane."

The tears threatening to spill are held back by sheer force of will, and my eyes burn with something far fiercer than grief.

Whoever took her will suffer a reckoning so complete they'll wish they'd never been born. Even if that means I have to find a way to ruin a god himself.

I *will* do it.

I'll even give Cypress whatever the fuck she wants. I'd do whatever task she had given Jane, and I'd even hold back on the bitching.

Jane is being used. Cypress put a fucking ruby in her skin.

Peering out the open window, now assuming she climbed out here, I lift my gaze to the ocean. That's all that separates me from the Order of Ash. It has to be where they're going; it's where I can feel Anya's very faint pulse of life.

I reach at my side, touching my mask before lifting it off of my hip to examine it. The chipped away pieces are still there, and for a moment, absolutely nothing exists inside of me; no fear, no love, no emotion, no rage. I simply exist, staring at a mask I earned through blood. *Others'* blood.

Only allowing clarity to guide my mind, my sole purpose is to unwind what happened, and figure out how to best proceed.

Lifting my gaze and staring out at the ocean, I put on my mask, the clay morphing until it's like a second skin. Immediately, I can feel Bones out there, and somewhere, in the distance, I can feel Anya, too. She's faint, though. More like remnants of her essence rather than *her*.

Jane isn't anywhere.

I'd behead a thousand men for her, if she asked.

I have a feeling I'll have to, no matter what.

———◈———

IT'S NOT clear to me how long I'm there before I sense Basilisk's presence, the man entering the shanty, strutting in with hands in his pockets like he has all the time in the world. "You just sat there," I remark. "When I sensed something was wrong."

His golden eyes flick up lazily. "I know better than to go near a trap set by Misery."

"Care to elaborate, at all?" I ask, my voice full of tension. Out of all the people present, aside from Ritter, Basilisk might be the most useful, and instead, he's like wielding a sword with no hilt.

All the time on the ship, Basilisk hardly moved. Came out only to exercise and refused to speak to another. I left him alone at his behest, because it didn't feel right to go near him.

Fuck my powers, and the way they've misguided me. I should have forced Jane to speak about the conversation she had with Cypress.

"I kept my distance because I'm better at following what my gut is telling me than you are."

"Oh shut the fuck up," I quip, squaring him up. "I don't have time for cryptic bullshit, and I'm tired of these shit powers that have been fucking useless lately."

Basilisk inhales deeply, nodding to the side like he guesses he will get this over with. "Misery is our god, Soren. Going near him is going to end badly, every single time."

Those words stop me cold. "*What?*"

"Well, he *was*. This bastardized state he's in has sort of unleashed us into unknown waters. But he still has massive influence if we're near him. Including leaving pockets of his energy that we can't go near without it killing us."

I move closer, each step deliberate, like I want to burst through my skin. Basilisk places a hand on his hilt, staring me down.

"You knew that," I begin, articulating slowly, my voice low and dangerous. "And didn't tell me when we were stuck on that ship? For *weeks*?"

Basilisk's expression hardly changes, and if anything, only his jaw sets like stone. There's a moment where he glances to the side. His energy is so calm I want to slit his throat, and I know he's hiding himself from me, just like I normally am from him.

"You're not going to like why I'm really here, either," Basilisk adds, his gaze heavy, and it's clear he knows his words are going to change everything.

"Get it out, *Rasmus*, because I have half a mind to fight you here."

His golden eyes flare. "I said don't call me that—that's twice now. *No one* survives the first."

"Then fight me, if it pisses you off. Do *something*," I grind out through gritted teeth, still not having processed that Misery is my *god*.

His lips thin, his glare sharpening. "I'm here, Soren, because Cypress called for me."

I step closer, his blade pulled out so the metal shines in the light. I don't bother reaching for mine because I want to beat someone bloody right now, and only with my fists.

"There's something from Cypress that I am quite desperate to get," he quickly adds. "It's a harpy killer. Potent. Useful for me and what I need to do. She called for me to be out here because you'd need my help."

"What the fuck are you talking about? You're going from a shadow cat to harpies?" I ask, everything about what he says feeling like the fucking truth.

If Cypress called for him, maybe there's an answer in there, somewhere. Something to help Jane—*Cypress came to her... yes... that's what happened, isn't it?* Guilt and rage are molten hot in my gut, but I need to know what to do with Basilisk.

"It's all related to someone. The cat is, too. I've been tasked to keep Jasmine alive, and there's harpies that will become a real problem for someone I'd rather not have problems at all. So, I'm *here*," he explains, his entire aura focusing on concealing the deeper meanings of that. "I thought this endeavor was even more than worthwhile, knowing it would help you, too."

I need to step away. Cypress is such a conniving bitch, and yet I'd literally do anything she told me, right now, if it ensured Jane's safety.

With more love...

I ignore Basilisk to stride away, back to the communal space, entering the sunlight once more. I'm beyond enraged he knew of this shit and didn't tell me. That *Jane* did, too. And that I trusted my instinct to leave her alone with that information.

It makes no sense why my magic would tell me to leave her be, if it was going to be connected to her *abduction*.

"We're not done," Basilisk says after me.

"Yes, we are."

"I know where they're taking her," he replies, his voice loud so it carries to me.

My vision is nearly being strangled from energy that needs to leave my body, almost uncontrollably. "Then fucking spit it out," I say, pivoting to face him.

"Order of Ash," he says, licking his lips. "My cat saw them depart, and saw who had Jane."

"You can talk to cats now," I state, feeling like I'm going crazy. Is *that* what's wrong? Has something in me been compromised?

"Shadow cats can when they imprint on someone." He glances my way, speaking as if these facts annoy him. "I, unfortunately, have to listen to everything she says. Including her severe judgement of most of humankind... and that the ship's rats were too sinewy." Basilisk, in all his rugged glory, doesn't quite match the caretaker of a *cat*. "You should probably go tell Tempest. Save that wrath, Soren. We'll have an opening. I feel it, and I know you do, too. I know you don't trust your gut right now; I've been there. Many times. But we are freed of Misery's influence, which means our powers serve *us* now. Including our heart, and our survival. If your instincts told you one thing, it was for a *reason*. We will find Jane. And I'll help you massacre them all."

"What do you mean, Anya's missing?" Bones snaps, his voice sharp with disbelief. His thoughts immediately flood to Kathleen, the image of a blonde woman saturating his mind. *He's worried she's in danger.*

"You're not worried about Jane?" I ask, briefly narrowing my gaze on the surrounding environment before focusing entirely on him.

He tuts, looking around the chaotic space. Dogs weave between broken branches and muddy footprints, noses to the ground, hunting for a trail neither Basilisk nor I can follow, seeing as the jungle nearly suffocates us. "I mean, sure," Bones mutters, his tone dismissive, but his aura betrays that with clear unease. "But it sounds like they can't kill her right away. *Anya* is dead weight to them," he remarks, genuine concern in his heart, his mismatched eyes meeting mine. "You said Cypress visited Jane? I bet that witch gave her a leg up, and Jane is crafty. It's not like we aren't going to go after her, either."

I don't reply. My mind and body are pulled in too many directions. Sure, he has a point. Jane isn't most people; I know that. And yet the thought of her suffering, of her enduring horrors I can't protect her from, drives a cold blade into my gut. When I get her back—*not if, when*—she might be a mess of scars. *I can heal her. I will heal her.*

I do hear Bones, too. Anya is at a massive risk of being murdered.

"How did this happen?" Bones asks, nodding to the shanty where a few of Tempest's men stand.

"While you were surveying the space, I was with the others when suddenly everything about Jane went *silent*. There was only one set of footprints, so she willingly went into the jungle. She left a note," I say, pausing when I remember how she signed it. "Said she heard sirens singing. She seemed to know it meant Misery. And that Cypress gave her a task."

"That batty old bitch just can't stop meddling."

"She *has* to be using Jane. The letter mentioned that if Jane told any of us about it, it would possibly get us killed. That sounds *convenient*."

"Jane's smarter than that."

"*I know*, which means I think Cypress didn't give her a choice. I think Cypress forced Jane's hand, and is going to use her like she fucking uses the rest of us." It doesn't matter what Basilisk said, the way I feel so much guilt for not forcing it out of Jane is nearly every other thought in my mind. I didn't protect her from Cypress.

I don't care if they're supposed to be related.

It's *just* like my sister; if I had demanded to know what lured her away...

"Can't believe the God of Misery is your deity," Bones comments, like it's an intrusive thought he couldn't control. His laugh falters when he realizes I find none of that humorous.

Basilisk, who leans on a building right next to us, clears his throat. "It's because, in the old days, he used people like *us* to figure out what made someone miserable, and we'd be in charge of ensuring they were tortured in ways that fed him most. People's misery is what fuels him."

I snap my gaze toward him, the implications of his words like cold water over a fire. "When did you learn that?"

"Across the Black Sea. There's Sensors that actually worship him. They're idiots though—he wants to off our kind. We're a threat, now that he's in his physical form. Our powers are essentially wide open to changing however the fuck they want to. He's an old, useless god, so not many know of him, at least outside of the sagas of his previous reigns. I had to search deep for those truths."

There isn't even a point to let Basilisk get to me right now, tensing at that revelation. Is that why Cypress's rubies affected me so greatly?

Ritter's arrival disrupts my spiraling thoughts. His energy is an absolute mess inside of him, his glare smoldering with unconfined fury. He's fresh from the jungle, his clothes streaked with dirt and sweat, and the murderous look in his eyes is a storm in of itself…

He returned right when the hounds showed up and disappeared into the jungle once more to help search for Jane, while I uselessly stand here, trying to deconstruct it all, piece by piece.

"Enjoying standing there?" he asks, everything about him pure venom, his words aiming to wound.

I meet his glare, holding my ground. "What's your point, Ritter?"

"I *trusted* you. *Jane* trusted you," he snarls, closing the distance between us in two strides. "You couldn't tell my daughter had that planned?" He's so close now I can see the dark circles under his eyes. "You forgot to *read* that?"

Now I just want to piss him off in return; the accusations slicing deep at an already open wound. I lean into my next words, my tone deliberately calm and taunting. "No," I say, shrugging slightly. "She told me Cypress visited her, actually. In *your* tunnels. Without any of us knowing. *You're* the one that brought that witch into this."

Ritter's eyes flare wide, then narrow to slits. His hands twitch at his sides, like he might actually try to strike me.

"We don't have a healer, now," I add coldly. "So think twice before stabbing me."

"You say that like you don't even give a shit," he hisses.

I get so close to his face that I can smell the jungle on him. "We are waiting on Tempest, and once we have a plan, you'll see how much of a shit I give when anyone *associated* with her disappearance is going to *suffer*."

Deathly cold eyes don't seem entirely convinced, but I can feel he doesn't quite know what to do, either. His energy is all over, scattered by a father's fear for his child—

Tempest.

The enigmatic oceanic pirate queen is nearby, but her energy is different. It's *incensed*. She feels like what I imagine a hurricane would if it had emotions. "Tempest is coming," I say to Ritter without even looking at him as I stare in the direction that she should appear in.

He bites back so much that he wants to sling my way, but clearly thinks better of it.

We're all ready for slaughter.

Tempest storms up the path, her dark eyes wide and scanning the area. The cutlasses of at least two dozen pirates glint at their hips as they follow behind her, but her fury outshines every blade. "Why do I have people telling me *Misery* was here?" she barks out, lowering her head to block out the sun rather than squint when she faces us. "And you're all just *standing* here."

"Maybe some conversations are best had in private," I suggest.

"Then get your asses in one of these shanties, *now*," she demands, motioning to any of them. "Just Ritter and Soren."

Ritter and I exchange looks, because Tempest scolding someone is more like being flayed alive by her words, and we're both already pissed off as it is. I pick the closest door to me, feeling no one inside, and enter it. The warm breeze of the ocean enters through an open window; such a contrast to the cold shore of Skull's Row.

We're far from home.

Tempest enters, her gaze flicking between us with lethal precision. "If Misery had access to my island and I didn't even know about it, *someone* is going to die."

"Then start digging a grave, because that's what happened," I reply, my mouth unable to shut the fuck up.

She gives a slow, languid blink, her eyes rolling under her lids to look at me, before she tilts her head. "This isn't Skull's Row, boy. I can flay your skin and make a rug out of you, and none of your men could stop me."

Boy? What is she, ten years my senior? Same age as Basilisk?

Everything in me tells me to be as succinct as possible with her, as if I have limited time to convince her not to kill me. "Misery is, apparently, my deity—" that doesn't seem to surprise her, not even a flicker of interest inside of her "—which means when I tried to follow Jane, the jungle made it impossible for me to stay. Basilisk has a shadow cat—"

"—yes, she visited me frequently," Tempest interjects, her hand slicing the air dismissively, as though this information bores her, and she wants me to get to the point.

"—and the feline saw what happened," I say, trying to maintain my composure. "Misery and Blackwell, along with their henchmen, took Jane and Anya on a longboat, both of them incapacitated. Basilisk claims they're heading to Ashfire—"

"RASMUS! Get in here!"

How the fuck does she know his name?

Basilisk enters, glaring hard at Tempest, who is the shortest in the space, and yet she seems to somehow tower over us with her energy.

"I have a reputation that no one says my name," Basilisk warns through tight lips, his eyes livid as his forefinger moves between us. "So stop *fucking* using it. If I kill any of you, I don't get my harpy killer, and I'm not leaving without it."

I swear one of Tempest's eyes twitches. "I don't give a fuck about harpies. What I *care* about is that I just heard they're going to Ashfire, and you know this how?"

My gaze drops to the mask at her hip, trying to cling to *anything* that might aid us here. But the connection between us feels useless, especially as her mask sits and waits. Just like mine.

The Council of Zenith feels entirely fractured now.

"When Jasmine saw they took her, there were a few with the fire emblem on their armor. I am piecing the puzzles together in my assumption."

I face Tempest, knowing I need her good side. "We will need

ships. I don't know what the plan is, but we will need *something* to get there."

"You want to use my ships to storm Ashfire?" she asks, like we're beggars asking for a crown. As if *no one* would dare suggest such a thing.

Ritter leans forward, and all I can feel from him is a desire to cut every ounce of fat from this conversation so he can focus on Jane. "Aye. Misery took Jane. If we don't go for Misery, he will fuck over the entirety of the Balar Coasts. You know this."

I glare at her to try and read her to the best of my ability. Tempest looks at me, as if she could *feel* that. "You're always trying to rip people's souls apart to read them better. What is *your* take on this?"

"Misery can't have the Balar Coasts. You've heard of the Tormented Ages."

"Aye. They were so long ago only the faintest scars remain of it," she says, but some of her confidence is waning like a crack in her veneer. Tempest sighs once more, touching the wolf fangs around her neck. "I aided you all because I owed *Ritter*. And I enjoyed fucking over Misery in the process. But *now*, he was on my lands, and I didn't even know. None of that would have happened if it weren't for *you* lot."

We all remain silent, and I don't know of many people who have existed next to two Sensors and remained a mystery.

"Something seems off," she states, flitting her gaze between the three of us as she paces. "Something is connecting all three of you. What is it? I want to know before I offer my ships. I run a bunch of pirates, not knights, and my ships come with *my* terms. If you want them, you'll need to earn them. Perhaps even beg for it with how much I'm about to risk."

Ritter aggressively laces his fingers together, jutting his jaw to the side, and says, "You've grown to enjoy flattery, I see. You used to abhor that behavior."

Her grin flashes a few of her gold-covered teeth. "I've grown to appreciate it," she croons. "I'll consider aiding you. Once you tell me how you know this information, then we can have a *real* conversation."

Jane is out there, right now, a prisoner of Misery. So is Anya.

"We need *more* than consideration," I press.

I can already tell that using the relationship of all three of us being a Zenith will mean nothing to her here. She's a pirate, in her own lands.

"Or what?" she scoffs. "You'll steal it?"

"You need us," I reply, my tone resolute. "Are you going to storm Ashfire alone? You're not far from the Fire Isles. This will greatly impact everything you do if Misery conquers us now."

Her lips hover open, licking the bottom one as she stares at me. "You need *me* more."

"This is fucking ridiculous," Ritter says, pacing in the small space. "Either you need us or you don't. And either you *will* give us your ships, or you won't. But I have to figure out what I'm doing with Jane's predicament, and preferably before the fucking sun sets."

Ritter reaches into his pocket, his energy completely silencing from me. It's like he's doing it subconsciously, the act barely intentional.

He's unraveling in there.

Tempest's eyes widen, her brows shooting upward, her expression a mixture of shock and fury. "The hells is that?" she hisses, her voice low and hateful, looking at his pocket. "Is that why I feel her? You brought *Cypress* into this?"

Pure, angry heat leaks from Ritter, his composure smooth like a scorpion's shell. But I can tell it's close to shattering, and I'm honestly amazed Tempest can recognize that. "What do you mean?"

"I can sense when her magic is around us, *especially* in use. Something in your pocket belongs to her."

"What's wrong with that?"

Tempest scoffs, the lines around her mouth deepening with disgust. "I won't work with her. She's *poison*. And you brought her to my island. Are you working with her? Is that what connects all of you? There's more to this than those earrings, isn't there? You *lied*."

I frown. "I hate the cunt just as much as the next person, but she's a means to an end."

Tempest growls at us, her breathing deep and heavy. "Get the fuck out of here, and don't ask for my ships ever again. I allowed the earrings because I knew it was sentimental. Anything else is a *betrayal*."

Ritter bites his bottom lip, the tension in the air changing in its undercurrents like violent riptides. "What are you talking about?" he spits out.

"Fuck Cypress and her magic," the ocean queen replies. "If she's involved, then this will all be ruined. She's as selfish as Misery, and I won't let her spin me into her webs." She throws her hand in the direction of the door. "*Out*. I won't tolerate this. I've already given you *two weeks* at sea on my ship. We are more than even."

The longer we stand there, the more I can feel our energy poisoning this relationship. The thought of Cypress is destroying Tempest, unraveling her like I've never seen before, like someone who has spotted a ghost and just wants to get away.

I motion for Ritter to leave, and Basilisk is already moving.

For a moment, it seems as if Ritter might remain and risk a fight. I understand that desperation, that deep need to beat sense into any and all around to get what we need. When Tempest's mask shifts on her hip, as if she might don it, Ritter heaves a sigh and storms to the door, busting it open with his shoulder to the point it's nearly ripped off the hinges.

Tempest yells after us, "If you break my door, you're paying for it, Ritter!" She steps out. "You lot have two days, and I want you off this island!"

I follow Ritter as he storms out of Tempest's room. "You better have a good explanation for why you put that ring on," I demand.

"It was mindless," he says, glaring at me. "I didn't want to feel your *invasion* any longer." A semblance of his control is breaking, his eyes giving that away. "I let Cypress do her work, and now Jane is in danger. More than ever. But I'm tied to her, and we *need* Tempest. So why the fuck did we leave and not even fight for those ships?" Ritter faces me, hand on his hilt, that ring of Cypress's gleaming as if that witch is proud of her chaos. "I'll gut you here and now if this leads to Jane's undoing."

I nearly laugh as I step near him. He means it, too. I don't need to feel him to know that.

"I'm already planning how to set that entire island on fire, Ritter. For every bruise, cut, or sad look Jane has from them, I will find those men and take them home with me so they can never know rest, after slitting the throats of the rest."

"The fuck you doing with my daughter?" he asks, like he's angry at himself for letting me near her, or determined to confirm I might actually be a source of salvation. "*Really* doing with her?"

Like hells I can admit what I really feel to *him*. I couldn't even say it to her. *With more love than I knew I'd have…* "She means something to me that no one else has, and it's not more complicated than that."

"Do you love her?" he asks, his voice almost desperate.

I'm so uncomfortable I might as well be sitting on a bed of nails, especially with Basilisk right here, even if that bastard knows the truth just through what he can feel. This is such an invasion of my heart and desires, striking at something so vulnerable in me, and it's her *father*. But I know—it bleeds from his gaze—that if I do, he'll trust me.

And we need each other right now.

"Clearly," I state.

The idea of her being alone, wondering if she believes if we're coming for her or not, or if she believes herself to be abandoned, twists my entrails like I'm being dried out.

"Then what is your plan?" he asks, like he's exhausted of always having one himself. "Now that we don't have ships and are stuck on this island."

"Tempest won't budge," Basilisk says, as enigmatic in his presence as his cat. "I felt her. We need to leave her be, or it will make everything worse."

Inhaling deeply and looking up at the puffy clouds above, I hope the very man I need is looking at the same ones right now. "I know where we can get a ship," I say, motioning to move forward and further from anyone who might be listening. "We need to act fast. Get our men out of here before Tempest turns hers against ours. As long as nothing has gone wrong, we'll get out of here on Storm's Fury."

My gaze finds the ocean.

I *always* have contingencies.

ONE OF THE tasks I gave Anya was to secure a ship that would trail our shadow until this was all said and done, to even offer as much loot as I possibly can—a chance at Blackwell's coffers.

The captain of Storm's Fury would *love* to steal what Blackwell has. The captain is a man named William Rackham, known as Liam. Our success hangs on a very fine thread, one that makes me far too uncomfortable. If the deal is still upheld with Liam, then that captain is out there. Waiting.

One of my men carries a hawk, something that we use for situations such as these. Like most things within my circle, the bird flies with magic in its wings. As long as someone has one of the beacons made for it, the hawk can find them.

By the time dusk is approaching, we're all sitting on the shore, listening to the ocean waves, the hawk having returned by now with a confirmation that he's out there, and he's supposed to be sending longboats.

We were not allowed to use the harbor.

"You're lucky I don't take you to an island and maroon you." It seems involving Cypress is *the* way to piss off the pirate queen, something I'll remind myself that could be used as a weakness should it come to it.

Although threatening Tempest is something that scares shit out of me, but I'd do it if it comes down to it.

"That's definitely a ship," Basilisk says. Relief allows me to breathe easier, fucking thankful for Anya managing to find Storm's Fury's captain in such a short span of time.

I'm coming for you too, Anya.

The cat standing next to Basilisk purrs, to which I glance over and stare into the feline's eyes, the yellow things harboring the same judgement as Cypress.

"Seriously, when did you get that cat?" That feline's energy like a prickly shadow, almost as if it can tell I'm not overly fond of pets.

"Someone gave her to me," he bluntly replies, the softer glow of a setting sun giving a golden cast on everyone.

"There's more to that story. We have time," I say, motioning to the ship that's still in the distance. I can't even see a longboat that will get us to it, just that the giant vessel *is* there.

"*Obviously* there's a story. Don't know if I want to share it."

"Why not?"

"Don't need a reason." He shifts his position, chewing on his lower lip before sighing. "I don't even know who you are anymore. You used to have a vendetta to save Serena, and now you seem to have abandoned that."

"*Don't*," I warn, not even wanting to proffer up a threat, not wanting to dive deep into those complexities, or how Cypress has basically forced me here even if I didn't want to be. "Things change."

"So they do," he comments, the cat purring against his leg. I can't tell if its presence makes him mad or not.

"That thing is obsessed with you," I pry, wanting to see what that stirs within him.

Oh. There's something *much* deeper in there, unrelated to Jasmine. "I'm very aware."

Basilisk's presence is such an odd one for me. It's like when nostalgia paws at the brain, but revisiting home just isn't the *same* anymore. The mentorship I had with him is officially in our shared past. And yet I value that asshole, because the experience he has is not one many survive to revel in.

I stare back out at the ship known as Storm's Fury. If I'm not mistaken, there's roughly five total vessels that are known to frequently cross the Black Sea, and this is one.

Basilisk even used it to get here.

I'm not a holy man, but I'll make whatever deal with whatever god is interested to *torture* Misery for an eternity if he actually harms Jane. Even if it's Tempest's god himself. *Even Cypress's.*

Heat sears my veins, so much so that I want to rip my shirt off and toss it to the cold sands, but I leave it on. It doesn't help that I'm sweating under these leathers, my vest and armor in a bag that I'm not ready to don yet. Swiping at my face, feeling the stubble that lines it, I can't calm down. I'm restless, agitated, and so fucking ready to kill someone.

I reach to my hip and feel the skull mask, gripping it to place it on my face. Anya's energy is so faint, but it hasn't disappeared. If they're in Ashfire—

I feel the energy of the men on the small boats before I see the top of their heads on the water, their bodies like dots until they're close enough that the waves beach their ships. Their presence means this is only a delay, not a setback. I close my eyes and exhale before making my way toward the boats.

You're not alone, Jane. I'm coming.

SOREN

Sails flap high above as our boats make their way to Storm's Fury.

The helm of it is of a kraken, its tentacles reaching back and along the ship, its hollowed out eyes fearsome underneath furrowed brows. The entirety of the ship is painted with a stormy gray, the sails a fresh, warm color—a sign they're new and haven't been bleached by the sun or salt.

Storm anchors are perched out of their holes, ready to be deployed. This one has more than any other ship, including the Sea Wolf. There's even holes for the cannons. So he *does* have them.

"How you think they manage to have such a large ship travel the Black Sea? The big ones always do terrible in storms," Bones asks.

"If I had to guess, some magic is involved," I say, because it's a *monster* of a ship.

The only one of Liam's crew not rowing leans over, the woman gazing around like she's in charge. "Fury is one of the fastest ships, next to the Sea Wolf."

"What are the storms like?" I ask, wondering what we're in for. I chose Liam for a reason, but if we're talking safety, it's *Tempest's* ship that I'd get on without question. We'll need every ounce of defense and luck to reach Jane.

"She takes a beating, sir, but she's reinforced. We take in the sails when it gets bad enough. There's no anchoring in the middle of the Black Sea, mind you. It's too deep." She downs something from her flask. "There's a kraken out there. You drop an anchor, and it'll find you. It's one of the few tricks, actually. Lots drop their anchors in those storms, especially when they spot an island and think it's shallow enough."

Bones groans. "I'm not meant for krakens."

She smiles with pride. "*We* don't worry about them. Liam made a deal with those beasts."

Bones scoffs. "I'm believing you less and less, lady."

She points to a section in the ship that's different colors than the rest—almost as if it was painted on a different day. "That right there is where the kraken first got us. Our captain took care of us ever since, making a deal with it."

I grit my teeth. I don't know why—maybe it's all the emotions as of late—but I uncomfortably find myself thinking of the useless fucker I have to call my sire. Tempest's ship was different, as she's a legend in her own right. But this crew reminds me more of traditional pirating, where my *sire* lived his days. I only learned he had been killed because of his tattoos, the ones seared into my mother's mind. When I finally tracked down the right crew, they had flayed the skin from his body before throwing it overboard—a sign he was disowned before being murdered. Seeing the design of a ship with sirens upholding it on dried flesh that was *supposed* to be related to me...

I still regret to this day that it wasn't me who killed him.

Liam stands atop the ship like a sentry, moving among the crew in a different manner than the rest. Calmer. As if he's a part of the very wood that makes Storm's Fury, the setting sun crowning him.

The longboats are raised on thick ropes, and as they're being tethered to the ship, we climb up the coarse ladders that will get us over to the deck. Sounds of sails flapping and ropes being pulled taught is a sound I'd like to stay far away from once this is all said and done.

"Welcome aboard," Liam says, wearing a black bandana over his dark hair, and a black, tattered captain's jacket; not a single adornment is on his. He's more gregarious than the rest, being a pirate that just *really* loves treasure. "Come to my quarters."

"I want a few others to join me."

He clasps his hands together. "As you request, Soren."

Rorge heads below deck with the rest, officially operating as the overseer of our collective mercenaries. Bones, Donna, Ritter, Basilisk, and I follow Liam, ascending the elaborate stairs to the floor above us, walking through a threshold to a set of double doors hidden from view. "The hawk you sent gave some information, and based on what I know, I already have an idea as to what you're looking for."

"Which is?" I ask, being led into a room with a large table in the center that's bolted to the floor, the walls lined with scrolls rolled and stuffed into shelves. If this ship were to ever catch fire, this room would be nothing but tinder.

"Well, right here," he motions to a large map that's already unfurled on the table. "You've paid handsomely, Soren, to have me trail Tempest and also sit in waiting. Now that you're in need of my actual *ship*, and that I happen to be of great use with my knowledge of the Fire Isles, shall we discuss what *more* payment looks like?"

"If we survive this, Blackwell's coffers will be up for looting, as well as the entirety of Ashfire... whatever will be left of it, anyway. We won't touch any of it." I glare at him, not wanting to negotiate with *pirates* right now. "I don't want what's Blackwell's."

My men will be paid with my own coin, with new lands and whatever homes Blackwell's mercenaries had in Skull's Row. I will throw everything I have at this to recover Jane and my sister.

I know how to rebuild, if necessary. Money isn't hard to make if truly needed.

His dark brown eyes reveal immense pleasure at hearing that. "I like those terms," he says, grinning to reveal a few golden teeth as he looks at the rest who enter his place. "I also used to visit Ashfire. They've ruined it, so I'd love to pillage what's left."

Bones struts about, hands in his pockets. "Lots of scrolls here."

"I collect *information*, not just trinkets. Everything in here has been copied by my scries and left on land," Liam proudly says. "I bet Blackwell has *amazing* scrolls in his coffers. Definitely will want access to the Spiraling Stone when this is all said and done."

"We can make that happen," Ritter replies.

"You wouldn't happen to have a map of Ashfire?" I ask.

He grins. "I do. *Many*." He moves along the table, his hand gliding on the wood before poking at the map. "This, in fact, is the very map you'll want to study. You can't take it with you, but you can look at it for as long as you'd like. I got it out once I read your letter."

"We need to infiltrate it," I say, looking over the papyrus that's scried with meticulous, inky lines.

His thick brows rise, slightly looking off. "Infiltration." He clicks his tongue. "That won't be easy. Not with the fire mages. They burn anything they don't like. Sort of impossible to get near them."

Not if you're Jane.

Ritter nears the map, touching it with his aged hands. "Maybe being butted up against the ocean is our answer. We can climb *one* of these walls. We can't enter through any of the gates, not without an entire army."

"I am not offering my men, before any of you ask," Liam swiftly says.

Ritter waves his hand in the air. "Fine, fine. Tell us where on this map then we should infiltrate from."

"Let me get us some drinks first," Liam offers, nearing a globe that opens to reveal rum and glassware. Not a single ounce of dishonesty emits from the captain of this ship, although that doesn't speak for any of the self-preservation he harbors. "Why did Tempest kick you off her island?"

"We're partially working with Cypress," Basilisk quickly answers. I glare at him, as that could very well get us kicked off *this* ship, too.

"The witch? Well, I don't have a problem with her, so no worries here." He passes a drink around before sipping on his now, sighing before standing across from Ritter. Basilisk *had* to know that was the case, and if so, I like that our odds are looking up. "Alright... infiltration... Well, here's a theory I can offer. I've been to Ashfire as a kid, when it wasn't the madness it is now. I know *this* apartment—" he points to the map "—and that the fire bastards have taken it over. It doesn't have many safeguards. They seem to think they're simply not a threat." He taps the map a few times on that structure. "Honestly, I'd get into their private quarters and kill as many as possible. You get rid of the mages, and the whole area is yours."

"What did they do before Misery?" Ritter asks, taking a drink for himself, licking his lips. "For protection?"

"They were just simply not bothered," Liam replies, shrugging his shoulders, strutting about while nursing his drink. His long hair is braided down the back, appearing as if it's been dried out by salt. "Merciless used to visit, and even has a home there. I think he kept them all away, as in all of his pirates. He might show up to support Blackwell, you should know. But if he catches wind of Tempest, he will clear out like the bitch that he is... but since she seems rightfully pissed, we should plan on him appearing at any moment."

I nearly laugh, thinking back to how he didn't even lift a finger during our skirmish. "Tempest has made it clear she's not involved, so good to fucking know."

"Well, then get to planning. You can have access to all the scrolls in here, as long as one of my men or I am present with you. I'll know if you take one," he warns, a cutthroat edge in his glare, like how Basilisk gets if someone threatens his cat.

"We appreciate the help," I say, nearing the map to stare at the apartment with the mages. I'll memorize every inked line, and infiltrate this bitch.

"Of course," he says, sliding his empty glass on an end table. "So, what are we after on this island?"

All four of us share an exchange of glances, to which Liam picks up on almost instantly, as if he can maybe decipher the face of one of us. Everything in me says he's safe, to which I nod to Ritter.

The Scorpion drowns his glass, too. "My daughter was taken.

The Order of Ash is planning to really fuck over the entirety of these coasts, and they plan to use her as a weapon."

"How?"

"The God of Misery," I reply. If Basilisk is honest, then everything in me screams to tell Liam this truth; it will only aid us. "Jane has the potential to be his undoing," I add, not willing to explain the *entire* truth. "But if they have her, they'll suppress that. Rescuing her is more than just because we want to. And as far as that's revenant to *you*, that means all the scrolls in the Spiraling Stone will go with it."

He inhales deeply, staring out the window. "I've heard of this Misery, mostly across the seas..." He throws his glare at me, the gregarious nature washing away. "Let's speak further, then. Because that's a serious allegation about the Spiraling Stone, if true."

JESPER
JANE

When I wake, I'm so disoriented I fully believe I'm sleeping in the small garden we had growing up, half expecting my mother to stand over me while offering some bread for a snack once I woke up after sleeping under a warm sun.

My gaze drifts to the dirt next to me, completely forgetting about everything, even though I know there's a life to remember.

As my heart rate increases, my mind returns to me.

Soren.

Lifting my head, I look for Anya—she's awake, sitting up against a tree, the bruising deepening in color on her face, even down into her neck. Trying my best to get back into a seated position, I grunt when digging my elbow into the dirt.

"You slept like the dead," Anya comments softly.

"My mom would say my body needed it, then." I finally manage to sit with my back against the tree trunk once more, my body aching so much that every breath is uncomfortable. I definitely kinked my neck lying there. My fingers are freezing, and I stick them between my thighs.

What in the hells would Mom think of me now?

Taking in the scene is disorienting, too, like I forget how to focus my attention. The fire is reduced down to smoke and charred wood, the morning light just barely illuminating the jungle. Many of the men start to rise, some hacking to clear their lungs and others walking off to shit loudly in the forest.

Misery's hood is dark until the orange light slowly burns again. So if he just sat in the same damn corner all night, his little flickering eyes burned out, does that mean he gets tired? Maybe even rests? Cypress mentioned how weak he is already. How he had to exhaust himself.

Maybe I can find a way to get close to him. Or butter up Blackwell and learn more about Misery. Take advantage of Blackwell's ego, stroke it *just* right so he slips a few things.

"Everyone up!" Blackwell shouts, walking through the underbrush. "Jesper is near."

"*Great*," Anya mutters.

"Who?"

"The leader of the Order of Ash."

Blackwell's gaze focuses on us, pointing two fingers our way and waving his hand. "And separate those two."

Anya and I are re-positioned by someone grabbing our ropes and yanking us to our feet. We're taken into the underbrush to relieve ourselves, never going past a totem pole.

I'm able to piss in peace behind a tree, the small reprieve a moment of opportunity. Can I use the solitude for something? Anything? Make a run for it?

You're not here to escape or be rescued, Jane.

Tying my pants back together with my hands in front of me, my bound arms severely limiting my ability, the man assigned to me drags me back to the camp where they allow me to eat cold meat and drink some weak ale.

The sound of a wagon being pulled makes me look down the

wide path we're camped next to; I'm shoved onto my knees, wincing when it jolts my broken body.

Can they fucking *not*?

A man I don't recognize approaches us all, leading the horse-drawn wagon, a troupe of about fifteen or so armed men accompanying him. I look up at the stranger who stands in front of me as if I'm supposed to be impressed. He has sharp, angular features. Deep-set, obsidian eyes bore into mine. "Jane." He squats down. "Jane, Jane, *Jane*."

Don't do it. Don't say something that will incite more pain.

"Looks like you picked her up after tumbling her off a cliff's edge, and then let her rot in her own waste," the man comments with disgust before glancing up at Blackwell. "How is her personality? Meek at all?"

There's an eagerness in his voice, and I'm not sure why he'd care that much. In that, I nearly tell him to pull his cock out of his ass, until it dawns on me—*meek*. I can play meek. I'll have the upper hand if he thinks I'm subdued, whoever this man is... probably the one named Jesper, if I had to guess. *Channel desperation.*

"Soren seemed to have control over her," Blackwell says. "And she's definitely not meek. That's why she's like that. Hasn't earned proper clothes."

Well, fuck you, asshole.

The man tilts his head to the side, his long black hair tied back, and sighs with the drama of someone who enjoys the sound of his own voice. "My name is Jesper, Miss Jane. I'm the leader of the Order of Ash." His voice drops to a near whisper, his gaze dripping with menace. "Let's see... are you aware of being immune to fire?"

"*Yes.*"

"Did you know your children will inherit that?"

I frown. "Yes."

Jesper grins, his teeth gleaming. "I see, I see." He pivots slightly. "There are other Cinders like you. If anything, I'd say you were created *just* for this purpose." He glides his hand along the side of my cheek, seemingly examining my face and I do my best not to act as repulsed as I feel. "We'll probably breed the women and use the few men as foot soldiers. The more are born with these powers, the more Morvock's legion will rise." He looks me over, from my sand-covered hair down to my boots. "And I'm rather interested in the female that Morvock needs to rebirth himself with. There's time for at least *one* birth from you. Would like to see you cleaned up."

The threat almost doesn't even faze me, because I *know* I wouldn't let that happen. I'd stab my womb ten times and heal the carnage without even a *thought* if I got so much as a *whiff* that he would seriously do that. "I know you need me to be compliant. Rape will *not* help you there," I tightly reply.

Be meek, Jane.

"Leave her be," Misery grits out, his grating voice making me shiver. "You cannot have her yet, Jesper. Not until we are in my lands, where *no one* can touch us. She is to be un-accosted until then, or else it will mar her rehabilitation."

At least *something* is in my favor.

"Now we just have to field the fact that Ritter and his witchy ally will be after Jane," Blackwell comments, while Jesper looks me over like he's examining a horse he's about to purchase. "Shouldn't be an issue since we made it here safely. Once Tempest gets any insight that Cypress is involved, she will be the last person to help Ritter or Soren; the pirate queen is crafty. She'll figure it out real fast. And then they'll be shit out of luck getting to us from *her* harbor."

My heart sinks at that statement. What does that mean? Where the fuck are we, anyway? Jesper stands, and I stare at his boots, much like I did to Soren when we first met. There's hardly a scuff on them.

"Is that why you were delayed?" Jesper asks.

"Partially. We figured it was best to have Ritter and Soren's men all with Tempest, where they won't be able to secure passage once the pirate queen learns who they're working with. Compared to Skull's Row where they could have taken *any* ship. It should buy us time. All we need is a little over two weeks before we can pass over to Morvock's lands. Merciless will be here to assist as well."

My deep breath spreads my ribs in a painful expanse, my gaze darting all over the sky that stars are slowly fading away from. *Oh, shit.*

"So who is this other woman?" Jesper asks.

"Anya. One of Soren's closest followers. She pursued us into the forest and did a terrible job staying hidden. We took her, wondering if we could use her against Jane. Or cut off parts of her and send them to Soren to get him riled up. Take advantage of his rage and let him burn himself first. It seemed like a waste of bait."

Will these people stop fucking using my friends? Or talking like I'm not right here?

"We need to move," Misery says. "Secure her at the castle, and then we travel in a fortnight. We shall begin Jane's mental rehabilitation immediately."

I nearly snort. *Okay. Rehabilitation my ass.*

It all begins to move, and I'm chucked into the back of one of two wagons, Anya and I pulled separately. The smell of damp hay fills my nostrils, mixed with the faint metallic tang of blood—mine, maybe hers, or someone else's. My fingers twitch uselessly, bound too tightly to offer any relief. My world tilts and jolts, and I do everything I can to strategize while I have *some* version of rest. I have two weeks, according to them. Two weeks to show them that I'm the spawn of Skull's Row and of a mother who was tougher than the rest, worthy of being the wife of a *Zenith*.

Two weeks to find these damn sirens, so I can metaphorically put a massive hole in their ship to let it sink, and then focus on returning *home*.

It's time to let them know who *Jane* Ritter is.

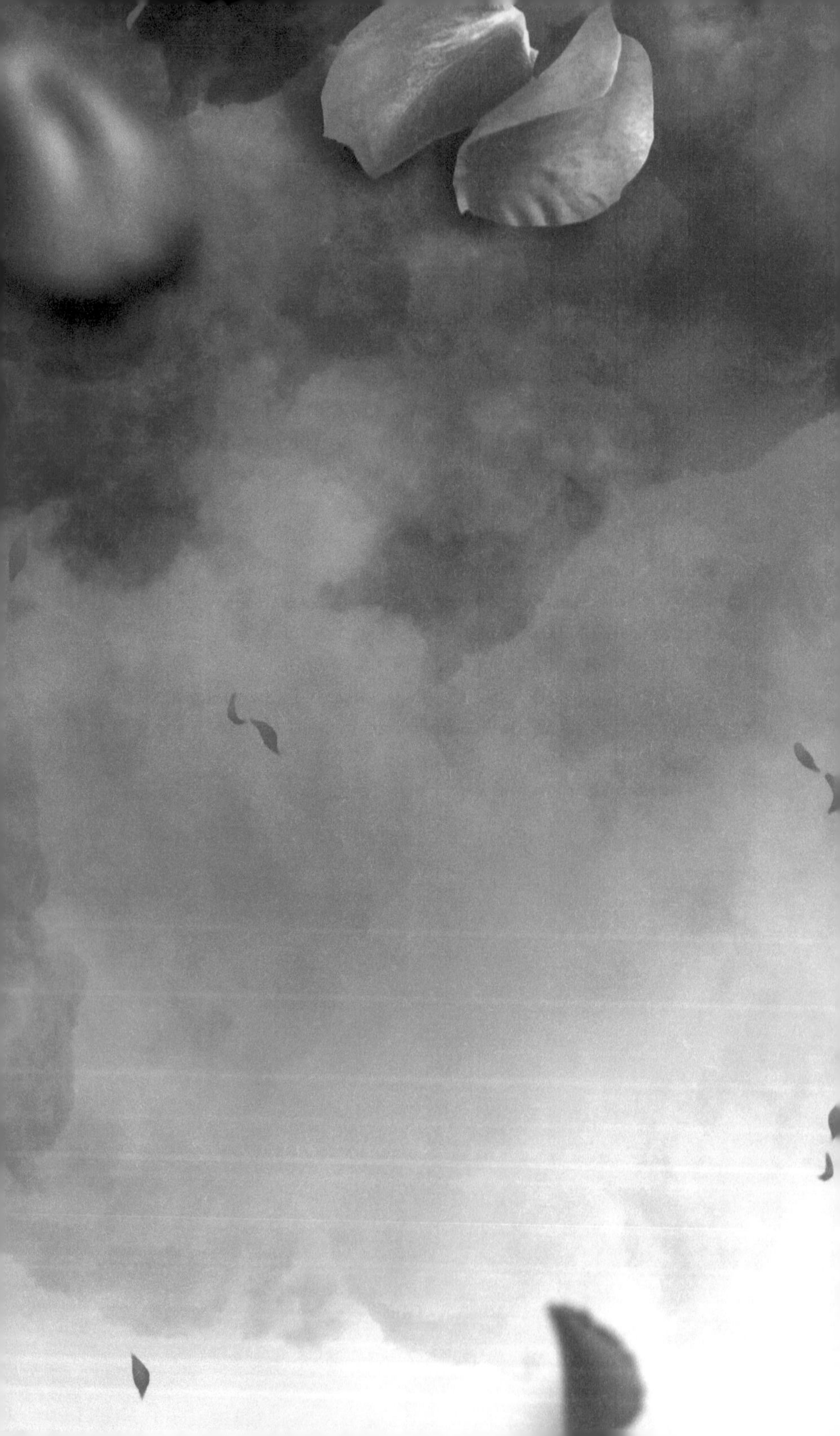

BELOW ASHFIRE

JANE

I admit my weakness once we're at the battlements of the castle, disappointed that I'm actually relieved. My legs are shaky from hours of being bound and hauled around, and my wrists throb where the rope has bitten into my skin, and I hope so badly I get to be freed, even if it's to a cell.

The castle appears to sprawl along the coast. Unlike the Spiraling Stone, which towers above the jagged cliffs, this fortress is squat and solid, built with practicality in mind. Its wide walls end at the ocean, as if daring the sea to claim it.

I risk sitting up to get a better lay of the land once we pass through a large, *thick* archway, the teeth of a portcullis pointing down right at me until I'm officially within the castle's walls.

Okay, free the sirens.

Whatever that means.

When no one barks at me to lie down, I can't stop *staring.* Whereas Skull's Row is a hot mess of humans, these ones are all dressed nicer, wearing the same black robes with an orange belt around their waists, the fabric evenly cutting off at their ankles. Sometimes, someone wears a white version.

There's even red robes, and my jaw drops when I think back to Blackwell and his fire mage—we're really in the Fire Isles, aren't we?

Curiosity overtakes my exhaustion as I turn to get a better view. The wagon moves beneath a colossal, decorative archway that acts as another entrance to the even more inner circle, its surface wrapped with flames. The structure is breathtaking, carved from pale, almost luminous stone. It depicts two figures—men or women, it's hard to tell—leaning against a massive circle at the apex of the arch. The fire that wraps around their sculpted forms is mesmerizing, licking up their bodies in continuous, living ribbons of flame.

Two fire mages stand in concentration at the base of either person, clearly in charge of ignition.

I can't help but find that absolutely fucking interesting.

Is this what the rest of the world is like? Vastly different from where I've grown up. Well, now I want to know what somewhere like Belstead is like. Or the Huntswood.

Or across the Black Sea.

Pale stone, along with polished wood, seems to be what the majority of structures are made from here, most of the edges crisp and the streets clean. The castle is made of the same materials, with more angles and rounded rooms, a massive circular piece in the center with a tall, pointed roof, windows lining it in rows, a few birds flying off of it to really exaggerate how large it is.

I'm a little angry this place is so beautiful.

When the wagons finally stop within the castle's inner courtyard, I notice the ocean stretching out behind the walls, a vast terrace ahead of me that one could reach after walking through a pathway made of arches. The entire opposite side of the fortress is open to the sea, the horizon vast and unbroken.

That's *one* way to escape.

And the sirens are out there.

Is *that* where I need to go?

Can Melona feel me? Is she angry at me for being a naive child who believed what she was told? If she's out there, and willing to help, I could literally just run for it and jump into the waters, fulfilling Cypress's task in under a day—

Stop trying to escape. You need to know where the sirens need to be freed from… the open ocean makes no sense.

Gods it's hard to change my thought process. I'm so used to fleeing as my only source of fighting, always dipping out of outposts near Coalfell if people from Skull's Row ever seemed to close.

I watch as Anya's carriage is taken further down, our gazes connecting for the first time in *hours*, her expression blank but her eyes sharp, assessing everything around her.

It's real, now.

She's officially taken somewhere else.

My attention snaps to the commotion behind me when the guards falter, their postures stiffening as though bracing against an unseen force—looking further over my shoulder, I catch sight of a carriage that seems to drain the light from the air around it. Its construction is menacingly sleek, crafted entirely from a black so deep it swallows details. Even the metal framework seems painted, as though polished with darkness itself. The people bow low, heads dipping in synchronized submission as the carriage creaks past.

A hand clamps firmly on my shoulder, the grip rough and impatient, yanking me out of my trance. "Enough, Jane," Blackwell's voice growls. "You'll have your day with Misery. *Lucky* you," he says, his mockery clear.

I don't reply and move forward as told.

"You have a lot less fire now," he comments, a guard guiding me to a side entrance.

"I'm just tired of it all," I reply, trying to lean into a meek personality, even letting my voice waver slightly. *Is that too dramatic? Probably is.*

"Oh, *really?*"

"I've heard that hunters will sometimes wound an animal and chase it until it just gives up. I'm tired of running. So good job catching me."

He has no idea of the undertones for me. And Misery can't read that, and while I might be tired of running, it's because I *badly* want to bring them all to their knees.

A strip of fabric is wrapped around my eyes before entering the castle, much to my disappointment. *Don't worry about that for now.*

I need to be complacent.

The air changes as we step inside, cooler and tinged with the faint, earthy scent of stone. My ears prick at the steady cadence of Blackwell's boots, accompanied by a chorus of obedient greetings, "Sir… sir… good evening, sir…" It's a long fucking walk to wherever we're going, and I just know Blackwell is probably getting hard at the idea of being so respected here. I don't need to be well-traveled to feel the energy is different here than at the Spiraling Stone.

Blackwell is getting a taste of *nobility*.

Eventually, we hit so many stairs, all in a circle, the stony steps unrelenting in how many there are. Each turn feels like an eternity, the muscles in my legs burning until I falter.

Blackwell lets out an annoyed grunt. "Carry her," he orders.

I'm chucked over a shoulder almost instantly, the pressure on my relatively empty stomach knocking the wind out of me, blood rushing to my head.

The unlocking of doors almost brings me relief, wanting to know what—I'm dropped back down on my feet, my knees buckling as the guard roughly grabs the rope around my arms to keep me steady.

Shoved forward, my body stiff as I worry I'll hit something, until the fabric is ripped off of my eyes and *finally* everything is taken off of me.

The space is actually quite nice, far from the dungeon I was anticipating. It's a circular room, and even has a hearth. A *bed*, with what looks like fresh linens. I raise my brows in confusion, shocked at all the amenities as there's even a rug on the floor.

Only one window, though.

As soon as I step inside to maybe look out and see where I am, the door is shut behind me. I don't bother turning around. The subtle click of the lock tells me all I need to know.

I'm alone.

For now.

It's been at least two days.

The only person to visit me is a woman that goes by the name of Marissa. She's a fanatic of Misery and probably thinks I'm royalty, and I bet would kill someone just to sniff his robe.

I already miss the noirs of Skull's Row.

I spend every moment plotting, planning. Devising backup plans to backup plans. Trying to decide on how I want to behave. Do I let Jesper do whatever he wants, knowing that I'm only working to foil him, and that I can take advantage of the rule that Misery said I am to remain un-accosted? Or do I fight him because, again, I can't be accosted?

It's on the third, uninvited morning that I stare at the cold, tower window for the entirety of the day, eyes raw and reddened from crying as I miss *everyone*, and it truly hits hard I have no idea when I'll see them again. What if freeing the sirens means once I'm *across* the waters?

For your family. For Soren's sister, who has suffered more than you.

The bite of loneliness reminds me that Anya has to be feeling these terrible emotions even more than me, as at least *this* is an official bedroom. No doubt she's in a cell; at least, I'd assume as much.

She needs me to keep my head straight.

I can do this; I *know* I can. I waited in Coalfell for all that time, didn't I? Maybe I'm more like my father than I realize, in that we're both extremely proficient in patience when it concerns the safety of others.

Patience doesn't matter, though, when I have *less* than two weeks before whatever happens… *happens*. I need to take advantage of these people not knowing me or my behavior patterns. I need to act, and *soon*. My fingers find the spot on my neck—*Cypress helped me. That has to count for something.*

I'm jolted out of my miserable thoughts at the sound of my locks being undone. The heavy sound of a latch is lifted, the door finally opening.

Marissa saunters in with her tight smile, which fades as she looks at me with such perplexity it's as if I've offended her. "Why do you cry? Is the food not to your liking? Has it given you a stomachache?"

My speaking is more controlled than normal, knowing that no matter what plan I create, being in good standing is my *only* way closer to Misery. "I am crying because I am not supposed to be here," I gently say, trying to play the victim with her.

"You will provide Jesper with the lineage needed to rule in Morvock's new world," she says, almost too softly, as if I'm a child that doesn't understand why wars happen. "If it's the babies you're worried about, they'll be completely taken care of when you've offered your skin to Morvock."

I pinch the bridge of my nose, suppressing an exasperated groan. "I—suppose," I let out, realizing empathy is not what I'll receive from someone who views me as lucky.

"Maybe you'd like some more tea," she offers with exaggerated kindness.

I know exactly what that tea is. One sip of it, and my energy zeroes out as I become a shell of myself. It's what they use when they want me to go anywhere or do anything, like take a bath. "Yes, that'd be great. I could use the forgetfulness," I lie. I'll just pour it out the window and let it trickle down the stone and then pretend to sleep.

It's so funny, because when Soren first took me, I was willing to fuck my way out of this. Now, that thought feels so juvenile and repulsive. I want to interact with everyone here as minimally as possible.

It's like something in me knew he was my person.

Time blurs once more as Marissa fetches my tea, only to once again swiftly leave the amber liquid sitting so peacefully in the white teacup. As soon as the footsteps fade away, I move to the window to dump the tea. As I slowly do it, so it's not pouring down in case it were to drip on something or someone, I lift my gaze to stare at the vastness of the ocean that my tower overlooks.

The doorknob jiggles, and I press the teacup to my lips and start to drink the *tiniest* sip so it might be on my breath. I'm surprised when I see Jesper, his presence drenching the room in discomfort.

This is nothing like Soren. I hate everything about this at such a deep level that I can't even express it.

"You drank your tea?" he asks, eyeing me curiously—almost suspiciously.

"It's better than having someone sit on me, pinch my nose, and nearly choke to death on it. Which seems to be a common tactic around here."

"You are abnormally compliant," he remarks, shutting the door. He's dressed in very formal attire, his black doublet custom-tailored and striking, with what looks like gold stitching. His dark wool trousers are tucked neatly into knee-high boots, the smallest sword at his hip.

Pompous.

"The tea is supposed to make you groggy, dull the sharpness of you. Not add compliance," he retorts, a smile in his eyes as if he's cornered me. "I'm highly suspicious of you."

I walk to the edge of the bed to sit, bringing my knees together to rest the empty cup on them. "Alright, fine. Maybe I'm *behaving*. I've seen plenty of kidnappings. Haven't seen a single outburst that ever saved someone."

He steps forward, and I watch him carefully as I swear he hasn't even blinked yet. "Morvock cannot read you," he states. "Which just makes this all the more confusing."

"That's a problem for himself," I say, knowing the tea is supposed to have an effect on me soon. "He's already examined me. Said it doesn't matter. He doesn't need to, in order to use me."

Jesper walks in front of the dwindling fireplace, hands tucked confidently in his pockets. "Should we use your friend? Carve her up? Maybe that'll get you to reveal your *true* self."

Don't show it. Don't show any attachment. "For a feast? Are you cannibals, too?"

He narrows his eyes, annoyance clear as day on his face. "I can't tell if you pretend to be cold, or if you just are."

"There *is* a draft," I say, waving my hand around the room, my eyebrow perking for a moment as if to indicate the joke.

He doesn't laugh; doesn't even blink or move a damn muscle. At least Bones might have entertained me. Soren would have snorted at the very least.

This is all wrong.

"Well, to test the theory on if you are hard-hearted, or *pretending* to be... I have something to show you," he says, like he's conducting a very swift transaction. "You see, I have a lot to gain in taming you... but I don't understand you at all. So, I'll work with what I know best—*fear*."

"If you insist," is my resigned reply.

He motions for the open door, swinging his hand toward it. I point to myself, still not seeing anyone other than a guard.

"Yes, rise and walk out."

My shoulders fall, dreading whatever the hells is going to happen. "Not going to tie me up?" I ask, although the weariness in my voice is palpable.

"If you drank that tea, it shouldn't be a problem," he quips, his dark eyes hoggishly gleaming.

My heart races and skips multiple beats as I stand, *loathing* uncertainties.

Jesper takes a step toward me, his eyes wild and primal. "Every single person on this island has been briefed that if they see you unaccompanied by either Morvock, myself, or Blackwell, to imme-diately apprehend you." He nears the threshold, his body moving before he takes his gaze off of me. "I want you to realize how I don't need to wrap you up to keep you here. Morvock insists your compliance is something to be *cultured*. Which means you don't have to fake that you drank the tea."

"I didn't—"

"*Don't*," he warns. "We can see you pouring it out."

My heart races, and I want to stab him right in the back for that. My nostrils flare as it's hard to agree and walk through that threshold willingly. Where would he want to lead me? Will it be to Anya, strung up and bloodied? Or someone else? What if they have Kathleen? Or someone else entirely?

The image of a mangled Soren barely clinging to life nearly makes the room go black as I stand and step forward. Picturing his muscled body as nearly lifeless, displaying the scars I've learned to trace in the dark gets me to move, because I'll do absolutely *anything* to keep him alive.

We descend the stairs that must be two to three stories in height, two landings giving reprieve for the person climbing up them, with bright windows making it almost inviting. It's a walled-in stairwell, and when we reach the bottom, the ceilings are immediately taller, the walls expanding out for more breathing room.

Oh, I'm not blindfolded.

Don't draw attention to that. Just observe casually.

As we pass by each window, I can smell the mist of the ocean. Everyone watches us, as if I'm a legend they've all heard of but took bets on if I exist or not. It's a sea of humans dressed in the same black robes, except everyone in *here* bears a fire insignia on their chest, whether through embroidery or metal.

Our descent is like moving through an expensive labyrinth—full of tapestries, paintings, rugs, unnecessarily gorgeous sitting spaces, and so much cabinetry. After an absurd amount of stairs, it's clear we've descended to the level of the ocean, my legs already shaking from the exertion. There's even a lovely sitting area with a piano overlooking the ocean. We pass by it right before entering a darker hall.

Even still, we go deeper.

I numb myself to the best of my abilities as he guides us to somewhere underneath the soil. At least, I assume we are underground, as there are no more windows.

There's something I don't like about that.

Finally, the stairs seem to end as we enter what appears to be a rounded corridor, only to realize to our right is a stream of deep, free-flowing water. It's like a giant stone pipe that's double my height, like how a bottle would look if filled a fifth of the way and tilted on its side, and we're walking on the side of it, the ceiling encompassing us, too. Fire sconces light everything we see.

There's even a wooden board with keys hanging on it, like the idea of someone breaking in here is preposterous.

"We call these tunnels the veins of the castle. We collect water from the ocean here, like a giant pipe. We boil it in massive cauldrons to use as fresh water, and we use the remaining salt for various things," he casually informs me. There are many inlets with elevated floors, and in one is a giant pile of salty chunks. He nears it, licks his finger, and runs it along one before giving a disgusting, languid swipe with his tongue. "Mm. That metallic, oceanic edge is something the inlands don't know what they're missing. Wouldn't you agree, Jane?"

Oh, no. He's crazy. "Yup," I stiffly reply. "That's what I always say."

He sighs, like we missed out on a good bonding moment, stepping out and holding an arm out down the tunnel. "Let's carry on."

The path is well-lit with many candles on the floor, melted wax forming uneven piles, every bit of flickering light dancing across the stone ceiling.

It's just us down here, which is quite nice for infiltration, but also *very* unnerving at the implications that *anything* could happen. When we round a corner, the tunnel curves as we walk alongside it, passing a small bridge to cross to the other side.

The inlets now have iron bars in front of them.

I don't like this—

My jaw drops, and I nearly *gasp* when I see what's inside one of them. I stare at the image as if it surely cannot be real. And yet, one of the tails *flops*, splashing water.

Sirens.

Every one of them has a fat, black metal collar on their neck, connected to a heavy chain that's unforgivingly bolted to the wall. Their striking, scaly tails rest in the water that's fed from the main tunnel, all sitting on edges, their chains too short to allow them *inside*. Many wooden buckets rest on the edges with them.

One siren uses a bucket to dip into the salty pool, leaning forward as far as the chain will let her. A long, thin arm outstretches to fill it, then pours it on herself, focusing on her gills.

"The sirens," Jesper begins, whispering in my ear as a few of the oceanic creatures look our way. "Are positioned *just* far enough from the water that only their tails can dangle in it. But they have been generously given buckets to splash water on themselves, as you saw," he says with a smile in his voice. "We're not *terribly* cruel, if we don't have to be."

I can't breathe.

In the corner, closest to the bars, is a siren with gray skin and hair so blonde it's nearly white, the usual wet strands totally out of place with how *dry* they are.

Melona.

Her gaze holds me hostage; those nearly black eyes widen as she stares at me like she sees a ghost. Her high cheekbones only add to the drama of her expression, broad lips parting to reveal her sharp teeth.

No emotion—don't show anything.

I owe Cypress for giving me that privacy.

"I'll leave you here for a bit, Jane. *He'll* be watching." Jesper waves a finger around, before using it to *poke me in the shoulder.* What a fucking weird person. Once his hand is off of me, my body loosens. My breathing is ragged as I'm shocked to watch Jesper walk away.

The sirens are completely silent.

Do I say anything? Do I move? *He* means Misery, right? There's no way he left me *alone* here.

"*Jane,*" Melona softly mutters.

A shudder seizes control over my composure, and I clasp a hand over my mouth to keep quiet, as if I've just given away my position. Another siren tilts her head to look me over. Her skin is a deeper shade of gray, her dried-up hair completely black and coiled, dangling over her shoulders. "Would have been better if it was Mother," she opines, her rich voice raspy like someone who needs a deep drink.

Inching closer to the sirens, my skull pounding from my rapid heartbeats, I touch the bars as if they might burn me. When I only feel the iciness of them, I grip it tighter as I look over every one of them—powerful tails, breasts out, claw-like fingernails tapping on the stone, their large eyes haunting, all of their hair so visually brittle…

I'll never get over the sharpness of their teeth, either.

My gaze finally lands back on Melona, as if saving her for last. I squat as if it will help quiet my words. "What has happened?"

She smells like a musky version of the ocean.

Melona leans forward until the short chain around her neck is taut. "Blackwell took us." Pointing to her arm where the flesh is raised in the design of a shark insignia, I can see it's healing terribly. "And branded us." She takes in a labored breath before dipping her bucket in the water and pours it slowly on her gills at her neck, the flaps opening and closing like one's nostrils would if starved of oxygen, and her chest moves as if breathing, but I swear only her gills move.

"What can I do?" I ask through tight lips.

Free the fucking sirens.

She almost chuckles at my clear naiveté, and none of the others join in; they all simply watch and stare. "If you know how to break steel bars, and all these chains, that would be a start. These tunnels have two openings, both leading to the ocean. We're very close, as these are the end of the tunnels before they spill back into the ocean. We just need freedom and time to get through."

Well, I can't fucking do that. There *has* to be *something* I can do for them. "How long?" I ask, nodding to the chains, trying to remind myself that Misery, apparently, is watching.

"Two weeks." Her voice is barely above a hush now.

"You will die soon," I say, looking over her very dry skin, the slits of her gills a deep pink, as if inflamed. "I'll do what I can. Even if it kills me."

Melona raises a thin brow. "You're acting as if there aren't those that will miss you."

"I can't think of them right now," I flippantly reply. Not that they suddenly don't matter, but if my mission is to free these creatures, then I'll do it by any means necessary. "I won't say more, though. It's just me, for now. Why did they snag *you* in particular?" I ask, afraid our time is paper-thin.

"I am close to the siren princess. And that's who they have," she says, motioning to the one with the darkest hair. "Jane. They'll be coming for you. The ones who miss you. They *will* come." Melona reaches out, but can't fully touch the bars. "Do not be reckless."

For the first time since being here, I genuinely chuckle, and her dark eyes soften. She used to say that to me every time she'd leave me in that cave.

"Why tell me that, out of everything you could say?"

She tilts her head to the side, looking me over. "It's something you have not considered."

Vague. That's her, though. She's like Cypress in that way.

"You should go now," she urges. "I think you just needed to see me."

How could she possibly know that? No, that's a dumb thought.

Melona is known as their Seer. *They'll come...* she wants me to focus on the fact that they'll come.

I give her a half-smile. "Did you know that I hate riddles?"

The smile she returns to me is so warm, and tears well up without *any* permission from me, reminding me so deeply of my mother.

A few clinks make me look over her shoulder, to see some of the sirens are trying to get a better view of me. I give the faintest nod, wanting to ask a hundred questions, while also wanting to do what's right for the moment. "Thank you, for helping me," I say, standing.

Trust.

Okay, fine. I'll fucking trust someone, if I have to. Trust that I'm placed here for a reason by Cypress, and that Melona can see it, too. That believing they will come for me is somehow a part of the plan.

And that freeing the sirens makes a lot more sense now.

I'm immeasurably grateful Misery cannot read me right now. In that, I find hope that Cypress might not be using me to my own detriment.

Hope.

Melona dips her head to acknowledge those words before looking back to where I am, motioning with her hand. *Okay, I'll, well, I'll try this trusting stuff, then.*

Maybe even trust Cypress, and that I *do* have a purpose here. If people are coming for me, then I can't waste time, either.

Walking along the narrow path that edges the water, I voluntarily leave the sirens behind, steeling my resolve as if I've never felt a single emotion, glancing back to look at them every few steps until they're finally out of view.

My head nearly slumps forward in relief when I sigh, so relieved that this is all for *something*. That I didn't risk my life just for the sake of bravado.

There's a real plan. A real web I'm stuck in. *One I have to strike a deal with its rubied spider before I can be set free.*

Around the corner is Jesper, the candlelight casting dark shadows on his face. We both stare at each other, the leader of the Order of Ash slightly moving his head as if to ask me what my opinion is. "Nothing to say? Not worth pleading for them? Or thanking me?"

"I *highly* doubt anything I ask for will be granted," I say, so much of my being fortified now.

He takes a step closer, clasping his hands together. "Morvock says that Cypress has helped you. Has she coached you to exist without emotion while here?"

He's studying me, like he plans to use my weaknesses.

"That witch uses any and all for her own gain." For the first time, it didn't feel right to speak ill of her. I'll be dead shocked if she was actually right, this entire time, that I would understand the entirety of her actions once I saw the whole painting.

Irritation flares across his features, and he leans into my face. "You're not as strong as you think you are."

Exasperation breeds both courage and imprudence within me. "Why are you complaining?" I ask. "I haven't fought you *once*. What do you want from me?"

"Come here," he commands, waving to me. Not an inch of me moves, so he narrows the space for us until his arm strikes out like a snake, gripping my hair.

Alright, I might chop this stuff off if people won't stop doing this. "What are you *doing*?"

"You are lucky," he warns, although his tone is as calm as ever, looking me dead in the eyes. "Morvock has a strict chain of commands for his use of you, which means I don't want these *un-accosted* times to get to your head. *I* am your salvation in this, Jane. If you try to grit and bear any of it, you will fail." I yell out when he pulls on my hair even more, almost growling as I try to claw at his wrists but I've chewed off the edges of my nails. He moves us both over to a brazier, and I try to keep his pace to take the pressure off my scalp. He holds my face *right* next to it, pressing on the back of my head so the flame licks my cheeks. I close my eyes and hold my breath... but again, nothing happens. It just feels like I've submerged myself into a very warm, bright wall of mist that makes me clench my eyes shut.

At some point, he pulls me back but doesn't release his grip on my hair. "Put your hand in."

I do so, wishing he'd just let go of me.

I leave it in there, the flames dancing through my fingers. The fire is warm; gentle. My clothes begin to singe, but my skin looks perfect. *Somehow, someway, this has to be useful to me…*

He laughs and lets go, tossing me so I stumble, hitting my knee hard on the ground. I wince with closed eyes, the pain sharp and stretching through my leg.

"Beautiful," he says under his breath. "Absolutely wonderful. One day, that power will be *mine*. And Morvock is right—your bravado is your weakness."

Something pushes my shoulder and I tumble over, getting really fucking tired of him doing this to me. *Don't fight him back.* I lift my head to face him, and Jesper slightly leans down. "When you bear me our children, you will sacrifice your skin to Morvock because you need to *save* them. Whether or not you live in misery between now and then is your choice. You might put on a facade, but the fear in your eyes when the fire gets too close reveals the truth. My men say you risked your life in Coalfell when they burned it down, searching for you, as we knew the flames wouldn't harm you. But you were afraid. The fear in your eyes was *real*." He squats down. "I should let you know that these sirens are not going to live for much longer. Every time one of them dies in there, I'll bring you her corpse; we sort of have a plan for their blood, but we don't need the flesh. We'll keep the one named Melona alive the longest, don't you worry. But we cannot save her once she is the only one remaining. Maybe even force-feed you some *fish* soup." He gives a shaky laugh. "Leave an eyeball or two floating in there."

Without much transition, he picks me up and pushes me forward. Angry words nearly spill out of me, but I clamp down my tongue, which turns into a weird growl.

They will be coming for you…

Free the sirens.

It's a long trek back to my tower, Jesper handing me over to guards while he walks ahead. My head pounds from residual trauma and the way he yanked on it just now, and I try not to make it obvious that I'm eager to memorize this place.

Once I'm returned to my cell in the highest tower of this castle, I stand there for a long time before sinking down onto the cold floor, right smack dab in the center of the room, over the rug. Mom's sunrise meditations come back to me, an act I'd skip because still-ness was never something I enjoyed. But as I sit here, staring at the fire in the hearth, an energy centralizes at my wrists.

My magic.

I'm not alone. I am connected to this healing magic. I look at my hands, then roll them over to stare at the blue tattoos. There has to be use in here, too. Cypress chose me for a reason. "Help me heal the sirens. Help me *free* them. They suffer in there, and I can get them out. I need *help*. Can you do anything?"

Embarrassment eats away at any hope that my goddess might be useful to me now, as only the sound of a crackling fire answers me.

Closing my eyes, I try to drown everything out as I focus on sending healing magic into my knee.

There *is* an answer here, somewhere.

I *will* find it.

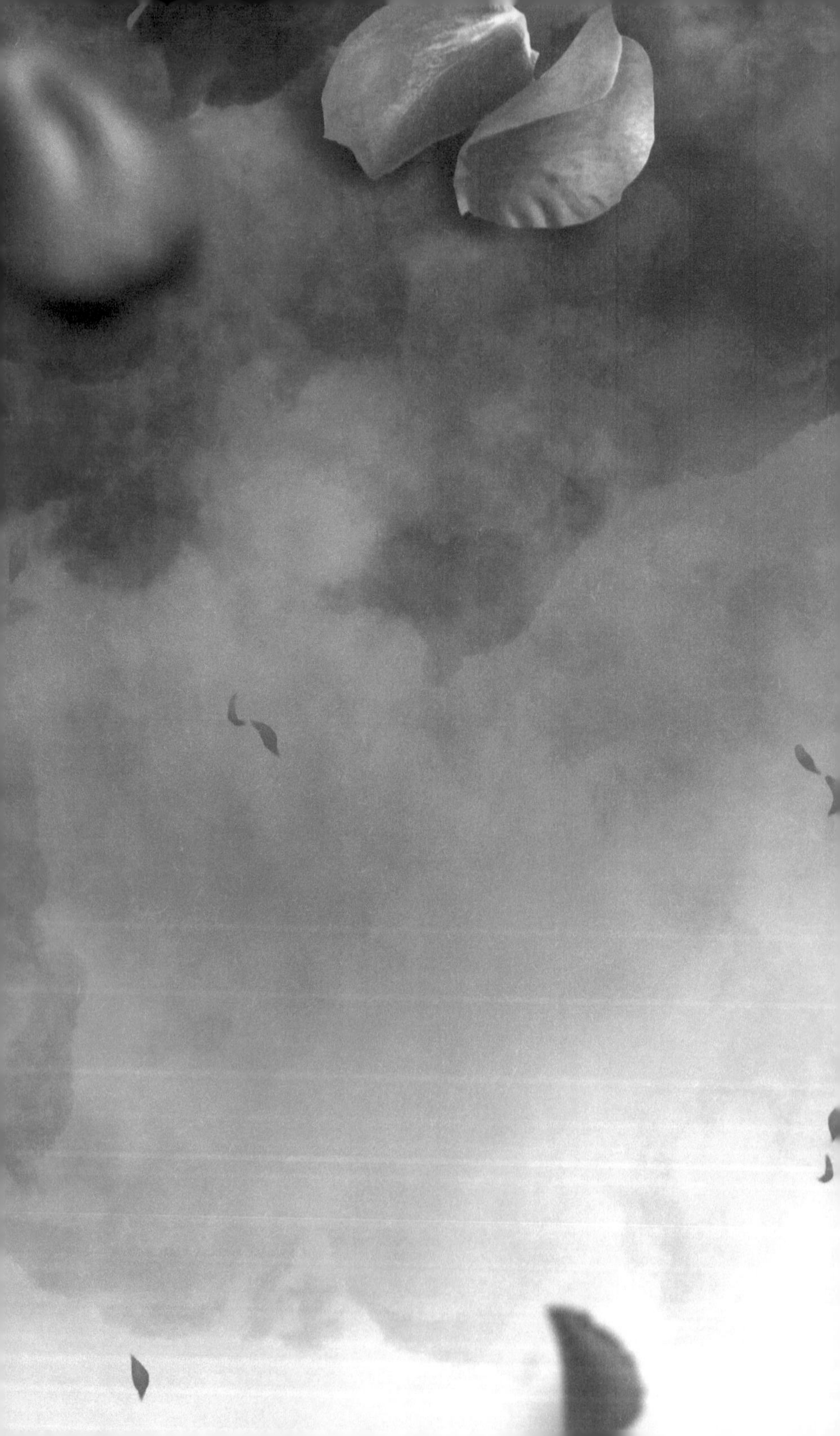

THE SONG OF A WREN
JANE

A few days have slipped by, to which I haven't left this room.
Do they plan to leave me here until it's time to do whatever the fuck they're going to do with me? I need access to that area below the castle. One way or another, I have to free the sirens from *there*. I still don't know why Melona once told me that for the siren's sunder, I could never visit Skull's Row. Or how that debt has been paid, but those obligations seem like they belong to another lifetime.

It's bizarre to consider how they once *ruled* my life.

It's on the third day since seeing the sirens that I hear the unlocking of the bolts on the door and not just the small flap where food slides under—the *'privilege'* of seeing Marissa revoked. I freeze when a disheveled Anya is chucked into my room, bound at the wrists, her reeking stench filling the space. I don't move. This feels so much like a trap that I don't even trust my distrust.

Jesper reveals himself from behind her, a smirk hidden under the shadow of his face. "Thought you could use the company."

Just as fast as she's tossed in here, Jesper shuts the door again. Anya and I both stare at each other in claustrophobic silence. Her hair is no longer slicked back—it reaches her nose, unkempt and dirty. The swelling in her eye is gone and replaced by horrible shades of blue and purple, her bruise blooming like a flower of pain. Dried blood seems to be matted in her short hair and neck, her body covered in grime.

When nothing happens to either of us, I feel somewhat safe to quietly state, "This is obviously a trap, right?"

"He's not very subtle."

The corner of my mouth crooks up, missing even *her*. "Should I heal you?" I ask, trying to sound as sincere as possible, taking a step near her. "Or is *that* what they want?"

"Just take care of the wound on my ankle." She hobbles to re-position herself, moving her ankle forward. "It's festering."

I examine the wound, which looks like a classic case of a rope, or even chains, digging too deeply into her skin, the surrounding flesh red and swollen. I fetch water from my pail and fill a cloth with it, indicating that she should sit on the bed—I don't care if she gets it dirty. She could probably use the moral support of sitting on something *soft*, as I doubt wherever she's at is comfortable. We don't speak as I kneel and look at what must have been a minor wound, but constant irritation has turned it into nasty trauma. I blot at it with clean water and clasp my fingers around it, eyeing my tattoos as they glow, ignoring how she smells; my mother would scold me if I let the state of someone get in the way of my duty.

Duty. I'm a healer who doesn't even know her goddess's name. I don't know the right words, either. *Please, goddess of healing, heal my friend. The world is sick with Misery. I need help. I need to heal.*

As I channel healing energy into her, I'm not sure if that made a difference or not.

"They have to be listening," Anya mutters. I glance up at her, and she leans down slightly—the poor thing looks like she's been in a fight with a molgrin. With cracked lips, she mouths, *"Do. You. Have. A. Plan?"*

My gaze drops back down to release my grip and take a peek at her ankle. I shrug. "Direction. Not a plan."

Anya leans down in my ear, and I feel terrible for wanting to hold my breath. "Make it happen *faster*."

"I'm sorry," I say, letting go of her ankle, not having realized just how much she was relying on me. "I can't say more. Are you okay? What have they done to you? Where do they keep you?"

"I'll endure. Don't apologize to me. *Fuck* these people." She repositions so she's right up on my ear, so close I can see the individual strands of hair on the side of her head. "I know Soren will come. I'll be the first one they'll kill when he does. Don't think twice about me."

"Don't think that way," I say before hearing what I'm saying.

Of course she'll be the first one to go.

"Don't be naïve," she sighs in my ear. Anya looks at me, close to my face. "I won't apologize for being difficult, Jane. It's my job to take care of Soren. And that's what I'm doing now by ensuring you get back to him. He'll be able to tell we're in the castle, okay?"

"Just, become another person and *flee*. Kill whoever. Get out of here."

She smiles, then coughs, and I go to get her some water to drink. I fill a cup and bring it to her like Soren did to me, but I take more care with the offering. When it dribbles down her chin and neck, Anya gulping like she's been stranded at sea, she adds, "I'm not giving up, Jane, but I'm not stupid. I'm ready to die if I need to."

My stomach knots as if a tourniquet binds it. "I'll find something." That's all I can offer as a reassurance. *It's all I tell anyone else, which means at some point, it's empty air.*

How can I tell her that I found the sirens, just like Cypress wanted? I *know* someone is listening. If I mention that to her, then they'll ensure I never get to go back down there again.

She motions for me to come close again, and she speaks in my ear, "Get the sirens out first."

It's the first time I lean closer to her, as if she read my mind. *"What?"*

"I can hear them. I'm not far from their cells. Tempest's daughter is among them. Set Moriganna free, and then Tempest will come. Once she's seen that Blackwell branded her daughter, Tempest will bring an entire armada."

Holy shit. "Her *daughter*?"

"Tempest is the queen of the ocean for a reason. Her daughter is a princess of sirens. And they have her right now. She's the key."

People will come… I nod, amazed at those details, gooseflesh rising on my arms. "You're fucking brilliant."

She laughs, the sound of humor befitting and out of character, all at once.

Anya pulls back, looking over me with sad eyes. There's something about the state of her, and knowing our days are numbered, that makes me terrified for her. "Can I ask why you owe Soren?"

Hopefully, the answer is something prying ears can hear.

She presses her lips together as she sighs, and then nods. "Don't care if they listen in on this… Soren and I were both in Death's Wing. My specialty is, well, you know what it is. I was, and am, exceptional at utilizing this talent, which is how I got in. We were in the same brigade, and he got to know me that way.

"I then took on a lover, once. She was the best thing that has ever happened to me," she says through a genuine smile, her usual stoicism completely unbound as emotion floods her eyes. "Amy was killed through a cycle of revenge. She looked *exactly* like a woman that had poisoned a very important man… so they killed her." Anya's lower lip trembles before she presses them together, sniffing, looking down at her fingers. "I became addicted to white poppy when all I wanted was to sleep. Then it all spiraled. I took so much that I was confident I wouldn't feel the water in my lungs, and dove off Dead Man's Cliffs. Soren, given how he can feel us all out… felt my intentions and waited at the bottom, probably mumbling under his breath that I was wasting his time while he waited on me," she says, letting out a weak laugh, still not looking me in the eyes, her hands trembling.

Something in my mind connects that this reminds me of a deathbed confession. "He found me in the waters through his powers and pulled me out. Took a week for my body to heal, and he even sat on me as my body overcame the sickness of recovering from that poison, holding me down so I wouldn't seek out the poppy. He told me that I wasn't allowed to die until I killed the man that killed Amy. *Then* I could make my decision on whether I died or not."

Her gaze finally connects with mine, and she's so entirely *human* in her expression. "I killed him, of course. The man who took my Amy. I came to him wearing the face of his concubine. He liked to have space and quiet, so no one bothered us for *hours*. I tortured him for *so* long. My emptiness remained, but it became different. Less painful. Quieter, maybe." She looks off, still messing with her fingers. "I appreciate that Soren gifted me the return of my clarity. If I die, I don't think I'd mind it. Not now. Not with my dignity in my hands." She slowly moves her gaze back to me. "I admit I see in you what he sees. If he's ever to love, it will have to be with someone as unique as you. I had it once... so this is my payment back to him—that he may find you and have your love for however long the fates allow it. It's... well, there's *more* to why I came, but..." Her eyes bore into mine as if to tell me not to ask her further.

I nearly hug her, but that might frighten her if I do. "This can't be worth that," I say, feeling as if I've interrupted something incredibly important, not realizing there are tears in my eyes. "I don't even know his mother's name."

Her laugh spreads across her face, tears welling in her dark eyes as well. "Oh, whatever. You two are annoyingly good for each other. You mean so much to him already... it'll grow. I know it." She digs into her pocket with shaking fingers, and pulls out a necklace, barely managing to hand it to me. "It's Amy's," she mutters softly, almost not audible. She looks me in the eyes, gesturing to me. "It's important to me that someone keeps it," she says, and I know if someone has their ear to the door, they wouldn't be able to hear that.

My frown overtakes my face, a single tear falling down my cheek as I glare at her like she's physically hurt me. "You're not dying, you idiot."

"I may very well be, Jane. There's Blackwell, Jesper, and a fucking God of Misery. I'm useless to all of them," she says, her breathing quickening. "I need to know someone has my last words," she says, looking at the necklace, as if hinting hard that she means *this*. It's the first time I've ever seen real, deep-seated fear in her eyes.

I clasp the pendant in my hand; it is a circle with the silhouette of a bird inside. I nod, not knowing what to say to keep this private between us.

"It's a wren," she says, almost like she's doling out her goods after being told she has a few days left to live. "Her favorite bird. I had it made after she was killed, and I've worn it every day."

I clasp it in my hand, my gaze darting around but focusing on nothing in particular. I raise a hand to place it on her knee, before looking up at her. "I don't know why they let you in here, but if something happens to you, I'll help take care of that *personally*."

Her grin is faint. "Good," she says, sniffing again. "I believe you." She lowers down into my ear again. "Do whatever you need to do, do you hear me? I want these cunts *dead*—"

The door opens, and Jesper struts in, dragging Anya away. Neither of us says a word as she looks at me before she's pulled down the stairs. Jesper sighs as if he literally has no choice in the matter. "So, Jane… you say you don't care, but you seem to be quite affected." He comes over and even touches the tear on my face. "Poor girl. You both had such a good talk. I can't wait to tell this *Soren* about how good I'm taking care of you."

I don't move. I want to know what they fucking have planned with this.

"You've been good this whole time, I admit. Keep it up, do you hear? If you do, I'll grant more moments like this for you. *Misbehave*, however, and we'll let as many men rape your friend while you watch. You'll have to clean her up and heal her between each session. It's a fate that can easily be avoided if you just listen to us, do you understand?"

I breathe heavier, staring at the linens that now have a little blood on them from Anya. The calamity of her life, used against me, can keep her alive. "Yes."

"That's all I wanted to say," he sweetly says, as if visiting me on pleasant terms. "I'm a little used to Morvock reading hearts for me, so it's because of your little trick with the neck that we have to be like this. I need to ensure I'm meeting the *real* you, not a facade."

He doesn't trust me. At all. But the *real* me would act out and be a pain in the ass, which seems like he'll just use as an opportunity to be violent with me. To lock me down further.

I need Jesper's trust. I need it to get back to the veins of this castle, not be caged even more.

When he leaves, it's the first time I *truly* cry since being here; the tears from a few days ago were more like stress relief. But now? The way it feels in my chest between each sob is like purging my body of all dread and fear. All while thumbing the necklace, staring at the bird.

I'm so pissed off they're using us like this. The wailing morphs into angry grunts. Maybe this is what Jesper needs to hear—that he has power over me. At least, let him think he does. In that, I don't hold a single tear back, so maybe someone can report to him that I'm torn up. Make him feel like he succeeded.

I'll free those damn sirens.

I *will*.

SOREN

I t's as if Cypress *wanted* this.

Wanted this misery.

Why else would she keep us all in the dark? Why would Jane be sent into such a situation, alone, when all of us could have done something? Formed some kind of *escape* route for her? I could have placed my mask in her neck, right next to the ruby.

A calm, almost apologetic energy within tells me I know the answer—we're not supposed to function to such a specific degree. For this to work *properly*, there needs to be chaos. Actions made within the heat of desperation.

I just hate believing those words, because it means Cypress is our puppeteer, and that terrifies me. She is not known for taking care of those who she makes dance for her.

"You're *sure* you can feel Anya?" Ritter asks, pulling me out of my damn head as if I was underwater.

That man's heart is readable once more. Maybe he chucked the ring, for all I know, after all the shit it caused. All that's clear is the sensation of Cypress's magic seems absent from him.

"She's at the castle. When I put my mask on, I can sense a dungeon," I answer, gripping the rail at the prow of Fury, staring out into the empty, dark night.

"What's that like? How can you tell it's a dungeon?"

Lowering my gaze to the pure darkness of the waters ahead, I try to find a way to describe what is something one can only understand if *felt*. "I get the overwhelming sense that if I looked around, I'd see stone walls and chains. The more I concentrate on envisioning Anya's face, the pain sharpens, especially in my chest and ankle, and all my mind's eye can perceive is *stone*. Then iron, metal. I assume that means a cell. *That's* how I know."

Ritter's energy stiffens, as if the crumbs of this truth are feeding a starving man. "And she visited Jane?"

"Maybe," I force out, a bitterness coating it. I felt so much change in Anya that I had to put the mask on, and it felt like she was broken again, like when I pulled her out of that river. "She was unusually sentimental, and I kept wanting to look for red hair."

It's too gutting to consider the notion that they could mutilate Anya, break her down.

"What are they doing to Jane?" His voice is lower, shaken.

"I don't know." The admission grates at me. I abhor that I can't feel her, no matter how I stare in the direction of Ashfire. And yet, I'm grateful Misery cannot touch her heart. "She's in a tower, though. It was a long journey Anya had to take after the sentimental feelings were cut off, and I kept getting the sense of being *lower*."

"That's impressive you managed to get your mask into Anya's skin."

"I got the idea from your ring. I just had the overwhelming desire to try it, and I was able to actually chip a piece off."

The mask has mostly been on my face the entire time, only removing it periodically. It's the only connection I have to Jane. To Anya, who is being forced to relive her darkest days. Misery. *I bet he has a Sensor, and is learning about her, trauma by trauma.*

I won't lose the trail this time.

Jane's dagger is even at my thigh. In the name of her reclamation, I'll properly bloody it for her with the life force of her enemies. I bite the inside of my lip harder when recalling how she knew she couldn't take it, because she didn't want it to be ripped from her and tossed away.

What are you planning, Jane? What information do you have that you withheld?

I want to help her.

I want—

My gaze drops, looking down at my arms that are crossed. "Ritter," I say, breathing slowly. "We need to speak with Cypress."

"I swear if we have to fucking look at her, one more time..."

"She knows what Jane has planned," I say, resoundingly. "We can't help her by being blind. Whatever task she was given... it *has* to be effective against Misery. What if... what if Cypress didn't involve us for a *reason*? I know it's hard not to consider the witch using us, but she's only appeared to help Jane and left us in the dark. She hasn't... I—I don't know how to describe it.

"My magic is calm. My heart is enraged, but my intuition tells me we're exactly where we need to be. Just like when I went searching for Jane initially. I knew she was south, and as long as I was moving in that direction, everything felt *calm*. Cypress knows we won't fucking sit around. She knows we will take action."

The words smooth something out within him, a sensation of control returning, even if small. "I *worry* she sent Jane to her death and doesn't give a shit. I know Jane is her kin, but I can't shake the worry that Cypress might sacrifice us for her god. Maybe it's some sort of *ultimate* sacrifice, or some bullshit. She could easily lie to us that Jane won't die."

Sure, it's a thought process I can't let go of myself. But if I really tease it all apart, then I know it's my *heart* worrying... not the powers that guide me. "I've been thinking about it a lot, and Jane knew something for weeks but didn't say a word. I know she doesn't want to risk us getting hurt, but if that was the true motivation behind her silence, she would have run away. I'm almost certain of that. She didn't say anything because something stopped her, and it wasn't just to *save us*."

"How does that help?" he asks, his tone exhausted.

"Everything in me screams to get to Ashfire with *this* ship. To use the plan you concocted with the sirens. Just even the acknowledgment in my heart that I'll commit to that calms my magic almost instantaneously. I think," I say, my sight heavy and sharp. "I think Cypress may have set this up to *help* us. I don't think Jane needs our rescuing, so much as she needs our *help*. Our manpower. We have a solid plan, a solid point of entry. And now that I know there's a tower that Jane is in, we can keep studying maps of the castle. We *will* reach her."

If my powers truly serve me, then my experience would say I'm fucking right about it.

We just need to get ourselves to the island.

The silence that now stands between us is so loud, raw emotions slamming through Ritter. I don't know if it's agony or fatigue in Ritter, but his more vulnerable side is raw to me. "It is so hard to trust Jane out there. Not because I don't believe in her, but because there's so much about the fucking world I was unable to teach her. I dread facing judgment that I failed her by the fates presenting me with her body—"

He goes quiet, and I don't press him.

Perhaps he and I are battling much more than just being worried for her. The world has burned us in ways that we can't see straight, because we know better. For now, I have to trust my desert rose can handle herself, and that soon, we'll be there for her.

And when this is all said and done, I'm never even *breathing* the air near a witch again.

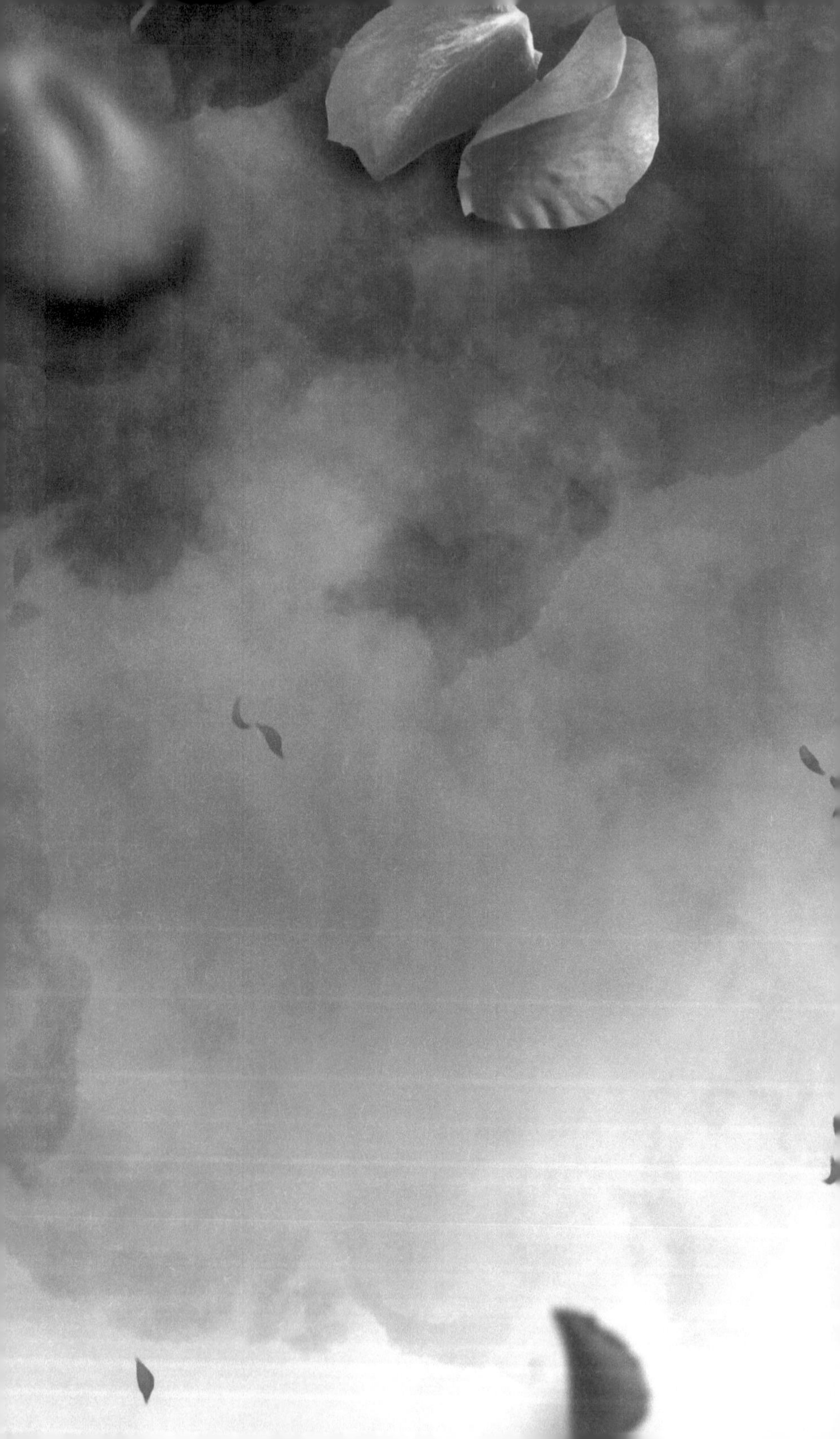

DINNER PLANS

JANE

I t's hard to get out of bed that following day.

I could hardly focus all night. Anya's raw emotions, mixed with a body that was broken and needed to be cleaned, made me feel like every breath I took was her taking the same one, but somewhere else. Somewhere darker.

I don't know what they're doing to her, but whatever I do next, *has* to be effective. If they catch me… *Jesper's threat…*

Sitting up, I stretch before rising to my feet, grabbing the sharp pebble from underneath my pillow that I found on the first day, making another notch next to the hearth, the warmth of it soothing me.

Seven.

I've officially spent seven nights here.

Seven nights of a bed, a hearth, and regular food, while many suffer in the bowels of this castle.

How does someone like me reach them and break through those iron bars? Melona said they just needed *time* to make it out. So I not only have to break them free, but also distract *Misery*. Or, well, I'm not sure about that. I haven't seen as much as his *shadow* since being here.

What if he's more incapacitated than they let on?

Time is running out, and I can start to feel my body losing weight, running my hands along the bony parts. I'm either too nauseous to eat, or too guilty. For a long time, I was just dropping bits and pieces of food out the window or burning the rest while consuming only the bare minimum: some bread here, a piece of fruit there.

This morning will be different.

I can't help anyone if my energy is shot because I haven't eaten properly in over a week. And after seeing Anya, it's clear I'm not a prisoner here. Not with the niceties of this room. Not with my clean hair.

That's *leverage*.

They need me.

When food slips through the flap at the bottom of my door, I stare at the eggs, some bread, and porridge, consuming what I can. Which, of course, makes me nauseous as the food stretches a starved stomach.

I sit by the door as I wait for someone to take the remainder of what I couldn't finish, only saving the bread in case I get hungry later. When there's the faint sound of feet climbing in a rhythmic *tap* up the stairs, my heart races with anticipation. The stepping stops, and then the flap pushes open—

"I have a request."

The hand that was reaching out pauses—small, dainty, and very clean; perhaps shaking slightly as if startled. Then I hear, "Uh, yes. I can ask for you. What is it?"

"I'd like to go back down to the main floor of the castle. There was a room that faced the ocean, and had a piano inside," I say, recalling the layout as Jesper boldly walked me through. "I'd like to go there. If Jesper is willing to let me visit that room, I'll be willing to have a *real* conversation with him. Hear him out on what he wants, and answer his questions with the truth."

I have a feeling he'll take *that* bait, but probably only once.

I'm uncomfortably aware that there's no room for error.

⋯⟡⋯

WAITING for Jesper's response is both exhausting and relieving; I can slightly relax, even if for a moment, knowing there's nothing else I can do while I wait, and that I've simultaneously taken action. So, I stare out the window, eyeing what my *true* target is with a calmer mind.

Placing my fingers on the stoney windowsill, I peek through and look down at the space I've stared at for countless hours, sometimes just watching the waves, memorizing every aspect of the castle I can see. I spot the large balcony, way down below, the one that faces outward to the ocean. To the right is the roof of what looks like the staircase we descended, the stone going into the soil. I remember those windows, which aligned with the view I saw when glancing out of them.

There.

That's my way in.

Well, this would sure fuck a lot of things up, wouldn't it? And if what I have planned works... I can save Anya, too. I don't know how this causes the metaphorical hole that Cypress wanted in all of this, but even Melona senses some of that potential. It's possible that with just the right *nudge*, a series of actions will cascade that are nearly unstoppable, and with a weakened Misery, there's *hope.*

I've been racking my brain for how it all connects; is it because the daughter named Moriganna can demand her mother to come? I don't even know why the sirens are being kept here—or how Tempest has a daughter that's a *siren*—but are they being used for something in particular? He mentioned their blood... Does that mean freeing them might create a massive dent in whatever is being planned? Like flooding the crops of a farmer about to reap what he sowed?

If I can create an opening to grievously wound the rest, and if people *are* coming for me…

One step at a time.

I squint, wishing I had a telescope to look closer. Right next to the main balcony is a much smaller one, and that's *directly* adjacent to a tower that seems to go *right* into the ground… I don't know why the piano room stood out so much in my mind, but there were other doors directly after it, *right* before descending.

If I can somehow gain access to that piano room, maybe I can access that smaller balcony and break into whatever room it connects to. I could *possibly* get near the stairwell and access the sirens without anyone noticing, especially if I can somehow be in that piano room with the door shut.

Anya's story of being alone with Amy's killer for *hours* before anyone noticed has stuck to my mind like sand to wet skin. *If I can get into that piano room, alone with Jesper…*

I need to visit it to plan anything further, though. I know better than to make plans on something I don't have eyes on, and given I've already seen that space, and can observe it from here, this is my best bet with the limited timeframe I'm allotted.

Pacing the room as I wait, I finally stop to sit at the edge of my bed, where Anya had been. I can't burn any more energy. I have a purpose now, and people are relying on me. Melona is. Tempest's daughter, too. Anya, as well.

When more footsteps precede someone entering the room, I'm immediately on my feet and stare up at the unforgiving eyes of Jesper when the door opens. "You want to go to a room with a piano?" he asks, although it's more like a statement from someone who is annoyed.

"Since Misery cannot read me, I know you're just going off my word." I stand straighter, hoping to convey sincerity. "You were right about my bravado." When his eyes glint with something that conveys intrigue, I hone in on it. "But I mean it when I say I *am* numb to this world, whether for better or for worse. And no. I don't know how to process the life I'm in right now. But I *do* know that I'm willing to work with you if it means more freedom for me and, more importantly, to protect those I care about. I don't want anyone else threatened on my behalf anymore."

I'll play him like he *wishes* he could play me.

He takes a few steps closer, no longer wearing any vests; his black, silk tunic makes it seem like he came up here rather quickly. *Eager*. "Blackwell tells me that he didn't trust you."

"Of course he shouldn't have. I had just been abducted, and taken to a place I was certain would kill me."

"There's no difference here."

I nearly snort at his admission that he knows what they're doing with me isn't an act of *service*. "Well, I beg to differ," I say, trying my best to transition my thought process. "There wasn't a god involved before. I—" I allow a pause, trying to sound broken. "I don't think I'm escaping this time, and I am *not* letting someone get hurt, abused, or *murdered* on my watch ever again. If that means working with you, then... I can at least *try*."

I can see his eyes gyrate like he's contemplating everything. "You cannot be okay with us taking you."

"Then what was your plan?" *What do I say?* "Please. I just need out of here, for a *moment*... I'll talk more, I promise. I need out of this damn space."

My desperation seems to tempt him into believing me more.

"And go where?" he asks, still examining me as if I may reveal how this is a trap, even in the smallest way.

"Let me go into the piano room, once a day. That's all I ask. I understand I can't leave the castle. But that room would be nice."

I don't plan to endure being here long enough for that to matter, but a feeling of victory steals my heart when he seems to believe me. "The piano room?"

"My mother played," I lie, and hope somewhere she understands I am using her to survive. "And I'd like to be relatively alone. At least, no more than one person in there with me."

He stiffens. "Why the limitation?"

I look at his sharp features, to the eyes that remind me slightly of someone who might be taken advantage of in Skull's Row; he's smart, but not cunning. "I know I can't be by *myself*. I just... I don't want an audience, either."

I swear something in his gaze suggests he's intrigued. *'I'm interested in the Cinder that Morvock needs...'* He's so arrogant *he* wants to be the one to make me bend.

So I'll dangle that in his face.

Jesper closes in the space between us, this whole encounter disgusting me. And I nearly show it. But at the last moment, I maintain my indifference as he reaches out to touch my hair, almost as if it's *his* to touch.

That's it. That's what he wants. He wants to be the savior that tamed the Scorpion's daughter.

Little does he know that title already belongs to another.

Soren… his pale gaze pierces my memory. Gods, no one will ever hold a flame to that man in my mind.

I can't refrain from the way my body stiffens, especially when thinking about where my heart truly belongs, but I let Jesper touch my hair as he wants. He twirls a strand of it before dropping his hand back to his side, his head rising up to further look down on me.

"There will be many outside the room."

"Understandable."

I focus on the relief it gives me, acting as if he's just granted me a lifeline, because in a way, he has. *Lean into that.*

"It will be at night."

"That's fine with me."

"You're plotting something," he adds, as if to rub in that he's more intelligent than me. That he will be harder to trick than this.

After being with Soren, though, I've learned that somebody doesn't need to state every time they don't believe you. They just let you dig that hole because they're *truly* confident.

Jesper's confidence is built on sand.

"Yeah, I mean, in a way, I *am* plotting something. I'm trying to understand where my life is going, and I need a moment of *clarity*, which I cannot get in *here*." I let the emotion break out from watching Anya, digging deep into what that made me feel. "I… I have been wrestling with this since the sirens… since Anya. I can't do it. I just can't watch someone suffer for me. Which means I need to at least *try* here. Accept that…" I trail off, hoping he believes me. "That for my life, people can't be close to me. They just can't. Which means I either live out these days in misery, or try to enjoy them… even if only a little."

His eyes flare with pride, like a hunter who is thrilled his trap has worked, as I hoped it would. I *hoped* he would think he's won by showing me all the prisoners they keep, so he can stop threatening them.

His ego will be the jugular I strike.

"I'll take you down there. *Any* misbehavior and you will be immediately returned. Anything more severe, and your friend will be tortured, as I already stated."

"Okay." *Misery… what of him?* "Will, um, *Morvock*, be present?"

The suspicion in his eyes nearly makes me hold up my hands to show I'm not meaning anything by it. "Is his absence needed for your scheming?"

A natural, genuine rise of my lips reveals a real smile, something only appearing because it's funny to me how little he knows of what I'm capable of. Of what I intend to do.

But… he takes that as, *flirting*? Almost returning the playful look… Oh, fuck no—*stop*. Let him think it's that. He has no idea the inferno he is toying with right now.

"I was just wondering… I'm not used to a *god* being in a room. If he is, I just need to compose myself. It's… intimidating."

His eyebrow perks as if his ego can't help but strut itself. "You get used to it. At least, *I* have." He looks me over, like some part of him recognizes he should be more careful, but he seems to be weak to this. Not to *me*, but the *idea* of this, like he thinks so little of my capabilities that it's worth it for him to risk. "I will return once the sun is down."

"Thank you," I say with as much sincerity as possible.

As he leaves, his gaze trails me once more, as if asserting he *can* because we both know I can't tell him not to.

When the door is shut, I place a hand on my stomach, nauseous from the insinuations of what would happen to me if I failed this. Of how that man will force himself on me once Misery tells him to.

Okay… it's okay.

What's my plan, then?

I don't fucking know, really. I just know when in the streets, I'd always survey the area before attacking, and that's the *only* area of this castle I know will get me below into those tunnels. Simultaneously, if it allows Jesper to open up and trust me to *any* degree, then even *better*. I need to know what I'm working with when it concerns him, and he clearly is very suspicious of my behavior. Will I have to sedate the madman with my healing powers while in there? I can do that. There's no way he sees that coming.

Just like Soren, I can only use it once. If Jesper can be rendered unconscious, I just need a solid hour head start.

It's actually genius to have him in there. He's *the* authority, next to Blackwell and Misery. People will just assume we're in there, having *alone* time. Just like Anya did when avenging Amy.

No one will bother to come in. At least, by the time they get suspicious, the sirens should be freed.

And so will Anya.

That's all that matters. I don't intend to escape what I am about to do. Misery can't kill me, so that means I won't die. And Jesper can't 'accost' me, at least not right now, and that's the only thing that might actually break me.

I can take a beating.

I can handle pain.

My heart races.

And like Melona said, I trust that the others are coming.

———◆———

A SHALLOW KNOCK comes to my door, Marissa returning with new clothes for me to wear, and some cloth to wipe myself down with, and even some oils to make me smell better.

I stare at the glass vial that smells like evergreens. Out of everything, *this* is the ultimate betrayal. Soren *loved* putting his preferred scent on me, which is so much more floral and sweet in its smell...

"Your hair is greasy at the roots. We need to braid it. There's no time for a proper bath."

"If you say so," I reply, placing the vial down in hopes she will forget to ensure I'm wearing it.

I kneel on the floor so Marissa can sit on the edge of the bed. Her rough strokes with a brush make me wince, and then she yanks hard on my hair. "Will you behave?"

Oh, *gods,* this is annoying. She wasn't like this yesterday. "Am I not doing so right now?"

She threads tighter. *Uneasy.* "You are lucky, you know."

I open my mouth, not sure what to say, breathing through my teeth when it hurts. *"Okay."*

She yanks again, pulling me back so she looks me in the eyes. They're wide, and disturbed. "Jesper is the chosen one from Misery. If you comply, you'll be courted by him... as you're about to be, tonight," she says, as if the idea is physically harmful to her. "And you'll get to live the best life before having the most meaningful end."

What the fuck is this? She gave off *none* of this over the last week. "Can you just finish my hair?"

Her jaw trembles, and she shoves my head forward again as I stare at the dwindling hearth. "I've been assigned to be your lady's maid, you should know. Permanently."

"I thought you already were, and you seemed so pleased by it..."

She lets out a puff of air, my mind spinning with trying to remember when this change occurred.

"Nope, the permanence was decided today. And I *was* excited to be a part of this great honor. Until Jesper spoke about you just now. He doesn't roll out the evergreen oil to *anyone*. I didn't think—I didn't think you'd get *that*."

Oh, well that's interesting to know. He's taking this seriously? That could either go well for me, or he could reveal how fucking weird he is and then I have to deal with *that*. "What did he say?"

"He *wants* you." She pulls my hair tighter.

"*Stop* that," I warn, raising my hands as if I'll do something, but I also don't want to ruin *any* opportunity for tonight.

She does nothing to stop, my scalp burning. "Stop acting like you're in danger. I'm not allowed to kill *you*."

"You say that like you've killed others."

"We're not having *that* conversation." She recomposes herself, or at least the mumbling under her breath stops. When she's done braiding my hair and I create as much space between us as possible, she looks at me like I disgust her.

"So who did you kill?" I ask, wanting to know what kind of crazy I'm stuck in a room with.

"Others." She's reminding me of a person that *just* received devastating news, like I'm the confirmed mistress of her lover. "I suppose we're like sister wives now."

I nearly laugh, my jaw dropping. *"What?"*

"I *know* Jesper." She looks at me like killing me *might* be worth it. Her eyes widen like that should terrify me, and she wants to see the power of having my fear. "Just know what he wants from you is Misery's fascination. Not *you.* Even if you smell like evergreens."

"I'll keep that *fresh* in mind." Gods I fucking hate these people. She should know the only thing I want with his dick is to cut it off and shove it up his own ass.

There's *so* much I want to say, but I swallow it all. *The sirens. Anya.* "Well, let me know when we can leave."

She frowns, like she's frustrated I don't fear her. "He will come get you," she spits out, turning on her heels to leave the room.

I stand there, my hair braided, and stare at the glass vial on the floor. I'm absolutely *not* putting that on. But I do undress from this rather simple, brown garb and slide on knickers and a thin, red, long-sleeve cotton dress, a belt at the waist to give it definition.

There are even sandals that wrap around my ankle for me to wear. I try to see it more as a warrior's outfit, like the dress I'm wearing to the liberation of others. I'm rubbing my eyes when I hear someone come through the door again.

Jesper.

I hate how demented this man is. Sure, my father and Soren might be killers, but they're not sadistic. They don't hurt others because it brings them joy to watch someone suffer who didn't deserve it. Shit, even Bones wouldn't threaten an innocent person with *rape,* and he's crazy.

"I don't think she likes me," I comment with a half-chuckle. "Marissa."

I'm so fucking ready to learn about Jesper's weakness. To see the piano room. Then, to knock him out and claim he passed out, but not before I get a *perfect* layout of the room. Of the balcony.

"She's a lady's maid. Too below me," he comments, as if that condensation would impress me, like I'd realize I'm being approached by someone *important.*

I just look away, not knowing what to say, trying to avoid how *gross* I feel.

"Let's go, Jane," he says, my spine nearly shivering at how wrong it is to hear my name in his mouth. Jesper sticks a slim arm out as if gesturing to go first, to which I do, relieved to see the endless sea of steps before me, eager for this bit of freedom.

I start descending when he nods for me to, and it seems like we're alone. For now.

"Did you ask for that implant to be placed in your skin?" Jesper asks. His fingers graze the back of my neck—I will *not* survive him beyond a few more weeks with how much I hate his touch. "It looks healed."

"I healed it because she forced it into my skin, and if it comes out, it will kill me. I figured it was best to heal rather than die a stupid death," I reply, touching the chilled stone of the walls.

"Morvock seemed more amused than angry. Like it's a residual mark of the witch. One last, failed attempt to overpower him. It will not matter in the long run."

My mind races freely with the gift Cypress gave me—no fear of my heart being invaded. "Where is Morvock when he's here?"

"Why do you ask?" he asks with a tight tone.

"He's a *god*, and you just mentioned him," I quip. He seems to trust me more with my sass involved.

"In *his* wing. He has to rest." The tone is still tight, and I get the sensation he doesn't want to talk about Morvock.

No, probably just wants to talk about himself.

As I see the end of the stairwell, I think of his answer—does that mean he's not watching me right now? Does Misery feel *safe*?

I *have* to make tonight count to its fullest.

Jesper takes the lead as we walk the same path as before: broad halls, lots of windows, tall ceilings, passing by *many* doors, fire light casting an orange hue all over.

After traversing a great hall, we bank to the left where the ocean is in clear view through the windows, even if only faintly visible with the moon, and then I see the large double doors, wide open.

Candlelight burns so bright inside; I can almost see why Marissa would be angry. It's as if he's officially courting me tonight. Planned everything out.

The only thing that carries me with confidence is knowing how, very shortly, I'm going to have *true* freedom… even attempt to make it down below.

Tonight.

Soren would tell me to strike when they don't suspect it, like I had done with him—I choke that thought off. I can't think of him, my dad, or Kathleen right now. I have *one* mission, and I breathe *only* for that—the sirens must be freed before anything else matters again.

Jesper is the first to strut in the room, at least half a dozen guards standing outside to shut us inside.

For a brief moment, I'm terrified he has something else planned. That Anya will be in here, or a siren will be served for dinner.

I survey every corner, looking for anything that would suggest such torture.

Nothing.

Except for some food—*real* food—on a table, along with a pitcher of wine. The scent of roasted meats makes my mouth salivate.

Then, the doors behind us are shut, and I make eye contact with Jesper.

This is not going to go how he thinks it is.

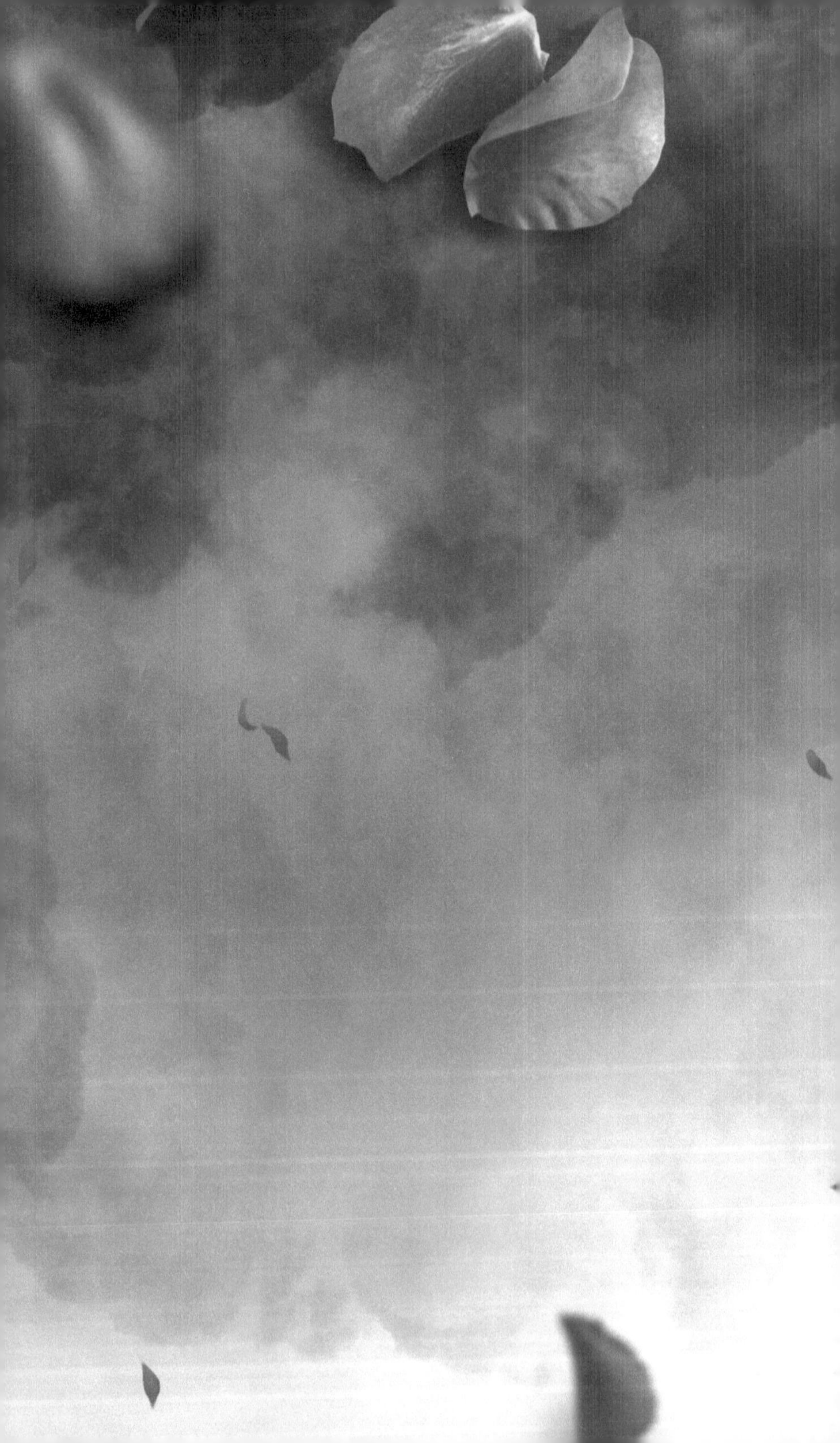

ORCHESTRATION

JANE

"You seem relieved," he casually states, that dark gaze roaming over me.

"I um," I stammer, trying to spin this in a way he might like. "I worried for a moment that I wouldn't like what I saw here."

His smile is thin, his hands sliding into his pockets as he paces around the room. "Come now, Jane. Like Morvock, those within my circle will know nothing but luxury and a good life. Cross me, and I will ensure I live up to his shadows. If I enjoy you, I may be able to extend your life even more. Morvock is not in a rush, you see… more so, in a rush to *secure* you. Once that has occurred, he can wait, if need be. You could become a queen and live a full life…" His eyes are dark and predatory. "If you submit properly."

Gods was this man born in the pits of Skull's Row? He's just *gross*. "I have not been known to be tamed," I say, slightly demure.

If I can even be such a thing.

Jesper's smile widens, a glint of amusement making my stomach churn. "Makes sense, given your father. That could create a strong lineage."

Not with you, fuckwit.

My breathing quickens as I move to the piano, the motion deliberate, almost too obvious, especially since I did it as if I forgot a line in a play.

"So, your mother played?" he asks, as if catching on. "I didn't know they had many pianos in Skull's Row."

"My dad has a way of securing unusual things," I smoothly reply, staring at the creamy keys, the painted wood slightly chipped in the corner, my vision honing in on it.

Jesper sinks into a nearby velvet couch, the color a bright red. His posture relaxes as he spreads both arms out on top, but his gaze never leaves me. "Can you play?"

"No," I say, running my finger along the smooth wood. It's cool beneath my touch. "I just… like to look at it."

I have no fucking idea how this thing works.

"Strange. She never taught you?"

"She taught me how to heal," I reply, my voice quieting as I try to recall my mother's face, focusing on her for my strength. She'd tell me I *can* do this and that I'll be okay. And to probably embarrass the shit out of him by following through with my plans. "I didn't want to learn the piano. It required too much sitting."

Grazing my fingers on the smooth keys, I hope the act makes me appear wishful. The weight of his scrutiny only grows heavier, and it doesn't help that I want to walk away from this thing to eat some food, my gaze drifting when I see there's even a *pie*.

"Please, help yourself," Jesper offers, his voice so kind and polite.

I trusted Soren not to poison my food when he said he didn't need to. This one, though? The doubt is *real*. The thought of acting tonight—right now, or very soon—sears my mind. Who knows when I'll get this again, if at all? I don't have to *escape*. I just need to free some sirens and then Anya, who can shapeshift and get herself out of here.

As long as I'm ready to stab a few guards, steal their keys, and act with precision, I can make this happen.

So, should I?

"What are you thinking about?" Jesper's voice cuts through my thoughts.

"I just don't know how much time I have. If I should spend it sitting here or eating some food."

I stare at the piano, not wanting to meet his gaze, still allowing my hand to roam, and even press down on a key every now and then, the sound singing through the wood.

"It's night. Blackwell is sleeping, and Misery is resting. We have time." There's something almost unintentional in his tone, especially the way his words tightened at the end, like he didn't mean to say that.

He talks easily.

I glance up and offer a smile, to ease his worries, because I *definitely* prefer him as a talker. "I'll eat, then."

He quickly rises to his feet, the low-cut tunic revealing a clean chest underneath; he's *too* clean. *No warfare for this one... an easy target?* He nears the table that has an obscene amount of food. The sight of it—so much richness, so much waste when Anya is probably starving—makes me feel even more like tonight *has* to be the night.

I honestly don't know if there's a perfect time, or if I'm simply letting my gut guide me. But I could eat up, get some energy and real food in my stomach, drink some *fresh* water.

Pulling one of the finely crafted chairs from the table, I sit on the velvet cushion, the candle flames at the table blowing all to the right; an ocean breeze even tugs at the heavy curtains. "Can I ask you questions?" I ask as I fill a plate.

Jesper's smile thins, his eyes hardening. "It's best if I am the one asking questions, Jane."

"Of course." I bow my head slightly and take a bite of the whipped potatoes. That buttery, salted flavor makes my eyes roll. The steak's fatty juices run on my plate, the meat tender.

If I weren't so determined to use this for my strength, I'd feel too guilty in indulging, knowing people I care about starve right below my feet.

Jesper collects a wide variety of food on his plate and pours a tall glass of wine for the *both* of us. "You know, I had a feeling this would work with you. I heard a story, once, about you being in chains, in public. And that you were surprisingly willing. I never forgot hearing about that."

My fork pauses mid-air. "With Soren?" I ask, surprised word of that spread all the way here.

More eyes are on you than you think, Jane.

Jesper stiffens, a wild flash of something erratic in his eyes. "I'd prefer not to mention him anymore. Not if we are taking this *seriously.*"

"Alright," I say, not fighting *that*. He's utterly lucky Soren isn't here right now. I bet this man would actually shit his pants if *my* Zenith appeared in that doorway. Gods help Jesper's actual *soul* if Soren finds me covered in someone else's preferred scent.

"He will never be relevant here; therefore best to leave it in the past," he explains.

"Understood." I take a bite of the potatoes, slowly mushing it around as my mind races, trying to deconstruct the undertones of *that*. Jesper's reaction isn't just dislike; it's a capricious danger. "Do you eat like this all the time?" I ask, motioning to the table, trying to shift the conversation to a safer place.

I'm still not sold on acting tonight, but I also don't want to waste this opportunity of freedom and solitude. I need to make this *count*, and he seems so gullible right now. If this is common, perhaps I can suggest dinner more often.

His smile returns, hung up by pride. "Perks of being me."

"Do you have a title?" I ask, instantly regretting it when he looks offended, like I'm making fun of him. I quickly recover, "I meant, I don't know if I should be calling you by something."

He grips his fork tightly, sighing as if he's doing *me* a service by being so patient. "Not yet. I *will* be a king, though."

Sure you will, buddy.

I nod, keeping my reaction neutral. Conversation with him seems risky at best. I could ask the wrong thing that sets him off, and then I'm sent back to my room until it's time to leave this wretched island.

This will have been a waste of opportunity.

"You are not wearing your scented oils," he comments, his tone accusatory, like I'm losing his interest.

"Oh, uh, yes. I set the vial down so Marissa could braid my hair, and I honestly forgot."

Jesper's gaze lingers on my face as I lower my gaze down to the table. "See to it that you don't forget again." He takes an aggressive bite of his steak, resting his hands together as he leans on his perched elbows, a fork and knife in either hand as his jaw works hard to tear apart the meat. "Marissa is an interesting choice, for someone to tend to you. She can be so jealous, but *very* loyal. Which is what *I* want." He puts his fork down, reaching into his pocket to retrieve a vial, placing it on the table. "I brought some, though. We can put it on after you eat."

"You really like that, then?" I ask, absolutely lost on how to converse with this man.

"*Very* much."

Gross. Officially, I hate the smell of evergreens now. I glance out the window as I eat, at the dark ocean that the moonlight casts scattering light across, like a mess of broken glass, and for a moment, it's beautiful to look at.

I need to get the sirens out there.

"You must enjoy the ocean," he comments, looking over his shoulder to the ocean at his back, returning his attention to me. "Given where you're from."

"It does have a sense of home," I reply, forcing a casual tone as I look back at my food.

"If it might help your compliance, I can have a cottage built on the coastline in Boneglass."

"Boneglass?"

"Where Morvock's lands are located."

"A secondary home," I absentmindedly say, my stomach twisting slightly as for a moment, I consider a reality where I *don't* succeed.

"There's a castle that currently exists there. We finished construction last summer, actually. I will spend my time between Ashfire and Boneglass as we build an empire for Morvock."

Nodding, I'm not entirely listening to him. I *refuse* to be taken there. I don't know what I'm looking for, or what sign I need. Technically, it's pertinent to act sooner rather than later.

So, why not tonight?

What if I fail?

"Where, um… where will *I* be? During all of this? Your travels?" I ask, trying to maintain his attention.

"Your behavior dictates *everything*." His demeanor then shifts, the air between us growing heavier. He leans forward, ever so slightly, looking me straight in the eyes. "You know… I hate to bring this up, but it might be relevant. Tomorrow, Blackwell is going to kill his first siren."

My eyes widen, the fork clattering on the plate as my hand falls to the table. "*What*? I'm being *good*."

Jesper shrugs. "He needs a few," he says, as if I just have to accept that, his tone dismissive. "I'll stop him after that." His gaze locks onto mine, unrelenting. "Make it worth my time, Jane, and I can see if he just sacrifices *one*."

"Please, don't," I whisper, my voice slightly trembling.

He raises his brows, as if amused by my desperation. *He likes the power he has over me this way.* "I have an idea. What about a massage?"

"*What?*"

"I've heard a healer's massage is to *die* for."

Oh, wrong choice of words. "You haven't received one before?"

"Okay, I *know* they're to die for," he admits with a smirk. "Show me it's worth having a bride that is also a healer."

I stare back down at my food, everything before me utterly repulsive now. What the fuck do I do? My mind reels, searching for a way out of this. Gods I miss my rugged mercenary so much it hurts, his energy so vastly different from Jesper; this dumbass doesn't even compare. "Let me know when you're done eating, then," I say, my tone hollow.

"No, I think you can go ahead and start now."

Well, do I do it? He's asking me to knock him out, basically. And a siren will die tomorrow?

In reality, if I don't commit now, there's no guarantee this will happen again. *Don't be reckless, Jane...* is this reckless? I stand with an awkward, loud scoot of my chair and near him, the man shrugging his shoulders like he's telling me he's ready, all the while he keeps eating his steak, his jaw flexing with each chew.

I don't know if it's my reckless heart or not, but everything tells me to do this. To risk it all, here and now. Going down to free the sirens, in any capacity, is daring beyond words. So what counts as *too* much?

Soren would know.

I tried to keep thoughts of him far from my mind, but I also know I'd trust any advice he'd give. *Jesper is the idiot letting you touch him without knowing your capabilities, like he was, once...* Perhaps my mind is officially losing itself, but I swear I can hear his voice as clear as anything else.

I escaped once, didn't I?

Fleeing this castle isn't even my prerogative, either. Which makes this task easier, less complications. Less tracks to cover.

Knocking Jesper out will at least give me a chance to explore, and if the door to the balcony or the interior door is locked once I'm in that room, I'll just go alert the guards that he passed out.

I'll gaslight the shit out of this man that it wasn't my massage, and I definitely don't know any siren songs; he clearly was hallucinating as he passed out. It's not as if they can read me, anyway.

Massaging him through his clothes as I tap into my magic, I feel there's an incredible amount of tension in his shoulders. With every knead into his muscles, I channel my powers, very gently, to help loosen and relax.

Meanwhile, my heart races so much it's making me dizzy.

"Aren't I supposed to not have clothes on where you touch, to make it more effective?" he asks.

Leaning down slightly into his ear, adrenaline saturating my veins with each rapid beat of my heart, I say, "Sure, if you'd like."

Before he can even reply, my magic morphs as sedation becomes my focus. I slide my hands to his neck, singing the song of the sirens so gently in his ears it's like a whisper.

"What are you..." food sputters out of his mouth, his body stiffening, but only for just long enough to almost rise from his seat as I hold him there, my magic flooding his body, the words of the siren so quiet in his ear the others won't hear through the wall.

As his body goes limp, so much faster than Soren's, I try to lean him over his food so he lies in it, finishing the song as I do so, trying to keep an even rhythm with my voice as I lay him down.

He breathes deeply, the muscles in his face so slack that I know this will work. For at least an hour. If not longer. *I never asked Soren how long it worked on him for, but I also poured way more magic into him than Jesper.*

The enraged part of me sees Jesper lying there, completely open for a nice stabbing. It would be so easy to slit his throat, but killing him might be the genuine death of me. I nearly grab the steak knife, thinking of the game from the Undercroft, but injuring him, even at all, would be the reckless part of tonight.

I may need his confusion when he wakes up.

Free the sirens.

I need to free these sirens.

ESCAPE ROUTES
JANE

I peer around as if the walls have eyes. I inspect every painting for holes, but I see nothing, careful not to touch a single thing. Rushing to the double doors, I peer through the keyhole—it's covered.

I don't even hear anyone outside.

No, shit.

I near the open doors to the balcony while Jesper sleeps in his steak, leaning out to peer around. It's so dark on this side of the castle, like it is every night when I peer out the window.

If I were up there, right now, I'd be able to see myself sneaking out. Well, perhaps not right *now*. The shadows are so dense… Will anyone else see me who could be watching? *Go. Time is wasting.*

My gut tells me that Jesper is having us meet in a *very* unofficial manner, which means very few eyes on us, even if he said other-wise. My gaze lands on the balcony that's—no fucking way.

They're connected.

Through a very narrow pathway, they're connected in a spot I couldn't see from high above. Moving as quickly as possible, I beat at the dress that flutters in the wind. This is why I wear *pants*. Creeping around the wall, I peer over, only for a moment, to see it's a straight drop down into the ocean.

Nothing I haven't faced before.

My lips part, the cooler air of night filling my lungs. And just as I saw earlier today, this side of the ocean is completely empty of people, the cliffs below a natural safeguard. Does that mean the sirens can escape there? Surely, it does.

If the timing is right, then maybe Tempest *will* come—I bet that's what Cypress wants. My heart is beating against my ribcage as I reach the other balcony. Misery might flee after this, seeing as it's almost time to leave, anyway. And if Tempest greets them in the open ocean…

The ocean god.

Cypress said Misery is weak to that energy.

That's how we'll trap him.

It *has* to be.

I peer out at the waters again, the waves moving with no care in the world about the dramatic humans inland.

Okay, then I need to act *tonight*. No doubt the minute they suspect Soren, or my father, are potentially on their way, these people will kill the sirens. Anya, too. All while I sit in a tower and feel gratitude for surviving? No.

I came here *exactly* for this reason.

Nearing the doors of the balcony while Jesper no doubt still sleeps in his steak, I eye the exterior handle of the balcony before turning it as quietly as possible, holding my breath as if it might somehow make it quieter, desperately hoping it isn't locked—it opens.

I open the door as gently as possible, and then shut it so a breeze doesn't blow inside.

There are drawn curtains on the other side, so I stand there with my back to the glass doors, creeping my fingers around the fabric that dangles in front of me, slowly moving my head so I can peek out, seeing nothing but darkness. It's dead quiet in here, the ocean the only muffled sound.

I slide through the fabric, worried this could be someone's private quarters and perhaps they're sleeping. It's so hard to see without *any* light, walking with my hands splayed out to touch anything I might run into. My hands graze stone, and then a wooden mantle—the hearth. I grab an iron poker for a weapon when my hands lay on one and look around once more, even if it's basically all black.

I don't even hear anyone breathing in here. Is it empty? Just another sitting room?

The only light I have is whatever bleeds through the bottom of a door, which, if I'm right, means exiting out of here will take me to a thinner hallway that will lead to the entrance of the dungeons, and then it's a straight shot down.

With the heavy poker in one hand, I use my other to turn the handle of the door for what seems like an eternity so as not to make a sound, holding my breath as I hear the faintest clicking sound of the internal mechanisms.

This is just like when I was a kid and stole from the unsuspecting, or tried to sneak into places I wasn't supposed to.

I can do this.

I literally escaped a Zenith, who admitted if he didn't have his powers, I would have gotten away.

My resolve steadies.

When the door is able to open, I don't let go of the knob. I've learned it's easier to repeat the same process and slowly return it back to neutral.

Now, I listen.

Whatever chatter is there sounds further away rather than close by. Risking it, I cringe as I wait for a possible squeak of the hinges.

They're clean.

When the door is open enough to squeeze my body through, I slip outside and slowly shut the door, looking around like I'm back in my childhood and about to get caught at any moment.

The hallway is still empty.

There are guards to my right, their backs to me as they chat with the others. Someone mentions something about it being odd that I'm not playing the piano.

Oh, fuck, I need to move, then.

Commit. Don't think twice.

Leaving the door *barely* ajar, in case I need to sneak back in, I strut down the lonely hallway in this stupid, flowing dress—sticking the poker between my thighs, I move as fast as possible to tuck the dress into my long knickers, right at the tied waistband. I didn't even think of this earlier because I don't know how to wear dresses.

So much better.

Moving swiftly and quietly, once more, I'm wondering what I'm to do about my appearance; aside from this very unorthodox style, I'm not wearing any of their robes. Should I kill the first person I meet and steal theirs? My hair being braided is actually of use tonight, both for movement and because it's not how everyone saw me when I was first brought in.

I don't care if I leave a trail. All these people support a world of terror that goes far beyond Skull's Row. At least in the city I was born in, there's freedom to partake or leave.

Not under Misery's reign, and they all support him, here.

They *will* catch me. But that's not the problem. I'm giving up my freedoms, my comfort, my dignity, *all* of it, in the hopes that I may succeed. If I can just get them to the ocean *before* I'm caught, it'll all be worth it.

Which means no holding back.

Moving quicker, I'm upon the stairwell that will take me down. I decide then and there that if I come across *anyone*, I'm maiming them. There's no way to do this without leaving a trail of blood, and I need to commit to violence *now*.

The world blurs around me until I come across a guard on the stairwell. A split second is nearly too long as guilt claws at me, but when his gaze trails up and then down my body, anger flashing through his expression as he's about to shout something, I stab the poker right through his throat to close off any ability to scream for help. As I pin him against the stone, he reaches for the metal rod as blood pours out like he's a barrel of wine with a hole in it.

For *Anya*.

She's counting on me, too.

Once the life is gone from him, I use my foot to push on his stomach and pull the poker out, slowing him down as he collapses and bleeds all over me.

I hurry down the remainder of the stairs, cursing myself for not grabbing one of his blades instead, but there's no time. I nearly trip with shaky legs and come across two *more*, wearing black tabards with a flame sigil. Leaping down two stairs to ram the poker into one, I immediately release and catch my balance, my gaze latching on the blade at his hip as I channel *everything* into ensuring I grab it —light fingers—as I spin to stab him in the mouth that almost screams out.

My *only* advantage—and the only one I've ever had—is no one really expects me to attack like this. Just as Bones said, and these two seemed more ceremonial than worth their armor.

This will only work until I come across someone like Soren or Bones, who knows how to fight. Who doesn't get lost in a wave of shock, and will know how to pin me down as they ask questions later.

I don't even bother to be quiet as I continue to run down the stairs, leaving three bodies behind me already. "I'm coming, Melona," I mutter.

I focus every bit of mental energy I have into my wrists, thinking of the goddess that's supposed to give me powers, and beg inside of my mind for the keys to the cells to be hanging up on the wall, just like they were when Jesper escorted me down here. Surely a healing goddess won't be overly fond of a God of Misery, right?

How can I use her?

I beg even more once I'm down on the level that Jesper took me to, pleading that this isn't for me and it's to save others. Aren't other lives worth this stroke of luck? If this goddess can only be summoned with a blue candle, I can understand why Mom thought she was rather worthless.

I nearly shudder when I see the keys *are there*. No fucking way. Darting to them, I grasp them quickly and hurry along the water, everything just as it was when Jesper took me down here: dark lighting, candles everywhere, the water calm and gently flowing.

This tension between being so close to success, and yet it hasn't happened yet, is something I've never enjoyed. It's a high that was only fun when it was sneaking around, but when lives are on the line—*numb it.*

I focus on nothing but the next foot in front of me, keeping every eye and ear peeled. When I round the corner, my gaze affixes to the cell where I can see sirens who look weak, slumped over, or leaning against the wall. I move as swiftly as possible, trying not to fall or trip, when one of them notices me, silently waking the others.

I don't say a word as I immediately begin trying different keys as each one clinks down against the rest when it's not it, knowing to think of nothing other than dexterity to try as many as possible—

Click.

The lock to the cell opens, and I swing the loud, rusty door out as wide as it can go, immediately leaning down to Melona to start the process of trying different keys again, her dark eyes wide as she pants through cracked lips, the smell of rotting scales enraging my blood. My heart races so fast I feel as if I'm in a fever dream, especially once the metal choker around her neck clicks open, Melona pulling away from the confines.

It's as if I've been doused in cold water, gooseflesh rising all over.

I did it.

"Go, Jane. Leave the keys so we can unlock the rest ourselves," Melona says through a hoarse voice, coughing as she does.

The one that has to be Moriganna leans forward. "We already know the way out. *Flee.*"

They start to murmur among each other in some kind of clicking, high-pitched whining sound. I watch as Melona works, rather than get moving. "There's nowhere to flee," I say. A part of me didn't even expect to succeed here, and what about the keys? How can I free Anya without them? "I need to wait, so I can unlock the cell door for my friend. Can we," I begin thinking out loud more than anything. "Can we come with you at all?"

Moriganna shakes her head. "We don't have marrowkelp on us, or we would take you with us and into the water. It's too cold without it; you'll last maybe an hour, but we'd need more than that. The closest growth of it is *miles* away, and if you have to remain above water, they could always spot us before we get you safely on a shore." Moriganna coughs through a dry voice.

"I'm willing to risk it," I press.

Melona glances at me. "Jane, it would kill you. This time of year, humans can last about one or two hours in the water. It will take an hour alone just to swim around the peninsula. There's a great chance you won't make it to shore, and even then, you'd need to be rewarmed immediately." She presses her dried lips together, motioning where I came from. "Another guard is down the opposite way. He always carries keys when checking in on us. They're different looking than this set. We will need these as there are iron bars at the end of these tunnels. It'll be faster to steal the others."

"What about if guards come upon you?"

"We can use the sunder if necessary."

"Why didn't you use that already?" I ask so fast the words nearly blur.

Moriganna leans forward as Melona works on her chains. "That is how one of us has been killed, already," the siren princess answers. "It won't matter if we can actually escape."

The tension in these confines is haunting, and I swear their beautiful, elegant features nearly turn monstrous. Oh, they want revenge. A *lot* of it.

Without questioning anything else, I rush back down the pathway, the sirens being extra quiet as they slowly work to free themselves.

"She's got to be here, somewhere," I mutter, darting my gaze around until I find what looks like traditional prison cells, barely taking in any details, moving my way down there, rounding a corner and—shit.

I make eye contact with a guard whose nose is so crooked, it's definitely been broken more than once, his dirty hand holding a battle ax like he's surprised to see me. He seems more prepared to fight than the others, but he doesn't have nearly the same amount of armor.

Quick, what—

Grabbing a torch on the wall, I ream it at him as he raises his ax. *Imagine this is sparring.*

I press the torch right into his chest, ducking low when I see his footwork steps toward me, weapon raised, which swings *right* over my head, just barely. He screams from pain as the fire effortlessly burns his clothes, and I pad around his hard, ale-laden waist until I've got a hold of another hilt, unsheathing it as he pushes me off of him, dropping his ax with a loud *clink*.

I stab him in the gut, then right in the jugular to make it quick, and to keep him quiet. *This is for you, Anya.*

Panting heavily as my arm feels entirely funny—almost like I can't even use it—I notice there's a nasty gash right in the shoulder, blood spilling down, and reach around so I can heal it as I make my way to Anya's cell—the keys!

Damn.

I return to the guard's body, the smell of burning flesh something I did *not* consider beforehand as he continues to cook—he's got a smaller rung, but there are a few keys. I hold the cold iron ring with the useless hand, finding it easier to fade into an emotionless state with the shock of his wound to my system, my blood pounding in my ears.

"*Jane,*" Anya mutters somewhere in the darkness of one of the cells, her voice full of fear. There's a clinking of metal on the stone floor, like the sound of chains.

"I freed the sirens," I spit out, panting, blood dripping down my hand as I hurry to her cell.

"*Nothing* about this is stealthy," Anya says, appearing in the faint light of the torches in here, her bloodied eyes glistening.

Seeing her utterly beaten makes me sneer, any guilt for what I just did *vanishing*. "There wasn't an option for stealth," I say, the lock finally clicking open as I enter her cell, the iron bars creaking. I immediately move to the shackles at her ankle; it works, the heavy weight of it hitting the floor as she's freed. "Go. They can't kill me. They need me alive and submissive. I'll survive until someone gets here. Cypress just wanted me to free the sirens, that's all. So that's what I'm doing. I knocked Jesper out in a private room like I did with Soren, so we have time."

A part of my heart, somewhere, had clearly hoped Anya would come up with a miraculous plan and take me with her. Instead, Anya's skin begins to change, bruises disappearing along with everything else as she takes on the appearance of a woman with brown hair that I don't recognize. I observe the process, accepting that as soon as she disappears, I'll be alone.

It's more bittersweet than I thought.

"Get to the ocean, Jane," Anya says.

"I can't," I pant. "The sirens won't take me. They don't have marrowkelp, so I'd probably freeze to death before they can acquire any or get me to the right shoreline. There's *no way* we can both escape here, but *you* can, with your skills."

"You shouldn't have come for me," Anya warns, the foreign face covered in grime even if the marring of her body is hidden.

"And leave you to rot?"

"I didn't anticipate I'd survive here, Jane. I came so Soren could follow our trail, and confirm we're here. And—well, I overheard your entire conversation with Cypress, Jane. I know Soren can't feel you, or Misery. Cypress came to me right after she left you and told me to follow. That… that I'd get *my* freedom. That it would help. That I wasn't to leave your side, and that my willingness to die here would help save the rest, while I'd get to finally let go of my pain. Plus, I can't leave you, because of Soren's mask—" The old, shrewd expression returns to her. "Yes, wait. I have a plan. I have a piece of Soren's mask in my arm, which I can put into you, so maybe he can track *you*. I need you to help get it out of me and into your skin. After this, it will be worthless in my corpse."

"*Anya*," I say, as if I can snap her out of whatever she's insinuating.

Her eyes harden. "Jane, *please*. I am aware of what I got into. Death doesn't frighten me. But dying without a purpose *does*." She sighs, the sound almost making me smile as it's so like *her*. "Think of it this way, if you're the priority, then it makes sense to give it to you. Since you can heal us, it should be quick."

"Then why in the hell did Cypress just not do *that*? Why couldn't I use Soren's help at all?" It's a rather pointless question, but it spills out nonetheless.

Pale, brown eyes stare sternly at me. "Jane, I think Soren getting involved would have made things worse. It would have risked him too greatly to get so involved, and I actually think Cypress intends for Soren to live. And I think my death, for whatever reason, ensures everyone acts in a way that ensures this."

Those words shine sunlight on a shadowed part of my heart I didn't realize was starving for the light. Cypress wants Soren alive?

The light, airy sensation that the witch *isn't* working against us darkens once more. "Cypress is letting you sacrifice yourself."

"It's not like I didn't agree to it."

The pendant, the one around my neck. It's why it was a death note.

Anya takes the dagger from where I dropped it and digs into her forearm, grunting and grimacing as she flicks something out. "Shit. We can't lose that—" She places the blade down. "Fuck, I didn't even think about it disappearing if it's not in me anymore. It's a part of Soren... maybe only he could remove it."

We both search in the dark, hands on the floor, and I present her a few pebbles, clicking my tongue when I realize they're not the mask. "What does it feel like?"

"You'll feel the magic—it's *here*. She faces me, the torchlight barely enough to see each other. "Where do you want it?"

I peer out the door. "Should we get out of here first?"

"Nobody comes down here. Not with the sirens. Only that guard was here and would periodically check, but he's deaf."

It's the perfect opening.

"Forearm works," I say, not wanting to waste this opportunity. "Just do it."

I bite down on my knuckles as she slices me open, shoving the piece of Soren's mask into my skin, and then the blue light of my palms emits in the darkness as I heal it in.

Soren.

"I don't get anything from this," I say, partially disappointed. "I can't feel him at all."

"Could be your ruby. It might still work. Let's go. I'll stay with you," she pants out, my mind tunneling as so many details are useless in the shadow of survival. I heal her arm as we step out, the body of that guard mostly burned at the shirt and chest.

"Anya, could you live if you left me? As in, now that everything is set into motion... You might as well try to run."

She peers down both ways. "Cypress said to stay with you as long as I could. I could try taking on your skin, maybe run as far as I can while they chase me..." Her eyes are more apologetic than I've seen them. "I won't get far, though. I've barely eaten in a week. No… I should remain, like the witch wanted."

This is really fucking hard knowing someone is likely to die, and I can't change it. As if *I* know what's best for her. *She's making this choice on her own. Somehow, I have to respect that.*

"Okay, well, let's go right then? Maybe we can exit through the other end."

It's a heart-racing chase through the tunnels as we go down a path neither of us has been, Anya limping at times. When we pass by what looks like water, she drinks until her belly is full. We then come across a wooden door, which is unlocked.

"This place isn't well secured," I mumble.

"Ashfire doesn't come under attack often, if ever," she whispers. "I bet after this, they'll change that."

We move through to what looks like a storage room, and there's even the smell of food. Anya faces me. "We both need new clothes. You look ridiculous. We can capture two people, tie them up. Take their stuff."

It takes a moment for me to chuckle when I realize what she just said, and as I look around the place, I realize this might be the storage area for the kitchen with labeled boxes, bags of rice and flour, and stacks of eggs. I recognize an open box of tea leaves, spelling just like the ones used on me. "If we can stew these, even in lukewarm water, it will make them dreary for hours."

"Okay, let's find some cups."

We're like two mice back here, rummaging around until we find things we want. Every now and again, we can hear orders being barked somewhere down the hall, mixing with the sound of kitchen prep work.

As we strain the leaves in with the tea through a cloth, little droplets the only sound between us, Anya lifts her gaze to look at me. "This is Amy's face, by the way." Her voice wavers, but only for a moment, that deep expression of emotion breaking through like a soul trying to leave a body. "I don't want to talk about it more. I just… it comforts me, and I wanted you to know."

"Uh, yeah. Thanks for telling me," I say, staring at her more than usual now. It's odd to think that this face was once someone that was to Anya what Soren is to me, and I'm sort of meeting this dead stranger. Anya keeps an eye out while I hide and strain; she's better at espionage than I am. I brew what I can, hoping some of the components seep out. When the water is dark, I figure it's good enough, placing the wet cloth full of moist tea leaves on the floor.

"How long do we have, with Jesper?" Anya asks. "Might be a while before we come across anyone since it's night, and I don't know who is down here. Might be worth moving forward."

"He wanted dinner with me—I know, it was awkward as shit—and I attacked him rather quickly. He'll be out for a few hours, but someone might check on the room before then."

Her eyes appraise me. "That was smart, Jane."

"I got the idea from you, and the time you wore the skin of that man's mistress," I reply, my smile almost painful as it feels conditional. Like at any point, she'll be wiped away.

Anya's eyes flush with gratitude, like her dying words really meant something, before she hushes me, and the voices of two women start to near us.

"You should apply to mornings, Bev."

Another one yawns. "I know, I know. I hate night shifts with *baking*."

"I've been up since the sun was down. Jesper had us make a giant meal."

"For *who*?"

The two women round a corner wearing black robes; one is older, and one probably younger than me.

Perfect. Those clothes will fit.

Anya and I both attack, placing our hands over their mouths with kitchen blades at their throats. "You can squeal, and we'll cut you. Or drink that tea, and you'll wake up alive," Anya says.

They both nod feverishly as we guide them to the tea, the women bringing the cups to their mouths as we remove our hands, both looking at each other like it might be worth— "Don't make this bloody," I warn, my blade still at her throat.

They both drink the tea, the effects happening so swiftly I hope I didn't make it *too* strong. There's something about killing someone who also has a weapon in hand, but it's a harder concept when it's two people who *look* innocent.

As they slump to the floor, Anya and I quickly disrobe them and change ourselves.

"You should know, Jane," Anya says, her words muffled when she puts her head through an underdress. "I'm severely weakened right now." Her gaze connects with mine, a slight desperation in there. "I'm stealthy, not a warrior. If you need to run, you *run*. I beg you to."

"Let's just go," I say, her words hitting my mind but none of them sinking in. I can't consider that right now. I couldn't even let Kathleen run into a fire without following, even when I thought that me getting caught would risk *thousands*.

We're slow and cautious as we move forward, working with hand signals and pausing frequently. Especially once upon the kitchen, which is staffed with a minimal number of people for prep work.

At some point, we actually make it past, having no idea where we're going, and then there are *stairs*.

Up.

A way out.

"How violent are we committing to be?" I ask. "I don't like stabbing people that don't look like they deserve it. I might freeze."

Anya looks back at me, her gaze moving all over this dark staircase. "I don't know." She shrugs, facing ahead. "If it was Soren, they'd all be spiked on the walls without a second thought... and since my job is to get you out, I'll do whatever that takes."

I breathe calmly, knowing it's my resolve that's needed now. Okay, I'll just do what feels right in the moment. Personal desires aside, Misery cannot have me. I have to really *try*.

Mom didn't get a choice whether she wanted to be involved or not.

When we open a service door at the top of the stairs, we're greeted by the livid, dark eyes of Jesper.

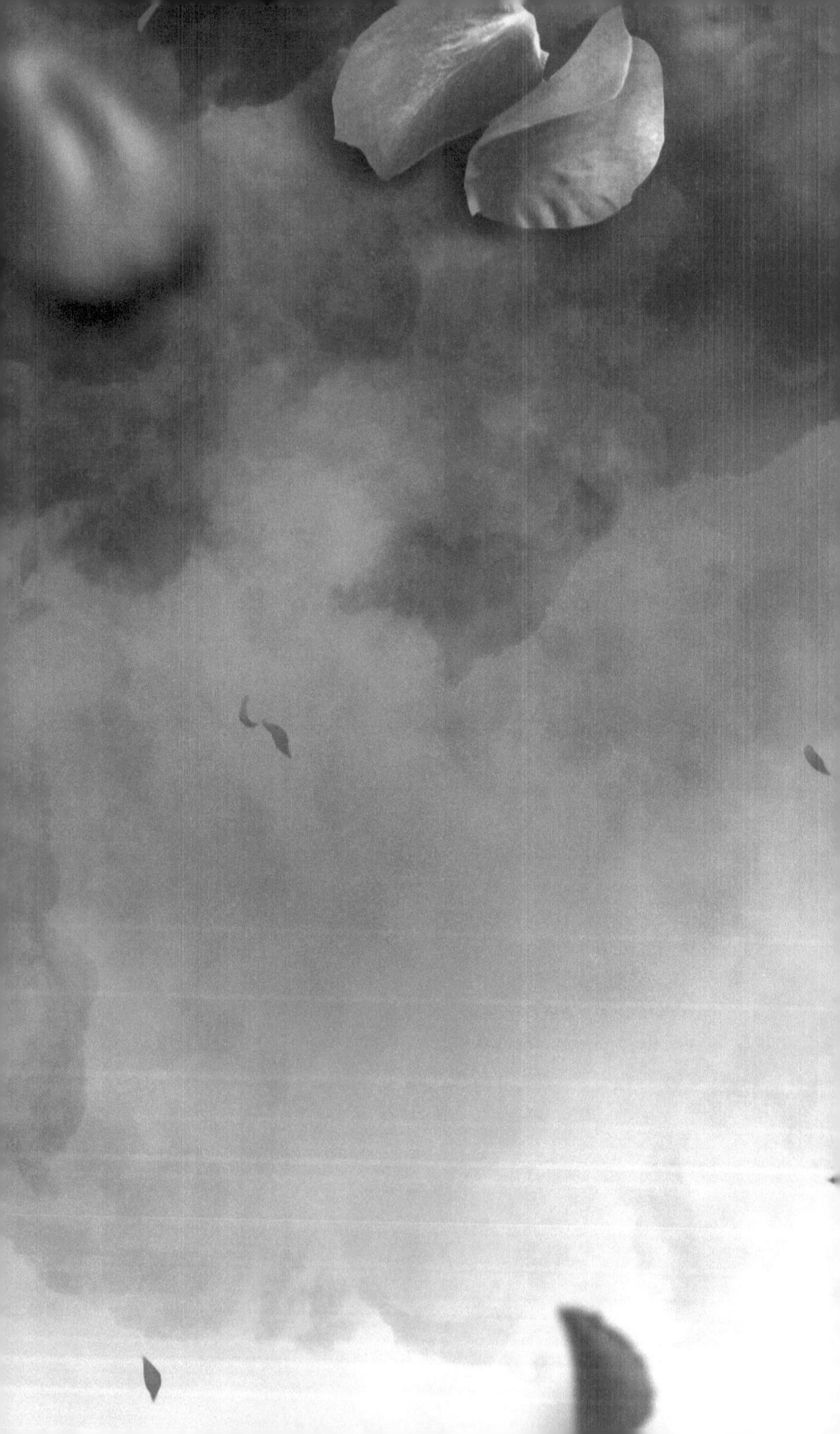

MAY HE REAP YOUR SOUL
JANE

I don't know how Dad ever managed this—facing his enemies without being scared shitless. Right now, my insides are coiled so tightly that I'm sure I'll vomit if I so much as exhale too deeply. My palms are slick with sweat, knowing that what is to follow will be the worst moment of my life.

They're going to hurt me. Badly.

How do I get Anya out of here?

Jesper's face is sewn together with threads of fury, his silken shirt covered in food stains. He focuses on Anya. "Grab her. Leave *Jane* to me."

We both rapidly descend the stairs, and I even skip a few steps as we reach the bottom, only to be greeted by the sound of many approaching. "She's this way!" The shout ricochets down the hall.

My pulse spikes, my heart hammering against my ribcage.

I stare at the long, dark pathway, the flickering torchlight the only movement until the shadows of at least two dozen guards move against the walls, and right behind me is Anya. It's either forward or up those stairs.

Shit.

It isn't even worth trying to fight, the guards converging on Anya, taking her up the stairs as she silently writhes in their grip.

For my lineage and my bloodline, I force myself to stand tall, and I wait. My back straightens, my chin lifts, and I allow myself to look up the stairwell and see Jesper slowly descending as Anya is carried past him.

The only benefit is knowing how *angry* he will be.

I *am* a daughter of Skull's Row.

And I fucking ruined his precious little plans.

I hear someone yell, "Thomas is killed, too!"

The gazes from all around lock onto me in increments, like they're shocked it was *me*. Jesper finally makes it to the bottom of the stairs, looking me over in disgust, before picking me up by the robes I stole and slamming me against a wall, seething. Pain explodes in my back and ribs as I gasp, struggling to stay upright. "What the *fuck* did you do to me?"

I meet his gaze, forcing myself to stay steady. "If you seriously think I was going to just sit in a tower, or casually eat dinner with you like my entire life never mattered, then I can't help you."

His expression twists, a grotesque mix of anger and amusement. "You will be punished for this." His wide eyes gyrate as they look all over my face, and yes... I am a little afraid. But I'm already numbing myself, disassociating. I must survive whatever happens. Anya needs me to. I can lie, say that I forced her out of her cell. Forced her to shift and to wear the robes. I don't know what good it will do... but maybe it'll help.

He lets out a dark, humorless chuckle. "Alright... you're right, Jane *Ritter*. There's no point in being angry at a dog for stealing food if it's on the table... but you *can* beat the feral beast." He motions down the tunnel, eyes connecting with guards. "Someone bring me the friend."

That's right. She wasn't looking like herself. He doesn't know...

A soldier rushes off, his boots pounding against the stone. Jesper looks back at me. "How did you do it? They said the sirens are gone."

I don't answer him and just glare, gripping his forearms to try and steady myself.

He shakes me. "You *left* me sleeping in my *food*."

"I know. You smell like steak."

He tosses me across the small space and into a wall, my breath clearing my lungs. That jolted my back so profoundly my hips feel out of place.

When it looks like Jesper might kick me, the same guard that took off returns, shouting, "She's gone! Sam is dead, too!"

Jesper's face is overtaken by pure shock, looking back up the stairs like he might see Anya there. His hand shoots out, grabbing the hood of my robes, yanking hard enough to make me stick my fingers between my neck and the fabric to prevent being choked, dragging me up the stairwell; the hood twists around as my knee slams into the edges a few times, trying desperately to keep breathing. I can't help but whimper at the searing pain. "If she fights me, someone stab her. Misery can deal with it, just like Blackwell can deal with his sirens," he commands, his tone *biting*. "We're going for a walk."

It takes all I have to keep up, moving quickly and at an awkward angle where I can't see much. I'm finally released when he tosses me onto the floor in what's clearly the grand hall, its vaulted ceilings and flickering braziers making the space feel cavernous and oppressive. I breathe deeply, rubbing my neck. *Many* are waiting, one woman yelling at me through sobs, "That bitch killed Brandon!"

They're free. Focus on knowing the sirens are free.

And where is Anya?

Accusations, curses, and sobs swirl together once they all feel like it's time to blame *Jane* for everything. Even Marissa is in the crowd, her eyes frenzied with glee. "She's not one of us! She never will be! We should just kill and use her now!"

Jesper shouts at them all to quit talking, his voice echoing against the stone before he stands over me. "I'm going to rape you, right here and now, then tie you in the dungeons. Every time we consummate, *everyone* will watch. And then after you've given me what *I* want, I'll let the men fuck you as many times as they please, right in this hallway… Oh, is that going to bother you? What, angry you can't heal your way out of *that*? Misery can deal with you being *accosted.*"

Silence, once more. I'll literally run straight into a sword, aiming for my womb, before letting that happen. *Don't let it scare you. You'll never live to see that.*

Right when Jesper yells in frustration, taking a step near me, someone else shouts, *"Enough!"*

Blackwell's presence is like a thunderclap, shaking everyone as many shoulders stiffen. "What the *fuck* is going on? Why did I have to wake Misery? Why do I hear that the sirens are missing?"

The oddest looking, dark furred monkey is perched on Blackwell's shoulder, the eyes completely circular and with orange, molten pupils. The monkey twitches, its movements unnervingly sharp, and then, without warning, it leaps from Blackwell's shoulder, scampering on the floor, its long tail coiling.

"She freed the sirens. And the *prisoner*," Jesper pants, his lips curled in against his teeth. "She escaped the piano room," Jesper adds, swatting at the monkey when it starts to approach him. "I think she used the balconies and crossed over on the servant's ledge."

"Why was she in there at all?" Blackwell asks, his gaze filled with rancor, his peppery hair tightly pulled back.

"She asked to go in there."

"Oh," he answers, the mockery almost embarrassing. "She *asked* for it, did she? And how the *fuck* did she get out of that room?"

"Her magic! Someone came in when I didn't answer, and a healer said she felt Jane's healing magic, which was used to *subdue* me."

Blackwell closes the space between him and Jesper, like a storm swallowing a weak sunrise; I hate Blackwell, but I can't deny he embodies authority forged in blood and hardship—his scarred, weathered skin displaying what he's earned through sacrifice, his outfit brimming with weapons that aren't for show but for survival. Jesper just looks like a spoiled twat next to him, his clothes polished and his unearned bravado feeble, covered in his *dinner.*

Fuck Blackwell for making me respect him, even if only because

I nearly want to laugh at how paltry Jesper is in comparison, and that's a good feeling for me.

"I warned you," Blackwell begins, his voice dipping low. "I told you not to trust this cunt. She's the daughter of the *Scorpion*. Do you think he bred someone *tame*?" He pushes Jesper on the shoulder. "You are immeasurably lucky that I have to wait for our god before doing *anything* to you. Those sirens..." his thin lips roll inward, vexation staining his gain. "You're such a spoiled cunt of an idiot. *She's* acting as I told you she would, and *you're* the one that let her out of her cage! The sirens being freed is on *you!*." His eyes seethe as he places a hand on his dagger's hilt, Jesper looking down with zero pushback. Blackwell holds a hand out like he might choke the pompous idiot, but refrains before turning to face me, the monkey hopping near Blackwell's feet to stare right at me, unblinking. "And *Jane*... you made a *mistake*."

"She didn't do it!" someone shouts from the crowd of onlookers. The monkey doesn't turn around and continues to stare me down. I remain lying on the ground, as I truly don't want to fight them now. I did what I came here to do, which means I need to focus on escaping. On surviving.

The guards bring Anya forward, who still wears the face of Amy. "Sir, she says she knows what happened."

Everyone stares at her, a few mumbling under their breaths as if they can't believe their eyes. Then, shoulder-length brown hair recedes and returns black, her round face lengthening to reveal Anya, the black robes slightly baggy on her now, her bruises all coming through as she breathes a sigh of relief, like it took too much effort to maintain that. "*I* freed the sirens."

"No," I mutter, the sound desperate, as I press up onto my knees.

"Don't listen to her," Anya coldly says. "She is under the impression that her father's life is dependent on you believing she freed the sirens."

"Anya!" I shout.

"*Jane*," she scolds, finally connecting her gaze with mine.

Jesper's voice breaks. "Someone get the *fucking* god by the name of Morvock. And not his *howler* monkey!" He advances on Anya, but she doesn't flinch, her calm demeanor unshaken even as the crowd parts to give him a clear path, the guards still holding onto her.

"Say that again," Jesper demands, towering over her while Blackwell watches on, his fingers twitching like he can't tell what he wants to do yet.

"I'm a skin shifter, and I'm loyal to Soren." She steps forward confidently. "You *are* going to die; you do know that? The more scars she has on her, the more torment is added to your miserable life. If she so much as *points* to you once Soren gets here, you will regret every breath after that, and he will ensure there will be *plenty* to endure. My only regret is I won't witness it."

I can't see Jesper's face from here, only that his shoulders stiffen. "Say it again about the sirens." Even though his voice is low, it carries in this stony enclave. "*Who* freed the sirens?"

"*I* did," Anya doubles down, her stance declaring no space for fear, shaking her shoulders as if to make the guards let go.

"No, it was me," I say, feeling like this is Maryanne all over again. What's the point? We're both caught now.

Anya's intense glare is thrown with such force at me that I actually close my mouth. What is she doing? *Taking the heat off of you, so you won't be punished.* I hate that I know the answer, because it's one I despise. Jesper throws his gaze between Anya and me, the stupid monkey still staring me down.

"I want the *truth!*" Jesper yells, pointing to the floor like he can command us.

Anya raises a brow, boredom clear in her eyes. "I'll wait for Misery."

"I'll get the god," Blackwell says, like he's fetching a pet. "Jesper, if you touch either one, I'll give you a taste of a Skull's Row punishment. To which I am *eager* to give, so don't—" he raises a hand, as if to stop himself as he storms off.

The Zenith stalks away, the monkey following him, jumping up onto his shoulder. I try to make eye contact with Anya as we wait, but she stares ahead, resolute. She's the shrewd one, isn't she? That's what Soren says. Is there more to this than meets the eye?

Remaining on my knees, the chilly floor starts to get to me, but I don't want to move. Silence weaves through us all until most of the heads bow down in respect. Through the hallway approaches the cloaked god, his candle eyes surveying the room, the staff clacking on the floor in a rhythm. The monkey returns on Misery's shoulder, continuing to stare at me, and I swear I'm contemplating how to stab it. Misery stops walking when at the center of this chaos, his unnatural fingers grip the staff tighter. "What is this?"

"She is waiting for you, my lord," Jesper says, failing to completely control the frayed seams of his mind. "The… the *sirens*… they've been freed. *She* claims to be the one who did it."

"It was *me*," I implore, Misery finally turning his head to stare directly at me. I lower mine just to avoid every aspect of his intensity.

"This isn't time for bravery, Ritter," Anya yells out. "I appreciate giving me the chance to go out on my own. I was never making it out alive, which is why, Jesper, *I* freed the sirens. Because I didn't give a rat's ass if I lived or died, but then your idiotic self took Jane, thinking *she* did it."

Misery removes his gaze from me, and I finally lift mine to look ahead, to assess.

Anya stares Misery down, completely unafraid. "That's right. It's not Jane. It's Cypress, actually. She holds Jane's father ransom, and she is the one that allowed Jane into the jungle. I followed and over-heard their conversation, which is how I knew the sirens were important to you—" Misery's grip tightens on his staff "—she told Jane that she had to free the sirens or else Jane's father would be murdered by the witch herself. I made the choice to come on my own, knowing it's what Soren would want. *I* freed the sirens, so Jane wouldn't get hurt by any of you for doing so. I came as her shield." She spins those half-truths so perfectly like a weaver, that *I'd* believe it, even though I was the one Cypress spoke to, and I know Dad was never a part of these conversations. "She did free *me*, I confess. But it's because I begged her for it. That's the only crime she has committed tonight."

Jesper watches as if he's ready to stab the next person to breathe funny, but bores his gaze into Misery, waiting for judgment. The broken god contemplates for so long it's as if he's unaware of his surroundings. "Why not flee, if you can take on the skin of anoth-er?" he asks, my brows furrowing at such a nonsensical question.

"Because I came to do the dirty work so Jane would live," she explains, and looks at me. Some part of my mind hears that she really is taking the fall for me, that maybe she *is* my shield, that maybe she *did* overhear Cypress giving me instructions, even if she partially lies about what was said. Which means Cypress *wanted* her to hear, knowing she'd likely take this exact path, protecting me after I freed the sirens like the witch asked… and yet, I cannot stand I'm in this scenario—again.

Useless.

It's not within my bones to watch someone take the fall for me.

"She's sad," Anya answers, right as I open my mouth. "If I had to guess, because her father will die now. You weren't supposed to know, you see. That was the deal. So she will proclaim I'm lying, no matter what."

It's such a smooth, believable lie. It makes me look like I'm acting out of desperation, not going on the offensive. It could literally save my life. Save my *dignity*. And yet it's not worth it, not for a second. I do *not* like the feeling of people sacrificing themselves for me.

Jesper releases a high-pitched, incredulous laugh. "Can we kill this bitch yet?"

"A lot of what she says is the truth…" Misery croons. "This feeble excuse for a body cannot allow me to see further. I need *my* lands," he growls, like he's growing impatient. "But we do not need this skin shifter. Dispose of her. I will ruminate more on what happened to the sirens before taking any action."

"*No,*" I protest, about to rise to my feet. I don't know how I'll stop them, but I can't sit still, either.

Misery throws a decrepit hand my way, and with it comes a gush of wind as nearby rope slithers over and crawls up me. I scream at the sensation until it wraps around my arms and gags me.

Anya looks at me with a crack of a smile before she faces Jesper. "Well, go on. Stab me, you weird fire prick. Get this over with."

It happens so fast that I barely notice it as Jesper unsheathes a blade and plunges it within Anya, her body eating the metal until it's mostly the hilt that sticks out.

I drop to my knees when blood spills out of Anya from her gut and her mouth, trickling down her chin, the woman barely moving in response, hiding her pain with perfection. My grunts are muffled by the rope, screaming through the threads that bind me.

Anya's eyes trail upward, and unlike my mother's eyes—full of disappointment and agony as she died—Anya's seem almost relieved.

Jesper removes the blade, and Anya slowly collapses as the guards let her drop, a glaze in her eyes as she looks at Jesper. She spits blood on his shoes before laughing. "Enjoy your life before Soren reaps your soul, you dumbass."

She pulls a blade out from somewhere—I cannot see—and slashes at Jesper's ankle, to which he falls over and cries out in pain, like the mayor's cousin did back in Moore's Inn; cowardice carries the shriek.

Blackwell unveils an obsidian blade and slits Anya's throat, her head slumping as her body ceases all movement.

They begin to strip the black robes she stole, and I thrash in my binds. I stop when I see the three marks on her back that Soren has —Death's Wing.

Assassins.

My father always told me people who join ranks like those are trained to die, to greet death rather than run. *Gods*, it doesn't make it better, but I do I breathe steadier, despite the tears that pour down, glaring at the back of Misery since he can't feel me, my furious gaze moving to Jesper. *Keep yourself together, Jane.* There's a whole new reason now to kill these fuckers. I *will* get revenge for her.

Marissa pushes a woman near Jesper, who begins healing him immediately with the same powers I harbor within me. That healer feels like a traitor.

"Throw her body into the ocean," Misery orders. "She is not worth anything more than that."

And like that, they pick up Anya's lifeless body and carry her away, blood dripping off of her fingers in a trail of red droplets. It's when her presence is gone that I feel the weight of being incredibly alone here.

The weight of *failure*.

FUTILITY

SOREN

It's been three days since I spoke with Liam, and I *loathe* this waiting. It's like dragging jagged knives across my chest, over and over. We've been arranging every last detail, obsessing over the possibilities, and scourging the maps of Ashfire that Liam possesses.

As soon as the sun had risen on the second day aboard, we landed on a part of the coast of the Fire Isles, far enough south the fire worshippers won't be here. Quite a few ships are anchored out in the ocean, the port filled with many people. The terrain is flatter, a permanent mist hovering over us like we've been slowly enveloped within another realm.

Misthaven harbor.

My mask is in my hand, and I stare at the small divot where I chipped off Anya's piece. The sensation of her, even if faint, completely disappeared a few days ago as if it had been ripped out.

And then *Jane.*

It took my breath away when all I sensed was a heart that I've ravaged more times than I can count. And there was *fear.* It struck me in the night while the others slept, and I put my mask on to try and understand what happened to her.

Jane had wept for the rest of that night.

How did those two come across an opportunity to implant that into Jane? What was going on in Ashfire? Why was Jane so frenzied like the day Blackwell burned Maryanne?

Jane...

Her heart is so faint across that ocean, but it's there. And it hasn't suffered anything new like it did all those days ago. In a selfish twist of my heart, I'm grateful I get to feel my desert rose over Anya, but that greed is quickly overshadowed when I know it can't be for a good reason. *Jane was weeping like someone was lost...*

What did you do, Anya?

I'm getting *really* fucking tired of waiting on this damn shoreline as Liam prepares his ship, ferrying goods to and from it, securing the rigging, and patching any holes. Ritter is supposed to be securing *the* most essential part of our plan, but it's starting to take too long. I need to know what happened in that castle.

To know if Anya is still alive.

"So," Bones says, sitting there as he hardly blinks. "You still can't feel Anya anymore?"

Anya going missing has disturbed the chaos within him.

We sit in one of the shanties on a deck, looking out at the misty ocean, the sound of the waves making me think of Jane's heartbeat, and how many times it's cycled a rhythm while she has no idea where we are, or if we're even coming for her. She is *burdened* with loneliness. *I haven't forgotten you, love.*

"I'm certain that Anya put the mask in Jane."

"Were they imprisoned together, maybe?"

"Anya always felt alone. It was clear when she wasn't. It's as if they found a way together, and then *that* happened."

If Jane acquiring the mask had been its own incident, I wouldn't be so worried. It's the grief that has me teetering on an edge, like I know I have to crash down the side and face the truth, but I don't want to. Not yet.

Ritter's energy precedes him, like a dangerous beast who grows more restless by the hour. There's no victory within that man, just an empty sort of weariness and exhaustion. What the fuck? Are we about to go *another* day without any progress?

When he approaches my deck, he shakes his head, his lips fidgeting with rage. "Something is wrong. I can't get the siren's attention."

I lean forward in my seat. *"Come again?"*

That was the cornerstone of our plan. Ritter would secure the sirens, as we *need* them to make this work.

Ritter's face is a mask of frustration and fatigue, his jaw tightening. "It's unlike Melona not to come when called. The stupid white eye can't even spot their energies in the water. Usually, I can at least see *traces* of them."

I don't even fucking know why the siren would come to him in the first place. "Do you want to give me half-truths or tell me what the fuck is going on? Why would she owe you anything? How severe is it that she hasn't shown up? What are the circumstances? You do realize I *still* cannot feel Anya anymore?" I connect my gaze with Ritter, as he knows this, although he seems to find more relief now that I can feel Jane. "Just because I'm connection to Jane doesn't mean the undertones of Anya's energy going missing aren't overlooked. It means the two faced desperation. We're losing our window of opportunity."

His eyes flash with barely restrained rage. This is a man who is unraveling, more than I think he realizes. He runs a hand through his hair, the gesture more desperate than deliberate, his gaze not focusing on anything. "Melona has my mask. My Zenith mask. Just like you trying to take pieces off of yours, and being surprised it worked, I was surprised I was able to depart without it returning to me." He pauses to shake his head, tutting. "I gave it to her so she could always find me. So she could feel me. She has the gift of *sight*, and that mask helped connect her to me. It was *always* my last resort with Jane—get her in the ocean and let the sirens take her somewhere remote." He looks off, fear and defeat weighing down his heart. "It's not right that she's not showing."

I listen very carefully, the words true. I listen further to feel out the impact of his words on the world around us, to see if I get a positive or negative feeling in that statement; I don't know what to fucking do because I don't feel a thing. "And what's stopping this siren from just deciding not to help you?"

"She made a blood oath with Cypress and me."

I laugh, the sound even a little high-pitched, while Bones remains still as a statue. "That fucking *bitch*. She's like a disease. I almost can't hate her anymore. She's infected all of us so perfectly; we might as well sit here until she appears to give us orders."

I lean back in my seat, staring off in the direction that is Ashfire, my indignation rolling into dangerous waves of energy.

Ritter stares at the sands below his feet. "Melona *has* to come as a part of the deal. She made the blood oath because she was worried for the siren princess, and wanted to protect her. Like how I did with Jane. Cypress must have seen our paths crossing, and decided to formalize it. It's why Melona was waiting for Jane when I took her to the coast, before I ran off to distract everyone from looking for my daughter... so I could... take care of *Nora*," he says, the pain even fresher in his soul.

It's like we're all damaged goods, and Cypress has offered to fill in the gaps in our hearts with her ruby crystals. If that bitch has used Anya, or Jane, and they die for it... I breathe steadier. Calmer.

No, I want *real* revenge. For that, I need to see *clearly*. I'll sit still like the Scorpion for however long I need to, if it means taking down whoever is to blame for all of this.

Ritter looks back at me, a pleading bleeding from his heart that his eyes can't express. "Melona can only give that mask back when the danger of her siren princess is gone, and I can only take it when Jane is no longer threatened by Misery. Which means..." He shakes his head. "Something happened to the sirens. It *has* to be."

"We *need* those sirens to infiltrate without Tempest," I warn, still staring off as far as the foggy veil will allow me. "Perhaps we get to deeper waters today, plunge a man in. Use it like a fishing lure."

That might work. Sirens don't frequent the coastlines, and if they do, it's not typically to *hunt*. They steal the flesh of men when they're out in open sea, devouring those that fall within a ship-wreck, and taking all the worthy ones back to shore—

Michael's energy comes rushing to me, full of something I do not want to feel. Why is someone like *him* scared? Gutted? "My *liege*," he says before making his appearance, Bones slowly lowering his head to look at our brother in arms. Michael's face is utterly crestfallen.

I don't like this.

"You need to come. You need to *see*."

Bones is on his feet before any of us, our footsteps sinking into the sands. Ritter yells out for Donna and Rorge as Bones and I hurry, walking out and to the shore, for what seems like an impossibly long time—

My heart rate picks up when there's a beached siren, waiting in the water, up on her hands as the waves wash over her tail, her long, nearly white hair wet and silky.

"Melona!" Ritter yells out from behind us, and the siren's wide eyes find him, only to drift sadly toward me.

Once close enough, it's clear she isn't alone. At least, not in the flesh. In front of her is a lifeless, naked woman's body, her flesh so pale and waxen it looks like polished stone, a deep stab wound in her gut marring the flesh, and then, as the wave pushes against the body, the head rolls to face us.

Bones shrieks, something more dangerous and deeper than anger flooding his body. I stop in my tracks, staring at Anya's neck wound, someone having slashed it—

Nothing surrounds Anya; her aura completely dissolved back into the ether.

The siren has a hand underneath Anya's head. "I can't move her further on land. But I know she belongs to you."

Even Basilisk comes hurrying over, slowing on the sands, wearing only a thin tunic and pants, staring on in surprise.

I stand in a haze of slow moving time, staring at Anya's body that is so devoid of anything human. All that history, all those years together, are completely gone. Not a single pulse of life is within her; her soul has been gone for some time.

Bones is the first one to kneel into the water, taking her body from Melona as Anya's head unnaturally slumps back with the injury to her throat; Bones repositions to hold it safely.

Slowly, I step closer.

My eyes widen further in shock when I squat down to see her face better, her fire completely burned out.

Anya...

My heart is pulled into too many directions, the grief of what I see like an untouchable emotion, while I'm so very afraid for Jane. I touch her face, her eyelids partially open to reveal the most lifeless gaze up at the sky. *Fuck.* My emotions are slung around so violently, a deep wave of mourning chilling *everything.* My vision even blurs without thinking. "Her necklace is gone..."

She filled a void when I was lost, a sisterly presence, even if clearly not *my* Serena. She was so fucking committed to each task, so *intelligent.* Her heartbreak at Amy's death broke something in her that day that not even *she* could mend.

That confirms that Jane's mourning is because she knows what has happened, here.

No.

This can't be.

Bones breathes heavily, wiping at his face. "Oh, you cunt, you can't die on me," he says through a shaky voice, pulling her body closer. "Who did this to you? What exact blade *did* this to you? I'll find it, Anya. I'll use it to carve whoever did this into *pieces* and make him eat his own flesh."

"*Melona,*" Ritter commands. "Where is Jane? What is happening? Where have you been?"

"Jane is alive at Ashfire," she quickly says, my gaze snapping up at her. "We were taken by Blackwell, and I left your mask in a safe place, just as I felt them take Moriganna. I knew I had to go with them. We were prisoners in there for *weeks,* slowly being starved and dried out. It was Jane that set us all free, she even got Anya out of her chains... who didn't make it."

A cold wave of shock too large to contain exits my body through a stupefied exhale—*Jane?* My breathing grows deeper, more unsteady. I stare the siren down, my eyes burning from not blinking. "*Jane* did that? Jane freed you?" I ask, my gritty voice steady. My blood pulses, my body breathing with purpose again; *Jane needs us. She shouldn't be fighting them alone. She's trying. She's fighting.*

The siren nods, everyone watching her with bated breath, even Bones, who still holds Anya's body. "Jane set us free, and then this woman here. We lulled the guard who carried her dead body with our songs and threatened him with our curse if he didn't tell us what happened. They were going to torture Jane, right in the halls of their castle—" a rage so uncomfortably hot boils inside of me "—Jesper, in particular. Anya took the fall for Jane, claiming it was *her* that freed us—Morvock wants our blood. He was to use the princess's in particular, like how he wants Jane. The two of them were supposed to make him untouchable in all of the Balar Coasts. Jane ruined *everything*. I heard the one named Jesper is suffering incredible punishment, and I think Jane will, too, if she ever reaches Boneglass."

I glare up at the direction of Ashfire, every pulse of blood from my enraged heart slowly changing as pure hatred seeps in, filling in every crevice within me. The images enter my mind of Jane in the castle, before everyone, *alone*, just as I feel her—

My teeth clamp so suddenly I nearly bite my tongue. I'm going to burn that entire fucking place down.

Ritter's concern is the loudest on this beach, the dread of a father facing that his child might endure something terrible screaming through his aura.

My heart can't seem to understand what to feel.

I'm in shock.

Not only with Anya, but that Jane is a fucking match for them. I'm not surprised she is… just surprised at how *useless* I feel standing here. She's battling them, all on her own. Anya tried to help her; I know it. That's what I had to have felt.

Glancing down, Anya's expressionless face pushes me further into the jaws of revenge. She died for Jane. My desert rose single-handedly fucked with an entire empire; *that's right, love. You are incredible. You ruined them all, you beautiful woman.*

"And to answer *you*," Melona says, nodding to Bones. "It was Jesper who stabbed her. And then Blackwell slit her throat."

"Jesper is *mine*," Ritter growls, the Scorpion in his full glory with the *death* that emanates from him. "I'll kill you for that. His order killed my wife and now, he has my fucking daughter. He. Is. *Mine*."

Bones's nose is red, but no tears are shed. "Fine, old man," he glances up at him. "But I *do* want to cut off his cock. I get to maim a *part* of him."

"Only his hands," Melona says. "We like to keep the rest intact for what we use them for. And I have a feeling Charles might want to deliver Jesper to us."

The Scorpion grunts in approval.

The energy of this beach is far too messy, too chaotic. There's no order to the violence that is *brimming* from our bodies.

We need to channel our focus.

Melona looks at Bones, who is like a viper everyone is afraid will attack, but just lies there; there's something more unnerving about the stillness. "She is at peace, Bones. I can feel it. Not a trace of her soul lingers, which means she was ready."

"You can feel that," Bones states, mockingly more than with hope.

She raises a brow. "Yes, we can."

The smallest sound escapes Bones, his hands slightly shaking. But I know the mad man, and I know his heart; he's like a hellhound who smells meat in the air and needs to *rip* at the flesh; he needs to *destroy* people for this.

He's becoming inaccessible in there.

I squat down and reach for Anya's hand, holding it up to see the bruises around her wrists. "A part of her has been dead for a long time, Dane." Everything within Bones stills, and I swear even his fucking heartbeat. I don't remember the last time I used his *real* name, but he needs to hear me. I need his savage chaos to pull this off, which means he can't lose himself to unsuppressed rage. "I felt it leave her when Amy did. Anya has been waiting for the right time, the right death. That's the only solace we can have, which means she'll have died wanting *us* to rip them *all* apart for her. But we can't lose ourselves, or her murder will be wasted. We owe her our steadiness."

I bring her hand to my lips and kiss the frigid skin, sighing with disappointment. "I hope you reveled in your death, Anya. Fly high and free." I lower it back to rest in the sand, some of the water rolling up to gently wash over the fingers. "I'm sorry."

I will properly mourn her later.

I know her enough to be aware she'd come back from the dead, just to stab me if I don't fucking figure this out by sunset.

And Jane needs me.

When I stand with a numbed heart, I face Melona. "How did Jane possibly free you?" I ask, refocusing myself. Anya's death will *not* be in vain. "Jane *has* to be under lock and key."

Melona wipes her arms in salt water, and then along her gills as if applying oils. "She risked a *lot* to get to us. They were *very* rough with her for it."

They have no idea how fortunate they are I was not nearby to gut them all. I'd make their deaths *hurt*. Touching Jane as if I'm not fucking right behind her.

"We need your help to reach the castle," I say, staring at the waves that separate me from her. This is the first time in a while I've been *afraid*. It will break me if it's Jane next—

I can't even fucking think of it.

Not when I can feel her.

"What do you have planned?" Melona asks, her smooth voice starting to crack as if she's parched. "You have our support. They *branded* us," she hisses, rotating her shoulder to reveal a shark burn mark on her arm, the ocean water rolling in to wash over her tail.

Blackwell.

"We're going to sail Storm's Fury close to the coasts, stopping just as the tip of the volcano is within view. We then plan to jump into the waters and have the sirens swim us to shore. There's one spot in particular that is the least guarded. Preferably reaching it in the middle of the night."

Her eyes widen with understanding. "You want to use marrowkelp," she says, her gaze roaming all over. "That will require a *lot* of it... but they won't see you coming. I encountered Morvock, very briefly. He is so very weakened. He's spent too much time away from his lands." She looks at me with something predatory in her eyes. "He's nervous, too. I can feel it when he's near."

"What is he afraid of?" Ritter asks, almost before she's even done speaking.

"The ocean god," she says with pride, her smile revealing sharpened teeth. "I think Morvock will be forced to leave the Fire Isles soon."

"Why would he fear the ocean god?" I ask.

"He branded Moriganna. At least, Blackwell did on Morvock's

orders," she replies, almost as if she's eager to see devastation befall them all. "She's our princess. She's the daughter of the ocean god."

Ritter frowns right away. "That's *Tempest's* daughter."

Melona's dark, doe eyes flash with ego. "Correct, Charles. Which means when Tempest finds out her daughter has been branded, Ta'Kan will no doubt rage the seas for Tempest. Misery will *not* make it home, and *that's* what he fears."

Purpose, drive, and rage are ablaze within me. "So then we flush him out," I say. "*Now.*"

Her smile stretches further, almost mischievous. "That's why I like this plan. Force him to leave *early*. He cannot set foot on his own soil until the solar eclipse. Which means the sooner we get him to the ocean, the sooner we make him vulnerable."

"Then let your sister sirens know," I order, rising to the call of Jane. "We'll send a hawk to Liam. He's still on his ship. We can be in the deep sea by sundown." I glance down at Anya, the act so out of habit, only to have everything in me halt.

Seeing her there is one of the most chilling sensations I've had in a very long time.

How the fuck did this happen?

Stop wasting time over me.

I nearly laugh at the memory of her, knowing that's exactly what she would say, but my face remains emotionless.

It's disturbing to see her dead.

"Melona," I say, staring at Anya's head. "Can you keep a body preserved?"

"Yes," she answers, confidence filling her energy.

"Please keep her body safe," I say. "She deserves a proper Death's Wing burial. It's her sacrifice that probably saved Jane."

"What exactly did Jane do to free you?" Ritter asks.

"She escaped, somehow. Was covered in blood—I assume not her own, not at first—and was incredibly rushed. She found the right key and unlocked our chains before taking off, where I assume she went to free Anya."

Tears burn my eyes, a sensation I'm not used to in the slightest. In all of this, I'm fucking proud of her. I love that about her, and she's alone. All fucking alone, yet her spirit is *far* from dead.

She's the fire no one can burn out.

I finally step away, knowing I can't linger, as even seeing Anya in my peripheral threatens my sanity. She wouldn't want me to, not right now. Her body is almost a call to action, as if she knew it would find its way home. I need to channel *everything* into action, and unleash my fury once in their castle walls.

It's when blood is spilled that I can begin to mourn.

I affix the skull mask to my face, and decide I won't take it off until Jane is safe.

FUTILITY

JANE

I've decided I don't like circular rooms. Or being thirsty. My lips are so dry they're like rubbing two pieces of linen together.

If my rations are being limited to make me go crazy, it's working. It feels like everywhere I look is a wall curving in on me, not a corner to be found.

Lying on the bed, I turn the silver pendant Anya gave to me, still hooked on a chain; every time I feel like being weak up here, I think of Anya. It's been three days since she was executed in front of me, and I still only *half* believe it to be true.

It's not fair she's gone. No one was supposed to follow me here. I eye the wren, the silent object the loudest thing in this room. I never had anything of my mother's to look at, no stagnant echo of a life that once burned so profoundly.

This pendant harbors many stories that I'll never know. I don't know *when* they met, only that it was in Death's Wing. Or who confessed their love first, or who flirted first, or what their favorite trait of the other was.

No, those details died with them.

I now hold their tombstone.

And for what? What have I done to deserve this sacrifice? Be of Soren's interest? She did this all of her own accord, and yet I can't help but wonder what I could have done differently.

There's nothing else to do in here but *sulk*.

I sigh, the muscles in my face heavy. I *had* to free her, even if maybe I should have left her. There's a chance she'd be rotting right now, but *alive*. I barely knew Anya, and yet this cuts deeply at me; my chest breaks with an emptiness, and the tears flow again. "Anya, you idiot, why did you do this?"

Her death has shattered me, in a way. I feel responsible to carry her shadow. I witnessed her last moments, and I can testify how strong she was, even to the very end. I tuck the pendant underneath my shirt as the new lady's maid named Iris should be approaching soon to bring me my food, based on the lighting of this room from the sun. I don't dare let anyone witness I have this.

Marissa has been reassigned, per *Blackwell's* command.

Once Jesper fell and was being healed, I was whisked away back up here and carried like a sack of potatoes, forbidden to leave under *any* circumstance unless escorted by Misery or Black-well. *"Pain is not a motivator for you like it is for others. Not having direction, I think, is a far worse punishment. You will stare at these walls until we are all leaving, Ritter. Jesper will suffer his own torment."*

In some way, whatever they're doing is working. There's been no beating, no punishment. Which confuses the shit out of me. So, I refused food for the first two days. On the third day, I had destroyed the room like back in the Black House, and they tied me up and forced food down my throat, pinching my nose so I had to chew just so I could swallow and breathe. They even brought a tube made of glass and poured bone broth down my throat.

How tempting it was to bite it and let it cut me from the inside.

But I didn't, because I will not let Anya's death be wasted. So, I complied as they cleaned my room, and not a word was spoken about punishment.

Misery is just letting everything *be*.

Stupid cunt.

I *hate* this.

It's a language I don't understand. I *know* violence. Corporal punishment. Torture, even.

Will Soren be angry that Anya died on my watch? That she technically died *for* me? Anya literally saved me from every kind of assault out there, as they apparently believed her. I've heard, through Iris, that no one believes *I* did it. It makes more sense that a Death's Wing assassin was responsible.

I fucking owe that woman.

Cypress had to know… she told Anya to come, so she could take the fall of the task Cypress gave me…

At some point, when do I see this free will the witch spoke of?

When the sounds of someone nearing the room pulls me from my mind, I sit up and wait for food to be pushed through the flap in the door, the one I've opened and stared through to watch the empty staircase about thirty times a day as a part of my routine.

The new lady's maid is silent and cautious with me, and I'm shocked when the door *opens*. I carefully rise to my feet, my body aching without any of the distractions to forget what it's been through.

Including my forearm that I barely healed with my depleted energy.

Soren.

Iris enters the room, her black hair tied back into a bun, her bumpy nose a little red today, and she's sniffing quite a bit as she checks the bedding for bleeding, along with my clothes in an undignified search for my monthly cycle; tracking of it begins *now*. "Bring in her food," she orders to a brute at the door. He carries a tray to me, smacking it on the bed as things jostle around.

"Traitor," he grumbles, glaring at me through bushy eyebrows.

"The only traitor here is *you*, because you won't bring me fresh water," I hoarsely say, coughing slightly, leaning over to grab the pitcher and show how empty it is. "Kind of hard for my body to work without it, like your precious god wants."

The guard's eyes flare as if I've called his mother a donkey, the man nearly backhanding me, but Iris holds her hands out in the air. "No! Don't. Morvock says not to touch her unless it's to make her eat."

"We won't be repeating *that*," I say through tight lips, taking a giant bite out of the bread, only to nearly choke when my mouth is so dry I can't swallow. "But seriously, water?" I ask, crumbs spitting out. "I need to be watered."

I'll forever think of it that way after Soren. *That man feels so far away now...* I almost glance at the piece of mask in my arm, but refrain in case they notice.

Iris purses her lips and grunts, taking the pitcher as she motions for the guard to leave, locking the door once more on her way out. Shadows at the bottom of the door tell me that the guard is still standing by, which he rarely does.

Interesting.

So far, I've been watching every move of this new guard and Iris, wondering if I could kill them to escape... except I have no idea how many guards are down the stairs after everything that happened.

Don't worry. Something will present itself.

I want to believe that Anya was right about freeing the siren, and that people will be coming. That Melona was right to suggest people *are* coming for me.

I eat my food once a pitcher is placed inside my room, right at the door, before it locks again. I drink leisurely, so as not to make myself nauseous. The food goes down easier, and I slowly eat my bread and apple as I stare out the window at the ocean, knowing I'm facing the wrong way. If they'll come from anywhere, it'll be south, or southwest. This faces north, toward an open ocean before we come across Misery's island. I know nothing about it other than it's *very* secluded, and apparently named Boneglass.

It's crossed my mind that I can find a way to end myself. Get rid of Misery's grand vision *and* save lives. Maybe commit to it as I take out another, like Blackwell or Jesper. *Some* way to make it worth it.

I just don't have it in me, yet.

Not yet. Not with Anya's sacrifice. Not with the oath I gave

Soren that I'd find his sister for him. She's suffered *too*, which means I can endure whatever is yet to come.

They'll regret ever taking me.

MOVEMENT

SOREN

Movement is never-ending as we prepare ourselves, a sense of finality overhanging us all. Some will not return alive, and these are the last days those hearts will beat. The unwritten nature of murderous conflict always brings a deep element of unfairness. There are those that will suffer simply as calamity on that peninsula, and they, too, unknowingly live their last days.

Only the other side of this will reveal who will make it.

I'm standing on the beach, the longboats nearing us that will take us to Storm's Fury, the sun having crossed the sky and is nearing the horizon line. The sirens are ready, and so is Liam. I sense out all the moving men behind me, still wearing my mask. There's a disruption within them, although I have not addressed it, yet.

Finally a few come near, one that is long standing with me.

Another is young, and the third has an evolving heart that started changing in loyalties once he had his children.

They don't want to be here.

The men all take a knee in the sand. "My liege, we want to speak," the one in the middle asks.

"Clearly."

"I've traveled with you for a long time, Soren," he says, connecting his gaze with mine; a spark of fear flares in his heart. "This is a lot to risk for Ritter's daughter. About a quarter just want to go home."

Lifting my gaze with a blink, I allow that statement to settle on my shoulders as I try to understand what to do with it. All my men are out on this coast, either eating, drinking water, putting on their armor, or sharpening their blades as we wait. I survey them; a weakness is plotted, very unstable in its grip.

I bellow out, "I hear some of you want to go home."

Everyone slows down to a halt, either with their water to their lips, or about to swipe a whetstone on their blade, all looking at me so the ocean is the only sound. Bones slowly moves my way, hands in his pockets, before turning to face the men with a mismatched gaze. Stubble lines his face; lines *all* of ours.

While my right side remains fucking empty.

"Did you all happen to notice we are missing someone?" I slowly pace around, my arms still crossed as I approach a man. "Are *you* wanting to go home?"

"No, my liege."

I can tell.

I go to another, one of the men has been affected since the murder of Silas and Mads. "But *you* do."

He is silent. Embarrassed.

"Do you think I'd call every one of you to risk your life for something personal of mine? Have I ever done that?" I think of Serena, and how even still, I don't demand my men's lives for that. "I could storm Ashfire with a dozen men, including the Scorpion, and get Jane out if I needed to." I point to them all. "You're all coming because this bitch named Misery plans to fuck every one of us over like we're some common wench he can use when he pleases."

I motion back to the opposite side of Bones, where Anya would stand; where her energy is so completely lacking. "He already *has* by killing Anya," I say, letting that settle on them, the statement striking through like lightning. "This is a fucking *god* that is trying desperately to reclaim a physical body. Right now, we are the only ones with wind of his goals that have any power and advancement to stop him. Blackwell is among him, so other Zenith can't be trusted." I slowly walk back to the three men, taking very deliberate steps as I stand in front of them. "Why the hesitation this time, when we've risked our lives before? This wasn't there when we entered the Undercroft."

I do not want them here if they are to feel this, but I need to know what's different.

"We *know* many are going to die."

"That's a shit fucking attitude."

This was never an issue within Death's Wing, but I understand those that follow me have not taken the same oaths I adhere to. I have a realm of people who are in my legion that want to *live* prosperous lives, at the risk of their own. Not live to *die*.

I pivot slightly, waving out at the ocean. "Go. Go home."

The young one's face scrunches. "As a *coward*?"

"I can't control how others will perceive it. I also understand a man that wants to see his family," I reply, the older one lowering his head further. "But I have absolutely no room for anyone that is going to fuck this up because he hesitates. Our collective goal is Misery. Jane is *mine*." I pace back around the hard sands. "If anyone thinks Mads and Silas dying has left my mind, then I *also* don't want you here. We are *the* group of men that can stop a hurricane before it *ravishes* our homes… anyone who is going to hesitate better be gone by the time I have my armor on."

I turn back to face the ocean, stopping near the canvas bag that contains my effects, including Jane's dagger.

Anya used to help.

Then Jane did.

Bones nears me, that violence contained exactly how I want it; I know once blades start swinging, it will be dangerous for *anyone* to get near. In some ways, when I feel that he's steadying himself, that blonde flashes in his aura again.

Maybe she's good for him, after all.

"Where do you want me in all of this?" Bones asks while I place a shoulder piece on, fingering at the latches.

"To be me when I cannot be. I want to burn this place down, to use that very fear that they inflict on others and let them suffocate in their own smoke... going through Liam's scrolls, it seems that only two dozen fire mages live on that peninsula, and they're housed somewhere near a statue of two people holding up a sphere," I reply, wishing we had more information. "We're targeting them, first. We will need to break up at times, and I need you to run whatever is going on like how I would.

"Ritter and I will go after Jane. She's in a tower, and I can feel her now. Which means I'll know how to locate her once we're closer. And if you see Blackwell, skin his hair for me, and bring me his knuckles."

"I'd love to bleach those," he comments.

I affix the rose dagger with the bright red hilt at my thigh, the leather fastenings barely fitting.

Jane.

Her solitude drives me, knowing she fights fucking tooth and nail. I'll find my desert rose, because she blooms even in a drought. Even when her roots are being actively culled, she'll survive just out of spite alone. I want to help her with every fiber of my being, to bloody her blade and give it to her so we can get her out of there.

And *this* time, she won't have to worry about losing it. Because she's worth it to me. Because I can't stop thinking about her opening up to me, to how it felt to let someone touch me so gently while being vulnerable.

If I fail here, she will disappear.

My heart is still torn in two directions as I worry for Serena, because once I'm in those waters I won't be able to turn back.

I've already lost Anya.

In every way but physically seeing it, I've lost Serena; the threads of my heart sharply echoing like when a violin screeches. That damn witch has meddled so much with my life, I don't know what to believe anymore. She claimed if I did this, she'll help me locate my sister. But what of Anya's death? She had to see that coming.

No hesitation. Jane will live. You know she will. She'll take care of Serena.

"It's weird to not have Anya," Bones comments, her emptiness hitting that vulnerability that's wide open in my chest right now.

Fuck it hurts if I let it sit for too long. If Misery wasn't a threat to everyone I know, I wouldn't sacrifice *any* of my men.

That's not a luxury we have, though.

"And they're going to pay for that."

"I still wonder how she got caught. Or why they took her, when everyone else was left behind at the shanty."

"I never once felt fear in her… I've been thinking on it. I almost wonder if she purposefully hid what she felt so I wouldn't be alerted." I breathe slowly, as if Anya left me a note that I have to decipher. "I think we're missing information, Bones. And that we just need to *act*."

A wave of violence crests at the surface of his aura, churning back into wherever he represses himself. Whenever he's this focused, so far on the edge of dissociation, he's like a lone man who happens to be on my side, guided by his own need for slaughter.

I'll need that.

If we can *halve* the fire mages, we can do enough damage to fuck this entire kingdom in one night to finish what Jane started.

⋯◈⋯

LEAVING behind the rowboats for the crew to raise and tether to the ship, we climb up the coarse rope ladders that will get us over to the deck. Sounds of sails flapping and ropes being tied and pulled taught mixes with the excited chatter of the crew.

Bones strides over, watching a few coiled ropes get neatly laid to the side. "I just don't get the attraction to all of this," he says, waving around. "We're stuck on this wooden contraption. *Again*."

I survey the slightly swaying deck. "It won't be for long."

Bone steps nearer, the twilight hours almost peaceful with the ocean water. "Are we really letting Ritter take Jesper?"

"Yes," I say without hesitation. "There's no doubt in my mind that he has been waiting for a long time to fuck him over. I wouldn't poke the Scorpion when it concerns that."

There's still doubt within Bones, and I eye his mismatched gaze, darker circles showing how little sleep he's gotten. Blankly staring off, he says, "It doesn't feel like she's dead."

It might be that way to him, but I feel it. There's a void that occurs when someone has left this world, their unique vibration utterly silent. It's one way I'm certain that Serena is still out there, as she doesn't feel dead to me.

Anya, on the other hand… I grip my jaw, running my fingers over the edge of my mask, and drop my hand. If she were here, she'd help us infiltrate the fire worshippers.

"We'll give her a proper burial. Death's Wing burial. I'll send her ashes back to the Steep, where she can be fully laid to rest next to Amy."

That comforts Bones, and I can tell he needed it. It's protocol that when anyone in Death's Wing dies, they're cremated, so new life can sprout in their ashes. A portion is *always* collected to return to the Steep, where we all trained and earned our stripes.

The vague image of a blonde woman flashes in my mind's eye once again, and I glance at Bones. "You better live, too. There's someone waiting for you to return."

That actually makes him uncomfortable. "I've never had that. Makes me feel guilty, honestly. And then I—" I don't think he knows what to do with those complex feelings. He furrows his brows, the sentence never finishing.

I don't reply, as I understand. He can't worry about her, not fully, or else it will wreck his concentration. It doesn't stop Kathleen from filling his mind in rapid flashes, though. Just like how Jane haunts every shadow of mine.

My purpose is different, as I'm *always* listening to the energies of my mask that's inside of Jane, her vibration felt in the direction that this ship sails in, and I'm so honed in on her I sometimes fail to read those around me.

My rage is only tamed by knowing that I'm *finally* on my way, and I can then unleash every ounce of rage that has festered in my soul for *decades*.

ONCE THE OCEAN is no longer visible in the darkness of night, we head down below deck. Ritter and my men sit together, having joined forces over the last few days as they've had nothing else to do but mingle. A few are passing around vials of poppy, tucking them away before we embark on our mission—I've made it clear that only those who are used to it are to consume it, otherwise it'll be the death of others.

Basilisk's energy approaches me as I lean in the ship's wall, sitting and bracing my core so as not to sway too greatly.

He joins me in this silence, his leather crinkling as he mirror's my position; we've never had a sentimental connection. We're two, very similar men with matching powers, and he was willing to take me under his wing for a while.

"What did Cypress tell you your purpose was here?" I ask, absorbing the energy around me, the ship creaking and groaning.

"Honestly?" he answers, leaning his back on the wall. "To be present. She just wanted me *around*," he says, rotating his finger in the air. "After helping your woman in the Undercroft, I'm assuming Cypress sent me here as an *assurance*, and since you know me, you won't reject me. She told me she'd give me what I wanted as long as I remained close until this is done."

At this point, I'm not going to ask any more questions. We're all being arranged within a dirty machination. "I don't feel your cat," I comment.

"I left her in the harbor. It's too volatile to bring her."

"How do you plan to find a *cat* after this?"

His sigh carries the edge of a growl, motioning his head slightly as if he can't hold something back any longer. "Jasmine is wearing the slimmest collar with a red ruby on it. It's lodged in her fur so you can't see it." He looks at me, nearly rolling his eyes as he looks away just as quickly. "I'm *very* eager to get my hands on a harpy killer, and *also* keep that damn cat alive. Cypress told me that if I had to leave Jasmine, that the necklace would keep track of her. Jasmine knows to wait."

I absentmindedly move a ring on my finger before suddenly releasing a breathy laugh. "What the fuck have you been up to, exactly?"

"Who knows how I got here. I don't think men like us are meant to live past thirty. If we make it, it's like we don't know what to do with ourselves. Somehow I'm on a journey with a witch's request to help you fuck over our own god."

"You're supposed to have a damn castle, an army, and a *harem*," I say, laughing more. "This is one hell of a detour."

He nods, like he's happy to hear that about himself. "Still have all that… they're all just patiently waiting on my return. Except the harem. Recently retired that."

I don't honestly want to know why.

"So then what is sending you on *this* journey? I know it's *something*. I can feel it," I say as if it's obvious, almost calling him Rasmus, but reframing.

He bites his lower lip, running a hand over his stubble that sounds like sandpaper. "It's over someone I haven't been able to forget about for, I don't know, ten years."

"Ah," I say. "You conveniently left that out."

He's silent for a while, and I can feel memories and emotions stirring inside of him. "A woman, of course," he finally says through a sigh. "She's the leader of an all female assassin group. Found that pretty fucking interesting. We had our time together. Then she left me, with her damn cat. Telling me if our time was worth anything to me, to take care of Jasmine."

I furrow my brows. "It's been ten years… you're still taking care of it?"

"Obviously." So many things flood his body, which are muted with precision. He has incredible control over his powers.

"So you're here because of *her*?"

He glares at me. "Does it matter?" He clears his throat. "I came over here to talk to you because you and me need to be careful getting too close to Misery. He can have a lot of sway over us, like we saw. I think we can plan as much as we want, but it's going to be a damn mess. We have no idea how many fire mages there are, either. If we can provide an escape for Jane, sounds like she can take care of that herself. That's probably the most we can do."

I think on that, agreeing with most of it. "Everything in me tells me not to worry. That the answer will come to me. My brain says fuck that, there's no guarantee. But it's like the concern melts away as soon as it enters, like I can't make it *count*."

"I don't think you ever get used to that," he replies, closing his eyes to lean his head back once more. "But if it feels like you can't even question it, then it's probably your powers telling you something."

Out of everything, it's the sensation of speaking to another Sensor that brings a calm to me I didn't know I was missing. He thinks like I do, observes his surroundings in the same manner.

"It's been all over the place for me," I retort, my voice so swift to move to the edge. "I got injured in the streets before we went to the Undercroft. Everything *screamed* in me to take the hit."

"I heard about it," he replies. "From the pieces I've gathered, I think it was worth it. I think it was your own magic tapping into survival, or the fates. Because that man named Shade acted like an idiot, and admitted he wasn't supposed to act when he did. If he hadn't, you may have walked right into an ambush instead of the Undercroft."

"So then I trust it?"

I know the answer. I need to hear someone confirm it; a person that *knows* what I go through. The stakes are too high, and Jane means too much. I need to know I can *trust* what my intuition demands of me.

"I feel it too. It's worth letting it go. Everything tells me we need to arrive, then we'll know what to do."

Basilisk looks over at a group of laughing men, who silence when they see golden eyes have spotted them. It's been rather hilarious to see the effect he has, as if getting too close is a curse. To touch Basilisk or even just brush against him is said to be akin to touching frostbite, biting cold and painful, because one knows death is coming—Tempest's crew was different, as it was clear they feared *nothing* but their own captain.

The pirates here still have a healthy dose of appreciation for who the rest of us are.

Closing my eyes, I try to find Jane's energy once again. It's still there, as if I have my fingers on her pulse. Her mood hasn't changed drastically, just ebbed and flowed in its sorrow.

It's okay, love. I'll be there, soon. You're so resilient.

Going to aid her feels like recalling something stolen from home. "Have you ever felt—*experienced*—being near a person, and their presence is almost like it's been there the entire time? At *our* level, anyway? With our magic..."

"Why do you think I'm taking care of someone else's cat, making deals with witches, and trying to kill Misery for?"

So, he feels that connection, then; it solidifies what embeds in my heart for Jane. "Except you and her have space between you... so why would that happen?"

"It was necessary. I was not right for her. Not then. I've fought that current for years, convinced it wasn't true. But now that it's so much later... I knew when we first met I couldn't have her. Not yet." He stretches his legs out and crosses them. "If you feel it with the Scorpion's daughter, it's because she *is* home for you. You're just lucky enough she wants to give it back. Some of us Sensors have to wait *years* once we have found that person."

That truth settles on me like I've been trying to hold my breath and finally *breathe*. Maybe if I was a romantic man, I'd have more delicacy in handling this.

How in the hells does someone like *me* handle that truth?

The two of us sit in silence, the undercarriage starting to fill with sleeping men, while I sit there awake. Perhaps I'll doze off for an hour soon, but I don't need more than that. No with what that witch did to me all those years ago; a sacrifice to reduce sleep so I could spend more time researching, traveling, and training.

I let Cypress read my entire soul so she'd grant me the ability to exist like I do, and that's how I learned she was poison.

I regret ever going to her.

All to find my sister, who I'm slowly accepting I may actually never see again, even if I survive this.

"Rasmus," I say.

He growls. "No one fucking listens when I say I don't want to be called that. Threats don't work on you, because I'm realistically not going to kill you. Why do you press that boundary I've *clearly* made?"

I ignore him, because what I want to ask is deeper than any moniker's title. I'll open up a piece of my heart, because I can feel death moving through these men, and I don't know which side of that coin my fate rests on. "I can't find Serena. At all. I can feel she is alive, but she is totally inaccessible. It's like when I think I'm near her, she's suddenly elsewhere. I've gone *mad* hunting her down. It's… it's why I'm here in the first place," I slowly breathe out, the words like cleaning out tension in my body. I can admit this to him, because he knows the angry, destructive young man I used to be.

"It's not failing, Soren, if someone is purposely hiding her. Which is what it sounds like," he says with annoyance, like he hasn't forgotten the use of his name.

Hope.

I hate that bittersweet bitch.

It's something I've considered before, but I'd allow it to blow away as soon as it appeared. It would mean she's *truly* inaccessible. "I always thought I'd find *something*. Use the Zenith and their network to man a hunt for Serena."

I know that Cypress has given me no choice, and that I truly do trust Jane to find her, especially after proving herself in Ashfire—*as long as I get her out*. Perhaps it's just impossible for me to uncurl my fingers that carry the responsibility of caring for my family.

It's not in me to *truly* let go.

"So, you're giving it all to Jane," he says with understanding, as if he just read me like how I read others.

The broken pieces of my soul are a little less jagged at that thought. "She feels like *mine*. Especially with my mask embedded in her. Her soul *connects* to me—" I stop, feeling incredibly uncomfortable to let another have that information.

"I know," he quickly replies. "I understand. You don't need to say more."

I don't even know if our conversation accomplished anything, and yet it seemed to help. The longer my magic is exposed to Jane, especially with this mask on, the more it feels entirely wrong to consider her not in my life.

In that, I understand Anya.

That's not a feeling you can ever forget, or move away from.

I rest my eyes at some point, finding peace in my duty here. I'm not even sure if I accomplished any sleep when my eyes shoot wide open as Ritter approaches us, along with Liam.

The captain of this ship stands in front of me, the man containing *true* pirating energy; as if any offer of the right kind will sway him.

"It's nearly time. When we can spot the tip of the volcano, we'll anchor and get every one of you into the waters. On land, once you're ready, light a blue flame. The bigger, the better," he hands both Basilisk and I a small bag, the two of us still seated. "That'll turn it blue long enough for me to spot it. We'll know that means it's time to ready the ship to leave. I'll get close enough so the sirens won't have to travel far to fetch you, and we'll then ready the cannons."

Cannons.

Something many have reported in ships further south in the summer trade lines. It'll be interesting to see them used here, if they're effective at all.

"And I double-confirmed with Melona," Ritter says. "The water is our ally. The sirens will be infesting them, called from all over. They'll be deep so they can't be ensnared, and as soon as they feel one of us plunge below, they'll grab us and use marrowkelp to get us back to the ship."

I stare out at the men who are trying to listen, some elbowed awake; they'll be formally briefed soon. When it's time to get their orders, I want it to be with the poppy in their system, their blood running *hot* with murder.

"It's time to get ready," I say.

VENDETTA
SOREN

The moon is barely a sliver in the sky. Heavy clouds cover the stars, a rumbling in the distance that promises a storm. The ship sways more with taller swells. I'm up on deck, my armor fastened, my weapons sharpened, Jane's blade at my thigh. My mask remains an extension of me, sensing out the peninsula just ahead. I can't quite pinpoint the exact sensation, but it's as if *right* ahead contains a massive amount of energy.

And Jane is there.

Oh, her feisty, determined heart is so much clearer, as if I could reach out and touch her.

I'm so fucking ready to get her home.

It's absolutely silent on deck. The men that remain are all here to

either die in glory, searching to keep their families safe, or are creatures of pure fucking madness.

None of us are noble men, and yet here we all are trying to save
the Balar Coasts.

I've felt Misery's powers too intimately to not at least *attempt*
cutting off this poison before it seeps into our world. If he can affect
me so greatly when he's weak, him at full strength, with an entire
cult behind him, would ruin *everything*.

This is even for my mother. A woman I wrote a letter to, handing
to the men that remained behind. For my sister, wherever she is. A
better world is never something one can hope will materialize, or
stumble upon.

Corruption is a permanent sickness that we have to physically
cull, and nothing is achieved without sacrifice.

I cannot leave this world knowing I failed two people that I love.
And Jane has fought so fucking hard—chills wash over me as I
think of what she's done. She *has* to know we're trying. That we
didn't forget about her, not for a single moment.

Someone climbs down from the crow's nest, my gaze lowering
slightly to peer at the blackness of the sea. "We spotted flickering
fire in the distance, sir! Probably best to anchor here."

Liam strolls the deck, peering around as if he can read details in
the wind. "Let's lower the anchors!"

My heart pounds, as it's happening. Our success, or failure, will
be unveiled very shortly. And I am *not* leaving that peninsula with
failure; I will either return to this ship with Jane or die on that soil.

Turning around, I address my men. "Move to the edges!"

I pass by Liam, who gives me a nod. "I wish you fair winds,
Zenith."

"Be ready for us," I reply.

There's a tunnel vision one gets; at least, I know I do. I have a
role to perform, and a task to achieve. *Nothing* else matters.

I move among the others as we near a gate the crew unlatches,
everyone shouting at each other to increase our energy.

Ritter and his followers, along with mine and Basilisk, all stand
and wait. Rorge is the only one to remain, along with a few that are
either sick or otherwise incapable of joining.

Ritter no longer has his long coat, and looks more like the mercenary I heard legends of. His energy finally vibrates with consistency; he's not only going to save his daughter, but *finally* claim his revenge.

"Do not fight the waters!" I shout. "The sirens are in there! Let your body sink and they will find you!"

I near the opening, ready to be the first to jump. I can barely see the swells that rock the ship, and even harder to spot are a few heads poking above.

The sirens.

It's officially time.

It feels entirely wrong to willingly jump overboard into an ocean so vast and powerful, but I'm so fucking ready for this.

Stepping out, my body is weightless as I plunge below, tensing as I fall into the icy waters, my body sinking with this heavy armor. As I hold my breath, hands grip me from all over, a few blurry sirens in my face, a small glowing orb tied around their necks and floating around their heads. One shoves something into my mouth, my body seizing as salt water enters my nostrils and lungs, swallowing the thick, globby mess. It's a substance that has to mix with the ocean water as it's consumed, and once it's down my throat, my body thrashes at the new sensation, gasping only to inhale water.

The sensation of drowning morphs into something almost pleasant, the pressure of the water eventually comforting. My throat burns on the outside, and I raise a hand to feel water suck in and push out from gills in my neck. My vision even sharpens. The frigid water is now refreshing. Two sirens keep me afloat as men drop through like pebbles, all sinking until sirens are among them and administering the transformation they need, the men thrashing until their bodies also adjust.

The sirens glide through the waters like the most elegant marine life, their hair effortlessly floating, swishing, and swirling. I'm handed a rope with leather around the handles, and a siren takes the other end as she begins to swim, pulling me forward. "We made these for your men, to make it easier to hold."

My eyes widen at the sensation of being pulled underwater without fear of drowning; it's such a weightless relief. The rope is long enough that I'm not directly in her wake, but I can feel the ripples of her tail.

The rest follow as we're guided through the darkness of the ocean. I can't even really tell that there are large swells above, or that a storm brews.

I glance back at the belly of Storm's Fury, barely visible in this darkness. I can sense that Ritter and Basilisk are close behind, along with Bones. There's a whole fucking armada of us being pulled to Ashfire, arriving under the guise of a storm.

The pulse of their collective energy grows more profound the closer we get, every one of their ripples a beacon of who is in the way of Jane. The razing of this place will be a message that if Jane's targeted, they're inviting my wrath.

And let this also be the clearest message to anyone even *thinking* about supporting Misery. He may be the god whose powers I use, but he wouldn't be the first sire I sought to slay.

The initial excitement slowly ebbs into uncertainty, as there's no marker for where we're at. No indication that we're actually making progress.

It's for a long time that we swim like this.

At some point, I swear I can see the bottom without much transition; it's concerning at first, thinking something from below was rising to us. Glancing up, I can see the waves above are no longer big swells but the smaller, collapsing ones with white peaks.

My heart thrums in my chest, my attention focusing. Breathing deeply, I ready myself for all the pain that will come, for the endurance I must call forth.

The depth of the oceans thins even more until the shoreline is upon us. My siren releases her rope, flipping in the water and moving like a snake to put her face in mine. "Walk out onto the shore, and the gills will be removed as soon as they touch air. The water from your lungs will spill out. Magic will remove it, so do not worry. It will be very uncomfortable, but temporary. You will not feel the effects of being cold once on land, either. This protection will last until your clothes are dry."

"Understood."

The discomfort means very little to me, not when Jane has faced so much. Not when Anya was tortured before dying.

The siren guides me until my feet touch the ocean floor, my leather boots walking over pressed sand. My head peaks through the waves, the salty ocean still filling my lungs. As soon as I intake the air, water pours from the gills, and I hurry forward to try and reach the beach. Saltwater drains from my mouth, nearly vomiting at one point until I gasp for air that feels just as clean as when my lungs filled with saltwater, choking and spitting out the last remnants of the ocean.

I stare up at the looming, craggy cliffs, and then higher still is the castle above, the ocean waves pushing against my body.

I can feel Jane.

Nearly laughing, I knew I'd fucking find a way into this land. That humor is quickly replaced by a growl as I trudge toward the shore, periodically glancing over my shoulders. Whatever moonlight breaks through barely touches the heads of the other men that surface.

The clouds rumble.

I near the man closest to me, pointing toward an alcove as water drains out of my vambraces. "We make for there once we all drain our armor. No speaking unless to spread the word."

Water drips off of me like I'm a creature of the ocean, and nothing about this peninsula feels like a threat. They really don't know, do they? We swiftly remove our armor once we're able, clearing out any fluids that will weigh us down, reattaching it just as quickly, as practiced.

I don't focus on what time has passed, only knowing that Jane is so fucking close and I won't mess this up by rushing. And as soon as we're out of here, if I'm still with her, we're removing that fucking ruby in her skin. It's just like with Ritter, where I can tell it's *him*, but there's no color to the aura, no crevices that emotions are hidden within. My mask only allows me to sense general emotions, not the complexities of Jane.

With as much love…

My teeth grind as there's so much worship for Misery here that it nearly drowns her out.

They picked the wrong god to obsess over.

Basilisk approaches my side, running a hand over his wet hair. "I want you to stay close to Ritter in this," I say. "He's not in his prime, and I want Jane to see her father after this is all done. Ensure he doesn't get killed."

"Babysitting the Scorpion," he comments, tilting his head side to side to get the water out. "What a task."

I motion for everyone to get closer, a wall of men surrounding me. Once we're all accounted for, I say, "We spare only children, possibly families that want nothing to do with us. Anyone with a red robe is to be killed under any circumstances necessary. Any person wearing armor is to be killed. And if you see Blackwell or Jesper, we want them *alive*." I take a small pause, to ensure they hear me. "We might just be the very thing that stops Misery from ruining *us all*. Don't forget that." Clinking spreads as shoulders bump together in unison. "It's time to fucking ruin these people."

A quiet hum of approval spreads through the four dozen that are here. As we discussed, I move first, striding along the rocky wall as we form a line. Rounding an edge, the small outpost with a giant bell on one of Liam's maps is far ahead, a bell that is no doubt to be rung if anything peculiar is spotted. A fire burns inside the building; a few braziers are lit around the surface of the stairs. The image of nearly fifty men rising out of the ocean's water is pretty fucking abnormal, and yet everything is silent; calm—save for the irritable clouds. I can feel a man is in that outpost, but his attention is extremely bare.

I turn behind me, searching for Bones's energy before motioning for him to come closer. "I'll go alone. Come if I call the signal or shout for your name."

"Can-fucking-do," he says, the pent-up rage finally singing smoothly inside him like the serenade of death. He's almost giddy at this.

I commit and move forward as quickly as possible, while staying low, pausing periodically to sense the man out; blank, again. Once I'm upon the stairs, I peer up, tilting my head to the side. I know I'm visible with the firelight, so I need to move quickly.

Placing a foot on the stairs to gauge the noise it makes, it creaks just enough that I bolt up, skipping steps, barging in as the guard is on his feet with a bottle of liquor in his lap. Pure terror seizes him, and I'm sure the mask I wear nearly makes him shit his pants.

He stumbles for the bell, but I unsheathe Jane's dagger and hold it at his throat as my other hand clasps over his mouth. "Answer a question, and I'll consider making this less painful."

He doesn't move.

"Where are the fire mages located?"

He tries to speak through my hand, and I gently lift my fingers as he shakily stammers out, "Inland. Near the outer battlements. There's a tall statue—"

"Where are they from *here*?"

"Up that path, head through the gates, then it's a long walk east, right at the base of the castle. Their buildings are right on the cliff's edge."

Perfect.

Jane's blade slides through his neck. His blood fills the grooves of the roses, and I help him down onto the floor without making much of a sound before cleaning the blade on his clothes. First barrier is out of the way.

I slowly move back to the line of mercenaries waiting on me, motioning for us to continue forward. We move along the walls of the cliffs, just as the map indicated, until they drastically reduce to reveal a dirt road, firelight more clear now in the distance as we can see smoke.

Now *that* is a full camp, and the shadows of night can no longer shield us there. I lift my gaze up to the tall tower still visible from here, where I can feel *her*. To the castle where I know Anya took her last breath, and where Jane fights for survival.

I come to a stop and get in Bones's ear. "The mages are exactly where we saw. We need to move past this and keep going. Should be dark up ahead, then we climb the cliffs."

We both touch each other's shoulders, and connect our gazes with a small nod, before I move forward and start the procession.

There was one building on the maps that was labeled as an apartment, one of the only ones along the cliff walls with no battlements. To which I brought rope and a grapnel. We'll climb the rocks to reach the blankest room that I can sense out, and infiltrate from there.

My heart pounds so hard, and yet it's alive with so much purpose.

One by one, we all cross into the darker path in this coverage of night, not an ounce of suspicion in these lands.

I'm here, Jane.

SOREN

I owe Liam after this.

It's just as he said, they're so fucking lax on security, the peninsula placing too much weight on Misery's presence and the power of the fire mages.

Just as the objects created to alter my powers caught me off guard, the mages vastly over appreciate their capabilities.

I'll gladly fucking remind them that they're not impervious.

Climbing up the frozen, jagged walls, it's one hand after another, the stone weathered and slick from the sea spray below. Thankfully, it's not very high. The building we're targeting is right on the edge of the small cliff. Windows exist like patches of darkness, unevenly spaced; they don't even have any glass in them.

I'm honed in on one that feels like the room is empty. I take a grappling hook and toss it up to the window ledge, catching it with a solid clang. I test the line—taut and steady—then swiftly scale the smooth surface of the building, every muscle burning with focus.

It's empty inside.

The wind whistles past my ears as I climb in. I grip the rope, pulling it into the room so I can use what's left at my waist to add additional length, knotting it tight. I search the room for a better anchor to handle more than one person at a time—a bed is right next to the window, and I wrap the rope through the framing, tying a knot and then tossing the rope out. Tension is placed on the frame, the bed creaking slightly as someone clearly climbs up. I stand against it to prevent *any* scratching of the posts on the floor, bracing my legs.

One by one, the room fills with more of our people, until a few sit on the bed to add weight so I can move forward through the old apartment.

Exiting the room and into a hall, I peer out a window that faces the street; a cleaner, sleeker version of Skull's Row, and much smaller. My whole body stiffens as I see a circular object being held up, flames wrapping around it like it's alive.

It's about fifty feet away, but its presence burns in my gut like a warning. This place *reeks* of fire mage magic.

At least we're in the right place.

I can't help but feel like there's another kind of person present here, the energies all mixing together, but there's a disparity. Whereas most exude a burning dedication, there are those who are tired, angry, and trapped. Perhaps workers, maybe?

Looking back over my shoulder, it's so dark it's hard to see who is near me, until I sense the man I want. As if he can tell, Basilisk looks my way and moves over, his gaze intensely eyeing the stone as if he can read the details of the place. "Do you feel other energy?" I ask.

"I do. I don't trust their lack of obsession; it's an abnormality. Let's get to them first."

We slip through the hall after taking Donna with us, since she's knowledgeable of these people. I come to a stop when that heavy sensation is powerful behind a door just to my right, a golden, glowing line below the door to signify light inside. It's unlocked as I turn the knob; people are chained to the walls, their bodies slumped on cots, faces pale with exhaustion. Their eyes snap to us as we enter.

"Speak a word and we stab you all," Basilisk says, almost lazily.

The captives remain silent, staring us all down.

"Why are you chained up?" Donna asks, while looking around the room.

They exchange uneasy glances and seem very confused, but also, nothing in them screams loyalty to this place. "Who took you?" I ask one man, my instinct pulling me to him. Looking directly into the skull mask momentarily empties his mind as wide eyes connect with mine, until my words seem to mean something to him. "We're Cinders. The men, anyway. The women are in the castle."

"What?" Out of every answer, that was not what I anticipated. "I'm here to find a Cinder myself. A woman."

The energy changes in an instant, intrigue flashing through them all, and one even motions with his hands for us to speak quieter. "We'll help you if you get us out."

"Where is their eternal flame being kept?" Donna asks, as if she has no patience. I don't disagree with her, so I look around to indicate that I'm waiting for someone to answer.

One seems eager to speak, the same one I first approached. "Five rooms down, there's an enclave which is guarded by them. That's where their stupid flame is. It's behind iron bars."

"How protected are the mages?" I ask, not liking that some of them are starting to get anxious; the energy is drastically changing in here.

They don't want to risk it.

"They ignite the floors if anyone gets too close. But it's usually just one or two at a time," he replies. "You can send me. I won't burn. They've... tested us." He speaks as if he's overly eager, but doesn't want to convey that *too* much. "I just want to go *home*. Please, I'll help. They're terrible at combat."

That's even more perfect. I turn to face Basilisk. "Let's weed out the ones who will hesitate. We'll use the rest to help."

We move through the group, gauging their resolve in ways only a Sensor could. One man barely reacts, his round face impassive as the two of us pass him by; his heart, on the other hand… it's *conflicted.*

I don't need to know anything more; sliding out Jane's dagger, gasps echo around the room like a window bursting open during a storm, the man in front of me only flinching as I cut at his garb and gag him, using some of the rope I have left to bind his wrists. He doesn't fight it, seemingly hating himself for that, and I re-sheathe my blade. "For your own good," I say.

When I'm about to turn to face another that I *know* will scream as soon as I make eye contact, I lunge at the man before I even look at him, hand at his throat as he claws at me. "We're going to gag you, and you'll shut the fuck about it. Do you understand?"

He nods, blood pooling underneath his skin, his bulging eyes wide as he can't breathe. Basilisk gets to work before I can even let go, forcing fabric into the man's mouth as we tie him up. He nearly slumps over when I release him, the color slowly draining from his face.

"Oh, thank the sirens," one breathes out. "Thought he was going to scream at any moment." It's the one from earlier, a man whose features I take in as he becomes relevant: blonde, small beard, dark eyes. He glares at the one we just bound. "I don't give a rat's ass, Merle, if you want to be *special*—"

"*Enough.*" I glare at the mouthy one, as we don't have time. "What is your name?"

"Roy."

I motion for him to stand on his bare feet, and he does so with hesitation, before I face Basilisk. "Stay in here with them. Keep them quiet until it's time to move."

A sinister play comes to life in his eyes as he scans the room, one of the Cinders lowering his gaze like he's petrified of this; he knows of Basilisk.

Go. Opportunity is right here.

I guide Roy out, who is so springy in his steps from pure excitement I wonder how long they've all been here for. I motion for Donna to follow, and I hand Roy one of the spare blades at my thigh. "Do you know how their magic works at all?" I ask. "And how to use one of these?"

He nods. "I do, to both. The mages need utter concentration. It can be broken so easily, which is what that statue is for. It's where they practice it, ceremonially, anyway. As long as you promise to come in behind me, I can get their concentration off, and you can finish them. I used to be a sellsword before they took me. I know what I'm doing."

I grin under the mask. "Done."

The effort is quick as he moves forward, the fire lighting up at Roy's presence. The mages let out a confused scream when they realize what's happening. When the whipping fires dwindle, I move forward, trusting every bit of this. It's so fucking hot in here, but I ignore it as I dispose of one, and the other is already stabbed in the chest by Roy. I help him ease the body onto the floor, searching for the keys.

Glancing up once I find them around the waist of a mage, I examine what is more akin to a vault guarded by steel bars. My eyes fall on the chalice, its molten glow of the fire pulsing like a heartbeat.

All I know is what Donna explained to me earlier, that it's a chalice forged in molten lava, cooled in sacred waters far from here. A mage donates their blood once a week to maintain the flame. To skip this step would be akin to injuring their god, and it's how they command their power.

Donna comes in behind me. "That's it. That's the flame... There's even the phoenix tears." She laughs. "Cocky fuckers to leave it right there."

"Are we sure it's it?" I ask, starting to unlock the doors. "I don't know shit about this. Could it be false?"

"Oh, it's real," Roy interjects. "It absolutely is. They leave it there in case they ever need to extinguish the flame, so they can restart it. Only if their god permits it, of course. But sometimes he does. Otherwise, they're a *slave* to it." His words sharpen with rage as he speaks, like he's eager to use it against them.

"We're going to hand that to you," I say. "And you will threaten to douse the flames if they don't cooperate. Do *not* extinguish unless we say so."

That seems to bring forth a piece of Roy's identity, the energy within him starting to even out in its collection of broken pieces.

Once we're through all the gates, I motion for the Cinder. "Take it, in case it burns us."

He seems to want to question it, only for a moment, but this man is so desperate to get out of here, all concern flees with his common sense. With hesitant hands, he grips it as his body is flooded with apprehension—nothing happens. "It's hot, but I can hold it," he says, breathing quickly.

"Then we start rounding up the mages, and you hold those tears near the flame and tell them they choose their god, or Jesper."

Roy is more than helpful, and the mages are like attracting a moth to flame, so careless in the way they enter this space as if it's *never* crossed their minds that they need to be careful. As soon as they witness what Roy carries, they all nearly crumble to their knees and beg for him to be careful, that he doesn't know what he's doing.

Every one of them denies to aid in the razing of this city, which doesn't matter to me. I just need them to be compliant, or dead. And if we can get at least *one* to help? It'll save all our energy for battle.

If not, their bodies can burn in the fires we start.

One by one, they all return to this building to investigate the flashing of defiant flames that periodically occur as they're snuffed out; some fire even grazes against my armor, but Donna was quick to ensure they didn't live long.

A woman slowly approaches, her head shaved like the rest. She sees the bodies of her comrades, inhaling deeply as if confirming the most dreadful assumption. "What—I don't. How did Misery not see this? Please, do not kill me. That would extinguish that flame," she manages out, her nostrils flaring as her jaw trembles.

Already, I can tell she is more of a fanatic than the rest, some part of her even resembling Cypress in that way. "I'm the only one left. The others are on Darkwater. Please, do *not* put out that flame. No one will be able to replenish it."

Darkwater? So they're all heading to Blackwell's ship already?

My heart races, my gaze moving to the windows to see the statue is no longer burning. *We need to fucking move.* "We want you to raze the city," I tell her. "Either agree, or we'll make it quick."

She looks crestfallen. "There are families here."

"That didn't stop your kind from ruining *mine*," I say, thinking of Jane and her mother. Of the people she cared about in Coalfell.

Roy seems as if he's about to pour water onto the heartbeat flame, and I have no intention to stop him. Fuck it. This is the last one relevant to us, and if he's a sellsword, he can take care of any others we come across.

"*Please!*" she shrieks, her palms flat out as she shows up her empty hands. "I'll burn the castle. I'll burn the homes, as long as we can warn the families to leave."

"You will target the stables, the stockhouses, the soldiers, and the entirety of the castle, except for anywhere that might contain a vault or treasure. If anything falls in its way, you do not stop," I press.

All she gives is a series of nods, the flame of her god reflecting against her eyes—

Jane.

My attention snaps in the direction of where she *has* to be, her energy morphing quickly like she's enduring something she'd rather not.

"Burn everything down to the harbor, then we target the castle," I command, knowing Jane can move through the flames to reach the ocean—the perfect cover for her. "Let's *move!*"

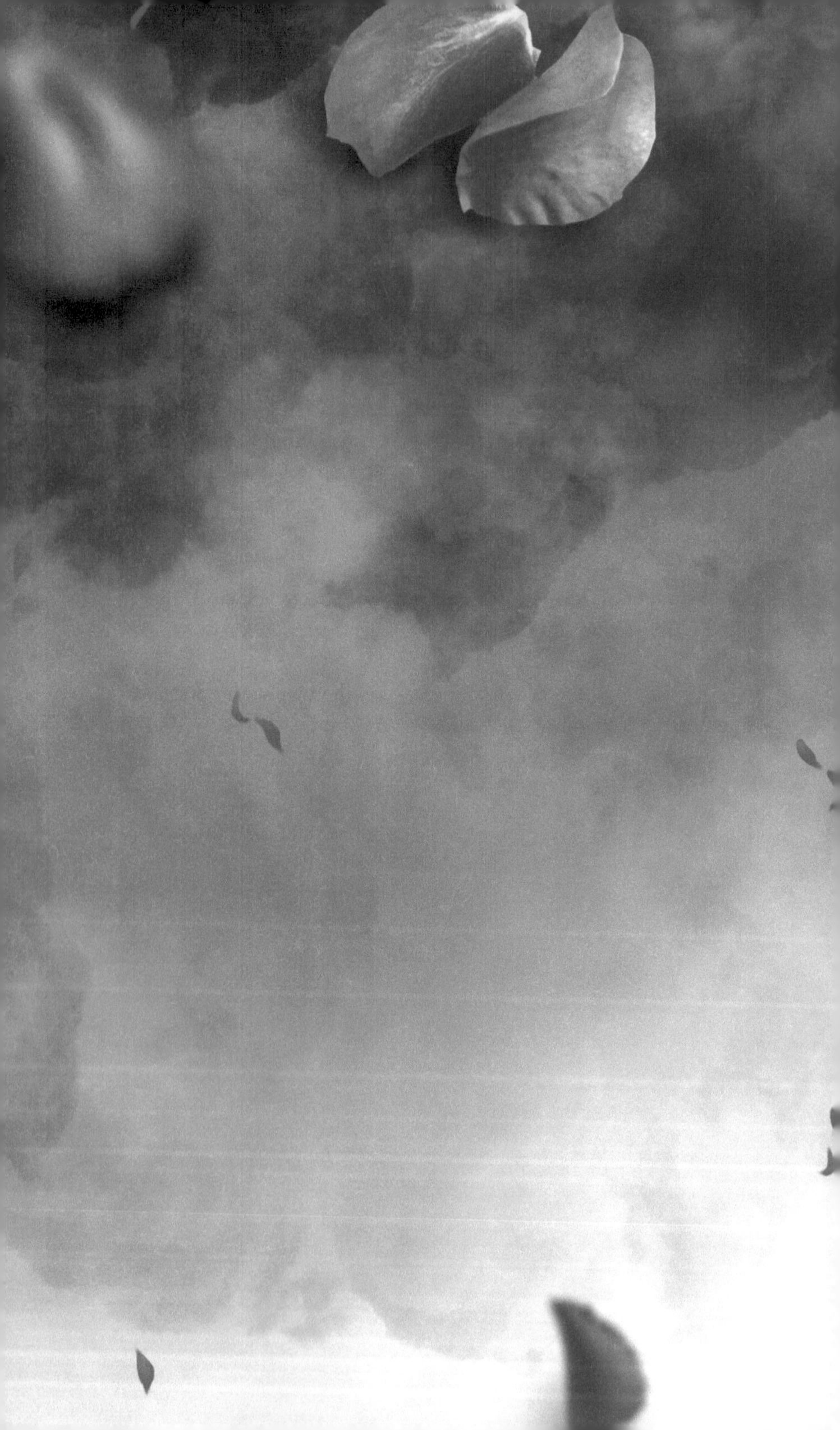

BRACE THE STORM

JANE

Moments earlier...

Frigid air washes over my skin as I'm yanked from a lovely dream where it was just Kathleen and me, having drinks by the river.

The very one that I hated taking cold baths out of.

Bringing my knees to my chest, I'm so out of it that it takes a while to process what in the hells is going on, and why this bed is suddenly so cold.

"Get up," says a voice that sounds familiar but I have no recollection of.

Opening my eyes reveals it's dark in here, and as I sit up, it slowly pieces back—imprisoned in a tower. *Anya is gone…* oh, fuck. It's like waking up *into* a nightmare.

Dread sours my stomach as I can't take waking up here much longer, realizing the blanket has been ripped off of me.

"Put on clothes. Hurry," Iris hisses.

I don't question and just do it, because if I have to hear her bitch one more time… plus, it's not like I have anything to be afraid of. Enemies in the distance? Perfect—I need the chaos if I'm to try and run for it. "Something interesting happening?" I ask as I lazily put on pants in the dark, the light of her lantern mixing with the moon's glow. "The sun isn't even out."

"Morvock has instructed us to get to the ship. He doesn't want to wait for the sunrise."

I go even slower to slide on wool socks, my mind processing as fast as hurricane winds.

I can't leave on a ship.

It's okay… the moment I get a chance, I'll jump into the waters. Right?

"Do you take *anything* seriously?"

I perch my elbow on my knee and look at her with incredulity. "Your shit stain of a leader killed my friend, wants to steal my babies, then *skin* me so his god can wear it like a creepy mask. *If* I took this seriously, I'd be insane. So, no. I think you're all idiots and don't take any of you seriously."

Her lips purse tightly, almost trembling, as she sucks her tongue to her teeth in a *click*. "Get dressed, and then you'll go with the others," she grinds out.

"What others?" I ask with annoyance, pulling my boots on.

"The other women like you."

I stop, staring at the stone floor. Slowly lifting my head, I stare at the moving shadows on her face. I have no idea why, but I hadn't fully considered there were others like me *here*. I look around the room, trying to make the pieces fit, but they don't. "What?"

She smiles smugly. "Didn't realize you're not special? You're just a womb to get us in Morvock's favor, and then your body will be used like compost to help him become reborn. Then, we'll be the chosen ones in the new world he brings, and no one will remember you."

I still don't understand, but I ask, "Where do the others stay? How long have they been here? I've seen the cellars. And women? I thought there were men, too?"

"It's not your business." She ushers me to the door.

My mind spins as if the gears have been oiled, eager to work out a riddle. I've been stagnant within these walls, but this is a lot of information that *surely* can help me, in some way.

Plus, are these women like me? Their freedom ripped from them? The chilling consideration makes my eyes widen that they may have already been subject to being *used*.

I dress quicker, not even wondering who is here. If it were Tempest, something tells me there would be more than Iris here to fetch me. Same with if it was Soren.

Soren.

It feels like I'm doing him a disservice to think he wouldn't come for me, and yet the concept is so vastly complex I cannot accept it. I don't want to miss a moment of opportunity if I squander my heart on *hope*.

What if it is him?

A peculiar feeling pricks at the back of my neck, almost whispering to me that I won't be returning here; it's the same thing I felt when my dad carried me away from my home.

Pay attention, Jane.

I have to escape.

I *must*.

⸺⸺◈⸺⸺

MY WRISTS ARE BOUND in a way that I'm growing quite familiar with, thankful every time that I can heal them after with how unforgiving the rope is.

Anya never had that luxury.

It's a shame such fanatics live here, as I'd be tempted to find this castle almost enchanting with its long corridors, beautiful windows, and balconies, something I can appreciate now that I'm not feverishly trying to analyze it.

Perhaps I feel different, too, because I no longer have to fake any part of me.

Blackwell waits for me at the bottom of the stairs, fully dressed in battle attire, leather straps all over, weapons adorned for easy reach.

Interesting.

I know someone like him has to have a lot of enemies, not just Tempest or my father. But, what if…

He doesn't even look at me as I'm guided through the castle. There's a certain, tight bustle to the people inside. Like how Skull's Row would get right before a hurricane—thinking that over, I notice that the curtains billow with more force, even rippling in the wind. Light rain begins to land on the sills, the stone shining.

My bones already feel soaked and freezing at the thought of going out into that. It even starts to smell damp—did I not notice this in my room?

Someone strides up to Blackwell, breathing heavily as if he rushed to get here. "Sir… Merciless is backing out."

Blackwell stops, the tension making me close my eyes as I nearly wait for him to blame *me* somehow. "And *why*?" Blackwell drolls out.

"Because of *her*."

Fuck, what did I do?

When I glance at the man, rather than indicating to me, he does so to the windows.

Wait, then who? There's no way it's Tempest. It feels too good to be true, honestly. Like why did Anya suffer so much just for Tempest to arrive days later? *And Merciless backed out? Was he going to join us?*

"Then we leave as soon as I say we're ready, and whoever doesn't make it, gets left behind."

I don't look at Blackwell's face as we start walking again, but if I were to, I can only imagine the expressions he must harbor as everyone we pass lowers their head in submission when they see his him; a little quicker than normal, like they're afraid.

"Can I even ask what's happening?" I inquire. He has no one to threaten me with now, so I don't have to *behave*.

"You set the sirens free," he says, too calmly. "Tempest is coming, and I suppose that's why Merciless is gone. But it's fine, you don't need to worry, Jane. We're leaving quite early as it is, before *anything* becomes a problem. You'll still get to have the *honor* of serving Morvock," he says, far too much condescension in his voice.

"Would hate to cause a problem," I say, my sleepiness completely staved off now.

Tempest...

Oh, I'll do whatever it takes to jump into the ocean. There *have* to be sirens in there. I'll even risk freezing to death over being with Misery.

Blackwell seems to buy that, and even *snickers*. "Enjoy breathing without fear right now, Jane. I don't envy you in the slightest. The sirens being freed is entirely Jesper's fault, and he's been punished *severely*. When it comes time to consummate with him, you will *hate* your life."

I won't let that happen. I need the ocean if I'm to get out of here. I have to hope one of the sirens is in that water, waiting on me with marrowkelp. If not, then... well, again, I'd rather freeze in the waters, and at least Soren can find his sister himself.

I also can't help but be happy to hear Jasper suffer.

"You seem rather calm," I state.

"I'm not the one who needed the sirens. And I mean what I said —your life will be nothing but suffering once on Darkwater. Jesper will never forgive you. I find a lot of solace in that."

Blackwell guides me to an area where I can see the shipyard in the far distance through a window, but before I can look further, I'm pulled to the opposite side as I walk through a threshold and stand on a landing, stairs in front of me to take us down to a circular entrance hall. My heart races when I spot at least a dozen women— ranging from what has to be late teens to even forties—standing in a row, wearing the same brown garb that I also wear, all with bound wrists and looking down at the ground, lined up.

I'm moved next to the women and placed at the end, with me being the only one to look around while they continue to have a staring contest with the floor. A few fire mages stand guard over us, each one with a different black marking on their forehead—from a diamond with a circle in the center, to three horizontal stripes. Their red robes stand out against the monotone grayish white of this place, their hands clasped behind their backs; they carry *so* much self-importance.

Blackwell moves around the room, surveying all of us, before walking to the only door here and opening it, the rain pattering at his feet.

"Great. There's a storm," he grumbles, although I'm not sure it was to anyone in particular. It's as if he's too lazy to be angry. Or maybe that's just how his confidence comes across, like he is certain that no matter what, none of this will stop him.

I lean into the closest woman next to me, whose lips are chapped. "My name is Jane."

The woman stiffens, shifting her gaze slightly at me before back down at the ground. Well, clearly they aren't the talking type, which means they were subjected to their own torture so far. I hear sniffing and lean forward, looking at one in the middle—the one who appears the oldest—who seems to be silently crying.

I badly want to speak, but I need to think before acting, for once. I potentially have an armada coming for me, and no matter what, I need to get away from Blackwell. From Misery. It's either I focus on those who would suffer under his reign, or these Cinders.

It's such a selfish feeling that saving my own life is more impor-tant than preserving others, especially when they're standing next to me.

It's necessary, though. I know this.

One of the mages goes under the stairwell, and I hear a door—I must have missed it. We're told to follow, the winds picking up as thunder rages in the sky. We're taken through a covered, open-arched walkway, *many* armed guards outside to escort us. I keep glancing out at the sea; a streak of lighting illuminates the entire ocean, revealing angry waves that bash into the coast.

Holy shit, is that Tempest doing this? I don't know why I assume it's her, but it *feels* like it could be her. The two mages even discuss it, mentioning how fast these storms appeared, and that usually they have more warning.

"Should we wait, until it passes?" one asks Blackwell, who is directly in front of me.

"I have a feeling the storm could turn into a hurricane if we don't move fast enough," he patronizes.

"We should wait," the other echoes, as if afraid of the water.

"Your leader and his poor decisions got us into this. Remember that when he tries to wear a crown." Blackwell looks over at one of them. "If we leave *now*, it will just be rough sailing. If we wait… You do not want to meet the pirate queen in this state. And Morvock has said we have to leave *now*. He's waiting for us on the ship. Quit your bitching, and keep *moving*."

My eyes widen when I remember it was a *shark* on Moriganna's arm—Blackwell's sigil. It's just as much his fault as it is Jesper's that Tempest is here, as I imagine Tempest will not be very forgiving of her daughter being branded; I nearly laugh when I realize he's throwing Jesper out onto the floor for others to trample on, while acting as if he had nothing to do with it.

Water sprays slightly on us when the winds push it in our direction; this is going to be *cold*.

The covered path takes us to an open, sheltered patio, one that then leads down to the harbor. The line of lit fires blows violently in the winds, and I stand closer to one to try and warm myself up. Those violent waters are no doubt frigid.

"*FIRE*! There's a fire on the peninsula!" someone shouts in the distance. Misery's mages look around, confused, one of them laughing. "Get a mage to fix it, you idiot," he mutters under his breath.

A man comes rushing our way, his entire body soaked with rain. "Mages! We need you!" He nearly knocks one of the Cinders over, a train of wet footprints behind him. "Ten buildings are aflame. And it's spreading! One of your kind is doing it, and we found at least, I don't know, two dozen dead in your quarters," he pants, his eyes wide with shock. "They've turned on us—I mean, I think something's *happened*."

The way Blackwell morphs from calmly moving about as if he's untouchable, to his lips parting and his eyes widening—he throws a look at me as if he chucked a dagger that *I* threw.

"I have *no* idea what's going on," I say, my voice a little high-pitched. "Don't blame *me*."

His lips partially move with each pant, curling in as he looks to the harbor, then back at where the man came. He pushes one of the mages. "Is this a coup?"

"Do *not* suggest such treason against me," the mage snarls, facing the man that came to us. "What do you mean, two dozen are dead? That's *impossible*. No one can get close without incineration."

The man steps forward. "Sir, please… there's a man with a black mask among them. A Zenith, I think."

Pure shock and horror nearly blanches Blackwell, that gaze falling to me. "GET JANE ON MY SHIP, *NOW*! Get her as *close* to Morvock as *possible*, under his fucking cloak if you have to!"

Panic consumes this place like wildfire, one guard grabbing each of my limbs, the other women subjected to similar treatment as they're ushered forward.

It's difficult to fight when at least half a dozen hands are on me, and all I can do is yell and thrash. Blackwell leads with a hurry, but remains very close to me. "Mages, stay with us! We'll need your power!"

The two mages mutter about how they could have been killed, and something about an *eternal flame*.

Rain streaks down my face, and I crane my neck to see that there's so much *smoke* in the air. It even rolls high like it did in Coalfell, so definitely from a fire mage.

Soren.

How the fuck is he here?

I thrash even harder, revitalized to know he's *here*. Who else would be in a black mask? I scream as loud as I can, my throat even scratching, but they don't stop my cries.

I'm carried further down, Blackwell's ship a massive, black construction with evenly placed braziers at the front, two mages standing near the flames. The bow is brightly illuminated, the front of the ship slightly resembling a shark's head with wooden teeth arranged so the bow is like the nose. Where the mouth opens up is a balcony.

Darkwater.

I can hear the ocean, smell her salt, and we near the vast emptiness ahead, Blackwell's stupid ship the only beacon in the rain. I transition quickly from that uncomfortable feeling of wet clothes to being utterly soaked by the time we reach the piers. Sails are being lowered, the fabric catching the wind with each gust.

Among the braziers at the bow stands a figure cloaked in black, the candle eyes visible from here, with Jesper standing right next to him.

As I'm taken closer, blinking rapidly to get the rain out of my eyes, that fire behind us isn't close enough.

They won't make it.

I don't lose myself to any of the misery; Anya's necklace is under my clothes, and I plan to fully fight for her memory. Soren is here, which means maybe my dad is too.

I'm not alone.

But as Darkwater is starting to rise higher above me, it means we are getting lower and closer to the ramp that will—

"Do not put Jane down. Do not let her, under any circumstance, enter that ocean," Blackwell commands.

Okay, well, that just confirmed for me that I *should* enter the ocean.

As they carry me up the ramp to Darkwater, a crack of lightning, along with a gust of wind, helps me see that there's a design from the fates. It's as if my mind has had many pieces floating in a murky pool of water, and suddenly there's clarity. There's a reason.

I'll have Blackwell and Jesper on this ship, along with every fucking asshole that follows Morvock's shadow, while the rest burn out. I'm not sure how to kill a god, but I know how to bleed a man. Stop his heart.

Burn him.

I'm immune to fire, aren't I? So are these women, then? What if I can set this ship on fire, out in the open, in tumultuous waters? Kill the mages so they can't put it out, just like Soren did? If Tempest is coming, it might buy her time. At the very least, I'd be getting rid of Blackwell and Jesper in one fell swoop.

As soon as my feet touch the deck's surface, someone grabs my soaking shirt and starts to tie ropes around my arms, to which two more guards are back on me to secure my wrists, too. As soon as I give a *little* fight, an arm is wrapped around my neck in a threat to choke me out.

They've learned not to trust me.

Can't fault them. I was *just* thinking about bolting to the edge of the ship and tumbling over into the water...

Jesper approaches Blackwell while I'm being bound, and he has what looks like bandages over his left eye, along with an eyepatch. It seems intentional that he won't look at me. "What is happening?" Jesper asks.

The man that came to alert us comes forward, and I'm placed down on the wooden deck. "We're under attack," the man says. "One of them has a mask like Blackwell's. But I thought we were told that none of the Zenith would follow, so I'm not sure. Nearly all of the fire mages have been killed."

Jesper finally looks at me with his one eye, that thing wide and locked in shock.

"Then it is as I feared," Misery says, his voice carrying unnaturally in the winds, his back still to us. "Not only is Ritter among those, but *Soren*. And *Basilisk*. I sensed them *too late…*"

"Get this ship out of the harbor!" Blackwell shouts, placing his mask on, the golden decorations of his design along the jaw and chin. "If anyone doesn't make it, then that's their shit luck. We leave *now!*"

The Cinders are all guided to the center of the ship, standing near the hatch to the stores below. A sword is poked into my back shoulder to nudge me forward, my torso completely useless. *I still have my legs… I could run—*

As soon as I try to dart, I'm yanked backward and slammed onto the deck's surface. Looking up in confusion, I see a guard holding onto a strand of rope like a leash, one that's intertwined in my bindings.

Shit.

There's an explosion that spirals into the sky near the castle, the flames consuming nearby homes, everyone jumping in surprise. I swear I can even hear the faint clashing of swords, and it's a struggle to stand so I can get a better look.

The flames now glow from *inside* the castle, reaching out the windows to stain the stone. Jesper screams loudly like a child who lost his inheritance.

One of the flames even turns blue.

"Get out of the harbor!" Misery cries into the air, the sound cracking through like a whip as Blackwell commands his ship.

"Where is Merciless?" Jesper shouts.

Blackwell pauses before ascending his stairs to stare down the petulant man. "He backed out like the cunt he is! Which means he must have seen the Sea Wolf."

Oh, I fucking like seeing them all concerned.

I'm poked with a sword once more and move forward. The deck is slick, everything set in motion to get us out of harbor.

Now that I'm up here and not worried about being choked out, I can see the devastation of the peninsula.

They've razed it.

People are running through the flames, some on fire despite the pouring rain. The fight edges closer to the ocean, the raging inferno consuming the east end of the castle, the blue flames mixing with the burning yellow and orange.

There's a silhouette of a figure looking out at the ocean right at the edge, wearing a mask.

Soren.

"That's the *fucking* castle on fire!" Jesper yells as the crew lowers the final the sails.

"What did you expect?" Blackwell yells back at him. "Soren has never been known to be gentle when angry, and we fucking pissed him off!" Blackwell shouts, motioning to me. "But he's stuck on that harbor, and we're on our way. Try not to piss your pants, *Jesper.* We'll be out of this shortly."

Blackwell begins to ascend the elaborate stairs, step by step, like his actions have articulation, climbing up to the wheel.

"Ride through the storm, Antony," Misery speaks, his words clearly unnerving everyone around with how it sounds like they're spoken right in our ear. "I'll exhaust what I have left to keep the ship safe and get us to Boneglass."

Everyone moves with immediacy.

Jesper grabs a telescope from one of the men, pointing it out to the chaos. With my head lowered so as to keep the rain out of my eyes, I glare through my lashes at Misery, who hasn't moved. The broken god continues to stand at the very tip of the ship as it begins to fully turn, veering north of the fire isles.

The morning sun is barely alive somewhere above the clouds, as there's *some* definition in the sky, the ocean *barely* discernible. My eyes widen when I get a full view of where we're heading, the heavy clouds a deep gray color that used to send Skull's Row into lockdown; storms were always perfect for murder, as everyone was too busy focusing on their dwellings, families, and self-preservation.

Skull's Row… my home. I can handle this.

The Cinders and I are guided below deck as Blackwell shouts, *"Brace for the storm!"*

BLOODY FLAGS

SOREN

A scream rips from my chest and blends into the winds when all this spilled blood isn't enough.

My body feels like it's wrapped by a lighting bolt, every nerve alight, every thought consumed by the sight of Jane. She's ushered on that ship, dressed in the same garb as the men, like they really think they can treat her like some cruel offering.

Even from this distance, I swear she's looking right at me.

Smoke billows around the harbor, thick and acrid, filling my lungs as I grip my blade so tightly my knuckles go white. My body is soaked in the blood of others, cutting down any guards that were bold enough to attack me if they made it through the fire.

The flames crackle and roar behind me, painting this early morning in blinding hues of orange and red, their heat pressing

487

against my skin. I take one step toward the edge of the harbor, as if sheer will could bridge the distance—

A hand clamps on my shoulder, the grip like iron.

"We'll follow on Storm's Fury," Basilisk grinds out. "We need to create an opening for Jane, not get us closer to Misery."

"She's right fucking *there*." My voice cracks with the rawness of being *so close*. "The sirens can get me to his ship. She just needs to be freed and into the waters. Misery can have me, then."

He gives my shoulder a shake. "You see Misery there? Right at the prow? That staff is about to become connected to that vessel, and the ship untouchable. Only ramming it with another will work. Not even the sirens can get their claws in it." His voice picks up the carnage and winds. "And there's a massive storm coming! That's Tempest's signature. Let's get to Storm's Fury before we lose our chance!"

Panting through the mask, my gaze leaves Darkwater to glance around as my powers search the area while my mind disassociates —I see it: a flicker of blue fire on the water in the far distance, pulsing and rippling in the wind. *Storm's Fury*. My heartbeat races, a fresh wave of fury and urgency surging through me. "Then, let's move!"

I do what I can to direct everyone, finding them in the mayhem, Basilisk moving to help corral everyone to the ocean as I search for Bones—my body bends as I feel an assault at my back, dodging without witnessing a single movement, only to see a man—his face a mask of rage—overextend from missing the blow. I don't hesitate. Jane's blade finds his neck, swift and merciless.

The fire makes it harder to weed out who is where, as if it's a barrier. *From the magic, perhaps?* As I near a corner of the courtyard, still feeling Bones in this direction, a woman in a black robe rounds the same corner, freezing when she sees me.

I felt her, but she's so insignificant—

Fear. She knows me. Why does she know me? Why does it feel connected to Jane?

I take a step directly toward her as she cries out, "No, *please*! I'm trying to flee, not fight you. I missed the ship. I just need away." She peeks around me, as if the sight of Darkwater is comforting, like she still has a chance.

"Why do you seem to know Jane?" I yell out, the cracking sound of wood preceding embers spiraling into the sky like a blizzard's inferno, somewhere far behind us. *Toward Bones.*

Her eyes widen, her black robes billowing in the hot wind. There's an echo of Jane within her, and before she can even hold her hands up to defend herself, I grip her by the collar of her clothes. "You know her enough to *loathe* her. What do you know? What happened to her while she was here?"

Her face pales, her mouth opening and closing as if searching for an answer. Dancing, golden light waves across her eyes, even glinting against her teeth.

Death. Murder. Jealousy. Her face warps into a sorrowful rage, tears welling in her eyes. "He *left* me, but then took *her*." Her eyes flare, this woman knowing she's lost everything she wanted; I can sense the depths of it. "I tended to her. I didn't even hurt her when I could have!" she yells at me, as if it will help. "Oh, how I *wanted* to—"

I slam her against the wall, her head cracking against the stone as she slumps to the ground, useless and in the way. I focus back on finding Bones.

Where is that lucky fucker? Why isn't he moving with the others?

Relief floods me as I exhale when he appears through the carnage, the fire mage clearing a path for them and the Cinder, who still carries that torch like it's priceless gold.

Bones is motioning to this building, or that one, and the fire mage follows his orders.

He's enjoying himself.

"Bones!" I shout, and he straightens, standing to attention. "We're getting in the waters, heading to Storm's Fury!" I motion for Roy. "You're coming with us. The other Cinders can find their way out. Take that flame with you."

The fire mage nearly lunges at Roy, who jumps back quicker than she moves.

"What if you don't make it back!" the mage yells out. "I need that back within the *week*!"

I watch as Bones guides Roy, and I feel out for anyone I may have missed. The energy of everyone relevant to me centralizes in the harbor, and as the mage looks like she might throw fire my way, I throw a glare at her. "You can have your chalice back once we're in the waters," I say, not having time for this. "Roy will be given a choice to go with us, or stay with you. Once we're far enough away from you, he will leave it in the harbor."

The Cinder looks back when his name is mentioned, and I can already tell he will choose to go with us.

It's a hustle forward, barely anyone around to challenge us. My attention is on the piers, then at the sirens that float in the violent waters. Darkwater is already sailing out, the back of her nearly turned all the way to us, flames still burning in the braziers at the prow.

As we make our way down to the piers, the water rocks them, and a few slip into the waters, only to surface and be pulled in the opposite direction of the current. One siren yells out to get my attention, the fires glistening against her skin. "Hold your breath! We will swim you to the ship, but not with marrowkelp. We are saving it!"

I motion for everyone else to get in. "I'll go last!"

One by one, everyone plunges into the water, the sirens pulling them swiftly away from the burning wreckage. Ritter is one of the first, the energy of that man nearly frozen by desperation as I can feel the *years* of build up, so close to getting what he wants.

Basilisk is lost somewhere in the middle, and Bones is one of the last men in as it's just me and the Cinder. "You will wait in these waters until we are far enough to not be in danger, then you place the chalice on any ledge."

Roy actually hesitates as he looks at the lapping water, and I push him in, his scream swallowed by the waves, before jumping in myself. A wave crashes into my body, and hands are on me to pull me under while I hold my breath, two sirens grabbing me and swimming swiftly in the waters before I breach the surface.

The icy grip of the water shocks my system, extinguishing the heat of the flames that warmed my skin. Two sirens have a hold of me, their hands cold and firm, and we plunge beneath the surface once more. I hold my breath, the pressure building in my chest as they propel me forward with incredible speed. When we break the surface again, the storm's wrath greets us as the heat of Ashfire is no longer on me. Rain lashes down in torrents, and the swells rise and fall like living beasts, tossing us like driftwood.

It was easy to forget about the storm with the inferno.

The harbor is a vision of hell. Flames devour Ashfire, their light reflected in the black waters. Smoke churns upward, mingling with the storm clouds above. Embers fall like fiery snow, carried by the howling wind. I stare at the devastation, my chest heaving as I struggle to process it all. All that effort, all that blood, and Jane is still out of reach.

The rain makes it hard to breathe, each gasp tasting of salt and ash. The sirens pull me onward, their strength unyielding. Finally, through the chaos, I see it—a massive ship looming ahead, its silhouette cutting through the storm that I completely missed, like it appeared right from the shadows.

The bow has a head of a wolf with silver on its teeth.

Tempest...

The Sea Wolf rises and falls with the waves, its red sails bright like bloodstains against the sky. Rope ladders dangle from its sides, thrashing wildly in the wind. One of the sirens surfaces beside me, her voice sharp and urgent. "Get on the ship! Tempest requests that you ride with her!"

"My men go first!" I shout. It's one thing to lead an attack, but this is to ensure they're all on board. I do my best to count as they all climb, Ritter going first, then Rorge, then quite a few more before Donna. Basilisk is among my people, with Bones the second to last before I'm upon the ship as it's in the water.

It feels entirely wrong to touch the outside of the ship's belly while out in the open ocean.

"Hang onto the rope loops if you hit a swell!" the siren yells.

I grab the rope, threading my freezing hands through a loop as a massive swell crashes over me, threatening to rip me away. My grip holds, and I climb as soon as I possibly can, each movement a battle against nature. It doesn't help that I can barely feel my fingers.

Hands pull at me to get me over once at the top, the blue fire of Storm's Fury close behind us. Boarding the Sea Wolf, in a fucking storm that's verging on a hurricane, wears me out more than the fighting we just did.

"You alright?" one of her crew asks. "Drink this—it's a fire tonic. It staves off the cold of the ocean!"

I down it right away, the tonic burning my throat as if I swallowed liquid flames. Sure enough, my body warms from the inside even though I'm soaking wet. "Tempest wants you at the wheel!" the pirate shouts.

Glancing over when Basilisk laughs, I see that he cranes his head up, the sound of pure joy contrasting the violence that's brewing in the air. "She's got the bloody flags raised!"

I lift up my head to gaze up at the sails that are all bright red, visible from the fires that rage in Ashfire. *Yes, the bloody flags.*

It means a pirate ship carries no mercy.

No. Fucking. Mercy.

In the underdeck, somewhere in the stores, the Cinders and I are all tied up to posts. I'm the only one who has her wrists bound so tight my elbows nearly hurt from this position; the rest simply have rope around their arms. It was a glorious few seconds to see Jesper's castle be ravaged by fire, his panic and anger like drinking fresh water after a long day in the sun.

This is what he gets for hurting those innocent villagers. For being behind the death of my mother, for giving Misery the worshippers he needs to even *attempt* building this empire.

The ship sways hard, the guards that are watching over us grabbing one of the many handles that now makes sense as to why they even exist—I'm just glad my stomach isn't lurching this time.

No, this is nothing like last time, when I'd just lie with Soren in a hammock.

I shudder with so much emotion at realizing that the man looking at this ship as we left might have really been *Soren*. He came for me. I don't know what to do with that gratitude—I glance down at my bound wrists, and then at the forearm that has Soren's mask embedded.

Can he feel me?

My body comes to life with purpose, with vengeance. It's as if any and all fear never mattered. He is busting his ass to help me, which how am I going to repay him?

I have to burn down Darkwater, that's for certain. So now, how do I get out of these ropes?

My eyes narrow with consideration when I see oil lanterns swaying with the waves that has us women—all but one—revealing we don't have much experience at sea with the way we're knocked around, even if we try to fight it.

Which gets me thinking… if I can spread oil around, it'll splash all over everything with how much this ship moves.

If the mages are dead, then it will be impossible to extinguish.

To think that Soren will be watching from somewhere nearby keeps me alert. It's as if every few thoughts circle around him. There's a massive part of me that wants to make him proud, to prove I'm worthy of being with someone as rough and intense as him. Almost as if this act is a part of a messed-up courtship.

I never doubted him, but I also knew I couldn't sit and wait for him to show. I still don't think I've processed that someone loves me enough to risk it all. Daydreaming about it is one thing, but seeing him actually *show up*…

The lantern that sways fiercely never spills any of its fire, and my mind hones in on it; I glance around at the barrels, and then at the giant hooks and metal rigging. Is this the maintenance deck? They need oil for maintaining things, right? And isn't a lot of this wood treated to keep water from getting in? I swear I remember Dad telling me to be careful with some of the buildings made out of pirate ships for that reason, because it's flammable.

One of the women looks up at a guard and asks, "Isn't that dangerous to have a fire lit during a storm?"

My lips press together like I'm trying to squish a bug. *Shut. Up. Lady.*

He blinks slowly and takes his time to face her. "Clearly, this is not normal fire." He waves his hands around. "Almost, and I know this is hard to understand, like magic from a *fire mage*."

Another woman says, "Leave it alone. You want to be bound in darkness?"

"All hands on deck!" starts to make its way through the ship, our guard remaining resolute. Another comes down, "You too, Heath. Orders from Misery."

He nods to me. "Even *that* one?"

"She's bound in Misery's rope. He'll know if it's been cut or if she tries *anything*."

We'll see.

The guard clearly has no more interest and heads to the door. When it seems like we're actually alone, one of the Cinders asks, "Did they just leave us here?"

"What's the worst that'll happen? We get to know each other?" another replies.

"Oh, shut it. You're the only one that wants this," the first one replies, her blonde hair braided down the middle, her knobby knees all red.

"At least we're not *her*," the protesting one says, nodding at me. "*She's* going to die at some point. We get to live. And be *revered*."

Shit, okay. So, she's our weak link. If I can somehow free myself, then she might scream about it. She lifts her head up as if to look down on us all. "We're going to have to all partake, one way or another.

Squeals and light screams begin to echo through us as the ship clearly dives down, nose first, over a swell, sending our bodies to really push against our restraints, some of the cargo sliding.

The blonde yells out, "Brace yourselves!"

I press back against my pole, digging my heels into the wood as the ship is then rocked dramatically in the opposite direction as if the front hit water and is now rising upward again.

That was *not* exciting. My heart skips a beat as I pant, the ship creaking and groaning.

"You work on a ship?" someone asks the blonde.

"Aye. I did."

Rope groans somewhere above us, and I feel like we're all stuck in a barrel that's adrift in a stormy ocean.

I waste no time in feeling around with my hands, trying to figure out what finger or bone needs to break in order to get out; I'll just knock the one out that seems far too interested in living in this new world. With just enough jostling, I realize a thumb should do it.

I sigh, accepting that I should probably break one and then heal it. Or, what if I don't have time? At some point, I realize I'm just sitting there, holding my thumb. I can just pull it out of place, yank with no mercy. But there's no guarantee I can get it out of the ropes.

There are a few false starts, but it's when we begin a dive over another massive wave, our bodies slung against the confines of our ropes again, that I nearly do it but focus so much on balance that I miss my window of opportunity.

As I look at the one who worked on a ship, I get an idea, but that other one is listening in. It might not be worth shouting these things out because then she'll share what we're plotting.

The blonde is the only one that's quiet, like the eye of a storm.

Okay.

Assess.

I work to bring my wrists to my mouth, right at the bindings. The first knot is a bitch, tied so tight that it makes my jaw tremble every time my teeth slide up the rough rope—the knot barely budges.

"What is she doing?" the loyal one asks. "Stop that!"

I don't reply. Instead, the blonde speaks for me, *"Quiet."*

The loyal one scoffs. "What is she going to do? Kill Misery, in a *storm*?" Her eyes widen. "Now, you better not fuck up my chance at a royal life."

Move quickly.

I connect my gaze to the blonde, and then up at the lantern, and then down at my confines. I hope she gets the message. If she's been on a ship, she'll know how to make it burn.

She lifts only her gaze, so as not to draw attention, and then nods.

Perfect.

She *has* to know.

If she can free herself, she'll have a better chance at succeeding than me—

Someone appears in the threshold, a dramatic groan escaping my lips when I see who it is. My eyes roll as I drop my head, turning to the side like my body has a sudden rush of energy, and I can't sit still.

"Morvock is calling for Jane," Jesper says, almost with too much joy.

"What the hells did I do?"

The loyal one motions to me with her head. "She is trying to escape."

He looks at her sweetly. "Yes, I know, dear. Morvock could feel it. Your loyalty will be noted."

Jesper nears me, but it's so awkward and tense to be near him after everything. It's as if he's slightly afraid of me, or like I'm a cursed object. "You just couldn't sit down here," he grumbles.

Somewhere in the distance, "*HOLD*" echoes.

Jesper backs off and grips one of the bars on the pillar I'm tied to, holding for dear life as the ship goes through another dramatic rocking back and forth, the cargo shifting with it again, held back by netting.

Once it passes, Jesper quickly finishes untying me from the pole before guiding me through the tight halls, pinning me against the wall when we hit another massive swell, putting all his weight on me so I can't do much; he even keeps his face away from mine. "Once we're on land, you are so *fucked*." he laughs. "Your stupid fucking Zenith killed Marissa."

My eyes widen.

"Yeah, I saw it on the telescope. Slammed her against a wall." He digs his elbow deeper into my neck so I gasp for air. "There will be a punishment for that."

"*You're* the one that left her," I manage out.

"Because he razed *my goddamn city*," he says, his one eye bloodshot and wide, his teeth baring at me. "Her worship was next to none, and now it's *gone.*"

I lean in as much as I can, and he pulls back further like I'm venomous, even taking the pressure off my neck. "Well, think of it this way. He killed Marissa, and all she did was tend to me." I pause, letting all of my chaos out that I've buried down. "Imagine what he'll do to the man that threatened to rape me in front of everyone? To the man who *killed* his right hand?"

Real fear flashes in his eye.

"Keep your *eye* peeled, Jesper. I know this storm wasn't caused naturally. Tempest is coming, isn't she?"

He yanks me up the stairs, the door opening to reveal rain that's blowing nearly sideways, a wet deck sleek from water, and a sky that barely has *any* light to it. In the very front is Misery, along with four fire mages, and all the braziers continue to burn to create a haunting scene.

He drags me quickly across the deck, the ocean momentarily scaring the shit of me.

The swells are *massive*—the size of this entire *ship*.

A quick glance shows Blackwell at the wheel, his mask creating a rather frightening image for a captain.

Jesper leads me to Misery without another word, his cloak billowing to create a lanky outline of a crouched body. The god reaches his bony hand out and touches my shoulder, my body rooting in the spot as my feet can't move, the ropes all falling off and rolling back to the ship. It's beyond unnerving to have something like *him* make physical contact with me, the knowledge that he is so beyond capable, and that he plans to use my flesh...

Those candle eyes...

We stand behind what is almost like an altar, a thick wall of wood coming to a point, stretching around us to incrementally get smaller, two mages on either side of us as Jesper returns to wherever he came. "My tolerance is low, Jane Ritter. So you will stand with me to ensure you do *nothing*."

What do I say to him?

Shut your mouth!

It's easy to remain speechless, especially when I realize that at some point, the ship will—oh, *fuck*. Two swells ahead seem to be on *either* side of us. Misery stamps his staff on the deck, the wood of the ship intertwining with it. The fire mages all seem to carry a mixture of determination and apprehension, their cloaks soaked now that I look at them.

The braziers almost make it hard to truly see the details of the ocean, like they're blinding my ability to perceive the dark.

I brace myself for what has to be utter destruction as the massive waves—that seem to move in slow motion—collide. Our ship raises up in the air, the prow pointing upward rather than down, and it's only when the ship begins to dip down again that I realize the two waves became one and raised us up to the top.

We roll over the massive wave, water spraying on all sides.

Misery lifts his staff and slams it down on the ship, a vibration rising through my feet as I feel like I'm a fixture of Darkwater.

I can't help but scream as the ship plummets down, Misery's grip on my arm surely bruising me at this point. I scream even louder when the tip of the ship is about to collide with water, as if I have just fallen off a balcony and into the ocean; I close my eyes and get ready to hold my breath—*no! Keep them open! You need to know when to hold your breath so you don't drown!*

Opening my eyes, I watch in horror as water hits us like a wall, consuming us instantly as the black void of the ocean envelops the front of the ship.

Pressure.

There's so much pressure as we enter the water's surface. I want to open my mouth and scream, or breathe, but then the pressure lightens and air graces my face once more. I open my mouth before my eyes. Water washes off of the deck as I breathe raggedly, somehow still pinned to this spot. Looking around, the swells of the ocean are like a giant beast coming to life, as if the ocean's surface is the skin of a demon.

Never thought I'd be so happy to be this close to Misery or to him holding onto me, as I could have been wiped away if not for him. I don't even register how soaked I am anymore, the braziers still bright and lit, keeping us warm. I pant as if I just ran through the entirety of Skull's Row.

This miserable god needs me to regain a body, so he can actually be powerful again, right? Which means he's a weak little shit now? I've never once seen him without his staff, so I bet he *needs* it. Could I just grab it when he doesn't see that coming? I flinch when I think of him feeling those thoughts, until Cypress's image comes to me.

Him not feeling me is the sole purpose of this.

It's as if I'm staring at a clear night sky and can finally see how the stars connect to form a constellation.

Cypress *is* on my side. Because of her god, and because *I'm* the one that could get closest to Misery without him killing me because he needs my skin.

Me choosing to take down Misery is essentially choosing to help Cypress's god, but at least he's not the one that plans to wear me like a jacket.

This is it.

This is *the* moment for me. And this ugly asshole is so focused, I can almost feel the fear in him. Something about Tempest unnerves the shit out of him, and he's focused on preventing that. I'd also be willing to bet he's helping Darkwater burst through these waves without crashing, as I don't know why else he'd be up here. It's clear he needs the help of the mages, so maybe the fire gives him power?

Either way, he's *vulnerable*.

I think of the tattoo on my chest and what the depth of it means. It's actually a unique design, what it might look like if it was actually for me.

It *is* mine.

Mine.

I'm surrounded by people with their own legends, and there's no reason I can't have my own. There's no reason I'm worthless, and so far, my magic has been used in ways *other* than to heal. *Maybe it will work here...* As we're about to crest over another swell and Misery lifts the staff, I throw everything I have at grabbing it.

I reach deep into every well of healing power and let it drain me as it bleeds from my hands, the blue glow matching the brightness of braziers that whip around underneath this masked sun.

A growl so demonic emits from the forgotten god, who then *shrieks*, his staff cracking apart as blue light seems to *emit* from it, the obsidian rock at the top glowing blue.

The boat tips over a wave, and a wall of water once again collides into us all.

It happens so fast and slow at once, the way the water overtakes me, and I get lost in it. It's freeing, almost, until my body slams into something hard. Instinct kicks in as I reach for anything, grabbing something metal and clinging to it for dear life.

When my knees are on a solid surface, and I feel my balance pivot to a center, I realize I'm not dead. As the water washes away, my hand immediately touches my calve that's bleeding from a nasty wound.

"BLOODY FLAGS!" someone shouts at the wheel, and it's not Blackwell. "The Sea Wolf has been spotted with bloody flags!"

A bell tolls.

Darting my gaze around, I can't spot the braziers anymore. Seriously? Were they wiped out, too? It makes sense if Misery is what was keeping us all planted there. *It's going to work.* I spot the door that could take me below deck, and so far, no one is coming for me.

It's my life's purpose now to set this thing aflame.

THE PIRATE QUEEN

SOREN

The three of us—Basilisk, myself, and Ritter—are guided up to the wheel while the rest go down below. Tempest glares out at the churning ocean with a fury that makes the hairs on my arms rise. Her rage feels elemental, as if she herself is part of the storm brewing around us.

"We're welcome back?" I yell out over the howling winds, lowering my head to keep the rain from pelting into my eyes. I grip the rail's handles like my life depends on it—which, to be fair, it certainly fucking does.

Her face contorts with rage that carves deep lines in her face, her grip fastened to the pegs of the wheel. "He. Branded. My. *DAUGHTER!*" Her scream pierces the storm, a flash of lighting briefly illuminating us all.

It's a shout that looks like madness, but the determination and primal hunt in her eyes, mixing with an aura that I've never felt so coherent, tells me exactly why *she* is the pirate queen.

Blackwell is absolutely *fucked* if she gets a hand on him.

"HOLD!" Tempest shouts, the few men around her all kneeling down and gripping the rails. We all do their actions, and the shout to hold echoes through the ship. She glances at the three of us. "Get your feet tucked in!"

My gaze falls to hers, and below her wheel is a place to insert her feet that's bolted to the floor. *Fuck.*

My body presses against the banister as the Sea Wolf pitches violently. I hold on to the best of my ability, my body jolting into the wooden barrier when it feels like the tip of the ship hits a wall, my boots losing any footing, even while sitting down, only for my weight to then be pulled *away* from the banister as the ship lurches *up*, before seeming to even out.

Basilisk shoots me a look of pure, unfiltered hatred for the ocean, and I couldn't agree more.

"Tempest!" Ritter shouts.

The pirate queen looks at him. "Get your sea legs, Scorpion! I called you three up here to say you can be on my ship as long as you all pledge your swords to kill any and all men on that fucking ship! Except Blackwell. He is *mine*! When it's safe, you can all go below deck."

The ship feels momentarily weightless once more, and I'm ready for it when Tempest yells for us all to brace ourselves.

"While we're here, what's the plan?" Ritter cries out, pressing against the rails to find a good position.

"We're ramming Blackwell's ship! The sirens follow us," Tempest declares, another crack of lightning reflecting against the wetness of her leather jacket. "If we fall into the water, they will save us. Do not fear the ocean!"

Basilisk tilts his head toward her. "Did you really fuck the ocean god?"

I look at him with the same glare I throw Bones when he's crossing lines, but to my shock, Tempest laughs. "He sired Moriganna! And he is *not* happy."

"Then why doesn't *he* just crash that ship?" I shout.

"Morvock is protecting it, and Ta'Kan doesn't take the flesh. Only on a full moon does he come to me, and Morvock sails on a nearly moonless night." She braces herself to steer the ship before adding, "So I will do it."

The ship undergoes another violent dip before rising again, and that's when Tempest shouts for us to go below deck. We move as quickly as possible on this ship, the raging sea utterly unnerving as it surrounds us in *massive* swells.

Everything swings that isn't fully lashed, like lanterns with no fire in them. Tempest's crew stands with determination, as if each wash of the ocean is rejuvenating and not fucking obnoxious.

The ship begins to dip once more, and I grip a pillar as the floor is removed from beneath my feet, Ritter and Basilisk both grabbing onto what they can as we ride through this wave before we're able to make our way to where everyone is lashing down.

I move to one of the few windows, able to see more clearly without the rain in my eyes. There aren't many times in my life where I feel genuinely uncomfortable.

Now is one of them.

The swells are so large, so striped with white cap water, and the skies so angry and full of lightning, it's as if even *touching* the ocean is certain death. Ocean water sprays against the side of the ship, and I'm convinced each time the wood will break.

So much *groaning* of wood and rope.

But even then, I can see the silhouette of Darkwater, the fire at the prow seemingly out.

We're coming, Jane.

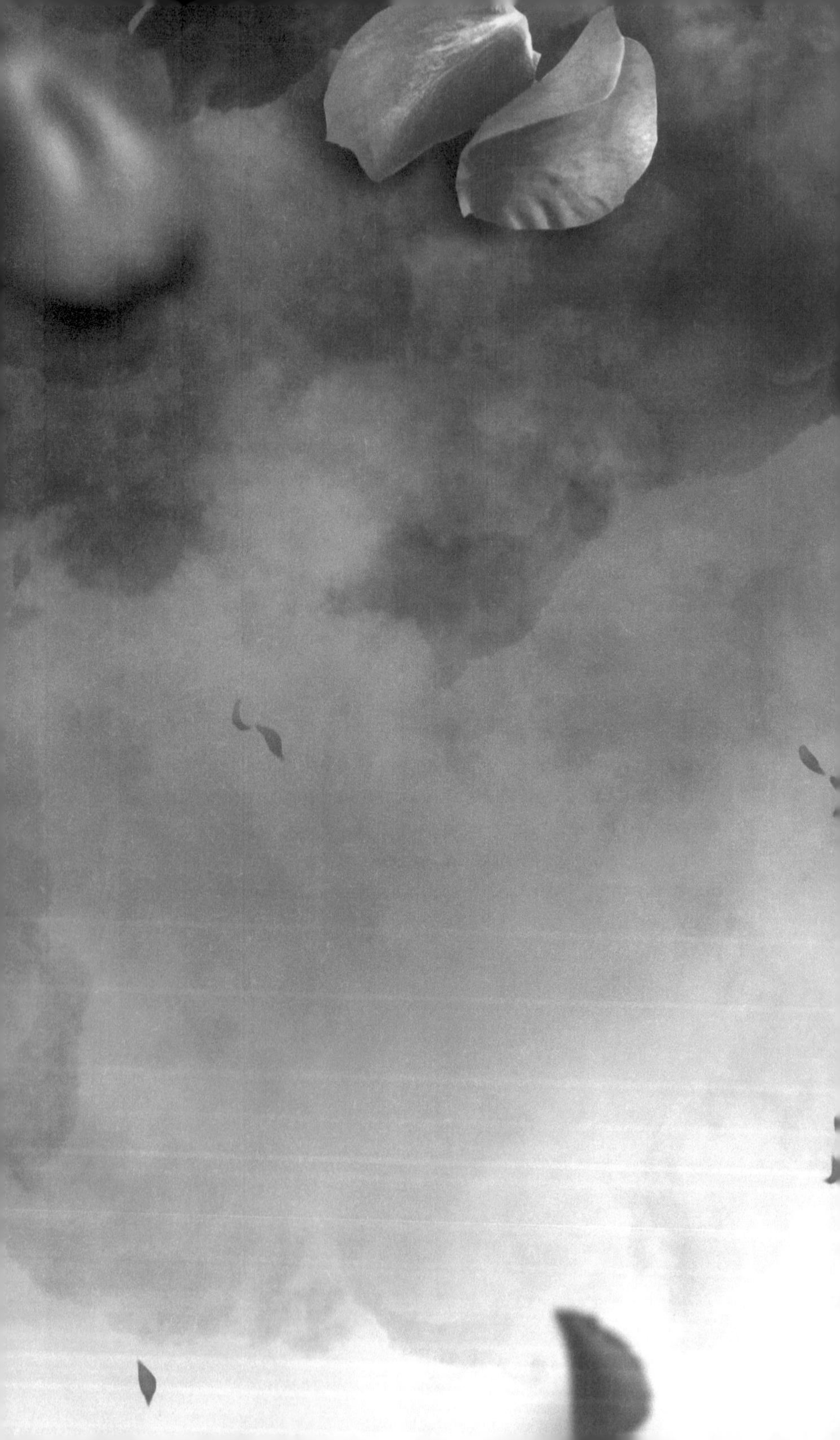

SOMEONE TO THINK ABOUT
JANE

Bolting down the stairs, I can't believe I'm free. I'm able to find the other Cinders, moving in a crouch position, ready to tumble or dive for support if the ship hits another wave.

I have no idea what happened to Misery but I'm not waiting to find out.

The Cinders are all shocked to see me, the loyal one starting to scream that I'm back and unbound. I go to her first, my knee stinging as it smacks into the floor, placing my hand over her chest. My well of magic is insanely low, but I'm also desperate to achieve this. Her cries become labored, and then she's out.

I pant as I pull my hands away, feeling as if I've been bled.

The ship dips once more, and I grab onto her body, clinging to it as my legs fly in the air, her hair getting in my face.

"What did you do?" someone yells as the storage boxes all press against the netting.

"Subdued her!" I shout, waiting on the ship to even out once again. "No time to explain."

As soon as I feel like there's an opening, I rush underneath the lantern.

Fuck.

I'm too short.

I start to feel the motion that might hint at the ship taking another dive, and I run over to a pole and hold it tight while the rest of the women scream. Every time I brace myself, it takes even more out of me, especially when I've exhausted myself so greatly already.

The blonde asks, "What are you doing?"

I ignore her to focus, to scoot a wooden box across the floor with labored breaths, quickly standing on it and nearly falling off from being lightheaded, and then unlatch the lantern. I smile with triumph as I hold the caged flame inside my hands. "Burning the ship down," I finally say, looking around the room and realizing I need to resecure the box before it slams into someone. I sway with my movements, saying, "We're immune to fire, and there are sirens in the water. I'm certain of it. They will protect us."

Two of them protest with something about, *'that's insanity'* or *'who asked you!'* But I don't care. This damn ship has to burn, and all the assholes within it. I don't owe these women any loyalty.

The blonde seems to be the only one who doesn't hate my plan and says, "Back that way. There are boxes stuffed with small barrels of oil. Spread it around. I saw it earlier when everything was sliding around. I realized what you wanted, so I kept a lookout. This wood is treated with pitch and tar."

"What's your name?" I ask, knowing she'll be helpful.

"Sheila—I know you're Jane. We all do."

Nodding, I grab a pole as the ship leans, the sound of splashing water nearly drowning out all conversation.

I carry the lantern with me, bypassing the netting as I search for a box, the lantern fire shining brightly to reveal all the labels. Behind me, the Cinders enter a heated debate about if they should scream for help or not, on how society always has its rises and falls so who cares if others will be hurt as long as *we* are thriving? I move faster, searching and coming up empty.

It's unnerving that no one has come searching for me yet—

The ship begins to dip again.

I hold the lantern against me, my body weightless and slinging around, my shoulder slamming into a box before my ankle lands poorly, and I wince loudly.

When I'm standing on a hobbling leg, my shirt is singing.

Oh, shit. My clothes.

I open another container just as one of them yells, "SHE'S SETTING THE SHIP ON FIRE! HELP!"

"*Cunt*," I whisper, my voice shuddering with joy when I see I've found the small barrels with corks at the top. I use all the strength remaining in me to uncork one and smell *oil*. I immediately begin dousing everything, my eyes flicking to the lantern with nearly every other breath.

I then get the idea to douse *myself* in it, just in case someone comes upon me. I partially smile while breathing through my mouth, waving at the flames. "Go, burn it all. Ruin this ship." I scoop up some of the flaming oil, amazed to see it not burn me as it washes over my skin, and splash it on one of the pillars, the flames climbing up. "This is for you, Anya." My brows are furrowed in a wild fury as I splash it on another one. "For *you*, Mom."

"What are you all shouting at?" someone asks, and I glance over to see one of the crew. I gingerly lay the lantern down, and the fire catches on a trail of oil. I laugh and get to work on another barrel.

"*FIRE!*" the guard shouts. "OIL FIRE!"

Like a mad woman, I dip my hands in oil and let them catch aflame, spreading it around like a child who is painting.

More men come in *right* as the ship dips. I scramble to pull out the cork, oil flying everywhere, even a little on my face, as I spill over the boxes. It's now golden and bright inside, the heat very appreciated after being up top. I glance up at the ceiling. The *ceiling*!

I take the small jar and sling it around lines the wood above us in streaks.

"Well, get her!" someone shouts.

"This bitch is on fire, too!"

The ship groans like a giant animal, the battering of rain echoing throughout, but at least it's no longer cold.

I stand among the flames as they roll upward, my body jerked around the boxes and barrels. The area reeks of burning oil and wood, and the panic begins.

A few of the women shriek as they're still tied to the poles, and the one that's knocked out begins to awaken and starts screaming her head off.

When I'm on my feet again, more men pile into the room.

Some begin to work on getting to the other women, the willing one being freed first as a few of the others protest.

Sheila's rope catches fire; she squints and holds her breath, as if waiting for the burn, but it's only the rope that's set aflame.

We dip over another wave.

I grab onto a pole and clench for dear life, watching as Sheila slams her body into the boxes as she's free from her confines.

The rest of the crew either scramble away as the flames overtake the space or fall into the fires themselves, screeching while they burn, the shock to their system swiftly overtaking them as they slowly collapse to the floor.

Where the fuck is Misery?

Sheila stands over a dead crewmate, a bloodied blade in her hand, probably stolen from him. She smiles at me. "I like your plan."

"And I like your attitude," I say. "Let's get the rest freed." Smoke overtakes the area, and while I choke on it, I can't help but notice it doesn't make me dizzy. It's the rancid smell of the space that makes me want to vomit the most.

With my back to the main entrance, I move to another Cinder after freeing one, Sheila helping another. Panic spreads on the face of the one I'm about to approach. "Careful!"

I glance over my shoulder to where she's looking, and the willing one from earlier is back, coming right at me with a dagger.

It—it takes me completely off guard.

The blade pierces my chest, and I'm almost shocked that this happened. I don't quite feel the pain, but rather the disturbance of everything suddenly not working properly.

"Maybe that will make you sit still," she grinds out. "Don't take it out, or it will kill you. I'm sure someone can heal you so Misery won't be mad."

My eyes flare, the taste of metal on my tongue. "But they won't heal *you*."

She knits her brows, the fire burning so bright I can see flames reflected in her eyes. I take a large step back and scream from the discomfort and agony as the blade is pulled from me, pressing forward once it's out to disarm her with my other hand, and stab her right in the heart. I lean over, labored breathing and blood spilling from my mouth. She struggles to catch her breath as she collapses to the floor, her arms lifelessly falling to her side, eyes remaining wide open.

I collapse to the floor, the Cinders all working to free each other as crewmates stand in the doorway, yelling hopelessly.

I place a hand on my chest, and it feels as if I'm drowning in one lung, like it's impossible to breathe on my left side. My mind can't focus as I'm next aware of Sheila trying to press onto my chest for me, the Cinders all standing together, over half their clothes burned off.

Lifting my gaze at Sheila, I shudder when I exhale. "Get to the ocean. Jump in. The sirens will get you to safety. They have to be out there."

I close my eyes and heal what I can when my hand replaces Sheila's, but this isn't like any injury before. My entire lung feels punctured, and it's a structural issue I haven't healed in my own body before. And I'm also *weak*.

I pivot to look at the men in the threshold, many of their eyes falling to my breasts.

"She's got a Zenith tattoo," one yells.

"Aye," I say, leaning my head forward to look up at them as I grind out, "I do."

Even Sheila looks down at me in shock.

"Let's fucking leave them!" one of the crew shouts, and the others. "We need to get sand from below and put out the fires!"

My senses become dreamlike, some survival in me able to stand when Sheila helps me. Who knows if this floor will cave in soon, and I can't get to the ocean stuck in here. At least, the sirens probably can't get to *me*, either, if I'm trapped in this wreckage underwater.

I only make it to the hallway, the sound of a panic somewhere so far in the distance, before I collapse on the stairs, breathing freely, knowing that they have lost.

"Go, Sheila. Get the rest out." I manage to get out, having no idea if she heard me or not. My inhale is ragged, every breath carrying a groan with it.

My eyes close as my body relaxes onto the stairs.

Drifting within my memories, I'm taken back to Soren's chambers in the Spiraling Stone, wishing I could lie next to him as tears begin to leak from my eyes. His grating voice is in the murky depths of my recollections, the corner of my mouth curling into a sad smile, the discomfort subsiding as his memory envelops my senses.

He came for me.

And now, I have someone to think about when facing death. And it comforts me.

SOREN

I narrow my eyes when it seems like there's something bright in the distance, and it's not the prow of the ship. It's hard to make sense of it when the waves continue to roll into view.

Someone comes down the ladder to the mess hall—a straight shot from up top—their legs flying in the air when we dip down before he's able to anchor himself on the bars. "Blackwell's ship is on fire!" he shouts.

As soon as we're able, we all stand, holding on as Tempest descends down the ladder after him. She's completely soaked, dripping all over the floors. "We're still boarding his ship!" she declares, holding onto the ladder as she looks around the space. "We're almost on him. If you fall into trouble, jump into the ocean. The sirens can feel human energy and will know immediately where you are.

"Liam Rackham will fire cannons just before we collide, and he will provide the escape ship as we ram Sea Wolf into Darkwater. Antony Blackwell is *mine*, and I'll kill the man that robs me of my vengeance. Do you all understand?"

"*AYE!*"

She walks over to us, leaning sideways as the ship dips more, although she doesn't need to hold onto anything. "Do *you* all agree?"

"I'm here for Jane," I state.

"I as well, and Jesper," Ritter replies.

Tempest nods, then looks at Bones. "I'm here for Anya."

"I'm literally here for the fun of it," Basilisk adds as she looks at him.

She doesn't seem amused. "Affiliation? Aside from the witch?"

"Death's Wing."

Even if the two rarely interacted, it's true that we rise to the call of each other when in need. And right now, Anya is in need of vengeance. Tempest tilts her head to the side, as if she accepts it. "Follow the crew when it's time to board. Get yourselves ready."

She climbs back up the ladder as the crew hoots and hollers. Heat sears my blood while I examine every possible outcome in my mind. Closing my eyes, I focus on the waves of energy around me. Everyone vibrates with eagerness, and I'm even able to sense out the utter chaos of Darkwater in the distance.

I swear Misery's energy is missing, always a source of something putrid. It's as if he's either shut me off, or he's not *there*.

Cannons fire—my eyes shoot wide open at the sound of them consecutively firing off, only having heard that once before.

There's a disturbance in my heart that overshadows the battle cries, my mask calling to me that something is wrong with Jane. Her life is in danger. I can sense out her fading heartbeat, like a precarious warning to what needs to be saved.

I engulf myself in the calm that is second nature to me, one that is purely guided by *years* of training in warfare. I don't question anything else, knowing I need to be surgical in my approach so I may reach her. Get her in the waters. I can't do shit for her when it comes to healing, but the sirens might.

That's my duty.

I *will* find her.

And the fucking world better hope she's alive.

I take over the directing of everyone to go above deck, looking at each man's face before they ascend the stairs while Tempest's crew climbs the ladder, keeping it quick and uniform, before I move up myself. Once up top, I don't even fully feel the rain that pelts against me.

Not when every step, every breath, is now fueled with a deep purpose. Every time my heart beats, I worry about Jane's. *We're moving too slow.* My eyes widen in shock when I realize what I saw belowdeck, only to blink as rain pelts in. The entire center of Darkwater is on fire, caved in right at the middle. The flames lick the air with a signature, as if imbued with the energy of the person who ignited them. Without thinking, I shout, "Jane set the fire!"

Ritter gives me his full attention as he stands to my right. "*What?*"

"I can feel it. Her energy, her anger, it's all over the flames." I peer around for Basilisk until I find him in the crowd, taking two steps toward him. "Do you feel Misery?"

"No!" Concern is etched in those golden eyes, furrowed brows hanging heavily over them. "I think we can risk boarding. I don't know what happened to him!"

We all reach for something to stabilize ourselves, the black expanse of the rolling ocean like the surface to another dimension. We're nearing Darkwater as if the winds have stopped brushing against Blackwell's ship, as if they *fuel* Tempest's more than before. I can even see Blackwell at the wheel, glancing at us before he leaves his post.

"HANG TIGHT!" ripples through Sea Wolf from Tempest's crew, and I glance over to the other side to see Storm's Fury is close enough to visualize the dots along his hull for the cannons.

No one outruns the Sea Wolf.

The sky above is torn apart in jagged streaks of lightning, light washing over Darkwater to reveal the damage. Sheets of rain lash at the ocean, reducing the horizon to a shifting, watery void. Crimson sails billow as if given one last burst of power, the wolf's head about to devour Darkwater.

We all cling to rough ropes, our faces and hair soaked.

I can smell the burning of Blackwell's ship, even the heat of the fire as the storm seems to hold its breath so the Sea Wolf can collide in an explosion of splintering wood, the fire nearly blinding after being in darkness for so long. Embers twist into the storm, the Sea Wolf groaning as it's firmly affixed to Darkwater, the crew immediately taking action.

Nearly two dozen pirates swing through the air on ropes, landing on the ship as they start slicing at Blackwell's crew, dancing around the fires, a few tumbling into the caved-in center.

Grapnel hooks arc through the stormy air as more pirates swarm the flaming ship, the war cries swallowed by the storm's howl.

The heat of the fire clashes with the cold sting of the rain, and I finally make my move, running to the prow to climb off of the wolf's head that's bitten into Darkwater, first trying to locate Misery.

The braziers are strangely empty compared to the rest of the ship, the broken god seemingly gone.

The pirates lead most of the fight as they're used to this terrain, my men slowly making their way over. Sliding down the wolf's head, I let my momentum carry me until I leap off onto Darkwater. I slide out two of my swords, moving forward to start slicing at the first unfortunate fucker near me. Ritter is on the ship, too, Basilisk landing on the deck, slicing his axes to chop two heads off at once; he keeps close to Ritter, just as we talked about.

I collide into many, intently focusing with my energy, feeling Jane *below* us. Every blow I deliver is to get me one step closer to her.

Tempest swings over on her own rope, her captain's jacket gone. After landing, she rises among the fire, the gold on her mask becoming translucent from the flames. "*ANTONY!*" she cries out, her voice carrying unnaturally in the winds.

Muscle memory dominates as I wade through the energies around me, sensing danger as if a puppeteer controls my actions. My steel collides with either flesh, bone, or metal. Two dangers come at me at once. Everything tells me to let the one in front hit me with the plank of wood he wields in order to avoid what's behind.

The man collides with my chest before I duck down, looking up to see a sword swinging over my head, cutting at the man's throat.

I gut the one behind me, his intestines slipping out of his body as blood mixes with the ocean's water on the deck.

Ducking down to a knee, I dodge another blow, striking up to cut that man's arm off.

A pause.

I seek Jane's fading energy—moving to the stairwell, I throw all my weight into elbowing the first man I see so hard his skull cracks.

I glare at the door, feeling what I desire just beyond it, and barrel into the wood. Blasting it off of the hinges, I confront two men standing on the other side, wide-eyed, water and blood dripping down my body onto the dry interior.

I don't give a fuck who they are or what their purpose is. I stab one right in the heart and pulverize the other so hard his ribs shatter.

They're in the way of Jane.

Going down the stairs, the blood in my veins feels as if it vanishes—

A body is splayed out right at the base of the stairs, red hair tangled around her face, most of Jane's body exposed as the rest of her clothes have clearly burned off. A wound is above her left breast, her body covered in blood.

"Jane," I say, dropping my weapons as they tumble down. I lean over her, pulling the hair out of her face; my hands are covered in bloody soot while her face is pristine, leaving dark streaks on her face. *The fires burned any grime away. This injury happened after.*

Relief. Absolute-fucking-relief exudes in her eyes as they barely part open. She smiles so big that she hardly seems to focus on my face, her teeth stained with blood.

"I," she tries, and coughs. "I missed you."

Overwhelming emotions gut me, my throat burning. "It's okay, beautiful," I say and gently cradle her in my arms to hold her close once more. "We're here to help finish what you started, and to get you off this ship."

"You were right," she mutters, coughing again before groaning. "It was nice thinking of you just now."

I grip her tighter, some of the fire burning me as it licks out from where she must have been, but I don't care, even if the temperature down here is nearly suffocating. "Stay with me, love." I pivot on the stairs, starting to climb, leaning on the walls for balance when I need to. "I'm taking you home."

She doesn't respond, her head unstable as it leans into my shoulder.

A man descends the stairs with a sword, and I grind my teeth as I give him my opposite shoulder, his blade piercing my skin and muscle as it cuts through some of my armor, my body blocking any access to striking Jane. I groan out and collide into him, resorting to the barbaric basics of using my sheer size to overpower him as he stumbles, stomping on his chest when he falls down, crushing him underneath me.

Jane is fading, and the comfort of not being alone almost has the opposite effect of keeping her alive. It's soothing her into that eternal darkness.

I enter the stormy night as the cold rain wets swiftly chills the steel of my armor, looking for the closest path to the ocean. Ritter spots the two of us, fear overtaking any and all fight within him.

One of the spars cracks at the base as, slowly collapsing in a warning to that it crush all those underneath. The rope around Ritter's leg spindles up quickly, but he doesn't notice; he's only focused on the dying woman in my arms. I can't drop Jane to save him, already knowing I'd choose her over anyone here if it came to it.

Ritter realizes what's happening, but it's too late.

I hold Jane closer, ducking her vision away from what's about to happen in case she can still see. Just as the rope nearly tightens around Ritter to slingshot him into the air, it suddenly doesn't, despite the spar continuing to crash down, taking out ropes and masts with it.

Basilisk dove to cut at the ropes *right* as it almost took the Scorpion, rolling into a standing position to brace himself to block an attack from another.

"*RASMUS!*" I shout.

Gutting his attacker, he moves quickly to me, his face darkened from soot and blood. "I need you to take Jane! Someone needs to be with her who can feel Misery. Keep her in the waters with the sirens until I'm with you!"

He doesn't question any moment of that order, receiving Jane as I pass her over, ensuring her head is supported until he has a secure grip. The ship sways again with a wave, and he lets himself slide right off the side off the ship, carrying away the precious woman that everyone severely underestimated, and I'll ensure that they reap the carnage of their mistake.

I won't leave this ship until I know *no one* is coming to haunt Jane again.

IT'S DONE, NORA

RITTER

A sense of finality struck me harder than anticipated as I watched someone *else* rescue my daughter, with the same fervor I once had when rescuing Nora, all those years ago.

I don't have time to thank Basilisk for saving my life just now, trusting that Soren knows what he's doing with Jane. *She's alive. The sirens will take care of her. Cypress promised.*

Cutting my way through those that remain, I re-center my aggression as I shout out to Jesper while he hides behind a wall of Blackwell's men. This damn body of mine is worthless without the training, knowing I can't get to him on my own—

The large figure of Soren enters my vision, pulverizing the pirates with either his weapons or his body, Bones right behind him, and then Basilisk joins.

It's a fast clash of wet steel, until I spot an opening to reach Jesper, who is bickering about getting into the reserve boat, only to yell out a counter point that the sirens will take them under if they touch the ocean.

"Where is Morvock!" one shouts as I near them while trying not to slide off the deck. I've earned the right to hone in on my target while the younger men handle the rest.

Jesper shouts, "He fucking left us!" They near the side of the ship, and one screams out, "There's sirens in the water!"

I laugh at their futility, the smile not reaching my eyes. My heart races faster, so damn close to the revenge my family needs.

Jesper glances around in a clear attempt to search for an answer until he spots me, fear washing over him as if he's never been truly terrified before. He fumbles for a dagger from his waist, rotating it inward on himself, and I know what he's about to do.

The siren's suicide; killing oneself is preferred to the siren's curse.

No he fucking doesn't.

I dive forward with my entire weight, my arm intersecting his blade right as it reaches his body, penetrating my entire wrist as I cry out when I see the metal sink into my flesh, severing the ability to use my fingers.

Jesper collapses to the ground with my attack as we both lie on the soaking deck. Jesper's laugh rents the air, his one visible eye manic, only for me to use my other hand to remove a blade at my thigh, cutting at one of his knees as his cackle morphs into a hollering pain. *Try escaping now, you cunt.*

I cannot die without knowing Jesper faces pure torment, and he will *not* be graced with the mercy of dying today. My wrist still bleeds profusely, the blade sticking out of my arm, but I'll plunge over the edge with him if I have to.

"What are you doing?" Jesper asks with panic, reaching for his knee.

"Giving you to the sirens," I declare, the raging inferno reflecting against his eye, his skin and clothes glistening as I slowly rise up to stand over him, his weapon still in my flesh.

"Please," he pleads, trying to move but Bones appears and stomps *hard* with his boot on Jesper's chest, whose mouth expands wide in a forced exhale. He tries to catch his breath, glaring at me. "Think of the life you're about to commit me to. The *misery*."

"And what about *my* misery?" I lean down, holding up my fucked up wrist as if to show *physical* pain means nothing to me. "My wife was *murdered* on your orders. And what of my daughter's life? Of *Jane's* suffering? Of the mother you robbed her of?" I spit in his face. "My only regret is I will die before you and be unable to witness your torture centuries from now."

Abject horror spreads on Jesper's face as I realize he sees Soren nearing us, as if the Zenith is death incarnate. Bones lifts his boot as Soren grabs Jesper by the neck, picking him up with one hand as the pompous cunt struggles to breathe. "You killed Anya," Soren rasps, and Jesper sputters something useless out. "And you planned to use Jane, to *assault* her. To destroy her dignity." Soren brings Jesper closer to his face, his mask utterly stolid but the striking eyes underneath are incensed with fury. "You were *never* going to survive that. *I* am your fucking reckoning, not the god you hid behind." Soren drops his gaze. "Go ahead, Bones."

Jesper is pinned to the railing, his hair splayed in wet strands over his face, the bandaging around his one eye sloughing off, slowly revealing a gnarled gash like he'd been mauled by an animal; red, swollen, and bruised. Bones unfurls Jesper's reluctant arm to immobilize with his boot, slamming an ax through his wrist, the hand nearly rolling away before Bones can grab it.

Jesper screams out in shock, trying to stand but his cut up knee won't take any weight.

"How polite to offer your hand in this," Bones says, laughing in Jesper's face before headbutting him so hard he becomes dazed, the mad man still in his face. "You're so fucking lucky you're going to the sirens. I would have tortured you until my last breath, *then* handed you over." He moves away, as if being near him anymore will force Bones to murder him. "I can't look at him."

Soren readjusts to grab Jesper by the collars, the Order of Ash leader beginning to cry, bleeding out all over the broken deck, his eyepatch sliding off to reveal eyelids that are sewn shut. Soren says to him, "You and I will never meet again. Enjoy your eternity."

He then lifts Jesper to toss him over, and I near the edge to ensure that the sirens greet him, just barely witnessing his body getting sucked into the waves. A few tails breach the dark water right where the ocean consumed him, like shark fins when circling a feast.

The relief that floods my body nearly has me collapsing.

Soren nears me, as if he can feel everything coursing through me. He probably can, and I don't think I'll ever get used to it. I look at him, holding up my wrist as blood drips down my arm, still unable to use my fingers. "I need to get in the waters. I'm bleeding out. I need the sirens. Pulling this out will kill me."

Nora always made sure to educate me on proper wound management.

Soren and I share a prolonged moment of eye contact, an aged Zenith staring at the younger, more capable one; it's officially time for me to let go. "Go ahead," Soren says, nodding to me.

With the next harsh jolt of the ship, I let my body fall overboard, weightless as I plunge below, watching flaming the deck rise higher above me as I tumble between the two interlocked vessels.

I did it Nora. I'm so sorry it took me so long.

My body collides with the surface to expel all air from my lungs, before gently sinking down, pale hair immediately floating around me, the fires above giving off immense, diffused light.

A part of me recognizes it's the sirens already tending to me rather than Nora's blonde hair, but in that moment, I wouldn't mind if I didn't wake up.

THE OCEAN GOD

SOREN

We all grip whatever's left of this vessel to stabilize ourselves with the swaying ship. Blackwell is pinned down at the front of the deck, the Sea Wolf's pearl eyes watching over him like it's a true beast having captured its prey. I near whatever's going on, along with Bones who still holds onto Jesper's stump of a hand.

Tempest stands over Blackwell, a figure made of ocean water joining her, its eyes glowing white. The surface of the ocean creature's body spins like a cyclone as if his ephemeral exists of fluid. *Ta'Kan.* Where his face should be, the rolling water gives vague impressions of sharp features. His hands, when they appear before recoiling back into the fluid flesh, are like claws made of brine. He gives off the same sensation as Misery or Cypress, like the mortals in this realm should not be witnessing their existence.

All the pirates around bow down immediately, the storm even letting up as Tempest stands with triumph over the fallen captain of Darkwater, who watches on in fright. "What are you doing?" he asks.

"You branded our daughter," Tempest says, tilting her head. "So I am going to reap your soul."

Ta'Kan's hand is defined once more, moving over Blackwell's mouth, the man starting to scream something high-pitched and primal—no ounce of decorum left—as a white, silvery essence pools in front of his face, shining brightly and almost with purity against the surrounding carnage.

Tempest holds out a vial, and the soul slips inside like silky air.

Blackwell's body shrivels as skin wraps tightly around his bones; the shell of a cunt who fueled all of this. Bones nears the corpse, rummaging through the weapons until he finds a blade that he unsheathes. The one that killed, Anya, perhaps?

Tempest's energy is as calm as the eye of a storm as she shakes the vial, the sound of a scream echoing inside like it's trapped within a hundred layers of glass. Tempest's laugh almost carries an edge of pity, like she knows Blackwell will suffer for a *very* long time. She faces one of her pirates, who is still kneeling. "Do a head-count on Storm's Fury once you make it over to her. The sirens will sort out any bodies, and I'll see if Sea Wolf is salvageable. I will be a *while.*"

The godly figure looks down at Tempest, the oceanic energy slowly engulfing her as her gaze connects with mine, the cyclone of water advancing up her legs. "Misery is gone for now, Soren. I don't know where he fled, but he's far from here."

The water slowly absorbs the pirate queen before Ta'Kan's gaze meets mine, to which I immediately lower my gaze.

I've had enough of the gods for a lifetime, and I don't need to interact with *any* more. I'll let her go do whatever the fuck one does with an ocean god. "Everyone, into the ocean!" I shout once the Ta'Kan's figure slowly pulls back beyond the ship, Tempest disappearing with him as if she's dissolved into salt water herself.

The ship tilts once more, and I let the momentum take me like it does with the remainder of these men. We all scuffle through the wreckage to reach the edge, and I catch myself on the banister before pivoting over, my body weightless until I crash through the water's surface. The sirens are on all of us, beginning to pull everyone away as they force marrowkelp into our mouths.

I let the uncomfortable process take over, still fighting it just because it's impossible not to. Once that pressure stabilizes, the waters are so calming compared to what was just endured above the water.

The sirens take me to a Jane, who elegantly floats in the water with hair gracefully drifting around her. I keep my eyes on her the entire time, as if my gaze is the chain that anchors me to her. Gills flex and contract in her neck, the sirens focusing on her chest wound.

One of them is Melona.

They weave something into her skin, another healing from behind with glowing hands. They won't let me touch her, but *do* allow me to float nearby, a few above paying attention to debris that slowly falls through. I even take off my mask, in case Jane's eyes open. I want her to see *me*, not the black skull.

At some point, I witness the belly of Darkwater sinking beyond us, bodies floating around it. The captain's quarters submerges into the ocean, slowly descending into the darkness, the entirety of that ship now destined to become one with the ocean floor.

The masts of the Darkwater are the last thing I see before the glowing orbs around the sirens are all that's left for light, the fires completely gone.

When they seem to be finished, Melona connects her gaze with mine. "Jane's wound is incredibly delicate. It holds well underwater, but above, she will need to remain nearly completely still for almost a week." She nods as one of the sirens hands me a canvas bag, which moves in slow motion compared to the creatures of the ocean. "In there are vials that will keep her barely conscious, just enough to drink water and maybe even eat. A human healer will need to care for her after."

"It will be done," I say.

They let me near Jane, and I hold her against my body as the sirens hook ropes under my arms to pull us to Storm's Fury. I hold her close enough that she's firmly affixed to me, but not so close that my abrasive armor will dig into her exposed skin. Her hair streams behind to reveal her sleeping face while we're being pulled.

Slowly—barely—I begin to accept I somehow survived.

With Jane.

SOOTHING TOUCHES

JANE

I'm so lost when I crack open crusty eyelids.

I first note the dryness of the bed I lie in, compared to the rains. Did I... did I dream everything? I clearly cannot be dead, for my body aches *far* too much. It's as if I got trampled on by a hundred horse hooves.

My neck is stiff as I barely move my head, staring out a window for a very long time, mindlessly watching a puffy cloud. Peaceful, golden rays beam through, my eyes moving to watch the floating particles in the air. My mind is absolutely blank, as if I know *this* is the dream, and I don't want to awaken.

Inhaling deeply, I whimper and lift my hand as if to touch my chest, but even *that* hurts. Breathing is also surprisingly painful, like each breath is dragging broken glass inside of my chest.

My lungs.

The ship.

My heart rate increases as I swiftly examine the small room I'm in—all of my concerns disappear when I spot Soren in the corner. He has a blackened eye, a new, deep cut on his lower lip and jaw, and bandages cross over his body underneath his loose tunic. His dark, grimy hair is pulled back.

His legs are spread as he sleeps, a hand on either armrest while his head leans against the wall behind him.

I'm too afraid to move—what if that breaks this dream? I nearly start to cry at the idea that I'm actually dead; does that mean he's dead, too?

His eyes suddenly shoot open, revealing the crystal clarity as he blinks and lowers his gaze to me, not moving anything else. He blinks multiple more times before recognition comes to his eyes, one of them bloodshot, and he leans forward while trying to cover a painful grimace. *"Jane,"* he says with that gravelly voice I love.

I can't help myself.

I crumble.

Tears flow, which morph into crying from pain as my chest *burns.* Soren comes forward, pulling me into his thick, strong arms. I start clinging to him out of pure joy, laughing and crying more.

Sometimes, I shudder and groan from how much it all aches and burns.

He holds me so tenderly I could melt, like I'm being embraced by love incarnate. "Careful. Your lung took a lot of damage. Some might be permanent. The sirens healed what they could, and there's no other healer on board."

"I'm so sorry about Anya," is the first thing I say. I pull back, prodding at my neck. "Her necklace."

"It's safe. It was around your neck, and one of the sirens took it off. I found it in a bag they gave me." He pulls me back in and gently kisses my head. "You're safe, Jane—"

"You came for me."

This man is now lodged so deeply within my heart, I don't ever want to know a world where he doesn't exist. There's something that burns between us that's brighter than anything I can explain, this love and gratitude so vast I nearly want to burst.

"Of course, I did," he answers.

For a while, we just sit there like this, leaning my full weight against him as I learn the rhythm of his beating heart. The faint thudding means I'm utterly safe. It's the sound of *home*.

"The others? What happened to everyone? My dad?" I ask when I realize they must have been there, too. "The other Cinders…"

"Only two Cinders died, but everyone else is live. Blackwell's soul was ripped apart; your father captured Jesper and I ensured the sirens took him. Tempest is alive, although her ship is now with the ocean. The hull broke at the bottom when colliding with Darkwater."

I pull back to look up at his face, at the bruising on his temple. I reach up to heal it even if it hurts like a bitch to raise my arm, noticing there's a large, scabbed wound below his ear.

Soren's hand engulfs my wrist and to bring it back down, almost in a scolding manner. "Your body needs to heal. If there's anything to tend to, it will be yourself."

I smile, fucking missing this man. "Back to the orders?"

"I have no problem asserting that your health is above the rest."

"There really isn't another healer?"

"No. She was taken under, and when the sirens got to her, she was already gone."

"I feel okay," I say, trying to hide a groan. "As in, I'm alive. I'll make it to wherever we're going, and I can be healed there. Others might need my help."

He pulls back and touches my chest with calloused hands that I'm so glad to feel against my skin again. "The sirens said their magic requires you to sit still." He looks me in the eye, the pale blue encased within dark lashes. "I'll tie you down in here if I have to. I already have the rope ready. I knew you might fight me."

My laugh turns into a coughing groan. "Are you in here to ensure that happens?"

He gives a faint, crooked grin, the stubble around his mouth deepening where his skin indents. "Yes." He looks over my face, the room so quiet I can hear the smallest sound of every breath he takes. It's a mundane detail that brings me more relief than can I interpret. "Did you really think of me when in that stairwell?" he asks.

The moment crashes back into my mind like the waves Misery

forced me to suffer through. "I thought of the nights when we'd lie together, when nothing else mattered," I answer through a voice that involuntarily grows shakier, tears blurring my vision; it's as if I fully realize I nearly died. "It was nice not to feel alone. And you brought me *so* much comfort."

Something deep and sentimental overtakes a face that's primarily unbending, his eyes perhaps wetter than usual before he pulls my forehead to his lips. I breathe him in, the traces of his unique scent covering up the rawness of my trauma.

"Sleep, my love," he says against my skin. "You need sleep."

THE WEIGHT OF THE TRUTH
SOREN

After helping her drink as much water as she could take, along with offering a biscuit and a pickled egg, I administered the vial to Jane under a slight guise; I told her it was to ease the pain, not render her unconscious again.

She can figure out the details of that later once she's *alive*, and with a healer.

As I stare out the window, an urge to open it overtakes me as I reach over a sleeping Jane to work the latch, fresh air wafting into the room once it's opened. While I'm up, I take one of the towels to lay underneath her, in case her body is unable to wake to relieve herself.

Sitting back in the chair, I lean my head back once more, dragging out a long, deep groan. My own body aches with a depth I don't care to ever feel again, my damn head pounding.

The way Jane broke down when she saw me just now and *knew* she was safe, flooding me with every ounce of love she had, and that she thought of *me* as she lied there on those stairs... *fuck*. That's what made all of this worth it. She was willing to die to save others, so it's important she realizes the same sacrifice will easily be given to her.

My body stiffens when a raven flies into the small room, the bird landing on a table next to Jane, eyes glowing red. Its beak opens as the form of Cypress rapidly expands until the witch is standing before me. "I'm here to remove Jane's ruby," she explains without wasting any time.

All I can do at this point is roll my fucking eyes and pinch the bridge of my nose. "Did you enjoy all of that?"

"I enjoyed that you all lived."

"Not *Anya*."

"She and I spoke. She understood her death was essential, and she was more than willing."

What? Why didn't Anya say anything? "Why was it *essential*?"

"Its *inspiration* is what was essential. For everyone. For Jane's dignity, as she otherwise would have greatly suffered. I always saw a decrepit Morvock would believe Anya." Cypress moves to examine Jane, who lies in one of the few beds on this ship, her chest slowly rising and falling in her sleep. "I can speak more freely now, Soren Latham. I don't enjoy being so cryptic, you know. But give too much information, and it could alter the visions."

When I don't say anything in return, she seems to take that as permission to continue. "I saw you in Jane's future long, long ago, to be clear. As soon as she was born, in fact. There are so many things I had to arrange just perfectly for you both to meet under the right circumstances. I needed to *ensure* Tempest would allow you on her ship, but that would be impossible if I involved myself, seeing as she and I go back over a hundred years."

I absorb every word the witch speaks. "How old is Tempest?" I ask, no longer fighting whatever current Cypress is dragging us through.

"Close to two hundred summers." I nearly laugh at that, as of *course.* "Her relationship with a god helps extend her life, like it does with mine. Although *my* god is not interested in me like hers is with her. Her capturing Ta'Kan's attention is an entire story in itself.

"Either way, I have worked myself backwards from there," she continues, looking at me as I remain seated. I just want her to keep talking, to explain *everything.* "Jane *needed* to be on that ship. *She* is who ruined Morvock, and sent him back to his lands, where he will be forced to slumber for a *very* long time. That's for a future not relevant to now. It will be *then* that he truly dies. In the meantime, he is not a worry for you. Not anymore." My eyes widen with this insight, wondering just how much she knows. "Jane used her healing powers and touched Morvock, sending every ounce of her goddess's powers into him. Healing is the opposite of misery.

"Getting her on that ship, and safely, is where everything became convoluted and I began the process of spending *years* plotting everything out. Perhaps one day you will know the specifics as to why." Cypress looks back down at Jane, and I admit the witch seems more mortal than usual in her expression. "For now, let me remove the ruby."

Cypress gently lifts Jane's head as I remain silent, just watching until, without warning, Jane's heart returns to me with such force that it makes me grip the arm rests, overcome with solace to be fully reconnected to her.

I'm still leaving that fucking piece of my mask in her, in case she ever disappears again.

Cypress holds the ruby up, the sun catching it just right as the center glows a bright red. "Let Jane know the debt she had to pay was simply staying in Coalfell until it was time to leave, and visiting me first gave me the chance to give her those ruby earrings that began Tempest's involvement, and that Melona didn't know the extent of her debt, only to relay my message—that's a burden Jane carried for a long time, I think.

"I also want you to tell her that what Misery wanted from her was *my* bloodline. I'm glad that information was able to be withheld from her, as being related to me would have clouded her judgment. And it wasn't just *my* bloodline he wanted, but he was also after Moriganna's, so he could claim power over the ocean god. The parents of either were too corrupted and intertwined with other deities. Ritter's body would have rejected Morvock, which is why he needed Jane so badly out of the two of them."

She points a finger up at the ceiling, but motions her hand toward me. "*You* were the catalyst, Soren. That injury at your neck was critical for everything." She laughs, as if she still can't believe it worked. "Morvock was set to attack your men at Rosmertta's within the week, but getting struck made Shade act carelessly. He so was utterly desperate to be the one to secure Jane. Morvock had always seen your injury as something he could take advantage of—he just didn't know *I* would take advantage of it, too."

It's the oddest fucking feeling to think all the free will in my life might have been orchestrated by another. "Then why didn't Misery just take Jane when we arrived?"

She grins. "He was *confident* he'd get her at Rosmertta's. He is fed by other's disparity, and the idea that letting *you* get attached—a Sensor who did not serve him—so he could crush your heart before your death, was simply inspired by greed. In *all* of my meditation, in *all* of my searching, *you* were the wild influence that he over-looked. Your role as a Sensor gave him false confidence that he'd know your every move. But he gave up that right as soon as he took the flesh.

"And now that Morvock is successfully back in his lands and suppressed for many more years, you can now know where your sister is."

I swear, even my heart stops beating as my body takes on an absolute stillness, staring at Cypress as I refuse to *blink*.

She eyes me like she's not sorry she inflicted this on me, but still understands how difficult she has made my life. "Your failed pursuit of Serena was *always* meant to be your motivation, one that would collide you with Skull's Row, and thus be sent to capture Jane rather than Blackwell, ensuring she would be on that ship *right* when Morvock was at his utter weakest—it's the only way her magic could truly work against him.

"And it was *me* that came to you all those years ago, disguised as a lord to lure your sister, and just as I have blocked you from feeling Jane, you have been unable to feel Serena. On the next full moon, you will discover her across the Black Sea. Basilisk is directly tied to the woman your sister now serves, which is my gift to you. I brought Basilisk here as assurance for everyone's safety, and also to guide you directly to your sister. He doesn't know that, however, but I trust you'll inform him."

I can't see straight as I stare her down.

"*You*… you're the one that made it so she has been *lost* for *years*?"

"I'm certain we will cross paths again, Soren. We can discuss this more then. Take care of Jane, please. She and her father are the only family I have left."

Without anything else said, her body folds in on itself as it turns into a flapping raven, flying out the fucking window *I* opened. I bet that bitch orchestrated *that*, too.

I aimlessly look around, processing everything she just laid at my feet. I'm numb. Utterly fucking numb. My gaze lands on Jane, who was completely out through all of that. Even though she's here with me, I feel alone.

For the first time since… since I realized I couldn't find Serena, I lean my head into my hand and let it all out.

— ◆ —

WHEN JANE'S still deep in her sleep and after I've rummaged through all the broken pieces of me, realizing that I have Jane *and* Serena, I exit the small room, coming across Basilisk, who sits outside our door.

"You're lucky to have her," he says, cleaning the grime underneath his nails. I don't even want to speak about what he might have just felt from me.

"Who do you have connections with that my sister will know?" I ask.

He drinks the water next to him. "Go on. I'll watch over Jane. Then we can talk about who I'm guessing Cypress is referring to."

I don't press Basilisk, knowing I need fresh air so I can think straight. It won't hurt to let my heart settle more before speaking with him further. The *need* to uncover information on my sister is so quiet I can finally just *exist*, finding relief in knowing her heart will be available to me, soon.

I stride out into the sun, noticing Ritter sitting against one of the mast's poles, his stump of a hand wrapped tightly. He had to chop the damn thing off, to which the sirens took care of.

We're *all* so beaten and bloodied.

I stand next to the man, kneeling down so he doesn't have to get up. "Jane has had the ruby removed. She awoke, too, but I put her back under. Thought you should know."

He nods, eyeing the tape of his wounded hand. "Thank you for taking care of her."

"As long as she'll let me."

Something has tamed within the Scorpion as well, and I can feel the acceptance of me that he thought he'd never give. "We are nearing Siren's Cove," he says, connecting his gaze with mine, the lines of his face deepened from the dryness of the salty air. "I have a few things to gather from the island. Things of Jane's mother. Will you keep Jane rested until then?"

"I'll manage her recovery."

His grin is unburdened. "She'll be pissed to learn she's being knocked out, over and over."

"Leave that to me to deal with," I reply, eyeing the men around that pass by us.

"I won't fight that," he croaks out before taking a swig of water. "She's not easy to negotiate with. Never has been."

"Truer words have never been spoken." My voice carries nothing but respect for her. I look down at my hands, at the rings I wear, focusing on the one that's the body of a serpent. The one my mother gave me when I left for Death's Wing. "She'll be taken care of when we reach my lands. My mother's a healer."

Ritter's eyes flash with intrigue, leaning forward slightly as if that *does* bring him relief, before his gaze drops back down, something nostalgic flooding him.

"Anyway, wanted some fresh air and to let you know," I say, standing once more.

"Thank you, Soren."

I grunt in reply, ready to head back to Basilisk as my head wanders down many different paths.

He and I have a *lot* to discuss.

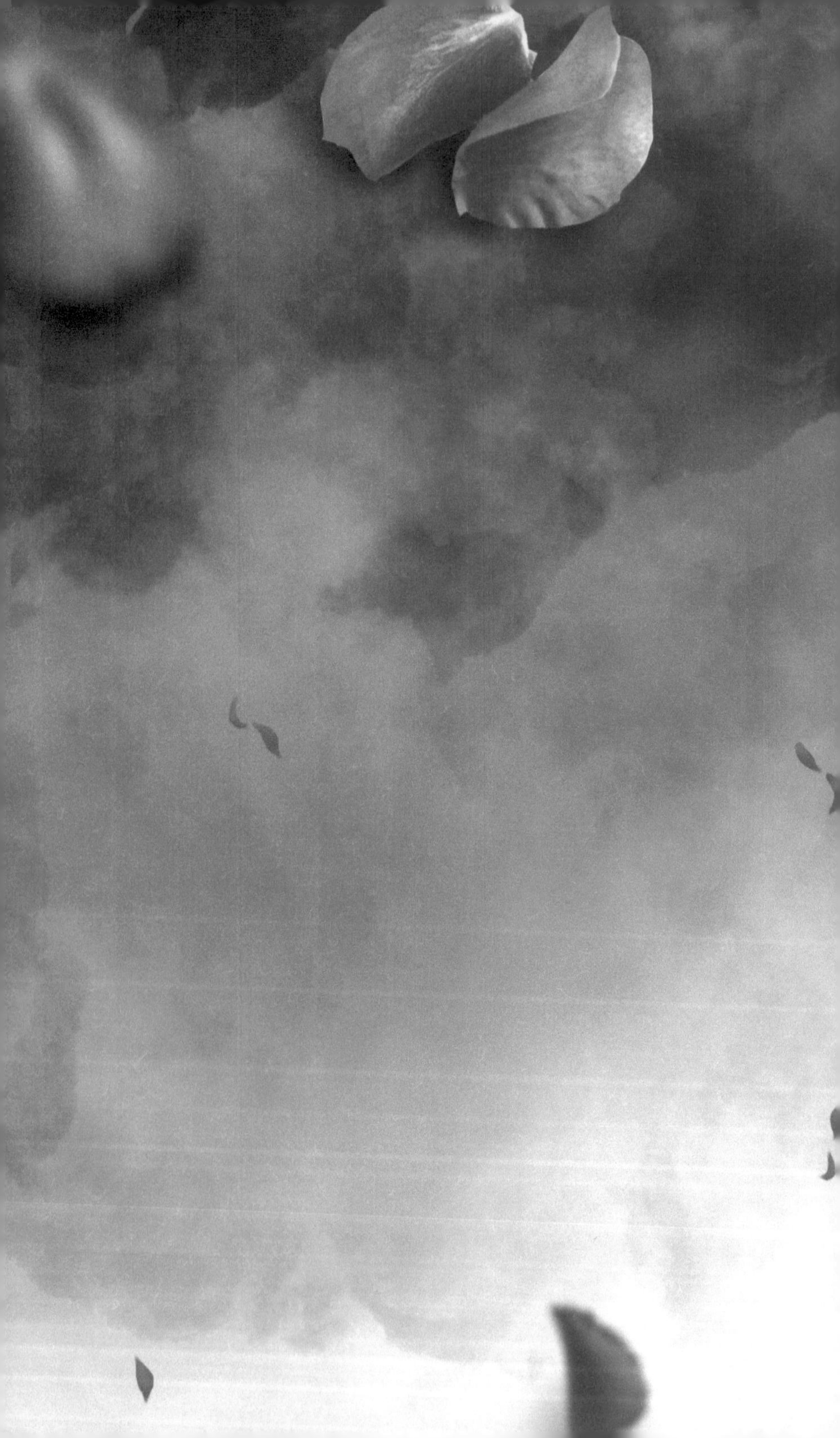

JANE

My mind is as a mess of memories that repeatedly collide. There's a vague awareness of drinking and eating, even of Soren cleaning my wounds only to re-bandage them.

But they're so blurry.

My focus returns when a woman with kind eyes leans over me, ones that have the same crystal coloration of Soren's. When she doesn't disappear, I start to accept that I'm awake.

"*Soren,*" I state, my heart racing.

"My son is well. I am taking care of you now," the woman comforts. Her voice is low and warm, dark hair streaked with white as it's loosely braided down her back. Her face is marked with age, but there's a certain vivacity to her eyes.

"You're his *mother*?"

"Yes." A strand of her peppered dark hair falls in her eyes as she moves away to tend to a bowl with a thick, gelatinous salve. "Your wound was very aggressive. I've been healing it for some time now," she says, waving a hand over my chest as her wrist glows blue. Pain mixes with relief as it's *slightly* easier to breathe, and I know that she must have helped some of the scar tissue heal.

She really is a healer. I don't know why, but that detail digs massively into my heart, as if it legitimizes everything that Soren has ever said to me. I knew I trusted him, because I *choose* to, but this confirms my difficult heart doesn't have to worry about him.

Not anymore.

He's *mine*.

"Why are you here?" I ask, looking around the small room that doesn't look any different than the rest, although there's a distinct lack of rocking from a ship. *Are we on land?*

"We're in Serpent's Crest. It's our home. It's where he was born," she replies, bringing the bowl over to me as her other hand finished sending her healing magic into my body. She then pulls a wet rag off my chest that rested underneath a tunic I wear, revealing the gnarled wound. There's a deep, red line where the compliant one stabbed me—

The flashback to what actually happened sends my head spinning, my heart racing.

"When did I get off the ship I was on? Soren was there," I ask with a high-pitched voice, trying to confirm I *am* off that ship. What if Misery is warping my dreams, and this is all his doing? Glancing back out the window with a pounding heart, I notice there are even leaves blowing gently in the distance.

"It's alright, Jane. It's all done. Soren got you off the ship, and I believe he had you sedated."

The burning ship… Like I always do, I numb it all. Press on so I drown in it.

So, he had me sedated? The memory of waking up comes back, along with my offer to heal others. My huff rolls into a painful cough. "Those assholes sedated me?" I ask without thought, nearly covering my mouth as I look at her while she gently rubs the salve over my sewn together wound. "Sorry," I say, holding a hand up. "No offense."

Her smile deepens the lines around her crinkling eyes. "He is smitten deeply with you. Gained a few new, deep scars just for you, too." She takes in a slow breath. "My son, unfortunately, has lived a very harsh reality. He can be a bit *too* blunt when he needs to be softer in his approach. Especially when he's passionate about something." She nods to me. "Such as drugging you to keep you alive without telling you. I can't say it was the wrong move, because you truly did need to lie completely still."

I take in the room all the more as a giant grin spreads across my face, getting the sense I might actually be in a normal dwelling, completely safe from everything that nearly tore me apart. "Was the injury that bad?

"This wound is stitched together with siren's kelp. It can heal nearly anything, but it's a very fragile bind. You were at great risk of re-traumatizing the wound. It seems to be a lung puncture, so yes, it was quite nasty."

When she's done applying the gel, his mother offers a hand with very short nails. "Let's sit you up and get some food and tea in you."

I grimace as I move, but it's nowhere near as bad as when I first awoke to Soren. His mother fetches me some tea and food on a table, and I find it interesting that she wears billowy pants, along with a loose tunic, her feet bare. She's not wearing a dress.

"Thank you for looking after me."

"Of course. Anything important to Soren is important to me," she replies, sitting back down on the floor with crossed legs, next to my cot. She pours me some steaming tea, and offers me a plate of spiced rice.

My jaw goes slack when I lock eyes with a few blue candles lit near the kettle. "Those! How do you use those?"

"The azure flame?" she asks, like this surprises her. "Oh, you just light them. It's done by gripping the candle and sending your healing magic into the wax. The flames only appear that way. You don't have to do much else, really. They're draining, though. So you can't leave them on for long because they give off a pulse of healing energy in the room, which takes from your energy."

"What's her name?" I nearly whisper, staring at the physical manifestation of the understanding I craved while locked away. "Of our goddess?"

"Azzara."

"*Azzara*," I mutter, a pulse of energy concentrating in my wrists. My heart almost breaks in two, desperately clawing at the memory of my mother. What happened that made her veer from our goddess? Her magic clearly saved me on that ship; my body turns rigid once more when recalling how the waves washed over me on Darkwater.

"Your mother didn't teach you?"

"No… um, she had a falling out with Azzara." Taking my gaze off the candles, I don't want to speak of my mother about something like that, as if I'm speaking *for* her. "What is it like having Soren as a son?" I ask, sipping on the tea that's thankfully *normal*, eager to have a conversation that roots me in reality.

She snorts, placing a hand on either knee as she looks me over. "Any man he kills deserves death. I won't hear otherwise."

Picking up the plate of rice after setting the cup down, I smile at her response.

"Eat slow. You didn't get to eat much on the ship."

Nodding, my growling stomach nearly tells me otherwise, but I listen to her and take my time.

"How did you do it?" she asks. "How did you set the ship on fire?"

I touch the back of my neck for the ruby—it's *gone*—and leave that part out of it. For better or for worse, Cypress may have actually saved me. "I… I used my magic and channeled every bit of it into Misery's staff, and then a wave washed over us, and he was gone. He screeched as if I had burned him."

Intrigue is etched into her gaze. "How did you do that? He should have seen that coming."

"I came with a suppressant. Misery couldn't feel a thing," I quickly say, the sensation of speaking about it in past tense quite odd on my tongue. "Why did that work so well? It was like me touching his staff was actual *poison*."

Her gaze trails off, canting her head to the side. "You touched him with another god's power, and in our case, *ours* is quite annoying to someone who is the God of *Misery*." She pours me more tea and motions to the bowl with the salve she used on me. "This is for inflammation, by the way. Your body has healed a great deal, but I'm afraid your lung will have some permanent injury. What that manifests as, I'm not sure. This will reduce whatever we can manage."

I look down, sighing like I've released a thousand worries. She places a hand on my shoulder, and it's been a long time since a motherly touch was given to me. "You will be alright, Jane. Get some more rest. There will be someone outside the door if you need anything. I'll let Soren know you're awake."

"Wait, what's your name?"

"You can call me Sera."

Downing the rest of the tea as she leaves, the quiet calm is almost too weird. Too out of place. It's something I lived with every day in Coalfell, but now I don't know what to do with it. Is it seriously over? Jesper is gone like he never existed? Blackwell's ship is at the bottom of the ocean? I may have had a hand in that, but... I didn't realize how much my heart had settled on going down with Darkwater.

Lie down.

Closing my eyes, I'm sure I fall asleep for some period of time, the lighting in the room seemingly brighter when I next open them. At some point, a lady's maid enters after knocking.

I sit up once more, my chest not nearly in as much pain as it was earlier. "Where's Soren?" I ask the woman, who is wearing a simple, red dress, her black hair pin straight and parted down the middle.

"In his chambers. He checked on you earlier. I'm here to see if you need anything."

"Am I near his room?"

"Yes. You are in the quarters adjacent to it. He wanted you here for pure peace and quiet until you woke up properly. If you'd like, I can take you to him."

"Yes, please. Let me put new clothes on."

It's a bitch to stand, but it also feels good to get my body moving as I strip off what I was wearing and find some new clothes; a simple, black dress with no sleeves. It's actually kind of hilarious that I don't hate it, compared to pants.

The lady's maid waits for me outside, guiding me—even slowing down when it's clear I can't move very fast. My bare feet smack on slightly chilled wooden floors until we reach a large archway, serpents carved all throughout. It's a sitting area of sorts, with a large window and couch, and a set of vast doors. Everything is of a dark shade.

"I can't go in, but I'm sure he's in there," she says, nodding to the doors.

I turn the thick, bronze handle of one, thankful that it's not *too* hard to open despite its size. When I step inside and shut the door behind me, I can't believe I was *just* sitting among other Cinders as fire consumed us, and now I'm somewhere that feels like it could become home. There's a peacefulness in here, a wind chime singing its song through the open windows, the curtain slightly rolling with the breeze. There's such a large sitting area with an impressive hearth. His chambers remind me entirely of the one in Skull's Row, even down to the colors.

And I love the view outside—a rolling pasture with tall, old trees, fences, and dirt pathways. Wild bushes break up the expansive green, a forest's edge in the distance.

It's like I died and went to another world.

It's when I hear the movement of water that I enter through another door, like I'm actually exploring this afterlife I've been sent to. Opening it reveals a man leaning against the side of an impressive, in-ground bath, windows lining the wall behind him. The texture of the glass makes it impossible to see out of, while still creating a bright environment. Both of Soren's arms are spread out on either side, displaying his muscles, his tattoos out for a full viewing as his wet hair is slicked back. He looks at me as if he expected this, a knowing smirk plastered on that handsome face.

I raise my brows and nearly laugh, which hurts my lung. "And *you* always got on me for the baths I liked!"

He tilts his head slightly at me, grinning darkly. "Get in."

He will *not* have to tell me twice. I near the waters, finding the act of stripping for him a little difficult at first. Stealing the fastest glance, he can *feel* all of that, and *gods,* I missed him. It's like my mind and body can just exist with Soren nearby, not having to speak a word of anything I feel. Of any of the trauma I can tell hasn't even settled on my heart.

He'll never ask *how I feel*.

"You are far from any danger, Jane. I, and many others, including yourself, have seen to that."

I need this more than I realized. The connection he has to my heart and soul, I now recognize, is not a crutch. It's how I *want* to live. It's the only way I can truly let go, knowing that someone stands in the darkest parts of me, aware of *everything*.

My dress drops to the floor, and I enter the warm waters, nearly wanting to cry from relief. Not only does this man know me, but he knows of my home. Of my family. He's seen me in my very last moments and brought me back to him.

Soren moves to me as soon as I'm close, running that calloused hand up my hip and back, wrapping me in his arms as he grips my hair from behind and looks me in the eyes. Staring into the palest blue, I know I'm home.

He has become my new home.

"Say it," he grumbles, that rough voice matching the trimmed stubble on his jaw and cheeks.

"What?" I ask, my hand rising up along his body, over scars I've memorized. If anyone tries to take this away from me again, I now *know* I can be their reckoning.

"I can feel it all through you," he adds, tightening his grip as his eyes look all over my face.

"That the water is a little warm?"

He doesn't budge, something ravenous overcoming his gaze. "Tell me you love me."

Those words rush through me in a sensation I have *never* experienced; to stare him in the eyes as he brings forth the word of *love* between us. The fact he *wants* my love, too. All right after I walked in death's shadow for weeks.

"I'll wait all day. You said you thought of me as you were dying," he says, boring that gaze right into me so the entire world is no longer relevant.

"I don't even remember the last time I told someone I love them," I remark without thought, finding it actually difficult to get the words out. I know I feel it, but confessing it is such a different task. Like saying the words will make this all disappear, and I'll wake up at the bottom of the ocean with the shipwreck. Next to fucking Blackwell and Jesper.

How have I been granted the chance to live so I can tell Soren I love him?

His gaze deepens with every bit of intensity in there. "Then you're definitely telling it to *me*."

A smile slowly spreads on my face, as I love the power I have over him. "*You* say it."

"Do you desire my love, Jane?" he asks, running his thumb along the nape of my neck.

"Oh, yes, I do." Those words effortlessly leave my lips.

He leans down and kisses me deeply, passionately, before parting to ensure I'm staring right into his eyes, so close our noses touch. "I love you, Jane Ritter."

My exhale is shaky; those words the salve that my soul needed, something immeasurably profound happening in my heart. "Of course I love you," I say through a rushed exhale, my brows upturned. He's already on my lips, his tongue spreading me wide. His free hand dips below the water to grab my ass so hard that I'm pressed right up against him, feeling his cock that's firmly hard between the two of us.

A new passion translates through our kissing, now that we both know how close we were to not having this. He moves us to the edge of the bath until he lifts me, gently placing me on a fur rug as if he knew where he wanted me when I came to him. Soren climbs out, the beautifully carved man dripping all over as he claims my lips once more. His cock grazes against skin that hasn't been touched by another since back in Skull's Row, the man completely ready to penetrate to claim what's his. I spread my legs further, *needing* him.

He rubs his stubble along my face as his mouth finds my ear. "Lots of things will change. You'll keep that piece of my mask, for starters." I breathe heavily, and he uses a hand to help guide him as his cock gently finds where it'll enter me, slowly stretching what's impossibly tight. "You're my love, Jane." His voice is a low rumble, filled with vulnerability. "It's all behind us, and *I'll* be the only one claiming you like this until our last breath. You can breathe easy with me."

My lungs might burn but fuck that injury. I run my hands along the backside of his arms, the two of us getting lost in each other from kissing, teeth gently scraping, or tongues roaming as he rocks his hips to deeply fill me, intertwining our bodies. I don't know why those words help settle the dust of everything that just happened, but they do. *I'm safe, now, and I trust Soren.*

He'll always find me.

"Touch yourself," he says into my mouth.

My hand lowers, rubbing my clit with so much purpose as my eyes fully roll with how it feels to have his cock deep inside while I clench onto the sensation of an orgasm rising. Every time I glance down, I glimpse his thick cock disappearing into my body, over and over. My other hand digs its fingers into his skin as I work so eagerly to let that feeling wash over me. It's not even really the sex I'm chasing, but rather that utter vulnerability I want him to have.

This means I'm *free*, and with *him*.

That pushes me over as I scream out, my body jolting. His cock *buries* inside as I do, and it's such a beautiful sensation to be physically and emotionally infiltrated by Soren after all that mayhem, this bliss turning that nightmare into something so far away.

Soren isn't far behind me, moaning as his body stiffens, the rocking ceasing as I can feel him pulse inside of me, the man pressing as deep as my body will allow him. He grunts and stiffens, his eyes slightly rolling as he suddenly slows down all movement, his cock twitching inside of me.

His forehead presses against mine as we both lie there, fully interlocked with the other. "Life isn't right without you, you know," I gently say.

Pale, beautiful eyes are so close to mine, so open and defenseless. "No, it's not," he gently says. "I need the vibrations of your soul, love. I couldn't function without it."

Well, fuck him, because now I'm almost crying again. When I press my lips firmly into his, the act is so slow and mesmerizing, my body filled to the brim with electric pins and needles.

"Thank you for fighting for me," I say into his mouth, the threat of crying fully returning. "Thank you," I say with a sniff, pressing harder into his forehead, those words stretching further than just rescuing me. For existing, for keeping my father alive, for taking care of Kathleen. *"Thank you."*

"Everything in me chooses you, Jane. I'll *always* take care of you."

OLD FRIEND

JANE

The calm after such a destructive storm is one my body doesn't know what to do with. Sometimes, I wake after a nap with a jolt and am convinced I still have to save Anya, while at other times, I stare at a brazier for far too long when passing by one in a hall.

Accepting that those memories *did* happen is one consideration, but fully embracing how close I was to a horrible life, or a tragic end, is not easy to manage. It's similar to when I first made it to Coalfell and started to realize I might actually never see my father again, and accepting how easily *I* could have been stabbed instead of my mother.

I *know* it's probably better for me to handle these emotions on my own, but the way Soren can spread through my heart and close off the chasms that threaten me… I let him. It's what I wanted when we first met, and I'm going to let someone have complete control over my heart if he wants.

My unique healing with him might create a dependency of sorts, but we're all dependent on *something*.

Who cares if my *something* is a behemoth of a killer?

I'm currently sitting in that very man's bed chambers, the ceilings tall, the walls dark, and quite a few windows overlook a shoreline that merges into a forest, whereas the sitting room faces the rolling hills.

Nothing has felt this close to home since the Silver District.

"That's the very shoreline I used to roam as a kid," Soren comments, catching me staring out.

"Who lived here before you?" I ask, putting my hands on my knees. I'm sitting on the edge of his bed after having just woke up.

"No one. I had this manor built when I took over Serpent's Crest in my twenties. It's completely mine. I tend to like things that way."

The corner of my mouth twitches into a roguish smile at his comment, before my imagination wanders to envisioning a Soren long before me. "Which came first, the name or you?"

"The name." He stands next to me as I continue to look out the window, touching my hair as I lean my head against his bare stomach. "There's a lot of snakes here," he explains. "I watched how they attacked and used it as a tactic before I was *properly* trained. Thought it was only fitting to make the name of this place my emblem." His fingers lace with my hair before smoothing his hand over the back of my head. "What makes you sad, love?"

"I miss *home*," I say, thinking of where *I* grew up. "I love it here, but I keep thinking of the Silver District... I'm just nostalgic, I guess."

"We can visit the Silver District, soon."

"I'll probably be wanted, after killing Matthias."

He chuckles, and I close my eyes as I lean against the thick muscles of his abdomen. "Corvus is said to take over. We could even have a home there, too."

My eyes flash open. "For the Zenith stuff?" That would be perfect. He could tend to the things he's obligated toward, and I get to put my heart back together after shattering all those years ago.

"I think I'm done with those cunts. I'll keep the mask though."

Soren steps away, and I want him to immediately come back. "We can get one just to have one."

"Corvus will be fine with that?" I ask.

"If he wants to keep using my ports and maintain an alliance, he will be," Soren says, moving to a dresser where he grabs a thicker tunic to slide on, his back and shoulders flexing with the movement. "Speaking of home, there's someone here for you that you should see."

"*Who?*"

"Bones immediately reclaimed Kathleen," he says with a partial grin, tucking the tunic into his pants before fastening them. "It would be good for you to see her."

I lower my gaze to my hands, to the mark on my arm where Soren's mask still sits underneath my skin. I have *so* much to share with her. "I'd love that."

"I'll take you to her."

⸺⸺◈⸺⸺

SOREN'S MANOR is nothing like a castle, and I'm completely happy with it. It's a large estate; formal with long halls, sitting areas, lots of hearths, and even a courtyard with an ancient oak tree casting the widest shadows. His mother lives in a beautiful cottage right on the property, with a pond, something I visited once when acquiring more of that salve.

Soren takes me to a room at the end of a hall, every piece of wood stained dark. When I enter, a pretty blonde presents herself as she stands from a chair. Kathleen wears a black cotton dress that's cinched with a corset, reaching under her breasts without binding them. It's too uncomfortable for her, otherwise.

"You two will have privacy for as long as you need," Soren says, connecting his gaze with mine before the doors shut.

While I'm ready to pounce on Kathleen in a long embrace, I hesitate when apology stains her green eyes. Bright lighting from the many windows means no expression left hidden, the silence deafening.

I can't tell if she's happy to see me or not.

"You're alive," I say, taking a step near, testing the waters.

"Jane, I have to tell you something. Or else I'll feel like a right asshole if I don't."

Dipping my head low, I nod a few times. "Okay. Yeah, go ahead, Kathleen."

Her jaw is slack as she cants her head. "*Jane.* You know you're *actually* my friend, right?"

Oh, I don't like this direction. "That's the impression I was under."

Her lips part before she looks around the room, returning to the chair she was in before I entered, leaning her elbows on her knees, her hands moving as she speaks. "I couldn't say a word." Familiar eyes flit to mine. "I swore him an oath."

An oath? She swore *who* an oath? "What is it, Kathleen?"

"I knew who Ern was this whole time," she confesses, unable to look at me.

The words mean nothing for a while, like my brain doesn't know what to do with that information. But the longer she sits in silence, her hands clasped like she's trying to squish away the guilt, I realize what she's *saying.*

My hands become fidgety, like I need to do something with them to alleviate the way my head spins. For a moment, I release my surroundings and get lost in my own mind as I deconstruct that, and honestly… there's a part of me that just doesn't care. Or maybe I do, but my desire to worry is completely gone. I've survived too much, reclaimed too much, to be angry at something like this.

Facing Kathleen, I steel my nerves and ask, "Can you just explain it all from the start?"

"You're not angry?"

"I don't know… maybe just explain it to me first," I press, sitting down, touching my arm where the mask is, comforted that Soren is always with me.

He's probably reading every wave of what I feel.

Kathleen's gaze drops back to the floor, silent tears running down her cheek; *that* breaks my heart. "It's been eating away at me, Jane. Ever since I heard your dad came back."

"Well… I don't know. I trust my dad, I think. I trust *Soren*, and he can read your heart—" I tut; *I bet he knows, that's why I'm in here* "—so, I'll trust you, okay?"

She nearly smiles at me, the expression shaky, like that takes her off guard. "Did they hit you on the head too hard?"

A laugh rolls out of me. "I think a *lot* of wounds finally closed."

That really does seem to ease her guilt, and she straightens her back before sighing deeply. "You have no idea how good it is to say this out loud. To even—well, let me go back to where it started. My mother," her voice shakes with emotion as she moves her thumb along her forefinger, over and over. "My *sweet* mother. Sorry, I don't mean to cry. I was thinking about her before you came in here. When mom died, I was only twelve summers, and the only work I knew was *Rosmertta's*, and I knew I didn't want that for myself. So I left, but I didn't get far before I was caught by men who used to keep an eye on her."

Kathleen connects her gaze with mine. I know her enough to know that I should remain where I'm at, rather than go to her; she wants the space. "I was born in Skull's Row, Jane. In the very house where we were kept for a while. Rosmertta gave us free shelter in exchange for my mother's services, and that just solidified as I got older and was willing to do the dishes, then the laundry, then clean. After Mom died, men who were willing to sell literally *anything* to make a coin caught me." Her voice thins with rage. "And so they took me to an auction. I *developed* early, as they said. I had a lot of people betting on me, then suddenly, my auction went silent as I was taken off stage and brought to the man that purchased me." She draws in a slow, steady breath. "It was your father."

My jaw drops with a disgust I wasn't prepared to feel. Kathleen raises her brows and shakes her head. "He immediately explained that he's not buying me for that, but rather for something else. He wanted me to go to Coalfell and live there to be *your* friend. Said a witch told him I'd be good for you."

Staring at my hands, I eye the tattoo on either wrist. To the goddess that may or may not have helped me, to thinking of Cypress serving *her* god. I simply never imagined *Kathleen* being involved in all of these secrets.

She sighs. "He then told me my gran lived there, which, turns out, she did. I honestly never knew, and apparently the entire time she had begged my father to learn about my whereabouts... your father told me that if I were to fail in befriending you, he'd send me back to Skull's Row, because he couldn't risk you knowing about him."

My natural smile fades, my gaze lowering.

"I'm so sorry that I knew, Jane. If I said anything, he'd take me away. And once we got to know each other, I realized how much you needed me. And how I needed you. Same with my gran."

Shaking my head, I say, "No... it's—I'm okay. It's so strange to think the Scorpion *orchestrated* my life, along with Cypress. And now I just feel..." I look at the tea table in a home that belongs to Soren, the details so comfortingly mundane. "Different."

"Well, I always thought you just needed a good fucking, but honestly Jane, I think you *do* need the violence to think straight." I throw my gaze right back at her, and she smiles. "You're so much more confident in yourself when hitting people. Maybe it's just who you are." She grins as if she's been eager to say this for so long, "Makes sense given it's in your blood."

I return the warmth, and it feels so healing to believe that in all of this shit, Kathleen is *still* my family. "So, if this is all true, then you knew my dad was Ern this entire time?"

Kathleen nods, reluctance returning in her green gaze. "Alright, fine. I'm really sorry, though, Jane. I mean it. I wouldn't have—"

I interject with, "It's okay, Kathleen. I—" pausing, as I'm about to admit words I didn't realize meant so much to me, "I understand. We do what we have to."

Her plump lips curl into a smile as she brings her clenched hands to her mouth. "He would also sometimes act as a merchant traveling through to check up on you. I was always so scared when he'd ride into town because I was afraid he wasn't going to be happy, but eventually I realized he just literally wanted you to not be alone.

"There was one time, when we were about sixteen, and you drank too much. Oh, he was so mad. Someone else had been slipping you extra ale when Ern—your dad, really—wasn't looking. He took me out back, and we got you on a carriage. I think he might have killed that man, actually."

My gods, it's real, isn't it? Something in me knows this is the truth, even if it's too much to grasp. "Yeah, Ern told me later that he was sorry it happened..." I whisper, speaking while emotionally removed. "He said he knew I hated being that drunk, which I still do."

"It was really sweet," Kathleen confesses, like she's been hiding a secret for so long and can finally talk about it. "He had touched your hair. He looked so sad."

There's something about that image that ignites everything in my bones, and somehow saddens me, because where is that man now? Where's that loving father? My nostrils flare, my lips trembling. The heavy rise and fall of my shoulders makes my injured lung hurt. Gods I'm ready to get all this healing over with so I can stop wanting to cry.

Kathleen pivots on her seat, but still doesn't rise. "Jane, I know you said it's okay, but I mean it—if I could have *hinted* at it, I would have. It killed me not to tell you. To play ignorant when speaking of your father. But then he told me, after a time, that it was a witch that bound him from seeing you, and that if the witch found out—and that she *would* if we spoke of it to you—then everything would fall apart. Including your own life. I played the role because I had to. But it was easy, because you *are* my friend. The only part that royally pissed me off was seeing how broken you were, and knowing *why*, but not being able to help you."

I crinkle my nose, touching my eyes and trying to control myself until I stand and near Kathleen. No words are said for her to understand that I want to embrace her, and the next thing I know, I'm gripping her like she might disappear. "I'm sorry those people tried to sell you," I say through a shaky voice, imagining killing them for her, especially now that I know I *can*. I'm not helpless anymore. I'm not *stuck*.

She laughs into my shoulder and pets my hair. "It's okay. I think Bones plans to kill them and make me something out of their bones. He was royally pissed when I told him."

I pull back and touch her hair that's on her shoulder as we face each other, brimming with new purpose. I'm also not alone, not with Kathleen. Not with someone who has known me for so long.

"Where did he stash you?" I ask.

"Stash me? Like I'm his acorns?"

We both share a deep laugh; I missed her so fucking much. "I asked about you, and he refused to tell me but reassured me he stashed you away nice and safe."

She looks away, shaking her head. "Oh, that man… I got taken to a small village in the Restless Peaks. They mine metals there, and he let me take my gran. We just said we were refugees from Coalfell. I dyed my hair and eyebrows for it. Spent five days washing it once I got the word that we were safe." Those green eyes finally look like the woman I know. "Everyone trusted us because Bones sent us with his cousin, who is a traveling merchant that frequents the area."

"His *family*?"

"She's the nosiest shit I've ever met, but damn if she didn't get word of something suspicious if it was over ten miles away. Once, we even left for a town over to run some errands for the village when she caught wind of people from Skull's Row checking out the village." She looks me over, at my arms and then the wound at my chest that's no longer bandaged but is clearly going to scar. "Jane, how *are* you?"

It's so much. I want to blurt out that Anya died, but then I'd have to talk about the entirety of being taken. "We definitely need to have a few days' worth of talking about it. Just… maybe not right now."

"Anya's *funeral* is later," she presses, as if she can't believe it.

It makes me want Soren. There's still something about Anya's death that gets to me in the middle of the night, even if we've been here for a week. Kathleen places a hand on my shoulder. "Hey, one day at a time, okay?"

I nod. "Yeah… yeah, how's your gran, by the way?"

My transition is not very elegant, but she goes with it because she's a good friend.

"Relieved to see me. Still upset about my dad being a dick, but she was happy to be with me. She wouldn't stop pestering me about Bones."

Yes, let's talk about him. "Did you know Bones is known as someone people actually pay good money to have him train them?"

"*Yes.*" Pride overtakes her expression. "He flexed that once or twice."

My eyes narrow slightly from how big I grin. "Okay, well did you know he and Soren met because Bones was hired to kill him?"

Her lips part in surprise. "*No.*"

"Bones couldn't hit Soren because he could feel Bones's intention, and apparently Bones is damn near impossible to hit. Then, Soren offered Bones more money to not kill him. Apparently, Bones just *loved* that and was Soren's man ever since."

Her chuckle that rolls into a slight giggle is a sound I missed more than I realized. "How'd you learn that?"

My smile falters drastically. "Anya told me."

There's that pause again, as if someone feels sorry for me. "What happened to her?"

I should probably fill her in a little, even if I'm genuinely struggling to speak on it.

"She got taken with me. And there was a whole fiasco in the castle, with Jesper—the leader of the Order of Ash." I pause, uncertain as to why this feels so *private*. "They were going to be *brutal* with me, but Anya took the fall for it all, and they killed her." I step away, my body heating up as if I drank molten hot soup. "It's actually hard to talk about."

The moment between Anya and me feels so personal. We both were locked away, and she was *tortured*; I even healed one of her wounds. We plotted desperate plans for freedom, and I have the necklace she gave me, her deathbed confession. No one, except maybe Soren, will be able to *feel* what it was like to live that.

"I hear the funeral today will be impressive," Kathleen says, as if to make me feel better. "Probably the safest we'll be with over half of Death's Wing here."

"The safest I felt was when I heard Tempest approaching with bloody flags," I blurt out, recalling the profound relief and gratitude. "I knew sirens were in the waters, then."

Staring at the ocean from this window... I actually wished it faced the forest.

"*Gods* that must have been wild, Jane. I heard that the Sea Wolf was lost at sea."

My breathing feels constricted, my lung even slightly burning as I never got to see that. I just remember Soren...

"It was bizarre," I force out, trying to divert my mind. "Misery even *touched* me."

It's easier to talk about that dumb god. Ruining him is my only *true* triumph.

"I feel like such a bad friend for just sitting casually in a village while you lived all of *that*," she says, and I can tell she means it. "I couldn't do anything for you. I didn't even know you were *suffering*."

"Are you kidding?" I ask, turning to face her. "I actually thought of you once, right when I wanted to give up. I kept thinking about how we promised we'd talk about this when we were older. Thought of you got me through it."

Kathleen gives a partial smile. "Alright, well, give me a bit to gain some grand tales to tell, too." Her face blanches. "I don't mean it like that because, you know, a lot of people died."

I'm just so ready to not have to talk about any of this with *anyone*. "It's okay, Kathleen. I know you don't mean it like that. And it's also okay that you knew all of that about my dad. I get it. Some things you can't share without hurting someone else." I think of Soren and knowing of his god before him. "Thank you for being my friend, even if that must have been hard to navigate."

She embraces me like it's a hug she's been holding back for years, and I return the affection. "It's good to have you back, old friend," she says.

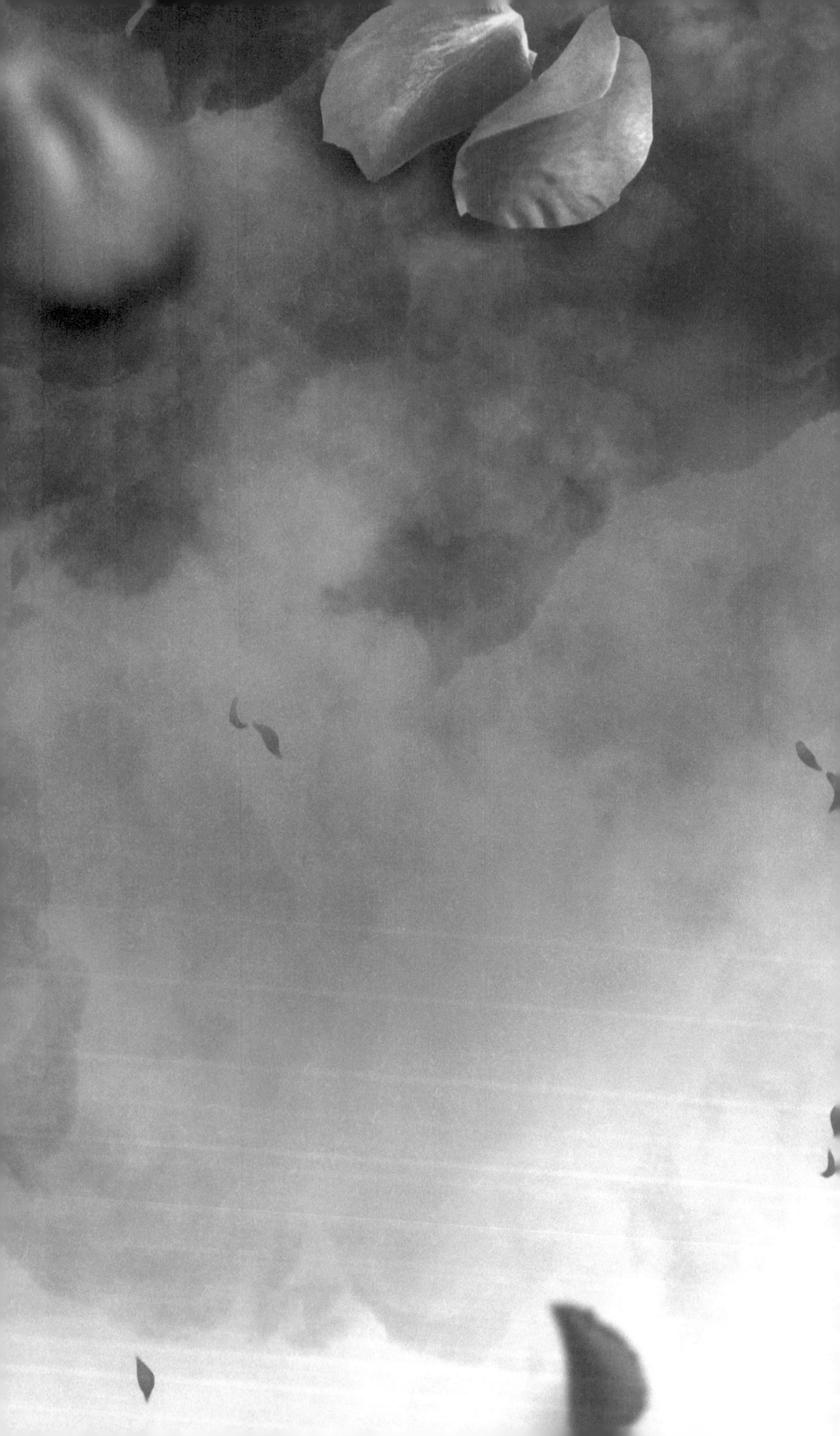

FLY HIGH AND FREE
JANE

Kathleen and I both wear red dresses as people in Skull's Row do when attending a funeral. We wait inside the mess hall of Soren's manor, the two of us sitting openly without any guards near us, like we're somewhere *safe*.

Members of Death's Wing have been slowly arriving to the gates of Snake's Crest, half of them arriving alone while the others come with nearly a full armada that's made camp outside the battlements. I even watched as one rode in a horse much like Phantom, the members shrouded in a cloak as thick vambraces peaked through while they gripped the reins.

Soren and the rest of Death's Wing sit at what can only be described as his throne, no doubt reminiscing on old memories. It's a fascinating group of men and women who are all wearing leathers, vests, and overall outfits custom made, and so many tattoos of all kinds. One woman even has her entire neck inked out, along with her lips.

Kathleen grabs the pitcher of ale next to us and pours some, the drink foaming at the top of my mug. "So, what are the tattoos for?" she asks. "The ones she's getting right now?"

I take a sip of the hoppy goodness, the alcohol burning down my throat even if it's weak ale. "Soren told me that it's a special ink that's temporary but lasts for the ceremony until Anya is burned. It connects the lines on her back. The outer two stripes will be finished down the backside of her legs, and the middle breaks off into two and stretches back up, then down the back of her arms. Apparently, they'll then draw elaborate works to depict what she's accomplished in her life."

Kathleen sips on her ale and looks at me as if she has just been served delicious gossip. "Wait, will she be *exposed* to see them? Lay her ass naked on the pyre? She didn't seem like that kind of person."

A chuckle rolls out of me as I shake my head. "Anya doesn't seem like the kind that would appreciate that." We both share a cheeky grin with the other before I add, "Soren said it's there for ceremony, hidden but present, just like their loyalty to each other is. It's all about formality and is supposed to honor the soul for its sacrifices. And then apparently they get the wings of a blood hawk —those giant birds in the Huntswoods—and put them on either side of her while she's dressed in whatever she chose while still alive."

Her green eyes soften. "What did she choose?" she asks with earnest. "I would ask Bones, but I think her death is hitting him hard. He's been enjoying talking about *my* time while we were apart, not really his."

"I don't know," I say, finding it interesting that both Bones and I share the same reaction to what happened to us all. I'm honestly eager to know what Anya chose myself, aware of how I only met the smallest glimpse of who she actually was. I barely knew her, and even *I* feel robbed in her early death.

She was just starting to get interesting.

A sad smile comes to my lips. I glance up Soren, the snake crest hanging above him as he listens intently with his Death's Wing troupe before flashing his gaze my way. I'll never get tired of that, I don't think. I could be seventy years old and he nearly eighty, and I know the hairs on my arms will still rise every time.

I return my attention back to Kathleen, not wanting to distract him. "What was it like to see Bones when he came for you?"

"I've never been so happy to see a madman in my life," she says through a sigh. "Hear me out—he's a sweetheart. A big, violent sweetheart. I mean, Jane, I'm pretty confident if I went to kill the bastard, he'd let me."

Fine, I guess I owe it to toad face to entertain speaking to him more, if he means that much to Kathleen. And for helping me.

"Well, it's good he made sure you were safe," I say. "It gave me a big peace of mind while all that shit was happening."

She lightly slaps her hand on the table. "I was so useless! That still makes me so *mad*. But, I guess I'm glad I wasn't in the *way*." She purses her lips. "Anyway… is it alright to ask what Bones was like? When fighting?"

I can't help but laugh at her wanting to see that side of him. "I can't tell you much about him, honestly. Well, he *did* train me, a little bit. But I never got to see him fight much. I just know wherever he was, people were *dead*."

She grins, pressing her palm against her cheek as she rests her elbow on the table. "It's alright. I can't help it. Something about watching him fight really does it for me." She looks off slightly. "Maybe I should challenge him to a duel…"

I laugh hard, even covering my mouth, to which she finally joins in before we both settle into a silence that I'm still trying to understand. It's like what happened has created a divide of sorts, but not in a negative way… just distance. Hopefully my saga is damn near over, and I can just enjoy Soren for the years to come. Help him find his sister, too.

As I stare at the blonde who looks off like she's thinking deeply of something, an idea strikes me—what will Kathleen do? Who will *she* become? "What do *you* want to do, Kathleen?"

She looks at me like she's never been properly asked that question. "What do you mean?"

Sipping more of the ale, I sigh before explaining, "We spent so much time worrying about *me* when in Coalfell. It's time to focus on you, now that your oath to my father is done."

Her green eyes widen as she blinks rapidly, the wit that always hovers behind her gaze diminishing as something somber replaces it. Looking up, her jaw flexes as she seems to really consider the question. "I don't think I've ever been asked that."

I frown. "Not even by Bones?"

She smiles, as if the mere thought of him lights up her misery. "There's been too much turmoil and fighting, I think." She looks at me seriously; then she seems inspired by something. "You know, the first thing that comes to mind is I'd love to return to Skull's Row. Help women out who were like me and nearly sold. Maybe a safe house, kind of like what Rosmertta had, but where they don't have to become petals if they don't want; not everyone is meant for that life. Somewhere with healers, too. Don't know how we'll afford it, but I'd love to tackle that challenge."

"Kathleen, that is an *excellent* idea," I reply, honing in on the possibilities. "Maybe once everything is truly calm again. I'd support you wholeheartedly in that."

⸻ ◆ ⸻

THE BELL TOLLS when it's time to attend the funeral, the sun just beginning to set as its intensity dwindles. We step outside, with Kathleen and I together as Soren moves among those belonging in Death's Wing. He dons his red leathers just like when I first saw him all the way back in Coalfell.

Walking along the trails to the beach, we're finally back near the ocean, a slight breeze toying with my dress. Where the sand is hardened by the ocean, a giant wooden pyre stands with a flat top and temporary stairs.

Even the sky is a burning red.

It's so calm and peaceful, as if the air carries forgiveness for all that occurred. It's neither warm, nor cold. Three men beat on a drum as another sings a deep, raspy song in a language I don't recognize, his voice dipping low into sounds that move my soul, before climbing higher to an emotional vibrato. Black paint streaks across their skin in delicate lines, like the ones on Soren's back.

Basilisk stands next to Soren, his black cat sitting by his side, the tail elegantly flopping back and forth. It dawns on me that all of these people have an idea of how their funeral will go, including Basilisk.

Including Soren.

When another bell tolls, everyone from Death's Wing looks behind them as if they know what to expect. I do the same and see four members wearing black wings carrying a large wooden plank and fur blankets draped on either side.

Anya.

The sight smashes through me, especially as I realize that I've never attended a funeral, let alone processed my emotions of losing someone in such a formal setting. Seeing her body on the plank steals the wind from my lungs. *She's truly gone, isn't she?*

Everything spirals, my chest heavy and exhausted, and it's like I'm back in that damn tower again, staring into watery, onyx eyes that pleaded for me to remember her last words.

If I were paying more attention, I'd register that Soren is watching me more than Anya. Even as my peripheral catches how he steps back a few times to get a better view, I'm keened in on the body being brought by us. She's nearly in front of me, and I can see she's wearing simple leathers, her black hair perfectly slicked back, tattoos rising up her neck in the decoration of waves, the shape of a wren morphing out of them.

I've never seen someone who died, long *after* their death. It's as if I'm looking at her all over again, bleeding out on the stone floor. Whoever took care of her body did miraculous work, as if she might take a breath, *any* moment…

I nearly jump when it's clear Soren is behind me, leaning down in my ear, that voice making me inhale deeply at the effect it has on me. "She wouldn't want you to feel guilt, Jane."

I could literally bury my head into his chest and close my eyes until the sun is fully set. How I *need* him. I look up to give him a small smile. "Thank you. Go ahead and be with your people."

He doesn't move, those penetrating eyes softened for me. "No, if I knew Anya, then I know she wanted me to experience what she felt with Amy. So honoring her means checking in with you when I feel anything wrong."

Tears beckon to fall, but are withheld by sheer exhaustion from doing it so much. I don't want to reveal my sorrows; no quivering, no sniffing, no hiccups from crying too hard. And yet, Soren knows *exactly* how I feel. It's a silent invasion that I could have used in Coalfall, the ability to connect with someone without having to speak a word. He touches the back of my head and kisses the top. I mutter, "Why did she choose that outfit?"

"She and Amy met while training. It's when she claims she was truly born, and when Amy was killed, Anya always said that's when she died. So she chose the outfit that we all wear before we've earned our stripes."

Soren's touch slides down my arm before he returns to his post, watching as Anya is guided to the pyre, the four men ascending the stairs on either side to position her over the construction. Once there, more men bring out giant, preserved wings and lay them on either side of her, the breeze gently rustling the tips.

They *all* begin to sing as her pyre is set on fire with a torch, and I've never heard anything so utterly emotional and yet beautifully painful. One of the men that brought Anya, the one who lit her pyre, stands in front of it. "Burn bright, Anya Lorraine! You were instrumental in our organization, and your loyalty to us is something we all dropped everything to come and honor your life.

"Your soul was shattered years ago, your flesh preserved by Soren's actions to keep you with us here. May you know peace now, Anya, of Death's Wing. Fly high and free."

The spiraling flames, for some reason, don't make me react like it did for last week.

Don't break Soren's heart…

She really did want me to love him. That gives me more resolve than anything else, and I know *that's* how I'll honor her sacrifice.

I'll take care of him, Anya. I hope you're with Amy, now…

I'm told it will burn for hours, long into the night, and remaining present is up to each person. When it's all said and done, her ashes will be collected to fertilize a garden that grows some of the deadliest plants that the organization uses, the rest given to any family that would claim it.

I imagine, one day, that will be the same for Soren.

The winds pick up, adding to the dramatic fires that burn away anything left that once identifies Anya as someone who existed here.

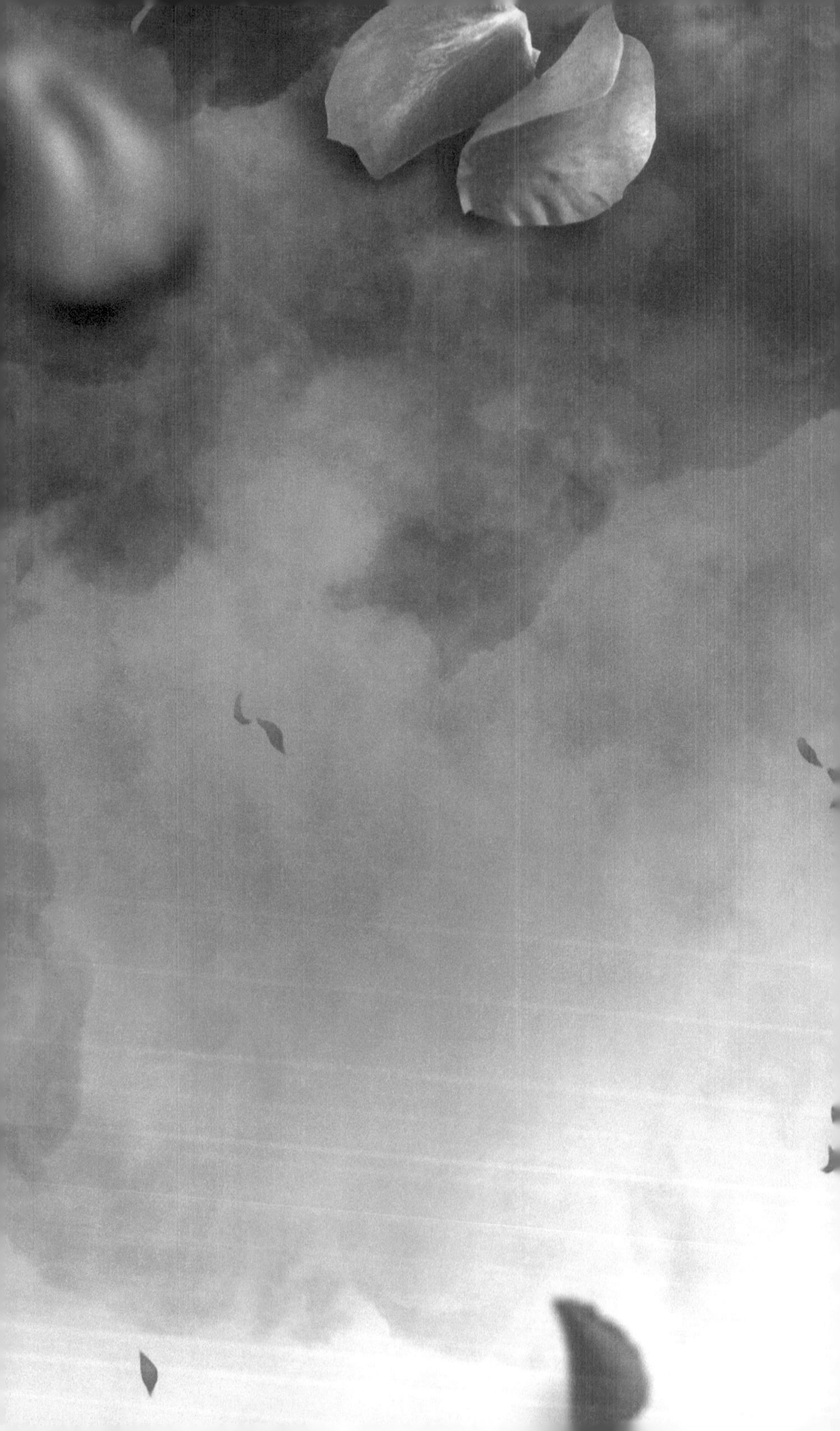

REUNITED

JANE

I'm truly happy for Soren that he gets to see those that share the same tattoos on his back. He mentioned it's always awkward at first, but as long as their hearts are loyal, it's like seeing a person who knows of a very rare language that not many can speak.

They've been through things that only *they* would understand.

I slowly back away from the small crowd; of course, Soren senses that and watches to see where I'm going, but when his attention is over my shoulder, I turn around to see my *dad*.

It's nice to see him with *his* face, even if he's now missing a hand. I heard how he sacrificed it to ensure Jesper didn't get to kill himself, the fucker somewhere in the ocean, suffering from the siren's curse. "I have something to show you, Jane," he says, something gentler in his voice.

583

"Yeah, okay," I say, my gaze meeting Soren's once more before I follow my dad, leaving Kathleen, who motions for me to go.

As he and I walk through the twilight sunset, along the beach toward what looks like a harbor with a few ships in the bay. His one free hand holds a lantern to guide us, squeaking slightly on its chains. I eye his bandaged stump. "How are you?" I ask.

He raises the rounded thing. "Well, at least every time I look at this, I know he's down in the seas, alive, and absolutely *miserable.*"

I admit, that gives me some comfort, too. "What will you do without it?"

"It's my left hand, so it's not as important as my right. Probably get a weapon to replace it." He lowers it to look me over. "I'll find help if I need it, don't you worry."

"Where?" I ask, my heart racing. "You're not leaving, are you?"

He takes his sweet time to reply as he surveys the path we're on, the gentle crashing waves of the shoreline right next to us. "I got a letter from Corvus. Skull's Row is in disarray, but not lost. Blackwell did a half-assed job at leading even if he was never chosen to lead. They want me to return, and I'll be taking Liam Rackham to pay off our debt for his help. I'll get my new hand there."

"Is it safe? What if they just kill you?"

"I don't think they will. I don't have to hide anymore, and with Donna and Rorge, we'll make it happen. They have a *large* network themselves. And... well, I'm *free.*"

Free. Free to leave me, I guess. I cross my arms, the air slightly cooler with the sun setting. "So you're really going back?"

"Aye," he says, and I realize we're not just nearing the harbor, but he's taking me along one of the piers as a ship is being emptied, the fading sunset silhouetting every line of rope. "Soren still needs to periodically visit, with all the shit that's gone down."

Dad is leaving me with him. In some way, it's nice to have the approval, but in another, it feels like he's just handing me off. "What about Matthias? We killed him. He has to have people there that will hate us."

"He was a cunt that only had two friends in there, and one was Blackwell. Either the other one accepts his place, or we'll exile him. Of which Soren will be a deciding factor. Tempest has also declared Corvus take the reign, and I don't think many want to challenge her right now, not since she wears Blackwell's soul in a conch around her neck. It helps I can see any auras that aren't friendly; I know how to disappear."

I don't know if I'll ever get over realizing my father isn't the man I thought he was, but at least I don't have to wade through those feelings alone. Not anymore. Of course, it's nice to have him after pining for him for over a decade. I just... had different visions for what that would be like.

Time to let that go, too.

We come to a halt on the pier as quite a few men unload a moderately sized vessel. I raise my brows when I see a necklace of wolf teeth around their necks. "Tempest is here?"

"Those are men she let me borrow as I regather mine. She was pleased to hear that Jesper was sent to suffer the siren's curse." He nears them as one carries something that looks like a painting covered in cloth, some of the wooden beams creaking underfoot. "And she's delivering things I stashed at her island many years ago." He looks down at me, the lantern casting long shadows up his face. "I half wonder if she's just giving these things back to me to get them away from her lands."

"Were you two friends, at one point?"

"Allies. Strained from Cypress, but a siren—Melona, specifically —told her that saving my ass would keep her daughter safe, one day. Since we helped with Blackwell, and since you saved Moriganna, Tempest is willing to put all that behind us."

Referencing back to my encounter with the sirens is odd, not having intended for that to create long-lasting debts to be paid. I just wanted them free, so I could fulfill whatever Cypress wanted out of me. Not once did it cross my mind that it would help me in the future. *A future I didn't know I'd have.*

We near the painting, and he hands me the lantern, not an ounce of self-pity in his eyes as we both understand it's because of his injury that he can only do one thing at a time. He lifts off the canvas fabric for it to reveal—

I clasp my hand over my mouth as if I've seen a ghost.

It's of my mother.

Probably when I was a few years old.

It's almost cruel to see her face, so stagnant and forever that way, dramatically lit with the lantern against the darker sky. I'd gut anyone who would even *attempt* to ruin this. Hells, if I had money, I'd pay an artist to recreate this for safekeeping. I kneel down in front of it, staring at the almond shape of her eyes, the artist capturing her smirking grin perfectly.

"What is all of this?" I ask, my head moving all around as I pay more attention to the things that are still being carried off, placing the lantern on the pier.

"Your mother's things. And some of mine."

"What?" I ask, my voice cracking as I look up at my dad, standing to face him, my lungs straining to breathe.

"After you had been secured with Melona, I returned to our home and had my men gather what I told them to. It would be important to your mother that you'd have it." His voice trails off, looking down at the painting behind me. "I hate how still she is. How I can't make her come to life. I—" he trails off, blinking rapidly as his jaw juts to the side. "I talk to her, often. I don't know if she hears me where she is… but I miss her."

I turn slightly so I can look back at it, my breath hitching for a second time at seeing her. "They even got the beauty mark on her jaw."

All he manages is a nod before sharply inhaling and moving over to a chest, opening it.

"It's not locked?"

"It was more for keeping things organized than safe. They're just made of wood. The thieves in Skull's Row would have broken in one way or another. It's about *where* you keep your precious things that's more important."

Dad opens it, the hinges creaking as it's almost like a coffin of my childhood. "Ah, this one has her healing stuff. It's got her candle that she used to light for healing before she lost faith in her goddess."

I near it so fast I nearly trip, stumbling as I reach back to grab the lantern to hold it closer. "She kept the candle?" I ask, staring at the blue wax, noting that the wick is even the same color. There's a divot around the wick, indicating it's been used. *The last time it was on fire was when my mother touched it…*

"She didn't know how to explain that she had lost a personal faith. You were still learning the basics of healing, so I didn't press how you needed to connect more with your magic. I'm not quite sure how the gods work, but I do know they can help connect your powers." He clears his throat, looking at me while I stare at the things that used to be kept around our house. "Soren's mother, I'm certain, would teach you."

I even spot a small bag, one I swear she used to—I pull out a pair of ruby earrings, my jaw dropping as if holding a precious memory snatched from thin air. I truly believed I'd *never* see these again.

"All of her jewelry is in there, too." He sighs, scratching the back of his neck. "I'm remembering now, I put all the special stuff in that one. The rest are her clothes…" He looks at the others.

"Are these safe to wear?" I ask, holding them next to the lantern as the fire flickers heavily. "I lost the ones I bought."

"I would maybe find another ruby jeweler, but they'd be fine to wear on occasion."

I laugh at the sudden humor, moving my gaze between the earrings and my father. "Do you trust Cypress, after all of this?"

"I trust that her god means more to her than any of our lives. I think it's best to stay far away from Cypress if we don't want to end up stuck in her web again, though."

I stare at the jewelry for such a long time, and Dad doesn't press me, all while Mom watches on through her painting. It's when I face him, so confused about all of this, and yet he still seems like a stranger—I'm stunned when Dad pulls me in for an embrace, the stumpy arm wrapping around to hold me there.

I don't know what to do, my eyes burning from how wide they are.

"I'm so sorry I was so distant, Jane. Cypress… it was all her. She told me I couldn't be close or show you any emotion. That it would throw you off. That if I broke that promise, she'd remove me from you. She said you'd be too attached to losing me again and not act how you *needed* to. I love you, Jane. I'm grateful I got to see you, for all those years, and got to do what I could to take care of you. Even from a distance. I'm just so sorry you felt so alone for so long."

I drop the earrings and wrap my arms around my father, crying like how I dreamed I would when still a child who trusted too much, burying my face into his chest as Mom's painting stands behind us. I wail into his chest like I'm a kid again, surrounded by my parent's effects, gripping him even tighter, as if to tell the lonely Jane that first arrived in Coalfell that it *is* okay; he *will* come.

He's already there.

It will just take much longer than anticipated to embrace him again.

"Enjoy this season while we have it, Jane," Dad says, and I can hear him sniff as his remaining hand pets my head. "Life is seasonal. You had an unusually rough one that lasted for a very long time, but it was bound to be reborn with new beginnings..." He sniffs again and kisses the top of my head. "I'm so proud of you, you know that? You took on a *god*, Jane. Your mom would be telling everyone of your legend." He laughs into my hair as I shudder more, burying my nose into his chest. "My *girl*."

THEN WE WILL
JANE

Some mornings, it's hard to appreciate where I'm at. If it wasn't for the scars or permanent pain in my lung if I breathe too heavily, I might have thought everything that occurred was simply a terrible nightmare.

The only evidence of what my life has been through is the way my heart has changed. How deep wounds are finally closing, and I actually have love for a man that I never thought possible. A love I *feared* I would lose.

Now that my life is starting to settle, I'm officially tired of the *fates*.

Of premonitions.

It's difficult when Soren lives within those confines, but he's learning to not frame it in such a way. I've missed feeling autonomy over myself, and predestined bullshit robs me of that.

At my mirrored desk that I use to pen letters to Kathleen and my dad, I sit with only a silk robe on and stare at the ruby earrings belonging to my mom, studded into a small cushion for display.

It will be a while before I wear rubies again.

Did Mom know that Cypress was watching her while wearing them? Questions about her invade me at least once a day, wondering all the way to what her childhood was like. We never got to talk about it much. Maybe it's something I can bring up when I go to visit her painting next, which Dad let me keep. Soren gifted me one of the rooms that overlooks the ocean—something I'm forcing myself to stare at. Despite the way ocean waves are like nostalgia, they're now stained with a complexity from enduring that storm, from standing next to Misery while rain pelted my face. There's bodies out in that water. Even my enemies are still alive, stuck in the siren's curse, just under those waves. My hope is that if I stare at them enough, surrounded by my mother's things, that maybe I'll somehow get over it.

That room even has Mom's brush with a few blonde strands in it, like she may have just visited.

Yes, I'll bring up her childhood next time I visit that sanctuary.

Properly dealing with her loss is an ache I've come to accept will always linger, and in that, I understand Anya better, understand my *father*. I can't imagine living with Soren for years on end, growing so used to him I forget what life was like before him, only to permanently lose him.

I drop my gaze, wishing Dad was here so I could talk to him about that. Ask him how *he* is, make sure he's healing, too. The next time I see him, he'll have a new weapon for a hand.

Reaching out to touch the rose dagger lying on the surface, I think of those that Soren bloodied in his reclamation of me. I've always craved special items of my parents, but never thought I'd ever have my *own*—

The door to this room opens, and I flash my gaze up at the mirror, seeing Soren stride in with dirt smeared all over and sweat glistening on his body.

Training.

When he meets my gaze through the reflection, peace rises within me like an ocean filling a cave at high tide, gentle and without rush.

I trust him completely.

His chest rises and falls to a heavy rhythm, as if the adrenaline still courses in his veins. I grin at him. "If I had your powers, what would I read in this very moment?"

He places a hand on either side of me on the table, which slightly shifts with his weight, looking at me through the mirror. "It would be a *lot* to take in, love."

The smile that man can spread across my face is my *true* healing in all of this. "Tell me you love me," I say, almost with a little *too* much sass.

Without skipping a beat, he confidently replies, "I love you, Jane."

My heart pounds away, heat pooling between my thighs, *needing* to be close to him. To smell his skin, and feel the warmth of his body. Soren's physical strength is a comfort I never thought I'd desire, like he's a literal wall of safety that reminds me as long as he's here, *someone* will come for me.

He raises his hand to thread his fingers at the nape of my neck, pulling my head back to fully expose my skin as he grazes his lips below my ear, sucking hard. "I can't tell what's best—*hearing* you say you love me, or the way your heart reaches out to me like I have a permanent invitation."

"Well, you're not wrong about that invitation. I think even if I hated you, I'd still miss you."

I swear the sound that comes out of him is almost like a pleased *purr*, deep and velvety, before positioning me so he can lean over to plant hungry, possessive lips on mine. I just let my heart go, no longer burdened by any debt or obligations.

He pulls me up out of my seat against his massive self. His tongue parts my lips to command my mouth, grazing against mine like it's his to claim. There's a depth to every movement, as if we're both aware of how every moment matters, and that he's already memorized every curve and scar of my flesh.

At least, I know that's what I've done with him.

His lips demand for mine to bend with him, the movements deeper, clinging to each other.

Gripping his neck, I melt into him as he lifts me, that internal, pleasurable vibration taking over my navel and spreading through like a pulsing heat. Soren plants me on the desk, my back resting on the wall as his hand spreads my legs, his rough touch contrasting against my inner thigh before sliding two fingers inside of me as I'm already slick for him. My legs straddle around his waist, the man rubbing my clit with his thumb in a motion that my body has grown to *love*, especially when he arches his fingers inside.

I'm so eager for him to fuck me. I've never known a high quite like watching him unleash himself and using my body for his pleasure, or to see his throbbing cock hard *because* of me.

As I cling to him for balance, his free hand works swiftly to unbuckle his leather belt, sliding it through to almost make a *pop*, dropping it onto the floor with a dull clink. I don't know why that makes me shudder, but I kiss him even harder as teeth slightly graze.

He darkly grins against my mouth.

Soren's affection moves as he kisses my jaw and then sucks hard on my neck, to which I whimper as I grip his hair, his thumb working perfectly in rhythm with my rising ecstasy. He unleashes an almost animalistic sound into my skin as my pussy is absolutely ready for him to take me. He just got here, and yet I can't control my damn self.

My fingers curl against his body, one hand digging into his shoulder as I arch into him, rolling my eyes as he controls the entirety of me, *right* between my legs.

He groans with longing as he continues to focus solely on me, and I know his determination isn't going to waver until I'm coming right on his fingers—I moan loudly as my muscles contract around him, panting into his skin.

He pulls his hard cock right out of his pants, using both hands to grip my hips as he grazes my clit with the tip of his erection before he finds my entrance, sliding in with one motion as my pussy slightly stings from the stretch. Soren rides in the wake of my climax, and he nearly rips off the silk robe as he lowers over me, kissing and licking my neck, fucking me hard as this desk hits the wall with a rhythm.

The pain is quickly gone until all that's left is Soren filling in spaces of me I didn't even know existed. "So fucking perfect," he rasps. "You feel *perfect.*"

I cling to his shoulders. "Yes I do, when you fuck me like this," I say, my mouth running away from my mind.

His growl is so primal I groan in response, moving my head forward so our foreheads are nearly touching. The man pants as his eyes slightly roll in his head, until his hips crash *hard* into me as he comes, remaining there to very carefully rock as he drains everything he has into me.

I've grown quite fond of our quick sessions that wet our appetite between the longer, more intense ones.

Soren reclaims my lips, licking my bottom one before he pulls back to carry me to the bed. I waste no time in getting settled into his arms as we both lie there, naked on the fur blanket, my eyes closing as there's not a single worry in my heart while Soren rubs his fingers on my skin.

His icy irises are what I saw at the brink of death, engraving himself deep into my soul when he appeared. I don't know if I could accept any other kind of love, honestly. I always feel like I belong when it's just the two of us.

"So, what happens to us next? To life?" I ask, not wanting to leave this reprieve, and yet I'm itching to visit Dad and Kathleen.

"Visiting Skull's Row seems important, given your ties there." He slowly inhales. "I'm nearly ready to find Serena. The dust is settling, so I could leave again, even if it takes me a few months."

I remember the first full moon appearing in the sky since I woke up here. Soren spent all night on the coast, staring outward over the sea, having told me everything Cypress shared with him.

He had felt his sister.

Finally.

And she wasn't hurt. Or afraid. He said she felt normal, as if living a real life. It took an immense amount of pressure off his shoulders, knowing she didn't *need* him to find her. Not with such urgency.

He could recover, first. Tend to the mourning families, and get his affairs in order.

"What about here?" I ask, knowing that travel is in our future, no matter where we go. "What goes on here when you're gone?"

"My mother runs it. I only trust her to do so. It's best done if I have a presence for a time, before leaving again."

I nuzzle into him, my arm stretching across his chest. "Serena is across the Black Sea, right?"

"Yes. Near Grimstone, where Basilisk lives."

"I'm going?" I ask, nearly tightening my grip as if to say I'll fight him over it.

His laugh is so calming as his chest moves against my head. "You already said you'd help me. You can't back out of that now." A deep sigh escapes him. "There would be rules."

"Of course," I mock.

"If you travel with me, and it's not for luxury, there's protocols for how we move as a unit. You'd have to adhere to it."

Like an addict, my heart is willing to agree to anything if it means being by his side. I mean, can this really be my life now? How is it fair that I live while someone like Maryanne is burned, her children still scorned out there?

Soren stiffens in a way that's akin to an unspoken reminder that I'm to tell him what bothers me—*unprompted*—which is a new concept for me. "First, I'd happily go and help you and do what needs to be done," I state with full confidence. "I just... I also feel, *wrong*. Guilty, maybe?" I press my lips together, trying to muster the words to leave my tongue. "Maryanne's children are out there, somewhere, bitterly enraged. I *know* that feeling. And I'm the reason their mother was killed."

His chest rises high before lowering with a deep exhale, my head moving with the motion as I can hear the faintest echoes of his heart beating. "That's why we never have peace. As long as there is revenge to be had, blood will be shed. It's why we enjoy the quiet while it exists."

I give a sad, bitter half-smile. I appreciate that Soren doesn't treat me like I'm all rose petals and no thorns, but the gratitude is weighed down knowing that he's right. So many were irrevocably damaged in the wake of whatever the fuck just happened to us.

"Do you think finding your sister will be dangerous?" I ask, wanting to focus on something else.

"Somewhat. The path feels clear. But not without fighting *someone*."

I move so I can glance up at him, Soren's chin dipping to he can lower his gaze to look at me. "We should bring back a pet," I suggest, trying to give him a sweet gaze.

He raises a brow, hiding his amusement. "A pet."

"Like one of those shadow cats. Basilisk *loves* his."

"He doesn't love it because he loves his cat, it's who gave it to him."

I frown, eyeing his stubble and the new streak of blank growth from a scar he gained when coming for me. "He was pretty passionate about that cat's welfare."

"It's because it's the only thing he possesses of the woman that gave it to him, and she wanted him to take care of it. I think he fucked something up, and he's trying to make up for it."

My eyes flash with intrigue. "Oh, well, this sounds interesting."

Soren's eyes hold no play. "He is what I would be if you left me. Took a *lot* to learn that from him."

I can't help but smile. "We definitely need to get a cat now." I lay my head back on his chest. "You're also not allowed to leave me, either," I state matter-of-factly. "I let you in, so now you're staying."

My heart is filled with so much peace that I kiss his chest, to which he turns us so I'm on my side, facing into his body as he also turns on his side, my head nestling into his chest. Those large, powerful arms wrap around me as one of my legs intertwines with his. I will never not love the girth of this man, especially when I'm up against the expanse of his chest.

"Don't worry, love. I feel your heart as if I'll know it for decades."

I breathe slower, my eyes closing as my body completely relaxes. "I'd like to grow old with you, Soren. My parents were robbed of that."

He holds me close, no need for anything other than love and adoration in his touch; it's pure affection. "Then we will."

END

The Heart of a Basilisk will follow *Basilisk* and his FMC, *Evie,* in an independent standalone. Evie is the leader of an all female assassin group named The Unsung, and she's thirty-three!

The woman who once loved him.
The woman who betrayed him.
The woman he could never destroy.

SOREN AND JANE *will make a cameo in this novel,* one that will also cover the conclusion of what happened to Soren's sister. It felt like the right way to really finish Serena's arc, while also exploring another couple that have a very loud space in my heart.

THIS BOOK IS SET to release late summer 2025. You can either sign up for my full newsletter, or just one related to the Basilisk.

Please visit www.charlottemallory.com for more info!
Find me on Social Media @cmalloryauthor

I HAVE TO GIVE A FEW SPECIAL THANK-YOU'S...

Erica for being an amazing beta reader. The way I laughed so hard at her comments, and the way she gave the best pep talks… thank you.

Baddie and Ashley, for tag-teaming a beta read. *Ashley* is a huge reason Bones and Kathleen have the chemistry they do, because her love for them made me want to keep dropping lines that would make her laugh. I think I owe that couple a book one day, just for her. *Baddie* is my PA, and she's like running a book through a sieve. She is wonderful for putting up with me!

Renee, my Aussie friend, for being a massive supporter of this series and my beta reader. Her enthusiasm really helped me push through this final edit, because I couldn't wait to get it to her. Her love for the series is very special to me.

Mae, who beta read this for me as the first one and gave me the boost I needed to power through my edits. I loved her feedback so much!

Heather, my editor and beta reader. She is such a massive supporter and I really am so grateful to have her on my team!

FINAL WORDS...

I am terrible at these, haha. It's like a microphone that's on with an audience who can't tell if the speech is over or not.

Tap tap.

Anyway, it also wouldn't feel right not saying *something*. This story is one that when I wrote the very first chapter, I knew where it was going. I had the 'I love you' scene already mapped out. Needless to say, this book really felt special to me.

This series is one where I made people's *top reads of the year* list. Soren is people's *book boyfriend*. There were *fan theories*. This book helped me cross of so many bucket list items, and the reality is, it can't do that without readers.

The fact that my book has seen so many highs, because of the collective interest of *thousands* of people, is still a humbling sensation. Thank you, from the bottom of my heart, for supporting me and this story. **In that, I'd really love if you made sure to review the next book you love.** I'd appreciate love for *this* one (lol), of course, but this energy is what is needed to propel other authors, too.

Anyway… yup. Guess I need to say something epic, right?
Okay, well, maybe something will come to me…

In the meantime, I hope to see you around in my other stories <3